Battle for Peace
<u>The Silent Champions (Book 2)</u>

By Andy Peloquin

Table of Contents

The Princelands

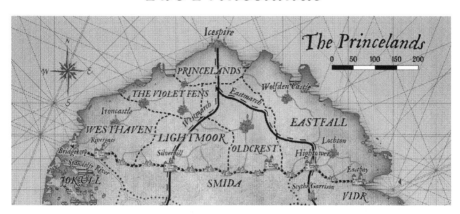

The Fehlan Wilds

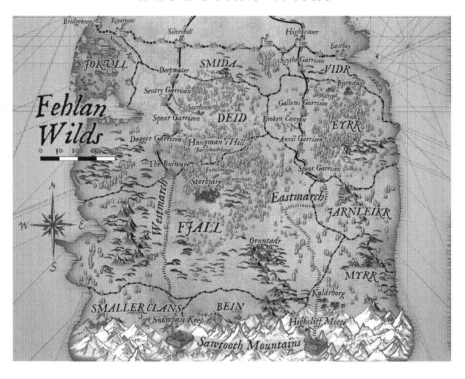

I do not advertise the nature of my work, nor seek recognition for my actions. I voluntarily accept the inherent hazards of my profession, placing the welfare and security of others before my own.

I will never quit. I persevere and thrive on adversity. If knocked down, I will get back up, every time. I will draw on every remaining ounce of strength to protect my teammates and to accomplish our mission. I am never out of the fight.

Brave men have fought and died building the proud tradition and feared reputation that I am bound to uphold. In the worst of conditions, the legacy of my teammates steadies my resolve and silently guides my every deed.

I will not fail.

-- excerpted from the U.S. Navy Seal Creed

Chapter One

"In and out without a sound." Captain Aravon spoke in a voice pitched low for the five figures crouched in the alleyway beside him. "No casualties."

Lieutenant Colborn grunted—Aravon couldn't tell if it signaled acknowledgement or disapproval, and the snarling greatwolf mask concealed the half-Fehlan soldier's expression.

Noll, however, made no secret of his feelings. "We're hunting a traitor, Captain." The little scout's words came out in a harsh whisper. "Seems to me a few bodies dropped would send a clear enough message about what happens to bastards who sell out the Princelands to the Eirdkilrs."

"No." Aravon's tone brooked no argument. "We've no proof that Duke Leddan is, in fact, in league with our enemies, only suspicion. Until we've confirmed it, he's still Duke of Oldcrest. Which means we go in using non-lethal weapons. Got it?"

Belthar and Skathi nodded. Colborn answered with another grunt, this one tinged with a hint of acquiescence. Zaharis shot Aravon the silent hand signal for "*Understood.*"

Aravon turned to Noll. "Are you clear on your orders, Noll?" He gritted his teeth, forced himself to remain calm. Noll, like most Legion scouts, had a stubborn, independent streak—the result of spending far too many days alone in the wilderness south of the Chain. That tenacity made him an invaluable weapon against the enemy, but an occasional thorn in a Commander's side.

Finally, the scout shrugged. "Yes, Captain," he signed. "But if he is the filthy traitor…" He needed no signals to complete his thought; his hand dropped to one of the three daggers tucked into his belt.

"If he is, the Duke will sort him out." Aravon turned to Colborn and Skathi. "You know your parts to play?"

Colborn answered with a nod and, turning, slipped down the darkened alleyway. His part of the mission led him away from Ironcastle's main avenue, off toward the eastern edge of nearby Ironcastle Keep.

Skathi unslung her horsebow and adjusted the strap of her black cloth-wrapped quiver. "Consider your backs watched."

The Agrotora disappeared into the darkness, heading west. She paused only long enough to glance up and down the main avenue before darting across and into the shadows of an alleyway opposite them. She, too, would follow the circumference of the high stone wall ringing Duke Leddan's fortress until she got into position.

Aravon noted the way Belthar's eyes followed Skathi's retreating figure. He owed Belthar a conversation the first chance he got, but time had been in short supply after the discovery of Silver Break Mine. The disappearance of an entire mining camp without so much as a trace took priority over Belthar's quiet infatuation for Skathi. As long as it didn't interfere with their mission, he'd have to let it slide one day more.

Swordsman, watch over us and guide our steps, Aravon prayed silently. He almost reached for the silver sword that had once hung around his neck, but stopped. He no longer wore the pendant. It had gone to the grave with Draian, the Mender slain in the battle for Bjornstadt.

A pang of sorrow twisted in his stomach at the memory of their healer's pale, bloodstained face as they set fire to his bier. Draian's death weighed heavy on him, as did the death of every soldier of Sixth Company that fell in the Eirdkilr ambush on the Eastmarch. It didn't matter that casualties were a part of war—he'd vowed he would do everything in his power to protect the men under his command.

Aravon's heart pounded an impatient beat as he waited for Colborn and Skathi to reach their designated posts. He shifted his leather mask, his fingers playing over the details of a snarling greatwolf etched into the alchemically-hardened surface. Yet another reminder of Draian. He'd had to wear the Mender's mask after an Eirdkilr sword had sheared through his own. Hrolf

Hrungnir, the bastard who had killed every man of Sixth Company, had nearly killed him again. Though the leader of the *Blodhundr* lay dead, his body rotting six feet underground, Aravon would carry the memory of the Eirdkilr chieftain forever.

His left arm, shattered in the ambush, would never hold a Legion shield again. The still-healing wound on his face would scar. And the burden of guilt on his shoulders would never truly lighten.

A hand on his shoulder brought Aravon back to the moment. "*Time, Captain,*" Zaharis signed in the silent hand language of the Secret Keepers.

With a nod, Aravon turned to Noll. "Go!"

The little scout slipped off into the shadows without a sound. After a moment, Aravon followed, with Zaharis and Belthar close behind them.

The shadows of the alley provided ample cover for their stealthy approach on Ironcastle Keep, though more than once Aravon grimaced as something squelched beneath his boots. A noxious miasma of mingled stale urine, stagnant water, and rotting food hung thick and oppressive around him. The odors seeped through his thick leather mask and twisted his stomach.

His heart hammered as a *crash* sounded from just around the next corner. He paused at the intersection, glanced toward the source of the noise. His white-knuckled grip on his sword hilt relaxed as a gaunt, mange-covered hound dashed past, scared by the flowerpot it had knocked over.

Drawing in a deep breath, Aravon steeled his nerves and continued his stealthy trek through the alleys of Ironcastle. He had only a few hundred yards to cover before reaching his goal: the towering walls of Ironcastle Keep itself.

Like so many other cities in the Princelands, Ironcastle had sprung up around the fortress—built to keep out enemy Fehlan tribes during the early days of conquest, when the Princelands were just forming. Ironcastle Keep had been well-maintained, its stone walls high and strong, its gate manned at all hours of day and night. The city around it, however, had been built for the comfort and convenience of those living and working in the fortress and its vicinities. Over time, it had grown from a single fortress in hostile territory to one of the largest cities on Fehl.

Yet with growth came chaos. The broad Legion-built avenue was the only truly *straight* road in the city; most of Ironcastle was dominated by a mind-boggling maze of alleys, back lanes, and side streets. Plenty of hiding places for soldiers sneaking toward Ironcastle Keep on a mission to hunt a traitor.

Ironcastle, more than a hundred miles north of the Chain, hadn't been attacked in more than three hundred years. Peace had lulled Duke Leddan's troops into a security that bordered on complacent inattention. They marched the rounds and held the keep's towers, doing their duties as Ironcastle's established city guard. Though a handful were veterans who had guarded Oldcrest's southernmost fortresses on the Chain, most were little better than adequately-trained militia. Those men trusted closed gates and high stone walls to keep out enemies—of which there were few.

Oldcrest had little industry, its primary commodities were grass, hay, and young men recruited into the Legion of Heroes. Duke Leddan wasn't particularly admired, feared, or hated. His personal fortunes, insubstantial to begin with, had taken a hard hit in recent years due to a combination of poor investments, a dearth of military-age men, and heavy drought.

That made him the perfect suspect for what had happened at Silver Break Mine. A fraction of its haul—according to Duke Dyrund, "the richest silver mine discovered in more than a century"—would be ample incentive for the fiscally struggling Leddan to consider selling the secret of its location. A secret known only by the five Dukes on Prince Toran's council, the Prince himself, and few others.

Aravon didn't want to believe that Duke Leddan was the traitor—or that *any* Princelander would sell out to the Eirdkilrs—but Duke Dyrund had insisted he and his company pay Oldcrest's ruler a visit to find out for certain.

As their steps led north, Aravon finally got his first glimpse of Ironcastle Keep. *It certainly lives up to its reputation,* he decided.

The keep's walls, built during the days of battle, stood more than fifty feet tall and three feet thick. Battlements ringed its top, with a guard tower at the four corners of the perimeter. Earlier that day, Aravon had gotten a good look at the southern entrance—once sealed, with the portcullis down, not even a battering ram would get through those enormous iron-banded wooden gates. And none had. Over fifty years of battle, before the Legion pushed the Fehlan tribes farther south, no enemy had ever breached that wall.

Beyond the wall, Ironcastle Keep itself rose to nearly a hundred feet tall, with four turrets overlooking the keep's interior and the city of Ironcastle itself. Pennants bearing the Duke of Oldcrest's insignia—a snarling hunting hound rampant on a field of sable—waved and snapped in the evening breeze.

Aravon scanned the keep's turrets. Colborn and Noll had both assured him they'd be empty—no need to man them in time of peace—but he had to be certain. The wrong pair of eyes in the wrong place, and they'd be spotted before they ever got close to Duke Leddan.

Darkness met his eyes. A full minute passed and he caught no sign of movement in either the southern or western turrets. Satisfied, he turned back to the wall. A younger, less experienced man might have insisted that they'd never get into the fortress unseen. But, as Aravon knew all too well, every stronghold had its weaknesses.

The Legion of Heroes sharpened the tips of the logs that made up its palisade walls, yet Eirdkilr furs were thick enough to protect the barbarians clambering over the top. Wooden gates could be harnessed to teams of horses and torn from their hinges, or battered down beneath a heavy ram or the onslaught of the seven-foot-tall Eirdkilrs. Keeps like Ironcastle had solid gates of steel and metal built to withstand heavy siege, yet there was always a way in. Bribe a guard, slit the throats of an unwary patrol, or steal a uniform and stroll in through the front disguised as an Ironcastle regular.

Had they had more time, Aravon might have considered two of those three options. But they couldn't spend days doing reconnaissance, scouting the castle's layout, drinking with the guards, and setting up their mission. Duke Dyrund had made the urgency of their mission plain—they had to find out who the Princelander traitor was *now,* before they sold any more confidential information to the Eirdkilrs.

Tonight was the last night of the new moon, which gave them ample cover of darkness for their mission. Perfect for finding a non-lethal way of getting past Duke Leddan's guards.

Aravon had little experience with this sort of thieves' work, but fifteen years in the Legion had taught him the value of letting the men under his command play to their strengths. Aside from his impressive brawn, it turned out one of Belthar's strengths was a surprisingly devious mind when it came to breaking into places. He'd formulated their plan of attack—with a few modifications from Noll and Zaharis—without hesitation. Aravon couldn't help wondering where the hulking Belthar had obtained such skills; one more layer to the man he had yet to uncover.

Now, however, he trusted that Belthar, Noll, and Zaharis' plan would work. He had no choice; none of the others had offered better alternatives.

A flash of movement from atop the keep's outer wall caught Aravon's eye. The hem of Colborn's cloak caught a glint of firelight as he crested the parapet and slid into the guard tower. Aravon tensed in expectation of a shout of alarm, tightening his grip on his sword hilt. Yet, after long seconds, only silence reached him, and his fist relaxed.

He turned to Zaharis, who padded along beside him, and signed, *"Seems your Sleeping Lily did its work."*

"I should be offended you doubted me, Captain," the Secret Keeper signed back. *"Then again, I was the one that said I wasn't certain it would, so that's on me."*

Aravon chuckled, but his rejoinder was cut short as a length of black rope dropped over the wall and Colborn's masked face appeared in the guard tower's window. The Lieutenant shot them the *"All clear!"* sign before ducking out of sight.

As planned, Noll went up the rope first, scaling the wall with the agility of a veteran sailor darting through a ship's riggings. Zaharis' speed put the scout's to shame; he seemed to run up the wall, his hands moving in time with his feet.

Aravon's ascent proved far less painless. His left arm had recovered strength enough to wield a spear, yet his elbow joint still pained him, twisted his muscles at an uncomfortable angle. The wounds he'd sustained in the battle for Bjornstadt had started to heal during their journey back to the Princelands, but five days was far from enough time for a bruised rib, pulled shoulder, and a slashed thigh to heal. The wound on his face throbbed with every hammering beat of his heart.

Gritting his teeth against the pain, he forced himself to keep climbing, one hand over the other. *Our company's only as strong as its weakest link, and I'll be damned if that's me.*

Sweat soaked his undertunic and streamed from his forehead, stinging his eyes. The muscles of his forearms burned, his hands aching from gripping the rope. He was breathing hard, nearly gasping for air, by the time he reached the top of the stone wall and clambered onto the parapet.

He half-threw himself into the guard tower and pressed his back against the wall, sucking in great lungfuls of air. *So much for stealthy!*

Thankfully, the guards in the tower were far too busy dozing to overhear him. Two men lay sprawled on the floor, while three more sat slumped face-down on a pile of cards, coins, and dice spread out atop their small wooden table.

Aravon shot a glance at Zaharis. *"How long do we have?"*

"An hour, give or take." The Secret Keeper shrugged broad shoulders. *"Without the time to test the Sleeping Lily powder properly—"*

"An hour will do." Aravon's brow furrowed. *"Will it harm them?"*

Zaharis shook his head. *"A mild hangover, at worst."*

"Good," Aravon signed. *"Better if no one but the Duke knows we're here."*

A quiet *scrape* sounded from the guard tower's rooftop, but Aravon didn't look up. Colborn would hold that position, out of sight of any guards below, and cover their retreat. In case of discovery, he could provide cover fire from above.

The rope creaked beneath Belthar's weight, and the big man grunted with the effort of climbing the wall. Aravon had *almost* insisted Belthar stay outside—he'd sustained more serious wounds than any of them, though mercifully none debilitating—but they needed the big man's expertise once inside Ironcastle. And, in case the mission went sideways, his size, strength, and skill would prove invaluable.

Aravon slipped out of the guard tower and onto the parapet, crouching low to remain out of sight of the guards below. He and Zaharis held the tower, but Noll slithered down the wall's inner steps in silence, skirted the men crowded around the brazier burning beside the gate, and crept through the shadows toward the keep itself.

A courtyard of paved stone stood between the wall and the keep, fifty yards of open space he'd have to cross to reach the shadows of the enormous building and its adjoining stables, warehouses, and smithy. If this was a Legion encampment, he'd never make that distance.

It's just the Swordsman's mercy we're not facing Legionnaires, then.

Aravon glanced to his left, toward the two gatehouses flanking the southern gate. Lamps shone in upper-story windows, and the sound of laughing, shouting men echoed from within. Doubtless drinking, gambling, and keeping out of the cold, as soldiers tended to do. Another dozen or so clustered around a brazier that burned near the keep's front entrance, a pair of iron-studded wooden doors nearly as heavy as the front gate. That same fire that kept the cold away blinded the guards to the darkness of the night.

As he prepared to follow Noll, Aravon glanced toward the roof of the southwestern guard tower. Darkness hid Skathi from his sight, but he knew she'd be crouched on the roof of that tower, opposite Colborn. The two archers would have a clear view of Ironcastle Keep—just in case they needed cover for their escape.

And, somewhere high above them, Snarl circled on his eagle's wings. With eyes as sharp as an eagle's and the night vision of his fox half, the Enfield made the perfect lookout. His yipping cries would alert Skathi in case of trouble.

It seemed an eternity, but couldn't have been more than a minute, before Belthar hauled himself through the window and into the guard tower. He flexed his huge hands, wincing at the pain in his muscles, but nodded to Aravon. *"Let's move,"* he signed.

Aravon hesitated only a moment before giving Zaharis the signal to take the lead. He had to trust Belthar could keep quiet as they descended into the keep and followed Noll's path into the shadows.

Zaharis peered out of the tower and held position a few seconds before motioning for them to descend the staircase. The guards never looked their way as they raced down to the courtyard, dashed across the open space, and ducked into the shadows of a squat wooden building. The smithy, judging by the stink of burned metal that permeated every wooden beam and stone pillar.

Aravon kept his breathing slow and steady as he followed Zaharis through the darkness, circling around to the east and heading north along the wall of Ironcastle Keep. Every step set his heart pounding—not in fear, but the nervous anticipation that came with knowing that they could face an enemy around every corner, in every shadow. Though it still felt odd to think that enemy could be a Princelander.

The muscles in his shoulders were knotted tight by the time he spotted Noll crouched next to the keep's rear entrance. *Seems Belthar was right,* Aravon mused. *Everywhere really does have a back door.* It appeared this one gave access from the keep's kitchens, providing the Duke's cooks a short path to reaching the reeking pile of rubbish heaped beside the servants' outhouses. *Not the most pleasant entrance, but at least we've got a way in.*

Noll turned to Aravon and shook his head. *"Locked,"* he signed. *"Heavy one, too."*

Aravon's jaw clenched, but Belthar seemed unperturbed by the news. He crouched in front of the door, eye level with the keyhole. After a moment, he nodded and drew out a small leather pouch. Aravon's eyebrows rose as the huge man selected long slivers of metal from within and inserted them into the lock.

After a few moments, the lock gave a loud *clunk* and Belthar pushed the door open.

Aravon couldn't help marveling at yet another of Belthar's surprising set of skills. *No wonder the Duke selected him for our company.* He'd never given much thought as to the Duke's choice—Belthar had been a valuable asset to their team from the first day, his courage in battle and abilities with his double-headed axe made him a good companion to have in the fight against the Eirdkilrs. Yet Belthar was one of the only members of their company that hadn't served in the Legion of Heroes. The why of that and how he'd come by such…unique skills filled Aravon with a burning curiosity to know who the big man had been before joining them.

But that would have to wait until after their current mission. *"Well done,"* Aravon signed to the big man.

Belthar nodded and stowed his tools.

Noll's fingers flashed. *"Who knew those banana hands of yours could do something so delicate?"*

Belthar said nothing, but Aravon noted the tension in his sloped shoulders. It didn't matter that it was the sort of ribbing and friendly banter common among soldiers; big man or no, he tended to be prickly when it came to Noll's teasing.

"Move," Aravon signaled to the scout. *"We've got an hour."*

With Zaharis at his side, Noll slipped into the darkened kitchens. Aravon followed, with Belthar bringing up the rear. They moved in unison, their steps light and quick, balanced on the balls of their feet to make as little noise as possible. Their weapons remained sheathed, on his orders, but Aravon knew Noll could draw his short sword and dagger faster than any Ironcastle guard. And Zaharis, well Aravon had faced the man in bare-handed combat one too many times to imagine the Secret Keeper would be anything short of lethal if it came to a fight.

Swordsman grant it doesn't. Even if Duke Leddan was a traitor, Aravon had no desire to leave Princelander bodies piled up behind him.

At the far side of the kitchens, a door opened onto a massive dining hall. Empty, with only a single lamp hanging on the western wall, above a throne-like chair that could only belong to Duke Leddan. Silent as wraiths, Noll and Zaharis led the way through the hall, slithering between the long wooden tables with the same grace that they'd cleared the obstacle course back at Camp Marshal.

A signal from Zaharis sent them scrambling into cover, ducking out of sight beneath the long table. The *tromp, tromp* of heavy feet echoed off the stone walls and high-vaulted ceiling, accompanied by a glimmer of lamplight. Yet the sound and light faded long before it reached them, the guards continuing on their patrol of the keep's interior.

Aravon drew in a deep breath to slow his racing heart, but kept his outward façade calm. His men needed to know he had the situation under control, even if he felt utterly out of his element. He was a soldier, accustomed to battlefields and shield walls, not sneaking and subterfuge. But he couldn't let *them* know that. They trusted him with their lives, and he couldn't give them even a hint that he wasn't up for the challenge.

"Let's move," he signed to Noll and Zaharis, *"before they come back around."*

With a nod, the two ducked out of the shadows and continued on their path across the dining hall, toward the staircase that led to the keep's upper floors. They'd have a long climb to reach the Duke's private chambers on the level just beneath the rooftop and turrets, and they had only a few hours to get in and back out before the sun rose.

The faint glow of oil lamps lit the stairwell, giving them more than enough illumination to see as they raced up the spiraling staircase. Aravon grimaced at the sound of his and Belthar's boots on the stone steps—it seemed terribly loud in the thick, all-pervasive silence. Yet he knew it was just his anxieties playing tricks on him. Fear made men jump at shadows or see enemies where none existed. If they truly *were* making too much noise, Noll or Zaharis would have warned them.

Just before they reached the second floor, Zaharis jerked to a stop, hand flashing up. Aravon slowed, his foot hovering over the next step. A moment later, lights appeared through the archway that led into the second-floor. The sound of muttering voices and marching feet grew louder with every hammering heartbeat.

The guards were headed right toward them!

Chapter Two

Zaharis moved before Aravon raised his hands to sign the silent order. Drawing a small cloth pouch from within his robes, the Secret Keeper wound up and hurled it down the hallway toward the guards. It struck the stone and thumped to the ground, giving off twin *puffs* of the fine-ground powder within. The dust-sized granules hung in the air directly in front of the approaching guards.

Aravon's gut clenched as three men marched into view. Right through the cloud of Sleeping Lily. Before the guards even raised their eyes toward the stairway, the alchemical powder took effect and they slumped to the floor, as senseless as their comrades in the guard tower.

Aravon turned to Belthar. *"Stow them out of sight, then follow."*

"Yes, Captain," Belthar signed.

Noll and Zaharis gave the floating dust a wide berth, holding their breaths as they slipped past the unconscious men and down the hall, deeper into Ironcastle.

The hallway led to another, smaller set of stairs. The Duke's private stairs. Aravon had never visited Ironcastle, but he'd spent enough time in Wolfden Castle to know that all early Princelander fortresses had two staircases: the primary stairs that led from the ground floor to the main residences of the billeted soldiers and their families, then upwards to the keep's rooftop and turrets; and the secondary stairs reserved for the castle's resident lord or Duke. Those stairs were set far back into the castle, with a long, straight hallway that would be easily defended in case of attack. Had this been a siege, Aravon would have found the corridor lined with soldiers ready to die defending their lord.

But in peace time, the halls were empty, the doors to the private chambers closed. The sound of heavy breathing and snoring echoed from within.

Down the hallway they ran, their boots near-silent on the rush-covered floor. Aravon's gut clenched as they passed one door after another, half-expecting them to burst open and disgorge an army. Yet the hour was late and the men within sleeping heavily. Not a soul stirred as Aravon and his men raced down the hall. Silence permeated the dimly lit corridors, and all was still as they rushed up the stairs to the Duke's private chambers.

The stairs ascended for two full floors, and Aravon felt the passage of every minute keenly. They'd entered shortly before midnight, which gave them the better part of four hours to get back out of the keep before dawn threatened. Even though it had gone smoothly thus far, he wanted to get the mission over with before anything happened. *And, knowing our luck, it's never going to be as easy as in and out.*

Finally, they reached the top of the stairs and found themselves confronted by the door to the Duke's chambers. The door was made of heavy Fehlan redwood and reinforced with steel, with no lock for Belthar to pick.

Noll gave a gentle push and shook his head. *"Locking bar inside."*

Aravon ground his teeth, a movement that sent pain flaring through his still-healing cheek. They'd gotten past the guards unnoticed and evaded detection, only to find themselves stymied here. When he glanced at Zaharis, the Secret Keeper shook his head. He hadn't had time to replenish his alchemical supplies beyond what he'd been able to forage on the journey home. They had been fortunate to find the small patch of Sleeping Lilies growing near the tar pits north of Blackden—or unfortunate, in the case of Belthar, who had stumbled into the flowers and gotten a firsthand taste of their drowsy effects—else they might have had to rely on lethal force to get into Ironcastle.

Belthar stepped back and drew in a deep breath, preparing to charge the door. Aravon stopped him with a shake of his head. Belthar was big, but no way he'd get through that much wood and metal without injuring himself and alerting everyone in the keep to their presence.

Aravon's mind raced as he tried to figure out their next move. They could improvise a battering ram from the heavy furniture below, but the Duke would hear them assaulting his door and raise the alarm. The towertop window into Duke Leddan's private chambers was far too high for any of them to scale, even with the steel climbing spikes Skathi and Colborn had used to ascend the keep's outer wall.

Noll solved the problem by reaching out and knocking on the door. "My lord?" He spoke in a feminine tone, high-pitched and echoing with the timidity of a servant. "My lord, a messenger has arrived from Icespire. Says it's most urgent, sir." The mask concealed his features, but Aravon would have sworn the little scout was grinning.

The sleepy grumblings of an irritated man echoed from within the room, followed a moment later by the *thunk* of a deadbolt being shot and the *clank* of the locking bar removed. "What's the—"

The door hadn't opened more than an inch before Noll drove his foot into its inner edge, slamming the metal frame into the gray-bearded face of the man who appeared within. Duke Leddan was hurled backward and fell to the ground, hard, his head *thumping* on the ice bear-skin rug beside his bed.

Noll leapt into the richly-furnished room in a heartbeat, dagger in his hand. He pounced atop the fallen Duke and pressed the razor edge of his knife against the man's throat. "Not. A. Sound. Traitor." He spoke in a low growl, fury tinging his words.

Zaharis moved a step behind Noll, hurtling across the large room in silence and clamping a hand over the mouth of the woman sharing Duke Leddan's massive four-posted bed. The woman, whose graying hair was a shade darker than her husband's, startled at the Secret Keeper's presence, her eyes flying wide. Yet her right hand darted beneath her pillow and lashed out at her captor. Zaharis barely managed to catch her wrist before the knife scraped off his armor.

Duke Leddan seemed equally disinclined to be murdered in his own bedroom without a struggle. He glared daggers into Noll's masked face, and his left hand scrabbled along the carpeted floor in search of anything he could use as a weapon.

Aravon stepped on the Duke's wrist, trapping it in place yet not applying pressure sufficient to cause pain. The man was, after all, a member of the Prince's Council and ruler of Oldcrest. They owed him respect right up until the moment he proved to be the traitor.

"Do your worst!" spat Duke Leddan. "I will not cower or beg for my life."

"We have not come for your life, Duke Leddan." Aravon pitched his tone deeper than normal, trusting the mask to muffle his voice. He'd met the Duke enough times that the man could recognize him—hence the masks, a necessary part of the deceit Duke Dyrund sold to the world. "Not unless you are in league with the enemy."

"In league with—" Duke Leddan's graying eyebrows rose and his ruddy face purpled with anger. "You dare accuse me of being a traitor?"

"If the codpiece fits…" Noll growled and pressed the dagger harder against the Duke's throat.

Aravon lifted his boot from Duke Leddan's wrist and crouched beside the man. "Silver Break Mine."

The Duke's expression never wavered. "What of it?"

"How much did they pay you for the secret of its existence?"

"Pay me?" Now confusion twisted Duke Leddan's face. "Who?"

"How much?" Aravon repeated the question.

Fire blazed in Duke Leddan's green eyes. "I don't know what you think you know, but—"

Aravon seized the man's face in a gloved hand and gripped tight. "*How much?!*" he roared.

"Not a Keeper-damned copper bit!" Duke Leddan met his gaze without hesitation. "Because I didn't sell any secrets. And definitely not to our enemies!"

"Your duchy is failing," Aravon growled. "Farmland is going fallow, your crops are withering, and your people are going hungry. All that silver from the mines could go a long way toward feeding the hungry here in Oldcrest."

Duke Dyrund had made that much clear: Duke Leddan cared for his people, and he'd only sell the secret of Silver Break Mine to fill his coffers to care for them. Yet that reasoning made him no less treacherous.

"Yes, it would!" Duke Leddan glared defiance into his eyes. "But that doesn't mean I'm a coward or traitor."

"You're telling me you wouldn't do whatever it took to care for those under your rule?" Aravon demanded.

"Damned right I would!" Duke Leddan growled. "Which is why I sold the better part of ten thousand acres to the Nyslians."

Aravon cocked his head. "The Nyslians?" The men of Nysl came from the mainland of Einan, far to the north.

"To grow grapes for their icewines." Duke Leddan's jaw clenched. "A deal that drives a dagger into the heart of every one of my ancestors who fought to claim Oldcrest, to build this very fortress. Yet times are changing, and I must change with it." The anger surged in his eyes once more. "But hear me when I say I would *never* sell anything to the enemy. Not one square foot of bog land, and absolutely not the truth of Silver Break Mine. A mine where *my people* were working!"

That was new information to Aravon. Duke Dyrund had told him Princelanders were mining alongside the *Eyr* clan, but that was all. No mention of what parts of the Princelands the miners had come from.

"Now," snarled Duke Leddan, "if you're done insulting me and accusing me of treachery, you'd better get your damned hands off my wife before—"

His words trailed off into a cough as Noll dropped a pinch of Sleeping Lily powder into his open mouth. A second later, Duke Leddan's head slumped against the woven woolen carpet, eyes closed in slumber.

Aravon stood and glanced at Zaharis. The Secret Keeper had removed his hand from Duchess Leddan's mouth long enough to dose her with Sleeping Lily as well. The gray-haired woman slept peacefully, dagger still clutched in her right hand.

"Orders, Captain?" Belthar rumbled from his place at the door.

"Down and out," Aravon replied without hesitation. "Once we're over the wall, we send a message to Duke Dyrund."

"You believe him?" Noll glanced down at the sleeping Leddan.

"I do." Aravon nodded. There'd been no deceit or treachery in the Duke's eyes, only genuine outrage at the accusation. "He's not the one who sold out Silver Break Mine."

Noll cocked his head. "So if not him, then who?" He rammed his dagger home in its sheath. "You saw the same thing I did. No tracks, no signs of a fight at all. The only people capable of something like that are the bloody Eirdkilrs. They couldn't have just stumbled across it, so how in the Keeper's twisted teats did they find out?"

Aravon had no answer for that question, yet he knew without a doubt that if they didn't unmask the real traitor soon, many more Princelanders would suffer. The wrong secrets whispered into Eirdkilr ears could not only harm the Princelands—they could turn the tide of battle against the Legion and open the way for the bloodthirsty barbarians to conquer all of Fehl.

Chapter Three

Aravon's hand dropped to his sword as a figure materialized from the shadows of the alleyway.

"Easy. It's me." Colborn spoke in a low, calm voice, his movements unhurried. "No one saw any of you leave the way you came in, and I left no trace of our presence."

Aravon nodded. "Good." His mind hadn't stopped puzzling over the mystery of Silver Break Mine since he left Duke Leddan's bedchamber. If the Duke of Oldcrest wasn't behind it, someone else had betrayed the mine's location—and the Princelands. Duke Dyrund needed to know as soon as possible so he could have his people look into the matter.

That meant waiting for Skathi and Snarl to rejoin them. Aravon had already scrawled out a short note—*"Leddan innocent"*—on a piece of the special parchment given him for sending messages. Much as he hated to be parted from the Enfield, Snarl was their only way of getting word to the Duke at once. The little fox creature's wings covered ground far faster than Aravon, even on one of Duke Dyrund's magnificent *Kostarasar* chargers. Snarl could get word to the Duke at Wolfden Castle within the space of a few hours, rather than days.

A quiet *flapping* of wings from above warned Aravon a moment before Snarl's weight crashed into his chest, knocking him off-balance. Aravon grimaced as his back struck the wall behind him, though he managed to both stay upright and catch the Enfield in his arms.

Snarl gave a happy yip and licked his mask and neck with a rough, wet tongue. The little creature saw Aravon as the alpha of his pack, and at just a few months old, Snarl was still over-exuberant in his affection. If Skyclaw, Duke Dyrund's Enfield, was any indication, the vivacity would diminish with maturity.

Most of the time, Aravon was happy for Snarl's eager antics. Snarl had a way of cheering him up in the gloomiest circumstances—the Enfield had been Aravon's source of comfort after Draian's death. Now, however, they were on a mission, so there was no time to play.

Aravon opened the metal tube secured to Snarl's collar, removed the cap, and inserted the scroll. Pulling out the strip of cloth covered in the Duke's scent, he held it up to the Enfield's nose. "Find the Duke, Snarl." Even wrapped in waxed parchment, the cloth would soon lose its scent. The Enfield would always recognize the trinkets attached to the cloth—a golden disc for Duke Dyrund, and another silver disc to direct him to Lord Eidan.

Snarl gave the fabric a little sniff, yipped quietly, and flapped his wings as if eager to be off. Those wings, grown larger and stronger in the last few weeks, batted Aravon's face with stiff feathers like those on an eagle. Grimacing, Aravon lifted the bone whistle that hung around his neck, placed it to his lips, and gave a short, quiet blow.

At the sound, the Enfield's sharp avian claws flexed in excitement and dug into Aravon's hand, and his furry face broadened into a vulpine grin. Paws scrabbled on armor as Snarl found footing on Aravon's shoulder and, with a single bound, leapt high into the air. The *flapping* sound quickly grew fainter as Snarl sped upward, cleared the nearby rooftops, and disappeared into the night.

"He's a good one to have watching over you." Skathi's voice greeted him from the opposite end of the alley. The archer hurried through the shadows toward them. "Though he's getting damned heavy."

"I'll say!" Aravon snorted. The Enfield's collision with his chest had set his still-healing wounds throbbing. "Anyone see you leave?"

Skathi shook her head. "Guards are still out cold in their watchtowers, and the ones in the courtyard are too busy getting warm to bother with checking up on them. We've got at least another half-hour before—"

The peal of an alarm bell shattered the stillness of the night and cut off her words. The ringing grew louder, echoed by shouts from within Ironcastle Keep's walls.

"Damn it!" Noll whirled on Zaharis. "I thought you said they'd be out for an hour."

Zaharis threw up his hands. *"Didn't have much chance to test it, now did I?"*

20

"That doesn't matter," Aravon interjected. "That alarm's going to have every guard in Ironcastle on the alert. And the six of us looking like this aren't exactly going to blend in."

"Good thing we've got lots of back alleys to get lost in," Belthar rumbled. "I've got an idea."

Aravon raised an eyebrow, an expression lost beneath his leather mask, but he had no time to indulge his curiosity. They had mere minutes before Duke Leddan's guards flooded the city. He had no desire to kill innocent Princelanders, especially those just doing their jobs.

"Go!" he said. "Anything happens to split us up, you don't stop running until you get back to the horses!"

His five companions nodded and, with Belthar taking the lead, set off at a loping run through the alleys of Oldcrest.

Aravon had always had a good head for directions, yet within minutes, he found himself losing all sense of surroundings as they raced through one alleyway after another. The back alleys of Ironcastle seemed utterly chaotic, with buildings thrown up haphazard. Crumbling shanties stood beside three-story stone buildings, and muddy alleys suddenly turned to larger, paved-stone streets that ran for only a few hundred yards before returning to muck-coated ground. Were it not for the occasional light of a candle or lamp streaming through open windows, Aravon would have run into houses, warehouses, and wooden shacks that seemed to spring up out of nowhere.

Yet Belthar moved without hesitation, turning down one muddy lane, darting along a side street, cutting back through a narrow gap between collapsing houses. He struggled to squeeze his enormous shoulders through two walls that had bowed inward, sagging beneath the weight of their thatched grass roofs. His head clipped a faded wooden sign that dangled from a fraying rope, eliciting a growled curse.

Colborn moved on the big man's heels, with Zaharis and Aravon behind then, Noll and Skathi in the back. A driving sense of urgency pushed them on; at any moment, they could be spotted by the guards. Already, a chorus of whistles and shouts filled Ironcastle, surrounding them on all sides. The baying of hounds filled the night.

Yet, as they followed down one side street and darted into a side alley, the sounds of pursuit grew closer. They'd barely taken ten steps before Belthar skidded to a halt. "Damn it!" he growled.

21

What had once likely been a thoroughfare was now surrounded by small stone buildings thrown up in a hurry to expand the city. Now, surrounded by solid walls, they had no way out.

"Back!" Belthar raced past them, back the way they'd come.

Straight toward the sound of hounds, shrieking whistles, and shouting guards, the light streaming from torches and lanterns.

Aravon's eyebrows shot up. *What in the bloody hell is he doing?* He opened his mouth to shout at Belthar—he couldn't let the big man attack the Duke's guards. They had to find another way out, a way that didn't leave bodies on the streets of Ironcastle.

With surprising speed for a man his size, Belthar hurtled down a narrow alleyway—one Aravon hadn't seen tucked between two wooden buildings. Instantly, Aravon was on the move, racing after the big man, the rest of his small company in tow. His eyes locked on the nearby intersection as the cries of alarm and the light of torches drew closer.

Aravon threw himself into the shadows of the alley just as the first of the guards appeared around the corner. He didn't slow, didn't stop to check if the others had gotten away clean. None of them could afford even a moment's delay in the cramped space between buildings. They just had to keep running, keep following Belthar and hope the big man could find a way out.

"This way!"

The shout sent Aravon's heart plummeting. The guards had spotted them.

Chapter Four

"They're headed into the marketplace!" a guard shouted from the street behind Aravon and his comrades.

"We'll cut them off!" came the answering cry.

Aravon sucked in a breath as he burst out of the alley and found himself in a wide, circular marketplace surrounded by solid stone buildings. The wood and stone stalls were shuttered and dark, but there was only one avenue leading in and out of the market.

"What's the plan, Belthar?" Skathi shouted. She was on the big man's heels, her bow gripped in one hand and an arrow in the other. "This looks like a dead end!"

"It's supposed to," Belthar called back.

To Aravon's surprise, Belthar never slowed, but charged through the marketplace, straight toward one of the stone buildings on the south side of the circular plaza. Yet instead of racing up the stairs to the heavy door, he headed toward the building's western edge—where its wall met the eastern wall of the neighboring house. Aravon drew in a breath as the big man pressed something in the walls and a narrow gap appeared where there had been solid stone a heartbeat before.

"This way!" Belthar stepped aside and motioned for them to enter.

A tunnel? Aravon had no time to question; the sound of the guards' whistles and the light of their torches brightened the main avenue, flooding the marketplace.

Skathi darted into the tunnel first, followed by Colborn and Zaharis. Aravon went next, ducking low to avoid scraping his head on the low stone ceiling. He cast a glance back in time to find Noll scrambling in after him, then darkness fell around them as Belthar's bulk filled the tunnel.

"Wait!" Belthar hissed.

Aravon froze in a half-crouch, leaning on the narrow stone walls of the tunnel. His heart hammered a rapid beat against his ribs as he waited, listening for any indication the guards had found them.

"Where in the bloody hell'd they go?" came a guard's voice, muffled by whatever Belthar had used to seal the tunnel behind them.

"Spread out, search every house in the area!" another guard snapped, a tone of command to his words. "They can't have gotten far!"

A grin broadened Aravon's face. *We'll see about that!*

"Go," Belthar rumbled in a low voice.

Aravon's legs soon burned from walking in a half-crouch, but he hadn't gone more than thirty yards before the tunnel widened and the ground sloped downward, with the low ceiling rising above his head. Ahead of him, a faint glimmer of red and blue light filled the tunnel. The oil burning in Zaharis' alchemical quickfire globes lit up a narrow passage of reinforced stone and wooden beams as wide as Aravon's outstretched arms and tall enough for all but Belthar to stand comfortably.

What in the fiery hell is this? The question pierced Aravon's mind. The hard-packed earth floor sloped gently downward and disappeared into the darkness far, far ahead of the faint glow of Zaharis' alchemical lights. *And how did Belthar know it was here?*

He turned to ask Belthar about the tunnel, only to find the big man shouldering his way past. "Keep going," the big man rumbled. "Can't stop. Don't know if the guards know about this, but we can't risk it."

Without waiting for an answer, he kept squeezing past Noll and Colborn until he reached Zaharis and Skathi at the front. He kept a steady pace, as if hurrying would keep the others from asking the same questions burning within Aravon.

Less than five minutes passed before a gust of fresh, chilly night air drifted up the passage toward them. Fifty yards ahead of Belthar in the lead, Aravon caught sight of the starry night sky beyond the mouth of the tunnel.

As he emerged from the tunnel last, he found himself on the grassy plains a short distance southeast of Oldcrest. The lights of the city lay far behind, with the shouts, whistles, and the baying of hounds faint, muffled by the houses that blocked the guards from view. When Aravon glanced around, he found the tunnel had let out far enough from both the southern and eastern highways into Oldcrest that it was invisible to any travelers, concealed from the city by the hill into which it had been dug.

Skathi removed her mask and whirled on Belthar. "What is this tunnel, and how did you know it was there?" Suspicion etched plain on her expression.

Belthar shook his head. "I-I didn't *know,* exactly. I…" He hesitated. "I just took a gamble and got lucky."

Aravon recognized the evasiveness in the big man's answer. Like everyone else in their small company, it seemed Belthar had bits of his past he didn't want his comrades to know about, at least not yet. It took time for soldiers to open up to each other. If Belthar didn't want to share this tidbit, Aravon and the others could respect his privacy. But there was one thing they all needed to know.

"Will the guards find the tunnel?" he demanded. "Are they coming after us?"

"No. At least, I don't think so. Not unless they use the hounds, but even then…" Uncertainty echoed in Belthar's voice. "We'd have heard them by now."

Aravon nodded. That confirmed what he'd suspected when the guards sounded surprised to have lost their quarry. Oldcrest, like all cities in the Princelands, had its fair share of secrets and mysteries.

"You didn't answer my question!" demanded Skathi. She stabbed a finger into the big man's chest. "How. Did. *You.* Know?"

Belthar recoiled from the intensity in her eyes and voice, yet he seemed unwilling to give up the one thing that would quell her distrust: the truth.

"Enough, Skathi." Colborn's quiet words rang with a note of command. "We're out of Ironcastle, but Duke Leddan's going to be spitting fire and pissing venom when he wakes up. Best to put some distance between us before then." He turned to Noll. "You remember where we left the horses?"

Noll removed his mask for the sole purpose of shooting the half-Fehlan a withering glare. "No, I've suddenly gone and turned into a forgetful idiot in the last twenty minutes."

25

"Then get hoofing," Colborn snarled. "Take Skathi and Zaharis and get the horses ready. The rest of us will follow once we're certain we're not being followed."

Noll opened his mouth to retort, but seemed to think better of it. "Yes, *sir*." Rolling his eyes, he replaced his mask and slipped off into the darkness. Skathi shot one last suspicious glance at Belthar before following. Zaharis never removed his mask, but he seemed unperturbed by this latest discovery. A man so accustomed to keeping a multitude of secrets likely expected others to do the same.

Colborn watched the others leave, then turned to Aravon. "I'm going to scout the way back to the highway, make sure it's clear." The look in his eyes held a depth of meaning; there was no need for any scouting, but he recognized that Aravon needed time to speak to Belthar alone. As the Lieutenant, it was his job to make sure his Captain got the chance to take care of his men.

Aravon shot him an appreciative nod. Once again, the half-Fehlan Lieutenant proved his worth, not only as a warrior, but as an officer. Other men might have needled Belthar for details, which would cause the big man to dig in his heels even more. Or, they could have tried to *order* the big man to divulge, an act that would drive a rift between them. The situation needed delicate handling, and Colborn had set Aravon up so he could do the heavy lifting, as expected of the commander.

Belthar's eyes followed the retreating figure of the Lieutenant, then turned to face Aravon. "Captain, I—"

Aravon spoke in a quiet voice, but his words were edged in steel. "There's only one thing I need to know, Belthar." Slowly, he untied the thongs that held his leather mask in place. "But I need you to look me in the face as you answer."

Slowly, Belthar removed his mask as well. His square jaw was set in a stubborn cast, a shadow behind his eyes. Yet he met Aravon's gaze without wavering.

"We all have our pasts," Aravon said, his tone softening a fraction. "Some we try to run from, others we try to forget. But the past always catches up with us, one way or another. So my question is this: will yours affect our mission?"

Belthar didn't hesitate. "No." He shook his head. "I…I left it all behind me, a long time ago." His expression darkened and his fingers toyed absentmindedly with the braided leather thong on his wrist. A faraway look flashed in his eyes, and he seemed lost in memories for a long second.

Finally, he snapped out of it, and a wry smile tugged at his lips. "And, like you, I'm dead, remember?" He lifted the leather mask with its ornately-tooled features of a snarling greatwolf.

A stab of pain and longing burrowed into Aravon's heart, but he pushed away the memory of Mylena, Rolyn, and Adilon. Now wasn't the time to dwell on his family—a family that believed he had died with the Sixth Company.

"To the world, perhaps." Aravon stepped closer and rested a hand on the big man's shoulder. "But not to us. Until this is done, we're all we've got. Whatever happened, whoever you were, there's no judgement here. Remember that, and remember that we all need to trust each other if we're to make this work."

Belthar held Aravon's gaze, mingled reluctance, fear, and gratitude in his eyes. Aravon had seen that in his father's eyes before; General Traighan had spent his life at war, and he wrestled with more than his share of inner demons. But the General had kept everything bottled up, until alcohol and sorrow over his wife's death brought it out in a torrent of vitriol and enmity—a torrent he had unleashed on his son time and again until Aravon was old enough to join the Legion and escape his father.

He couldn't let Belthar go down the same path.

"Promise me, Belthar," Aravon said, gripping Belthar's massive shoulder tighter. "Promise that when the time comes, when you feel ready, you'll trust us."

Belthar nodded. "I-I will, Captain." The guarded look remained, yet Belthar seemed to relax slightly, the tension draining from his shoulders.

"Good." Aravon clapped the big man on the arm. "We trust each other with our lives. It's important to know who we're trusting."

Belthar swallowed, but managed a jerky nod. "I understand."

As if on cue, Colborn's dark figure appeared in the moonless night, slipping across the rolling plains toward them. A moment later, the quiet *thump, thump* of horses' hooves on grass-covered earth echoed from behind. The mounted Noll, Skathi, and Zaharis reached them at the same time as Colborn. The Agrotora had replaced her mask, but Aravon caught the glint of suspicion in the gaze she shot Belthar. Noll and Zaharis seemed far less perturbed and said nothing as Aravon, Colborn, and Belthar mounted up.

27

The chargers, bred specially by Duke Dyrund himself, had broad withers, deep chests, with muscled shoulders and long, powerful legs. Their double coat would keep them warm in even the coldest Fehlan winter, and their name—*Kostarasar*--was Fehlan for "fleet-footed". After weeks spent riding, there was no doubt in Aravon's mind that they were the fastest horses on Fehl, perhaps even the mainland itself. Horses worth a fortune, entrusted to them by the man who had recruited them for his special company.

Aravon replaced his leather mask—it had the added perk of keeping out the night's chill and road dust as well as concealing his features. *"Lead the way,"* he signed to Noll. *"To Wolfden Castle."*

With a nod, Noll dug his heels into his horse's flanks, and the beast leapt into motion. Riding at night on the grassy plains could be dangerous; even with the horse's excellent night vision, any number of hidden obstacles—from gopher holes to sudden drop-offs in the terrain—could snap a horse's leg or cause them to stumble and throw their rider. They'd have to keep their pace slow and steady, riding toward the highway that led away from Ironcastle to the east.

Aravon glanced back at Belthar, but a wall had gone up in the big man's eyes. Belthar had told him as much as he was willing to for the moment. It would take Aravon time to pry more details from him; for now, he'd have to leave well enough alone. They'd have enough time on the road to Icespire—or wherever the Duke wanted them next—to dig deeper.

Dawn found them riding hard up the northern highway, fifty miles away from Ironcastle. Only then did Aravon call for a halt, certain they were far enough from Duke Leddan's city that they had no fear of pursuit.

They made camp on the leeward side of a sharp hill that concealed them from any traffic on the highway. In silence, they spread out their bedrolls and shared a cold meal of trail rations. Skathi's gaze fixed on Belthar, suspicion burning in her eyes. Colborn, too, seemed curious, but after a single questioning glance at Aravon, he let the matter rest.

Belthar alone forgot to remove his mask—forgot, or refused. Used it as a shield to protect the secrets he wanted to hide from the rest of them.

Zaharis, however, seemed unperturbed. He sat hunched over one of his many books, pausing every few minutes to jot down some note or annotation in his illegible Secret Keeper script.

Noll's face was a mask of contemplation. Instead of his usual banter, he simply sat in silence. Aravon didn't know if he was occupied with thoughts of Belthar or the outcome of their mission.

If it wasn't the Duke that betrayed the presence of Silver Break Mine, who was it?

There was always a chance that the Eirdkilrs had simply stumbled upon it, yet not even Aravon could believe that. Not after seeing the camp perfectly still, undisturbed by any sign of struggle. There had been no bodies, no burned tents, not even a drop of blood. Simply…nothing. Silence. Emptiness.

And that odd note in the overseer's journal. *"Why does it glow?"*

Aravon had no idea what it meant, and without the man himself, no way to find out. That only made the total absence of any Eyrr or Princelander miners and guards there even eerier.

The quiet *flapping* of wings shattered the silence. Aravon's eyes darted upward and he scanned the brightening sky for the Enfield. Snarl's orange and white-furred body grew larger with every passing second, his wings spread wide as he soared through the glorious hues of pink and blue filling the dawn sky.

Aravon braced himself for impact as the Enfield plummeted toward him. Though Snarl was growing larger, he still hadn't mastered landing. The weight of the little creature slammed into his chest, but this time he was ready and managed to stay upright.

"Hey, Snarl!" Aravon scratched the scruff of the Enfield's neck, and Snarl licked his dusty face. "Let's see what you brought us."

Removing the cap of Snarl's collar tube, he plucked out the tightly-rolled parchment. The message, printed in Duke Dyrund's neat handwriting, was succinct. *"Camp Marshal."*

The word sent a little chill down Aravon's spine. The message gave no explanation as to what the Duke wanted or why he re-directed them to Camp Marshal, and that only added to Aravon's curiosity.

Whatever the reason, if their path led to the clandestine camp in the marshes near Wolfden Castle, that meant the matter was something both important and of the utmost secrecy.

Chapter Five

The shout of "Riders!" echoing from the wooden watchtower beside Camp Marshal's gate brought a strange tightness to Aravon's stomach. Everything from the heavy gate to white-haired Clem the watchman to the marshlands surrounding the secret camp brought back memories.

Memories of mourning the men of Garnet Battalion's Sixth Company and struggling with the burden of guilt over their deaths. Of pain as his shattered bones and torn flesh healed. Of battling with the Duke's request, his question of Aravon's loyalty—to the Legion of Heroes he served or his home in the Princelands. Of meeting his companions for the first time, training beside them, becoming a company not just of fellow warriors, but soldiers with a common goal.

And of Draian, the Mender who had nursed him back to health. The same Mender who had trained beside them, and died fighting with Duke Dyrund.

Once again, the weight settled on Aravon's shoulders. He knew he'd done everything in his power to keep Draian safe; the Mender was just one more casualty in the brutal Eirdkilr Wars. Yet that didn't make it easier to ride through the gate and into the encampment where he'd helped turn Draian from a healer into a killer—a transformation that ultimately led to his death.

Noll, riding in the lead, reined in his mount just inside the gate and leapt from his saddle. The little scout was born to sit a horse and appeared no worse for the last two days of travel. Aside from the road dust that covered them all from helmeted head to steel-booted toe and the exhaustion of weeks without more than four hours of rest a night, of course.

The others of Aravon's small company moved more slowly, fatigue dragging at their muscles as they drew their horses to a stop, dismounted, and removed their masks. They hadn't had a proper night of sleep since they first rode out of Camp Marshal almost a month earlier. Every one bore wounds in various stages of healing, and the ceaseless travel had taken a heavy toll on each of them.

A shadow flashed over Aravon's head, and a little figure with orange fur and dark brown wings swooped toward the obstacles erected in the middle of the training field. Snarl landed on the climbing wall with a little yipping bark and sat proudly grinning down at Camp Marshal. Despite his exhaustion, Aravon couldn't help smiling at the young Enfield's exuberance. *At least one of us is excited to be here, however long we stay.*

He suspected they wouldn't be getting much time to rest. Duke Dyrund would only call them here and risk Camp Marshal's discovery if it was truly important.

"Welcome back, Captain." Aravon turned to find Clem, the grizzled guardsman, grinning up at him. The gray-haired man's smile revealed five teeth—it seemed he'd lost one in the weeks since their departure, though his single eye appeared as sharp as ever. "I'll see to your mounts, sir. Polus'll be wanting to get his hands on your weapons, make sure everything's in order."

"There's no chance he'll spare us the lecture on proper maintenance, is there?" Aravon asked.

Clem shook his white-haired head. "Not a chance."

Aravon grimaced. "Give me a suicidal ride into enemy territory any day over a blacksmith's tongue-lashing." Every man in the Legion of Heroes had to endure the griping of master craftsmen bemoaning the pitiful state of their armor and weapons—a rite of passage, of sorts, but one that never grew more enjoyable. "Thankfully, command comes with a few perks."

He turned to Belthar and Noll. "You two, get our weapons to the smithy. Make sure Polus gives them a thorough going-over."

Noll groaned. "Really, Captain? A night ride, no breakfast, *and* we have to put up with the smith's whining? That's cruel, even for you."

Belthar was too tired to protest; he simply climbed down from his horse and set about collecting their weapons: Colborn's Fehlan-style longsword and shield, Zaharis' spiked mace, and the sword that had once belonged to Draian. The big man winced when Aravon drew out the two halves of his spear. A blow of Hrolf Hrungnir's greatsword had shattered the shaft in the middle, though the Odarian steel spearhead and the extendable iron spike built into the spear's butt were still good. Aravon was glad someone else would bear the brunt of Polus' harangue.

As Belthar and Noll carried their armfuls of weapons toward the smithy at the back of the stone barracks, the front door opened and three figures stepped into the noon daylight.

"Aravon." A tired smile brightened Duke Dyrund's face. "You made good time." Taller than Aravon himself, the Duke had the broad shoulders and chest of a career soldier, blue eyes gleaming with intelligence, and only the first hints of gray and white dusting his hair and beard.

"Of course, Your Grace." Aravon gave a respectful nod. "Anything important enough to take you away from Icespire or Wolfden Castle has to be important."

"Important is right." The Duke's expression grew grim. "And if Lord Eidan's reports are to be believed, I fear things will only grow worse before we can take action."

Aravon's eyes shifted to the lean, well-dressed man in the Duke's shadow. Lord Eidan looked every inch the Duke's aide, from his hooked nose and prominent cheekbones to his permanent frown and his long, slim fingers.

"Captain, I wish I had better news." The only oddity was Lord Eidan's voice, which had the deep, rich boom of a career Drill Sergeant. "I'm certain you are all exhausted from your travels, but the situation must be addressed at once."

"Of course." Aravon inclined his head.

"And when that is done," said the third figure, a tall, broad-shouldered man with the heavy features and braided blond hair and beard of a Fehlan, "I will see to your wounds."

Rangvaldr had been the *Seiomenn,* or "shaman", of Bjornstadt, but when Chief Ailmaer of the Eyrr refused to send aid to the embattled Legion, he'd chosen to leave his home to take up the fight. With the Duke's blessing, he had joined their small company. A welcome addition, if an unusual one. He'd proven his skill in battle and bore the scars to prove it, yet his true value lay in his abilities as a healer.

Around the *Seiomenn's* neck hung a pendant set with a brilliant blue gemstone—an Eyrr holy stone. Aravon had seen Rangvaldr bring a man back from the brink of certain death with that amulet. He didn't understand how it worked—the Fehlan hadn't explained the "magic" of how it healed, only that his faith brought forth the gods' power stored within the stone—but it was enough to know that it did. With their Mender slain, they could use a healer.

"Thank you, Rangvaldr." Aravon's smile held genuine warmth. During the few days he'd spent in Bjornstadt and traveling alongside the *Seiomenn*, he'd come to like the man. Like him, Rangvaldr had sacrificed everything to be here, to help fight the Eirdkilrs alongside him. That earned him a great deal of respect as well. "Start with Belthar and Colborn. They need it the most."

"All due respect, Captain, but you should be tended to first." Colborn's face took on the stubborn, determined look that characterized his nature perfectly. "I'll wait my turn."

"Belthar first, then," Aravon insisted. "He's gone with Noll to the smithy. He'll definitely be needing some tending to after one of Polus' dressing-downs."

Rangvaldr's smile broadened. "Of course, Captain." He gave a Legion salute—surprisingly crisp, his form precise, for a Fehlan—and strode around the stone barracks toward the smithy.

"Come, Captain, Lieutenant." Duke Dyrund beckoned for them to follow, his expression somber. "We have much to discuss, and little time left."

A heavy dread settled in Aravon's stomach as he fell in step behind the Duke. The last time Duke Dyrund had looked so solemn, an army of fourteen hundred Eirdkilrs had been preparing to assault Gallows Garrison. They'd barely arrived in time to prevent wholesale slaughter.

What could it be this time?

He followed Duke Dyrund into the barracks. Made of brick and stone, the building was solid with a hint of chill that felt drafty for the breeze blowing through the windows. Nine doors flanked the long, straight hallway. It was to the first of those that Duke Dyrund led him.

Nothing in the War Room had changed since Aravon last stood in the chamber. Someone, likely Clem, had dusted off the heavy oaken table, displaying the detailed topographic map carved into the surface in perfect clarity.

Yet, before Aravon's gaze rose from the map to the heavily-laden shelves that lined the wall, he caught sight of a figure standing hunched over the table. His eyes flew wide. Even with his face downcast and his eyes locked on the map, there was no mistaking the familiar features of Prince Cedenas Toran, Prince of Icespire.

"My Prince!" Aravon dropped to one knee and bowed his head. Beside him, Colborn did likewise.

"Come, Captain." Prince Toran's voice was relaxed, almost familiar. "Only the living need kneel before their ruler."

Aravon's brow furrowed, and confusion flashed through his mind for a long moment before he understood the Prince's meaning. As Duke Dyrund had explained, he was dead to everyone outside these walls.

"Of course, My Prince." He stood, though he fought back the urge to salute.

Prince Cedenas Toran stood a few inches shorter than him and narrower in the shoulder, yet had the strong build of a man accustomed to fighting. Older than Aravon by a decade, he exuded an air of confidence and command that not even a blind man would miss. On the few formal occasions Aravon had crossed the Prince's path, he'd been awed by the authority that rang in the man's voice, the way he dominated his surroundings without being overbearing or arrogant. A ruler Aravon had been honored to serve, and one who had surpassed all of his ancestors at advancing the conditions in the Princelands.

Prince Toran seemed to size him up for a long moment, his lips pursed in contemplation. "How long has it been since last we crossed paths?"

Aravon's brow furrowed. "Six years, Sire."

"Of course." The Prince's lips quirked into a smile. "That horrendous soiree at Lord Kytur's, shortly after you earned your Lieutenant's commission."

Aravon's eyebrows rose a fraction. *He remembers?* He had been just one more junior Legion officer among those brought in to entertain the noblemen and women—the women, especially—of Icespire.

"I never did thank you for knocking Lord Achdan on his arse that night, did I?" Prince Toran's smile grew. "Almost made the evening tolerable, the way that boor kept blathering on about his amorous conquests." He sighed. "Some men just don't know how to hold their tongues."

Aravon struggled to mask his surprise. He hadn't expected the Prince to know his name, much less remember so many details. Yet when Duke Dyrund had recruited him, he'd mentioned that Prince Toran had requested him specifically. Perhaps it had something to do with the fact that he was the son of Traighan, one of the Princelands' most celebrated Generals.

35

"And now, it seems you're doing much the same with the Eirdkilrs." The Prince's smile grew sly. "Sammael has filled me in on your actions at Gallows and Anvil Garrisons, as well as the battle for Bjornstadt. I had to come in person and meet the men who have given everything. To look them in the eyes and let them know of my deep gratitude for their actions." He turned to Colborn. "Not just those born to the Princelands, but *all* the brave soldiers fighting to end this war."

From the corner of his eye, Aravon saw Colborn stiffen, a flush of color rising to his cheeks.

Prince Toran stepped toward the Lieutenant. "I know your father, and I have little doubt that being his son held its share of…challenges."

The muscles in Colborn's jaw worked, yet he remained silent.

"It is not my place to apologize for him, but I will offer my sincere thanks for your choices." He held out his hand to Colborn. "And the promise that when this is all over, we will speak of your place in the Legion and the Princelands."

Colborn's eyes widened a fraction and he shook Prince Toran's hand. "Thank you, My Prince." His voice resonated with the same respect Aravon had heard when Colborn first called him "Captain".

The Prince released Colborn's hand, then turned to Duke Dyrund. "While you fill in our Captain and Lieutenant, I will go and speak to the others. They, too, deserve the gratitude of all the Princelands."

"Of course." Duke Dyrund gave a little bow. "I trust you will join us for dinner? While I doubt our simple fare can rival the feasts of Icespire, I'm certain we can cook up something half-edible."

Prince Toran chuckled. "Make it fully edible and I shall be there." He turned to Aravon and Colborn. "Until later, gentlemen." Turning, he strode from the War Room and closed the door behind him.

Long seconds passed as Aravon struggled to comprehend what had just happened. The Prince, here in Camp Marshal, all for the express purpose of speaking with them! Aravon had accepted the mission without expectation of gratitude or recognition, but knowing that Prince Toran cared enough to make the journey filled him with pride. Pride to call himself not just a Legionnaire, but also a Princelander.

The Duke's voice cut into his thoughts. "Much as I wish that was the *only* reason I summoned you here to Camp Marshal, there is a matter of great urgency we must discuss."

Aravon's momentary elation faded, and the Duke's solemn tone and dark expression brought reality crashing back down on him. "Of course," he said, steeling himself.

Duke Dyrund and Lord Eidan stepped toward the oaken table dominating the War Room, and Aravon and Colborn joined them in study of the map of Fehl carved into the table's surface. The details were breathtaking, with elevations for the mountains, depressions for valleys and canyons, even winding paths depicting the various rivers that snaked throughout the continent. The topographical map displayed everything from the northern tip of Icespire to the steep Sawtooth Mountains far to the south of Fehl.

"Thanks to your actions, we now hold Anvil Garrison." The Duke tapped the carved wooden figurine of a tower that represented the stone fort the Eirdkilrs had once occupied, and which Aravon had helped Jade Battalion drive out. "Gallows Garrison will be receiving reinforcements day after tomorrow, with half of Amethyst Battalion dividing their forces between Gallows and bolstering the four hundred of Garnet Battalion stationed at Scythe Garrison."

Aravon frowned down at the map. "What was the final casualty report from the Battle of Broken Canyon?"

Duke Dyrund turned to Lord Eidan with a questioning glance.

The nobleman flipped through a notebook for a moment and cleared his throat. "Between the cavalry, the Agrotorae, and the Legionnaires," he read, "six hundred and thirty-five slain, with two hundred and twelve wounded, eighty-seven mortally."

Aravon forced himself not to think about the pale, lifeless faces of the men that had fought beside him at Broken Canyon—doing that would only bring back the weight that dragged on his shoulders, the burden of command. Instead, he occupied his mind by doing quick sums, losing himself in the cold calculation of mathematics. With half of Amethyst Battalion, Commander Oderus had more than a thousand soldiers spread between Anvil and Gallows Garrison, with an additional eight hundred or more stationed a hundred miles north at Scythe Garrison. Months ago, before Hrolf Hrungnir had attacked along the Eastmarch, that many men would have been excessive. Now, with the Eirdkilrs potentially planning to assault Eyrr lands, it could prove too few.

"The good news," Duke Dyrund continued, "is that the assaults on Anvil and Gallows Garrisons appear to be nothing more than the actions of one Eirdkilr chieftain."

"Hrolf Hrungnir," Aravon growled. The leader of the crimson-cloaked *Blodhundr,* the Eirdkilr who had ambushed and killed every man of Sixth Company—save for Noll and Captain Aravon himself.

The Duke nodded and removed the blue-painted piece representing Hrungnir from the table. "With him eliminated, the east is once again quiet. Jade and Amethyst Battalions have strict orders to monitor the surrounding Eyrr and Jarnleikr lands, and we will never again be caught unaware by a force of Eirdkilrs attacking in the east."

Though Duke Dyrund's voice rang with confidence, Aravon knew they had nowhere near enough Legionnaires to properly patrol or watch all of eastern Fehl. Yet with the majority of the battles taking place on western Fehl, there were only so many men to pull away from the front lines.

"With Hrolf Hrungnir's failure in the east," the Duke went on, "it appears the Eirdkilrs are ramping up their efforts in the west." His finger traced along the map toward the Westmarch, the broad highway that stretched from Icespire all the way along the western half of Fehl toward Snowpass Keep in the Sawtooth Mountains—the jagged, near-impassable mountain range that was the only thing preventing the Eirdkilrs from flooding Fehl wholesale.

"They have redoubled their attacks on the Bulwark and Dagger Garrison, forcing us to commit more troops to those strongholds."

The two named fortresses straddled the Westmarch as far south as the Legion had ever gone, which put them closest to the enemy—the first line of defense against the Eirdkilrs.

Aravon frowned. "That makes no sense. Eirdkilrs don't bother with sieges, not unless they know they can win. No one's broken the Bulwark since it was founded, even back when the Eirdkilrs pushed us all the way north to the Chain."

"Correction," Lord Eidan interjected, once more clearing his throat before he spoke—a habit that hadn't grown less irritating since their last encounter. "The Eirdkilrs *didn't* bother with sieges. It seems they are once again shifting their tactics."

Aravon narrowed his eyes. "How?"

Duke Dyrund tapped on the two wooden fortress figurines for the Bulwark and Dagger Garrison. "The Eirdkilrs have laid siege to both, but it seems to be nothing more than a distraction to tie up Pearl, Sapphire, and Diamond Battalions." His finger indicated the Fehlan clan lands surrounding the two southernmost strongholds. "With the three battalions tied up holding the walls, the Eirdkilrs are free to roam the Fjall lands. And to launch attacks on the Deid."

Colborn stiffened, so slightly Aravon only noticed it because he happened to be looking in the Lieutenant's direction. Curiosity burned within Aravon, but he tucked it away until later.

"And what of the men in Hammer Garrison, Sentry Garrison, and Deepwater?" Aravon gestured toward the two northern fortresses. "Surely with Beryl, Emerald, and Moonstone Battalions holding the strongholds, there should be men to spare!"

"A month ago, I would have agreed with you." Duke Dyrund's expression grew grim. "But recent battles have taken their toll on all three garrisons. Emerald is at half-strength and a bout of the Bloody Flux has one in five men of Moonstone Battalion either ill or dying. The Menders and the Ministrants of the Bright Lady are doing what they can, but…" He shrugged. "There are no more to spare from the western garrisons."

Aravon's eyes traveled across the map, studying the arrangement of the Legion troops across Fehl. Each Legion battalion had one thousand Legionnaires, give or take a few dozen, a contingent of cavalry from two to four hundred strong, and a staff—including Menders, carters for supplies, and commissioned officers—of up to two hundred. With the companies of attached Agrotorae irregulars—typically between one and four hundred, depending on the terrain where they'd be stationed—a battalion at full strength had roughly fifteen hundred fighting men. That meant more than sixteen thousand Legionnaires, cavalry, and archers currently distributed around the continent.

Sixteen thousand men, and not one to spare. The thought added to his grim mood, which grew bleaker by the moment.

"The good news is that Onyx Battalion is back in commission." Duke Dyrund tapped on the black-painted shield figurine situated beside Icespire. "The last of the new recruits shipped in last fortnight."

39

Aravon grimaced. "Full of untrained, untested men." Even experienced Legions could crack in the face of an Eirdkilr charge; raw recruits were far more likely to break and flee.

The Duke inclined his head. "Perhaps, but those untrained, untested men may make all the difference when it comes to a battle. A battle the Prince and his Generals anticipated after the attacks on the eastern garrisons, which is why Onyx Battalion began the march ten days ago." He moved the black shield marker from Icespire toward Hammer Garrison, two hundred and thirty miles from the Chain. "If we send Onyx Battalion here, they can free up the veteran Moonstone Battalion to march south, toward Dagger Garrison and help break the siege. Once Dagger is freed—"

"They can help defend the Bulwark." Aravon nodded.

"Forgive me, Duke, but what about Deepwater?" Colborn put in. He tapped the fortress a hundred miles south of the Chain. "Shouldn't the recruits be as far from the front lines as possible?"

Duke Dyrund and Lord Eidan exchanged grim glances. "That is why I have called you here. You must know of the situation at Rivergate."

Aravon cocked an eyebrow. "Situation?" Rivergate was one of the sixteen fortresses that formed the Chain, the heavily-defended boundary between the Fehlan territories and the Princelands. Rivergate sat astride the Standelfr River, which ran from the Deid lands in the heart of Fehl northeast through the lands of the Smida and Jokull clans.

Duke Dyrund's expression darkened. "According to our last report, the Eirdkilrs have finally turned the Jokull against us. Rivergate is under siege, and there is nothing the Legion can do to help them."

Chapter Six

Aravon's eyebrows shot up. "Under siege? By the Jokull?"

The Jokull clan lived just south of the Chain, far to the west of Fehl. They alone of the northern Fehlan clans remained hostile to the Princelands. Even after the Legion conquered two-thirds of the continent, the Jokull remained a stubborn holdout, hiding in their swamps and marshes, launching raids against both Deepwater and Hammer Garrisons.

The Standelfr River provided both a natural defensive barrier against the Legion and a clear demarcation of their territory's limits. They had never expanded east beyond where the fast-flowing Feigr River joined the Standelfr, confining them to a tract of land less than two hundred miles wide and long—one of the smallest Fehlan clans, yet still the most fractious.

According to admittedly limited Legion knowledge, the Jokull had fewer than two thousand warriors, mostly raiders and reavers. The Jokull controlled much of Fehlan's western coast, their narrow longboats providing them access to both food and their Deid neighbors to the south. Westhaven, the Princelands' westernmost duchy, had built up a navy to counter Jokull raids, and after a series of fierce sea battles nearly four hundred years earlier, the Jokull had been reduced to little more than the occasional nuisance.

Rivergate had been built specifically to keep a watchful eye on the querulous clan. Situated on the southern side of the Standelfr River, it gave the Legion a toehold in Jokull land, a solid defensive stronghold to prevent the Jokull from crossing the river in their longboats and launching raids on Westhaven.

The thought of the Jokull—a clan of fishermen, marsh dwellers, and sea wolves—laying siege to a fortress the size of Rivergate seemed impossible to imagine. Yet the Duke's grim expression told him it was very real.

"Five days ago, the Jokull launched a surprise attack on Rivergate," Duke Dyrund said. "All twenty-three hundred of their warriors, it seems, with more than eight hundred Eirdkilrs supporting them."

Aravon's gut twisted. That made sense. The Jokull wouldn't besiege a fortress, but it seemed the Eirdkilrs' shift in tactics included an alliance with the hostile Fehlan clan and an attack on the Chain itself.

"In the course of battle, the combined Jokull and Eirdkilr forces managed to overrun Rivergate's outer wall." The Duke's expression darkened. "The people of Rivergate retreated to the inner keep, but the men of Topaz Battalion and Duke Westhaven's regulars sustained heavy casualties in their retreat. Less than eight hundred of our men remain, according to our intelligence." He glanced at Lord Eidan, who gave him a confirming nod.

Aravon sucked in a breath. "But if they stormed the outer wall, that means they've captured Rivergate Bridge!"

Rivergate Bridge provided access across the Standelfr River, straight into the heart of Westhaven. If the combined Eirdkilr and Jokull forces controlled it, nothing stood between them and the Princelands.

"Fortunately for all of us," Lord Eidan put in, "the Legion Commander..." He glanced down at his notes and cleared his throat. "...Commander Rheamus, had the foresight to bring down the bridge before sounding the retreat." His expression grew grim. "Though it cost a full Legion company, Rivergate Bridge was collapsed."

Relief mingled with the sorrow in Aravon's chest. A hundred Legionnaires had given their lives to protect not only the people of Rivergate, but all the Princelands. A noble sacrifice, yet no less painful a loss to both the Legion and every family on Fehl and Einan that had sent their sons, fathers, and brothers to war.

"But with the collapse of Rivergate Bridge and the retreat into the inner keep, the garrison was forced to abandon most of their supplies." Duke Dyrund's jaw muscles clenched. "Our eyes in Rivergate report that there is less than a week's worth of food stored within the inner keep, while the Jokull and Eirdkilrs feast on the bounty pilfered from Rivergate's warehouse."

42

"And," Colborn put in, "without Rivergate Bridge, there's no way to send reinforcements, either." A statement, not a question.

Duke Dyrund nodded. "The people of Rivergate will starve in a week, and with the Eirdkilrs in Jokull territory, we can't afford to spare anyone from Deepwater and Hammer Garrison." He tapped the two northernmost fortresses on the Westmarch. "Duke Olivarr of Westhaven *might* be able to pull a few hundred irregulars from his other strongholds along the Chain, but it would take more than a week for them to reach Rivergate." His expression soured. "Without Rivergate Bridge, their only route would be to travel a hundred and fifty miles south along the Westmarch, then double back and head northwest, through Jokull territory—territory that appears to be crawling with Eirdkilrs, it seems."

Aravon shook his head. "Sending such a small force into the Jokull wetlands would be a waste." The heavily-armored Legionnaires would get quickly bogged down in the deep mud and marshes, easy pickings for any Jokull or Eirdkilr raiding parties.

"Which is why I said there is nothing we can do to help the garrison at Rivergate." Duke Dyrund fixed him with a piercing gaze. "Nothing, besides sending you."

Aravon's eyes narrowed in thought. "The seven of us. Against three thousand enemies surrounding Rivergate. With no bridge to get us across the Standelfr, and no reinforcements." He shot Colborn a glance.

"Sounds like a party," the Lieutenant replied, a cynical grin cracking his stern expression.

A smile tugged at Aravon's lips, but the impossibility of the mission wiped away any hint of mirth.

"There are *some* reinforcements available." Lord Eidan's deep, booming voice echoed in the War Room. He cleared his throat and tapped a finger on the over-sized fortress figurine representing Highkeep, the capital of the duchy of Lightmoor. "Two companies—Second and Third, Topaz Battalion—at near-full strength were rotated out with the last batch of Legionnaires shipped from the mainland. Many of them, however, chose to remain in the Princelands rather than return to their homes in…" He consulted his notes once more. "…Nysl and Drash."

Aravon cocked an eyebrow. Drash and Nysl were two mainlander kingdoms, thousands of miles away in the heart of the continent of Einan.

These Legionnaires were far from home, yet they had chosen to remain. Likely career soldiers, men with no prospects beyond battle and the military. He could understand that—his father had given forty years to the Legion, and had seemed lost, cast adrift in the turbulent sea of civilian life in Icespire, once he was retired.

"How many?" Aravon asked.

"One hundred eighty." Lord Eidan's lips formed a small frown. "Half are veterans, but the other half are mostly raw recruits, or those recovering from bouts of the Bloody Flux."

Aravon had seen the plague spread through Legion encampments like a deadly wind, decimating companies and killing even the strongest of men. The fact that these *recovered* meant they were fighters in spirit as well as body.

"They marched out of Highkeep last night." Lord Eidan ran a finger along the map toward Eastland Tower, Westhaven's capital, situated seventy-five miles from the Chain, then continued further south. "You will rendezvous with them here at Bannockburn, five miles north of the destroyed Rivergate Bridge. From there, it's up to you to figure out the best way to deal with the situation."

Aravon's brow furrowed. Even with nearly two hundred men at his back, they faced three thousand enemies. No access to Rivergate itself, no way to safely cross the fast-flowing Standelfr River, and the knowledge that every day's delay meant starvation and death for the besieged Legionnaires, regulars, and citizenry of Rivergate.

"There is no doubt that this is an impossible mission." Duke Dyrund fixed Aravon with a solemn gaze. "Yet, after Bjornstadt and the Battle of Broken Canyon, I have faith that you and your men are up for the challenge."

Aravon exchanged glances with Colborn. The half-Fehlan Lieutenant frowned, the wheels in his mind already at work.

Duke Dyrund raised a clenched fist. "Whatever supplies we can make available to you, tell us and it will be yours. But you are Rivergate's only hope. Without you, every one of them dies."

A weight of responsibility settled on Aravon's shoulders. Though he and his small company had trained for this precise purpose, confronted with a task so daunting, he found himself wavering. The odds were beyond hopeless.

Yet, with the help of every member of his team, he had achieved the impossible before. Duke Dyrund and the Prince had faith in not only him, but the soldiers under his command. Together, they would find a way. They had to—as the Duke had made clear, the fate of Rivergate rested in their hands.

Chapter Seven

The knocking at Aravon's door pulled him from his dour contemplation. Snarl perked up at the sound, leaping off Aravon's blanket-strewn bed and racing toward the small room's only entrance.

"Enter," Aravon called.

Colborn appeared in the doorway. "Dinner, Captain."

Aravon's eyebrows shot up. *Already?* He'd retreated to his chamber after the briefing with Duke Dyrund and lost himself in thought, puzzling over their mission. Snarl's playful antics hadn't pulled him from his grim mood, but as the Enfield calmed down and dozed off, Aravon had sat stroking the creature's soft orange fur. It didn't lift his spirits, but it provided a few moments' distraction from what lay ahead.

Now, he could hide from it no longer. He had to leave his room, face his soldiers, and tell them what was expected of them. A conversation he'd dreaded for hours, yet a necessary one. He hadn't yet come up with a solution to the problem—together, with each of their minds working at the problem from a different angle, they had a chance, however faint, to succeed in this mission.

He rose from his bed, grimacing at the knots in his muscles. Zaharis' alchemical concoctions had sped up the healing process, but the wounds in his shoulder and face still ached. The stiffness in his left arm would never truly heal—a reminder of the toll the Eirdkilr Wars had taken not only on him, but every man, woman, and child in the Princelands.

"By your bright smile, I take it you've solved our problem." Colborn's voice held a hint of droll humor. "And here was me worried we had a challenge on our hands."

"Sure." Aravon gave a dismissive wave. "I also figured out how to end the Eirdkilr War tomorrow and cure the Bloody Flux."

Colborn snorted. "Now *that's* asking the impossible."

Aravon found his lips quirking into a ghost of a smile. "You had any strokes of genius this afternoon?"

Colborn shrugged. "Nothing yet, but I'll keep you apprised." He stepped out of the room and fell in step beside Aravon. Together, they strode down the short hall toward the barracks' mess hall.

"Did you say anything to the others?" Aravon asked.

Colborn shook his head. "Figured I'd give them one proper night of rest."

Aravon nodded. Knowing his company, they'd be curious, but Colborn's decision to hold off on revealing their mission meant they could enjoy tonight, at least.

"For what it's worth, Captain," Colborn said in a quiet voice, "we've got the best shot of dealing with this as anyone on Fehl. And even if death is what's in store for us, we're all marching by your side."

The words surprised Aravon. It was the closest the stoic Colborn would come to paying him a compliment.

"Except for Belthar." Colborn grinned. "He's been getting into the beer, and you know how that makes him."

Despite his mood, Aravon couldn't help a small smile. "Swordsman! Best keep him downwind at all costs."

"Who knows, maybe that'll come in handy for this mission." Colborn chuckled. "We'll just set him to gas the Eirdkilrs to death."

At that moment, the sound of laughter drifted from the open door of the mess hall. Aravon and Colborn entered a scene of merriment and revelry. Noll had clambered onto one wooden table, an overflowing tankard in one hand and a chicken drumstick in the other. He danced in time with the clapping, stamping, and horribly out-of-key singing echoing in the room. Even Prince Toran smiled and sang along with the bawdy, raucous lyrics of "The Soldier Down Under", a song known in every Legion encampment but one Aravon thought foreign to the lofty halls of Icespire.

Duke Dyrund sat beside Zaharis, and their hands flashed in the Secret Keeper hand language almost too quickly for Aravon to follow. Belthar led Clem and the two Camp Marshal servants in chorus, his huge boots stamping the ground with such force Aravon feared an earthquake. Skathi sat in a corner, apart from the men filling the mess hall, nursing a tankard of ale. A small smile cracked the Agrotora's usually stern, fierce demeanor as she watched Noll make a complete and utter fool of himself—as he tended to do.

The song ended with a final ringing shout, and the room broke into enthusiastic applause for Noll. As he bowed, he upended his tankard, spilling half its yeasty contents over the table and bench. The little scout stepped down, right onto the ale-soaked wooden bench, and promptly slipped, falling hard onto the table. Much to the amusement of everyone in the room, especially when he popped back up to his feet with another broad smile and bow.

Aravon filled his plate with food—oat and barley bread with a generous helping of herb-and-goat-cheese stuffed venison, Clem's specialty—but stayed away from the keg of ale. He needed a full belly and a sharp mind for what lay ahead. Plate in hand, he slipped onto the bench beside Duke Dyrund, who shot him a greeting nod before returning to his conversation with Zaharis.

As Colborn took his seat near Skathi—close enough to be companionable, but not so near as to invade her personal space, Aravon noted, a very conscientious Colborn thing to do—Prince Toran rose and climbed onto the table Noll had just evacuated.

"Gentlemen, lady!" He nodded to Skathi. "Let us raise our cups in a toast. A toast to each one of you, brave champions of the Princelands."

Belthar and Noll cheered, pounding their tankards on the table. It seemed they'd gotten into the ale shortly after delivering their gear to Polus, and appeared unlikely to stop drinking anytime soon. Aravon didn't begrudge them their merriment. Zaharis' potion—aptly called Drunkard's Salvation—could prevent all but the worst hangovers, and Noll's tolerance for alcohol was a marvel to behold, a rival for the hulking Belthar despite his small stature. They deserved a few moments of revelry before facing their next mission.

Prince Toran's smile dimmed, his expression growing somber. "I know what is being asked of you, my friends, and there are no words to convey my deep gratitude for the sacrifices you are making and the risks you are taking in the name of our home. Though the world may never know what you have accomplished in the name of peace, I swear, by the Swordsman, that your deeds will never be forgotten."

He raised his tankard once more. "To you, brave warriors, my silent champions! May the Swordsman strengthen your arm and guide your steps."

"The Swordsman!" echoed every man in the room, and even Skathi joined in.

The Prince drank deep, emptying his full tankard in a single pull and earning a round of cheers from Belthar and Noll. He descended from the table and took his place at the table, where he was quickly dragged into a rousing rendition of "How Low Do They Hang?", an even bawdier drinking song—one to which he seemed to know every word.

A somber silence hung over Aravon as he ate his food. He couldn't bring himself to join in the merriment, though it felt good to see his men laughing, smiling, and enjoying themselves. Colborn had engaged Skathi in a quiet conversation, leaving Aravon as the only man sitting alone. Well, except for Lord Eidan, who sat on the far side of the mess hall, sipping a glass of wine and picking sparingly at the carcass of a chicken breast.

Aravon was about to go over and join Lord Eidan—he was interested in finding out more about the Duke's aide, the man who furnished them with information amassed through the Prince's network of spies—but the nobleman finished his meal, gathered up his notebook and parchments, and strode from the room. It seemed the business of espionage and intelligence-gathering kept him busy.

But Aravon found himself following Lord Eidan's example. Pushing back his plate, he stood from the bench and left the mess hall. He might not be able to sleep, his mind busy worrying over the problem of their next mission, but his body could use a few hours of rest.

He stepped into the cool, welcoming darkness of the hallway and strode toward his room.

"Aravon!" Duke Dyrund's voice echoed in the corridor behind him.

Turning, Aravon found the Duke emerging from the mess hall, an intent look on his bearded face. "Duke?"

"I wanted to speak with you earlier," the Duke said, "but after our briefing, I could see you needed time to wrestle with thoughts of the mission."

Aravon cocked his head. "Speak with me? About what?"

"Duke Leddan." Duke Dyrund fixed him with that piercing stare of his. "Your note didn't give specifics. What did he say?"

"Oldcrest *is* suffering, but he'd rather sell his land than sell our secrets to the Eirdkilrs."

The Duke's eyes narrowed. "Sell his land?"

Aravon nodded. "To the Nyslians. For growing icewine, he said."

"Hmm." Duke Dyrund pursed his lips. "I'll have Eidan look into that, confirm he actually made the sale. But it sounds right. It wasn't more than a month or two ago that a Nyslian approached me about the same thing."

"It's definitely worth verifying the story," Aravon replied. "But when I looked him in the eyes, I saw nothing that hinted at treachery. Even with a dagger to his throat and the promise of certain death."

"Good." Relief pierced the Duke's solemn expression. "I'd hoped it wasn't him. Leddan and I may rarely be on the same side of political matters, but I always admired his dedication to his people. Takes after his father and grandfather in that way, both men my own father spoke highly of."

Aravon had no reply to that; he was a soldier, son of a General, with little experience in the world of Princeland politics. But he *did* have experience reading men. First, as a low-ranked Legionnaire watching the volatile moods of his Drill Sergeants and Commanders, then as an officer trying to keep his company in line and follow orders while doing his best to protect his men. Everything he'd seen in Duke Leddan's defiant reaction made him believe the man truly was innocent.

"Of course," he said, "I find myself asking, if not the Duke, who is the traitor?"

The Duke frowned. "Leddan was the only member of the Prince's Council with any *visible* motive for selling out Silver Break Mine." He ran a hand through his beard, which seemed shot through with more strands of gray with every passing day. "I've tasked Lord Eidan with digging into the matter of the ledger. I'll have him probe deeper into the Dukes' retinues and aides as well, along with anyone else who might have had access to the information. He's like a bloodhound, he'll always sniff out the truth." A wry smile tugged at the Duke's lips. "Makes him invaluable, truth be told. Just like his father, grandfather, and every Eidan since the foundation of the Princelands."

Aravon cocked an eyebrow. "I've never heard of any Eidans until we met here."

Duke Dyrund nodded. "That's by design. Denever, first Prince of Icespire, knew he needed someone to keep an eye on his enemies, so he recruited his best friend, Lysekel Eidan, to run his spy network. Every generation of Eidans is raised to the same calling—one they are all well-suited to. From a long line of bright, cunning men, Ardenas Eidan is among the brightest and most cunning. It is thanks to him and his family's eyes and ears around the Princelands and Fehl that we know what we do."

Aravon inclined his head. "Then I'm glad he's on our side."

"Indeed." The Duke smiled. "Anyways, I wanted you to know that we'll keep looking into the matter, keep digging until we find out who is guilty. They will not escape punishment for their treachery!"

"And the missing miners?" Aravon asked. "What of them?"

Duke Dyrund remained silent a long moment, his frown deepening. Finally, he shrugged. "I'll have Eidan put out feelers among his Fehlan contacts, and I'll do the same with my own. But if they *were* taken by the Eirdkilrs—and there's no other explanation I can think of that makes sense—then I can't begin to guess at the horrible fate that awaits them." A shadow flashed behind his eyes. "We can only hope the Eirdkilrs made their deaths quick and painless, but you and I both know that's not likely."

Acid surged in Aravon's throat. It was a cold, dark day when a speedy execution was the *best* possible outcome.

"One more thing," Duke Dyrund said.

"Sir?" Aravon cocked his head, curious at the strange, strained tone in the Duke's voice.

"It's..." Duke Dyrund hesitated. "It's your father, Aravon."

A fist of iron gripped Aravon's heart, cutting off his breath. "What of him?" A mélange of emotions roiled in his stomach, as was the case every time he thought of General Traighan.

"He's fallen ill." The Duke fixed Aravon with a solemn gaze. "Nothing too serious, according to Prince Toran's healers. A cold and cough that has settled in his lungs, one which should heal in a few weeks. But it's *how* he fell ill that matters."

Aravon's mouth had grown suddenly dry. "They found him wandering again, didn't they?"

Duke Dyrund nodded. "Yes." He drew in a deep breath. "Swimming, actually, in Glacier Bay."

Aravon swallowed, hard. His father's retirement from the Legion hadn't been because he was physically unfit for duty. Instead, it was his mind that failed him. Forgetfulness, confusion, and sudden changes in mood coupled with bouts of poor judgement made him an unreliable commander. He'd lost one battle too many because he simply *forgot* to give an order or couldn't remember the strategy he'd laid out for his men. He'd grown worse over the last year, a part of the reason that Aravon had chosen not to return home on his last leave. His father had always been an angry man—the loss of his wife, his experiences during the war, and now his failing mind only compounded the issue.

"But Prince Toran has made certain he is receiving the care he needs," Duke Dyrund continued, his voice quiet. "He has a Ministrant of the Bright Lady with him at all hours of the day. And Mylena and your boys are with him."

Aravon's breath caught in his lungs. He couldn't imagine Rolyn and Adilon enduring half of what General Traighan had subjected him to during his own childhood. Yet Mylena knew the truth of Aravon's history with his father—if she had chosen to remain with him, she had to believe it the right choice for her sons as well as her father-in-law.

"And all your family's financial needs are being met." Duke Dyrund placed a hand on Aravon's shoulder. "They want for nothing, Aravon."

A lump rose to Aravon's throat. "Thank you, sir."

"I know it's poor comfort, given what is being asked of you." The Duke's face was solemn, sorrow sparkling in his eyes. "But I promise that the Prince is looking after them, as am I." His grip on Aravon's shoulder tightened, a paternal, comforting squeeze. "I will care for them until the day you can return home."

Swallowing once more, he nodded, but no words came out. Throat thick with emotions, he could find nothing to say.

"Go," the Duke said, releasing his shoulder. "Get what rest you can tonight. Tomorrow, you do the impossible."

Chapter Eight

"So that's our mission." Aravon met the eyes of each of his company in turn. "Any questions?"

Noll's hand shot up. "Yeah, how in the bloody hell are we supposed to pull that off?" As Aravon had explained the Duke's instructions, the little scout's expression had gone from questioning to skeptical to full-on incredulous. "I'm all for doing the impossible, but some impossibilities are just too…" He trailed off, fishing for the word.

"Impossible?" Belthar put in helpfully.

Noll shot the big man a withering glare, but shrugged. "Good as any way to say it, I guess." He threw up his hands. "Us and fewer than two hundred Legionnaires have about a spark's chance in a frozen hell of pulling this off."

"*Six of us took on twelve hundred Eirdkilrs before,*" Zaharis' hands flashed in the silent hand language. "*Seems much better odds this time around, if you can do the math.*"

Noll's face drooped into a scowl. Numeracy, along with literacy and genteel manners, hadn't been included in whatever education life had given him. He could get an accurate enemy count and do the basic calculations for distances to march or ride, but anything more complex than asking him to split a crust of bread between himself and his companions was beyond him.

A fact Zaharis had taken upon himself to correct. Despite the scout's recalcitrance, the Secret Keeper had begun teaching him the rudiments of letters and numbers—just one more of the many skills they'd need on their new mission for the Princelands.

55

"Here's the Swordsman's honest truth." Aravon's voice was solemn, his expression grave. "I've no Keeper-damned idea how to do what needs to be done. Neither does Duke Dyrund, Prince Toran, or anyone else with a military or noble title in front of their names. But now it's *our* job to figure it out. So that's what we're going to do. On the march. We ride for Bannockburn in three hours. That's enough time to gear up, collect any supplies we need—" He shot a meaningful glance at Zaharis, who nodded in response. "—and get underway. Duke Dyrund's sending maps of Rivergate and the surrounding terrain with us, and thanks to Snarl and Lord Eidan's man inside the city, we'll have the best possible intelligence to guide our steps."

He drew in a deep breath. "But everything else is on us. Us, and those one hundred and eighty Legionnaires that will be following our commands. That means we've got to come up with a damned good plan in the five days it'll take us to get there. Because by the time we reach Rivergate, the garrison and citizens there will be running out of supplies. Starving men can't fight, which means the Jokull and Eirdkilrs have a better chance of overwhelming their defenses with every passing day." He raised a clenched fist. "Every hour counts!"

Colborn, who had stood silent at Aravon's right shoulder throughout the briefing, now stepped forward. "You heard the Captain. Gear up, pack your belongings, and get the horses ready to ride."

"Yes, Captain." Skathi stood and, raising her right hand, gave him the Agrotorae salute: forefinger and pinky finger bent, ring and middle fingers ramrod straight. An archer's insult to their enemies, but a promise—"*My bow and arrows at your command!*"—to their allies.

Belthar followed suit, snapping off a sloppy yet enthusiastic Legion salute, banging one ham-sized fist against his barrel chest. Noll rolled his eyes and muttered something under his breath, but nodded his assent.

Zaharis' fingers flashed. "*We'll be ready, Captain.*"

"One final thing." Aravon's voice stopped the four of them mid-step. They turned toward him, curiosity etched on their expressions. "We'll be seven once more."

Three eyebrows—belonging to Belthar, Skathi, and Noll—rose at those words. Zaharis' lips quirked into a smile. The Secret Keeper doubtless knew what Aravon planned to say. Colborn's face held no hint of surprise; Aravon had filled him in before they rode out of Bjornstadt.

56

"Rangvaldr will be joining us." Aravon fixed them each with a solemn stare. "He'll be our healer, replacing Draian." The name sent a pang of sorrow through his chest, but he kept his expression impassive. "And he knows a thing or two about Fehlan battle strategy. Not just Eyrr, but every clan."

Noll's eyes narrowed. "No offense to the *Seiomenn*, who did right by joining the fight for Bjornstadt, but are we sure we want a Fehlan on our team?"

Colborn stiffened, his jaw muscles working.

Noll seemed to realize what he'd said and color rose to his cheeks. "W-What I meant to say…" He swallowed, his eyes darting toward the Lieutenant. "A Fehlan we *don't* know. Someone we're not sure we can trust fully. He's no coward, that much is clear, but how can we be sure of his reasons for joining us?"

"I'm certain he has his own reasons." Aravon nodded to Colborn, and the Lieutenant strode from the War Room. "Why not ask him yourself?"

At that moment, Colborn returned, with Rangvaldr a step behind. The Eyrr *Seiomenn* was a few inches shorter than the Lieutenant, but he carried himself with an air of authority, an almost mystical aura enhanced by the glowing blue gemstone hanging around his neck. The fact that he wore the same camouflage-patterned armor that Polus had fashioned for their company made him appear far more dangerous—the warrior he'd once been before he donned the shaman's furs.

"Rangvaldr, the floor is yours." Aravon gestured for the man to speak. "Why would a Fehlan, and a *Seiomenn* no less, want to take up arms against the *Tauld* clan?" He used the name once given to the barbarians that now called themselves "Eirdkilrs". "Why should we, whose forefathers invaded your home and claimed your lands, trust you to stand shield to shield with us, rather than turn and join our enemies?"

A tad dramatic, Aravon knew, but it was the underlying cause of Princelander distrust of all Fehlans. Most Princelanders feared that the clans of Fehl perceived them exactly as he'd just described—invaders to be hated and, if possible, driven off the continent. The Eirdkilrs were one of the few clans taking action, but far too many Princelanders believed that all Fehlans harbored similar sentiments.

Rangvaldr's solid face creased into a smile, which set the bones and stones in his braided beard jangling. "A wise question, Captain." He turned toward

Noll, Belthar, and Skathi. "And one I expected coming from the moment Duke Dyrund agreed to let me join you."

One of Noll's eyebrows raised a fraction and he shot a questioning glance at Aravon. Clearly he hadn't known of the Duke's stamp of approval on the *Seiomenn's* presence, though he *should* have guessed it from the fact that Rangvaldr had been in the heretofore top-secret Camp Marshal.

Rangvaldr clasped his hands in front of his waist. "Before I was *Seiomenn* of Bjornstadt, I was a warrior of the Eyrr, one more among many in the shield wall. I watched my brothers fall to our enemies or succumb to old age." He gestured to his beard, a wry smile tugging at his lips. "A fate I was prepared to share until the Eirdkilrs attacked my home and slaughtered my people."

His smile faded, his broad face growing serious. "And in the moments of quiet following our battle for Bjornstadt, I heard the voice of Nuius speaking in my heart." He tapped his broad chest. "My god has called me to take up arms to protect my people—not only the Eyrr, but all Fehlans who suffer at the hands of the *Tauld*. Those who are determined to wreak slaughter and death rather than sue for peace."

Now the shaman turned to Aravon. "It is your Duke's example that I follow. He seeks the path to end the bloodshed and war. An impossible dream, perhaps, yet a dream that I share. That I have shared since the day I accepted the *Seiomenn's* mantle." He stroked the shining gemstone pendant with a strong, scarred hand. "*That* is what brings me to join your cause. To heal any who I can, and to do everything in my power to bring my land and people through this time of violence, of turmoil and into an era of peace and prosperity. For Fehlans and Princelanders alike."

A solemn silence settled over the room as Rangvaldr's words trailed off. Noll's expression remained pensive, but all hint of suspicion had fled his eyes. And how could it have been otherwise? No one in the room could have doubted the conviction that rang in the *Seiomenn's* voice, that shone in his eyes.

Rangvaldr broke the silence. "And, of course," he said, a smile broadening his face, "if I can convert you all from that swill you call ale to proper *ayrag*-drinking men, I will consider my life's work fulfilled."

"Hah!" Noll straightened and slapped Rangvaldr on the shoulder. "*Please* make Belthar your first disciple! Anything's better than hanging around him after a few pints of ale."

Belthar colored and mumbled something about "indigestion", which only made Noll laugh all the harder. Skathi smiled and shot Rangvaldr a nod, which Aravon took as her approval.

"*Welcome, Seiomenn,*" Zaharis signed. "*If nothing else, your presence means I have a chance to study that 'magic stone' around your neck.*"

Rangvaldr closed a protective hand around the amulet. "Oh no you don't!" A look of mock severity flashed across his face. "I want none of your 'science' around my magic, you skeptic."

"*Skepticism is the first step toward rational thought,*" Zaharis shot back, his round, pale-skinned face breaking into a smile. "*No wonder you are still such savages. Next you'll be telling me you worship the mud and pray to the lightning.*"

Rangvaldr threw an arm around the Secret Keeper's shoulders. "Now that you mention it, that reminds me to speak to you about the mercies of Umma, goddess of pig's feet and cow tails. It's said that…" The *Seiomenn's* voice trailed off as he and Zaharis strode from the War Room.

Aravon turned to Noll. "Satisfied?"

The little scout hesitated, then inclined his head. "For now."

Aravon raised an eyebrow. "You doubt him still? After that?"

Noll shook his head. "Not that we can trust him, trust his motives." He gave a little shrug. "We've only seen him fighting for his home. I'm just not certain how he'll fight when it's someone *else's* home he's protecting." He held up a hand as Aravon opened his mouth to speak. "I'm all for giving him a chance, don't get me wrong. But it'll take me a bit before I'm comfortable putting my life in his hands."

Aravon nodded. "Fair enough." He couldn't *force* Noll to trust anyone, especially not a Fehlan. Just as Aravon had had to prove himself to his men—as they *all* had to prove themselves to each other—Rangvaldr would have to do the same.

"Captain." Inclining his head, Noll strode from the room.

Skathi had already left, and Colborn was disappearing through the door as well. Belthar had remained seated throughout Rangvaldr's speech, but as he stood, Aravon stepped toward the big man. "Stay a moment," he said in a quiet voice.

Belthar's shoulders knotted, worry flashing across his blunt, solid face. Skathi and Noll seemed to have forgotten his actions in Ironcastle—or at least let the matter lie, for now—but Belthar clearly hadn't gotten over their reactions. The previous night had been the first time since leaving Ironcastle that Belthar had appeared comfortable around his comrades.

Aravon waited until he was certain the others were out of earshot before speaking. "What you did back in Oldcrest, finding that tunnel—"

"Captain, I—"

Aravon held up a hand. "As I said, I trust you'll tell us when you're ready." He shook his head. "That's not important right now. What I want to know is if you can do the same in Rivergate."

Belthar's blocky features creased into a frown. "You mean find a B—" He swallowed whatever word he'd been about to say. "—a tunnel into the city?"

Aravon nodded. "Yes." He cocked an eyebrow. "Anything like that we can use to get in, or get people out?"

Belthar remained silent for a drawn-out moment, his expression pensive. Long seconds passed before he shrugged. "Sorry, Captain. Never been to Rivergate, so I can't tell you for certain."

"You'd never been to Ironcastle before, either." Aravon took care to keep any hint of recrimination from his tone. Belthar could be…sensitive, and he'd get defensive if Aravon said the wrong thing.

"I know." A shadow flashed across the big man's eyes. "What I mean to say is that I can't know for certain *until* I get there. See the…signs for myself."

Curiosity burned with Aravon. *Signs?* He replayed his memories of the desperate flight through the streets of Ironcastle, but he couldn't remember seeing anything out of the ordinary. Perhaps Belthar had a sharper eye, or he'd simply known what to look for. That raised even more questions, but Aravon had promised to let Belthar open up at his own pace.

"So once we're near Rivergate, you'll be able to spot any tunnels like that?" he asked.

Again a moment of hesitation, and another shrug of Belthar's huge shoulders. "No promises, but I'll keep an eye out."

Aravon nodded. "Good." That was the best he could hope for—until Belthar told him how he knew about the tunnel's existence, he'd have to settle for that answer. "Then I'm trusting you'll tell me if you see anything that could help us get in and out of Rivergate unseen."

"Yes, Captain." Belthar saluted. He was getting better, but he still couldn't quite manage the crisp, military precision of a Legion salute.

"Thank you." Aravon clapped the big man on one huge bicep. "Now, let's get geared up. We ride out in two hours."

* * *

"Ye bring that back broken again, don't bother showing yer face in my smithy!" Polus' shout followed Aravon from the forge. "All the time and effort spent crafting a masterpiece, and ye damned fools…"

The closing door silenced the last of the blacksmith's tirade, which had gone on the entire time Aravon had spent in the smithy gathering his gear. But, at least there was one bright side to enduring that haranguing: his spear was once again whole.

On the return journey from Bjornstadt, he'd felt naked with nothing more than his Fehlan-style longsword. Years spent behind a Legion shield had trained him to fight defensively as much as offensively, but his injured arm meant he could no longer carry a heavy shield. His six-foot-long spear with its Odarian steel head and metal-capped end had become his defensive weapon. The extendable iron spike in the butt had given him an extra weapon to wield—one that had won the battle against Hrolf Hrungnir.

Now, with the spear in his arms and his sword by his side, he felt once again complete. Or, as complete as he could be without a hundred pounds of solid wood and steel to protect himself. He was still growing accustomed to the more offensive style of fighting demanded by the spear.

"Keeper's teeth!" Colborn gave a quiet whistle. "Did he even pause for breath?"

Aravon grimaced. "Worse than a mother black bear guarding her cubs, he is."

"I'd take the bear over a pissed-off smith any day," Belthar muttered.

"That's because you're about the bear's size." Skathi shot him a fierce grin. "But Polus'll rip you a new bunghole far faster."

It seemed each of them had also had to endure the blacksmith's lecture over their "piss-poor care for my works of art", as he'd put it. Belthar worst of all. He'd had the unfortunate lapse of judgement to use the wooden butt of his oversized crossbow as a weapon, and Eirdkilr faces had left bits of bone, bloodstains, and scuff marks on the stock. To hear Polus tell it, he had just defaced a masterpiece on par with a de Stigar painting or the sculptures of Dendur Ariss.

But at least they had all emerged unscathed from the tongue-lashing. Armed and armored, his six men were busy stowing the last of their gear. Aside from the standard Legion-issue supplies—flint and steel, waterskin, dried trail rations, wooden bowl and spoon, a fresh tunic, and three changes of socks— each of them carried their own "extras".

In Belthar's case, that meant three additional days of rations. For Noll, that usually meant a waterskin or two filled with wine—little better than vinegar, but the scout liked his vintages rough. Skathi carried two additional oilcloth-wrapped quivers of red-fletched arrows and a dazzling array of knives, plus the glue, twine, turkey feathers, and beeswax required to maintain her bow and craft new arrows.

Colborn traveled light, as befitted a Legion officer, which left space for Zaharis to saddle him with additional alchemical potions, pouches of dried herbs, clay jars filled with powder, and more Secret Keeper paraphernalia. Behind his own saddlehorn, Zaharis strapped a wooden chest with a lock that Noll declared "an Illusionist-damned nightmare" after just one glance.

Aravon's only extras hung around his neck: two small, oval silver pendants displaying the Prince's torch-and-sword-wielding griffin insignia—his own, and the one he'd taken from around Draian's neck—and Snarl's bone whistle.

The little Enfield scampered around Camp Marshal, barking at squirrels, leaping into the air to chase butterflies and blackbirds, and scurrying between the horses' hooves, much to the mounts' discomfort. Finally, Aravon climbed into his saddle and summoned Snarl with a short blast of his whistle, which brought the fox-like creature running at full dash.

"Come on, Snarl!" Aravon braced himself and caught the Enfield without falling from his saddle. Snarl looked up at him with shining amber eyes that gleamed with intelligence. The Enfield was smart enough to know that something big was underway, and he was eager to be part of it. He yipped and licked Aravon's face with a rough, moist tongue.

Aravon stroked Snarl's head and scratched under his chin, just the way the Enfield liked it. As soon as they rode out the gates, they would once again be back on duty, off to a battle they had little hope of surviving, much less winning. He would enjoy this moment with Snarl—it could be his last for a long time.

As ever, his thoughts returned to Mylena and his sons in Icespire. It had been too long since he saw nine-year-old Rolyn and Adilon, the "baby" at age seven. Closing his eyes, he shot up a silent prayer to the Swordsman. *Keep them safe, and watch over them.* After a moment, he added. *My father as well.*

The Duke's news of his father's illness had added to the burden on his shoulders. At least he could console himself knowing the Prince and Duke were both looking after his family. One day, the missions would be over and he could return home. Hopefully, not before his father forgot him completely.

"Captain." Colborn's quiet voice sounded at his elbow. "It's time."

Aravon opened his eyes. His six men sat their horses around him, their faces expectant. They waited for him to give the order.

Drawing in a deep breath, he steeled his resolve and pushed away his worries, along with the aches and pains of his recent battles. Now he had only the mission—impossible, yet one he had to somehow complete. Until it was done, nothing else mattered. Nothing else *could* matter.

He reached up and tied his leather greatwolf mask in place over his face, his movements slow and precise. Each of his men did likewise. Once again, they became the faceless, nameless warriors, the silent champions of the Princelands.

"We ride." With a nod, he spurred his *Kostarasar* charger to a gallop and rode out Camp Marshal's front gate.

Chapter Nine

The hours of riding passed in a blur of blinding sunlight, pounding hooves, and the mounting worries tightening in Aravon's shoulders. With Noll to guide their path and Colborn and Rangvaldr flanking him to the right and left, he had nothing to do but keep his mouth closed against the road dust kicked up into his face. That, and wrestle with the matter of Rivergate.

He and his six warriors prepared to face close to three thousand enemies. Even against just the eight hundred Eirdkilrs, they'd have an impossible task. Add to that the twenty-three hundred Jokull, and Aravon felt as if they rode to certain death.

But this wouldn't be the first time. They had achieved the impossible first in Anvil Garrison, then again with Jade Battalion in Broken Canyon and in Bjornstadt. Not him alone, but *all* the brave soldiers around him. The burden didn't rest solely on his shoulders. This was a problem they all had to work together to solve.

That didn't stop him from puzzling over the impossible task they'd been given. He'd grown accustomed to the *Kostarasar* chargers' impressive speed—ten miles per hour at a steady pace, a smooth, rolling gait the specially-bred mounts seemed able to sustain for up to twelve hours a day with infrequent rests—and years spent in the saddle allowed him to ride instinctually while his mind worked.

For the hundredth time since riding out of Camp Marshal five hours earlier, Aravon went over the map of Rivergate he'd committed to memory. Rivergate, like so many other cities built along the Chain, had a fortified outer wall surrounding the city proper, the dwellings, marketplaces, warehouses, and other buildings occupied by the populace that made their homes in Rivergate and served the Legionnaires and Westhaven regulars guarding the city. The outer wall had also been built up to the banks of the Standelfr River, protecting the Rivergate Bridge.

The inner keep at the center of the city, however, was intended only to house the Legionnaires stationed there, alongside the regular forces conscripted and compensated by the Duke of Westhaven. Their families lived in the city, and only the soldiers active on duty were stationed there. The keep was solid, built of river stone and raised on a foundation of bedrock far enough back from the Standelfr that the ground would never be undercut by the deep river's fast-moving current.

But, the problem was that the inner keep was too small to house all the people of Rivergate—more than four thousand, according to Lord Eidan's sources within the garrison. Not only the families of the Legionnaires and Westhaven regulars, but the usual assortment of merchants, artisans, smiths, and tradespeople that dwelled in Rivergate. All men, women, children, and the elderly, people who would occupy space in the keep and consume the meager stores without doing much to aid in the keep's defenses.

Lord Eidan's report indicated that the inner keep held enough supplies for a week, on the outside. It would take Aravon and his companions the better part of five days just to reach their rendezvous with Topaz Battalion's reinforcements at Bannockburn. Once they did, they'd still have to find a way to break the siege with fewer than two hundred men.

Aravon's studies with Lectern Kayless had included siege tactics, both offensive and defensive. Given time, he had little doubt they could break the backs of the Jokull surrounding Rivergate—perhaps *before* the Eirdkilrs received reinforcements. But time was against them. If they delayed even two or three days, the people of Rivergate would starve. And that was gambling on the fact that the men of Rivergate could hold the inner keep that long. They would be fighting to protect their families, but even that might not suffice in the face of so many enemies.

Which explained Aravon's dour mood. Even if they arrived in time, he couldn't be certain their actions would save Rivergate. Harrying the besieging army would do little more than anger the Jokull and Eirdkilrs, perhaps even divert a few hundred away from Rivergate's wall. But nowhere near enough to make a difference for the Legionnaires and Westhaveners trapped on the opposite side of the Standelfr River. There would be no retreat, nowhere to run.

The stone walls of the inner keep were all that stood between those brave Princelanders and certain doom.

Yet, even as the sun began to dip toward the western horizon, Aravon still hadn't found an answer to the matter of the siege. His disposition grew steadily worse until Colborn finally called a halt two hours after sundown. Aravon bit back an angry growl—it would not do to push the horses harder, else they'd risk stumbling in the dark. And, much as he hated to admit it, he welcomed the rest as much as any of his men. The wounds sustained in the battle at Bjornstadt hadn't fully healed. His face, in particular, throbbed fiercely—the result of clenching and unclenching his jaw all day long.

Colborn seemed to sense Aravon's disposition, and he took care of assigning the watch shifts. They had little to fear nestled amongst a dense thicket of old-growth pines and oaks common in Oldcrest, yet the Lieutenant knew better than to take risks with their safety.

Rangvaldr and Zaharis drew the first watch, leaving Belthar, Noll, Skathi, and Colborn to join Aravon at their little campfire. Aravon sat hunched over the map of Rivergate, studying the layout of the garrison *again* in the fire's flickering glow. Skathi ate and worked at cutting new arrows in silence, Snarl curled around her feet where he could receive the occasional handout from the red-haired archer. Colborn dozed against the trunk of a particularly thick oak tree, his chest rising and falling in a steady rhythm.

Belthar sat across from Aravon, belt dagger in hand, whittling at a branch he'd picked up from the myriad strewn around the campsite. His eyes strayed toward Skathi from time to time, a frown furrowing his blocky face. When Aravon happened to catch the big man's wandering gaze, he opened his mouth to say something to Belthar—Swordsman knew the archer didn't appreciate the attention, much less encourage it—when he stopped.

The stick in Belthar's hands was long and straight, the same dark, sturdy wood Skathi was using for her arrows. He wasn't whittling as Aravon had thought; instead, he stripped the branches, carefully sliced off the outer layer of bark, and worked to straighten the shaft.

Aravon's eyebrows rose a fraction. *He's making arrows for her?*

"Skathi," Belthar's voice rumbled over the *crackle* of the flames, "am I doing this right?"

The red-haired Agrotora looked up from her work, her eyes narrowing.

Belthar held up the stick. "I thought…" He hesitated, tension suddenly squaring his shoulders. "I thought, given what we were going to be facing at the end of the road, you could use more arrows." His big hand swept a hasty gesture toward Noll and Colborn. "All of you."

Skathi's jaw muscles worked, her expression going tight. She said nothing for a long moment as she fixed Belthar with an inscrutable stare, forest-green eyes piercing.

"Never mind." Belthar's face reddened and he tossed the stick aside. "Stupid, I know." He turned his eyes back toward the fire, the color in his cheeks burning as bright as the glowing embers.

To Aravon's surprise—and Snarl's dismay—Skathi didn't return to her work. Instead, she stood and extricated herself from the little orange-and-white bundle of fur and wings at her feet. In silence, she strode over to the stick Belthar had discarded, retrieved it, and held it out to him.

Belthar took a long moment to turn toward her, shame burning in his face. His eyes widened as he saw her holding out the stick and he took it in a hesitant hand.

"Not bad." Skathi's voice held no anger or scorn. Instead, a tone of encouragement—barely a hint, yet enough Aravon couldn't mistake the gesture—echoed in her words. "But you need to cut the nock a bit deeper and wider. Otherwise, it'll stick when you release the string. Just for a fraction of a second, but that's enough to throw off your aim. So do it like this."

Belthar listened in silence, his face a mask of studious interest as he watched her widen the groove in the nock of the arrow, then imitated it with another of the sticks he'd collected.

"Good." She nodded. "An archer can never have too many arrows." A wry grin crooked her lips. "Maybe tomorrow night, we cut down one of these oaks to make you another bolt for that crossbow of yours."

Belthar smiled, a chuckle rumbling from deep in his belly, and ducked his head. With another nod, Skathi returned to her place against a tall, slim pine tree. Snarl gave a little whine of protest as he curled up around her feet and resumed his nap. Skathi stroked the Enfield's neck, setting his wings rustling in delight, before picking up her own discarded arrow shaft and setting to work on it.

Despite himself, Aravon found his mood lifting slightly. He'd been worried about Skathi, given the attention both Belthar and Noll had shown her since her arrival at Camp Marshal. She'd straightened them both out on multiple occasions, and both men had learned to treat the archer with the same respect they showed Aravon, Colborn, or Zaharis. Yet it was still good to know that Skathi was starting to feel more relaxed around her companions. That was vital for the formation of a cohesive bond between all of them. Without that, they'd never survive what awaited them at Rivergate.

Aravon had just turned his attention back to the garrison map when Noll's whispered question drifted across the fire. "Does she know you've already got a girl waiting for you?"

From the corner of his eye, Aravon caught Belthar stiffening. "What?" he mumbled. Color blazed in his face once more.

A mocking grin broadened Noll's face. "The way you're always playing with that bracelet, almost like you're thinking about stroking its owner with the same tenderness." Mischief sparkled in his dark eyes. "You can't tell me you didn't get that from someone awful special."

Fire blazed in Belthar's eyes and his fingers went to the braided leather thong at his wrist. He caught himself mid-stroke, his flush deepening. "It's not like that." His voice came out in a low growl.

"Ain't it, though?" Noll dug a finger into his hawkish nose and rooted around, then flicked his findings into the fire. "Lots of things a man carries into battle. Weapons mostly. Rations, particularly for a big fellow like yourself. But something like that..." He thrust his sharp chin toward Belthar's wrist. "...that's the sort of trinket you carry to remember a lady love by."

"Sort of like that scar you've got running down your right side?" Colborn's voice cut into the conversation. It seemed the Lieutenant, like most soldiers, had a gift for light sleep.

"Hey!" Noll held up his hands defensively. "I didn't *ask* for that kiss, but when the woman planted it on me, what else was I supposed to think?"

"That she tripped and got unlucky enough to be falling in your general direction," Colborn shot back.

"Ouch!" Noll mimicked a dagger thrust to the heart. "She didn't seem to mind it all that much—"

"Until she put a knife in your side to register her protest," Belthar rumbled.

Noll shrugged. "Whatever. So I misread the situation, that's all."

"Good thing you didn't *misread* yourself into an early grave." Colborn's lips quirked into a grin. "Seems to me there's a lesson in there for you, Noll."

The little man scowled. "Never flirt with a Lightmoor tavernkeeper's wife."

"Wrong lesson." Colborn sat up and leaned forward, eyes fixed on the scout. "Push your luck too far, and you may find it runs out."

Noll snorted. *"That's* what you got from—"

"Your watch, Noll." Aravon spoke up. "Time to replace the Secret Keeper and *Seiomenn*."

Mumbling under his breath, Noll stood and headed away from the fire to relieve Zaharis and Rangvaldr. Colborn followed suit, pausing only long enough to fix Belthar with a meaningful look. Gratitude shone in the big man's eyes as he sat in silence, his fingers twirling the braided thong around his wrist.

Aravon couldn't help wondering at the meaning behind the bracelet. *Just one more of Belthar's mysteries.* He hadn't forgotten about the secret tunnel at Ironcastle and Belthar's skills at breaking and entering, but he *would* leave it alone until the big man felt comfortable. Noll's poking and prodding, even if it was the sort of well-intentioned, spirited ribbing between comrades, wouldn't help the situation.

A few moments later, Zaharis and Rangvaldr returned to the fire, rubbing their hands and taking the seats recently vacated by Noll and Colborn. The Secret Keeper dug into his pack and produced a bundle of rations, which he set about eating with relish despite their bland taste. Aravon made it a point not to watch—he had seen the mangled stump of Zaharis' tongue, carved out by his order of priests, enough for one lifetime.

He found his eyes drawn to Rangvaldr, instead. From the moment he'd met the *Seiomenn*, he'd been drawn to the man. Not only the authority he emanated in his role as holy man and loremaster of the Eyrr, but the way he seemed at ease with his place in the world—a world that had grown increasingly more violent, threatening his home and clan in the process.

Rangvaldr had fought to protect his home, yet all the bloodshed, death, and suffering hadn't diminished his merriment or put a damper on his upbeat nature. He had knelt over the bodies of slain comrades one moment, then smiled at his surviving friends and family the next. That was something Aravon, languishing under the burden of guilt over Draian's death and now his mission to rescue Rivergate, envied immensely.

"Be careful, Captain." Rangvaldr's booming voice interrupted his thoughts and snapped him back to attention. "It's said among the wise women of my clan that men who frown too much go gray in the hair and in the mind."

Aravon cocked an eyebrow. "They do, do they?"

Rangvaldr shrugged. "I personally believe it's simply a wives' tale. After all, look at me." He swept a hand toward his beard and hair, flecked through with gray and white. "All my smiling and still I can't stop the graying."

Aravon couldn't help chuckling. "I'll try to remember that next time."

A grin broadened Rangvaldr's Fehlan features. "Knowing you, next time will come all too soon." He took a bite of his food and fixed Aravon with a piercing glance. "Thoughts of our mission ahead weigh on you."

Aravon nodded, but couldn't bring himself to say the words aloud. How could he tell his men he had no plan to free Rivergate? He was the *leader* of this company, and they trusted him to give them orders. They'd help him enact whatever plan he came up with—fiery hell, they'd likely improve on anything—but he couldn't reach Bannockburn with nothing to go on.

Rangvaldr leaned back against the tree and broke off another piece of trail biscuit. "Let me tell you a story, Captain."

"A story?" Aravon cocked his head. Perhaps the *Seiomenn* wanted to distract him from his worries with a fable.

Rangvaldr spoke around his mouthful of food. "About the *Hveorungr,* an ancient creature said to live in the wilds south of the Sawtooth Mountains."

Aravon resisted the urge to roll his eyes. The Eirdkilrs were monster enough without bringing fictional creatures to life. Yet, something about Rangvaldr's enigmatic smile and his calm self-assurance stopped Aravon from retorting. He simply nodded and gestured for the man to speak.

"Legends of my people's past tell of the *Hveorungr,* a creature that haunted men's nightmares. The *Hveorungr* would find a man, latch on to his deepest fears, and nurture them, drawing its victims deeper and deeper into those fears until they consumed not only his dreams, but his every waking thought. And the *Hveorungr* fed on that fear, growing stronger as its victims weakened, until finally, the man would die, consumed from within by his own terrors."

Aravon raised an eyebrow. "So this story has a lesson, does it? Not to let my worries or fears for our future consume me?"

Rangvaldr shrugged. "I was simply telling a story. But now that you mention it…" A ghost of a smile played at his lips.

Despite himself, Aravon couldn't help a little grin as well. Rangvaldr's smile was infectious.

"Listen, Captain." The *Seiomenn* leaned forward. "According to the legends, the only way to defeat the *Hveorungr* was to face your fears and defeat them. In doing so, you deprive the *Hveorungr* of its strength, until it weakens away and turns to dust." His expression grew solemn. "Your Duke told me of what happened to your men. You faced your fears and defeated your *Hveorungr* at Bjornstadt."

"Hrolf Hrungnir." Even the name left a bitter taste on Aravon's tongue.

Rangvaldr nodded. "But the problem with the *Hveorungr* was that if even a small part of him remained, he would come back and find a *new* fear to latch on to. And, as my ancestors discovered, there were always more fears, so the *Hveorungr* always had a new source of strength."

Aravon digested the words. "So it's a constant battle to face our fears."

"Right." Rangvaldr took another bite of food, leaving trail biscuit crumbs dangling in his long, braided beard. "There will always be another fear to face. All we can do is keep fighting."

His deep green eyes went to the map in Aravon's hand. "You are not wrong to fear what will happen in Rivergate. Only a fool would go into that battle without a measure of unease. And you, Captain, are no fool."

Aravon found the words, spoken in a tone of such confidence, surprisingly reassuring. He'd only known Rangvaldr a few weeks, yet in that time, his respect for the man had taken deep root. If Rangvaldr shared that respect…

"But you cannot feed the *Hveorungr,* my friend." Rangvaldr gave Aravon a knowing smile. "If you do, it will consume you alive."

"How do you do it?" Aravon asked. "How do you face the unknown ahead and *not* feel fear?"

"I feel it," Rangvaldr replied in a quiet voice. "I, too, am no fool." The humor flashed through his eyes and disappeared in a moment, replaced by earnest sincerity. "But it is my faith in Nuius that keeps me fighting." His hand went to his shirt, and he drew out the glowing blue pendant hanging around his neck. "I have only to look down and see the work of his hand. I have only to close my eyes and listen, and I hear his voice."

"You...*hear* him?" Aravon couldn't help his incredulity. *Seiomenn* like Rangvaldr were the loremasters, priests, and wisemen of the Fehlan clans, the equivalent to the Swordsman Adepts, Secret Keepers, Lecterns, and other priests that served the Thirteen gods of Einan. Yet only the highest-ranked priests ever claimed to hear the words of their gods directly. Aravon had spent his life serving the Swordsman, god of heroes, yet he had never come close to actually hearing the god's voice.

"Not like I hear you now." With a chuckle, Rangvaldr tucked the pendant back beneath his leather armor and undertunic. "But there is a feeling, in here." He tapped his chest, above his heart. "I do not need to hear a voice in my ears to know that I am heard."

Aravon's brow furrowed. The sincerity that sparkled in Rangvaldr's eyes and echoed in his voice was as fervent as anything he'd witnessed from any Princelander priest. A quiet faith, yet incredibly deep-rooted and genuine.

"When I feel the *Hveorungr* coming for me," the *Seiomenn* said, a smile on his face, "I simply turn to Nuius with my fears. That is enough, for I know I am heard. And that knowledge banishes the fears and starves the *Hveorungr.*" He fixed Aravon with a meaningful look. "Perhaps that might work for you, too."

Aravon nodded. "Perhaps."

Silence stretched on around the campfire, broken only by the sound of Belthar's ponderous snoring and Snarl's quiet whining. Rangvaldr leaned back against his tree and set about finishing his evening meal, that knowing smile still fixed on his lips. Yet, he made no attempt to belabor his point with Aravon. He'd said his piece and knew to leave well enough alone.

After a moment, Aravon rolled up the map of Rivergate, stuffed it into his pack, and lay down. He had the next watch, between midnight and the third hour of the morning, in just over two hours. He needed sleep if he was to make it through the next days and reach Rivergate in any shape to fight.

Worries continued to whirl in his mind; he couldn't shut out his concerns over the battle to come and his lack of plans. Yet, as Rangvaldr's words echoed in his thoughts, he closed his eyes.

Swordsman, hear my prayer and guide my path. The way ahead is dark and dangerous, and I have but my earthly eyes and ears to navigate it. Strengthen my arms and lead my feet aright, for the sake of my comrades, my friends, and loved ones.

A simple soldier's prayer, lacking the eloquence of the Lecterns that held noonday services in the Master's Temple in Icespire. Yet those words seemed to lighten Aravon's burden. The problem of Rivergate remained, but a part of him, deep down, took comfort in knowing that *someone* had heard him. If not the Swordsman, then Rangvaldr, at the very least, knew the difficulty he wrestled with.

True to the *Seiomenn's* words, as Aravon finished his silent prayer, he felt the weight indeed lifting from his shoulders.

Chapter Ten

"What do you think, Captain?" Skathi's voice cut into the late-night darkness.

Aravon shot a glance over at the Agrotora. Even after their second full day in the saddle and too few hours of rest, she appeared calm, almost at ease perched on a fallen log a few feet to his right. She held her short horsebow in one hand, an arrow resting lightly on the string. Doubtless she knew as well as he that there was little chance of being assaulted here, deep in the Princelands. Yet relaxed or no, she could nock, draw, and fire that arrow in less time than it would take Aravon to stand. That was enough to fill anyone with an unassailably calm confidence.

"About what?" he asked.

"Rivergate." Long seconds passed before she continued. "And what's waiting for us there."

Aravon's jaw muscles clenched. Rangvaldr's words the previous night had helped him sleep, but another day spent riding had brought all the worries crashing back down atop him. He hadn't spoken more than a few words through the entire day. The others seemed to have sensed his mood. Their meager dinner around the pitiful campfire had been a quiet affair. Even the usually-energetic Snarl seemed subdued, curling up around Aravon's feet as if to offer the comfort of his presence.

After a moment, Aravon sighed. "I'd be lying if I said I wasn't worried." Skathi didn't typically go out of her way to speak to him—to any of them— except on matters relevant to the mission. Much as it felt uncomfortable for a Captain to admit he was clueless how to win an impending battle, opening up to her might be the only way to get her to open up to him in turn. "Try as I might, I can't figure out what to do."

Skathi nodded sagely. "Standelfr's going to be a pain to get across. Then there's the matter of all the Eirdkilrs and Jokull camped inside Rivergate's outer wall."

Aravon drew in a deep breath. "That's exactly what's got me worried." He no longer needed to look at the Duke's map to see the image of the garrison; he'd studied it so thoroughly every inch of the streets were burned into his mind. "Rivergate Bridge was our best way in, but Commander Rheamus had no choice but to bring it down. Without the bridge, we're going to have to assault the outer walls just like the enemy did."

The archer grunted acknowledgement. "And with just two hundred of us, we've got about as much chance of success as Noll's got with Princess Ranisia."

Aravon couldn't help chuckling. Princess Ranisia, wife of Prince Toran, was considered the most beautiful woman in the Princelands. Noll, on the other hand, was a damned good scout...but he was still Noll.

"Well, maybe our odds aren't *that* bad," Aravon shot back.

The night was dark, the moonlight obscured by the canopy of the beech tree under which he and Skathi sat watch, but he would swear he saw a smile tugging at her lips.

"Is that what's got you gloomy?" Skathi asked. "Or is it..." She trailed off, then gave a dismissive wave.

"What, Skathi?" Curiosity burned within him. "Is it what?"

The archer drew in a deep breath and, after a long moment, said, "Your father."

Her words drove a dagger of ice into Aravon's gut.

"I'm sorry, Captain," Skathi said quickly. "I didn't mean to eavesdrop, but I couldn't help overhearing what the Duke said to you when he followed you out of the party, back at Camp Marshal. I just thought..." She ducked her head. "I was worried, we all are, that maybe your attention's divided."

Aravon's spine stiffened. "You're *all* worried?" Acid surged in his throat. "Everyone else knows?"

Skathi nodded. "Somehow Noll found out, and you know how he tends to run his mouth."

Aravon clenched his jaw, his fists curling tight.

"But when he told us, it wasn't because he was trying to gossip about you or anything. He was just making sure we all know so we could…" Her eyes dropped away. "…help pick up the slack, I guess."

Aravon's jaw fell slack—not only at his surprise to hear Skathi actually *defending* Noll, but at the concern in her tone. "You all…worried about me?"

"Yeah." Skathi nodded. "You're our Captain, after all. If your head isn't on straight, we all end up dead." She shrugged. "Rather fond of staying alive, most of us are. Which means we want to make sure your head is on right before we head into battle."

Aravon's eyes burned, and he found his throat strangely thick. Hearing this—not only from the usually close-mouthed Skathi, and about his men— brought a sudden upsurge of emotions within him. He was fiercely loyal to those under his command, but it always felt odd to hear his soldiers expressing the same devotion to him.

"It's not that," Aravon said. "Or, at least, it's not *just* that." He swallowed to clear his throat. "Yes, the Duke's news of my father has me worried. Or, it did until we set out on our mission. Then there was no time for worries about home. But what's got me concerned is the fact that, like you said, we've got an icicle's chance in the fiery hell that we're pulling this off."

"Sounds kind of like Anvil and Gallows Garrison," Skathi offered. "And Bjornstadt, for that matter."

"I know, and that's the only thing that's keeping me from turning tail and riding in the opposite direction." Aravon clenched and relaxed his fists. "I can trust that Mylena's looking after my father, but…" He hesitated a long moment, finally blowing out his breath. "I'm worried that you'll all end up like Draian."

Skathi stiffened on her seat beside him, her expression growing tense. She'd only known the Mender for a few weeks, yet, like Aravon and all the others, she had grown fond of the man. Though Skathi hadn't said anything, Draian's death had hit her hard.

"Commander Rosaia has a saying." Skathi spoke in a quiet voice. "Once the arrow's left your string, all you can do is pray you aimed true."

Aravon cocked his head. "The wisdom of the Agrotorae."

Skathi shrugged again. "We're the arrow, Captain. We've left the string, so there's no going back. All we can do now is aim true." She chuckled. "Not the best saying, as arrows don't really have a mind of their own, but—"

"No, Skathi." Aravon shot her a grateful nod. "It's just what I needed to hear."

He sat back, and he felt the tension draining from his shoulders. The worries about Rivergate remained—he still had to figure out the way to deal with the Eirdkilrs and Jokull surrounding the inner keep, impossible odds under the best of circumstances, and these were far from perfect—but he felt better knowing his men not only trusted him to lead, they *cared* about him enough to worry. For a commander, that was the greatest feeling in the world.

"There's no chance you've had a brilliant idea on how to pull this off, is there?" Aravon shot her a sly grin. "It'd make my day a whole lot easier if one of you happened to solve it for me."

"Nah." Skathi shook her head, setting her braided red hair whipping around her face. "Clever shite like that's something I leave to the lot of you. Me?" She ran an affectionate hand across her bow. "I just care about picking my targets. Simple archer's work."

"You're *anything* but simple, Skathi." Aravon fixed her with a piercing gaze. "Skill at arms aside, you're as fierce and courageous a soldier as I've ever marched with. And, I suspect, a lot like my Mylena, deep down."

"How so?" Skathi's voice held a strange note of curiosity.

"You should have seen her when we first met." Aravon smiled, warmth flooding him at the long-ago memory. "Cooler than a Frozen Sea glacier, elegant as a duchess, and with a tongue sharp enough to kill every barbarian between here and the Sawtooth Mountains. I can honestly say there were days I'd rather stand up to an Eirdkilr charge than face her down. Stronger than a tidal wave and twice as devastating if you got on her bad side."

Skathi chuckled. "The woman of your dreams, eh?"

"Every damned day." Aravon nodded, his voice ringing with sincerity. "Beneath that icy exterior she presented to the world, there was a beautiful, wonderful, caring, loving woman. Took me a long time to find my way through her walls, but when I did, I fell in love with her even more."

Skathi said nothing, her expression inscrutable, and her fingers toyed with the smooth wood of her horsebow.

"What I've seen of you, Skathi," Aravon said, "that's what made me think of Mylena. When the day comes that you find the right someone to open up to, to let them in, I think you'll find exactly what I did. Her vulnerable, tender, emotional side didn't make her weaker. Instead, they made her even stronger. Letting people in can be hard, but it's worth it."

For long moments, Skathi held her tongue. "Until it's not," she said in a quiet voice. "Sometimes vulnerable is just that."

Aravon sensed a deep well of hidden meaning in her words. Something had happened in her life to cause her to erect those defensive walls around her heart and mind. But, like Belthar, she seemed unwilling to fully open up. But what she'd shown of herself, even that tiny glimpse, was enough. For now. He had to prove that he was someone she could trust, and he'd do that by letting her speak her mind when she was ready.

"Fair enough." He shrugged and leaned back against his tree trunk. "But just so you know, it might be worth giving *someone* a chance. I won't say who or when—that's up to you—but none of us can get through this on our own. Only way we survive is together."

"Thank you, Captain." The words sounded strained, yet they echoed with a hint of relief. "And just so *you* know, none of us think what happened with Draian is on you. All's shite in love and battle, a friend of mine used to say. Let it weigh on you too long, and it might drag you down."

Aravon swallowed and found his throat too thick to speak. Instead, he reached down and scratched at the scruff of Snarl's neck. The little Enfield gave a delighted whine and turned his gleaming yellow eyes up toward Aravon. Trust radiated within the fox-creature's gaze, and he leaned against Aravon, his weight and the warmth of his body comforting.

Again, Aravon felt his shoulders lifting, his breath coming easier. Skathi's words had lightened the burden weighing on him. He still had an impossible mission ahead, but he didn't have to carry the weight of command alone. His men cared about him as much as he cared about them.

"Shared burdens grow lighter," his father had always said. If he wanted to get through this mission, he'd have to do it with *their* help. He had to share his burden and trust his men wouldn't think him weak because of it.

Chapter Eleven

"Damn," Noll swore, shaking his head, "and here was me hoping you'd have this all figured out neat and tidy by the time we reached Rivergate."

Colborn drove an elbow into the little scout's ribs. Noll's armor absorbed the blow, but the impact sent him staggering into Belthar—and rebounding off the solid wall that was the big man.

"What Frog Face here means to say," Colborn growled at Noll, "is that we understand." He shot a warning glare, and Noll threw up his hands defensively. "The Duke knew how impossible this was when he asked us to do it, so none of us are expecting a miracle here. But we *all* know you'll do your damnedest to pull it off. That's all any of us can do."

Aravon's heart soared as six heads nodded in agreement, even the sarcastic Noll. In that moment, it seemed the pre-dawn light grew a little brighter, the murky fog permeating the Oldcrest forest a little thinner. The exhaustion from two days spent in the saddle diminished in the faces of his men's confidence in him.

"Some puzzles demand many minds to solve," Zaharis signed. *"Especially when those minds are as useless as Noll's."*

"Say that again, Secret Keeper, and I'll show you useless." Noll shook a fist at the pale-skinned Zaharis—an empty threat, everyone around him knew. Zaharis could take the scout apart before Noll threw a second punch. Yet, after a moment, a hint of a smile cracked Noll's scowl. He dished out a hefty dose of ribbing, especially aimed at Belthar—it seemed he could swallow his fair share as well.

"Thank you." Aravon nodded, meeting the gaze of each of his company in turn. "I guess it's going to take some getting used to this new company. In the Legion, there was a strict chain of command. I've grown so accustomed to carrying the burden of leadership that I forgot who I was leading. Not just Legionnaires following orders, but men and women capable of great things in their own rights." He placed a hand over his heart. "By the Swordsman, I swear I won't forget that again. I may bear the title of Captain, but you are *not* my subordinates. We are equals in this mission."

"Aye," Belthar rumbled. A flush of color had risen to his cheeks. "Last thing I ever expected from a Legionnaire Captain, so I won't say I mind hearing it."

Aravon knew the Legion's disdain for the Princelander regulars—even those who served under Duke Dyrund. "You've more than proven yourself, Belthar." His eyes roamed across the six faces before him. "All of you have."

"As have you, Captain," Colborn put in. All around him, even Rangvaldr, added assenting nods.

"Thank you, Colborn." Aravon smiled at the half-Fehlan lieutenant. "So I guess it's time we stop worrying about trying to prove ourselves to each other. Instead, what say we turn our attention to proving to the Eirdkilrs that we're a force to be feared?"

"Damn straight!" Skathi raised her bow. "Let's show those bastards what happens when they mess with us!"

"Aye!" Belthar and Noll echoed. Zaharis and Colborn simply smiled, and even Rangvaldr added his assent.

"Together," Aravon said with a grin. "The seven of us against three thousand enemies. Odds are about fair, don't you think?"

All around him chuckled, and Aravon felt his spirits lift even more. At that moment, he didn't care that he had no solution to their problem at Rivergate—what mattered was that he would work it out, with his small company of warriors to share the burden every step of the way.

"That brings to mind a favorite legend of my people." Rangvaldr spoke up. "The saga of Gunnarsdottir, slayer of the *Farbjodr*."

Noll groaned and opened his mouth to protest. "Not another bloody sto—"

Belthar silenced the little scout by clamping a huge hand over his mouth. Noll tried and failed to squirm free of the big man's grip.

Rangvaldr shot Belthar an appreciative nod. "While it would take hours to sing the full saga in all its glory, I will save that privilege for another time. And a less...boorish audience." A sly smile tugged at his lips, and his eyes pierced Noll.

The little scout shot back something, doubtless crude and insulting, muffled beneath Belthar's huge fingers. Yet he cringed, his squirming falling still when Belthar fixed him with a warning scowl. Perhaps the little scout knew better than to push someone with hands large and strong enough to crush his skull. When Belthar finally removed his hands, Noll remained silent, though he shot a sullen glare at Belthar.

Rangvaldr drew himself up and folded his arms across his chest, and once again Aravon was struck by the air of wisdom that emanated from the *Seiomenn*. Rangvaldr's rich voice rang clear as he told his tale.

"It is said the *Farbjodr* was a creature of the vast wilds south of the Sawtooth Mountains. A thing of nightmares, with the tail of a serpent, the fangs of a greatwolf, and a hide hard as stone. A monster from the darkest hell, it was whispered, bringer of death, bane of the *Tauld* clan long, long ago."

An instinctive shiver ran down Aravon's spine. The timbre and cadence of Rangvaldr's voice echoed with the fervency of an experienced storyteller, and he could almost *picture* the creature in his mind.

"The mightiest warriors of the *Tauld* sought to defeat the *Farbjodr*, yet though every farmstead, village, and town sent their bravest sons against the beast, they could not slay it." Rangvaldr's eyes sparkled as he lost himself in the marvel of his story.

Everyone, even the cynical Noll, leaned forward, expressions rapt, as they were drawn into the tale by the *Seiomenn's* resonant voice.

"A thousand warriors stood shoulder to shoulder, a wall of bronze and wood, yet the *Farbjodr* roared in derision and threw itself against the shield wall. Hundreds died beneath those rending claws and snarling teeth. For a day and a night they fought, the proud sons of Fehl against the solitary creature of nightmare. But when night fell, the *Farbjodr* stood alone on the battlefield. The *Tauld* broke, their courage sapped in the face of a creature that could not be slain. The *Farbjodr's* howls pursued them home. The sounds of snapping bone and tearing flesh echoed through the night as the *Farbjodr* feasted on the fallen."

Aravon's heart hammered a beat. He had little trouble imagining the deep-rooted, visceral fear of such a beast. It was the same terror every new

Legionnaire felt their first time in the shield wall, and it never truly fled no matter how many times they faced an Eirdkilr charge.

"But one among them stood tall. Gunnarsdottir, shieldmaiden and daughter of the *Tauld* chieftain." Pride echoed in Rangvaldr's voice, and a smile pulled up his lips. "She would not cower in her hut and wait for the *Farbjodr* to come for her, to tear her flesh from her bones and suck out the marrow. So, she devised a plan to defeat the *Farbjodr*. It could not be killed, but she had no need to kill it."

"What did she do?" Belthar's words came out in a whisper, his expression clearly enraptured by the *Seiomenn's* story.

"Gunnarsdottir strode onto the battlefield alone, shield and sword in hand, and faced the *Farbjodr* with no one to guard her back." Excitement sparkled in Rangvaldr's green eyes. "The *Farbjodr* laughed and taunted her, but she would not back down. When it came for her, she fled, not in retreat to the safety of her home, but toward the icy heights of the Sawtooth Mountains. The *Farbjodr* gave chase, taunting her all the way. Steeling her ears to his mockery, Gunnarsdottir led him into a deep canyon between two cliffs, where the Svellberr River once flowed. There, she turned to face the *Farbjodr* with a smile on her face and a battle song on her lips. And there she fell, the *Farbjodr's* claws in her throat, sword buried into its side."

Aravon's heart sank; a grim ending to the saga, as was the case with so many Fehlan legends.

"But as the *Farbjodr* feasted on her flesh, Gunnarsdottir raised her voice one final time and unleashed a mighty shout. Then the men of the *Tauld* appeared atop the cliffs, as she had instructed, and brought rock walls crashing down onto the *Farbjodr*. Seizing the beast's massive limbs, she held it fast as the mountains collapsed atop them both, burying them forever."

The sinking feeling in Aravon's stomach gave way to triumph at Rangvaldr's words. Despite impossible odds, facing a creature of nightmare, Gunnarsdottir had proven victorious. Even though it had cost her life, her people had won.

"Some versions of the legend say that Gunnarsdottir did not die that day," Rangvaldr continued. "But that Bani claimed her before the ice collapsed atop her. For her bravery, he carried her to Seggrholl, where she waits to return on the day that Fehl most needs her courage and—"

"Keeper's teeth!" Aravon sat bolt upright and sucked in a deep breath.

"Captain?" Colborn turned to him, brow furrowing.

Aravon's mind raced. The idea that had sprung fully-formed into his head might work. *Might*. Whirling, he dug the map of Rivergate from within his pack, his movements almost frantic as he unrolled it and studied the city's layout. His thoughts were a seething, chaotic mess, but the first hints of a desperate plan came into clarity as he stared at the map. Rangvaldr's story echoed in his mind and filled him with hope.

"Yes!" He rolled up the map and raised his eyes to his men. Curiosity and worry etched into their expressions, but Aravon met their gazes with an elated smile.

"Mind cluing the rest of us into whatever's going on in that brain of yours?" Noll put in.

"I've got an idea that could work to take back Rivergate." Aravon's grin broadened. "A crazy, suicidal idea that's barely a hint of a plan, but if we put our heads together, we've got a real shot at winning this!"

"What are you thinking?" Colborn asked.

Aravon turned to the Lieutenant. "We need a Gunnarsdottir of our own." A laugh burst from his throat at the incredulous look on Colborn's face. "And I know just who will play the part!"

Chapter Twelve

Aravon reined in his horse as the village of Bannockburn came into view at the bottom of the hill. One by one, his men drew their mounts to a halt and turned their masked faces toward him.

"You all know your roles to play?" he signed in the Secret Keeper hand language. *"Once we assume command, you've got your tasks."*

Six helmeted heads nodded assent. The fragments of Aravon's plan—inspired, in part by Rangvaldr's story—had come together over the last two and a half days of travel. Everyone in their company had contributed to the battle strategy and though plenty of details remained to sort out, at least each of those under his command knew their part of the mission.

Drawing in a deep breath, Aravon turned back toward the Legion encampment below. *And it all begins with Captain Lemaire.*

Worry tightened his gut; after his less-than-delightful encounter with Commander Oderus of Jade Battalion, he was leery of what lay ahead. But he *had* to take control of Topaz Battalion's Second and Third Companies, and quickly. The more time wasted convincing Captain Lemaire of his bona fides, the greater the risk that Rivergate's supplies would run out or the Eirdkilrs and Jokull overran the weakening defenses.

Aravon grimaced beneath his mask and, tapping his heels against his horse's flanks, set the charger into motion. Colborn fell in beside him, flanked by Belthar, Skathi, and Rangvaldr, with Zaharis and Noll bringing up the rear. Down the hill they rode, seven faceless, nameless warriors wearing strange mottle-patterned armor and bearing the Prince's personal seal.

A shadow wheeled above Aravon's head, and he caught a glimpse of widespread wings and orange fur circling high over the Legion encampment. Snarl had been too energetic to remain in hiding, and the nearest tree cover had been more than a mile from Bannockburn—too far for the sound of Aravon's bone whistle to travel. He could only hope Snarl didn't tire himself out flying; they might need to get a message to Duke Dyrund, and an exhausted Enfield would serve them no good.

Bannockburn was a medium-sized town located at the crossroads where the Marshway intersected with the road that led to Bridgekeep, Westhaven's westernmost fortress. Home to a few thousand souls, it thrived on the herds and cattle that grazed the hills north of the town, as well as the trade that flowed through on the way to and from Rivergate.

But Aravon's course led east, away from the village itself and toward the cleared stretch of ground upon which the men of Topaz Battalion had made their camp. Though there were no trees to provide shelter from the winds, the broad swath of grassy flatland near the village made an excellent location for a camp. There, the sea of dull brown canvas tents spread out in the precise, neat layout universal to every Legion encampment.

Aravon rode straight toward the broad pathway that led to the heart of the Legion camp, mud flying from the hooves of their fast-moving horses. The sentries on guard straightened at their approach, raising spears and tightening grips on their shields.

One, a man bearing the insignia of a Sergeant with the unshaven jaw, broad face, and growling voice to match, held up a hand. "Stop right there!"

Aravon recognized the accent—Nyslians spoke in a rounded, flowing tone far softer than harsher Voramians or Praamians, or the clipped, fast-speaking Drashi—but not the man. Then again, he had only come in contact with Legionnaires from Nysl once, and that briefly during his years as a Lieutenant.

"Sergeant." The mask muffled Aravon's voice, but he'd learned—as they all had—to project their voices to get past the thick leather covering their faces. "Take us to Captain Lemaire."

Without dismounting, he drew out the Prince's silver griffin pendant and held it up to the Legionnaire. Sunlight glinted off the bright, shining metal, and recognition dawned in the soldier's eyes. Clearly he, like the rest of the Legion, had heard of Prince Toran's instructions to defer to them.

Yet still the Sergeant hesitated. Like any well-trained officer—even a non-commissioned one—he didn't just follow orders blindly, no matter who they came from. Years of experience had apparently taught him to rely on his own intuition as well. His eyes narrowed and he fixed Aravon and his companions with an intense scrutiny that bordered on suspicious. But, as his eyes flashed back toward the pendant in Aravon's hand, he seemed to make up his mind.

"Straight down the middle." The Nyslian Sergeant stepped aside and motioned for them to pass. "You can't miss him. Look for the oversized bruiser and Captain Lemaire will be the fellow in his shadow."

Aravon cocked an eyebrow—an expression rendered useless by his mask—but nodded. "Thank you, Sergeant."

The Legionnaire gave him a crisp, military salute as he rode past.

A familiar longing surged within Aravon as he cantered down the muddy avenue toward the Captain's tent. He'd spent the last fifteen years of his life in camps like this, living in cramped tents, eating food that could barely be considered edible at the best of times, and sharing every part of his life with soldiers just like those around him. Men who sat sharpening their weapons, throwing dice, or napping in the shade of their tents, or watched Aravon's silent company pass with curiosity burning in their eyes.

The *clang* of a blacksmith's hammer echoed somewhere in the distance. On the western edge of the camp, the officers' horses stamped at the ends of their tethering ropes. Soldiers swore, shouted, laughed, and barked orders—or, in the case of one unfortunate platoon, dug latrine trenches. Downwind of the camp, of course.

All around him, soldiers lived their lives for the only today guaranteed them, making the most of their life in camp, knowing that at any moment they would be summoned to battle. A battle from which many of them would not survive or walk away unscathed. This, Aravon knew, was the calm before the storm. He and his men brought the storm with them. By nightfall, this orderly encampment would be uprooted and packed as the Legionnaires prepared to march on Rivergate.

Sorrow tightened his chest. He'd been here before, had watched men laugh, shout, and doze one day and buried them the next. It never got easier, no matter how many times he lived it.

"Soldiers do as soldiers must," his father had always told him. That knowledge filled their eyes with a grim determination, despite the smiles on their lips and the bragging, jesting words rolling off their tongues. The veterans of Topaz Battalion laughed harder, shouted louder, and boasted bigger than the raw recruits. They knew what lay in their futures and they were determined to squeeze every drop of life out of their day.

Yet, he forced himself to keep riding, to sit tall in his saddle. If he didn't give the orders that sent these men to face death, Rivergate would fall. He would put his life on the line beside these men, for the sake of their comrades and the Westhaveners trapped in Rivergate.

He steeled himself as he approached the Captain's tent, but his jaw dropped in surprise as he caught sight of the man standing guard at the entrance. Taller than Aravon, taller even than Belthar by fully half a foot, he was a towering wall of steel and muscle defending his commanding officer. He stiffened at Aravon's approach and dropped a hand to his short sword—little more than a dagger in his massive fingers.

"State your business," he growled.

"The Duke's business," Aravon said, though it took effort to keep the surprise from his voice. Even atop the oversized *Kostarasar* charger, he felt dwarfed by the giant of a man.

The soldier's face creased into a pensive scowl as Aravon drew out the silver griffin pendant and held it up. After a moment, he nodded. "Captain!" he called without turning away. "We got company."

Seconds later, a man—normal-sized, almost appearing small in the shadow of his huge sentry—strode from the tent. He took one look at Aravon's pendant, armor, and mask, and gestured for them to enter the tent.

Aravon dismounted, which made him feel even slighter as he strode past the giant and followed the Captain into his tent. A simple tent, with only a cot, canvas camp chair, foldable table, and wooden chest containing all of his belongings. The only personal item was the round, wax-covered bottle tucked sitting beside the leg of the Captain's chair.

Captain Lemaire stooped, retrieved the bottle, and poured wine into a tin cup. "Drink?" He held out the cup. "It is not the best white, but it is Nyslian, so it cannot be too bad." He spoke with the same soft, rolling accent as the Nyslian Sergeant, and he failed to conjunct his words like Princelanders or men from the mainland's southern cities.

Aravon shook his head. "Thank you, Captain." He reached into his pocket and drew out Duke Dyrund's letter.

Captain Lemaire scanned the letter—a simple message proclaiming Aravon's right to command Topaz Battalion's Second and Third Companies—glanced at the Duke's seal at the bottom, and nodded. "Good enough for me." He rolled up the letter and tucked it into the official Legionnaire dispatch pouch. "You are here to lead us to Rivergate, *oui*?"

"I am." With deliberate movements, Aravon reached up and untied the two straps holding his mask in place. His face uncovered, he held out a hand. "You may call me Captain Snarl." He'd grown to like the nom-de-guerre, an easy one to remember.

"I wish I could say it was a pleasure, Captain, but that would do the both of us a disservice." Captain Lemaire's mustachioed face grew grim as he shook Aravon's hand. "It's nasty business we're facing. Three thousand enemies, and just the two hundred of us. Half of whom are greener than a ripe Anjou."

Aravon shrugged. "From what I've heard of Nyslians, I've no doubt their metal will hold strong when it comes time." He actually *hadn't* heard anything particularly special about the men of Nysl—Princelanders held few mainlanders in high regard—but a bit of encouragement to the Captain could build confidence, which would trickle down to his Lieutenants, Sergeants, and Legionnaires.

"Your words are kind." A smile broadened Captain Lemaire's handsome, angular face. "I trust my men will do you proud."

"Given it's their comrades holed up in Rivergate, I've no doubt." Compliments given, Aravon moved on to the matter at hand. "Have you scouted along the Standelfr?"

"*Oui*." Captain Lemaire nodded. "I've had men up and down the river for ten miles east and west."

"Excellent." Aravon found his own confidence increasing; it seemed Captain Lemaire was at least *fairly* competent. "Have them give a report to my man Foxclaw. The little one at the back." He used Noll's code name—after adopting the nom-de-guerre of Captain Snarl for himself, he'd assigned similar sobriquets to the rest of his company.

The Captain shot a glance past Aravon. "Of course, Captain."

"And I'll want to see Rivergate Bridge for myself as well, once night has fallen."

"Captain?" The officer cocked his head, curiosity etched into his aquiline features.

91

"I've the beginnings of a plan, but in order to know more, I'll need to see the bridge personally."

"As you say." Captain Lemaire tugged at one corner of his dark brown moustache. "I will send Private Woryn along as a guide."

"Good." Aravon shot a glance over his shoulder. "Also, I need you to pass the word to your men that I and my men are now in command of Second and Third Companies."

Again, Captain Lemaire's brow furrowed, this time a hint of worry showing in his eyes.

"We're not here to stay, Captain," Aravon said. "But while we prepare for the battle at Rivergate, I need it to be clear to everyone that the orders I and my men give are to be followed immediately, without question."

After a moment, Captain Lemaire inclined his head. "I shall make it clearer than Nyslian crystal, *mon Capitaine*."

"Thank you." Aravon fixed the man with a piercing stare. "And there is one thing I need *you* to understand, Captain."

Captain Lemaire's face grew serious, a shadow passing behind his eyes.

"I have no intention of throwing your men's lives away." Aravon spoke in a quiet voice. "The danger we face, the monumental impossibility of the task laid at our feet, I fully understand the risks that you and those under your command are taking. And, we *will* be asking a great deal of all of you in the battle to come. We will all face certain death against an overwhelming enemy. You have my word that I will do everything in my power to give your men a fighting chance."

Captain Lemaire digested the words in silence, his expression pensive. Like any Legion officer with battle experience, he had to know that Aravon couldn't promise anything more. Men died in war, no matter how much their officers, comrades, and loved ones wished otherwise. Yet there were two types of commanders: those who fought for an objective, and those who fought for their men. The mission always mattered, but a good officer knew not to let it outweigh the lives of the soldiers bleeding, sweating, and dying to complete it.

"Thank you, Captain." Lemaire held out a hand once more. "That is all I can ask for." The tension drained from his face, and he inclined his head. "I will assemble the Lieutenants so you can relay your orders."

"Good." Captain Aravon nodded. "And while you are gathering your men, I will speak to mine." Replacing his mask, he strode from the tent.

Outside, he found his men had dismounted—all but Colborn and Zaharis, who hadn't moved from their saddles. *"Go,"* he signed to the two. *"But be back an hour after dark."*

"We'll do our best, Captain," Zaharis' fingers flashed. *"But I've always found Dragon Thorngrass to be notoriously stubborn."*

"Get what you can, then get back here," Aravon commanded. *"I need both your eyes and minds at Rivergate Bridge."*

"Yes, Captain!" Colborn saluted and, turning his horse's head, galloped down the avenue toward the edge of the Legion encampment. Zaharis followed, and the two soon disappeared among the sea of tents and soldiers.

Aravon turned back to his remaining men; he, Noll, Belthar, Skathi, and Rangvaldr had their own tasks to attend to. His fingers flashed in the silent hand language, but Noll paid him no attention. Instead, the little scout was busy staring up at Belthar and the hulking sentry.

Belthar stood head and shoulders taller than Noll, yet the top of his head barely reached the giant's eyebrows. The Nyslian sentry frowned down at the masked man, sizing him up just as Belthar did. Despite the size difference, the breadth of their shoulders were comparable, and Belthar's heavy musculature was a match for the giant's.

"Corporal Balegar!" Captain Lemaire's voice sounded from beside Aravon. "Get Aterraign, Dellare, and the others here double time. Rayoque as well."

The big sentry hesitated a moment, eyes still locked on Belthar, before snapping a crisp salute. "Yes, *Capitaine*!" His huge fist *clanked* against his breastplate and he strode off, lumbering at a surprisingly speedy pace for his size.

Aravon snapped his fingers, and the sound brought the enraptured Noll spinning around.

"Noll, liaise with the companies' scouts and find out as much as you can about the Standelfr," Aravon signed.

"Yes, Captain." Noll's nimble fingers formed the hand signals easily.

Aravon turned to Skathi. *"Find out what sort of archers you can scare up among Second and Third Companies."*

A noise suspiciously akin to a snort echoed from beneath Skathi's mask. *"I'd be surprised if there's anyone even half as good as Noll."*

The little scout straightened at the compliment, and Aravon could almost imagine the bright smile beneath Noll's mask.

Skathi's fingers flashed once more. "*So none of them will be able to hit anything smaller than the Sawtooth Mountains.*"

Noll's hands formed the rude gesture Zaharis had taught them—one that Aravon had *purposely* avoided learning the meaning of, due to its extreme vulgarity—but Skathi had already turned away.

"*Belthar, you and Rangvaldr get into Bannockburn and see what supplies you can find. Lumber, steel, iron, anything else we can use. If nothing, a few dozen axes. We'll cut our own lumber if we have to.*"

"*Aye, Captain.*" Belthar saluted—it was getting better, Aravon had to admit, and he couldn't fault the big man's enthusiasm as his fist *thumped* on the alchemically-treated leather breastplate—and hurried away, Rangvaldr beside him.

Aravon watched the two men go. The previous night, Rangvaldr had approached him with an unusual request: he wanted to visit the Mender's tents and offer what aid he could to any ill or wounded Legionnaires. Aravon had seen the power of his glowing holy stones, the way they'd healed an Eyrr warrior on the brink of death. Yet he doubted the Menders, healers and priests of the Swordsman, would welcome "Fehlan magic". Many Princelanders regarded the Fehlans as heathens, little better than savages. He'd determined it was best to keep the power of those holy stones a secret, for now.

We may need them yet, given what we face, Aravon thought.

He turned back to Captain Lemaire, who remained standing at the entrance to his tent, a worried look darkening his angular features. Aravon, too, felt the same concern over what lay ahead, despite his confidence in his men's abilities to carry out their plan. Yet he couldn't let it show. Even with the mask to conceal his expression, he had to exude assurance. Soldiers looked to their commanders' examples, and even a hint of uncertainty or self-doubt in the battle that lay ahead could spell the difference between success and failure—death for not only the Second and Third Companies, but all in Rivergate.

Drawing in a deep breath, he strode into Captain Lemaire's tent, removed his mask, and steeled his courage to relay his orders—orders that the military-minded Legionnaires would see as insane.

Chapter Thirteen

As Aravon had feared, the Standelfr River truly *was* as impassible as he'd been warned.

The fast-flowing river had carved deep into the earth on its way west toward the Frozen Sea. Cliff walls thirty feet high bordered the river to the north and south, continuing unbroken as far as Aravon could see—according to Captain Lemaire's scouts, at least twenty miles east and five miles west.

Even if they could manage to build a boat and lower it to the river, crossing the Standelfr river would be next-to-impossible given the river's racing current. They'd waste precious time and energy trying to fight their way across in little boats and trying to scale the thirty-foot southern cliff. And all that beneath the watchful eye of the enemy.

From his position in the trees clustered twenty yards from the northern riverbank, Aravon had a clear line of sight into Rivergate. Eirdkilrs with blue-stained faces and clad in the filthy white pelts of wasteland icebears rampaged through the city, filling the air with their howling war cries. Beside them, the smaller, ragged figures of their Jokull cousins set fire to wooden homes, brought down stone walls, and wreaked havoc through the shops and markets of northern Rivergate.

But not *all* of the enemy was distracted in looting and destruction. Of the two hundred enemies Aravon could see, more than half were focused on the wall of Rivergate Keep itself, surrounding it and keeping the Princelanders locked up. Another thirty held the southern end of the Rivergate Bridge—they might not have to worry about soldiers marching across the destroyed bridge, but whoever led them clearly wasn't going to take chances.

Damn! Aravon gritted his teeth and let out a long breath. *And here I was hoping they'd make it easy for us.*

He turned to the little figure crouching beside him in the late-night shadows of the trees. "Well?" he asked. "Tell me Rayoque and his scouts found something."

Noll grunted. "Maybe." A long moment of silence passed as the scout contemplated. "It's not much, but there *may* be a spot around ten miles upriver where we could get a few dozen men across and into Jokull territory. And I say *may* with extreme hesitation. I saw it myself and it's going to be a bloody nightmare."

"Can you do it, though?" Aravon stared at Noll, his gaze piercing. "Pretend our lives depend on it."

"Keeper's teeth!" Noll snorted. "Won't take a thespian to pull that off." After a second, he shrugged and threw up his hands. "Best I can say is we'll do our damnedest. With the Secret Keeper, Colborn, and Rangvaldr, we've got a half-decent shot. If Colborn can handle the Jokull marshes like he handled the bogs back at Camp Marshal, it might not be totally impossible."

From Noll, that was about as positive as it got.

Aravon shifted to his right, his head swiveling to the figure on his left. "Thoughts, Skathi?"

The archer's eyes were fixed on the walls, buildings, and streets on the other side of the Standelfr River, across the crumbled remains of what had once been Rivergate Bridge.

"Range isn't ideal," she muttered at last. "Two, two hundred-fifty yards, at least. Belthar's crossbow will handle it, but he's no marksman. Even perched right on the cliff's edge, I'll be lucky to hit four out of five targets at this distance if I have to shoot fast."

Aravon raised an eyebrow. He'd never heard Skathi admit even a hint of inability, much less within hearing range of Noll. Yet the scout made no comment; he was far too concerned with his own role in their desperate plan to spare any scorn.

"From what I hear, Woryn's not half-bad with a bow," Skathi said. "He's no Agrotorae, but maybe, between us, we've got a chance of picking off a few targets."

"If Colborn's crew play their part," Aravon said, "a *few* is all we'll have to worry about."

Skathi nodded, though her expression remained unconvinced. Finally, she shrugged. "I'll do what I can."

Aravon clapped her on the shoulder. "Best I could ask for." Without rising from his crouch, he scrambled backward, deeper into the densely packed trees that grew alongside the Marshway. Leaves rustled as he passed and twigs *snapped* beneath his feet, so loudly he worried the enemies holding the bridge would hear him. Tension tightened his shoulders with every step, and the darkness seemed to press in around him, adding to the burden on his chest.

Yet he forced himself to remain calm, to push back the worry. *We have the plan, now it's time to work it through to completion.*

A hundred feet back from the forest's edge, he reached the small clearing that he'd designated the meeting spot for his companions scouting the river. Zaharis, Colborn, and Rangvaldr stood waiting for him in silence. All three turned at his approach.

Aravon addressed the Secret Keeper. "Now that you've given it a good look, Zaharis, do you think you can make it work?"

Zaharis inclined his head. "*Between all the materials Belthar and Rangvaldr came up with from Bannockburn and what the Legionnaires can chop down tomorrow, it ought to come together well enough.*" His fingers moved calmly, yet his unmasked face revealed far more worry than Aravon had ever seen. "*But I'm not sure it's best for me to leave this half of the plan to Belthar.*" He shot a glance at the big man. "*No offense, but building's not exactly your strong suit. Especially not something this specific.*"

Belthar's face tightened, but he held his peace. Zaharis truly *didn't* intend offense; he simply stated a fact. Thankfully, Belthar's temperament wasn't so prickly he couldn't recognize and admit his limitations, at least to those he considered his friends. And, without Noll nearby, he didn't have to worry about being mocked for any shortcomings.

"I wanted you here, too, Zaharis," Aravon said. "But I need you with Colborn and the others. That half of the plan carries twice the risk and thrice the difficulty. Without you and that Dragon Thorngrass, they'd be going into battle with nothing more than steel."

Colborn nodded and smacked the Secret Keeper on the back. "Your fault for proving yourself so damned indispensable at Broken Canyon and Bjornstadt."

Despite the solemn nature of their discussion, Aravon couldn't help a small grin. Zaharis' alchemical "tricks" had given Jade Battalion a chance to retreat, preventing a wholesale massacre by the Eirdkilrs.

"We'll make it work," Belthar said. "I've already conscripted half a dozen Bannockburners into helping me, men who *actually* know their way around building tools. With Legionnaire hands to help, we'll get it done in time."

After a moment, Zaharis inclined his head. "*So be it,*" he signed. "*I'll get you the final plans shortly after midnight. Follow them exactly—*" Fire flashed in his eyes. "*EXACTLY, down to the inch, and maybe it'll save you all from a watery swim.*"

Belthar nodded. "Down to the inch." His eyes flashed past Aravon toward the edge of the forest where he knew Noll crouched, a wry smile tugged at his lips. Mention of "inch" seemed to have given him an insult or retort to use against the little scout next chance he got.

Aravon turned to Colborn and Rangvaldr. "Think you can do it?" he asked. "Think you can get the better part of a hundred Legionnaires through Jokull territory in time to attack from the south?"

Colborn and the *Seiomenn* exchanged glances. They appeared calm, no trace of uncertainty in their eyes. Battle-hardened men both, with years spent navigating the Fehlan wilds—Rangvaldr as warrior and shaman of the Eyrr, Colborn as half-Fehlan of…Aravon wasn't certain which clan. Yet, they both appeared confident in their abilities.

"Aye, Captain." Colborn nodded. "We'll get where we need to go."

Aravon drew in a deep breath. "Then, by the Swordsman's grace, we attack Rivergate tomorrow at midnight."

Chapter Fourteen

Aravon sat beside the small fire burning in the center of their small camp, a hundred yards south of the Legion tents, and stroked Snarl's fur absentmindedly. The Enfield was fast asleep, exhausted from a day spent circling the Legion camp and trotting through the shadowy woods after Aravon, Skathi, and the others scouting the Standelfr River. His wings gave a little flap in time with his scratching back leg, as if he dreamed of pursuing a particularly plump rabbit or tasty pigeon.

Despite his own fatigue, Aravon found it difficult to calm his racing mind enough to sleep. He wouldn't get another chance until the following night's battle had been won, but his whirling thoughts spun about in a seething, chaotic maelstrom that kept rest at bay.

Is this the right plan? He asked himself the question for the hundredth time. The rest of his company hadn't come up with any better plan—though their additions to *his* strategy had increased their chance of success—but he couldn't help worrying. There had to be something he'd missed, forgotten, overlooked, or simply didn't know. The cleverest plans rarely survived the clash of swords. The last thing he wanted was to be caught off-guard or surprised in the middle of the battle.

Finally, he gave up any hope of rest and stood. Snarl didn't so much as stir as Aravon extricated his feet from beneath the Enfield's furry belly and left the comforting warmth of the fire. He couldn't sit idle or rest with so much hanging in the balance. The only way to find peace was to get up and *do* something.

Maybe I can help Colborn. After a moment's thought, he discarded the idea. Colborn didn't *need* any help; the half-Fehlan Lieutenant might see his presence as interference, or an indication that Aravon didn't trust him. That was the last thing he wanted. Colborn had proven himself worthy of Aravon's confidences every time. Letting him do his job was the best way to ensure it got done.

Aravon welcomed the cool, dark silence of the night. Away from the fire, with the Legion's main encampment three hundred yards to their east, the only sound he heard was the whistling of the wind, the gentle rustling of the grass that grew thick on the flat land. He closed his eyes and drew in a deep breath, willing his mind to calm.

The sound of creaking leather and quiet conversation echoed behind him. Aravon opened his eyes and glanced back. Rangvaldr was strapping on his armor and adjusting the cinches on his leather breastplate, while Zaharis rummaged through the contents of the wooden chest he'd carried all the way from Camp Marshal. Noll sat beside the Secret Keeper, trying to peer around Zaharis' body to get a glimpse into the chest's contents.

"What's this?" Noll held up a small object that looked like a studded metal ball. "Some sort of steel apple?" He shook it around, earning a frantic look from the Secret Keeper

"*It's called an Earthshaker, Noll.*" Anger etched Zaharis' face as he snatched it from the scout's hand. "*Shake it around too much,*" he signed one-handed, "*and we'll all find out why it's got that name.*"

Noll's eyes widened and he leaned back, as if from a striking serpent. "Damn, Zaharis, and you just leave that lying around?!"

"*No, I don't.*" Zaharis' jaw clenched, his face reddening with irritation as he stuffed the Earthshaker into the chest. "*I'm trying to find the specific ingredients needed to save your ass once we hit the Eirdkilrs and Jokull. But you're making it damned difficult and nearly getting us killed in the process!*"

"Easy!" Noll threw up his hands in a defensive gesture. "Forgive me for taking interest in your 'magic', Secret Keeper."

As Noll had no doubt intended, the jab struck home. Zaharis' fingers signed insults that would have made even the hardest Icespire sailor cringe, and the scout's eyes flew wide beneath the barrage.

"Whoa, Zaharis, take it easy." Noll recoiled beneath the force of the Secret Keeper's anger. "I was just playing around here."

Zaharis breathed through his nose, his face a mask of fury. "*Don't you have some getting ready to do?*"

"Nah!" Noll gave a dismissive wave. "I packed hours ago. Then again, I'm not carrying half as much stuff as—"

"Noll." Rangvaldr's deep, authoritative voice cut into the scout's words. "Maybe we give Zaharis a few moments to himself, yes?"

"Sure," Noll said, a hint of sarcasm tingeing his words. "I'll do that." Standing, he turned away from the Secret Keeper and strode toward Rangvaldr. He came to stand face to face with Rangvaldr—face to *chest,* more like, given that the *Seiomenn* towered over the little scout—his jaw thrust out in that stubborn, defiant expression of bravado he adopted when trading boasts with Belthar or trying to out-retort Colborn.

"Then again, maybe *you* explain what in the fiery hell you're *really* doing here, eh, *Seiomenn?"* He spat the last word like a curse. "Oh, you talked a fancy game back in Camp Marshal, but I'll believe you're being straight when I see it with my own eyes."

Aravon hurried toward the two men. "Noll this isn't the time to—"

"No, Captain!" The scout whirled on Aravon, the dim moonlight turning his scar bright white against the deep, angry red of his face. "Now is *exactly* the time. Now that we're going into an impossible battle with him by our side." He thrust a finger at the *Seiomenn.* "He said he'd have no trouble killing Eirdklrs, but we're going up against the Jokull as well." He turned back to Rangvaldr. "Can you really swing your sword knowing it's one of your own people dying at the opposite end?"

"If I must." Rangvaldr's face and manner was serene, yet his expression had grown serious. "The Jokull have chosen to align themselves with the Eirdkilrs. They have chosen the path of war and bloodshed."

"And you're all sunshine and smiles?" Noll snarled. He jabbed a finger into Rangvaldr's chest. "Isn't what *you're* doing exactly the same? Killing them before they kill you!"

Rangvaldr met Noll's fury with icy calm. "There are battles and there are battles, young man." He leaned forward, looming over the scout. Yet no anger blazed in his eyes; instead, a deep, almost sorrowful shadow settled onto him. "I fight the battle for peace, to put an end to the war on Fehl. I and my people have no quarrel with the Princelanders. We want nothing more than to coexist, to share the bounties of this world with which Nuius has blessed us. But the *Tauld,* and now the Jokull, fight for the sake of war and death. *That* is why I fight. Peace not only for the Eyrr, but for all on Fehl. Fehlan and Princelander

101

alike. Even the Eirdkilrs, if they managed to see past their hate and lay down their weapons."

"Bloody little chance that'll happen!" Noll spat.

"Indeed." Rangvaldr inclined his head. "And that is why I choose to take up arms against those who were once my people." Anguish darkened his expression. "Even as I grieve at the senseless death, I will do what I must to protect my home, my land. As do you. As do we all. *That,* young man, is the mission that unites us all."

Noll's face hardened in a scowl, but he could find no reply. "Pah!" he finally spat, then turned on his heel and stalked off into the darkness.

Aravon was about to pursue the scout—Noll needed to get over his innate distrust of Rangvaldr if they were to fight side by side—but Rangvaldr's quiet voice stopped him.

"Leave him, Captain." The *Seiomenn* sighed and shook his head. "Truth be told, I do not resent his suspicion. Had I not known what manner of man Duke Dyrund is, I, too, would have been suspicious of your motives for joining the fight at Bjornstadt."

Aravon turned a questioning gaze on him.

"Fear not, Captain." Rangvaldr gave him a small smile. "The Duke is not the *only* Princelander I have come to respect. Your courage in defending my home was what made up my mind to join you. And, as I have sworn to you and the Duke both, you have my loyalty to the end."

"I know that." Aravon put a hand on the Fehlan's shoulder. "And I'm sorry about Noll. He's been a soldier too long. Trust comes hard to a man who's known war and death all his life."

"Speaking from experience?" The little smile on Rangvaldr's face held warmth as he studied Aravon. "You seem to have survived your years as a soldier surprisingly unhardened."

"Blame Mylena for that." Aravon shrugged. "It's hard to hate with someone so loving in your life."

"You're more fortunate than most, Captain." Rangvaldr chuckled. "From the Duke's words, you alone among our company are blessed with family."

"I…" The words caught Aravon off-guard. "I guess so." He hadn't given it much thought—he'd simply accepted the soldiers as his to command without digging into who they were beneath the armor. But it made sense that the Duke had only chosen those without familial ties. Easier not to exist with no one around to care about you.

"And you?" he asked. "Any family waiting for you in Bjornstadt, or among the lovely ladies of the Eyrr?"

Rangvaldr chuckled. "More than a few ladies." Mischief twinkled in his eyes. "Being the *Seiomenn* has its perks, after all."

Aravon couldn't help smiling.

"But no." Rangvaldr shook his head. "No wife, no sons or daughters. Only the burden of my past as a warrior of the Eyrr, and my duties as *Seiomenn* to my people. All Fehlans, not just the Eyrr."

His tone of voice grew heavy, as if a burden weighed on his shoulders. Aravon had a pretty good idea as to its source. Noll's accusation might not have been too far off the mark.

"Can you do it?" he asked quietly. "Can you kill the Jokull, your own people?"

Pain flashed across Rangvaldr's face, but he stiffened. "Of course, Capt—"

"No." Aravon gripped the man's shoulder tighter. "I ask this not as your commanding officer, but as a fellow soldier. A friend." He drew in a deep breath. "You were right when you said that carrying around the guilt of Draian's death will consume me from the inside. But if killing the Jokull will do the same to you, I want to know. Maybe there's another way. A way that doesn't force you to raise sword against Fehlans."

A sad smile played on Rangvaldr's lips. "I thank you, Captain. Truly. Your concern does you credit." He drew in a long breath, exhaled slowly. "Truth be told, I had thought of asking you just that. I *could* stay back from the battle, find a way to help where I am not forced to bear the burden of Jokull deaths on my conscience."

"But?" Aravon cocked his head.

"But if I did that, I would be no better than Ailmaer."

Aravon's eyes widened. Ailmaer, Chief of the Eyrr clan, had cowered in the longhouse—claiming to "protect" the women and children—during the battle of Bjornstadt. Any man who had fought as bravely as Rangvaldr could never be considered craven.

"Ailmaer hid from the difficult choice," Rangvaldr said, his voice quiet. "He faced an impossible decision but rather than choose a path, no matter how

103

difficult to walk down, he opted for inaction. In avoiding that responsibility, he proved himself a coward."

"And you will not hide from the difficult choice here." Aravon nodded understanding. "Even if it burdens your heart?"

"My heart will be strong, knowing I am doing the right thing for my people." The words seemed to cost Rangvaldr, yet he spoke them nonetheless. "I will carry the burden, as is my duty as *Seiomenn*, for the sake of the Eyrr and all Fehlans. With it, I also carry the hope that one day—soon, if Nuius is good—I will once again put down my sword never to pick it up again."

"That is the hope." Aravon gave Rangvaldr a warm smile. "And that is why Duke Dyrund selected us, and now you, for this mission. If we can find a way to put an end to the Eirdkilrs, Fehl will once again know peace."

"And I will do everything in my power to hasten that day." Rangvaldr let out another long breath. "Even if I must carry the weight of Jokull deaths on my conscience."

"I never doubted you." Aravon rested a hand on the *Seiomenn's* shoulder. "Given time, Noll and the others will feel the same."

"Indeed." Rangvaldr's expression grew grave. "But, perhaps Noll was not as far off as he believed."

Aravon cocked his head. "Oh?"

Rangvaldr shook his head. "I am not the only Fehlan that will raise a hand against their own in this battle." He turned his palms upward. "Colborn will find himself facing a difficult choice in the mission ahead. One I am not certain he is prepared for."

Aravon's brow furrowed. "You think Colborn's going to have a problem?"

Rangvaldr shrugged. "It couldn't hurt to ask. He is a strong man, yet even the mightiest oak will bow beneath the weight of a mountain."

Aravon opened his mouth to reply, yet stopped himself. He had no doubt Colborn would do whatever was needed to win the battle, no matter what. But what manner of commander would he be if he ignored the *Seiomenn's* advice?

Finally, Aravon nodded. "I will speak with him about it."

"You are a good man, Captain Aravon of the Princelands." Rangvaldr returned the grip, fingers strong and firm around Aravon's forearm. "A good man, and a better commander."

Aravon flushed beneath the praise, warmth burning bright in his chest. His respect for the *Seiomenn* had only increased after this conversation. Rangvaldr knew the truth of his actions, yet he bore the weight of his position without hesitation. That strength and sincerity of spirit shone in his eyes, echoed in every word.

After a long moment, Rangvaldr released his hand and stepped back. "Now, Captain, by your leave, I will go help Colborn prepare the Legionnaires to march."

"Of course." Aravon nodded. "May the Swordsman guide your steps and strengthen your arm, Rangvaldr."

A warm smile broadened the *Seiomenn's* face, and his hand went to the gemstone pendant around his neck. "And may Nuius' wisdom light your path to victory." With a little bow, he slung his pack over his shoulder and hurried toward the Legion encampment.

Aravon watched the man go. If he'd had any doubts about the man before, they were erased now. Fehl or not, no matter what happened, Rangvaldr would stand beside his companions.

A hand on his shoulder brought Aravon spinning around. Zaharis thrust a rolled-up parchment at him. "*Make sure Belthar doesn't stray from my exact instructions,*" the Secret Keeper signed. "*Whatever his talents are, architecture isn't one of them.*"

Aravon chuckled and took the parchment. "I'll impress upon him the importance of being precise."

Zaharis turned to leave, but paused mid-step. He shot a glance over his shoulder at Aravon. "*He's right, you know. Rangvaldr.*"

"Right about what?" Aravon asked.

"*You are a good man, Captain.*" The Secret Keeper smiled. "*Anyone who cares about his men like you do is worth following. Even on a half-baked, suicidal plan like this.*"

Aravon was so stunned by Zaharis' words that he failed to form a coherent reply before the Secret Keeper had drawn too far away.

"Captain?" A quiet voice from immediately behind him snapped Aravon from his thoughts.

Aravon spun and nearly jumped as he found Noll standing two feet away. Noll returned from wherever he'd stomped off to, his anger had faded, and with the return of calm, he once again moved with the stealthy grace that made him such an effective scout.

"Swordsman!" Aravon swore. "You'd give Colborn a run for his money, sneaking up on a fellow like that."

A grin broke Noll's expression, but disappeared a moment later, replaced by a frown. "You really trust him?" His eyes darted in the direction of Rangvaldr's retreating back. "He's a Fehlan, after all."

"A Fehlan, yes," Aravon said, "but one who's joined our cause. The cause of bringing peace to Fehl and putting an end to this war with the Eirdkilrs."

Noll's expression grew pensive. "So if our places were switched, and *you* were going out into enemy territory, you'd want him in dagger-range of your back?"

Aravon nodded without hesitation. "Yes. Beneath the warrior is the healer who saved lives back at Bjornstadt, the *Seiomenn* who cares for his people. He believes in what we're doing, and why we're doing it. That's enough for me, and it ought to be enough for you, too."

The scout's eyes narrowed in thought, and he remained silent for a long moment. Finally, he shrugged. "So be it." He fixed Aravon with a piercing stare. "You might be a shite archer, respectfully sir, but you've proven yourself a half-decent judge of character."

"Thank you?" Aravon raised an eyebrow. Leave it to Noll to insult and compliment him in one breath.

"Don't mention it." Noll shook his head. "Ever. You tell anyone I said that, I'll deny it up and down."

Aravon chuckled. "Your secret's safe with me."

"Good." Now a small smile broadened Noll's face. "See you tomorrow night, Captain."

"Swordsman be with you." Aravon clapped the little man on the shoulder. "Now get hoofing, or you'll never reach your destination in time for us to kick Eirdkilr arse!"

Chapter Fifteen

"Captain Snarl, I mean no disrespect, but I am obliged to question this course of action." Captain Lemaire turned toward him. "Is it truly wise to send my Legionnaires into enemy territory with only their weapons?"

Aravon stifled a grunt; he'd expected resistance from Captain Lemaire the moment he'd suggested the plan.

"Yes, Captain." He spoke to the Nyslian officer without turning his masked face away from the column of men marching into the pre-dawn darkness. "The weight of their armor and shields will drag them down in the wetlands. They need to be as light as possible to get across the Standelfr, through the marshes, and into position in time for the attack."

Even leaving now, at the fourth hour after midnight, they'd be cutting it close. A Legionnaire could march close to four miles per hour loaded down with armor and pack. With their burden lightened, they could fast-march as much as five miles per hour—on good terrain. The distance to the crossing was ten miles, and they *had* to be across the Standelfr River before the sun fully rose, else risk being spotted by Jokull scouts. Setting a quick pace, Colborn and his men would complete that first leg of the journey in good time.

But once they crossed the river and entered the marshlands, their pace would slow to a crawl—one, perhaps two, miles per hour. Aravon had no idea how far out of their way Colborn's company would have to go to evade Jokull watchers. Stealth was their priority, not speed. They had to remain invisible to the enemies until the moment they attacked. Depending on how vigilant the Jokull were, that could tack hours onto a journey of at least ten miles wading through deep marshes, muddy bogs, and quicksands. Not a journey to rush if they wanted to arrive alive and undetected.

Aravon had set his best soldiers to the task. Colborn and Rangvaldr were Fehlans, experienced in the ways of hunting, tracking, and moving through

rough terrain—though the Eyrr lands on eastern Fehl were far less inhospitable than the Jokull marshlands. Zaharis and Noll had both excelled under Colborn's tutelage at Camp Marshal. The four of them had the greatest chance of reaching their destination in time.

But could they do it with a hundred and thirty of Topaz Battalion at their backs? Colborn had hand-picked the men, yet worry had been evident in his eyes as he set off at the head of their column. Aravon could only trust that the Fehlans, scout, and the Secret Keeper could pull this off.

If they don't, Rivergate will fall.

Aravon turned to Captain Lemaire. "I know you're only thinking of your men's safety, Captain. As am I."

"Sending them into battle against the Eirdkilrs with no armor or shields?" Skepticism flashed across Lemaire's face. "That is not exactly what I would consider safe, *Capitaine.*"

Aravon couldn't fault the man his disbelief. Truth be told, that was his *least* favorite part of their plan. Sending unarmored Legionnaires against the Eirdkilrs went against every rule of warfare he'd learned over his fifteen years of service. Everyone, from the highest-ranked General to the lowliest, latrine-digging Private, knew that the Legion's strength lay in its armor, its shields, and its ability to fight in synchronicity as a cohesive unit.

But this wasn't time for "standard", tried-and-tested tactics, not in this battle. Against such impossible odds, they had to take a big risk if they wanted any hope of success.

"It's not." Aravon shrugged. "But if I know one thing about Legionnaires, it's that they *never* back down from a fight if there's a chance of winning. Especially one their Captain is confident they can win." He turned to the Nyslian officer. "You don't know me well, Captain, but you should know that I would *never* send others into a battle I wasn't willing to fight. The only reason I'm not going myself is that I'm not the right man for the job. My people are, and they'll do everything in their power to see your men get through this alive. You and me and those of us left here, it's up to us to do our parts. Rivergate is depending on us, Captain. Your comrades, friends, and families. We're their only hope, faint as that may be."

A long moment stretched on as Captain Lemaire studied Aravon's eyes, the only thing visible beneath the leather greatwolf mask. Finally, he inclined his head. "As you say, sir." He looked as if he wanted to say more, but seemed to think better of it. "With your permission, I will check up on our *other* project?"

"Thank you." Aravon nodded. "Make sure my man's instructions are followed *to the letter.*"

"It shall be as if he built it himself, *Capitaine.*" His fist *thumped* against his breastplate in the Legion's salute and, with crisp movements, he turned on his heel and strode back to camp, toward the distant sound of ringing hammers and whirring saws.

A quiet whining echoed from the nearby bushes, and Aravon caught a glimpse of two amber eyes. Brow furrowing, he hurried toward the thicket and ducked into the shadows of an overhanging beech tree.

"Snarl, what are you doing here?" He knelt and scooped up the Enfield—a task that had grown much more difficult, given how fast Snarl had grown over the previous few weeks. "You're supposed to be with Colborn!"

Snarl gave a soft whining bark and licked Aravon's mask. His wings flapped as he nuzzled his face against Aravon's leather armor, pressing his furry body close.

"I know you don't want to leave." Aravon scratched Snarl's scruff, so soft and silky. "But I need you to."

He didn't know if Snarl understood what he was saying—sometimes the Enfield was little more than a wild animal, and at other times he stared up a Aravon with such intelligence in his eyes that Aravon almost believed the animal would speak—but he trusted in Snarl's training. Duke Dyrund had shared the simple words of command that gave the Enfield basic instructions like "Stay", "Go", or "Follow".

Aravon had instructed Snarl to follow Colborn, and the Enfield had obediently trotted off into the darkness in pursuit of the Lieutenant. Yet now, he stood here, snuggled in Aravon's arms, clearly unwilling to leave him.

"Go, Snarl," Aravon whispered into his ear, stroking the Enfield's soft fur. "Go, and keep my friends safe."

Kneeling, he set Snarl onto the ground and spoke the command words to "Go" and "Follow". The Enfield turned those brilliant, yellow-glowing eyes on him, and for a moment, Aravon thought he saw sadness glimmering there. Snarl's pink tongue flashed out to lick Aravon's hand and, with a little whining bark, he turned and padded off into the darkness after Colborn.

A lump rose in Aravon's throat as Snarl disappeared into the foliage. He hated being apart from the Enfield, but he needed to send Snarl with Colborn in case they had to send an emergency message or call off the attack. He would have to trust that the Enfield could avoid Jokull archers, that he'd be safe in enemy territory. Like Aravon, Colborn, and the others, Snarl was one more soldier on a mission for the Princelands. He had his own battles to fight.

Thoughts of Colborn brought Rangvaldr's words to Aravon's mind *Damn it!* He ground his teeth in frustration. He'd been on his way to speak with Colborn when the Nyslian captain sidetracked him, and now the Lieutenant had departed.

He'll be fine, Aravon tried to tell himself. The words felt hollow, but it was too late for him to call the Lieutenant back. *He's got the mission to keep him focused.*

Aravon stood and strode out of the bushes, back onto the open ground south of the Legion encampment. He had just turned to follow Captain Lemaire—he figured it was high time he check up on Belthar's progress on Zaharis' construction—when a call stopped him short.

"Captain!" Skathi's voice echoed from the south, in the direction of Rivergate Bridge.

Aravon's heart leapt into his throat as he spun toward the archer, who raced across the field toward him. He'd left her at the bridge to keep an eye on the Eirdkilrs and Jokull guarding the crumbled bridge, and to figure the best position for her handful of archers. The only reason she'd abandon her post was if something serious had happened.

A thousand dire scenarios flashed through Aravon's mind. The Eirdkilrs and Jokull had stormed the inner keep and overwhelmed the defenders. The enemy had somehow managed to cross the Standelfr and now surged toward their position, a howling wall of fury and steel. Rivergate had fallen, the people slaughtered to a man. The tone of urgency in her voice only compounded his fear.

No! He swallowed the surge of acid rising to his throat, tried to shake off the icy hand gripping his neck. He couldn't allow himself to think the worst.

"What is it, Skathi?" Aravon forced his voice to calm, striding toward the archer at a fast clip despite his desire to break into a full sprint. He couldn't let the Legionnaires of Topaz Battalion see him worried—even the slightest crack could shatter their faint hope of winning the battle.

Skathi pulled up short in front of Aravon, gasping for breath at her five-mile run. "Message…Captain!" she gasped. "From…Lord…Eidan."

Aravon snatched the proffered strip of paper—thin and lightweight enough to be rolled into one of the message tubes secured to an Enfield's collar—and tried to read it in the faint light. Growling in frustration, he hurried toward the Legion encampment, leaving Skathi panting and leaning on her knees behind him. He only stopped when he drew within the illumination of a nearby brazier and could finally read the message.

The words, scrawled in Lord Eidan's neat, precise handwriting, sent a chill down his spine. *"Rivergate's supplies exhausted,"* the message said. *"People starving. Break the siege, or the garrison falls."*

Chapter Sixteen

Dread coiled like a serpent in Aravon's gut. *It can't be!*

Crumpling the note in his hand, he raced back to Skathi. "When did you get this?" he demanded. "And how?"

"Less than an hour ago." The archer had recovered enough wind to speak without gasping. "Skyclaw delivered it."

Aravon's eyebrows shot up in surprise. "Skyclaw?" His mind raced. *The Duke's personal Enfield, here?*

Skathi spoke quickly. "He found me in my hiding place by the river, delivered the message, and took off. I don't think Woryn or any of the other Legionnaires noti—"

"What is Skyclaw doing delivering messages to *you?*" Aravon's brow furrowed. Duke Dyrund had said the communiques would be sent to him, which explained why Snarl had been given to him as a kit, nestling, or whatever Enfield young were called. Aravon was the alpha of Snarl's pack, so Snarl would always return to him.

"After the Duke saw how much Snarl took a liking to me," Skathi explained, "he gave me this." From beneath her armor, the archer drew out a bone whistle much like the one hanging from Aravon's necklace. "And he took a bit of cloth with my scent, so his Enfield messengers could find me. He figured you had enough to deal with, and he wanted a backup in case…" The leather greatwolf mask hid her face, but an odd strain tightened her words.

"Of course." Aravon nodded understanding. Draian's death hadn't just hit *them* hard; it had shown Duke Dyrund the real-life consequences of what had, until Bjornstadt, been nothing more than theory and strategy. If, Swordsman forbid, something happened to him, Duke Dyrund wanted to be certain he could get messages to someone else in their company. Necessary redundancies, given the dangers they faced.

"Did you read it?" he asked.

Skathi nodded. "Which is why I ran all the way here. Figured you'd need to see it on the double."

Aravon's jaw clenched. "And there's not a damned thing I can do about it!"

He'd acted based on Lord Eidan's intelligence, the report that the people of Rivergate had less than a week's worth of food. He and his company had pushed themselves and their mounts hard to reach Bannockburn in just under five days, which left them one additional day for Colborn, Noll, Zaharis, and Rangvaldr's crew to get in place for their attack.

The problem with any intelligence reports, whether carried by Legion horseback messenger or Enfield wings, was that circumstances could change in the space of hours or even minutes. Anything could have happened to reduce Rivergate's supplies: unexpected food spoilage, rats in the storehouse, or simply hungry men, women, and children wolfing down incorrectly calculated rations. With no food, the soldiers of Rivergate would weaken. The inner keep would fall and the Eirdkilrs would slaughter everyone in the garrison.

But Aravon could do nothing about it. He could race after Colborn and likely catch up to the marching Legionnaires before they crossed the Standelfr, but then what? Their entire battle plan hinged on Colborn's attack from the south, behind enemy lines. Colborn needed time to navigate the marshes and get into position. They had no choice but to wait until the following night.

From the grim look in Skathi's eyes, it was clear she'd come to the same conclusion. The people of Rivergate would go hungry another day. Wounded soldiers would fall prey to their wounds, and the ill, weak, and very young could starve. And Aravon had no choice but to let it happen. It was the only way to save Rivergate, and it broke his heart.

He crumpled the message in his fist but resisted the urge to hurl it away. The action would do little to ease his frustration, the feelings of helplessness coursing through him. No, he needed to be calm, his attention focused on the task at hand. The only way out of this terrible situation was *through*.

Aravon drew in a breath through his nostrils and nodded to the archer. "Thank you, Skathi."

"Of course, Captain." Her voice was quiet, her tone subdued. "I'll get back to my post, then, sir. Make sure everything's ready for tomorrow night."

"Good." Aravon clenched his fists, fighting back the anger. He hated this feeling of impotence, of being forced to wait and do nothing while others suffered. Yet acting rashly now would benefit no one. "How go the preparations?"

"Slow, sir." Skathi's grip tightened around her longbow. "Woryn's not a half-bad archer, for a Legionnaire." A high compliment, given Agrotorae skill and their disdain of the few men of the Legion who tried their hands at archery. "As for the others, I've seen better, but I've seen worse, too. As long as there aren't too many enemies…" She shrugged. "Best I can say is we'll do our damnedest."

"That's all anyone can ask." Despite the tension tightening his shoulders, Aravon forced his voice to sound calm, confident. "I've seen what you can do, and I have full faith that you'll pull it off. Impossible be damned, right?"

"Bloody right, sir!" Skathi straightened and, snapping a quick salute, turned and padded off down the grassy hill, back in the direction of her post at Rivergate Bridge.

For long moments, Aravon wrestled with an overwhelming sense of frustration. He wanted to lash out—preferably at a lot of Eirdkilrs—but finally managed to get his anger at the situation under control. Every one of them was playing their part, doing their best to win a fight against odds they all knew were insurmountable.

If he gave in to the irritation, he'd be no good to anyone. But, he determined, he could channel his feelings of powerlessness into doing something useful. Right now, that meant helping Belthar make sure Zaharis' building project turned out *exactly* as the Secret Keeper had designed it.

Turning on his heel, he stalked up the hill toward the Legion encampment. The din of hammers, saws, creaking ropes, shouted orders, and braying donkeys had grown steadily louder in the last few hours. At their steady rate of progress, with the remaining Legionnaires of Topaz Battalion to pitch in, Belthar should have the construction completed before nightfall.

That creation was the final piece of their puzzle, the critical element to their battle plan. Without it, Colborn's men would be walking into a death trap.

Aravon *had* to ensure it was completed and that, when the time came, every man and woman at his heels was ready to cross the Standelfr and hit the enemy hard. The people of Rivergate were counting on them.

* * *

"Captain Snarl!"

At the sound of his name—the alias he'd adopted for interactions with the Legion—Aravon looked up from the wooden log he was busy stripping of branches and found Captain Lemaire striding toward him. The light of the bright noonday sun seemed to cast shadows on the Captain's angular face, and worry turned the bags under his eyes a deeper shade.

The Nyslian officer drew closer and spoke in a low voice. "A word, *Capitaine?*"

Aravon released his grip on the one-man saw and nodded. "Of course, Captain Lemaire." Gesturing for a resting Legionnaire to take over for him, he followed the officer out of the sawdust-strewn construction area. Sweat streamed down his brow and soaked into his undertunic, and Aravon found himself stifling beneath his heavy leather mask. Yet he dared not take it off, even to wipe his face. He hadn't recognized any of the men of Topaz Battalion, but there were enough veterans of the Eirdkilr Wars that one of them could recognize him.

Captain Lemaire didn't slow until the sound of whirring saws and rapping hammers faded to a muted hum behind them.

Aravon raised an eyebrow as the Nyslian Captain turned to him. "What's the matter?"

"While I understand the need for all this—" Lemaire waved his hand at the strange-looking skeleton of logs, planks, and ropes that had sprung up overnight. "—I question the wisdom of keeping the men working through the night and day." His jaw muscles worked. "Tired soldiers will be no good to anyone. And many are still recovering from wounds or illness, while the rest..." A grimace twisted his aquiline features. "Let us simply say I was not given the cream of the Legion crop. After all, until a week ago, Rivergate numbered among the Chain's best-defended cities."

Aravon nodded. The Legion sent new recruits to the strongholds less likely to see battle, allowing them to gain experience and train without putting them

116

on the front lines. Their presence on the walls of the northernmost fortresses along the Eastmarch, Westmarch, and the Chain freed up the most able-bodied, experienced soldiers to join battle on the front lines.

"Most of the *true* soldiers went with your men across the Standelfr," Captain Lemaire continued, his expression tight. "But if we push those remaining too hard, they may be too exhausted to join battle come nightfall."

Aravon drew in a long breath, basking in the warmth of the morning air, the feeling of the gentle breeze cooling off the sweat soaking his body. He had joined the men working on Zaharis' construction, filling his time with hard work to speed up the project. But they would be fortunate to finish before night fell. And, to have everything in place when the time came for their attack, every one of the Legionnaires remaining in camp would be needed.

Yet that didn't mean Captain Lemaire was wrong. The Legionnaires hadn't had a moment's rest since the previous night, and they'd worked hard under Belthar's watchful eye and barked orders. Strong men and trained soldiers they might be, but even they needed to rest from their labor in order to be fresh enough to fight the coming battle.

"I've received word from inside Rivergate, Captain." Aravon spoke in a voice pitched low for Lemaire's ears only. "Their supplies are exhausted. The food has run out."

The officer's eyebrows rose sharply, disappearing beneath the rim of his Legion helmet. "How could you—?" He cut off, as if he knew the question wouldn't be answered. "You are certain?"

Aravon nodded. "If we rest, they starve. Their only hope is for us to be ready for tonight's attack. That means every one of us working to complete this."

For long moments, Captain Lemaire's eyes remained fixed on Aravon, his expression pensive. Suddenly, he whirled and stalked toward the building area. "Put your backs into it!" he shouted over the sound of hammers and saws. "This thing will not build itself, *mes Légionnaires!*" As he moved, he stripped off his heavy officer's cloak, helmet, and unbelted his weapons. He reached the spot Aravon had recently vacated and, seizing a saw, set to work with abandon.

Aravon smiled behind his mask. Many commanders he'd met would have simply driven their men harder; it was a mark in Captain Lemaire's favor that his response was to pitch in and toil alongside his men.

The smile faded as Aravon studied the ever-expanding framework of Zaharis' project. It had begun to take shape, slowly at first, but more quickly now that he'd recruited able-bodied men from Bannockburn to join the Legionnaires bending their backs to the task.

Belthar moved among the working soldiers, calling orders, throwing his shoulder beneath heavy logs, and pulling on ropes that creaked beneath heavy burdens. His huge muscles and strong hands made him perfectly suited to the task—finesse might not be his strong suit, but they had carpenters for that.

Aravon's eyes roamed toward the only figure in the encampment larger than Belthar. The Corporal, Balegar, matched Belthar's tireless pace. Together, the two men hoisted a log that would have taken a team of horses and a rope winch to lift, settling it into place with loud grunts of effort. Working side by side, likely competing with each other under the guise of their task, they stood a good chance of actually finishing the construction.

Zaharis' parting instructions flashed through Aravon's mind. Instead of returning to sawing logs, he strode toward the huge man leading the project.

Belthar caught sight of him as he approached, and Aravon's fingers flashed a silent request to talk. Nodding, Belthar called out one last order—"Shore up that beam before it crushes you, you damned fool!"—and marched toward Aravon.

"Progress report, Ursus?" Aravon used the big man's code name.

Belthar's shoulders tightened. "Some, but it's not as fast as I'd like." His huge head swiveled toward the toiling Legionnaires and he thrust a thick finger toward one man wearing the stripes of a Corporal. "We got lucky with Radalle over there. Father was a builder, taught him the tricks of the trade before he joined the Legion. A few of the others can swing a hammer without killing anyone. As for the rest..." He shrugged. "We'll make do with what we've got, sir."

"Good." Aravon nodded. "The Duke sent word. Rivergate's out of time. We *have* to attack tonight. Will you be ready?"

A long moment of silence elapsed, and Belthar's eyes darkened in thought. Finally, he let out a long breath. "Not much choice, is there, Captain?"

Aravon gave a harsh chuckle. "That's what I hoped you'd say. Have you had a chance to rest, grab a bite to eat?"

Belthar shook his head. "My hands are a bit full at the moment. Only way we're going to meet the deadline is if we push all day long."

"I know." Aravon grimaced. "But I need *you*, especially, fighting fit tonight. Let the Legionnaires shoulder the weight of the work here; you're far more useful swinging your axe than a hammer, especially against the Eirdkilrs."

"All due respect, Captain," the big man said, "but if we're going to ask them to work and fight, I ought to do the same."

"No question about it." Aravon met Belthar's gaze steadily. "Yet I need you to promise that you'll take a few moments to rest and refresh yourself before we march out at sunset." He held up a hand to forestall the big man's protests. "You know what caliber of soldiers we're fighting with. Good men, brave men, but can you truly say they're a match for you when it comes to taking down Eirdkilrs?"

Belthar hesitated, but shook his head. "No, Captain." Not a boast, simply a statement of fact.

"You've trained specifically for the battle we face tonight, but these men haven't." Aravon fixed Belthar with a stern gaze. "I'm not asking you to shirk your duties or lounge in comfort while the Legionnaires work. But I am asking—I'm ordering, if I have to—that you take care of yourself. Against the Eirdkilrs, you are Topaz Battalion's best chance of staying alive. Got that?"

After long, silent seconds, Belthar nodded. "Yes, Captain." Despite the tightness in his voice, Aravon saw a hint of something akin to mingled pride and gratitude sparkling in the big man's eyes.

Aravon clapped the big man on the enormous, heavily-muscled shoulder. "Now, unless you've found one of those secret tunnels…?"

Belthar shook his head. "Nothing I could find here, Captain." A shadow passed across his eyes. "But they're *supposed* to be damned hard to find for anyone not a B—" Again, he swallowed his words. "—not in the know. I didn't see any signs."

Aravon fixed the big man with a questioning look, remaining silent for a few seconds to give Belthar a chance to expound. A wall had gone up in Belthar's eyes, yet there was shame mixed in. The big man felt driven to keep his secrets, yet doing so left him guilty.

Finally, Aravon shrugged. "No tunnels, which means that's our only way in. Let's make it happen." He turned and set off toward the construction area. "The people of Rivergate are counting on us."

* * *

Worry twisted in Aravon's gut as he glanced at the sky for the tenth time in as many minutes. The light of the setting sun bathed the wispy clouds in a glorious mélange of purple, orange, and red tinged with brilliant gold. Princelanders loved to say that the sunsets on mainland Einan could never match the beauty of Fehlan twilight. The descending sun filled the air with a glorious array of deep reds and fiery oranges, with hints of delicate blue and purple darkening the edges.

Yet all the beauty in the world didn't stop Aravon from pacing a rut into the top of the grassy hill overlooking the Legion encampment. Fifty Legionnaires stood arrayed in ranks, their armor polished to glistening, shields forming a solid wall of red and gold that glimmered in the light of the setting sun. They remained silent, motionless, heads held high and backs straight. Waiting, as they had for the last half hour.

Yet Aravon couldn't give the order to march, not yet. His eyes strayed toward the south, again. Nothing. No hint of wings high in the sky or a flash of orange fur blazing in the sunset glow.

What's taking them so long? Why haven't they sent word yet?

Any number of things could have gone wrong. Colborn and the others could have drowned attempting to cross the Standelfr River. Jokull scouts might have spotted them and slain them in the marshes. Quicksand would drag the Legionnaires to a muddy grave. An Eirdkilr arrow could bring Snarl down—the thought drove a pang of sorrow into Aravon's gut.

No matter how much he wanted to appear calm to the Legionnaires, he couldn't help his worry. Only something truly dire could have kept Colborn from sending Snarl with the message that his men were ready.

No, Aravon told himself. *You can't think like that! It's not dire—they just got delayed.*

They'd expected the fifteen-mile trek across the marshlands to take the better part of the day, and Colborn's pace would slow as they approached the Jokull and Eirdkilr camps south of Rivergate. It could be nothing more than a slower-than-anticipated travel speed, a particularly difficult stretch of marshes to cross, or any number of things that didn't involve his men or his Enfield lying dead.

Yet, as Aravon glanced up at the sun—now disappearing behind the western horizon—one last time, he knew he could delay no longer. Even with every draft horse, ox, and donkey they'd commandeered from Bannockburn, the five-mile journey to Rivergate Bridge would take the better part of three hours. Tack on the time required to maneuver Zaharis' construction into position, and they would barely be in place ready to attack by midnight. The time for waiting had passed. Now was time to act.

Turning on his heel, Aravon stalked down the hill toward the Legion camp. The moment Belthar caught sight of him, he began shouting orders—orders that every Legionnaire had been expecting for an hour. The *crack* of whips echoed loud, followed by the lowing of heavily-burdened oxen and the braying of donkeys. Ropes creaked, men shouted to each other, and the clatter of armor filled the air as the fifty Legionnaires of Topaz Battalion's Second and Third Companies prepared to march to battle. A neat, perfectly ordered column of row after row of disciplined men following the command of Captain Lemaire, who rode at their head. A hundred and eighty brave men marching off to a battle from which many—far, far too many—might never return.

Though it took every shred of willpower, Aravon kept his gaze away from the sky, his eyes fixed on the men below him. Snarl *would* come. The Enfield had the keen vision of an eagle and the hearing and smell of a fox. He'd trained to find Aravon anywhere on Fehl. Colborn had no need of tucking a written note into the tube on Snarl's collar—the little creature's presence would be all the message he needed.

And, when the message came, Aravon would be ready. The future of every Legionnaire and Westhavener in Rivergate depended on it.

Chapter Seventeen

This was the part Aravon hated most. The calm before the storm of blood, flashing steel, and flesh. The breathless, heart-pounding moments of silence leading up to the battle horns ringing, the first shouted orders to "Forward march!"

After the frenzied hurry of getting everything into place—the heavily-cloaked Legionnaires tucked away in the shadows of the forest bordering the Marshway—they had nothing to do but stand ready. And wait. Wait for Colborn's attack from the south, an attack that none of them *knew* for certain would come.

The waiting always seemed interminable. Expectation, tension, and fear of the inevitable clash added to the anxiety boiling like a thundercloud within Aravon. Sweat trickled down his forehead, stinging his eyes, and turned his palms moist. He clenched and unclenched his fists, willing himself to remain calm, stay crouched out of sight of the enemy holding the bridge.

The Jokull and their Eirdkilr allies were alert. Thirty-five fur-clad barbarians had taken up station at the bridge, backs turned to the chaos howling through Rivergate, eyes fixed on the darkness north of the Standelfr River. Despite their certainty that no one would cross the ruined Rivergate Bridge, the experienced warriors took no chances. If anything moved on the Princelander side of the river, they would spot it.

Well, not *anything*. Aravon and the Legionnaires remained well back from the swaths of open ground bordering the Standelfr and the Marshway, trusting the tree cover and shadows of the night to conceal them from enemy eyes. Yet Skathi, Woryn, and the five men she'd deemed "not quite rubbish marksmen" had already begun their slow, steady move toward the cliff's edge bordering the Standelfr.

Aravon's eyes went to the bush-looking forms that had now advanced within fifty feet of the riverbank. Colborn had taught her the Fehlan tactic of weaving together a screen of boughs and using them to disguise their movements. The deception worked best at night, when the shadows blended with the branches and leaves to conceal their forms.

But even with their figures camouflaged, their movements were glacial, little more than a forward crawl anytime the Eirdkilrs' attention wavered or the Jokull turned to glance at the burning city behind them. They had been on the move since the last light of twilight faded to night. Three hours to cross two hundred feet of open space and get into position on either side of what had once been the Rivergate Bridge.

That required a degree of patience Aravon wasn't certain he possessed. His heart hammered a rapid beat against his ribs, his pulse pounding in his ears. Every second brought them closer to the inevitable attack. But, until the signal came, they had no choice but to wait.

And wait.

Someone muttered in the woods to his right, eliciting a hiss from one of the Sergeants. Armor clattered, a shield *thunked* against the trunk of a white-barked birch, and a leather-wrapped sword sheath *clanked* on the ground. The Legionnaires grew impatient, nervousness growing with the expectation of the coming battle.

And still they waited.

Aravon tried to push the gruesome images from his thoughts—he'd already envisioned his companions' deaths a half-dozen times, each more creative than the last. As Mortius, his old Swordsman Adept trainer, had loved to say, "What you don't know is always more terrifying than what you do." The imagination had a tendency to fill gaps in knowledge, inevitably turning to the grim and ghastly. Not knowing what had happened to Colborn's company led his mind deeper into darkness.

His only hope was to focus on something else. At the present, that meant yet *another* scan of northern Rivergate. The city's outer wall ended at the riverbank five hundred yards east and west of Rivergate Bridge, the circle broadening the farther one went into Rivergate itself. The northern edge of the inner keep stood close to a thousand yards south of the bridge, the area between populated by the homes, shops, and businesses of Rivergate's populace.

The inner keep occupied less than one-quarter of Rivergate's surface area, dominating the center of the city. The Marshway ran in a direct line from Rivergate Bridge toward the gates of the inner keep, and a marketplace had sprung up alongside the broad avenue. Now, however, the shops were empty and dark, the wooden stalls shattered and canvas roofs destroyed beneath the assault of Eirdkilrs and Jokull.

The piercing, bestial war cries of the enemy rang off the city walls, and a thick pall of black, choking smoke rose from the burning buildings, blotting out the stars. The Eirdkilrs and Jokull had finished their rampage through the city hours earlier; Rivergate had been one of the smaller fortresses along the Chain, a fact the enemy had taken full advantage of.

Fires blazed among the homes of northern Rivergate. It seemed the barbarians didn't just intend to starve out the Princelanders; they would destroy everything they held precious, including their possessions, merchandise, and valuables.

Anger surged within Aravon, setting energy coursing through his muscles and scouring any last traces of fatigue. *Just you wait, you bastards!* he snarled inwardly. *Let's see how you celebrate once we get across!*

Yet, even as he watched his enemies destroying Rivergate, heard their delighted cries and the shouts in their guttural tongue, he could do nothing but wait. Wait for Colborn to give the signal.

And then it came, a blinding flash of light that illuminated the darkness beyond Rivergate. Fire sprang into the night, a wall of gold-and-orange flames that stretched burning fingers skyward with such intensity that Aravon had to shield his eyes. A *whooshing* so loud that it echoed above the screams and shouts of the enemy. Yet even as he turned away from the fire, elation surged within him.

Yes! He would have laughed aloud, if not for the necessity of remaining hidden. That didn't stop him from driving a clenched fist into the soft earth. *By the Swordsman, they've done it!*

Quiet gasps echoed from the woods around him, silenced immediately by hissing Sergeants that whispered threats of floggings and endless latrine duty to any fool careless enough to draw attention.

But the enemy paid them little heed. All thirty of the Eirdkilrs and Jokull guarding Rivergate Bridge spun at the sudden brilliance, the shouts of alarm and confusion that echoed through the city. All eyes turned toward the towering mass of flames that consumed the land south and southwest of Rivergate.

Zaharis had come to play.

Aravon would have given anything to see what manner of "magic tricks" Zaharis had conjured up with his Dragon Thorngrass—he'd described the effects as "a little spark to get their attention", an understatement of the highest magnitude—but he had his own part in this charade.

Triumph blossomed bright in his chest as the Eirdkilrs and Jokull rampaging through northern Rivergate loosed a howling war cry and surged south, in the direction of their new enemy. Even half of those holding Rivergate Bridge joined in the frenzied stampede, leaving fewer than twenty men guarding the rear as they raced toward the enemy. They wanted Legion blood, and if they couldn't get at those within the keep, they would slaughter the fools that dared to attack from within their own territory.

Aravon spared a worried thought for Colborn's company. Noll, Zaharis, and Rangvaldr were capable warriors in their own right, and they had more than a hundred Legionnaires at their backs. Unarmored Legionnaires unaccustomed to fighting outside the standard Legion shield wall, but brave soldiers nonetheless. If anyone could pull this off, it was the half-Fehlan Lieutenant and his hand-picked men.

Our turn.

He had no need to give a signal or call an order; Skathi knew her business, and she'd prepared her chosen archers for their moment. The archers at the edge of the riverbank leapt to their feet and cast off their camouflage. Six longbows bent and, with only a breath of pause, released the arrows with a *thrum* of bowstrings.

Two hundred-fifty yards separated Skathi and her archers from the enemy. Shadows sliced the darkness, leaping across the distance in the space of a single heartbeat.

Three Eirdkilrs fell in silence, arrows buried in their throats, chests, and, in one case, an eye socket. Skathi's shot, no doubt. Even as the first volley found their targets, the archers loosed a second flight of shafts. Six more arrows sliced the darkness of the river and buried into Eirdkilr and Jokull flesh. One fell with a piercing cry, the red-feathered fletching protruding from his gut. Another toppled forward off the cliff, landing in the fast-flowing river with a muted *splash*.

But before the third volley flew, the enemy had already been alerted by the agonized cry of their comrade. The ten remaining men—five towering Eirdkilrs and their smaller Jokull cousins—spun toward the attack, raising their round wooden shields to ward off the next flight of missiles. Five of the six arrows clattered off the leather-bound shields. Only the sixth arrow found its mark, slipping just above the steel rim of an Eirdkilr shield and buried into the man's throat.

Cries of alarm pierced the darkness, the Jokull crying out for reinforcements. Bowstrings *thrummed* again and two more enemies fell, but still seven remained. Five Jokull and two Eirdkilrs blocking Aravon's way to help the people of Rivergate and his men beyond.

The Jokull clustered together, forming a wall of interlocked shields that kept Skathi's arrows at bay. The two Eirdkilrs, however, turned and raced south, deeper into Rivergate.

"Skathi!" Aravon's voice echoed across the cleared space. "Take them down!"

Before the words finished leaving his mouth, two bowstrings *thrummed* in perfect unison. Twin streaks of black streaked through the night. One of the Eirdkilrs fell without a sound, a red-fletched arrow buried in the base of his spine, just beneath the metal rim of his helmet. The other cried out as the second arrow punched through his leather leggings. He stumbled and fell hard, a stream of Eirdkilr curses mingling with his cries of pain. Skathi silenced him a moment later with an arrow to the chest. The Odarian steel head punched through leather armor, furs, and flesh. Blood sprayed from the man's lips and he fell to the cobbled road of the Marshway.

But the five Jokull remained. One howled in agony as an arrow drove through his exposed calf, but it did little to stop him from retreating with his comrades, one step at a time, still locked in the shield wall. The arrows loosed by Skathi's archers clattered off their shields or *spanged* on their metal helmets.

Damn it! Aravon's mind raced. He could give the order to advance, but there was no way they'd get across in time to stop the Jokull from escaping and summoning reinforcements. They had seconds before—

Movement flashed in the corner of his eye. A huge figure burst free of the woods and raced toward the river's edge. Belthar, sprinting at an impressive speed for one so large, held his cocked and loaded crossbow in both hands, his long legs eating up the ground. The big man ground to a halt beside one of the archers—broad-shouldered, with long red hair hanging in fierce war braids—and raised the crossbow.

Polus' special creation, the "artisan's masterpiece" of which he was exceedingly proud, had metal limbs six feet across—far too large for a man of average size and strength to carry, much less load and shoot. Belthar was anything but average. His huge shoulder muscles corded as he raised the crossbow, took aim, and pulled the trigger.

The *whomph* of the releasing crossbow sounded like a ballista being loosed. The bolt, three feet long and two inches thick, with an Odarian steel tip, leapt in a blur across the Standelfr River. Two hundred and fifty yards was a long way to shoot for an inexperienced archer, but Belthar didn't need Skathi's pinpoint accuracy. Not with the Jokull packed so tightly together in their shield wall.

Belthar's crossbow bolt punched through the centermost shield with a massive *crack* of splintering wood and tearing leather. The missile hurled the Jokull back a dozen yards, and the dying man's flailing limbs and shield brought down two of his comrades. More than that, it broke the shield wall, giving Skathi, Woryn, and the archers an opening.

Six arrows whistled toward the Jokull. Two men fell with agonized cries, arrows buried in their legs and guts. A third died a moment later as Skathi's follow-up shot, loosed with the impossible speed and precision of an Agrotora, punched through his armor, buried in his chest. Five more arrows rained down around the last Jokull, still staggered by the blow from his flailing comrade's shield. One caught him in the shoulder and spun him around, while another buried in his back. His legs flopped uselessly, spine severed. He died with a cry of pain on his lips, the shaft of an arrow from a Legionnaire—likely Woryn—blossomed in the side of his head.

Silence fell, breathless, excruciating, punctuated by the *thump, thump* of Aravon's pounding heart. He found himself suddenly exhaling, air bursting from his lungs. He sucked in a lungful of air, his eyes scanning the darkened streets and marketplace of north Rivergate. Nothing moved, not so much as a breeze fluttering the canvas of the ruined stalls.

No reinforcements would arrive to defend the bridge crossing. The first half of their plan had succeeded.

Chapter Eighteen

Triumph burning in his chest, Aravon turned to Captain Lemaire—who stared wide-eyed at the archers and Belthar clustered at the river's edge—and gave the order. "Now!"

To his credit, Lemaire recovered from his shocked surprise in an instant. He whirled to his left, toward the Legionnaire who had remained by his side for this very purpose. "Go!"

Mudden, a Third Company Legionnaire with the harsh accent and dark brown hair of a Drashi, leapt to his feet and raced off east, deeper into the forest. He'd been chosen for his speed, and within a few seconds, Aravon lost sight of him within the dense tree cover opposite the highway.

Come on! They hadn't had time to test Zaharis' construction; either it worked and they got across, or it sank like a stone and Colborn's company faced the enemy alone.

Aravon turned back toward Rivergate and studied the city once more. The stillness of the night was broken only by the dull roar of the fast-flowing Standelfr and the distant cries of the Eirdkilrs and Jokull scrambling to comprehend the fiery attack from the south.

Colborn had bought them a few minutes at best. They had to make the most of it.

"There!" Captain Lemaire's sharp intake of breath echoed in the darkness.

Aravon spun toward the east, and his eyes scanned the dark, rushing ribbon of the Standelfr. His heart leapt as he spotted the hulking shape racing toward them, carried along on the icy, fast-flowing current.

Calling it a boat would be an offense to every shipwright on Fehl; the construction looked less like a proper barge and more like an enormous system of builder's scaffolding mounted on dozens of shallow-draft boats. Boats that had been cobbled together so quickly they would sink if not for the sheer number united in the effort to remain afloat, and a massive keel in its center as a counterbalance to keep it stable. Forty feet tall, a hundred and eighty yards long, and five yards wide, the thing was, for all intents and purposes, a massive pontoon bridge, raised on beams and supports to create a flat "roof" that the Legionnaires could march across. Belthar had dubbed it "the Coracle", a name the rest of the grim-humored Legionnaires had quickly adopted.

Fifteen Legionnaires ran alongside the riverbank, struggling with the five tow ropes secured at various intervals along the length of the Coracle. They could never hope to compete with the river as it dragged the enormous boat-thing downstream; their only task was to keep the prow from pulling too far away from the northern bank of the Standelfr.

A single figure stood atop the Coracle, a hulking giant of a man that seemed somehow perfect for the gargantuan monstrosity he rode. Balegar, the Nyslian giant, had volunteered for the position—better to risk one soldier's life than the three Legionnaires required to carry out the most important task of all.

Come on, Balegar! Aravon's fists clenched so tightly his leather gloves creaked. The Coracle floated downstream at a tremendous speed, racing toward the four massive piles that had once held the Rivergate Bridge aloft. Each of the supports were made from water-hardened river stone, easily fifteen feet thick around. If the Coracle plowed into those pillars, the Standelfr River would turn the wooden vessel to splinters—and the enormous Legionnaire with it.

Aravon's mind raced as he tried to calculate the Coracle's approach, speed, and distance from the piles, but gave it up. He was no sailor or riverboatman. This was the part that Zaharis had been *most* specific about; a single second's delay could spell the end of their plan.

Closer, closer, closer, one hammering heartbeat at a time; the floating wooden monstrosity raced along on the Standelfr's current, racing toward a stony doom—or the salvation of Rivergate.

Then Balegar moved. Stooping, he bent his back to the massive stone anchor secured just beyond the prow of the Coracle. For a second, Aravon feared the weight too ponderous for the giant. Yet, as Balegar strained, the stone anchor slowly lifted and toppled off the side of the wooden boat. It hit the river with a loud *splash* and plummeted to the bottom of the Standelfr. Coils of rope snaked off the side of the Coracle, then snapped tight as the anchor struck riverbed. The prow of the boat tilted, dipped, and veered violently to the right, pulled toward the northern cliff face by the force of the river tugging against its anchor line.

Aravon's heart leapt into his throat as rope creaked and groaned beneath the strain. The Legionnaires on the riverbank hauled hard on the rope attached to the bow, pulling it closer to the northern cliff face. Five enormous logs attached to the Coracle's prow, like the teeth of a naval ram, slammed into the stony riverbank with earth-shuddering force. Two gave a loud *crack* and shattered beneath the impact, but the remaining three held fast.

Zaharis' design held true. The Coracle's bow remained unmoving, secured to the stone anchor, but the stern floated free on the current. With the ponderous lethargy of a Frozen Sea glacier, the stern swung outward. A slow shift, yet faster and faster as the river clutched the Coracle in its watery grip. Pivoting, its bow locked in place by the anchor rope and kept from slamming into the bank by its prow. One hundred and eighty yards of hulking, floating wooden scaffolding swung outward and floated toward the stone piles of Rivergate Bridge.

Aravon's eyes snapped to the figure of Balegar, racing along the flat top of the Coracle. His heavy boots thudded on the wooden planking as he raced the one hundred and fifty yards to where the second stone anchor sat waiting to be released.

A fist of ice clutched Aravon's heart. *He's not going to make it!*

The huge Nyslian moved with impressive speed for someone his size, yet he was no Belthar. His lumbering steps would never cross such a distance in the seconds he had left before the side of the pivoting Coracle slammed into the stone piles.

Dread sank like a stone in Aravon's gut as he watched the scaffolding-like construction floating toward its doom. He could do nothing but wait, breathless, his stomach in knots, as Balegar raced against time and the force of nature.

Yet somehow, impossibly, Balegar reached the anchor just in time. The Nyslian giant threw his shoulder against the heavy stone and heaved. It seemed an eternity before the boulder toppled off the side of the Coracle and dropped out of sight into the Standelfr. Within the space of a second, the rope snapped

131

tight and the boat jerked to a shuddering stop. Less than five yards from the stone pile that would have shattered it and Balegar with it.

The huge Nyslian was thrown from his feet by the sudden force and flew off the side. He barely managed to seize the anchor rope as he hurtled over the Coracle's edge. Aravon let out the breath he'd been holding as Balegar pulled himself back up and onto the boat.

Yes! Hope once more bloomed in Aravon's mind. The two anchor ropes had held thus far. As Balegar scrambled back onto the Coracle, he rushed back along the wooden planking toward the anchor set in the middle of the huge construction. Pausing only long enough to heave the last anchor over the side, he turned and raced toward the tow ropes the Legionnaires had used to keep the boat in position.

"Move!" Aravon called the order. Even as Captain Lemaire relayed the order, Aravon burst from the forest and raced toward the Legionnaires on the riverbank. By the time he reached them and took up a rope, Balegar had unhooked the tow ropes from their hooks and now knelt to secure the ropes to another pair of hooks set into the two hooks at the end of the plank bridge.

"Heave!" Aravon hissed to the men. Together, he and the six men leaned their weight against the ropes, and the plank bridge slid out from the prow of the Coracle toward the riverbank. Belthar was suddenly there, and with his help, the Legionnaires pulled out a wooden plank bridge thirty yards long—long enough to span the distance between the riverbank and the bow of their wooden construction.

Captain Lemaire and ten Legionnaires were already at the riverbank, ready to race across the plank bridge and onto the Coracle. With Balegar at their head, they sprinted toward the stern of the huge construction and set about extending the plank bridge on the far end. But instead of designing the stern bridge to slide outward, Zaharis had insisted Bannockburn's blacksmith secure this one on massive hinges that secured one end to the stern of the Coracle—the only way it could span the distance without ropes secured to the southern riverbank.

Four knelt to unhook the tow ropes on the aft end, secured the ropes to the aft plank bridge, then helped Balegar, Captain Lemaire, and the others heave the bridge upward. Wooden push poles had been placed atop the Coracle for the precise purpose of shoving the plank bridge higher, higher, one hammering heartbeat at a time. Balegar and the ten Legionnaires beside him pushed until the bridge stood straight up. Gravity did the rest and the plank bridge dropped onto the riverbank—with the ropes to slow its descent and prevent it from breaking. It still *crashed* onto the stony ground, and Aravon winced at the sudden noise.

Yet there were no Eirdkilrs or Jokull nearby to hear them; all enemies still living were too busy with Colborn's distraction.

Aravon was the first to race up the plank bridge and into Rivergate. Belthar thumped up the plank bridge on his heels, with Captain Lemaire, Balegar, and the remaining men following. Aravon barked out quiet orders, sending Legionnaires scurrying toward the shadows between the darkened houses that bordered the Marshway. In less than a minute, all the Legionnaires had crossed and taken up positions in two alleys on the eastern and western sides of the main avenue. Only once he was certain Skathi and her small company of archers had crossed did Aravon join the men gathered in the alley west of the Marshway.

He drew in a deep breath, grim determination hardening within him. Fifty men was a pitiful force against close to three thousand enemies, but two solid shield walls of twenty-five Legionnaires—supported by Belthar, Skathi, Woryn, and four archers—could do serious damage to an enemy caught unaware.

And, thanks to Zaharis' brilliant and devious mind, they would hit the Eirdkilrs and Jokull from behind.

Fifty-seven soldiers, fewer than half a proper Legion company, but if the men at his side fought with even a fraction of the anger that burned with Aravon, the enemy stood no chance.

Chapter Nineteen

Aravon shot a quick glance at the twenty-five Legionnaires formed up opposite him, crowding in an alley on the western side of the Marshway. Belthar stood in the rear beside Captain Lemaire, ready to relay Aravon's orders. Skathi and two of the archers held position in the big man's shadow, arrows nocked and gripped tight.

Woryn and the other two archers had taken up identical positions behind Aravon, who had a hulking bodyguard of his own. Balegar, the giant Nyslian Corporal, held a Legion shield in a loose, easy grip—it seemed to weigh nothing, and offered scant protection for his enormous, heavily-muscled frame—a hewing spear in his right hand. A standard-issue Legion short sword would be little more than a dagger to the big soldier. With his reach, the long-bladed polearm gave him a significant advantage over the smaller Jokull, and certainly put him on par with the seven-foot-tall Eirdkilrs.

Right now, they'd need every advantage they could get. Aravon hesitated only a moment before giving Belthar the silent hand signal to advance. Zaharis' fire wall still blazed bright south of the city's outer wall, but there was no telling how long the conflagration could last in the muddy Fehlan swamplands. Or how long the Eirdkilrs and Jokull would remain focused on the fire and the inevitable surprise attack by Colborn's company.

They had to take advantage of that distraction to launch a surprise attack of their own.

The Legionnaires marched out of the alley as quietly as heavily-armored men carrying heavy shields could manage. The shouts and howling war cries of the Eirdkilrs provided ample cover. For now.

Aravon signaled to Belthar. *"Slow and steady."* His eyes flicked to Skathi. *"Keep a sharp eye."*

The Agrotora nodded but didn't release her longbow and the nocked arrow. Her grip was loose, her shoulders relaxed, but Aravon knew she could draw, aim, and loose in less time than it would take him to call out an order. He trusted her—and Belthar, beside Captain Lemaire—to handle their business. He had only to focus on his own platoons.

"Stay ready," he told Woryn.

"Nothing gets past us, sir." The man spoke in a low voice that echoed with a confidence that matched the easy way he held his bow. For a Legionnaire, he seemed remarkably comfortable taking up an archer's weapons. And, as Aravon had seen first-hand, he was a deadly shot. Not quite as good as Skathi, but a damned sight better than most. Aravon doubted Noll or Colborn could outshoot the man easily.

Then there was the enormous Balegar looming over him. Captain Lemaire had made the Corporal's duty as plain as the thick Nyslian nose on his face: "Keep Captain Snarl safe, no matter what." The Captain had given Aravon a wry grin. "Easier than trying to explain to the Prince why I let his special envoy fall in battle."

Aravon welcomed the hulking Corporal's presence. Since the ambush on the Eastmarch, he hadn't been able to lift a Legion shield. He'd grown adept at wielding his Odarian steel-headed spear, but now, marching in a proper Legion battle line, he had to fight like a proper Legionnaire. That meant using the spear the way a Legionnaire would—to stab over the front ranks and bite back at any enemies locked against the shield wall. But that left him exposed to Eirdkilr arrows and Jokull slings. With Balegar on his left, he could duck behind the big soldier's shield and shelter from missile fire.

He *hoped* the enemy wouldn't have the time to bring their ranged weapons to bear. The plan was to hit hard from the rear and keep hitting until they pushed the enemy out of Rivergate. Simple, inelegant, but their only solution for retaking Rivergate and saving the starving Princelanders.

Sweat soaked Aravon's palms as he marched in silence behind his men. With ranks only eight wide and three deep, they had to rely on speed and surprise to carry the day.

And one important element the Eirdkilrs hopefully aren't expecting. A desperate addition to an insane plan, but their only hope.

136

He sought out Skathi. "*Do it!*" he signed.

As he turned his attention back to the road ahead, he caught the quiet *thrum* of the Agrotora's longbow and the whistling of the arrow speeding off into the night.

Please, he prayed to the Swordsman, *for the sake of the innocents trapped within the keep, let this work.* He no longer reached for Mylena's pendant—the trinket had burned as a "grave gift" for Draian, a Fehlan custom. Instead, he tightened his grip on the smooth wooden shaft of his spear and clenched his jaw against the inevitable tremors that set in the seconds before battle. Fear kept a man's mind sharp, but give in to it and it would turn to panic—panic that got men killed, not just the one losing his nerve, but everyone around him.

The tension of every man in his small force was palpable as they marched down the Marshway toward the walls of the inner keep. Fires still blazed in the homes and shops bordering the broad avenue, lighting their way and painting the debris-strewn, bloodstained city streets a gory brown and black. Smoke thickened the air around them, a sharp bite in Aravon's lungs that threatened to set him coughing, and billowed high into the night sky. Gritting his teeth, Aravon kept his pace steady, his steps quiet, moving in time with his men.

Closer and closer they drew, until they could see the blood and gore staining the sealed keep gate, the marks left by Eirdkilr axes and clubs as they tried to batter the gate open. A rough-hewn log lay beside the gate, the improvised battering ram abandoned as the Eirdkilrs and Jokull turned away from the siege to burn Rivergate.

Aravon sucked in a quiet breath as they reached the keep. No defenders stood atop the battlements, no calls to identify themselves or stand fast echoed from above. Silence and darkness greeted them from within.

Clenching his jaw, Aravon turned to Belthar. "*Be ready for anything,*" he signed.

Belthar saluted, a gentle *thump* of his fist against his alchemically treated armor, and turned to join Captain Lemaire and the rest of his company in taking the road that went along the eastern edge of the inner keep. Aravon's company turned right, toward the western avenue. This was the moment of greatest peril. The forces divided, separated by the walls of the inner keep, they were vulnerable to counterattack. Yet they couldn't risk taking just *one* of the roads that circumnavigated the inner keep. Hitting the enemy from both sides gave them the best chance of doing serious damage.

Heart hammering in his chest, Aravon matched the steady pace of his Legionnaires. Step by agonizing step, the walls of the inner keep on their left flank and the dark alleys of Rivergate on their right, they marched toward the enemy. An enemy that far outnumbered them, but who they hoped to catch off-guard.

Their plan was nearly foiled before they'd traveled half the distance around the keep. Three Jokull raiders stumbled out of a nearby house, drunk off whatever liquor sloshed within the clay pitchers they'd pilfered from Rivergate's tavern. The blond-bearded, fur-clad Fehlans stopped short at the sight of the oncoming Legionnaires and opened their mouths to cry out.

Woryn's arrow took one in the gaping mouth, punching into his brain and dropping him like a sack of rocks. The other two archers loosed a heartbeat later, their shafts whipping past the formed-up Legionnaires and hurtling through the night to slam into the second enemy. The man fell, feathered by a pair of missiles in his throat and groin.

The third, however, managed to turn and flee south, in the direction of their camp. A howling war cry burst from his throat.

A flying spear silenced his call. The thrown polearm struck him with such force it knocked him forward, sending him sliding across the cobblestones. The Jokull never rose, but the shaft of a familiar hewing spear quivered in its sheath of muscle and bone.

Aravon turned a surprised glance on Balegar. The big man's arm was fully extended forward, and he had just begun recovering from the throw. A throw that, Aravon realized, had sent the spear a full eighty yards. And not the sort of spear designed for throwing; no javelin this, but a full-length hewing spear that had to weigh upwards of ten pounds, shaft to head.

"Good reflexes," Aravon said, approval echoing in his quiet voice. He'd once more fallen into the role of a Legion Captain, trusting his men to deal with individual enemies while he focused on the battle at large, so he hadn't even thought to throw his own spear. Not that he'd have had much chance of hitting the Jokull from this range. Balegar's cast was a feat few in the Legion—even the massive Belthar—could have replicated.

Balegar accepted the compliment with a grunt as he drew the Fehlan-style longsword that hung at his hip. With a whispered command, Aravon set their small company in motion once more.

His eyes went to the dead Jokull lying on the cobblestone street. Blood pooled around the bodies in an ever-widening pool, darkening their blond beards and staining their furs. He'd never seen a Jokull up close—they resembled the Deid and Smida, though with much leaner, gaunter features and more ragged furs. The Jokull marshes were harsh, with little dry ground to grow crops or raise livestock. The wetland clan's diet subsisted chiefly of fish, frogs, eels, and other water-bound creatures they could catch. Not a life of prosperity, made even harder by the Legion's presence on their eastern border.

No wonder they joined the Eirdkilrs! Aravon shook his head as he stepped over the first body, his boots *splashing* in Fehlan blood. *Anyone would seize a chance to claim not only Rivergate, but as much of Westhaven as their warriors could capture.*

Only Commander Rheamus' quick thinking had stymied the plan. Now, Swordsman willing, Aravon's men would push them back. Perhaps once the Jokull had lost, they would consider diplomacy. Then again, a loss could only compound their hatred of the Princelanders—the "half-men" their Eirdkilr cousins hated with such ferocity.

Either way, that doesn't matter now. Aravon tightened his grip on his spear. *All that matters is that we win here.* Diplomacy and relations with the Fehlan clans was a concern for politicians like Duke Dyrund, not a simple military man.

The howling of the Eirdkilrs and Jokull warriors grew louder as they approached the inner keep's southern edge. Aravon slowed his men—this close to the enemy, they had to move slow and quiet to avoid discovery until the right moment. The Legionnaires squared their shoulders and tightened grips on their weapons. Balegar had paused in his advance long enough to rip his hewing spear free of the slain Jokull; now, he hefted the polearm, bloodstained tip dripping along the cobblestone street.

Aravon drew in a deep breath as they reached the southwestern corner of the inner keep's wall. *The moment of truth.*

As they rounded the bend in the road, Aravon had a full view of the chaos gripping southern Rivergate. A sea of Jokull and Eirdkilr warriors stood between them and the outer wall's south gate, which had been thrown wide. Through the open gate, Aravon caught sight of the blazing inferno Zaharis had used to lure the enemy away.

Brilliant flames of red and orange licked at the swamplands south of the city, bathing the land around Rivergate in blinding light. And there, limned in the glow of the raging fire, stood Colborn's Legionnaires. One hundred and thirty strong, arrayed in six ranks twenty men wide, with Colborn, Rangvaldr, Noll, and Zaharis at their head. They wore no armor, carried no shields, but they threw themselves at the Eirdkilrs and Jokull with a roar that echoed off the stone walls of Rivergate.

Aravon's heart leapt to his throat. Colborn's men had no chance of winning the battle against so many enemies. They hadn't taken more than a half-dozen steps before they were swarmed by towering Eirdkilrs and howling, ragged Jokull. If they stood fast, they died.

But Colborn was too wily to stand. Before the enemy could fully surround them, a blinding *BOOM* split the air in the middle of the Eirdkilr ranks. A pillar of fire burst high into the sky for a brief instant. That instant was all it took for Colborn's Legionnaires to break off and flee. The one hundred and thirty men split in half and took off east and west, racing along the wall of burning flames and disappearing into the darkness beyond.

The Eirdkilrs' howls of rage split the night, echoed by the Jokull war cries. *"Death to the half-men!"* The Eirdkilrs' battle chant rang off the walls of Rivergate, and the thunder of their feet set the ground trembling. A rolling tide of enemies—more than a thousand Fehlans and barbarians—surged through the gates to give chase to the fleeing Legionnaires.

Aravon's heart leapt as he watched the enemies streaming through the flung-open gates. Every passing second diminished the forces arrayed against them until, when the flow of pursuers finally slackened off, the number of the remaining besiegers had been slashed. Of the twenty-three hundred Jokull assaulting the city, Aravon guessed nearly half had raced after Colborn's men. Two hundred Eirdkilrs had joined in the pursuit. That left a thousand enemies in Rivergate.

A thousand against the fifty Legionnaires divided between Aravon and Captain Lemaire's companies. *That's what Noll would call shite odds.* A wry smile crooked Aravon's face beneath his mask. *Let's see if a surprise attack can turn those in our favor.*

He had just opened his mouth to sound the attack, when a roar erupted from the southeastern corner of the inner keep. Aravon's heart leapt to his throat as he caught sight of Captain Lemaire's company charging down the avenue that led toward the inner keep's south gate. He'd intended to attack first, bearing the brunt of the Eirdkilr and Jokull in the precious seconds it took for the rear assault to divert the enemy. But the run-in with the drunk Jokull had slowed them down, meaning the Nyslian Captain had the unenviable privilege of springing the trap.

Aravon would be a step behind.

"Charge!" he hissed, as quiet as he could manage.

All Eirdkilr and Jokull eyes had turned away from the gate, in time to see Captain Lemaire's men burst from the shadows along the eastern edge of the keep. So stunned were they by the presence of Legionnaires in their midst that they failed to meet the charge. Skathi's arrows flew as fast as the Agrotora could fire, scything down the enemies clustered in front of the inner keep's gate. Legionnaires hurled their hand axes at Jokull and Eirdkilrs too shocked to raise their round, steel-rimmed shields. Fifty enemies fell in the space of seconds.

But those seconds were all it took for the enemy to recover. Surprise gave way to rage, and Eirdkilr howls echoed with delight at a *new* foe to slaughter. After days besieging the inner keep's stone walls, they finally faced flesh and blood. The war cries of *"Death to the half-men!"* thundered through Rivergate and echoed off the high walls.

Towering Eirdkilrs charged the clustered Legionnaires, waving enormous axes, spears, and clubs large enough to shatter a man's skull and helmet in a single blow. The smaller Jokull raced in their larger cousins' wake, waving spears rusted by years of fishing and frogging. Yet in such numbers, they could have fought bare-handed and overwhelmed Captain Lemaire's forces.

Aravon's Legionnaires broke into a run, crossing a hundred yards toward the main avenue before the enemy spotted them. One Jokull half-turned, caught a glimpse of them, and fell with Woryn's arrow in his throat before he could cry out. But the man's three comrades, clustered around a brazier, saw the new threat and raised their voices in alarm.

The time for stealth and subterfuge had ended. Aravon raised his voice in a roar. "For the Legion!"

The three archers on the flanks sent a stream of shafts at the enemy, loosing one arrow after another, emptying their quivers into Fehlan and Eirdkilr bodies. As one, the soldiers drew their swords and lowered their shoulders into their shields.

The wall of Legionnaires collided with the dispersed, surprised Eirdkilrs and Jokull with a deafening *clash* of steel and wood on flesh. Blood sprayed in the air as Legion short swords punched through ragged furs, leather armor, and enemy muscle and bone. Eirdkilr howls turned to cries of agony as the

Legionnaires bowled through the scattered barbarians, and Fehlans fell beneath the charging Princelanders.

Caught off-guard, attacked from both sides, the Jokull and Eirdkilrs seemed confused, disoriented. Of the thousand remaining enemies, only two hundred or so managed to mount any sort of defense. Eirdkilrs raised their huge shields in time to repel Legionnaire swords, and a handful of Jokull threw themselves against the solid wood-and-steel wall arrayed against them. Aravon's men scythed them down in twos, threes, and fives. Facing a cohesive barrier of shields—with Legion short swords behind to bite back—the disorganized mass of barbarians stood no chance.

Yet, slowly, one man at a time, the Eirdkilrs recovered from their surprise. Five, ten, twenty more joined those streaming toward Aravon's shield wall. The huge barbarians threw themselves against the Legionnaires with howls of rage and flashing weapons.

The first casualty came less than ten seconds into the battle. A Private of Third Company in the front rank fell, skull crushed by an enormous Eirdkilr axe. Even as the Legionnaires closed ranks and brought down the barbarian that slew their companion, a wild-eyed Jokull threw himself into the gap. Aravon thrust his spear into the man's face, opening his cheek to the bone, and the Sergeant anchoring the center of the second rank drove his shield into the stumbling Fehlan, hurling him backward. But when the non-com officer moved forward, he stepped into the path of a driving Eirdkilr spear. Bloodstained steel exploded out the back of the soldier's head, spraying Aravon with hot gore. The Eirdkilr howled and, tearing his spear free, swung around for another attack on the Legion line.

Balegar's hewing spear sheared through the barbarian's neck, separating his head from his shoulders. A Legionnaire in the third rank stepped up to close ranks, and the soldiers behind him filled in the gap he'd left. Yet they'd lost a tenth of their number in the space of a few heartbeats, and scores more Eirdkilrs streamed toward them.

The forward momentum of their charge slowed as the Eirdkilrs and Jokull crashed into their line. Slowed, then stalled completely. To Aravon's horror, as more and more of the enemy joined the battle, he and his company found themselves forced to retreat. Such a small, ragged shield wall couldn't stand against ten times their number of the seven-foot barbarians.

"Captain!" A shout from beside Aravon brought him whirling around, in time to see the giant Balegar raising his shield. An Eirdkilr arrow *thunked* into the shield, a steel-tipped head punching an inch through the wood.

Aravon had no time to thank the man, or to search out the archer who had loosed the shaft. His world filled with the snarling faces, howling war cries, and flashing weapons of the enemy. The fires burning outside the walls filled the air with thick, noxious smoke and splashed the Eirdkilrs in a light that turned their faces hideous, bestial. The ringing chant of *"Death to the half-men!"* rang in his ears until it was all he could hear, all he could think.

A Legionnaire in the front rank crumpled beneath the crushing blow of an Eirdkilr club, then another to a savage thrust from a Jokull spear. The Legionnaires tried to close ranks, tried to re-form the shield wall, but there were too few against far, far too many. Even a single instant of inattention could cost the few men left to him their lives.

Aravon's spear was a stabbing, thrusting blur of steel that sprayed blood with every attack. The archers' bows had fallen silent; they'd run out of arrows, and now joined the ranks of Legionnaires stabbing short swords at the enemy pressed up against the shield wall. Yet even as he drove the Odarian steel spearhead into an Eirdkilr's chest, Aravon knew the battle had turned against him.

Balegar grunted beside him, and from the corner of his eye, Aravon caught sight of the Nyslian giant crumpling, an Eirdkilr axe carving a deep gash in his face. Two more Legionnaires fell, borne to the ground beneath the crush of enemy flesh and metal. The Nyslians screamed as the Jokull and Eirdkilrs tore them to shreds.

Aravon's heart sank, dread writhing like acid in his gut. The time had come to sound the retreat, before the Eirdkilrs and Jokull slaughtered them all.

He opened his mouth to cry out, but his words were drowned beneath the roar of an Eirdkilr charging their ranks. The huge barbarian burst through the weakened shield wall, axe swinging, shearing through one Legionnaire's upraised sword arm and crushing another's armored shoulder.

Before Aravon could bring up his spear to defend himself, the Eirdkilr's backhanded attack crashed into his chest. The alchemically-treated leather held, but the force of the blow knocked the breath from his lungs and hurled him backward. Aravon's boot slipped on blood-slicked cobblestones and he fell hard. Gasping for breath, pain shooting through his torso, Aravon could only look up, unable to move in time to dodge, block, or deflect the enormous Eirdkilr axe descending toward his head.

Chapter Twenty

Time slowed to a crawl as death came for Aravon. Hatred twisted the blue-stained face of the Eirdkilr standing above him. The steel axe head glinted in the light of the burning Rivergate homes, bits of blood and gore darkening its enormous half-moon edge.

Impossibly, the axe halted mid-air. An enormous hand gripped the shaft just beneath the crimson-stained head, arresting its downward swing. Snarling, a bloody Balegar held the Eirdkilr at bay for a brief second.

Just long enough for Aravon to recover and explode upward. The Eirdkilr had just turned his hate-filled glare on the Nyslian Corporal when Aravon's spear punched through his throat. The blow, driven upward from a half-seated position, lacked the force of a proper thrust, but the Odarian steel spearhead sliced through flesh, gristle, and blood vessels. Hot, wet crimson gushed from the man's throat and splashed onto Aravon, the arterial spray spattering Balegar's face. Yet the giant soldier seemed not to notice; baring his teeth, he tore the enormous axe from the crumpling barbarian.

Aravon scrambled to his feet, trying his best to ignore the ache in his chest and back. Clambering over the fallen Eirdkilr, he hurried to take his place in the re-forming line. The shadow of the giant Balegar towered on his right.

The attacking barbarian had opened a gap in the shield wall, but the Legionnaires had managed to close ranks, lock their shields once more. Eirdkilr and Jokull axes, spears, and clubs battered at steel-reinforced Legion shields, and two more soldiers fell before Aravon could bring his own spear to bear. The attack had reduced his company to just over half their strength, and more enemies streamed toward them with every second, bestial cries of rage and glee filling the air.

Then a new sound greeted him: the *groan* of enormous hinges. A roar of "For the Legion!" drowned out the Eirdkilr and Jokull cries, and a flood of armed and armored men burst from within the slowly-opening gates of the inner keep.

Topaz Battalion had joined the fight, Duke Westhaven's regulars at their backs.

"Bring the fish-fuckers down!" A shout rang out across Rivergate. A hundred hand axes hurtled through the air, striking down scores of Eirdkilrs and Jokull caught off-guard by yet *another* surprise attack. Enemies torn by the desire to attack the two small companies on their western and eastern flank found themselves beset from the north. In the confusion that gripped the Eirdkilrs and Jokull, a swarm of Legionnaires stormed out of the inner keep's gates.

The foremost company—a full hundred men strong, formed up in a solid wall of armor and steel twenty men wide and five ranks deep—rolled over the enemies clustered before the gates. Straight down the broad avenue they charged, a hammer of fury and determination barreling toward Rivergate's wide-open southern gate.

The second company out of the gate wheeled left, falling onto the Eirdkilrs and Jokull hammering at Captain Lemaire's soldiers. Seconds later, a third company rushed out and swiveled right, toward Aravon's men. The two hundred Legionnaires crashed into the backs of their enemies, and Legion swords took a heavy toll before the Eirdkilrs or Jokull could fully turn to meet the charge.

Triumph surged within Aravon's chest—Commander Rheamus had received Skathi's arrow-borne message in time—but he could spare no attention for the battle. The Eirdkilrs' howls doubled in pitch and volume at the sight of their enemy and the thrown-open gates of the inner keep. Those attacking Aravon's men fought a desperate battle, torn between their desire to slaughter the pathetically tiny group in front of them and the need to wheel and face the full-strength company at their backs.

Aravon's spear flashed in the fire-lit night, its razor edge punching through Eirdkilr armor, opening Jokull throats, knocking aside weapons aimed at his men. With his ranks reduced to fewer than twenty, he had to buy the men under his command a few more seconds until reinforcements arrived. Enemy weapons battered at the Legionnaire's shields but the soldiers, raw recruits and veterans alike, weathered the storm of fury.

Help arrived in the form of furious, hungry-eyed Legionnaires of Topaz Battalion. The Eirdkilrs and Jokull had no choice but to break off the assault on Aravon's slowly-retreating force. Too late. Even as they turned to face the larger threat, the Legionnaires of Rivergate crashed into them with a deafening roar of steel and wood striking flesh. The smaller, leaner Jokull were hurled backward, stumbling into their comrades and entangling with their larger Eirdkilr allies. Enemies stumbled on prone bodies or blood-slicked stones, falling beneath flashing Legion swords.

At that moment, a new sound pierced the din of battle: a resounding, rumbling *BOOM*. It was the sweetest thing he'd heard in a long time. He spared a glance to the south, found the men of Topaz Battalion formed up within the now-closed gate, the heavy iron portcullis dropped into place.

Triumph surged within him. *Yes!* Commander Rheamus had heeded the order scrawled on the slip of paper Skathi had shot over the wall. His men had retaken the outer wall, held the gate against the enemies inside and outside the city.

The tide of the impossible battle had turned in their favor.

"Forward!" Aravon roared, waving his spearhead at the enemy. "Hit them hard!"

His small force, now reduced to just seventeen, closed ranks—a ragged wall of shields six men wide and two ranks deep, with Aravon, Balegar, and the three archers in the rear—and charged the enemy.

Aravon's small company punched into the rear of the Eirdkilr and Jokull ranks. Legion short swords thrust between gaps in heavy shields, finding exposed legs, throats, arms, and blue-painted savage faces. One bloody step forward at a time, the cobblestones slick and sticky beneath their feet, the Legionnaires under Aravon's command fought to bring down the enemies already locked in combat with the men of Topaz Battalion. Only a handful ever managed to turn and attempt to repel the assault—they died beneath a storm of Legion steel.

Balegar's enormous axe whirled above the heads of his comrades, his massive arms swinging the weapon with enough force to shear through Eirdkilr and Jokull necks, limbs, and bodies alike. Aravon's spear darted forward time and again, a striking snake that left Fehlans and barbarians dead in its bloody wave. All the while, the twelve Legionnaires in the shield wall absorbed the brutal punishment, trusting in their shields, armor, and courage to stand strong. Even when one fell, then a second and third, the men reacted as they'd been trained, closing ranks, locking shields, and facing their foes as a unit.

Then there were no more enemies. The last Eirdkilr fell, so suddenly that Aravon's small company staggered. A small gap stood between Aravon's men and the shield wall of Topaz Battalion. Eighty of the original one hundred remained, men with gaunt faces and eyes filled with hate for the enemy that lay dead at their feet.

In the momentary pause after the battle, Aravon shouldered through his now-ragged ranks of Legionnaires.

"Who's in charge?" He had to shout to make his voice, muffled by the leather mask, heard over the din of the battle raging within Rivergate's walls.

"Me." A tall, broad-shouldered Legionnaire with a drooping moustache and an ugly-looking gash along the right side of his face stepped forward. "Captain Nyaro, Fifth Company, Topaz Battalion."

"Captain Snarl," Aravon replied simply. "Good to see you got my message."

Captain Nyaro nodded. "Almost thought it was a forgery, except the damned Eirdkilrs can't write such neat letters." A grin split his bloodied, exhausted features. "Whoever sent that arrow over the wall is one hell of a shot."

"You can thank her later," Aravon replied. "But now, we've got a battle to win."

His eyes slid past Fifth Company. The remaining two companies—short a few dozen Legionnaires, doubtless fallen to illness, hunger, or wounds—had joined combat, laying into the Eirdkilrs and Jokull occupying Rivergate between the inner and outer walls. The company that had gone to help Captain Lemaire's men seemed to have a handle on the enemy occupying eastern Rivergate, and the gate to the inner keep was held by the three hundred men of Westhaven.

The Legionnaires at the outer gate, however, fought a desperate battle. Fully two hundred Eirdkilrs and Jokull had survived the driving rush to close the gate, and their howls of fury echoed loud as they tried to carve their way through the Legion's shield wall. If they couldn't get that gate open, their comrades outside—those off in pursuit of Colborn's company—would be trapped outside, and they'd be trapped within.

"There!" Aravon thrust his finger toward the gate. "We help them!"

Captain Nyaro snapped a salute without hesitation. "Aye, sir!" He might not recognize Aravon—the unusual armor and the greatwolf mask saw to that—but it appeared he was smart enough to understand that Aravon was in charge. At least until the battle was over and his fellow soldiers were safe. Then Commander Rheamus could sort out proper chain of command.

"About, turn!" Captain Nyaro shouted. Instantly, the Sergeants under his command took up the call, relaying it down the line of eighty Legionnaires. With the precision that made the Legion of Heroes the greatest fighting force on Fehl, the men of Topaz Battalion raised their spears and pivoted in place, turning. In less than five seconds, they had re-formed ranks, this time facing the enemy at the southern gate.

Aravon's surviving handful hurried to join the lines of Legionnaires, and Aravon took his place in command position at the rear of the company, with the hulking Balegar towering over him. Blood streamed from a deep gash in the huge man's face, yet his expression revealed no hint of pain, only grim determination and fury. He gripped his weapon, the axe he'd ripped from Eirdkilr fingers, and squared his enormous shoulders in anticipation of battle.

Aravon raised his bloody spear. "For the Legion!"

"For Rivergate!" The men of Topaz Battalion roared and, at their Captain's orders, marched to meet the enemy.

Backed by the might of Fifth Company, Aravon felt his confidence mounting. The *clash* of steel, the howls of war cries, and the screams of wounded and dying men rang off the stone walls of Rivergate, underscored by the crackling of burning homes. Smoke thickened the air and stung Aravon's lungs. The chaos of war held the city in a firm grip, and death rampaged through Rivergate tonight.

Legionnaires fell beneath the mighty blows of Eirdkilr axes and clubs. Jokull spears slipped between momentary gaps in the shield walls or *spanged* off Legion helmets. Short swords stabbed out, biting deep into Fehlan and barbarian flesh. Blue-painted faces contorted in agony and Jokull howled as the shield wall advanced, inexorably, crushing them beneath its might.

One look at the swirling tide of combat told him that they had a real chance of winning this. Westhaveners held the inner keep's gate, repelling the

149

scattered Jokull attacks and driving back the towering Eirdkilrs beneath a storm of arrows. The Legionnaires of Topaz Battalion stood firm, their shields and strong arms more than a match for the disorganized fury of their enemies. Fewer than a hundred Eirdkilrs remained, and half the Jokull had already fallen. The battle would be over in minutes at this rate.

We just have to hold the gate!

Aravon ached to break into a run, to sprint down the main avenue that led to the city's southern gate and help the beleaguered Legionnaires there. Yet the Legion's strength lay in its cohesion, its unity, the strength of its shield wall. That meant he had to keep his men moving at a fast march, yet no faster, if he wanted to strike with maximum efficiency.

Anger surged within him as the company under his command closed the distance to the gate. A hundred yards. Seventy. Fifty. Twenty. He felt a roar building in his chest and he unleashed it, a mighty war cry that rang above the din of battle. A hundred Legion throats took up the wordless call as they *clashed* with the enemy trying to re-take the gate.

The Eirdkilrs and Jokull fought—like demons out of the fiery hell, how they fought—but they had been caught flat-footed by the successive flank assaults. Captain Lemaire's sneak attack had reduced the number by a few score, and Aravon's men had done likewise. The charge from the inner keep slashed the enemy numbers by more than three hundred within the first minute, and the Eirdkilrs and Jokull, caught off-guard and disoriented by the repeated pummeling, never managed to form cohesive ranks or any semblance of a battle plan.

They didn't die easy. The seven-foot-tall Eirdkilrs wielded enormous axes, spears, and clubs capable of crushing Legionnaire limbs and smashing through shields. The strength of the shield wall was all that kept the massive barbarians from overwhelming the smaller Princelanders. They gave no quarter and asked none in return. A wild light shone in every Eirdkilr eye, twisted their war-painted features. They would kill every Eird or die trying.

The Jokull, however, appeared far less slaughterous than their southern cousins. As Aravon's commandeered company scythed through the ranks, fear pierced the battle frenzy burning on their faces. A few threw down their weapons and tried to surrender, only to be cut down by Eirdkilrs or the furious Legionnaires who had watched their comrades slaughtered, their city destroyed, and their homes torched.

"Let them surrender!" Aravon shouted over the clash of weapons, the shouts and cries of battling men.

Captain Nyaro took up the call, as did the Lieutenants under his command. The order flew down the lines as Sergeants shouted at their platoons. Too late for scores of Jokull, who died where they stood even after they threw down their rusty spears, but in time for the last forty or fifty Fehlans who had tried to re-take the gate. The shouts seemed to reach the Legionnaires holding the gate. A few Fehlans died in the attempt, many of the soldiers too caught up in the fury of battle to restrain their bloodlust, but by the time the last Eirdkilr fell, thirty-five Jokull knelt empty-handed on the crimson-stained street before the gate.

Sweat soaked Aravon's face, tunic, and hands. His chest ached from the blow he'd forgotten about, and blood and gore caked his armor, sliding down the alchemically-treated leather and seeping into his boots. He squelched with every step and his arms felt heavy—so, so very heavy, to the point that lifting his spear seemed an impossibility.

Yet the battle wasn't over yet. Behind him, knots of Jokull and Eirdkilrs locked in combat with the solid shield walls of Topaz Battalion and Duke Westhaven's regulars holding the inner keep. Through the smoke hanging in the air, Aravon caught sight of Captain Lemaire at the rear of the company that had gone to his aid. Belthar's hulking frame hovered at the Nyslian officer's side, his enormous double-headed axe crusted with Eirdkilr and Jokull blood.

Dread thrummed within Aravon as he searched the ranks for Skathi, but saw no sign of the Agrotora. He forced the worry from his mind and turned his attention back to the battle at hand.

"Captain Nyaro, see that these men are properly restrained," Aravon commanded, "then start going through the streets and clearing them out, thoroughly. No surprises!"

"Aye, Captain Snarl." Nyaro saluted.

"Any enemies that try to surrender, let them." Aravon fixed the man with a piercing gaze. The leather mask hid his stern expression, but his eyes and the command in his voice made the message clear.

The Captain hesitated a long moment. Aravon understood the man's recalcitrance. He, like everyone else in Rivergate, had suffered at the hands of the Jokull. They might not be as bad as their Eirdkilr cousins, yet the Fehlans had harmed Nyaro's fellow Legionnaires and Rivergaters.

Yet, Nyaro was a Captain of the Legion first and foremost. Despite his personal feelings, he had been given an order. "Aye, Captain." Whirling, he set about barking orders to his men. Half of Fifth Company set about collecting the Jokull weapons and herding the surrendered Fehlans off to one side. The other half, including those who had accompanied Aravon, split into four ten-man platoons to clear the streets east and west of the south gate.

Aravon glanced back at the battle in front of the inner keep. Topaz Battalion and the Westhaven regulars were mopping up the last of the enemy. The Eirdkilrs died to a man, often taking two or three Legionnaires with them in their battle frenzy. However, the Nyslian Captain seemed to have the same idea as Aravon, and any Jokull that threw down their weapons were allowed to surrender.

Confident in the Legion's ability to handle the battle, Aravon turned and raced toward the gate, shouldering through the exhausted, gaunt-faced Legionnaires guarding it. He sprinted up the stairs set into the stone wall, taking them two at a time, until he reached the battlements.

His eyes scanned the marshlands south of Rivergate. Zaharis' fire still blazed bright—impossibly, considering the fact that it seemed to consume only marsh water and damp logs rather than any fuel normal flames would feed on— though it had gone from a towering inferno fifteen yards tall to a low-burning line barely higher than a grown man's knee. Yet it still provided ample illumination for Aravon to see across the space cleared around the city walls.

Nothing moved beneath the shadows of the wetland trees. The howling war cries of the Jokull and Eirdkilrs echoed through the darkness, too faint and distant for Aravon to determine how far they were.

Now, with the battle in Rivergate won, Aravon could spare thought to worry for Colborn, Rangvaldr, Noll, and Zaharis. They were out there somewhere, with a hundred and thirty Legionnaires of Topaz Battalion's Second and Third Companies at their backs. So few, hunted by ten times their number of Eirdkilrs and Jokull. Enemies intimately familiar with the marshlands, their own territory, accompanied by savage barbarians intent on slaughtering every Princelander they pursued.

Come on, Colborn! Aravon's hands clutched the stone parapet tight, his knuckles turning white. *Where in the fiery hell are you?*

Long minutes passed in silent vigil. The sounds of battle grew faint behind him, the clash of steel falling silent, until only the shouts of Legion officers and the cries of the wounded and dying echoed through Rivergate.

And still Aravon watched, hoping, praying to the Swordsman that his comrades would find their way home.

He whirled at the presence of a figure on his right, but relief flooded him as he caught sight of familiar tight-braided red hair.

"Captain." Worry twisted Skathi's strong features as she stared out across the marshlands. "Any sign of 'em?"

"No." Aravon shook his head. Acid writhed in his stomach. *They should have been here by now.* Only one thing would stop his men from returning. Aravon tried to push aside the image of Colborn's unarmored, lightly-armed company surrounded by Jokull and Eirdkilrs, slaughtered to a man. He half-expected to see the swamplands stained red with Princelander blood, or the gently-flowing tide carrying the bodies of men he'd sent to their deaths.

A flash of movement to the southeast brought him spinning around. Hope surged within him as he spotted a tall, lithe figure in mottled leather armor racing toward the gate. Zaharis moved at a dead run, arms and legs pumping, sending mud flying everywhere.

Then another figure appeared through the trees, unfamiliar to Aravon, but wearing the mud-stained undertunic of a Legionnaire.

More burst from the trees, five, then ten, then thirty and more. Fifty became a hundred, then a hundred and twenty. Aravon's heart leapt as he caught sight of Colborn's broad shoulders moving near the rear of the pack. Yet his brow furrowed. *Where are Noll and Rangvaldr?*

A howl of "*Death to the half-men!*" drove a dagger of ice down his spine. Eirdkilrs burst from the marshlands fifty yards east of Colborn's running men. To the west, directly south of the city gate, Jokull raiders splashed across a shallow stream, speeding toward the dry ground.

Then two more figures burst from the trees, far behind the rear of Colborn's column. A broad-shouldered man in mottled leather armor, with a smaller, compact man in similar armor limping along beside him.

Aravon's heart stopped mid-beat. His eyes went to the Jokull and Eirdkilrs converging on his men. In that moment, he knew beyond a shadow of a doubt that Rangvaldr and Noll would never make it to safety in time.

Chapter Twenty-One

Aravon spun toward the archer on his left. "Skathi—"

"On it!" She was already racing past him and heading east, drawing an arrow from the nearly-empty quiver on her back.

Aravon dashed down the steps that led from the parapet to the ground below. "Open the gate!" he shouted.

The Legionnaires stationed in front of the gate turned questioning glances on him, but none moved. Second and Third Companies had accepted Aravon's command based on Duke Dyrund's letter and the Prince's pendant, but the rest of Topaz Battalion had no idea who he was. He'd saved their asses and fought beside Captain Nyaro, sure, but to them, he was just a man in a snarling greatwolf mask and strange-looking armor.

Aravon had no time for the delay. Even as he raced down the steps, he scanned the ranks of Legionnaires until he spotted the two he sought. "Corporal Balegar, Ursus!"

The two huge soldiers looked up from where they stood, at the base of the stairs, near the two enormous wheels that raised the portcullis.

"Get the bloody gate open!" Aravon shouted. "We've got friendlies outside."

Belthar obeyed first, no hesitation. The giant Balegar moved a fraction of a second after him. Together, the two of them set to work turning the winches that typically required four soldiers to work. Yet as soon as they bent their enormous backs to the task, the *clanking* of chains echoed loud in the night and the portcullis slowly rumbled upward.

"What you doing?" A Legionnaire bearing the insignia of a Captain rushed through the ranks formed up before the gate. "We just got the damned thing closed!"

"My men are out there, with more than a hundred of Second and Third Companies." Aravon brushed past the officer and raced toward the gate. He shot the bolt holding the wicket gate closed and ducked beneath the slowly-rising portcullis. "The enemy's on their heels, and if we don't go out there, they're dead. So let's go, Swordsman take it!"

He didn't wait to see if the officer followed his orders; the men racing toward the gate couldn't afford even a second's delay. As Aravon dashed onto the hills outside Rivergate, he scanned the night for his men. Zaharis alone was in sight, a mere thirty yards away, but he'd stopped to help a fallen Legionnaire to rise.

"Get in here!" Aravon yelled, racing down the slope toward the Secret Keeper.

"*Working on it,*" Zaharis signed one-handed. "*Company's not the most pleasant.*"

Aravon's gaze slid past the Secret Keeper toward the Jokull and Eirdkilrs spilling out of the marshlands. "I can see that. Get your men to safety. We'll buy you time."

If Zaharis signed a response, Aravon didn't bother looking. He had eyes only for the column of muddy, unarmored soldiers streaming up the hill. His jaw clenched as he leaned into the mad dash, forcing his lungs to work despite the ache in his chest. Those at the front would reach safety, but the slower Legionnaires were cutting it close. As for Noll and Rangvaldr…

Come on, damn it! Aravon tightened the grip on his spear and spurred himself to run faster. He gave the stumbling, exhausted Legionnaires a wide berth, instead turning his steps west, toward the Jokull. They'd reach the Legionnaires first, but Aravon just needed to buy a few seconds for the men to reach safety.

The Fehlans howled in delight as they spotted the lone figure racing toward them. Raising their spears, they splashed through the shallow stream and charged up the hill.

Right into Skathi's arrows.

The foremost Jokull fell in silence, a red-fletched shaft sprouting from his eye. Two more followed in quick succession, arrows feathering their scrawny, exposed chests and throats. A fourth screamed as a missile punched through his ragged breeches. He fell, hard, face into the muck, and his flailing limbs bore down the two Fehlans racing alongside him.

But Skathi had a limited supply of arrows, and the stream of Jokull only grew thicker as more and more returned from their pursuit of the Legionnaires. Furious shouts and insults, barked in the sibilant marshlands dialect of the Fehlan language, pierced the night as scores, then hundreds of Jokull rushed into view.

Aravon could never take them all on alone, but he didn't need to. He just had to bring down the fastest of the lot, those close enough to catch his men before they reached the safety of Rivergate. Without hesitation, he raised his spear and unleashed an echoing war cry of his own. "For the Legion!"

The first Fehlan died with Aravon's spear in his throat. Aravon's forward momentum drove the dying Jokull backward into the man behind him, and Aravon ripped his spear free, whirled it over his head, and *cracked* the iron-capped butt against the side of the man's head. The Jokull fell, skull crushed.

Aravon blocked a savage spear thrust, disemboweling the man with a whirling strike that carried him into a deflection of the next Jokull's attack. The weighted end of his spear swept the Fehlan's legs out from beneath him and shattered a kneecap. Before the man could rise, Aravon spun the spear and drove the tip into the fallen man's chest. Odarian steel punched through ragged furs and filthy flesh, snapping bones, driving into the Jokull's heart. He died with a venomous curse on his lips.

In the second between enemies, Aravon risked a glance over his shoulder. The fastest of the Legionnaires had reached the open gate and had begun streaming through. Zaharis, ignoring Aravon's orders, had returned to help another slow-moving soldier up the hill.

Aravon had no more time to look for Colborn, to check for Noll and Rangvaldr's position. The howling cry of a Jokull brought him spinning around. He whipped his spear around, knocking aside an enemy's fishing spear, slicing through Jokull flesh. Crimson sprayed from the man's ruined throat, splashing Aravon's mask.

Hot blood stung Aravon's eyes and he staggered backward, frantically pawing at his face. He managed to open his left eye just as a Jokull leapt high into the air, spear raised for a thrust.

The spearhead *crashed* against bright Odarian steel. Colborn's sword hacked through the wooden shaft of the spear, the wrist beneath, and finally the man's head on the return stroke.

"Captain?" Colborn shouted. "You good?"

"Blood in my eyes!" Aravon called back as he tried to scrub the gore from his mask.

"You don't need to see to run!" A hand gripped Aravon's arm and spun him around, half-dragging him back up the hill toward Rivergate.

"But Noll—"

"Rangvaldr's got him." Colborn was breathing hard, a sign of how exhausted the usually-robust Lieutenant was. "We've...got to look after...ourselves!"

Aravon allowed Colborn to drag him along for a few steps, his feet moving of their own accord as he wiped at his mask. Tears streamed from his eyes, washing out enough of the blood that he could finally see where he was going. He and Colborn had covered a third of the distance to the wide-open gate. Just thirty yards to go, and most of the Legionnaires had reached safety.

But, as his eyes snapped toward the two figures laboring up the hill, Noll stumbled and collapsed. Rangvaldr stooped, lifted the little scout to his feet, and hauled him along through sheer force of will.

Without hesitation, Aravon sprinted east, toward the two men. A loud curse echoed from behind him, but Colborn's footsteps pounded along in his wake.

The Eirdkilrs were closing the distance to Noll and Rangvaldr fast, their long legs eating up the ground far too quickly for the two to reach safety. Skathi's arrows whistled downrange, bringing down first one, then a second giant barbarian. Yet even as the shafts flew, Aravon knew the slow-moving Noll and burdened Rangvaldr wouldn't escape.

Suddenly, a loud, high-pitched barking sound echoed in the night. A dark shape swooped down at the Eirdkilrs with a flap of feathers and raking talons. Blood sprayed from blue-painted faces and the Eirdkilrs cried out. A few slowed long enough to fumble for the bows still slung on their backs, but most were too focused on their prey to pay attention to the small, fox-sized Snarl in the darkness.

158

Aravon couldn't see the Enfield, but hope surged within him. It didn't matter that Snarl hadn't delivered a message from Colborn—all he cared was that the little creature still lived!

Snarl's attack slowed the foremost Eirdkilrs. Just a few steps, but enough to buy Rangvaldr and Noll precious seconds. And, in those seconds, Aravon and Colborn reached the pair.

"Need a hand?" Aravon shouted. Without hesitation, he bent, hauled Noll onto his shoulder, and whirled to race back up the hill. Noll's armor was light—the alchemically-treated leather weighing far less than chain mail or Legion half-plate—and the scout himself was short, compact, the result of years spent in the saddle. Though Aravon's lungs burned and fire coursed through his calves, he refused to slow as he carried his wounded soldier up the hill.

Aravon's eyes fixed on the slowly lowering portcullis. He had seconds before it slammed shut and trapped him outside forever. Eirdkilr howls of delight grew furious, and the Jokull seemed to redouble their efforts to reach the fleeing survivors. Gritting his teeth, Aravon leaned into Noll's weight and the angle of the incline, his boots churning the mud as he sprinted toward the gate.

The portcullis rose once more, and a rush of armored Legionnaires burst through the wicket gate. Thirty men of Topaz Battalion rushed from safety to form a protective shield wall around Aravon and Noll. Just in time. They'd barely closed ranks when a smattering of Eirdkilr arrows rattled against the shields.

Aravon staggered through the wicket gate, slipped on a patch of ground turned muddy with blood and heavy boots, and staggered to the side. He crashed into the wall but managed to remain upright, still clinging to Noll. He craned his neck and spotted Colborn and Rangvaldr stumbling into the city, followed by the brave Legionnaires. One at a time, the soldiers retreated through the wicket gate. The resounding *BOOM* of the dropping portcullis set the ground trembling, but filled Aravon with triumph. His elation doubled as the howling cries of the Jokull and Eirdkilrs echoed outside the walls.

Gasping, exhausted, Aravon sagged against the stone wall. Belthar materialized at his side, broad arms offering support and lifting Noll's weight from Aravon's shoulders.

"Hah!" Colborn fell to a knee beside Aravon, laboring for each breath. "Nice night…for a little swim…isn't it?"

159

Rangvaldr, equally winded, snorted beneath his mask. "Always did love…the marshes after dark. So…peaceful and…quaint."

Aravon shook his head. The two men were covered in mud from head to toe, and bits of marsh scum, water grasses, and swamp vegetation hung from their armor. "Glad to see…you enjoyed it." He was too exhausted to laugh, and the exertion of running and fighting had amplified the ache in his chest. "Next time…we can send you both…alone."

"Nothing like a dinner of raw fish…to lift a man's heart." Colborn recovered his wind first, though he remained kneeling, leaning on the wall beside Aravon. "Good to see you pulled this off, Captain. For a moment, you had us worried."

"Worried?" Aravon shook his head. "Three thousand enemies against us? They never stood a chance."

"Hear, hear!" Rangvaldr chimed in.

Aravon found himself fighting back a laugh. It held little genuine mirth. Before the mission, these words would be little more than bravado to push back worries over what lay ahead. Now, after the battle, they echoed the relief of men who had prepared to die and found they'd somehow come through the impossible alive.

Chapter Twenty-Two

A dark shape materialized before Aravon, and he looked up to see Zaharis standing over him. "*Sorry, Captain,*" the Secret Keeper signed. "*I'd have done more to cover your asses, but I used up everything alchemical I had to make that fire and to get out of the marshes alive.*"

"Are you kidding?" Noll's voice echoed from where the scout lay on the ground, Belthar hovering over him. "You set the bloody marsh on fire! That's more than enough where I'm concerned. Besides, I had my own special guardian watching over me." His masked face lifted as Skathi rushed down the steps toward them. "See?" he told the archer. "I knew you liked me!"

Skathi snorted beneath her mask. "Dream on, little man. I just didn't want our only healer to wind up dead. Belthar's got a scratch that needs looking after."

Noll muttered something under his breath, muffled by his mask, but Belthar perked up.

Aravon studied the archer. She still held her longbow, and only a single arrow remained in her quiver. However, she appeared unharmed, concern for her companions foremost in her mind.

Belthar's scratch, however, was far worse than Skathi's flippant tone hinted. The big man had a long gash running down the side of his face, across his jaw, and along his neck. Aravon sucked in a quiet breath—the wound had come within a finger's breadth of slicing the artery. Only the Swordsman's grace kept him alive.

"Stonekeeper." Aravon addressed Rangvaldr by his code name. "Get Ursus and Foxclaw somewhere out of sight and see what you can do for their wounds."

Rangvaldr nodded. "Of course, Captain Snarl." No question echoed in his voice; he knew as well as Aravon that the secret of the Eyrr holy stones was one best kept precisely that.

Aravon turned to Skathi. "Redwing, get back across the Standelfr and get word to Bannockburn as quickly as possible. We need those supplies here yesterday."

"Aye, Captain." Skathi stood and, with only a quick glance at the departing Belthar, Rangvaldr, and the injured Noll, hurried north, deeper into Rivergate, in the direction of their makeshift barge bridge.

"Need something for the pain, Captain?" Zaharis signed.

Aravon grimaced as he climbed to his feet. "If you've got it, I'll take it." He'd gotten off lucky in this battle—despite the throbbing ache in his chest, he considered a single semi-grievous wound good fortune. Better than far too many Legionnaires.

"I'll get something mixed up. But first, I'll go see if I can do anything for Noll and Belthar."

Aravon nodded. "Thank you."

With a little salute, Zaharis strode off in the direction Rangvaldr, Belthar, and Noll had gone.

"Captain." Colborn's voice was quiet beside Aravon, a solemn tone to his words.

Aravon turned a questioning glance on the Lieutenant.

"About the message." Colborn actually seemed hesitant. "I know we were supposed to send it with Snarl, but I didn't want to risk it." He drew in a deep breath. "Too many Eirdkilrs and Jokull around by the time we got into position. Couldn't take the chance he'd get shot down. I know it messed with your plan, but—"

"It is no matter, Ghoststriker." Aravon gave a dismissive wave. "What matters is that you did what you needed to do. Impossible odds or not, you carried the day. And got most of your men back alive."

"Yeah." A heavy gloom seemed to settle over Colborn, weighing on his shoulders.

"How'd you do it?" Aravon asked. "How did you pull it off?"

"Zaharis' fire did most of the work." Colborn shrugged. "And Rangvaldr's plan did the rest."

"Plan?" Aravon cocked his head.

"Playing to the Jokull's expectations," the Lieutenant replied. "They've studied our tactics, like every other Fehlan clan, and they'd know that Legionnaires don't flee unless they're routed. That was all it took to lure them out, and the Eirdkilrs with them." He let out a long breath. "I couldn't be sure how many would actually give chase…if it'd be enough."

"More than enough!" Aravon clapped the man on the shoulder. "Pulled more than half away from the city."

"Good," Colborn grunted. "After that, it was just a matter of hiding when the Jokull expected us to run." He chuckled. "We've all had enough marsh scum in our mouths, noses, and skivvies for a lifetime. But there are plenty of places to hide if you don't mind a bit of mud."

Aravon chuckled. "Mud's better than being Jokull fish bait."

"Aye." Colborn nodded. "But we couldn't all hide…" His head seemed to droop, his spirits sagging.

"How many?" Aravon's voice was gentle, firm.

A long moment of silence passed before Colborn responded. "Forty-five."

The words struck Aravon a blow to his gut. He'd been an officer and leader of men for years, but losing men never came easy. "I'm sorry, Colborn. That can't be—"

"Captain Snarl!" A familiar voice cut into Aravon's words. "Just the masked man I was looking for!"

Aravon turned to find Captain Lemaire marching toward him. Beside him strode a lean man with a pockmarked face, neatly trimmed gray beard, and piercing green eyes. Behind the Nyslian Captain was the looming shadow of the giant, Balegar.

From the corner of his eye, Aravon caught sight of Colborn slipping off down a side street. He wanted to call after the Lieutenant, but Captain Lemaire spoke before he could.

"*Capitaine* Snarl, permit me to present you to Commander Rheamus."

Aravon thrust a hand—still covered in Eirdkilr blood—toward Commander of Topaz Battalion. "Commander." If he offered a Legion salute and a "sir", it would establish Rheamus' authority over him. This way, he showed the man respect while tacitly sidestepping the matter of who, precisely, was in command here. Now that the battle had ended, he had no reason to wrest control from the Commander, Prince's orders or no.

Commander Rheamus fixed him with a stern scrutiny, suspicion plain in his eyes and weathered face. His brow furrowed, pulling his thick, close-cropped hair into a perfectly straight line. After a long moment, he accepted Aravon's hand. "Captain Snarl, it seems Rivergate is in your debt."

"Just doing our job, Commander." Aravon shrugged.

"Indeed." Commander Rheamus' green eyes flashed to Captain Lemaire, then back to Aravon. "You're the Prince's special envoys, yes? The ones mentioned in the official dispatch we received last month?"

Aravon nodded. "That's us." He drew out the Prince's silver pendant and held it up just long enough for the Commander to get a good look before tucking it away.

"According to the Prince, we're to defer to your orders." The words seemed to rankle, but there was only a hint of grimace on the man's face. He, it seemed, had swallowed the news of Aravon's authority far more easily than Commander Oderus of Jade Battalion. Perhaps the fact that Aravon had just saved his city made it more digestible. "What are they, exactly? Other than doing our jobs and holding the walls against the howling bastards outside."

Aravon chuckled. "Seems you've got things under control again, Commander. I doubt you'll need us to do anything more than sit back and let you handle things. Though I might advise you to send a message west to Bridgekeep, warn them the Eirdkilrs might try something there."

"Understood." Rheamus actually looked relieved; he had no idea who "Captain Snarl" truly was beneath the mask, and a Commander of Rheamus' years likely loathed the idea of answering to someone younger and less experienced. With a nod to Aravon, he turned to Captain Lemaire. "We owe your boys of Second and Third Companies for what they did. It's only right you lot get the pleasure of stringing the fish-fuckers up and hanging them from the walls."

Aravon's eyebrows rose. "Commander?"

Commander Rheamus' head swiveled back to Aravon, a slim gray eyebrow cocked.

"You're ordering the Jokull *executed?*" Aravon asked.

"Best way to deal with them." Rheamus nodded. "Nothing sends a message to the bastards like the sight of a few score bodies stripped and strung up. And, after everything the lads have endured these last days, they'll settle for nothing less than blood!"

"Commander, these men surrendered in good—" Aravon began.

"All due respect," Rheamus said in a voice that held next to none, "I've been holding Rivergate for the better part of a decade, which means I've had to deal with these reavers every day since." His words dropped to a low growl, anger darkening his eyes. "The only way to *stop* the attacks is to send a clear message in blood."

"That *message,* Commander, will only make the Jokull hate us more." Aravon's jaw clenched and he straightened, meeting the officer's eyes without hesitation. "Every one of the men who surrendered is someone's son, father, or brother. If we kill them here, all of the Fehlans still howling outside these walls will have twice as much reason to continue the war."

"They've already made their stance clear, Captain Snarl." Rheamus' tone was measured, tinged with barely-restrained anger. "They threw in their lot with the Eirdkilrs against us. There's only one answer to a statement like that."

"No, there's not!" Aravon stepped closer, looming a full half-hand taller than the Commander. "Answering cruelty with more cruelty will only continue this war long after the Eirdkilrs are defeated. Fehl will *never* know peace if we keep killing each other."

"Peace!" Commander Rheamus snorted and threw up his hands. "The words of a dreamer, not a soldier. You're Duke Dyrund's man through and through, no doubt about it."

"And proud of it." Fury blazed within Aravon's chest. His fists clenched by his sides, but he bit back a sharp retort. "I understand that you are angry, Commander," he finally said through clenched teeth. "I would be, too, if I watched my city burned and my men slaughtered."

Aravon *had* been angry after Hrolf Hrungnir slaughtered his men on the Eastmarch. Had it been the Eyrr that killed them rather than the Eirdkilrs, he might not have been able to hold his peace or join the battle in Bjornstadt. But that was beside the point. At the moment, all that mattered was preventing Commander Rheamus from slaughtering Jokull who had surrendered.

"If you kill them," Aravon insisted, "there's no chance we'll ever put an end to the war or convince the Jokull we're anything but the monsters they believe us to be."

The Legion Commander's jaw muscles worked. "So what, pray tell, do you suggest we do?" he growled, eyes blazing.

"Imprison them." Aravon met the Commander's eyes, pouring every shred of authority into his gaze. "And send word to the Prince in Icespire. Let *him* decide what to do."

Commander Rheamus' eyes narrowed, and Aravon could see the wheels in the officer's mind turning. Prince Toran was commander-in-chief of all military forces—Legion, ducal regulars, and irregulars—in the Princelands. *Technically.* The Prince usually left matters of war up to his two Generals, Vessach and Tinian, with the five Dukes as advisors. Commander Rheamus received his orders from Vessach, general in charge of the war's western theater, not the Prince. To a military man, Prince Toran was nothing more than a politician, one who ought to spend his time focused on running his kingdom and leave battles and strategy to "men of war".

But sometimes "men of war" needed "men of peace" to restrain them. Duke Dyrund had impressed upon Aravon the importance of what came *after* the Eirdkilrs were driven off Fehl, a belief shared by Prince Toran. And if that belief could spare a few hundred Fehlan lives and pave the way to potentially opening negotiations with the Jokull clan, it was one Aravon would choose to espouse in front of Commander Rheamus.

Long moments passed as Aravon locked eyes with Commander Rheamus. He had the authority to simply *order* the man to carry out his instructions, but if he did that, he ran the risk that he'd have to stay in Rivergate to see it was enforced. But if the Commander *chose* to heed, even if he felt he had no choice, Aravon could trust it would be carried out. Career soldiers like Rheamus rarely survived long if they disobeyed orders.

Finally, Commander Rheamus nodded—little more than a tiny jerk of his head, but grudging acknowledgement flashed in his eyes. Grunting, he turned and stalked off north, back toward the inner keep.

Aravon resisted the urge to let out a long, relieved sigh. Captain Lemaire and Balegar hadn't moved, and he didn't dare show any sign of uncertainty or weakness in front of the men. He'd learned long ago that a good officer held himself with confidence and authority. That didn't prevent him from taking the advice of the men under his command or admitting his mistakes, but he never backed down from doing what he believed right.

Captain Lemaire's eyes followed the Commander's retreating back. "Thank you." He spoke in a quiet voice, not turning to Aravon. "There has been death enough for one night, *Capitaine* Snarl."

The words surprised Aravon. He'd half-expected disappointment from the Nyslian Captain; after all, it had been the men of his battalion that suffered at the hands of the Jokull and their Eirdkilr allies. Yet, it seemed the "man of war" standing before him had a hint of peace lurking in his heart.

"Agreed." Aravon nodded. For a moment, he remained silent. The howling of the enemies outside the gate hadn't fallen silent, and thick smoke still rose from the burning houses throughout Rivergate. All around him, Legionnaires rushed toward the gate and climbed the steps onto the parapets, preparing in case the Eirdkilrs and Jokull decided to force an assault. Wounded men cried, screamed, or groaned. Syrupy rivers of crimson flowed across the cobblestone streets and stained the icebear pelts, marshland animal furs, and Legion armor of the hundreds that lay silent and still on the streets.

Yes, there had been enough blood spilled for one night. If he could prevent more senseless deaths, he would do so, even if it earned Commander Rheamus' ire.

"Sir." Captain Lemaire gave Aravon a sharp Legion salute and, turning on his heel, strode north after his Commander, the hulking Balegar at his heels.

Chapter Twenty-Three

Aravon cast a wary glance over his shoulder and, content no one watched his movements, ducked into the narrow alley that led toward the southeastern corner of Rivergate. The ache in his chest had settled into the bone, and even breathing proved painful. He'd almost sought out Zaharis, but thought better of it.

Duty first, he told himself. The battle had been won, but his task was not yet complete.

After the noise and chaos of combat, he welcomed the quiet darkness away from the rushing, marching, shouting Legionnaires guarding the gate. The Jokull and their Eirdkilr allies hadn't left—their howls, edged with fury and frustration, echoed outside the high stone walls of Rivergate—but no attack had come yet. Doubtless they were regrouping and preparing for another assault, yet the lack of siege put them at a severe disadvantage against the dug-in, alert Legionnaires. Aravon wouldn't be surprised if the enemy slipped away before sunrise.

But it would be a long night until they did. He guessed it was the second hour after midnight—the battle had lasted less than an hour—but with Commander Rheamus and Topaz Battalion occupied with the Jokull prisoners, Aravon had finally found a moment to slip away and call Snarl.

Finally, satisfied that he was far enough from people that the Enfield wouldn't be spotted, Aravon drew out the bone whistle and blew a short blast. He listened intently for the sound of rustling feathers, the high-pitched yapping of the little fox-creature. The noise of Snarl's approach reached his ears just in time for him to brace his feet to catch the Enfield.

"Ow!" he groaned as Snarl's full weight collided with his injured breastbone. His grimace turned to a full-on hiss of pain as Snarl's paws scrabbled against the armor atop his chest, each movement sending fresh torment through the bruised muscle and bone. Yet, he'd take all the pain in the world if it meant Snarl was alive.

The Enfield yipped in his ear, rough tongue flashing out to lick Aravon's mask.

"Easy, boy." Aravon pulled the Enfield out to arm's length. "Else you might end up with a mouthful of Eirdkilr blood."

Snarl answered with a joyous bark, squirming in Aravon's hands and his wings flapping. Somehow, despite everything, the Enfield had *far* too much excited energy for the exhausted Aravon.

"Settle down, Snarl." He lowered himself to a seat against the wooden siding of a building that had escaped the flames and stroked the Enfield's soft fur with a gentle hand. "You had me worried back there, you know? When you didn't show up…"

Snarl refused to sit still, but leapt to his feet and darted over Aravon's legs with all the enthusiasm of his vulpine relatives.

A smile broadened Aravon's face as he watched the energetic Enfield scamper around. He truly *had* been afraid for the little creature when Snarl didn't show. Then, when Snarl threw himself at the Eirdkilrs—an action that had bought Noll and Rangvaldr precious seconds—he'd feared an unlucky arrow would bring him down.

His worry had been for naught, and the sight of Snarl's boundless antics left him relieved—a relief compounded by the knowledge that they'd won.

By the Swordsman, we actually pulled it off!

It still felt surreal to him. Calling their plan "audacious" was an understatement on par with calling Belthar "husky" or Noll "a bit of a pain in the arse". Yet somehow, despite the odds, they'd managed to complete their mission. Rivergate was once again under Legion control. From the grim determination sparkling in the eyes of the Legionnaires and Westhaven regulars, Aravon felt confident that the Jokull and Eirdkilrs would have a fiery hell of a fight on their hands.

As for the matter of the starving populace and soldiers, Skathi had gone to solve that problem. The people of Bannockburn would be sending supplies across their makeshift pontoon bridge. Though the villagers had little enough to spare, it would suffice to feed the starving Rivergaters until Duke Olivarr could send more.

And all Aravon had to do now was send Snarl with a message to the Duke. The note, penned by the light of a Legion brazier, was succinct. *"Mission accomplished. Send reinforcements and supplies."* The moment Duke Dyrund read those words, he'd send word to the Duke of Westhaven. Food and, Swordsman willing, additional regulars from Westhaven would likely already be on their way now.

Yet, to get that message to the Duke, Aravon had to send Snarl away. At the moment, after everything he'd just endured, he needed a few minutes of peace and quiet with the Enfield. Snarl's enthusiasm and delight was contagious, and his antics always lifted Aravon's spirits.

The little creature seemed to sense his mood and came over, settling down atop Aravon's legs. He pressed his nose into Aravon's hand—his signal demanding that Aravon stroke his scruff. Aravon complied. The Enfield's fur was so soft, his body so warm. He lay with his head in Aravon's lap, gaze lifted. Those gleaming amber eyes held a look of such simple trust, as if Snarl knew that the alpha of his pack would take care of him.

Aravon had tried to be worthy of that trust, not only for Snarl, but for all the men under his command. Yet, no matter the effort, he couldn't prevent casualties. Fifteen of the men in his small force had died facing the Eirdkilrs and Jokull. Forty-five more would never leave the marshlands. Aravon hadn't had the heart to ask Captain Lemaire how many of his men had fallen. Add to that the hundreds slain in the initial battle for Rivergate and the Legionnaires that fell bringing down Rivergate Bridge, and the death toll was far too high for Aravon's liking.

But that was the way of battle. Noll's words, spoken after the battle at Bjornstadt, flashed through his mind. *"Sometimes it's easier to blame a man than to accept that shite happens, even to good people."* Surprisingly wise, coming from the little scout.

Aravon had blamed himself for Draian's death, and long hours of miserable self-flagellation had passed before he finally came to terms with it. Shite did happen. Men died in battle, no matter how much he wished otherwise. All he could do was his best to keep his soldiers alive.

That understanding made the burden of command only slightly easier to bear. When the final death toll was counted, he'd have to live with the knowledge that *he* had given the order. That sort of weight rested heavy on every officer and commander's shoulders.

Sighing, Aravon gave Snarl's scruff one last good scratch and, reaching into his armor, drew out the scrap of parchment. Snarl seemed to perk up at the sight. His head lifted, back arched, and his wings snapped out, eager to fly.

Aravon rolled up the message and stuffed it into the metal tube secured to Snarl's collar. Drawing out the strip of cloth heavy with Duke Dyrund's scent and the golden disc, he held it up to the Enfield's nose. "Take this to the Duke, Snarl."

Snarl sniffed the fabric and, with an excited bark, leapt a few feet into the air, wings flapping. Drawing out the bone whistle once more, Aravon trilled a longer note. Yipping quietly, Snarl gained altitude quickly and, turning north, disappeared into the night sky.

Swordsman be with you. A lump rose in his throat; he was sorry to let the Enfield go, to be apart from Snarl. Yet, as always, duty came before desire.

Aravon watched the starry heavens for long minutes after the Enfield disappeared. He knew what awaited him once he left the shadows of the city's back alleys. A heavy burden, a final honor that every commander owed to those who fought and died under his command.

Finally, he could put it off no longer. With a heart that ached far worse than any bruised breastbone ever would, he stood and marched back toward Rivergate's inner keep.

171

Chapter Twenty-Four

"It is said the Legion of Heroes once stood shoulder to shoulder with the Swordsman himself." Commander Rheamus' solemn voice echoed across the courtyard of Rivergate's inner keep. "Brave souls, men of honor and valor, warriors willing to face the hordes of demons that invaded Einan under the banner of the Great Destroyer. Warriors who died to a man. As the Swordsman fell facing Kharna, so too the first Legionnaires sacrificed themselves to protect mankind."

A thick blanket of silence hung over the paved stone courtyard. Seven hundred Legionnaires and Westhaveners stood mute, still as statues. The gentle breeze had died, the night owls fallen quiet, and even the howling of the Eirdkilrs and Jokull seemed hushed beneath the solemnity of the occasion. The quiet farewell to the soldiers who had fallen in battle.

"Yet, despite their noble sacrifice, they remained nameless, faceless, forgotten to time." Commander Rheamus shook his head. "No, never forgotten. To the world, perhaps, those who take for granted their peaceful lives. But those of us who serve in the Legion, who take up the Swordsman's mantle and grave duty, statues are but a trinket, a trifle. We wear our badge of honor on our belts—"

He drew his sword, and seven hundred soldiers followed suit.

"—on our bodies—"

The Commander's fist *thumped* against his steel breastplate, and a thundering chorus echoed his movements.

"—and in our hearts."

"For the Swordsman!" Hundreds of throats shouted in unison.

"For the Swordsman," Commander Rheamus intoned.

Aravon's eyes roved over the bodies arranged in neat, military precision on the cobblestones. Three hundred and seventy-eight Legionnaires and Westhaven regulars, the men that fell in the battle for Rivergate. Men who had given their lives to bring down Rivergate Bridge, to hold the walls of the inner keep, and to re-capture the city.

The soldiers laid out here were only those recovered in the aftermath. Forty-five brave Legionnaires of Second and Third Companies would rest forever in the marshlands, their blood, flesh, and bones claimed by the Fehlan wilds. According to Commander Rheamus, twenty more had drowned bringing down the bridge, their bodies dragged away by the Standelfr River.

Yet the ceremonial words were spoken in their honor as well. They had earned their rest at the Swordsman's side.

"So, though no statues will be erected in their names, no engraved stones bear the record of their actions, let us be the monument to their courage and sacrifice." Commander Rheamus straightened, giving the fallen soldiers a final Legionnaire's salute—fist to chest, crisp and precise. "We bear witness to who they were, and we will never, never forget."

"Never forget." Seven hundred voices echoed the words.

Silence fell once more. A lump rose to Aravon's throat as he studied the pale faces, glassy eyes, and bloodstained figures of the fallen soldiers. Many had been stripped, their armor stolen by Jokull and Eirdkilr warriors, their lifeless flesh desecrated by barbarian knives. Some were mangled beyond recognition, heads and faces crushed beneath Eirdkilr clubs. Others missed limbs, their legs, arms, or heads severed by enormous axes.

Yet Aravon had no doubt that every man and woman on the ground would be remembered by someone still living. It was the way of the Legion—to honor the memory of the brave fallen in battle. Soldiers carried those memories forever, long after they returned home and put a life of war behind them. But, for Legion dead, it was enough. They would go into the afterlife to spend an eternity with the Swordsman, an army of soldiers to be summoned by the god of war and heroics on the day of his return.

A soldier coughed, another groaned at the pain of his wounds, and the moment shattered. Suddenly, sound seemed to return to the world, and the thick blanket of solemnity lifted. The simple ceremony had ended and life for the Legionnaires still living went on.

Aravon glanced around the courtyard and found few familiar faces. Captain Lemaire had gathered the remaining men of Second and Third Companies—barely more than a hundred—and was in the process of reorganizing them into a single company, dispersing the rawest of the recruits among the rest of the battalion.

Balegar towered behind the Nyslian Captain, a looming shadow with hooded brows and dark eyes. A thick bandage covered his ruined nose; he hadn't been the prettiest Legionnaire, even before the wound. At least he, unlike so many of those he'd marched with, had survived. And come away with a trophy, it seemed. He'd left his hewing spear and kept the Eirdkilr axe, which now hung from his back. The way he'd wielded it in battle, it was definitely a weapon worth keeping.

Aravon owed the Nyslian giant thanks. The hulking Corporal had saved his life at least twice. He moved toward Captain Lemaire and Balegar, but he hadn't taken three steps before he caught sight of Zaharis hurrying toward him.

"*Captain,*" Zaharis' gestures were quick and sharp, an urgency sparkling in his eyes. "*We need you.*"

"*What's the matter?*" Aravon signed back.

"*It's Colborn.*"

* * *

Eerie, savage laughter pierced the darkness, sending a chill down Aravon's spine as he hurried in Zaharis' wake. Belthar, Noll, and Rangvaldr clustered around the mouth of the alleyway, radiating palpable waves of tension and worry.

"They found him like this," Zaharis signed

Aravon's brow furrowed, but nothing could have prepared him for the sight that met his eyes. Colborn sat in the middle of the muddy alley, legs splayed in front of him, his upper half reeling like a ship caught in a storm. His mask hung loose, revealing cheeks flushed a deep, drunken red. The contents of the clay jug in his hand sloshed as he waved toward the figures seated against the alley's eastern and western walls.

175

No, Aravon realized, not seated. Propped up, even after death. The broken shaft of a Jokull spear protruded from the throat of the Legionnaire to Colborn's right, and the man's pale features had long ago gone slack in death. Colborn's Fehlan-style longsword was buried in the chest of the Jokull on his left. Blood pooled in a congealing puddle around the Fehlan, sticky and wet, filling the air with a metallic stench.

Aravon's attention snapped back to the Lieutenant. *By the Swordsman, he's blind drunk!* Not just drunk, but shouting in a mixture of Fehlan and Princelander tongue, singing the funereal dirge Rangvaldr had performed in Bjornstadt with the words of the Legionnaire ceremony mingled in.

"Sorry, Captain," Noll muttered as Aravon pushed past. "Thought it was best to let you handle it."

Aravon nodded. "Good call." Colborn was always so reserved, so in control of himself and his emotions. No telling what he would do in this state.

Colborn's song faded and he turned to the dead Jokull, raising his jug high and shouting a slurred "*Skaal, Cousin!*" he shouted in Fehlan. Tilting up the clay jug, he drank deep, liquor trickling from the corners of his mouth and down his chin. Belching loudly, he saluted to the Legionnaire. "Drink up, Brother!"

Aravon's jaw clenched. Colborn was well beyond rational thought, yet he had to find a way to get through to the Lieutenant somehow.

Reaching up, he loosened the straps holding his mask in place and pulled it down. "Colborn." He spoke in a quiet, calm voice, slipping closer to the drunken man. "Colborn, can you hear me?"

Colborn's head whipped around, so fast he lost his balance and swayed, nearly falling onto his back. His free hand *splashed* in the crimson-stained mud, but he managed to remain upright. Barely.

"Captain!" His voice rang out through the alley, an almost manic edge to his words. "C-Come to have a drink with ush?" The effects of the liquor slurred his words. He tried to rise, failed, then tried again, only to slip on the mud. He crashed back down to the alley floor hard, and that harsh, piercing laugh echoed off the walls. "I...I think..." He burped, switching languages to Fehlan mid-sentence. "*...need to catch up, Captain.*"

Aravon pushed aside the proffered jug. The potent reek of Nyslian brandy rose from the jug's wide mouth and wafted off the drunken Lieutenant in noxious waves. "Colborn—"

"Look, Captain!" Colborn's hand flashed out and snatched at the collar of Aravon's armor, pulling him close. He spoke in a harsh whisper. "Look at him. He looksh jusht like me!" A drunken finger waved unsteadily at the dead Jokull.

Aravon glanced at the Fehlan. His long blond hair hung in braids far dirtier and lanker than Colborn's, his beard sparse, his features narrower and leaner. Yet even in death, there was no denying the blunt, wide Fehlan face, the solid jaw, and the ice blue eyes.

Colborn's hand tugged at Aravon's collar again and he gestured at the Legionnaire. "But sho…sho doesh he!"

The Legionnaire had skin far darker than Colborn's, and his features—either Praamian or Voramian—bore little resemblance to the Lieutenant.

"It'sh the a…armor." A hiccup interrupted Colborn's words, accompanied by a noisy belch that blasted alcohol-soaked breath in Aravon's face. "M-My armor! I wore that, too. Sho long. Y-Yearsh. But all the time, I looked like him. Why, Captain?"

The question caught Aravon by surprise. "Why what, Colborn?"

"Why?" Colborn shook his head. "Why did I do that?"

Aravon's brow furrowed. "Do what?"

"Kill them!" Colborn's shout echoed off the stone walls, setting Aravon's ears ringing. "I killed them! And they look like me. Just like me." He shook the jug hard, splashing brandy across Aravon's face, but his eyes were locked on the dead Jokull. *"Just like me,"* he said in slurred Fehlan. *"But they're not, are they? No one'sh like me."*

Aravon's gut tightened. Rangvaldr had warned him that Colborn might struggle with killing Jokull—Fehlans, just like him. He'd intended to speak to the Lieutenant but hadn't gotten the chance before Colborn departed. Now…

Colborn's face whipped around, his gaze locking with Aravon's, and a wild light entered his eyes. "You can't undershtand, Captain!" he shouted. His grip tightened around Aravon's armor, pulling the collar so tight it cut off Aravon's breath. "No one can!"

Aravon sighed. "Forgive me, Colborn." Twisting in his crouch, he threw a quick hooked punch to the drunken man's face. The blow rocked Colborn's head to the side and spun him around. The strike, which the half-Fehlan Lieutenant might have shrugged off under normal circumstances, dropped him hard. He flopped to his back and lay still, covered in mud and the blood of the Fehlan and Princelander seated beside him.

177

Aravon checked Colborn's pulse. Slightly accelerated by the effects of the potent liquor, but otherwise steady.

"Belthar." Aravon spoke without turning away from the prone Lieutenant. "Help me with him, will you?"

Heavy footsteps sounded behind Aravon and Belthar appeared at his side. With careful movements, the big man stooped and picked up Colborn. The half-Fehlan Lieutenant was tall, only a few inches shorter than Belthar with broad shoulders, but Belthar carried him like a mother cradled an infant.

"Noll, find us somewhere quiet."

The little scout slipped out of the alleyway and took off down the street, glancing into the open doorways of burned and crumbling homes until—

"This one!" Noll gestured to a house built of stone rather than wood. The door had been smashed off its hinges and the furniture inside destroyed by the rampaging Eirdkilrs and Jokull, but at least the structure was sound. And, as Aravon discovered as he entered, the straw-tick mattress had only been slashed, not scattered.

"Set him down there."

Belthar lowered Colborn gently onto the pile of straw.

"Allow me, Captain." Rangvaldr knelt beside Colborn's head and drew out his pendant. The *Seiomenn* pressed the pendant to his lips and whispered quiet words, and the blue gemstone began to glow with an inner light. The soft azure brilliance bathed Colborn's face and lit up the darkened room as Rangvaldr touched the stone to the Lieutenant's bearded jaw. After a few long seconds, he removed the still-glowing pendant and tucked it beneath his armor. "That will ease the pain, at least a little."

Zaharis produced a small pouch from within his oilskin pack. "*Water,*" he signed to Belthar. The big man took off, and Zaharis turned back to Aravon. "*It'd dissolve better in wine, but I think he's had enough for one night.*"

When Belthar returned, he carried a Legion-issue canteen half-filled with water. Nodding his thanks, Zaharis dropped in two pinches of the dark brown powder. After a vigorous shake, he held it out to Aravon.

"*Drink half,*" he signed one-handed. "*Give him the rest when he wakes. It won't take the pain away completely, but it'll help.*"

Aravon accepted the canteen. "Thank you." He turned to the four men in the small stone house. "I'll stay with him. You've earned some downtime. Go, enjoy it while you can."

"Not much trouble we can get up to while wearing these." Noll gestured to the leather greatwolf mask. "Makes it mighty hard to drink."

"We'll figure it out." Belthar clapped a huge hand on the scout's back, hard enough to knock Noll forward a step. Together, the two of them turned to leave.

"Given Colborn's current condition, maybe a drink's not our best choice," Zaharis signed.

"Hey, just because he can't hold his liquor, that doesn't mean we're all going to end up…" Noll's voice faded as he and Belthar strode from the house, the Secret Keeper a step behind.

Rangvaldr hesitated, worry in his eyes.

"Go," Aravon told him. "If you don't want to drink, at least you can get a few hours of rest."

"And you, Captain?" Rangvaldr cocked his head.

"I'll stay with him." Aravon lowered himself to a seat beside the pile of straw. "As his Captain, it's my duty to see to him."

"But perhaps more than *just* his Captain, yes?" The *Seiomenn's* tone was kind, filled with concern. He stared down at the half-Fehlan Lieutenant. "The counsel of a friend may go a long way towards calming the tempest raging within him. He carries a great many weights, not just those of war. Sometimes, it does a man good to know he is not the only one struggling beneath a heavy load."

Aravon nodded. "Go, Rangvaldr. Rest, for only the gods know what tomorrow will bring."

"May the words of Nuius flow through your lips, Captain." With a little bow, Rangvaldr turned and strode from the house, leaving Aravon alone with the unconscious Colborn.

Chapter Twenty-Five

Colborn's groan snapped Aravon awake. He sat upright, dragging himself back into wakefulness despite the sleep that hung heavy on his eyelids.

"C-Captain?" Colborn's words were thick, his voice still tinged by the receding effects of the alcohol. "Wha—" He grimaced, a hand rising to his jaw. "What happened?"

"You don't remember?" Aravon raised an eyebrow. "Sitting in that alley, drinking…" He drew in a deep breath. "…talking to corpses?"

Colborn's heavy, bearded face creased into a frown. After a moment, his eyes widened a fraction and his gaze darted up to Aravon. "Keeper's teeth!" he groaned, and slumped back against the wall. "So I *didn't* dream that."

Aravon shook his head.

Colborn's eyes darted around the small, sparse room. "Which means the others—?"

Aravon nodded. "They were the ones who came and got me."

A shudder ran down Colborn's spine and he pressed a hand to his eyes. "Of course." Shame set his cheeks flaming red hot. "Of course that's how you all had to see me."

Aravon hesitated, uncertain how to broach the subject that had weighed on him all night. He'd expected Colborn to be reeling from the loss of so many of his men—fully a third of the soldiers under his command, a heavy toll for even experienced officers. Yet this, this was something Aravon had *not* been prepared for.

"Do you remember what you said?" he finally asked.

After a long moment, Colborn nodded silently.

"Was that...the first time?" Aravon spoke in a quiet, gentle tone.

"Yes." Colborn's voice came out in a hoarse croak. "Never had to kill a Fehlan before. Never..." He drew in a shuddering breath. "...one of my own people."

Aravon had never heard Colborn refer to Fehlans as "his own people". In the few weeks he'd known the Lieutenant, Colborn had only mentioned his heritage once, on the only occasion Aravon had gotten him to speak of his past before the Legion. Even then, it had only been in passing, an explanation as to how he'd grown skilled at Fehlan woodcraft and tactics.

But last night, he'd seen another side to the usually stoic Lieutenant. The loss of his men, the effects of the alcohol, and the Jokull raider he'd slain in the alley had all combined to shatter the strong, composed façade. Perhaps this man, the one torn between two peoples, was the most *honest* version of Colborn he'd glimpsed yet.

"I always knew it'd happen. Always knew I might have to do it." Colborn didn't meet Aravon's gaze, but kept his eyes down, locked on the leather mask he picked up from beside his bed. His fingers toyed with the material, traced the snarling wolf etched into the surface. "But knowing and actually *doing* it..." He shook his head. "I-I thought I was ready."

"The fact that you weren't doesn't make you weak." Aravon's voice held no recrimination, no disdain, only acceptance. Swordsman knew he had struggles of his own; Colborn's quiet words had helped him cope with the loss of the Mender, Draian, which had only compounded his guilt over Sixth Company's fate. Now, it fell to him to return the favor. "What it does is make you human. Anyone would hesitate, question, feel pain at their actions. You?" He shrugged. "You just did it a bit...louder than any of us expected."

He tried to chuckle, to laugh it off as a joke, but his words had the opposite effect on Colborn. The Lieutenant's face went ashen, disgust twisting his features.

"Listen, Colborn." Aravon spoke quickly. "What you had to do yesterday is something *no one* should be asked. If someone asked me to take up arms against the Legion or my fellow Princelanders, I don't know if I could do it." He thrust a finger toward Colborn's chest. "The fact that you're feeling it means you're a good man. Only a good man would feel that pain you're feeling now."

"Pain!" Colborn snorted. "Pain's all I've ever known. Why should this be any different?" His face twisted into a snarl and he lifted his eyes, blazing with fire, to meet Aravon's. "All this proves is that *he* was finally right about me in the end!"

The vehemence of the Lieutenant's voice surprised Aravon. He raised an eyebrow. "He?"

Colborn's jaw muscles worked, but no words formed on his lips. Instead, his lip curled up in disgust and his hands clenched and relaxed a half-dozen times. When he finally spoke, his tone was little more than a harsh whisper. "He loved to say it, almost as much as he loved beating it into me." His right hand closed as if around a sword hilt, so tight his knuckles turned white. "Said I was too much a savage to be a proper Princelander. A proper *man*. A hundred times, more probably, he threatened to drag me to the Chain and throw me across, back with 'those ferocious bastards' where I belonged. Nearly did it, more than once. He would have, if not for the fact that the Captain of his guard took a liking to me."

He lifted his gaze to Aravon's, and a shadow darkened his ice blue eyes, turning them the color of a storm-tossed ocean. "Leish, his name was. The Captain, I mean. A good man. Former Legion, returned home to Whitevale and took a post with my father."

Aravon's brow furrowed. He'd never heard of anyone by the name Leish, but he knew only a few of the irregulars serving in the various duchies.

"Leish saved me more times than I could count." Colborn's words were quiet, his face a torrent of emotions. "The day he died, I did what my father wanted. I went south, lived among the 'savages'. But they didn't want me, either."

Though Colborn's voice never changed tone, something broke in the man's eyes, his expression. His shoulders drooped and the grimace on his face had little to do with his aching head.

"No matter where I went, they only saw the Princelander." He clenched his jaw. "And when I came back, all they saw was the Fehlan."

"Belonging to both worlds and neither." Aravon nodded. "An outsider among your own people."

"Who are my people?" Colborn gave him a bitter laugh. "I'm no Princelander, not looking like this!" He gestured to his blond hair and beard, braided with bones in the Fehlan style. "And the one time I tried to seek out my mother's family, they treated me the same way my father did." He shook his head. "That's why I took up the Duke's offer to join. Not because I gave two shites about his mission, but because it meant I could be dead to the world." Again, the grim chuckle. "Colborn of Whitevale is dead, and not a damned person will mourn him."

"I'd mourn you." Aravon fixed him with a piercing gaze. "And I know the others would, too."

Colborn gave a dismissive wave. "You *have* to say that." His expression grew cynical. "A Lieutenant who cracks under pressure's no good to anyone. Especially not what we face."

"Of course." Aravon inclined his head. "And if I thought for a single moment that last night had cracked you for good, you *would* be no good to us."

Colborn's face turned hard, stony, his eyes glittering icicles.

"But the man I saw last night is a man burdened by the same things we *all* have to deal with." Aravon held Colborn's gaze without hesitation. "A man who faced an impossible situation and didn't crack under pressure. You not only completed your mission, you got most of your men back in one piece."

Colborn's lips twisted bitterly. "Forty-five men lying dead in the marshlands might beg to differ."

"But the eighty-five still living won't." Aravon drew in a deep breath. "After losing Sixth Company, I very nearly died. Not from the wounds, but from the burden of guilt. I told myself that I was the reason that the soldiers under my command were dead. Men I had marched beside and served with for years."

Colborn snorted. "That's idiotic." He shook his head. "I read the reports of the ambush. No way your hundred could have stood against that many Eirdkilrs."

"Four hundred and eighty of them." Aravon's jaw clenched; even after all this time, the memory still weighed heavy on him. The screams of pain, the pale faces of his slain men, the stink of blood and bile hanging thick in the air all remained to plague his dreams. "But is that any more idiotic than to feel the same guilt because you lost forty-five unarmored Legionnaires in a battle against nearly two thousand Eirdkilrs and Jokull?" He shook his head. "If anything, your casualty rate makes *you* a better leader than me."

Colborn's pale blond eyebrows rose a fraction.

"My point," Aravon continued, "is that a good leader *feels* the deaths of his men. He doesn't just write them off as casualties of war, but he does his damnedest to keep his soldiers alive. The way you hung back last night, stayed to the end to help me buy time for Noll and Rangvaldr, that proves you're a good leader. Back at Camp Marshal, that first night training in the marshes, you said you never wanted command. Your actions over the last few days and your pain now, that's the mark of a leader."

Colborn's expression grew somber, pensive.

"As for the matter with your heritage…" Aravon drew in a long breath. "I'm not the one best-suited to help you. But, perhaps the words of a wise man might help." A smile tugged at Aravon's lips as he remembered his conversation with Rangvaldr the night they left on the mission. "We fight a battle for peace, to put an end to the bloodshed on Fehl. Our hearts must be strong, and we must carry the burdens of our actions—*all* our actions—as our solemn duty. We were chosen by our Prince to bear the weight."

The Lieutenant's eyes grew dark. "And what if the weight is too heavy?" His gaze dropped to the wolf mask in his hands. "What if—"

"There is no what if, Colborn." Aravon reached out a hand and gripped the man's thick forearm. "We bear the weight because we must. Not for ourselves, but for the people of the Princelands, and the Fehlans. My people and your people."

After a moment, the stony sharpness of Colborn's expression softened.

"But remember, you do not bear it alone." Aravon met the man's gaze. "No matter your past, all that matters is the present. Now, today, you ride with friends at your side. Friends who would fight beside you and *for* you, against impossible odds." He thrust out a hand. "We are your family now, Colborn. The six of us. And together, as you proved last night, we can do anything."

Colborn held his eyes for a long second, and gratitude brightened the shadows there as he returned Aravon's grip. "Thank you, Captain."

They remained like that, hands clasped, warriors and brothers in battle sharing a silent moment of camaraderie. Men who bore heavy burdens placed on them by their pasts, yet who fought on for the sakes of those they cared about.

Then the moment passed and Colborn released Aravon's hand. A loud groan escaped his lips as he slumped back against the wall.

"Here." Aravon reached for the canteen Zaharis had left him. "This will help your head." Already, the ache in his chest—courtesy of an Eirdkilr axe—had diminished, thanks to whatever the Secret Keeper had added into the water.

Colborn accepted the canteen with a nod and, pulling out the stopper, drained it in a long pull. "Keeper's teeth!" He spat, disgust twisting his face. "Warn a fellow next time, will you?"

Aravon grinned. "Consider it payback for letting me fight the Secret Keeper bare-handed." He'd borne the bruises of that sparring match with Zaharis for long, painful days.

"I guess that's fair, then." Colborn's grin was crooked, strained, but slowly the tension in his face faded. "Whoa!" He sat up, blinking hard. "Damn, that stuff really works!"

Aravon nodded. "We certainly don't keep Zaharis around because he makes for great dinner conversation."

Colborn gave him a laugh. "If that was the standard, we'd have to get rid of Noll, too." His smile widened. "And Belthar, for that matter, especially if beer's being served."

Chuckling, Aravon stood and offered a hand to help Colborn up. The Lieutenant accepted with a grateful nod and pulled himself upright. He swayed, somewhat unsteady, and leaned on the wall for long seconds until his skin had returned from sickly, nauseated to its usual Fehlan pallor.

"Next time, keep me far from the brandy, yeah?" Colborn hawked a gob of phlegm, spat, and swallowed hard. "The Nyslians make great wine, but damn if that brandy doesn't pack a punch."

"Lesson learned, eh?" Aravon grinned. He turned to the door, but stopped just before leaving. "Can't forget this." Stooping, he picked up his mask—still stained with Jokull and Eirdkilr blood.

Colborn looked down at his own leather mask, clutched in his free hand. "It's easier when we wear these, you know. Easy to forget who we are beneath."

"Or, who we're *trying* to be." Aravon pursed his lips. "I think it was Taivoro who said, 'The mask does not hide us from the world; it simply strips away pretenses to reveal who we truly are.'"

"Taivoro, eh?" Colborn's eyebrows shot up. "Didn't take you for a lover of erotic plays, Captain."

Aravon scowled. "I've Mylena to blame for that. Always loved his poetry, though she sometimes broke out the saucier things when…" He trailed off, aware of a flush of heat rising to his cheeks and the smile growing on the Lieutenant's face. "Not everything Karannos Taivoro wrote was as bawdy and carnal as you'd expect."

"Aye, sure it's not." Colborn's grin only widened at Aravon's discomfiture. "Your secret's safe with me, Captain. But if you ever need a few minutes alone with one of his plays, you just say the word and—"

"Thank you, Lieutenant," Aravon snapped, though he couldn't *truly* be mad at the man. Irreverent, caustic Colborn was far better than the drunken, howling man he'd found in that alley the previous night. "Now, get that mask on before we head out to find the others."

Colborn seemed to hesitate mid-step, his foot hovering in the air. His expression had gone as rigid as his spine, his face a mask of anxiety. "The others…"

Aravon understood the reason for his tension. Colborn had always been the officer, Aravon's second-in-command, in control of himself and everything around him. And now, after the previous night's events, he likely feared the shift in their opinions. Officers needed the respect of the soldiers serving under their command. Without it, they were little better than politicians.

He turned to face Colborn fully and placed a hand on the man's shoulder. "They'll understand. They just need to know why."

Colborn's jaw clenched, but he nodded. "I owe them that much, eh?"

"As much as pertains to last night. As for the rest…" Aravon shrugged. "We've all got things in our past we'd rather leave there. But the only way we'll be effective is if we share the burdens together."

Colborn drew in a long, heavy breath, then blew out his cheeks. "So be it." He stared down at the leather mask in his hands, his gaze intense. "The truth, then. Come what may."

Aravon tied on his own mask without a word. None were needed.

After a comfortable night of rest, the mask felt stifling, stiff from all the blood. *Come to think of it, I feel damned stiff all over.*

He glanced down at his armor. Zaharis' alchemical treatment didn't just harden the leather; it also coated it with a slick sheen that repelled water. And blood. Long streaks of crimson tracked the path that the Eirdkilr and Jokull blood had traveled as it rolled off him. Yet enough of it had dried on the leather's surface that it *cracked* with every movement.

Grimacing, he turned to Colborn. "What say we find a well and wash off? After the night you've had, I bet a bit of fresh water will go a long way."

Colborn nodded. "I've got mud in places I didn't know I had places."

Aravon chuckled. "To the well, then!" Turning, he strode toward the door and pushed it open.

Outside, a wall of noise and light assaulted him. The thick pall of smoke from the previous night had dissipated to little more than a gray haze. Sunlight bathed the city of Rivergate in brilliance and warmth, pushing back the feeling of gloom that had hung over the besieged city. All around him, Rivergaters hurried through the streets or worked to clear the rubble and ashes that had once been their homes. Platoons of armored Legionnaires toiled beside the citizens, helping to restore order in the wake of the Jokull and Eirdkilr attack.

But the sounds that greeted Aravon's ears filled him with hope. The *clatter* of bricks, the *thumping* of heavy logs and roof beams, and the low murmur of conversation. Not, however, the wailing, howling war cries of the enemy.

The battle seemed to have ended, the world moved on without them. And after the tension of the previous days, it was the most glorious discovery of all.

Chapter Twenty-Six

"Ba-le-gar!" The shouts and cheers echoed from within the inner keep long before Aravon and Colborn strode through the gates. The source of the noise became immediately apparent: a crowd of Legionnaires had formed off to one side of the inner keep's courtyard, around two enormous figures seated around a Nyslian wine barrel.

A masked Belthar was locked in an arm wrestle with Balegar, the Nyslian giant. Their forearms looked like twin oaks, flesh red from the massive quantities of blood flowing through their tensed muscles. The leather greatwolf mask covered Belthar's face, but his enormous shoulders were tensed, his barrel chest bulging. Sweat poured down Balegar's forehead and stung his eyes, but the enormous Legionnaire never looked away from his opponent.

"How long have they been at it?" Aravon asked one of the Legionnaires in the crowd, the archer Woryn.

"Twenty minutes." Woryn shook his head. "The odds started out five-to-one in Balegar's favor, but now...?" He shrugged. "It's anyone's guess which one will give out first."

Balegar had a crowd of soldiers cheering him on, but only one figure hovered at Belthar's back. Like Belthar, Noll had washed off the blood and mud that had covered him from head to toe the previous night, but his excited voice held no trace of exhaustion.

"Come on, Ursus!" Noll shouted Belthar's code name. "Don't let the damn bastard wear you down!"

"Shut...up...Foxclaw!" Belthar grunted with the strain. "Gotta...focus."

189

"I'll give you focus!" Noll called. "Think of a pretty redhead, smile for days, eyes the green of a Fehlan forest and tongue sharper than your ax—"

"Graah!" Belthar's roar drowned out Noll's words, and his arm inched forward, pushing Balegar back a fraction of an inch.

Much to the dismay of the watching Legionnaires. Even Woryn lent his voice to the shouts encouraging the Nyslian giant.

Aravon *almost* didn't intervene—Swordsman knew he wanted to find out which of the two would prove victorious as much as the men around him—but, sadly, they had better things to do. Pushing through the crowd, he strode to stand over the two grunting, straining men.

"Ursus." He spoke in a quiet voice. "We've got to get a move on."

"Sorry…Captain," Belthar growled. "Can't…lose. Too much…riding on—"

"Now, Ursus." Aravon turned to the Nyslian giant. "It's over, Balegar."

"He quits…I win." Balegar struggled to speak against the strain.

Aravon hesitated. He knew Belthar well enough to know the big man would *never* back down from a fight, especially not one like this, in front of so many Legionnaires—men he'd always admired, a brotherhood he'd wanted for years to belong to. They might not be cheering his name, yet he was the center of attention. Not ridiculed or derided, but applauded for his strength. Giving up now, well that was something Belthar could never do.

With a sigh, Aravon stepped back. "Finish this, Ursus. Quickly."

"We hit…thirty minutes," Belthar gasped, "and…the payout…doubles."

"End it," Aravon growled. "That's an order, soldier!"

The muscles in Belthar's enormous forearm and bicep rippled, and blood rushed up his arm toward his hand. He grunted, his free hand clenching into a fist, and leaned into the effort. Balegar rumbled low in his throat and tightened his grip on Belthar, trying to push back against the renewed assault. Belthar answered with a growl, which rose to a full-throated roar as, with a final effort, he drove Balegar's arm down against the barrel top with an audible *thunk*.

Groans rose from the crowd, but Noll threw himself into the air. "Yes!" His fist pumped wildly and he slapped Belthar on the back. "Told you, big guy!"

From the stoop of his shoulders, Aravon could see Belthar's exhaustion, yet he stood and held out his left hand to Balegar. "Good match, Legionnaire."

Balegar's face had gone dark. He stared up at Belthar with an angry expression, a scowl twisting his face. Slowly he stood, looming half a head taller than Belthar, seeming to cast him in the shadow of a boiling thundercloud.

Aravon tensed, anxiety thrumming within him. Big men with volatile tempers could be *very* dangerous.

The moment passed. A wry grin split Balegar's enormous face and he gripped Belthar's hand in return. "Good match, indeed."

Now the crowd's groans and jeers turned to applause, resounding cheers echoing through the inner keep. Many slapped Belthar's back and offered commendation for his strength. Noll, slipping along in Belthar's shadow, collected the winnings of their wagers.

Normally, Aravon might have frowned on such things. As he'd said, he and his men had better things to do than gamble on feats of strength. But after the tension of the previous days, he welcomed a chance to let his men blow off a bit of steam.

With the arm wrestling match ended, however, they could get on with whatever came next. He'd been so concerned with Colborn that he hadn't given much thought to what that next was. Now, he bent his mind to how they proceeded.

"Where are Zaharis and Rangvaldr?" he signed to Noll and Belthar once they'd pushed through the crowd and exited onto the main avenue outside the inner keep.

"Secret Keeper's holed up somewhere studying something." Noll shrugged. *"Didn't say what, but got mighty antsy when I asked him about it."*

Aravon raised an eyebrow—an expression lost beneath his mask—then tilted his head. *"Any idea where?"*

Noll jerked a thumb over his shoulder. *"Little place on the north side. Said it's quieter there, away from the Legion taking back control of the gate and holding off one last desperate attack."*

"The Sei—" Belthar's thick fingers, exhausted from his wrestling match, fumbled the letters for *"Seiomenn"*. *"—said something about saying prayers for the fallen Jokull. Last I saw, he was headed up to the wall. But that was hours ago. He could be anywhere by now."*

"You and Colborn," Aravon signed to the big man, *"see if you can find him."* His mind had already begun to work at their next move. *"Once you do, bring him*

191

over to the north side, to the bridge. We're headed across the Standelfr and back to Bannockburn."

"Oh?" Colborn's fingers signed.

Aravon nodded. *"Snarl's delivering our news to the Duke, which means he'll be back soon with more instructions of what to do. When they come, I want to be mounted and ready to ride. That means collecting our horses."*

The *Kostarasar* chargers had been left in the care of Bannockburn's wealthiest farmer, who had promised a plentiful meal of hay and oats. That had brought a smile to Aravon's masked face. *If only he knew how much the beasts ate!* Much of Belthar and Noll's recent winnings would go to compensate the man for his generosity.

He turned to Noll. *"You, lead me to Zaharis. We'll collect him on our way back to the bridge."*

"And Skathi?" Belthar signed.

"She'll be supervising the teams crossing the supplies," Aravon replied. He'd sent her shortly after recapturing the city, but she'd had to travel back to Bannockburn, then return with food from the town and get it across their makeshift bridge. The task would likely take another few days, which meant Skathi would be right where he wanted when they returned to collect their horses.

With a nod, Belthar turned and strode off down the main avenue, south toward the gate they'd just retaken. Colborn's eyes flashed toward Noll and he looked as if he wanted to speak, but seemed to think better of it. Turning, he hurried after Belthar.

Aravon hesitated only a moment before heading in the opposite direction. Colborn would get a chance to explain himself to everyone, but only *after* they got out of Rivergate.

"Lead the way," he signed to Noll.

Noll hurried north through Rivergate, taking the eastern road. The brick and stone houses in eastern Rivergate had evidently survived most of the Jokull and Eirdkilr devastation, though more than a few wooden buildings, thatched roofs, and market stalls smoldered, leaking thick black smoke. Yet the farther they went from the main avenue, the more houses Aravon found still standing. Plenty of wrecked furniture, broken windows and doors, and valuables discarded by the looters, yet less wanton destruction.

Noll led Aravon to one single-story stone building a short distance from the eastern edge of the outer wall. He pushed open the door and entered without a word. Within, Aravon found Zaharis seated on the floor amidst a sea of debris—overturned furniture, shattered crockery, and half-eaten foodstuffs. The Secret Keeper had cleared a small island of calm in the chaos, and spread out a collection of alchemical items: a stone pestle and mortar, leather pouches stuffed with dried herbs and noxious-smelling powders, glass tubes, bright-glowing heat stones, and a neat pile of blue flowers.

Aravon's jaw dropped. *Is that…?* The question died unformed in his thoughts. Zaharis had described ice saffron, the plant he'd spent the last decade hunting, as pale blue with bright crimson threads, but these were closer to the near-purple of a hyacinth, dotted with spots of yellow, orange, and red.

"These again?" Noll groaned. "Nearly got us caught collecting these, Zaharis."

The Secret Keeper didn't look up from his work, crushing a pair of deep blue petals in his mortar. The fingers of his left hand signed, "*You'll be glad we got them.*"

"Oh?" Noll folded his arms. "Does Belthar really smell all that bad?"

Now Zaharis lifted his eyes to the scout. "*Yes, but that's not what these Squatting Crocuses are for.*" He removed the pestle and took a long sniff of the contents of his mortar. "*Once properly dried, these little beauties will make a wonderful addition to my collection of things that set fires. A single spark, and you've got a big blaze that'll make the Dragon Thorngrass oil look like a match in comparison.*"

"Very useful." Aravon's mind flashed back to the alchemical tricks Zaharis had used against the Eirdkilrs at Anvil Garrison, Broken Canyon, and Bjornstadt. The more he had up his sleeve, the better as far as Aravon was concerned. "But you'll have to keep digging into it later. For now, we've got to get across the Standelfr and regroup with the others."

"*Plans, Captain?*" Zaharis signed.

"None yet." Aravon shook his head. "But Snarl should be back before nightfall, so I want to be ready for whatever the Duke'll ask of us next."

Nodding, Zaharis set about stowing his pestle, mortar, and the rest of his alchemical oddities in the heavy pack he always carried.

"*By the way,*" the Secret Keeper signed one-handed as he packed his bag with the other, "*I left our marshland friends a little treat.*" He turned long enough to shoot a wicked grin at Aravon and Noll. "*Funny thing about the leaves of the*

193

Squatting Crocus plant, they're terribly poisonous when left in water. Turns even clean drinking water bitter and undrinkable. Anyone unlucky enough to get a bellyful's going to spend so much time soiling their trousers they'll be too busy to think about sieges. Hence its name."

"Damn, Zaharis!" Noll's eyebrows shot up. "Remind me never to piss in your boots, yeah?"

Zaharis chuckled as he set about gathering up the dark blue flowers and stuffing them into his pack. Finally, he'd gathered the last Squatting Crocus and slung his satchel over a shoulder. *"Ready when you are, Captain."*

Aravon had just turned to leave when a shadow darkened the door. The figure who stood there was a man, bald like Zaharis but with only a pencil moustache above his upper lip and a long, thin goatee hanging from his chin. He stood a full head shorter than Aravon, slightly taller than Noll, but his arms were corded with muscle.

Aravon's blood ran cold as he caught sight of the man's clothes: the unmistakable muted brown robes of a Secret Keeper.

The man's dark brown eyes slid past Aravon and locked on to the man behind him.

"Hello, Zaharis," he signed. *"And to think Arch-Guardian Nalroth insisted you were dead."*

Chapter Twenty-Seven

Every muscle in Zaharis' body went rigid and he froze mid-step. The leather greatwolf mask concealed the Secret Keepers' face, but his gray eyes went ice cold at sight of the man in the doorway.

"*Darrak.*" Zaharis' fingers signed the letters slowly, as if unwilling to form the gestures.

Aravon's blood turned to ice, and a long ago conversation with Zaharis flashed through his mind. "*If the Secret Keepers even suspected I still lived,*" the man had said, "*they would hunt me down and kill me. And you. And Duke Dyrund, and everyone I've ever spoken to.*"

He took a step to the right, interposing himself between Darrak and Zaharis. Darrak's eyes never left Zaharis' face—he ignored Aravon much as a donkey ignored a dozing gnat.

Aravon leveled the tip of his spear at the brown-robed man, but a hand on his shoulder stopped him. When he turned, Zaharis gave a slight shake of his head and stepped past Aravon to stand empty-handed in front of Darrak.

"*You've gotten more creative with age.*" A fleeting ghost of a smile cracked Darrak's stern façade, disappearing so fast Aravon almost thought he'd imagined it. "*That wall of fire, Dragon Thorngrass oil with a touch of Weeping Serpentvine?*"

After a long moment, Zaharis nodded, but his fingers remained silent.

"*Saymech would've been proud to see it.*" Something akin to sorrow flashed in Darrak's eyes. "*Proud, and disgusted by what you've done with the Mistress' secrets.*" The man's lip curled upward. "*Such knowledge is to be guarded at all costs, not—*"

"*Used to save your life and those of every man, woman, and child in Rivergate?*" Zaharis' fingers formed the words with sharp, angry gestures. "*That's something the Arch-Guardian never could see. None of them could. The secrets we gather aren't to be hidden away, not if they can make this miserable, wretched excuse of a world better.*"

"*Aye, I remember this Zaharis.*" Again, sadness darkened Darrak's face. "*The idealistic dreamer. Champion of lost causes.*" He snorted. "*Just like your fruitless search for ice saffron.*"

Zaharis stiffened, and anger radiated off him in waves. "*Not fruitless!*"

Darrak cocked an eyebrow. "*So you've found it, then?*"

From the corner of his eye, Aravon caught sight of Noll edging along the wall one slow, cautious step at a time. His hand hovered a few inches above the hilt of his belt dagger, and despite his casual stance, his muscles were coiled and ready to strike. Keeping his gaze fixed on Darrak and Zaharis, Aravon, too, began sliding left.

Neither he nor Noll knew how this encounter with the Secret Keeper would end, but if it came to blows…

"*…just a matter of time,*" Zaharis' fingers were saying. "*And I've found so many more species of flora. Plants no one in the Temple of Whispers could have dreamed of!*" He took a step toward the man in the doorway. "*My mission on Fehl is not over. The Council was too blind to see that, but please, Darrak, tell me you can think beyond what the Guardians tell you.*"

Darrak took a half-step back, raising his hands defensively. "*My oaths are binding,*" he signed, his face a mask of stone. "*As were yours, until you broke them. But I will not turn my back on the Mistress or her secrets. I guard them with my life and my silence, until the end.*"

"*Then, for the sake of what we once shared, Darrak, let me go.*" Zaharis' stance seemed pleading, almost desperate. "*The world believes I am dead. Let that be the case. What we are doing—*" His gesture included Aravon and Noll. "*—is saving lives. Rivergate would have fallen if not for us. So let me remain dead to the world.*" He reached out a hand, as if aching to touch the man. "*Dead to you, as you swore the day we last spoke.*"

Pain flashed across Darrak's face. For a moment, he actually seemed to soften, moved by Zaharis' entreaty. His right hand moved toward Zaharis', an unconscious, familiar gesture. But the moment passed. Darrak's face hardened and he shook his head.

"*I cannot.*"

196

The two words, a simple hand gesture, seemed to shatter something within Zaharis. His shoulders sagged, a fraction of an inch, yet for the Secret Keeper, it was as if he'd collapsed.

"*Your display outside the gate was too visible,*" Darrak signed. "*Word of it will reach the Temple of Whispers, and when they hear I was here, in the city, they will demand to know why I revealed our Mistress' secrets to the world.*"

Aravon glanced at Noll without moving his head. The little scout had almost closed to within striking distance. Just another step, a few inches closer, and he'd be in a position to blindside Darrak.

"*They will listen when you explain that it was to save Rivergate!*" Zaharis' fingers flashed so quickly Aravon struggled to keep up. "*It is forbidden for us to share our knowledge, but not to use it for the good of mankind.*"

"*But they will know it was not me.*" Darrak shook his head sadly. "*After all, such alchemical marvels are your specialty, while mine is—*"

Noll leapt, dagger flashing from its sheath and driving toward Darrak with the speed of a striking serpent. Aravon attacked at the same time. He swung the iron-capped butt end of his spear up and thrust it forward, a blow aimed at the Secret Keeper's midsection.

Darrak moved far faster than expected. He flowed out of the way of Aravon's spear and inside of Noll's outstretched arms. His left hand slapped Noll's dagger wide while his right drove into the side of the little scout's neck. Noll stumbled backward, reeling from the blow to the artery. A second lightning-fast strike knocked the wind from the scout's lungs.

The third punch never landed. Before Aravon could recover from his thrust, Zaharis caught Darrak's driving fist an inch away from Noll's throat. Darrak leaned into his blow, snapping an elbow into Zaharis' face, but Zaharis was no longer there. He slithered around behind Darrak with impossible speed, wrapped an arm around the man's throat, and twisted him around to throw him over his hip.

The throw, which had brought Aravon crashing to the ground on numerous occasions, sent Darrak into the air, but the man threw his body into the spin and landed on his feet. His right hand drove into Zaharis' chest with staggering force. Zaharis twisted his backward stumble into a spinning kick, his heel crashing into Darrak's shoulder.

Darrak rebounded off the wall, slapped Aravon's attack wide, and drove an open-handed blow at Aravon's face. Aravon managed to snap his head backward to avoid the nose-shattering strike, but Darrak's follow-up blow to the groin would have landed had Zaharis not deflected the attack with a kick to Darrak's shoulder.

"*Back!*" Zaharis managed to sign in the heartbeat between blows. "*Mine!*"

Aravon hesitated. He couldn't let Zaharis fight alone, no matter who he faced. Yet, he'd battled against and beside the man long enough to know that in hand-to-hand combat, no one bested a Secret Keeper.

No one but another Secret Keeper.

Darrak launched himself at Zaharis, arms and legs flying with such speed and grace that Aravon could only watch, mesmerized by the two. It reminded Aravon of a dance, the twisting, spinning, whirling movements that never seemed to slow or stop. But this dance ended up with one of the two Secret Keepers dead.

Aravon watched the two men, spinning, kicking, punching, and striking at each other. A flurry of blows, almost too fast for him to follow, sent the pair back and forth across the small room. Anger burned in Darrak's face, but a grim resolve burned in Zaharis' eyes.

Darrak was the first to land a blow. His low kick slammed into Zaharis' left knee, knocking the leg out from beneath him. Zaharis, off-balance, stumbled back, and Darrak pressed the advantage with a barrage of rapid-fire punches and strikes.

But Darrak made the mistake of losing sight of Aravon. Reversing his grip on the spear, Aravon swung the iron-capped butt end across in a powerful sweeping strike. The ash shaft slammed into Darrak's back knee just as he lifted his front foot in a kick aimed at Zaharis' head. Cartilage *crunched* and his knee gave way. His collapsing bulk crashed atop his leg, shattering the bone with twin *snaps*. A horrible, piercing scream burst from Darrak's tongueless mouth

Zaharis recovered his balance and leapt forward, both hands coming around for an open-handed blow to the sides of Darrak's neck. Instantly, the wordless screams fell silent and Darrak collapsed, unconscious.

Aravon and Noll stared wide-eyed at Zaharis, who stood over the senseless form of the Secret Keeper. He gasped for breath, clutching at his left side where Darrak had landed a vicious kick. Yet, instead of anger, only sorrow burned in his eyes. And moisture, bright and sparkling, that disappeared beneath his leather mask.

"Zaharis—" Aravon began.

The Secret Keeper lifted his gaze to meet Aravon's, and Aravon was struck by the depth of misery radiating off the man. This exchange had held a far greater meaning than Darrak's silent words could ever convey. A look of utter betrayal and guilt darkened Zaharis' eyes.

"Please, Captain," he signed. *"Give me a moment with him."*

Aravon hesitated. Everything he knew about Secret Keepers told him that a broken leg wouldn't stop Darrak from coming after Zaharis. Their best hope was to get as far from Rivergate as possible before the unconscious priest awoke. It was only a matter of time before every Secret Keeper on Fehl—and on Einan—knew of Zaharis' presence. The runaway priest would have few places to hide north of the Chain. Even the Fehlan wilds might not be large enough to conceal him from the silent, tongueless priests of the Mistress.

Yet in that moment, he saw the look in Zaharis' eyes. Beneath the pain shone a love, deep and abiding, even after everything that had just transpired between the two men. Realization dawned on him. *This isn't just any ordinary Secret Keeper. He meant something to Zaharis.*

Though Darrak was a threat to their safety and the secrecy of their operation, Aravon had no doubt Zaharis would fight *them* if it meant keeping Darrak alive. Ordering the Secret Keeper's death would turn Zaharis against his companions. He wasn't willing to fight that battle.

He gave a little nod. "A moment, no more." Zaharis deserved a few seconds to tend to his fellow Secret Keeper, a man who'd clearly meant something to him in the life he'd left behind.

Zaharis turned back to the pack, which he'd dropped in the scuffle. The pestle had slid out from beneath the flap, a glass bottle shattered, and a pile of the blue flowers scattered across the floor. Crouching, the Secret Keeper rummaged in his satchel and carefully extracted two pouches. He opened one, drew out a pinch of the dark red Sleeping Lily dust within, and dropped it into Darrak's nostrils. *"He will sleep until long after we are gone,"* he signed without looking up.

The second pouch, he placed gently beside the man's head. *"For the pain."* He remained crouched beside Darrak a long moment, his shoulders slumped. Finally, he gathered the scattered items back into his pack and stood.

"What the fiery hell, Zaharis?" The words burst from Noll's lips, curiosity burning in his eyes. "Why didn't you tell us there was a Secret Keeper in Rivergate?"

"I didn't know." Zaharis' face was dark, shadowed by pain and anguish. *"And I never expected…him."*

"We need to kill him and be—"

"No!" Zaharis cut him off with a slashing gesture. *"His life is not ours to take."*

The scout rounded on Aravon. "Captain, if these Secret Keepers really are as dangerous as he says…"

"Enough, Noll. Go find the others and get them across the Standelfr," Aravon ordered. "Meet us at the first mile marker north of Rivergate Bridge."

Noll's eyes fixed on Zaharis, and he made no move to leave.

"Now, Noll!" Aravon's voice cracked like a whip.

Now Noll turned to Aravon, his posture stubborn, defiance blazing in his eyes. "All due respect to our Secret Keeper here, but—"

"The time for explanations will come later, Noll." Aravon held the man's gaze firmly, his tone brooking no argument. "Now, we've got to move quickly. Get. The. Others."

A long moment passed before Noll nodded. "Aye, Captain." He gave the fallen Secret Keeper a wide berth as he left. His leather mask obscured whatever he muttered, but the tension in the little scout's posture told Aravon that Noll would *not* let this lie any longer than necessary.

Once Noll had gone, Aravon turned to Zaharis. "Tell me why we shouldn't kill him. The Secret Keepers already want you dead. If they find out you're alive, it puts our mission in jeopardy. Puts *you* at serious risk. The smart play is to put an end to him n—"

"We cannot, Captain!" Zaharis' eyes blazed, a fire of mingled defiance, fury, and sorrow. *"The death of a Secret Keeper will draw too much attention from the Temple of Whispers. They will demand reprisals and hunt us through every corner of Fehl."*

Aravon cocked his head. "Didn't you say they already wanted you dead?"

Zaharis nodded. *"It's…complicated."*

Aravon's jaw muscles worked. A part of him wanted to demand an answer now, but he held the questions in check. Pain was etched into every line visible behind Zaharis' mask—the sight of his fellow Secret Keeper had brought up memories best left in the past. At that moment, getting the bloody hell away from Rivergate was their best way forward.

"I do expect an explanation later, Zaharis," Aravon said, "as will the others." *After* the Secret Keeper had time to process the emotions roiling through him. If Zaharis was willing to risk everything to keep Darrak alive, they would all need to know the reason.

"Of course, Captain." Zaharis gave a little nod. *"I never…"* His fingers fell silent as he turned to look at the unconscious Darrak. *"I knew he was on Fehl, sent to search out creatures of legend. Like Snarl."* When he turned back to Aravon, moisture glimmered in his eyes. *"Every time I see Snarl, I'm reminded of him. Of what we once had, until I ruined it. All for the sake of Keeper-damned ice saffron!"*

Zaharis' fist punched out, striking a wooden wall hard enough to splinter the roof beam and shatter the boards. The explosion of emotions surprised Aravon; he'd never seen Zaharis lose control before.

"Tell me, Zaharis." Aravon spoke in a quiet tone. "Do you believe ice saffron is real?"

Zaharis hesitated a long moment before turning back to Aravon. *"I do."* Despite the slump in his shoulders, confidence gleamed in his tear-rimmed eyes.

"And do you believe that with it, with the Elixir of Creation, you could end the fighting and make our world a better place?"

Zaharis nodded.

"Then trust that it will be worth the sacrifice." Aravon placed a hand on the Secret Keeper's shoulder. "No matter what anyone else says, if you listen to your heart, it will never lead you astray. You fight for something bigger than yourself, even than this company or this war. You have found your guiding star. Let it guide you unerringly to your destiny, wherever that may lie." He tightened his grip, a reassuring squeeze. "And know that we, your friends and family, march at your side."

Again, tears sparkled in Zaharis' eyes, but a glimmer of gratitude pierced the darkness. *"Thank you, Captain."*

With a nod, Aravon turned and strode from the small house, Zaharis on his heels.

Chapter Twenty-Eight

As Aravon and Zaharis hurried northwest, toward the crumbled remains of Rivergate Bridge, he couldn't help noticing that life had begun to return to the stronghold.

Men, women, and children moved among the broken remains of their lives, picking up the pieces of shattered furniture, fighting fires, collecting their scattered belongings. Many had eyes red-rimmed from crying—likely mourning their friends and family slain in battle—yet they moved with resolve. The battle had passed, their city had been recaptured, and their lives moved on. Surrounded by blood, carnage, and the memories of all they had lost. Yet the people of Rivergate would rebuild, one day at a time.

As Aravon approached the destroyed Rivergate Bridge, the sound of shouted orders echoed loud in the brightening daylight. Two familiar figures stood on the southern riverbank, one calling instructions and coordinating the movements of the Bannockburners bringing supplies across the makeshift pontoon bridge. All along the hulking length of the wooden barge, carpenters set about strengthening the ropes holding the stone anchors and reinforcing the scaffolding-like structure. It would take long months to rebuild Rivergate Bridge, but until then, the Coracle would serve as Rivergate's source of supplies.

"Captain Lemaire?" he called out as he approached.

The Nyslian Captain and his ever-present giant shadow, Balegar, turned toward him. "Ah, *Capitaine* Snarl." A smile broadened his face. "I was hoping I would have a chance to speak to you before you disappeared into the mists."

"It's a bright, sunny day." Aravon gestured at the grassy riverbank, the white-churned ribbon of the Standelfr, and the lush green forest north of the river. "Not a lot of mists around."

Captain Lemaire chuckled. "You know what I mean. I had figured you might leave with about as much fanfare as you arrived. I believe I owe you my thanks in person. The Swordsman knows Commander Rheamus won't make it a priority."

"Your thanks?" Aravon cocked his head.

"*Oui.* You and yours are the only reason Rivergate still stands," Captain Lemaire said. "Were it not for you, things would have turned out rather…differently."

Balegar snorted. "Understatement," he rumbled.

"Just doing our jobs, Captain." Aravon shrugged. "And, if I recall correctly, it was your men of Second and Third Companies that did the heavy lifting. We just hung around in the background looking pretty."

"Now that," Captain Lemaire grinned up at Balegar, "was the *real* understatement." He turned back to Aravon with a shake of his head. "Your modesty does you credit, *Capitaine.*"

"As does your courage." He thrust out a hand. "It was a privilege to fight by your side, Captain Lemaire. May the Swordsman strengthen your arm."

"And guide your steps." Captain Lemaire finished the soldier's incantation and shook Aravon's hand.

Aravon turned toward Balegar. "Seems I owe you my life. If I didn't already have a big man of my own, I'd be tempted to steal you away from the Captain here."

Balegar shot a sidelong glance at Lemaire. "Make me an offer."

Aravon chuckled and gripped Balegar's hand. "I might just." His gloved fingers looked tiny enveloped in Balegar's, which were as thick and long as sausages. "But that would deprive Second Company of their best soldier."

Balegar's huge cheeks flushed under Aravon's praise.

"How soon do you think you'll have the bridge restored?" Aravon asked Captain Lemaire. "The barge will only hold out for a few days, at most."

A frown creased Captain Lemaire's face. "I could not say for certain, *Capitaine.*" He tugged at the tip of his moustache. "Weeks, certainly. Perhaps a month, depending on how quickly our carpenters and stonemasons work."

"Hopefully not too long," Aravon said. "Duke Westhaven will likely be sending supplies as soon as he hears the battle is won. I'm certain everyone in Rivergate is looking forward to a proper meal once more."

"Indeed." Captain Lemaire grinned. "Though if what I hear about the Duke is true, he will more likely be interested in getting his precious freight back to the safety of his lands."

"Freight?" Aravon cocked his head.

Captain Lemaire jutted his chin toward a small, square wooden shed built up against the northeastern end of the wall. Within the shed stood three carts covered with thick canvas, though one corner of the canvas had been slashed and ripped free. Beneath, Aravon caught a glimpse of glittering black stone. It appeared as if the enemy had tried unsuccessfully to haul the two-wheeled carts away, then abandoned them in their assault on Rivergate.

"Tribute from the Jokull, according to Commander Rheamus." Captain Lemaire pursed his lips. "Not too likely, given their attack." He dropped his voice to a conspiratorial whisper. "From what I have heard around the city, someone has discovered silver in the marshlands. What you see here is just one load. The third such. It could be a rumor, but the fact that it arrived *two days* before the Eirdkilr attack tells me there may be more than a little truth, *oui?*"

Aravon pondered the statement. "Too much of a coincidence that the Eirdkilrs *happened* to attack here and now, isn't it?"

Memories of Silver Break Mine flashed through his thoughts. He'd pushed aside the images of the abandoned, silent mining camp to focus on his mission here in Rivergate. Yet now, with the battle over, he had spare room to give it thought.

Much as the military propaganda tried to suggest otherwise, the Eirdkilr War had begun over the resources abundant across Fehl. Early Einari had only begun to colonize when they discovered gold, silver, and precious stones—a vast fortune untapped by the "savage" natives. That had led to their incursion deep into Fehlan territory, and the Eirdkilr's efforts to drive the interlopers off the continent.

Silver Break Mine was just the *newest* of the many silver, gold, platinum, and gemstone mines around Fehl. Prince Toran could only afford to bring in Legionnaires by offering the mainland cities a share of the profits of his mines, or using the wealth pulled from the depths of Fehl to pay the Legion fees. A smart Eirdkilr commander—one like Hrolf Hrungnir had been, or one clever

205

enough to plant spies in the Princelands and among the allied Fehlans—could easily conclude that the mines were the Princelander's key to victory. Kill the miners and steal the resources, and Prince Toran would be hamstrung.

A question flashed through his mind. *What was the real reason for the attack here?* Had the Eirdkilrs and Jokull come hunting the silver, only to find themselves unexpectedly in possession of Rivergate and besieging a dug-in force of Legionnaires? Capturing the city would give them access to the Princelands, but had that been more happy accident than the original intention of their attack?

Whatever the case, they had failed, thanks to men like Captain Lemaire and Balegar. Yet something the Captain said niggled at him.

"You said that's a load of silver, yes?" he asked.

Captain Lemaire nodded.

"So why does it look like the wagons are heaped high with coal?" From where he stood, nothing but black stone was visible.

"Ahh, that." The Nyslian Captain gave him a wry smile. "A clever deceit to conceal the truth from the Jokull, and any Fehlan spies in our midst." He winked at Aravon. "From what I hear, the black stone—Ghoulstone, some call it—is little more than worthless gangue mixed in with the gold and silver mined on Fehl. Too soft to use for building, shatters too easily to make it of any worth for floors or stone facades. Pretty parchment-weights at best, but it serves to disguise the silver piled beneath."

Aravon raised an eyebrow. "Interesting."

"Even more mysterious," Captain Lemaire continued, "the first load seemed to vanish the day after it arrived. No one saw it crossing the Rivergate Bridge. Poof!" A sardonic smile twisted his handsome face. "I don't believe in spirits, *Capitaine,* but clearly someone wanted it spirited away unseen."

"Is that so?" From the corner of his eye, Aravon noticed Zaharis slipping toward the wagon. The Secret Keeper peered at the black stone and, with a speed that any thief would envy, pocketed a small chunk. He turned back to Captain Lemaire. "What did Commander Rheamus have to say about it?"

"Officially, nothing." The Captain's smile turned wry. "Unofficially, however, he made it clear that we are to look anywhere else. Pretend it doesn't exist, even."

That set off Aravon's suspicions. Duke Dyrund had kept Silver Break Mine a secret even from Aravon, only clueing him in when absolutely necessary.

Perhaps he'd given Commander Rheamus similar orders. With the future of the war resting on their ability to mine resources from the Fehlan countryside—and with the Jokull's enmity toward the Princelands, even before this attack—he might have kept it a secret for the sake of protecting it.

And given what happened at Silver Break Mine, he might have been right to do it.

The miners had disappeared completely, with nothing even hinting at their fates. Had the miners working in the Jokull territories suffered a similar end? Until he spoke to Duke Dyrund, he couldn't be certain.

"Then allow me to honor Legion policy and join you in the pretense." Aravon adopted a nonchalant tone. "I saw nothing, heard none of the rumors you certainly didn't share with me."

Captain Lemaire chuckled. "Clearly you are accustomed to a life of politics, *Capitaine*. Perhaps, one day, I will have the honor of meeting the man beneath the mask."

"By the Swordsman's grace." Aravon gave the Nyslian officer a respectful bow and, with a nod to the hulking Balegar, strode toward the Coracle.

The river crossing took less than three minutes. Carpenters had secured the land-side end of the plank bridge to stakes, and the stone anchors held the Coracle mostly steady as they strode along its length.

Skathi stood waiting for them on the Standelfr's northern bank. Her green eyes watched the Bannockburners and Legionnaires hauling supplies across, but she nodded as Aravon, Zaharis, and Noll approached.

"*Horses are waiting by the first mile marker,*" Skathi signed. "*I figured you might want to slip away quietly, so I restocked supplies from the food delivered to Bannockburn.*"

"*Good thinking.*" Aravon was glad his mask hid his surprise. He'd known she was clever—she'd proven that many more times than he could count. Yet to anticipate his order and have the confidence to act on it, that took a degree of prudent forethought he hadn't expected. "*Noll's gone for the others. We'll get on the road as soon as they arrive, then find somewhere to hole up come sundown once we've put some distance between us and Rivergate.*" The longer they hung around the city, the more likely Commander Rheamus or another inquiring soul would begin to ask questions. Better to, as Captain Lemaire had put it, melt away into the mists.

The mystery of heavily-laden wagons plagued Aravon as he marched up the Marshway. It didn't make sense that the Jokull would pay tribute to Westhaven or the Prince, only to attack them a few days later. Far more logical

207

was Captain Lemaire's theory that silver had been discovered in the marshlands and someone in the Princelands had found a way to mine it.

And, if the Eirdkilrs knew about it, he reasoned, *it made sense that they'd try to disrupt that flow of valuables, perhaps even capture it for themselves.* The attack on Rivergate could have served multiple purposes—not just punching through the Chain and invading Westhaven, but denying the Prince valuable resources that could be used to bring in more Legionnaires.

Damn. Aravon shook his head. *The Eirdkilrs are playing it far smarter than ever before.* Something had changed—the Duke had suspected as much since the attack on the Eastmarch, but the siege of the Bulwark, the abduction of Silver Break's miners, and now this surprise assault on the Chain itself only confirmed their suspicions.

Aravon intended to raise the topic with the Duke next chance he got. *We've got to figure out what they really want—aside from all of our scalps, of course—if we want to have a chance of stopping them.*

At the first stone mile marker north of Rivergate Bridge, Skathi led them into a dense alder thicket. There, seven enormous *Kostarasar* chargers stood saddled and waiting.

"Farmer fed 'em well." Skathi spoke aloud. With no one around, they had no need to use the silent hand language. "Probably as well as the Duke would've. Almost made up for his complaining that they nearly ate him out of seed hay for the next year."

Aravon grimaced. He'd seen the huge horses eat; they rivaled Belthar's enormous appetite and, like the big man, cared more about quantity than quality. "Next time I speak to the Duke, I'll make sure he gets compensation."

He turned to Zaharis. "Go keep watch on the road for the others."

With a nod that seemed far more subdued than normal, Zaharis slipped off toward the highway.

"What's with him?" Skathi asked. "Seems gloomier than usual."

"He ran into a ghost from his past." A solemn mood fell over Aravon. He held up a hand to stifle Skathi's question. "He'll explain later." And Zaharis wouldn't be the only one. When they made camp for the evening, Colborn also owed an explanation to their company.

Worry about the Secret Keeper thrummed within him. Not *his* Secret Keeper, but Darrak, the one they'd fought in Rivergate. It would only be a matter of time before every Temple of Whispers in the Princelands heard of Zaharis' presence on Fehl. That could complicate their mission.

A faint, familiar sound reached his ears: the flapping of wings. He glanced up in time to see Snarl crashing through the thicket, wings tucked against his sides.

Aravon's heart stopped as the Enfield dropped toward him, apparently exhausted from the flight. His amber eyes seemed to have lost their glimmer, and Snarl's wings drooped with fatigue. He plummeted rather than swooped low, landing heavily in Aravon's arms.

Worry gnawed at Aravon's stomach. There was only one reason Snarl would be so exhausted.

Aravon reached for the scroll tube and, wrestling the cap loose, fished out the small rolled-up parchment within. Nine words were all the message bore, yet the sight of them brought the knots back to Aravon's shoulder.

"Find contact behind Rivergate's Shouting Tankard Inn, noon. URGENT!"

Chapter Twenty-Nine

Aravon read the message again. It was written in the Duke's hand, not Lord Eidan's. That filled him with a strange sense of anxiety, compounded by the sight of an exhausted Snarl in his arms. The Enfield's wings drooped and his head hung low, nuzzled against Aravon's arm. Snarl would only fly to the point of exhaustion if the Duke's message was urgent.

"Look at this." He held the note out to Skathi.

Frowning, Skathi took the message and read it. "The Duke's hand, correct?"

Aravon nodded, surprised by the fact that she could differentiate between the Duke and Lord Eidan's handwriting. Agrotorae education was as varied as that of Legionnaires—that was to say, dependent entirely on their military rank and their lives before joining up. Then again, he shouldn't be surprised that Skathi was more than simply literate. She'd proven herself far too capable to simply be "one more archer". Skill alone wouldn't have caused Duke Dyrund to select her for their special company. Though the Duke hadn't filled him in on his reasons for choosing each, they had all, in their own way, illustrated the reasons for the Duke's confidence in them.

"Whatever it is, it's got to be important." Skathi handed the note back. "I'll be back before the others—"

"No." Aravon shook his head, stopping the archer in her tracks. "This is a job for Noll."

"Noll?" Skathi's posture went instantly rigid. When she spoke, her voice was hard, edged with the anger that glimmered in her green eyes. "All due

211

respect, Captain, but I can get across that bridge, to the inn, and back here without breaking a sweat. Unless you don't—"

"I more than trust you, Skathi." Aravon held her gaze, sincerity echoing in his voice. "But I need someone who doesn't stand out." He gestured to her long red braids. "Won't take much for one of Captain Lemaire's company to connect you with the same archer who fought beside them."

"And what does that matter?" Curiosity echoed in Skathi's voice. "We're on the same side, aren't we?"

"We are. But right now…" Aravon drew in a long breath. "It's better no one recognizes whichever of us goes back into town."

Skathi's eyes narrowed. "Why?"

"Zaharis' ghost," Aravon replied simply. "Right now, suffice it to say that we're better off going into Rivergate incognito, *without* our masks this time. Colborn and Rangvaldr are out of the question, and I can't take the risk anyone in town knows me. Belthar's huge frame and your hair are unmistakable. No one's quite as unnoticeable as Noll."

Skathi snorted. "True that."

The scout was slight of build, his most remarkable feature a hawkish nose and a scar that ran from his chin to his right ear. Once out of his armor, he could pass for just about any Princelander. A shifty-eyed, conniving, light-fingered Princelander, but as inconspicuous as a farmer or stablehand.

Aravon suspected that had factored into Duke Dyrund's decision to choose the man—that, and the fact that Noll had served under Aravon and had personal motivation to put an end to the Eirdkilrs that slaughtered his company. But when they needed someone to blend in among the Princelanders, Noll was their perfect option, just as Colborn would appear perfectly at home among the Fehlans.

"As you say, Captain," Skathi finally admitted with a nod just short of grudging. "Let's just hope he hurries up." She shot a glance at the sky. "Noon's not far off, and after a couple of sleepless nights, I feel like *him.*"

Aravon glanced down at Snarl, nestled in his arms. The Enfield had fallen asleep, snoring quietly. The journey through the marshes and the flight to and from Camp Marshal—or wherever Duke Dyrund was at the moment—had taken a heavy toll on him.

The same toll that days of travel and battle had taken on all of them. Colborn had gotten a night of rest courtesy of Aravon's fist and too much liquor. Aravon guessed he'd snatched about three hours of sleep before the Lieutenant awoke. Knowing Noll and Belthar, they'd likely spent the time among the Legionnaires of Topaz Battalion. Zaharis rarely slept, yet the encounter with Darrak seemed to have left him drained, almost listless.

Rangvaldr's actions were the most curious. According to Belthar, he'd gone to pray over the fallen Jokull. As *Seiomenn* of the Eyrr, it fell to him to administer the final rites to his clan's warriors slain in battle. Aravon had been in Bjornstadt as Rangvaldr commended his fellow Eyrr—and Draian with them— into the arms of the *Roskvaettr,* the revered ancestors that escorted the slain to *Seggrholl,* the afterlife of heroes.

But the fact that he prayed over the Jokull came as a surprise to Aravon. The marshlanders had been his enemy. Perhaps not *personally,* for they had no reason to hate the Eyrr—aside from their dealings with the Princelanders—yet they would have slaughtered him as readily as they would the Legionnaires beside him.

It took a special kind of man, a man with deep-rooted faith in his god, to offer such prayers for men who had taken up arms against him only hours earlier. Not only did that show what manner of man the *Seiomenn* was, but in many ways, it proved that he'd spoken the truth when he explained his reasons for joining them. Rangvaldr, more than any of them, fought a battle for peace. When the war with the Eirdkilrs ended, it was his hope—as with the Duke and now, increasingly, Aravon himself—that the Fehlans and Princelanders could find a way to coexist, to share the richness of Fehl.

As if on cue, the man himself appeared through a gap in the alder thicket, accompanied by Zaharis, Colborn, Noll, and Belthar. While the scout pushed through the dense stand of trees and scrub with no difficulty, Belthar's helmeted head and armored shoulders displaced the branches and set them rustling.

"Ready to move out, Captain!" Noll called out, his voice just a little too cheery. Aravon couldn't help noticing the way the scout's eyes darted toward Zaharis every few seconds. Clearly he wanted that explanation now.

He was in for a disappointment.

"I just got word from the Duke." Aravon held up the note. "Noll, you're going back into Rivergate, now."

Noll cocked his head. "But we just came from—"

Aravon thrust out the note to Colborn and relayed the message's contents to the scout.

"The Duke's man inside Rivergate is the only reason we knew about the siege when we did," Aravon said. "If the Duke's wound this tightly about something, it's got to be important."

Colborn nodded agreement.

Sighing, Noll shrugged. "So be it. While I'm there, maybe I'll see about a bottle of that Nyslian brandy."

Aravon *felt* Colborn wincing beneath his mask. Brandy had been the cause of the Lieutenant's undoing the previous night, and had left him with a vicious hangover—or would have, if not for Zaharis' alchemical marvels.

"No." Aravon shook his head. "In and out, quick and quiet."

Noll muttered something that sounded suspiciously like "no fun", which Aravon chose to ignore.

"And you're going in without your armor," Aravon said.

"What, you mean *naked?*" The scout's eyes darted toward Skathi. "This your idea? All you'd have to do is ask."

"I'd rather gouge out my eyes and drink acid," Skathi snarled.

"Don't be an idiot, Noll," Colborn snapped. "No one wants to see your shriveled—"

"You're going in unarmored, in your plain clothes because we need to keep out of sight." Aravon inclined his head toward Zaharis. "Can't risk *anyone* recognizing you."

"Ahh." Noll nodded understanding and, with no decorum, set about unbuckling his armor right in their midst.

Colborn rolled his eyes and Belthar made a show of groaning and grimacing. Skathi, Aravon noticed, paid the little man no heed—much to Noll's disappointment once he'd finally stripped down to his undertunic and removed his mask.

"Go," Aravon told Noll. "Get to the meeting, find out what the Duke's contact wants, and get back here." He fixed the man with a piercing stare. "No distractions."

"Aye, Captain!" Noll snapped a smart Legion salute and, turning, padded off through the thicket toward the highway that led south to Rivergate.

Aravon watched the man go in silence. During his years as officer of Garnet Battalion's Sixth Company, he'd seen Noll out of his light scout's armor enough to recognize his scout's stealthy walk. *Let's just hope no one else here sees him for what he is.*

He turned to the others. "While he's gone, let's get ready to ride. Grab some food, drink water, and do whatever else you've got to do. The moment he's back, we're out of here."

Chapter Thirty

Time seemed to drag on for an eternity as Aravon waited for Noll to return. Colborn, like a true Legionnaire, had fallen asleep with his back against a broad alder tree. Snarl dozed as well, nestling against Skathi's feet. The archer sat working on crafting new arrow shafts to replace those used in the battle. Knowing her, she'd likely taken time to cut as many of her Odarian steel arrowheads out of the slain enemies as possible. Aravon had spent enough time around the Agrotorae to know that they *always* carried a small pouch of replacement arrowheads, just in case.

Rangvaldr sat in silence on the northern side of their small circle, his eyes closed but his posture upright. With his mask hanging around his neck, his face appeared surprisingly serene—surprising, given that he'd just killed Fehlans the previous night. Perhaps he was praying to Nuius, casting his burden onto the shoulders of the Eyrr's god. If that helped him, Aravon envied him that peace of mind.

Zaharis, however, was a stark contrast to the *Seiomenn's* tranquility. He sat beside Rangvaldr, his pale face dark, a ceaseless whirlwind of activity. He chewed at his lower lip, plucked at the grass beneath him, and turned the black stone he'd taken from the silver wagons over and over in his fingers. His eyes fixed on the stone yet he seemed not to see it.

Aravon paused in his pacing. Worry for Zaharis thrummed within him. The encounter with Darrak had changed something within the man, and now it left him a bundle of nervous energy, a stormcloud of emotions locked away deep in his brain.

"Zaharis."

The Secret Keeper's head snapped up.

"Come." Aravon inclined his head toward where the horses stood. "Help me go over the gear one last time before we ride."

Zaharis' brow furrowed but he stood smoothly, rising from his cross-legged position to his feet with agile ease. He hunched slightly over his left side; evidently his dark mood wasn't the only thing Darrak had left him.

Aravon led the Secret Keeper around the horses, as far away from the others as he could get within the dense thicket. *"How concerned should I be about Darrak?"* He spoke in the silent hand language.

A scowl deepened Zaharis' expression. *"First thing he'll do when he wakes is send a report to the Temple of Whispers in Westhaven and Icespire. From there, it'll spread to every other city around Fehl where my order has priests. Within the week, every Secret Keeper in the Princelands will know I'm alive and here."*

Aravon's jaw clenched. *"So where does that leave us?"* He fixed the man with a solemn gaze. *"Can you continue by our side, or do you need to run?"*

The Secret Keeper grew pensive, his brow furrowing in thought. After long moments, he shook his head. *"I ride with you, Captain, as I swore to Duke Dyrund. But every day I remain in the Princelands puts me in greater danger. You and the others with me."*

"And if we ride south?" Aravon asked. *"How many of your brothers roam the Fehlan wilds?"*

Again, the contemplative frown. *"South of the Chain, there is little chance of discovery. I will not lie and say they will not find me, but the land of Fehl is vast and men are hard to find. Especially men who make it their mission to remain hidden."*

Aravon nodded. *"I make no promises, but I will see if the Duke has anything that can take us south."*

"And if not," Zaharis said, *"I swear that I will do everything to ensure that my brothers do not find me. I will not let my past affect our mission."*

"That is all I can ask for." Aravon met the man's gaze. *"But I cannot be the only one who knows the full extent of the danger we face in the Princelands."* He gestured toward the figures seated around the thicket. *"You owe them the truth as well."*

Zaharis' face hardened, but he inclined his head. *"I will tell them all."*

"Knowing them," Aravon said, *"they will stand by your side. But they cannot hope to fight an enemy they do not know is coming."*

"*Yes, Captain.*" Zaharis half-turned, then paused and shot a glance back at Aravon. "*A lesser man would have ordered the truth. I can see why the Duke chose you to lead.*" With that, he turned and strode back toward the camp.

The words caught Aravon off-guard. Such a thing from Zaharis was high praise, indeed.

Before he could give it any more thought, a slight figure slunk through the gap in the thicket. Aravon had half-raised his spear before he recognized Noll. Even as he lowered his weapon, he registered the puzzled frown on the little scout's face.

"What happened?" Aravon asked as he strode around the horses toward the man. "Did you find the Shouting Tankard?"

"Aye, Captain." Noll nodded. "But when I went, no one was waiting for me."

Aravon cocked an eyebrow. "The Duke's man?"

Noll shook his head. "Not so much as a starving mouse. I waited for a full half-hour and still no one showed." Reaching into his tunic, he pulled out what looked like a chunk of crimson wax. "But there was this."

Aravon took the object from Noll. It *was* wax, the sort used to seal letters, bearing the imprint of a signet ring Aravon didn't recognize: a carbuncle, eight radiating rods that formed an interlocked cross and saltire.

"Where did you find it?" Aravon asked. A scrap of fragile parchment still clung to the chunk of wax; something this delicate wouldn't have survived long left out in the open, which meant someone had placed it somewhere safe, away from the elements.

"Dead drop in the stone wall." Noll shot a glance at Belthar. The big man had stiffened, his expression frozen. The same reaction he'd had while detailing a surprisingly crafty plan to break into Duke Leddan's stronghold.

"Dead drop?" The term was unfamiliar to Aravon.

"Sneaky way of passing messages. A hidden page in a book, loose brick or stone in the wall, something like that," Noll explained. "Sort of like the caches we scouts use to leave supplies when ranging far ahead of our Legionnaires. Only it's done in cities and towns."

Aravon turned the wax seal and its attached scrap of parchment over in his hands. He had no idea what the insignia meant or which noble House of the Princelands—or of mainland Einan—it belonged to. The fact that the Duke's agent had taken pains to hide it meant it *had* to be important. More worrisome, however, was the man's absence. If the Duke's contact within Rivergate had an Enfield to send and receive information—a fact that seemed very likely, given the speed with which the updates had been delivered to the Duke and Lord Eidan—the message would have taken less than a day to get from Rivergate to the Duke to them.

Which makes absolutely no sense. Aravon's brow furrowed. *That means the message would have been sent the same night we attacked Rivergate.*

The Duke's agent wouldn't have *known* they planned an assault, as evidenced by the message that the city's supplies had run out and people were starving. Yet, if the man had been present during the battle, he'd have to have seen Aravon and the others in their strange, non-Legion armor. A man who reported to the Duke personally would likely know who they were, and would have sought them out in person long before the Enfield delivered his message.

Unless he was already dead by the time we attacked. Cold dread sank in Aravon's gut. That was the only explanation he could think of.

He lifted his eyes to his men. "While you were in Rivergate, did any of you hear about suspicious deaths *before* we broke the siege?"

Six pairs of eyes narrowed. "Suspicious?" asked Noll.

"Not deaths by enemy arrows or by starvation." Aravon's mind worked at the problem. "The only reason the Duke's agent would miss the meet is if he *couldn't* make it. And, given the quick arrival of the message—"

"He'd have to have sent it off yesterday." Skathi seemed to have reached a similar conclusion. "Not long before the battle, for that matter."

"Which means he's either dead or wounded," Colborn finished.

Aravon nodded. "If he was wounded, he'd have done everything in his power to make that meet." There were plenty of injuries that could render a man unconscious or immobile, and that could be one explanation. But the other…

"The fact that he didn't means something happened to him, you think?" Noll screwed up his face, an expression that made him look startlingly like one of the voles that ran rampant around the Princelands. "Yeah, that tracks."

"You suspect foul play?" Colborn asked.

"Between him sending that message and now," Aravon said, "the only men who died in battle were Legionnaires."

"And no Legionnaire would play spy?" A sneer twisted Skathi's face. "Not all soldiers are as virtuous and noble as you, Captain."

Those words held a far greater depth of meaning, but Aravon had no time to dig in to it at the moment.

"Legionnaires *can* be spies," Aravon replied, "but were that the case, I believe that the Duke would have told me to be on the lookout for a particular soldier. He'd have tasked me to do my best to ensure his agent got out of the inevitable battle alive."

"Which leads you to believe that the Duke's agent *isn't* someone who would be put at risk in battle," Colborn finished. "Someone *else*. A Rivergater, one of the regular citizenry. Someone who wound up dead for another reason. Murder."

Aravon shrugged. "Given the information we've got, that's my best worst guess." He glanced around the circle. "Unless any of you have another theory."

The six exchanged glances, then shook their heads.

"Which leads me back to my original question," Aravon said. "Did any of you hear of any strange or suspicious deaths?"

A long moment of silence elapsed as everyone contemplated.

"Oh!" Belthar's rumbling voice broke in and he turned his huge face toward Noll. "Before the wrestling match with Balegar, did you hear the two Legionnaires of Fifth Company talking about Turath?"

"Yeah!" Noll's eyebrows shot up. "Yeah, that *was* suspicious."

"Turath?" Aravon asked.

"Local tavernkeeper," Belthar replied. "Lost his wife and daughters in the initial attack, then his youngest during the siege." His huge face darkened. "Fell ill and never got better."

"One of the Fifth Company officers was dressing down a loudmouth for suggesting that Turath snapped and lost his marbles." Noll shook his head. "Said he took a long walk off a short parapet. Blind drunk and mad with grief."

"Only the officer said Turath never touched his own merchandise." Belthar frowned. "He slung the liquor but kept his whistle dry. Last I heard was the Legionnaire retorting that even a good man like Turath could go batty. That was when Balegar challenged me to an arm wrestle." Pride shone on his face. "And you all know how *that* turned out."

Aravon gave the man an approving smile, but his mind was already working on the matter of Turath. He hadn't wanted to believe his own theory. It was easier to think that the Duke's agent had simply died in battle, but if—and it was a huge *if*—Turath had been the one sending messages, that "walk off the parapet" might have been more of a "thrown". The alcohol could have been nothing more than the murderer's ruse to distract from the truth of his crime.

Which left the question burning in Aravon's mind. *Who knew the Duke had an agent in Rivergate, and who would want him dead?*

The same thought seemed to be brewing in everyone's thoughts. The faces of those around him darkened, expressions growing grim.

Since Silver Break Mine, Aravon had known that someone in a position of power was working against Duke Dyrund. Only a traitor would have revealed the mine, a secret known to a select few of the highest-ranked people on Fehl. Their visit to Ironcastle had written Duke Leddan off as a suspect in regards to the mine. Blaming the Duke of Oldcrest for this particular death seemed far more than a stretch of logic.

Duke Dyrund had told him that Lord Eidan would investigate the matter. As the Prince's spymaster, Lord Eidan's reach extended throughout the entire Princelands. It was likely the man killed had been a member of his spy network, reporting to both him and the Duke. Aravon would make sure Lord Eidan learned of his agent's death. Unmasking the culprit behind Turath's murder would likely point fingers at whoever was responsible for Silver Break Mine.

"Send me back into Rivergate, Captain," Noll said. "Let me do a bit of poking around, see what I can learn about Turath's death."

Aravon hesitated. The matter of Darrak remained fresh in his mind, and Zaharis' statement that all the Secret Keepers on Fehl would soon be looking for them definitely added a new wrinkle to their mission to operate behind the scenes. Sending Noll into Rivergate was a risk; not only was it an added delay to their departure, but there was a chance Darrak would awaken and come after them, broken leg or no.

Yet he couldn't simply leave the matter alone. If Turath was the Duke's agent and *if* he'd been murdered, the best time to look into it was now. The more time that elapsed, the greater the chance that someone would forget a vital detail of the matter. Even if they only got hints and clues, it could be enough to set Lord Eidan's investigation on the right track. And, knowing the nobleman and the Duke to whom he answered, there *would* be someone sent to find out what had happened.

Finally, Aravon nodded. "Go. You've got two hours, then get out of there."

"Got it, Captain!" Noll saluted.

"Belthar, stay here and wait for him. The moment he's back, I want you two riding north. We'll be waiting for you at that spot where we camped the night before we arrived in Bannockburn."

"By the waterfall?" Belthar's eyes lit up.

"That's the place."

"Aye, Captain!" Belthar saluted as well—he was getting better, Aravon noted.

"As for the rest of us," Aravon said, turning to the remaining four, "we get on our way, get camp set up and dinner ready for when they arrive."

"Ah, dinner!" Delight sparkled in Rangvaldr's eyes, and a smile broadened his face. "After these weeks of hard trail rations and meager Legion fare, I find myself longing for a proper Fehlan suckling pig roast."

"No promises," Colborn said, "but I could swear I saw grouse tracks near the stream." He shot a glance at Skathi. "At least *one* of us ought to be able to bring a few down."

"Winner gets the first watch." Skathi raised an eyebrow.

"Deal!" Colborn shook her hand. "I'm already looking forward to a good night's sleep and a half-decent dinner."

"Half-decent?" Zaharis signed. *"You get me grouse, and I'll produce a feast fit for a King."* His dour expression cracked, a hint of a smile tugging at his lips. *"Or, fit enough for a handful of savages like you."*

Despite himself, Aravon couldn't help mirroring the grin. "Looks like we've finally got something to look forward to tonight."

The five of them mounted up and rode out within five minutes. Snarl was too tired to fly or run alongside them, so Aravon carried the little Enfield curled up in his arms. That forced them to set a slower pace, but it was worth it to have Snarl rested and ready to fly once Noll and Belthar caught up with them. They might have to get a message to the Duke in a hurry.

Thoughts of the Duke's missing agent pushed Aravon's momentary good mood aside. Such accidents didn't simply *happen* by chance. Someone had killed

Turath and covered it up to look like he'd thrown himself off the keep's ramparts.

An enemy—Eirdkilrs, one of the Duke's political opponents, or the same traitor that had revealed the location of Silver Break Mine, Aravon couldn't begin to figure out—had murdered the man.

The question was: who? And what was the meaning of the strange heraldic symbol? With every pounding step of his horse's hooves, Aravon felt the sense of wrongness penetrating deeper into his bones.

If they didn't find out who was behind all of this and *soon,* the Eirdkilrs might not be the only foe threatening Duke Dyrund, Aravon and his men, perhaps even all the Princelands.

Chapter Thirty-One

The sound of drumming hoofbeats snapped five heads toward the south. Aravon reached for the spear resting on the grass by his side, Skathi nocked a freshly-made arrow to her bow, and a seax appeared in Rangvaldr's hand. Colborn, on watch under the shadows of the trees, was invisible to Aravon's eye, but he had no doubt the half-Fehlan was ready for anything.

Snarl, curled around Aravon's feet, perked up, lifting his little furry head. But instead of leaping toward the newcomers or barking out a greeting or warning, the Enfield lay back down and snuggled closer to Aravon's boots—a comforting warmth after the long days and nights they'd endured.

Zaharis seemed not to notice the sudden tension. The Secret Keeper appeared lost in deep, dark thoughts, his brow pulled so tightly thick furrows formed all up his brown-haired head. His lithe, strong fingers turned the small chunk of black ghoulstone over and over mindlessly.

Aravon released the grip on his spear as he caught sight of the two riders—the towering giant astride one of the few horses on Fehl strong enough to bear his weight, and a small, compact man riding in his shadow.

Noll reined in and leapt from his saddle with the easy grace of an experienced rider. "Please tell me you've got that fancy feast Zaharis promised," he said, removing the straps that held his mask in place.

Aravon gestured toward their small fire, and the spit that held three plump grouse. "Saved one for you." He shot a glance at Belthar, who dismounted much more slowly than the scout. "Other two are for you. Extra-spicy, just the way you like it. Eat up, then tell us what you've found."

Belthar's stomach rumbled in appreciation as he, too, removed his mask and strode over to take a seat beside Noll. The scout had already snatched the spit from the fire and dug his knife into the meatiest of the birds. He'd barely put a piece of stringy dark meat into his mouth before he started panting.

"Keeper's teeth!" He gasped for air, fanning his face with his knife hand. "How the bloody hell can you eat it so hot?"

"How can you *not?*" Belthar took a giant bite out of the next grouse on the spit, the one slathered in the bright red spices popular among the men of Eastfall. "Anything without spice is just boring. Like *your* dinner." He slid the third grouse, which had a light dusting of salt and pepper, off the spit and handed it to the blowing, wheezing scout.

"Water!" Noll sucked in deep lungfuls of air, struggling to breathe.

"Behind you, fool." Skathi gestured with an arrow to the waterfall beside which they had made camp.

Noll was on his feet in a flash, whirling and racing the two steps to the cascade's pool. He plunged his entire head, helmet and all, into the cool water and held it there for long seconds. When he finally came up for air, he was drenched, red-faced, and only fractionally less agonized than before.

"Here." Rangvaldr held out a long, thin stick. "Chew on this. An old Eyrr remedy."

Noll snatched the proffered stick and stuffed it into his mouth. He chewed with gusto, his face slowly contorting in disgust. "*Blech!*" He spat a mouthful of saliva, bark, and gnawed-up twig. "Tastes awful."

"Yeah." Rangvaldr's face was serious, but Aravon could swear he saw a hint of a smile tugging at the man's lips. "That's what does the trick."

For long seconds, Noll continued chewing, all eyes locked on him. Finally, a snort echoed from the cover of trees, a sound that shattered the calm. Rangvaldr descended into a fit of laughter, accompanied by Skathi, Aravon, and Colborn.

Noll's face deepened into a scowl and he spat the twig. "Very funny!" He fanned at his mouth. "Now I'm not only burning up, but I've got a mouthful of whatever the hell that was."

Rangvaldr doubled over, his booming laughter echoing through the small campsite.

A slow smile spread Belthar's face as he caught on. "What was it?"

"A bloody stick!" The *Seiomenn* struggled to speak around his guffaws. "Just picked…it up off…the ground!"

"Your face was priceless," Skathi said, a broad, nasty grin stretching her face. "I'd give all the gold in Aegeos to have an artist immortalize that stupid look in stone."

Noll snarled a curse and rounded on Rangvaldr. "Traitor!" His eyes flashed. "And here I thought we were good after we saved each other back in the marshes."

"Way I remember it," Colborn's voice drifted from the shadows of the trees, "the *Seiomenn* here saved *your* ass. When, exactly, did you return the favor?"

Noll's scowl deepened. "That's beside the point." He gave a dismissive wave. "We had each other's backs, and now you pull this?"

"Forgive me, Noll." Rangvaldr still struggled to contain his laughter, despite the scout's angry face. "It was just too perfect to pass up."

Noll whirled on Aravon. "Can you believe this, Captain?" His eyebrows shot up. "I thought he's supposed to be a holy man of the Eyrr! Little more than a juvenile prankster."

Aravon plastered a solemn expression on his face. "You're right." He stood slowly, fixing the scout and *Seiomenn* with a stern frown. "I'm disappointed in you, Rangvaldr. Especially because you knew *this* would be the cure for his problem." He waved a handful of freshly-plucked grass in front of the scout.

The *Seiomenn's* laughter redoubled and he fell back, clutching at his stomach. Skathi, Belthar, and Colborn joined in, and a smile shattered Aravon's mock severity.

"Not you, too, Captain!" Noll threw up his hands. "Watcher's beard, you lot are worse than a group of drunk one-legged Morris dancers. And that's saying a lot."

"Don't be a sore loser, Noll." Belthar nudged the man's leg. "You have to admit, it was pretty damned funny."

Noll glared at the big man. "Next time *you're* the one with something of yours burning, we'll see how funny you think it is."

"Ahh, but something tells me Belthar's smart enough to stick with the *cleaner* bawdy houses," Colborn's voice drifted from the woods.

Noll's face darkened, but Belthar's turned a bright red. His eyes darted to Skathi and a protest formed on his lips. But the archer was too busy laughing at Noll's angry expression to notice.

"At least I can count on Zaharis not to pull sneaky shite like that, eh, Secret Keeper?" Noll shot Zaharis a sidelong glance.

The sound of his name seemed to snap the man out of his trace. His eyes lifted to Noll, a blank expression on his face, and his fingers moved in a silent, questioning hand gesture.

"I said you wouldn't pull anything sneaky on me, right?" Noll raised an eyebrow.

"*Sure.*" Zaharis' hand gesture was half-hearted, absent-minded.

"Although, speaking of sneaky shite," Noll pressed, "maybe it's time you explain what in the fiery hell happened back there? Who in the Keeper's name is Darrak and what does he want with us?"

Pain flashed across Zaharis' face. Confusion and puzzlement twisted the expressions of the three seated around the fire. A rustling from within the shadows of the nearby woods told Aravon that even Colborn had moved closer.

"Tell him, Captain." Noll never took his eyes from Zaharis. "Tell him he owes us the truth."

"Noll," Aravon said, a warning tone in his voice. "Let him be. He will speak in his own—"

"No!" Now the scout rounded on Aravon, eyes flashing. "I've held my tongue long enough. First, we got Colborn wailing drunk and partying with corpses, then Zaharis' buddy nearly kills us." He stabbed an accusing finger at Aravon. "You're the Captain, so it falls to you to make sure everyone's in their right minds and focused on the mission at hand. Right now, it feels like anything but!"

Aravon opened his mouth to speak, but Zaharis cut him off with a slashing hand gesture. The Secret Keeper stood, slowly, his expression a mask of shadows and anguish. "*You're right,*" he signed to the little scout. "*I promised you the truth.*" His head swiveled to face the rest of their small company. "*I owe it to all of you.*"

"Truth about what?" Skathi sat up, her arrows and bow discarded as she leaned forward in curiosity.

228

Zaharis' fingers moved slowly. *"About my reasons for being here. Not just on Fehl, but among all of you."*

"Ice saffron, right?" Belthar rumbled.

"Something to do with an elixir of some sort." Skathi frowned in thought. "Elixir of Creativity."

"Elixir of Creation," Zaharis corrected. He'd given a simple explanation on their journey from Bjornstadt to Gallows Garrison, after he'd broken away from the company and run off on his own. *"And yes, that is the truth of what I am searching for. Yet you also deserve to know what I am running from."*

Rangvaldr was the only one who didn't appear surprised at the Secret Keeper's words. The two had known each other before Zaharis joined Aravon's small company; perhaps he'd shared more with the *Seiomenn* than simply a few dozen horns of potent *ayrag* liquor.

"In my role as priest to the Mistress, I have uncovered many marvels of this world. Marvels that offer immense power in the right hands," Zaharis explained. His expression grew grave. *"What I did with the Watcher's Bloom back at Anvil Garrison or the Dragon Thorngrass here at Rivergate, that was just a taste of what I've learned over the years of studying Fehlan flora and fauna."*

'Still waiting for the part where one of your own tries to kill us," Noll muttered.

"As you know, the Temple of Whispers guards their secrets with fanatical zeal. They will kill to protect the wealth of dangerous knowledge gathered over the years." Zaharis' shoulders seemed to droop beneath a heavy weight. *"Even their own priests are not safe."*

Belthar's eyebrows shot up. "Your own…?" He let out a long, low whistle. "Swordsman's bony elbows, that's cold."

"Cold, and sometimes necessary." Zaharis inclined his head. *"It is not an understatement to say that some of the secrets locked within the Mistress' temples around Einan and Fehl have the power to shape the world. Or destroy it."*

"And you've got these secrets?" Skathi's voice was tight, controlled. "Planning to destroy the world, are you?"

Zaharis shook his head. *"But that won't stop my order from hunting me anyway. Temple policy."* His lips twisted into a frown. *"Preserve the Mistress' secrets at any cost."*

"And Darrak?" Noll asked. "Where'd he come from?"

229

"*From my home in Voramis,*" Zaharis replied. "*When I was evicted from the priesthood, I fled the city to escape certain death. I came to Fehl because I believed it was where I'd find ice saffron, and because I hoped it was far enough away that I could remain hidden from the Mistress' priests while I searched. Here, no one knew my face, my name, or who I was, save a select few I knew I could trust.*" His eyes darted toward Rangvaldr, who hadn't moved or spoken a word in all this time.

"Until now." A somber note echoed in Noll's voice. "Darrak recognized you immediately. Mask and all."

Zaharis' fingers flashed. "*He recognized my alchemy. Secret Keepers are, in our own way, artisans and artists, masters of our chosen craft. For Darrak, it was always the study of legendary creatures. His drawings, produced from ancient depictions and the animals he discovered on his travels, were true masterpieces, all of which will never see the light of day. My art, however—*"

"Turning innocent plants into things that go *boom.*" Belthar's lips quirked into a smile. "That was some art at Bjornstadt and Broken Canyon, no doubt about it."

Zaharis inclined his head. "*My realm of expertise extends to all plant life, not just the ones that, as you say, go boom.*" His finger mimicked the explosive pillar of fire that had thrown back the Eirdkilrs and brought down the walls of Broken Canyon.

"We've all benefitted from your expertise, Zaharis," Aravon said. "Hells, we'd all be *dead* without it." He shot Noll a meaningful glance. It was no exaggeration; the Secret Keeper had saved them all on numerous occasions. Not just the six of them that marched alongside him, either. Both Jade and Topaz Battalions owed him for their survival.

Noll seemed to understand the hint, and the sharp, angry edge to his face softened a fraction. "But now Darrak knows you're here." He raised an eyebrow. "Should we be expecting hordes of Secret Keepers to chase you?"

"*Us.*" Zaharis' face hardened. "*Because of your association with me, my superiors at the Temple of Whispers will assume you've learned more of the Mistress' secrets than they want getting out. If they find me, they'll deal with you just the same.*"

Noll burst into a string of curses that had Belthar's ears blazing as red as the glowing embers of the campfire.

"So why in the bloody hell did we leave him alive, then?" The little scout rounded on Zaharis, eyes blazing. "We could have put an end to him then and there, blamed it on the Eirdkilrs!"

"It wouldn't have worked." Zaharis' face hardened, his teeth clenched so tightly his jaw creaked. *"Too many people in Rivergate would have seen him alive after the battle. When the Secret Keepers came asking questions—and trust me, they will come hunting the truth of their priest's death—they would find out about our presence just the same. Everyone in Rivergate saw what I had to do to turn the battle against the Eirdkilrs."*

Zaharis had the right of it. His alchemy, setting the marsh water on fire, would doubtless remained burned into the memories of every Legionnaire and ducal regular in Rivergate. A detail like that would immediately arouse the suspicions of any Secret Keeper who dug into the matter of a Secret Keeper's death.

"The Secret Keepers will know it was me, one way or another. The only question is how long it will take them to find out." Zaharis' eyes darkened. *"Killing Darrak would have delayed the discovery by a week, perhaps two. But when the Temple of Whispers learned the truth, their retribution would have been far worse had we taken Darrak's life."*

Of that, Aravon had little doubt. Secret Keepers had a reputation for savagery in their protection of the Mistress' secrets. He could easily imagine how fiercely they would carry out their goddess' punishment on any who dared to take a priest's life.

Yet, the look in Zaharis' eyes as he stood over Darrak's broken, senseless form had made the truth clear. There was history between the two men. Love that had endured—within Zaharis, certainly, and the way Darrak had hesitated indicated he, too, still felt the same—even after Zaharis was expelled from the Secret Keepers.

"But…" Zaharis hesitated, his fingers faltering. After a long second, he managed to continue. *"But, no matter the threat to my life—to our lives—"* He winced at the words. *"—I could never kill Darrak. Never stand to see him killed, not by my hand or any other outside the temple."* His gaze locked on Noll, meaning etched plain in every line of his face. *"If it means I must disappear, must leave your company to protect all of you, so be it. But this is one line I will not cross."*

A tense silence descended over the camp, broken only by the quiet splashing of the waterfall behind them. Long seconds passed as each of the soldiers around the fire contemplated Zaharis' words. They all shared the same thought, Aravon knew—how would this new wrinkle affect their mission?

If the Secret Keepers hunted them because of their association with Zaharis, their fight to protect the Princelands would prove even more difficult.

However, the fact that they kept their identities a secret and were constantly on the move gave them a decent chance of staying ahead of their pursuers.

Aravon had pondered the matter since riding out of Rivergate. He'd come to the conclusion that they needed Zaharis. Even if that meant they'd have Secret Keepers looking for them, Zaharis' alchemical knowledge, ingenuity, and skill in battle had saved the day time and again.

But he couldn't make the decision for his soldiers. Couldn't force them to accept the consequences of Zaharis' choices and the danger inherent in the Secret Keeper's presence in their company. He needed to give them a chance to come to their own conclusions, whatever they may be. Skathi spoke first. "Fuck 'em."

Aravon's head snapped toward the Agrotora. She hadn't risen, but remained seated, eyes fixed on Zaharis. Yet there was no recrimination in her eyes, only calm acceptance.

"Fuck them all in their tight-clenched arses." Skathi's words came out in a growl. "Let them come. They'll find we're not some shrinking violets that can be intimidated or threatened into hiding."

Aravon almost opened his mouth to contradict her—he'd fought beside Zaharis and against Darrak, and Secret Keeper combat skills were no joke. Yet, at that moment, the point she was making mattered far more than him telling her just how much danger she was in. After all, she'd faced Zaharis in the training ring and defended Bjornstadt with him. She had to know exactly what came for them.

Skathi rose now, leaving her bow and arrows on the ground, and came to stand before Zaharis. "Like he said." She jerked a thumb at Aravon. "We'd all be dead without you. Seems like the least we can do is stand by you when you need us."

Gratitude sparkled in Zaharis' eyes, and a small smile pierced his stony expression.

Skathi thrust out a strong hand. "Those brown-robed bastards mess with you, they'll end up like my Nana's pincushion. Agrotorae don't abandon their friends, through fiery hell or rushing riptides."

Zaharis accepted her hand, the lean muscles of his forearm cording as he returned her grip.

Belthar was next to his feet. "Let's see how those Secret Keepers like the taste of axe." He hefted his huge double-headed weapon in one enormous hand and clapped Zaharis' back with the other. "We've got your back."

"So we do." Rangvaldr shot Zaharis a reassuring smile.

Colborn materialized from the shadows of the trees, coming to stand beside Zaharis. He rested a hand on the Secret Keeper's shoulder. "All of us."

Aravon turned a questioning glance on Noll. The little scout hadn't moved, and a recalcitrant expression twisted his lips into a frown. Long seconds passed as Noll stared in silence at the Secret Keeper.

Finally, he stepped forward. "On one condition." He jabbed a finger into Zaharis' chest. "*You* promise to help me get revenge on the *Seiomenn* for that vicious trick." He turned his head to the side and spat. "It's going to be weeks before I get the taste of the damned stick out of my mouth."

The words snapped the momentary tension, and a smile wreathed Zaharis' face. "*Deal!*" he signed. His eyes darted toward Rangvaldr. "*Careful, old man. Make sure to check your bedroll carefully. Never know what'll end up in there.*"

"My man!" Noll barked a laugh and smacked Zaharis on the shoulder. "You and me, Zaharis, taking on Eirdkilrs, priests, and tricksters."

Everyone around the camp chuckled. From the looks in their eyes, Aravon knew the true depth of what Zaharis had just told them—the threat that could lie in wait around the next corner, or the next. And yet, despite that, they had responded exactly as Aravon had hoped. As a team, a company of warriors united in not only the mission for which they all strived, but the bonds of friendship and camaraderie that made soldiers put their lives on the line for each other.

"I believe I, too, owe you all an explanation." Colborn's quiet, somber voice cut into the momentary good humor. "About last night."

A knowing look flashed across Rangvaldr's face, but Belthar, Noll, and Zaharis grew somber. Even Skathi appeared curious; she might not have been present the previous night, but Aravon had little doubt Noll or Belthar had told her of Colborn's...reaction.

"I..." Colborn began, but nothing came out. He seemed to struggle to form words, to explain to the others the pain and emotional anguish that had finally been unleashed.

Rangvaldr stood and came over to stand beside the Lieutenant. "You are not alone in your struggle, Lieutenant." His gaze locked with Colborn's ice-blue eyes. "Perhaps your particular burden is one that none of us share. Yet we all wrestle with our own questions and inner turmoil."

Colborn swallowed, hard, and his voice came out barely above a hoarse croak. "Thank you." His usual stoicism seemed to give way before the *Seiomenn's* gentle reassurance. "But you all deserve better than that mad, raving lunatic you saw last night."

Rangvaldr shrugged. "We all process feelings in our own way." A kind light sparkled in his eyes. "Perhaps not quite so...theatrical."

Something between a strangled sob and a harsh chuckle burst from Colborn's throat. His lips twisted into a bitter smile, which seemed to accentuate the bluntness of his Fehlan features.

"It is never easy for a man to take a life." Rangvaldr turned to look at the others around the camp. "Harder still when it is one's own blood being spilled."

Skathi nodded, and even Noll seemed to agree with the *Seiomenn's* words. Belthar's face, however, grew hard, his expression darkening as if he, too, knew the toll such a death could take on a man's soul.

Yet another layer to peel away, Aravon thought. The more time he spent around Belthar, the more he realized he had to learn about the man beneath the easy smile.

Colborn drew in a deep breath. "But, be that as it may, I vow that what happened last night will never happen again. No matter..." He swallowed and tried again. "No matter what enemies we face from here on out."

Aravon nodded approval, and Zaharis shot Colborn a silent hand gesture of reassurance.

Noll threw up his hands. "Keeper's beard, you think *that's* what you need to explain?"

Colborn's eyes darkened, narrowed.

"No!" Noll shook his head. "You need to explain why in the bloody hell you drank all the good brandy." A grimace twisted his lips. "Thanks to you, Lieutenant, Belthar and I had no choice but to drink that rubbish rose wine Nyslians seem to love."

"Like fruity piss," Belthar grumbled.

"Worse than swill!" Noll snarled. "We need something with real legs, else we might as well just drink..." He shuddered. "...water."

The shadows lifted from Colborn's eyes and a small smile tugged at his lips. "Then next time I find myself drowning my sorrows in drink, I'll make sure to stop while there's still enough for you two."

"That's all any good soldier could ask for." Noll punched the Lieutenant in the arm, earning a scowl from Colborn. He held up a hasty hand. "Er, sir."

Colborn nodded. "Now, tell us what you found out about Turath's death." He raised an eyebrow. "Unless you spent all your time in Rivergate searching for something good to drink."

"Not a drop, honest!" Noll's crooked grin belied his words. "Even when the men of Eighth Company were raising toasts to the 'Grim Reavers'!"

Aravon cocked his head. "Grim Reavers?"

"That's what they're calling us, sir." Noll's smile broadened until it stretched from ear to ear. "Seems it's traveled from Anvil Garrison in the last few weeks. Has a nice ring to it, doesn't it?"

Colborn rolled his eyes. "Screw the name. What'd you find out about Turath, Noll?"

"Not a bloody lot." The scout shook his head, his smile fading to a grimace. "A couple of Sixth Company's platoons were watching that section of wall on the night in question, but they were more focused on the enemy outside the keep than anyone moving around inside. Didn't see or hear anything, they say. No one noticed Turath missing until the next day, and he wasn't discovered until *after* the battle ended."

"So nothing we can use?" Aravon's heart sank. He'd wanted to confirm his suspicions, to have something to relay to the Duke. But by the sound of Noll's report—

"Well, there was the matter of the dagger wound."

Aravon's eyebrows shot up. "Dagger wound, after a drunken man walks off a parapet?"

"Mad suspicious, right?" Noll jabbed his thumb into his side. "While it's not impossible for a man bleeding out from a thrust to the vitals to jump off the wall of the inner keep—"

"I'd say it's pretty damned unlikely." Aravon chewed at his lip, a hand stroking the non-regulation beard that had grown uncomfortably thick since leaving Camp Marshal. "You're sure about the wound?"

Noll nodded. "Saw the body myself. All it took was a sob story about his being a relative of mine, and the Legionnaires allowed me to 'pay my respects to my dearly departed uncle'."

Aravon drew in a long, slow breath, letting his mind tug at the dangling threads of information. A dagger thrust to the side would kill a man in seconds, minutes at best. With the Legionnaires focused on the besieging enemy, someone with intimate knowledge of the inner keep *could* conceivably find a way to dump a dead body over the wall unnoticed. All evidence pointed to murder.

The question was why. Why had Turath been murdered? A quarrel with a fellow Rivergater, or was someone hunting the spies working for Lord Eidan and Duke Dyrund? And, if that was the case, how had the killer known Turath was the planted agent? More questions with no answers.

No way we can go back to Rivergate, not with Darrak there. That meant he'd have no way to dig deeper into the matter in person. All he could do was send word to the Duke and let him sort it out.

But one look at Snarl told him the Enfield was nowhere near ready to travel. Snarl had returned to the comfort of Aravon's blanket and, after finishing off the scraps of grouse left for him, fallen fast asleep once more. He'd likely sleep until midnight, but he wouldn't be ready to travel until morning.

Nothing we can do but wait, then. Aravon sighed, but he couldn't feel too disappointed. Since leaving Camp Marshal, they hadn't slept a full night through. Now, with the battle won and the threat passed, he and his company—*the Grim Reavers,* he thought, with a chuckle, *what a name!*—could afford to spend the night resting here. Come morning, he'd send Snarl winging off to the Duke with a message. They'd wait here until the Duke sent instructions on how to proceed.

As far as places to wait and rest went, they could be far worse off. The nearby thicket of fir trees provided ample cover for their little camp, as well as wood for their fire and soft boughs to use for a bed. With the warmth of the flames and Snarl's furry body curled up around his legs, Aravon barely felt the night's chill.

The campfire crackled in time with the gentle sound of splashing water. Moonlight gleamed on the little waterfall, dappling the ripples that ran through the small pond formed at the cascade's base. The quiet rushing and the sight of the glittering water brought to mind a fond memory. Long ago, a much younger

Aravon had snuck away with the most beautiful woman in Icespire to enjoy the peaceful beauty of a place much like this.

Thoughts of Mylena filled him with a familiar longing. A longing for home and family, a family he hadn't seen in far too long. He'd grown adept at pushing them out of his mind when the din of battle or the duty of command occupied him, but it was in quiet moments like this that the yearning struck hardest.

He tried to distract himself by studying the people sharing the camp with him. Noll, who lay sprawled in his bedroll, already fast asleep. Zaharis, hunched over one of the Secret Keeper books he carried everywhere he went. Rangvaldr, lying with his back turned to the fire, doubtless trying to rest before his midnight watch.

Aravon's brow furrowed as he studied Belthar. The big man's fingers toyed with the leather thong wrapped around his wrist, yet his gaze drifted time and again to Skathi, who sat opposite him, fletching the arrows she'd spent the evening preparing. Aravon had seen the look in Belthar's eyes far too many times—the man was moonstruck.

I'll have to have a talk with him. Skathi would set Belthar straight should the big man cross any lines—the archer could more than handle her own problems—but Aravon wanted to be certain it never came to that. Such things could interfere with the cohesion and solidarity of their company. Given the challenges they had faced thus far, they'd need to be strong, their unity as solid as the towering Icespire itself.

Belthar had drawn the last watch of the night, so Aravon would use the time alone for a private conversation. After seeing the reaction to Colborn and Zaharis' words, perhaps Belthar would be willing to open up. If not to the entire company, then at least to Aravon.

But not yet. Aravon yawned, his eyelids drooping. *Not until after a few hours of rest.*

Snarl gave a little whine as Aravon's movements disturbed his comfortable resting place. Yet he was more than content to snuggle under the blankets with Aravon, curling his furry body against Aravon's chest.

Closing his eyes, Aravon allowed the emotions of the day and the worries for what lay next drain from his mind. His muscles seemed to uncoil, the knots relaxing and the tension within him uncurling. Snarl's warmth and the sound of his breathing comforted Aravon, lulling him into a deep, peaceful sleep.

Snarl's movement snapped Aravon awake. Even as the little Enfield leapt to his feet, Aravon was reaching for his spear. Years as a soldier had trained him to sleep light; he was awake and alert the moment his eyes snapped open.

Cool, silent darkness hung like a blanket over their campsite. The fire had died to glowing embers, the faint light barely illuminating the five forms sleeping in their bedrolls. Save for the quiet, merry splashing of the waterfall, no sound met Aravon's keen ears. The shadows of the night were deep, with the moon already disappeared behind the western horizon and a thin cloud of fog blurring the glow of the stars above.

Yet Snarl was fully on the alert, his wings outstretched as if to leap into flight, his gleaming amber eyes locked on the sky to the east.

Then Aravon heard it: the quiet *flap* of wings, a rustling of feathers so quiet it seemed barely more than a trick of the wind.

A dark shape dropped out of the sky and landed lightly on the grass ten feet from Aravon. Another Enfield, with a thicker body, darker orange fur, and wings with lustrous golden feathers that extended nearly twice Snarl's wingspan. Skyclaw, Duke Dyrund's personal Enfield.

With a delighted *yip,* Snarl raced toward Skyclaw, greeting him with happy barks and racing around the older Enfield. Skyclaw, however, ignored Snarl. Instead, he padded toward Aravon and sat on his haunches, wings curling up around his dark orange-furred body. He barked, deeper and throatier than Snarl's youthful yaps, and lifted his head to show Aravon his collar and the attached steel message tube.

Aravon hurried to open the tube and extract the rolled-up parchment within. The note, scrawled in Lord Eidan's handwriting, was succinct. *"Meet the Duke at Deepwater, second mile marker north, in three days. His mission promises to turn the tide of the war."*

Chapter Thirty-Two

What could possibly bring the Duke south of the Chain once more so soon after Bjornstadt? Three days and nearly four hundred miles of riding hadn't offered Aravon an answer to the nagging question. *And to the western arena, of all places?*

As the Prince's foremost political councilor, Duke Dyrund's place was in Icespire, or in his home duchy of Eastfall. Doubtless he had a myriad of matters to attend to in the Princelands. Which could only mean something of *monumental* importance drew him south.

Yet what that "something" was had escaped Aravon, though certainly not for lack of trying.

Since the moment he relayed the Duke's message to his company, they'd indulged their imaginations and come up with a wild range of theories. Noll maintained that Duke Dyrund wanted to personally lead the army marching south to break the siege at The Bulwark. Belthar, with his usual rock-solid stubbornness, insisted that the Duke had a secret mission to head up an assault on Snowpass Keep, deep in enemy-held territory. Skathi maintained that Duke Dyrund was traveling to solidify their alliance with the Deid, an opinion shared by Colborn. Zaharis had offered no speculation, saying only, *"He'll let us know when we need to know."*

Aravon shared Rangvaldr's suspicion that the Duke intended a visit to the Fjall. A conversation he'd had with Duke Dyrund echoed in his thoughts. *"If the Eirdkilrs refuse to speak of peace, we must drive them out of Fehl once and for all. And the only way to do that is if all the clans join us. The key, my boy, is the Hilmir."*

Eirik Throrsson, Chief of the Fjall, had taken advantage of the fact that his clan was the largest and most powerful on Fehl, adopting the title of Hilmir.

The appellation—a Fehlan equivalent to "great King"—had not been used on Fehl since the first Einari invaded and defeated the clans north of the Sawtooth Mountains. Yet, if Throrsson had claimed the title, it meant he'd gained enough confidence to assert his dominance—not only over the Deid to the north and the Bein to the south, but perhaps even over the Eirdkilrs invading his homeland.

If the Duke can actually manage to get Throrsson on our side, we've got a shot at this!

A faint hope had blossomed within Aravon's chest over the last few hundred miles, and he'd nurtured it silently. Little else could matter enough to cause the Duke to risk his life.

Aravon gripped his reins tighter, leaned lower over his horse's mane. The Duke's failure at Bjornstadt notwithstanding, he was the one best-suited to represent Prince Toran in any negotiations with the Fjall. *If anyone can talk some sense into the Hilmir, it's him.*

With the Fjall marching beside the Legionnaires, there was a real chance the combined armies could push the Eirdkilrs back across the Sawtooth Mountains. Peace could once again return to northern Fehl.

With the *Kostarasar* chargers riding hard, the miles seemed to flash by. This far south of the Chain—nearly one hundred and twenty miles—the terrain bordering the Westmarch had transformed from Smida-held grasslands and hills to the thicker forests of the Deid clan. To the west, the Standelfr carved a glistening ribbon of blue through miles of greens and browns as it snaked its way through the land on its way downriver toward Rivergate, Bridgekeep, and the Frozen Sea beyond. To the east, legions of alders and birch trees stood solemn vigil beside the stone-paved highway. Towering cypresses and willowy, drooping sallows were interspersed with maples of vivid red, orange, and yellow.

Overhead, the sky sparkled a brilliant blue with only the occasional hint of lazy white clouds, the sun beaming golden warmth down on Aravon and his men. The dazzling brilliance of the day only added to the sense of impending excitement growing within Aravon.

His men seemed to sense it as well. Though he knew *all* were exhausted—they'd ridden hard to cover nearly four hundred miles in three days—there was no trace of fatigue in their postures, the wariness in their eyes. They, too, knew the importance of whatever the Duke had summoned them for.

240

The bond between them had grown stronger over the last few days of travel as well. At night when they made camp, they appeared more relaxed, the conversation coming with greater ease. In the wake of the battle at Rivergate, Rangvaldr had assimilated among the others so quickly that even Noll seemed to have forgotten his initial suspicions.

There had been a noticeable wariness among them all as they crossed Silverhill, the Lightmoor city through which the Westmarch ran. Every one of them had cast darting glances, heads on a swivel, doubtless searching the shadows for hidden Secret Keepers. And Noll had made it a point to procure a bottle of brandy and offer it to Colborn with true Noll theatrics—earning a scowl and the midnight watch as a reward.

Yet now, as they approached the mile marker where they were to meet the Duke, all trace of playfulness and leisure faded. Only grim determination and steel-eyed resolve remained. A serious group of professional, highly-trained soldiers off on a mission for their commander.

Aravon's brow furrowed as they reached the stone mile marker as instructed. Two miles south, the solid sharpened palisade walls of Deepwater rose high in the sky. Yet the Westmarch was empty, with no sign of the Duke. No men or horses moved through the broad-leafed poplars bordering the highway.

Aravon signed silent orders to his men. "*Colborn, Noll, spread out and—*"

A high, piercing whistle echoed from the thick forest to the east. Aravon's head snapped toward the sound, his eyes narrowing as he scanned the dense trees. Nothing but smooth white tree trunks and a thick wall of broad, dark leaves.

"High in that big cottonwood," Colborn muttered beside him. "Fifty yards south."

Aravon lifted his gaze toward the tree the Lieutenant had singled out. "You sure?" Colborn's eyes had to be better than his, for he could see nothing.

"He's there, and he's good." Colborn's voice was quiet. "Fehlan good."

Aravon's mask hid his surprise. The Lieutenant had learned woodcraft and tracking from the Fehlans, and his skills far surpassed any of theirs. Coming from him, those words were the highest form of compliment.

Just then, a hint of movement flashed through the forest. So quickly Aravon nearly missed it, had he not been looking right at the tree. Slowly, as his eyes adapted to the colors of the forest, he caught sight of a leaf-and-branch covered shape slithering down the trunk of the cottonwood. The man wore the same Fehlan camouflage Skathi and her archers had used to approach Rivergate Bridge.

Noll whistled. "Good thing he's on our side." He paused, then, "He *is* on our side, right?"

"If he was Eirdkilr," Skathi told him, "you'd already be dodging arrows."

The bright, sunny day seemed to grow suddenly chilly at the words. A memory flashed through Aravon's mind: *the thrum of a hundred bowstrings, a hail of arrows streaking from the thick trees bordering the Eastmarch road.* Acid churned in his gut, and he swallowed hard to force it down. He and his men of Sixth Company had spotted the Eirdkilr ambush too late.

"We're too far north," Colborn said. "And too close to Deepwater for them to risk it."

Not long ago, Aravon might have accepted that statement as given fact. "Then again, after Rivergate, we can't be certain of anything."

Colborn grunted agreement. The Eirdkilr-led Jokull assault on Rivergate was just one more indication that the enemy could and would strike in unpredictable locations. *Fiery hell, they're even laying siege to Dagger Garrison and The Bulwark!*

"Eyes peeled, weapons loose," Aravon said. He rested a casual hand on the spear strapped next to his saddle. Given the Duke's instructions, he could be fairly certain the man ahead was friendly, but the days of taking such things for granted were long past.

"Aye, Captain." Wood *clacked* quietly against wood as Skathi slid an arrow into ready position across her bow.

The branch-covered figure appeared from the woods and strode toward them, arms spread wide to reveal empty hands.

"The Duke's expecting you," the man called. Though thick leaves and sturdy branches concealed his face, his voice rang with calm confidence and he spoke with the unmistakable accent of Icespire. "This way."

Aravon shot a questioning glance at Colborn, who answered with a shrug as if to say, "*Who else could it be?*" After only a moment's hesitation, Aravon nudged his huge horse forward and rode off the Westmarch, across the thirty-yard stretch of cleared ground bordering the highway.

Before they crossed half the distance to the forest, the man turned and slipped back through the forest. Between the Fehlan camouflage and the dense undergrowth of the forest, Aravon found it difficult to track the man's movements.

"Colborn, sharp eyes in the lead," he called.

"Aye, Captain." Colborn spurred his horse faster, riding in front of Aravon and slowing to match his pace.

The horses pushed through a thick wall of forest ferns without hesitation, but soon the tall poplars gave way to low-hanging cottonwoods and willows, forcing all but the diminutive Noll to duck to avoid the branches. Though Aravon couldn't see the man, he followed Colborn, who rode with confidence. He trusted the Lieutenant to guide him aright.

Less than three minutes of riding from the road, they broke into a small clearing. The low-hanging willow branches had provided such excellent cover Aravon didn't spot the figures sitting around the cleared space until he was nearly on top of them. Colborn's quick hand signal barely warned him in time to rein in.

Ten men sat in the clearing. Eight had the hard eyes, grizzled faces, and broad shoulders of men accustomed to battle. They wore mottled brown robes, fur cloaks, and leather armor, but the lack of insignia or distinctive ornamentation marked them as hired swords.

Aravon narrowed his eyes. *Mercenaries?*

The ninth man in the clearing rose as they entered. "Ah, Captain Snarl." A broad smile split the Duke's face—delight at seeing them or amusement at the codename, Aravon couldn't tell. "Just in time."

"You called, sir." Aravon dismounted and, doing his best to ignore the aches of too many hours spent in the saddle, marched over to the Duke. "Here we are."

"I'd pretend surprise," the Duke said, clasping Aravon's forearm, "but those are my horses you're riding. I trust you've taken care of them?"

"Better than we've taken care of ourselves, sir." Aravon couldn't help relaxing around the Duke. Despite his position and the responsibilities that had to weigh on him, Duke Dyrund had an easygoing nature. Aravon had always felt comfortable when in the Duke's presence—something he *couldn't* say for his own father.

The Duke had been General Traighan's best friend during their days in the Legion, but they couldn't have been more opposite. For as long as Aravon had known him, Duke Dyrund had been the sunshine to the General's gloom, the smile to Traighan's frown. Stern and authoritative were good characteristics for a military commander, but Duke Dyrund's welcoming, empathetic nature made him a perfect choice to serve Prince Toran in more political endeavors.

Duke Dyrund beamed at Aravon's six companions as they dismounted and took up positions behind Aravon in silence. "Glad to see you all made it through in one piece. According to reports, it was a close thing."

"Never doubt Legionnaires, sir," Colborn said. "Especially those fighting for their homes and families."

"Indeed." The Duke's smile cracked slightly as he turned to the ninth man, who had remained seated. "Allow me to introduce you to Lord Myron Virinus of Icespire."

Lord Virinus rose to his feet and strode toward them. "Captain Snarl." The man's voice had a distinctly nasal quality, barely above a perpetual whine. He thrust out a hand to Aravon. "If even half of what I've heard about you and your men is true, it's an honor to ride beside you."

Aravon met the nobleman's eyes, blue and cold as Frozen Sea ice, without hesitation and returned the grip. "My lord."

Virinus had a face far too narrow and angular for the ears protruding from the messy brown hair that hung lank down to his shoulders. His fur cloak had once been the pelt of a brown bear, and its voluminous mass made his slim build appear slight. At his hip hung a long, slim sword of the style popular among Voramian and Praamian fencers, its hilt gilded and far too ornate to be more than decorative. Then again, the scabbard showed some signs of wear.

The name Virinus was familiar to him. Lord Aleron Virinus numbered among Icespire's wealthiest noblemen, and Myron was his second oldest of five sons. His presence here confused Aravon, but he let no trace of that puzzlement show on his face, mask or no.

"Scathan, take Barcus, Torin, and Urniss and see to the horses," the Duke ordered. "As soon as I've filled Captain Snarl in on our mission, we move out."

"Sir." The man who responded was tall, with a dark brown beard cropped close to his face, hair that hung in a long tail down his back, and eyes the same color. He had the appearance and accent of an Eastfallian—Aravon would place him as a man of Eastbay, the easternmost fortress in the Chain. Turning, he and

244

the three other men named hurried toward the horses, which stood placidly munching forest grass and fallen leaves a few yards east of the small clearing.

"Captain." Duke Dyrund gestured for Aravon to take a seat, a gesture that included the rest of Aravon's men. Sitting, Aravon leaned forward, nervous anticipation tying his stomach in knots as the Duke drew a canvas map from within a nearby pack and unrolled it across the springy grass.

"We are here, just under a hundred miles south of the Chain." Duke Dyrund tapped a finger above the black-inked square marking Deepwater's position on the map. "Our journey leads us here."

Aravon's heart leapt as the Duke's finger slid southward along the Westmarch, to the vast wildlands of the Fjall. "Five days ago," Duke Dyrund said, "I received word from Storbjarg. The Hilmir's ready to talk."

A smile broadened Aravon's face beneath his mask, and he exchanged an excited look with Rangvaldr. They'd been right.

"The Fjall have grown tired of the Eirdkilrs running wild on their lands," the Duke continued, looking up from the map. "Eirik Throrsson will hear what the Princelands have to say, and decide if our offer is worth entertaining. Which, if you read the meaning beneath the message and the fact that he reached out to us, means he's seriously considering throwing his lot in with the Legion."

Aravon cocked his head. "Desperation, from the Fjall?" He frowned. "Given the size of their warband, shouldn't they be playing it a bit more coy?"

"Yes." Duke Dyrund nodded his head. "But they think we don't know about the Wraithfever."

Aravon had never heard of it, but Zaharis stiffened, wincing beneath his mask. "*Wraithfever?*" he signed to the Secret Keeper.

"*An ancient malady, one long ago eradicated from Einan,*" Zaharis responded, his eyes darkening. "*Far worse than the Bloody Flux or anything we've seen in the Princelands as far back as anyone can remember. And, one with no known cure.*"

"Not according to the High Ministrant of Wolfden Castle." Duke Dyrund's lips quirked into a knowing smile. "Let's just say it's not the first time we've heard of its presence on Fehl. The problem is one the Prince has had certain people working on for a few years in anticipation of its return."

Even with the mask hiding his features, Zaharis' surprise was evident. "*Impossible!*" he signed.

"That was the original belief." Duke Dyrund shot Zaharis a knowing smile. "Until a Secret Keeper stumbled across a particularly potent plant with a foul-smelling root."

Zaharis sucked in a breath. *"You mean—"*

"Yes." The Duke nodded. "Your discovery of Fetidroot was the key. When combined with other ingredients suggested by the Ministrants of the Bright Lady and the Bloody Minstrel's Trouveres, it not only slowed the fever, it cured it altogether." He pulled a bottle from within his cloak. "And this will be the proof of it."

Zaharis' eyes widened, his gaze locked on the glass bottle and the dark red liquid swirling within.

"This is what we bring to the table for the Hilmir." Duke Dyrund's smile widened. "Not just an alliance against a common enemy, but a hope for saving his people. According to the reports I've gathered, Wraithfever has already laid low more than fifteen thousand Fjall. Including three thousand of the Hilmir's warband."

Now it was Aravon's turn to suck in a sharp breath. "Three *thousand?"*

The Duke nodded, his expression growing grave. "And hundreds more falling ill with every passing week. If nothing is done to stop the illness, the Fjall will weaken until they are too decimated to hold off the Eirdkilrs. They, once the strongest clan among the Fehlans, will be the first crushed beneath the enemy's boot."

The gravity of that statement struck Aravon like a physical blow. The Fjall had served as an example of Fehlan resistance to Eirdkilr dominance for more than a hundred years—since the Battle of Vigvollr, bloodiest clash in Fehlan history. There, near the Fjall capital of Storbjarg, ten thousand of the Fjall warband stood against twelve thousand Eirdkilrs. Fifteen thousand warriors had fallen on both sides and though the outcome favored the Eirdkilrs, the Fjall survivors had remained numerous enough to give the southerners pause. Nothing but a tenuous peace and the threat of the Fjall warband—returned to its original strength of ten thousand—kept the Eirdkilrs at bay.

But with three thousand dead and more fallen ill, the Fjall are weak, vulnerable to Eirdkilr attack. It would be a simple matter for the Eirdkilrs to break off their sieges of the Bulwark and Dagger Garrison, and they'd be numerous enough to launch an attack on the debilitated Fjall. *And if the Fjall crumble, so will every other clan. Even our allies among the Deid and Jarnleikr will have no choice but to side with the*

246

Eirdkilrs or else face destruction. The war would be over, and the Eirdkilrs would drive the Princelanders north behind the Chain—and, if they had their way, back across the Frozen Sea.

Aravon's fists clenched. "Then we ride, and hard, sir." He stood, determination echoing in his voice. "If getting this to the Fjall is enough to convince them to join us, then by the Swordsman, we'll reach Storbjarg, even if we have to fight through every Eirdkilr on Fehl."

Chapter Thirty-Three

"Duke Dyrund, a word?" Aravon signed.

Raising a curious eyebrow, Duke Dyrund indicated the woods beside them with a thrust of his chin. In silence, Aravon followed the Duke deeper into the forest until two thick walnut trees hid them from view of the camp.

The Duke turned to face him, his fingers flashing in the silent hand language. *"Speak your mind, Aravon."*

"You know how deadly Wraithfever is, Your Grace, and yet we're riding toward *it?"*

The Duke's lips quirked into a smile. Clearly he'd expected the question. *"The Ministrants and Trouveres swear that the fever is only contracted when someone comes in direct contact with the death miasma of those infected."* He shrugged. *"I'm assured that if we steer clear of anyone too close to the Long Keeper's arms, we have nothing to fear."*

Aravon grimaced. *"Still, sir—"*

Duke Dyrund held up a hand. *"It's a risk, I know. But one worth taking if it sways the Fjall to our cause."*

Much as he wanted to, Aravon couldn't argue with that logic. He made a mental note to tell his soldiers to steer well clear of wherever the Fjall kept their ill. He'd have to have a conversation with Rangvaldr, most of all. The Seiomenn would doubtless want to minister to the sick and dying, just as he had in Bjornstadt. His prayers for the fallen Jokull spoke to his character—he might be willing to put himself in the plague's reach if it eased the pain and suffering of those afflicted. The Duke might have eased his first concern, but he had a few more to raise.

"And mercenaries, sir?" Aravon cocked his head. "And Lord Virinus? Not that I've cause to doubt Your Grace, but—"

"But you're doubting anyway." A wry smile twisted the Duke's lips. "And for good reason, given the danger we face."

Aravon nodded, but his fingers remained silent.

Duke Dyrund's smile faded into a tired frown. "After what happened in Bjornstadt with Syvup, Astyn, Farrell, and Rendar, I found myself in need of men I could trust to keep my secrets. Lord Eidan suggested these men. It seems they have served the House of Eidan faithfully for years." He grimaced and scrubbed a hand over his face. "Much as I would rather have men of Wolfden Castle or even Hightower by my side, my forces are stretched too thin. The recent attack on Rivergate has given me reason to suspect the Eirdkilr assault may soon strike closer to home. Duke Olivarr isn't the only one scrambling to send his men to man his southern borders. Just as he had to pull men from the Westhaven fleet to reinforce Rivergate and Bridgekeep, I've been forced to strip Wolfden Castle's garrison as bare as I could risk it. It's the only way to have enough reinforcements to send to Eastbay, Lochton, and Hightower, just in case."

"Can they be trusted?" Aravon narrowed his eyes. "To guard your secrets and to faithfully watch your back?"

"According to Lord Eidan, yes." The Duke shrugged. "My aide thoroughly researched these men—sellswords of the Black Xiphos—and swears they have no idea who you and your company are."

"Which means even if they saw our faces, they could not reveal our identities." Aravon glanced through the trees in the direction of the clearing. The mercenaries moved with the calm confidence of men who knew their business. The leather wraps on their hilts were faded from use, their leather armor maintained yet clearly well-worn. They had the look of professional sellswords and two of them, including the man Scathan, emanated the certainty of a Legionnaire. He turned back to the Duke. "And the fact that they're for hire?"

"The Black Xiphos has been paid enough to assure their silence and loyalty. They are all men of Westhaven, I'm told, but the fact that they are mercenaries and thus have no direct connection to me gives us a better chance of evading suspicion. After all, if our enemies somehow discovered my presence and my reasons to travel to Fjall, I have little doubt they would make it a high priority to find and capture me."

Aravon chuckled. "Such modesty, Your Grace."

"Indeed." Duke Dyrund's expression grew strained. "Reluctant as I am to rely on the services of mercenaries, let us call this the best worst situation." His jaw muscles worked as he continued in the silent hand language. *"But I trust you and your company implicitly. I would have no one else by my side, watching my back on this dangerous mission."*

The unspoken meaning was clear: Duke Dyrund needed Aravon to not only keep an eye on the Fjall or watch for Eirdkilrs, but to pay close attention to the mercenaries. No matter how much Lord Eidan insisted otherwise, the Duke had to be certain the men around him were trustworthy.

"Understood, sir." Aravon straightened. *"We'll keep our eyes open and our swords ready."*

"I've come to expect no less." Duke Dyrund clapped him on the shoulder.

"And Lord Virinus?" Aravon cocked his head. *"The second son of an Icespire nobleman isn't exactly the man I'd imagine you bringing on a secret mission to the Fjall."*

"Princeland politics at its most delightful." The Duke's mouth twisted into a grimace. *"When old Aleron tells the Prince that he wants his son to study diplomacy—a way of getting his second son out from underfoot as he passes the family mining business on to Gravis—Prince Toran has no choice but to think long and hard about how he's going to answer the request from the Princelands' wealthiest family and biggest contributor to the war effort."*

Aravon shot a glance at Lord Virinus. *"Not an ideal answer, is it?"* He'd never met the second oldest son of House Virinus, but he hadn't exactly heard the man's praises sung through the streets of Icespire. All the nobility knew of the clever, business-minded Gravis Virinus, but Myron had remained in relative obscurity in his older brother's shadow. Perhaps *this* was the nobleman's means of making his own mark. Playing a part in the negotiation and, by the Swordsman's grace, ultimate peace treaty with the Fjall would be a golden feather in a cap that had, until now, remained featherless.

"I've made it clear that he's to be seen and not heard," Duke Dyrund continued. *"Especially when it comes to negotiations with the Hilmir. Everything I've heard about Throrsson leads me to believe he's a man of fire and passion, far more warrior than statesman. But, if Lord Virinus is content to listen and observe, he may come away from this experience a far wiser man."*

"Let us hope he has wisdom enough now to know his place." Aravon clenched his jaw. *"We can't afford any dead weight, not so close to enemy territory."*

"Every man on this journey will stand watch, share in his load of the camp duties, and pitch in." Duke Dyrund's lips tugged into a smile just short of sardonic. *"Thus far,*

he's proved an…adequate traveling companion. Not more than a dozen complaints about the lack of comforts or the long hours of travel."

"The Swordsman is often merciful." Aravon chuckled.

The Duke grinned, but his expression sobered quickly. *"I know this isn't ideal, Aravon. Truth be told, Lord Eidan and I had no choice but to throw this together at the last minute. I had no time to protest the Prince's request for Lord Virinus to come with me because I knew the threat that Wraithfever poses to the Fjall's might. The sooner we reach them and make peace, the more of the Hilmir's people we will be able to save."*

"Not just his people, but his warriors," Aravon replied. *"Warriors that can help us push back the Eirdkilrs."*

"Precisely." Duke Dyrund nodded. *"Skyclaw had already winged off toward Wolfden Castle before I rode out of Icespire. By the time we reach Storbjarg, the Ministrants, Secret Keepers, and Trouveres will have large quantities of the Wraithfever cure ready to deliver, loaded onto wagons prepared to depart the moment I send word that the treaty has been signed."*

Aravon's eyebrows rose. *"Swordsman's teeth, you've thought of it all!"*

The Duke grinned. *"I've been working at the Fjall for years, Aravon. They are the key to restoring peace to Fehl and driving out the Eirdkilrs. There's no chance in the fiery hell that I'll let an opportunity like this pass us by."* He winked. *"It's no accident that Throrsson learned of a potential cure for Wraithfever among the Princelands. I had people whispering it among the Fjall clans weeks before I actually discovered it."*

Surprise coursed through Aravon. That was precisely the sort of forethought and tactical thinking that made the Duke an invaluable member of the Prince's Council. A military mind like Aravon's—or minds like Generals Traighan, Vessach, and Tinian—were unlikely to conceive of such stratagems. They saw only the military, the ebb and flow of battle, the movement of soldiers on both sides of the war. It took a man like Duke Dyrund to think beyond the shield wall and Legion garrisons.

"Speaking of whisperers," the Duke said, *"I trust the meeting with my agent in Rivergate went well?"* His fingers toyed with the heavy signet ring on his left hand—the ring of his office as Duke of Eastfall.

Aravon's brow furrowed and he shook his head. *"The man never showed up."* He drew out the scrap of parchment and crimson wax and handed it to the Duke. *"But Noll found this at a dead drop."*

Duke Dyrund's eyes narrowed as he took the seal. *"I don't recognize the insignia, though I feel as if I've seen it somewhere before."* His lips pursed into a frown as

252

he looked from the imprinted wax to Aravon. *"And you said my man didn't show up? That's not like him at all."*

"Turath, the tavernkeeper?" Aravon asked.

The Duke nodded, then seemed surprised. *"If he never showed up, how did you kn—"*

"Noll did some digging," Aravon replied. *"Found out that Turath died during the siege of Rivergate."*

The Duke's fingers flashed a series of sharp, harsh gestures that Aravon didn't understand—though the vitriol in the signed expletives was clear.

"Lost his wife and children to the enemy." Aravon shot the Duke a meaningful look. *"Which was why no one thought it suspicious when he threw himself off the parapet, when no one was looking. After stabbing himself fatally in the side with a dagger."*

The Duke's eyes widened. *"Murdered?"*

Aravon inclined his head. *"That's our belief. We didn't have a chance to find out more. Things in Rivergate got...complicated."*

Duke Dyrund cocked his head. *"Explain."*

"Ask Zaharis." It wasn't Aravon's place to share the man's secrets, though he suspected the Duke already knew the full truth behind Zaharis' eviction from the Temple of Whispers.

The Duke nodded, understanding written in his eyes. *"The fact that you had only three days to get here also had to factor into it."* He tugged at his white-dusted brown beard. *"If you'll lend me Snarl, I'll send a message off to Lord Eidan, let him know about Turath. He's got another agent in Westhaven who can dig around a bit, find out what happened."* He tucked the wax seal away and, after a moment's thought, removed his signet ring and added it into his pouch as well. *"I'll look into the matter personally when I return to Icespire."*

"Of course, sir." Aravon reached for his bone whistle. *"After the last few days, I'm sure Snarl's eager to have something to do."*

The little Enfield was circling high overhead, close enough to come when Aravon called yet following orders to stay out of sight. After recovering from his exhaustion, Snarl had become his over-energetic self once more. With his eagle's wings, he'd had no trouble keeping pace with the horses, and his exuberance had proven a lot for Aravon at the end of a long day of riding. It would do the Enfield good to put that energy to use.

Drawing out the whistle that hung around his neck, Aravon blew a short, sharp blast to summon the Enfield. Within a few seconds, a bright orange shape streaked through the canopy and dropped toward Aravon. Snarl's wings snapped out at the last moment to slow his descent, yet he still crashed into Aravon with bruising force. The little fox-creature hadn't yet mastered the landing, and Aravon's chest would continue to suffer until he did.

Aravon set Snarl down on the ground and straightened, catching his breath. Snarl gave a happy *yip* and trotted around Aravon's legs, shaking the feathers of his wings, his vulpine face breaking into a broad smile.

The Duke studied the Enfield with a grin of his own. *"He's getting bigger. Soon enough he'll be properly grown into his wings."*

"Yes, sir." Aravon gave the Duke a little bow. *"I'll give you a moment to pen your message, and I'll make sure everything is in readiness for our journey."*

Duke Dyrund gave no answer, for he had already drawn out a strip of parchment and a charcoal writing stick and begun scribbling his note to Lord Eidan.

As Aravon returned to the clearing, he found the mercenaries had packed up their camp and made ready to ride. Eight of the men sat in their saddles, and the ninth was just finishing stripping out of his Fehlan branch camouflage. Lord Virinus had also mounted up and now sat beside Aravon's men, who hadn't dismounted through the entire exchange. All but Colborn, who stood holding the reins to Aravon's horse.

"Explanation?" Colborn's fingers flashed as Aravon approached, and his eyes darted toward the mercenaries and the Icespire nobleman.

"Not ideal," Aravon replied, *"but no other choice. I'll fill you all in later."*

With a little shrug, Colborn handed the reins to Aravon and climbed into his own saddle.

A quiet flapping of wings echoed from behind Aravon as he mounted up. He turned in time to catch a fleeting glimpse of bright orange fur before Snarl was lost in the thick canopy.

Watch over him, Aravon prayed to the Swordsman. *And bring him back safe.* Snarl had become a part of his company as much as any of the others riding beside him.

Duke Dyrund emerged from the trees a moment later, hurrying toward them and taking his own seat atop his horse, a compact, heavily-muscled

Kostarasar charger. Turning to Aravon, he flashed the silent hand signal to move out.

With a nod, Aravon relayed the order to his own men. "Go."

Noll and Colborn kicked their horses into motion. Within the space of a minute, they disappeared among the dense forests.

Now Duke Dyrund glanced at Lord Virinus and the mercenaries. "You all know your positions, your roles to play in our mission. We ride, for Prince Toran, and for peace on Fehl."

Simple words, yet it was all that needed saying. Long miles separated them from their destination, but Aravon felt a surge of hope that, at the end of this journey, they truly *would* have hope that the Duke's dream of peace would become reality.

* * *

Aravon leaned back against the magnolia tree trunk and closed his eyes, grateful for a few hours of rest. One more long day of riding after so many others had taken a toll on his muscles. Thankfully, he'd mostly healed from wounds sustained in battle at Bjornstadt and Rivergate, though a dull ache still radiated through his chest.

The sounds of their small camp broke the peaceful silence of the forest around him. Mercenaries laughed, carried on quiet conversations, sharpened weapons, or tended the pot hanging over the fire. Lord Virinus had gone off a few minutes earlier to tend to the horses, and the Duke had taken Zaharis into the forest for a silent conversation—likely about the events of Rivergate.

The others of Aravon's company were silent, each absorbed in their own task. Colborn had drawn the first watch, and now stood somewhere among the trees near their camp. Rangvaldr sat with his eyes closed, likely in prayer to Nuius, his hand clasped around the pendant at his neck. Skathi had taken up the evidently eternal task of making arrows, and Belthar fumbled his way through whittling a long, straight branch to make an extra bolt for his crossbow.

They appeared relaxed, yet Aravon knew they were as alert as he. One sound out of place in the forest, one *crack* of a twig trod underfoot, and they'd be armed and ready. This far south of the Chain, enemies could lurk behind every tree.

Their route to reach Fjall lands only made the chance of stumbling across enemies even greater. On Duke Dyrund's orders, they had kept to the smaller trade trails and hunting paths through the Deid lands. Though the Westmarch would have been the faster, more direct route south, the recent Eirdkilr attacks—on both Rivergate far to the north and Dagger Garrison and the Bulwark—necessitated greater caution. They couldn't risk being caught on the highway by Eirdkilrs planning an ambush on the Legion. Out here in the Fehlan wilds, with Noll and Colborn riding scout, they had the best chance of covering ground unseen.

However, that meant speed was sacrificed in the name of stealth. The smaller back ways through the woods often meandered, following the path of game, the dips and rises in the terrain, or the banks of rivers and streams. When the trails turned east or west, their small company had no choice but to cut straight south through the dense trees and bushes of the Deid lands. They couldn't push the horses beyond a jog trot, and the uneven, unfamiliar terrain forced them to slow their pace.

Aravon did a quick calculation of the distance left to cover. Since passing Deepwater just before noon, they had made good time—close to fifty miles, thanks to one broad, deep-rutted wagon trail that led south, deeper into Deid lands. That left roughly three hundred miles more to cover on their trek to Storbjarg. They'd be lucky to make the journey in fewer than three days—even after they found a way across the Standelfr River, a great deal of forest, hill country, and the vast watery expanse of Cold Lake stood between them and the Fjall lands.

"That's my seat."

The nasal pitch of Lord Virinus' voice snapped Aravon from his thoughts. He lifted his gaze to find the nobleman standing in front of Rangvaldr, hands on his hips.

Rangvaldr looked up. "What's that?"

"My seat." Lord Virinus stabbed a slim finger at the log upon which Rangvaldr sat. "I was sitting here earlier, but left for a few moments to tend to my horse."

"Right." Rangvaldr's flat, toneless voice revealed nothing, his face still covered by his leather greatwolf mask.

Lord Virinus drew himself up. "I demand that you vacate my seat at once."

The *Seiomenn* flashed a questioning glance at Aravon. At Aravon's nod, the Fehlan stood. He towered half a head above Lord Virinus—a fact not lost on the nobleman, who retreated a half-step. Yet Rangvaldr spoke in a calm voice. "Of course."

Lord Virinus seemed to recover, the *Seiomenn's* easy acquiescence bolstering his confidence. "Thank you." His voice held no trace of genuine gratitude, only the icy, courtly courtesy of an Icespire nobleman. Sweeping past Rangvaldr, he bundled his heavy bearskin cloak under himself and took a seat before the fire.

"Serve me a bowl," he demand of Urniss, the Black Xiphos mercenary tending to the fire.

Urniss' jaw clenched but he complied, ladling a small portion of the stew into a wooden bowl and handing it to the nobleman. Lord Virinus sniffed at the food and a grimace twisted his face. With barely concealed disdain, he took the bowl to "his seat" and set about spooning it into his mouth.

Rangvaldr strode around the fire and settled on the ground beside Aravon. "*I didn't think he was serious about that,*" he signed. "*Not the sort of thing I'd expect from someone on a diplomatic mission.*"

Aravon gave a little shrug. "*Far be it from me to speak ill of my land's nobility,*" he replied in the silent hand language. "*Wealth and power have their privileges, but they can twist the minds and hearts of those who wield them.*"

"*Reminds me of Ailmaer.*" Rangvaldr shook his head. "*I left Bjornstadt to get away from men like that.*"

Aravon nodded. "*I'll have a word with the Duke when he gets back from talking with Zaharis.*" He glanced in the direction of the low-hanging willows where the Duke and Secret Keeper had disappeared a few minutes earlier. "*It seems Lord Virinus' lessons in diplomacy will start in earnest long before we reach Storbjarg.*"

"*Good.*" Rangvaldr settled back against the knotted, twisted trunk of the tree behind him. "*Because if he keeps this up, it's going to make our days of travel feel like months.*"

Chapter Thirty-Four

The next day, Lord Virinus' disposition seemed to improve—courtesy of a quiet conversation with Duke Dyrund. At least, he no longer complained about the food. He still carried himself with the hauteur bred into young noblemen, looking at all around him with the silent disdain that sprang from an inflated sense of superiority. Even his words echoed with forced courtesy, politeness that ran only skin-deep.

But as they pushed deeper into Fehlan territory, Aravon had no time to worry about the young nobleman. Such matters were better left up to Duke Dyrund. As long as Lord Virinus didn't interfere with their mission or piss off Aravon's men, he could be as quietly disdainful as he wanted. Aravon and his men learned to give Lord Virinus a wide berth. Easier to avoid the man than have to deal with his unspoken scorn.

The farther south they traveled, the closer they drew to enemy forces. By sundown on their second day of travel, they had nearly reached Saerheim, one of the largest cities in Deid lands. The Deid numbered among the Princelanders' strongest Fehlan allies—a fact the Eirdkilrs had not let go unpunished. Even with the bulk of their forces committed to the siege of Dagger Garrison and the Bulwark—a siege that had left both Eirdkilrs and Legionnaires locked in a stalemate that neither seemed willing or able to break—they still launched regular raids on the Deid lands.

That meant Noll and Colborn had to be particularly cautious as they scouted the way ahead. They rode less than a mile to the southwest and southeast of the main company, alert for any signs of enemies among the Deid lands. The knots in Aravon's shoulders grew tighter with every hour that the two men remained out of sight, yet even when they returned to report or for food and rest, he couldn't stop worrying about Eirdkilrs lurking in the shadows.

Tension hung thick over their small camp, and even the Black Xiphos mercenaries sat in silence, all focused on their tasks—among them, sharpening the short, heavy, black-handled swords that had earned their company its name—and on watching the surrounding forests. All knew the dangers that could lurk in the shadowy woods.

Only the Duke's voice broke the stillness. "Tomorrow, we reach the *Yfir* crossing. That'll put us a few hours north of Saerheim. We'll be well-received by Elder Asmund." He grinned and patted his belly. "I don't know about you, but I could use a night's rest in a proper bed and a good meal."

From the corner of his eye, Aravon caught the sudden tension in Colborn's posture, the rigidity of his spine. He'd reacted the same at mention of the Deid clan, and the shadows in his eyes had darkened the moment they rode into Deid territory.

Until now, Aravon hadn't found an opening to ask Colborn about the Fehlan half of his heritage. The stoic, reserved Lieutenant had revealed a few details of his Princelander father—a man who, it seemed, had inflicted all manner of cruelties on a young Colborn. Yet the only mention of his Fehlan blood had been the night in Rivergate when they'd found him drunk and raving beside a Jokull corpse.

But now, curiosity blazed within Aravon. *Is Saerheim home to Colborn's Fehlan family?* The Lieutenant hadn't spoken of his mother or anything to do with her side of his heritage, except to say that they had treated him the same way his father did, as an outsider, an outcast. *If that's the case, no wonder he has no desire to enter the city.*

"While I'm all for a bed and meal," Aravon said quietly, "perhaps it's best we push past Saerheim." He ran a finger along the Duke's canvas map and tapped the broad blue circle of Cold Lake. "If we rest in Saerheim, we'll have to ride around Cold Lake to continue south. Seems we're better off crossing at *Yfir* and skirting Cold Lake to the west, avoiding the wetlands east of Saerheim. It'll certainly make it quicker to reach Storbjarg, even if that means another night sleeping on the ground."

The Duke's face creased into a frown. "Well, damn. Trust you to use logic and the needs of our mission to talk us out of a few creature comforts."

Aravon inclined his head. "That's why you brought me, Your Grace."

His gaze darted toward Colborn. The Lieutenant had relaxed, the tension leaving his shoulders, but a shadow darkened his ice-blue eyes.

Colborn's mood hadn't improved by the time morning dawned—cold and windy, with a thick bank of fog rolling through the forest. Though the mask covered his face, Aravon could tell the man hadn't rested much. He moved a step slower than usual, his shoulders stooped as if beneath a great weight. But before Aravon had a chance to speak to him, the half-Fehlan rode out of camp, off to scout their path to the southeast.

Noll snapped awake at the sound of Colborn's departure. Leaping to his feet, the little scout hurried to stow his bedroll and gear behind his saddle and mount up. He was still scrubbing sleep from his eyes as his horse disappeared into the forest, heading southwest.

Aravon, tired from the last watch shift of the night, made little conversation as the rest of their small company awoke. The same tense silence from the previous evening hung over the Black Xiphos mercenaries and Lord Virinus. After a quiet breakfast, they broke camp and rode out with little fanfare.

Yet, as the day wore on, the thick bank of mist retreated, pushed back by the warmth and brilliance of the sun. Puffs of lazy white clouds dotted the cerulean sky, and Aravon felt his spirits lifting as the world brightened from dusky gray to a glorious medley of greens and browns. A sense of reverence hung over the old-growth forests of the Deid, a timelessness found in trees that had watched over the land for hundreds, perhaps even thousands of years. There was an ancient beauty here—similar to the shimmering blue surface of Icespire or the glittering diamond-hard ice of the Frozen Sea glaciers—that couldn't be ignored.

They forded the Standelfr at the *Yfir* crossing just after noon, pausing only long enough to refill their waterskins from the fresh, ice-cold flow of the river. Rangvaldr's silent offer of a birch stick to Noll—accompanied by the hand signal for "Hungry?"—brought a smile to Aravon's face. By the time they reached the western shores of Cold Lake, Aravon found his spirits greatly lifted.

Who could possibly feel maudlin in the face of such beauty?

Cold Lake was vast—stretching nearly fifty miles east to west, closer to forty miles north to south—an expanse the color of the purest Twelve Kingdoms' turquoise. The mirrored surface reflected the sunlight with dazzling

261

brilliance, shining so bright Aravon had to shield his eyes. An icy wind rolled off the lake, carrying a crisp scent of clean, fresh water.

Aravon grimaced. *Almost makes me wish I hadn't talked the Duke out of visiting Saerheim.* Saerheim, built on the northern shore of Cold Lake, would doubtless offer views of the sunset and sunrise to rival those of Icespire.

With reluctance, Aravon turned his horse away from the lake, resuming their trek south. They hadn't come for the panorama, no matter how breathtaking.

The trail they followed meandered along the lake's shore, then ascended into the gently-rising hills that bordered it to the west. It was there, among those hills, that the Duke called a halt to make camp for the night an hour after the sun had set.

Their small company spent another evening in silence, and neither Colborn nor Noll returned. Aravon trusted that meant the path ahead was all clear, but he couldn't help worrying about the two scouts. Even Noll's cleverness and skill had its limits, as he'd learned during the fateful ambush on Sixth Company. And if Colborn was too distracted with the burdens that weighed on his soul— burdens that had seemed to grow heavier as they rode into Deid lands—he could find himself in hot water.

When morning dawned and still the two scouts hadn't returned, Aravon found his worries increasing. *"Eyes sharp,"* he signed to his four companions.

"Noll and Colborn not back yet?" Belthar's fingers asked.

Aravon shook his head.

"Probably just ranging far ahead, Captain." Skathi appeared unperturbed. *"All they missed was whatever the fiery hell it was that Torin served last night."*

Aravon grimaced; his stomach hadn't appreciated the watery stew or the chunks of uncooked meat and raw vegetables floating in the lumps of duck fat. For once, he couldn't help agreeing with Lord Virinus' visible, if silent, contempt for the meal.

"I'm sure they're fine." Aravon couldn't quite *feel* the words, but he had to try for the sake of his soldiers. *"All the same, just keep a watch. Never know what's hiding out there."*

"Aye, sir." Belthar caught himself before saluting—Aravon had made it clear that there could be no association with the Legion once they entered Fjall lands—and managed to restrict himself to a nod.

As the sun rose high, dappling the thick tree canopy with its golden brilliance, Aravon kept a close eye on their path for any hint of Colborn and Noll's passage. He doubted he'd see any, not with Colborn's woodsman abilities, which he'd passed on to Noll. Yet he still looked all the same.

An hour before noon, they reached the southern end of Cold Lake. Aravon shot one last glance backward at the turquoise perfection of the lake. One day, when the war was over, he'd bring Mylena here. She'd love the sight of such beauty.

Then he turned away, pushing back the thoughts of his wife and the future he didn't dare dream of. He had the present to focus on. The mission was all that mattered now.

Yet, as he pushed deeper into the woods bordering the lake, he caught sight of a feathered figure speeding across the watery expanse. Turning in his saddle, he craned his neck upward, watching the approaching creature. High in the sky, it flew on eagle's wings, but Aravon caught a flash of orange.

Snarl had returned, and judging by his speed, he carried an important message.

"Your Grace," Aravon called out. When the Duke didn't hear him, Aravon tried again, louder. "Your Grace!"

Now, Duke Dyrund glanced back, then slowed his horse to a walk when Aravon's silent signal caught his eyes.

"*Snarl,*" Aravon signed.

"*Where?*" the Duke asked.

Aravon jerked his head to the east, toward the forest. "*Push on, I'll catch up.*"

Duke Dyrund nodded and turned back to the hunting trail.

Aravon drew in his horse and slowed to a walk, turning toward the dense forest bordering the path. The Black Xiphos mercenaries riding behind him shot curious glances at him as he pulled away from the column, but Skathi and Belthar, riding at the rear, made to follow.

Aravon shook his head. "*It's just Snarl,*" he signed.

With a nod, the two returned to the small column, keeping pace at the rear of the line of riding men.

Aravon pushed his horse off the track and through the dense undergrowth of the hazel trees. Duke Dyrund had insisted on keeping Snarl's existence a secret from Lord Virinus and the sellswords, a decision with which Aravon

263

agreed heartily. After Silver Break Mine and the murder of the Duke's agent at Rivergate, he would take every possible precaution to keep all under his command safe. That included Snarl.

A few dozen yards from the trail, Aravon stopped and dismounted. He glanced over his shoulder and, certain he was out of sight of the column, drew out his bone whistle. A short, sharp blast was all the Enfield needed to locate him.

Snarl swooped toward him, dropping through the thick canopy of the towering hazel trees. His wings snapped out to slow his descent, and this time, he managed to land without slamming into Aravon.

Delight gleamed in the Enfield's amber eyes as he leapt on Aravon with a happy *yip*.

"Hey, good to see you, too!" Aravon laughed, rubbing the creature's furry back. "You were gone a long time."

Icespire and Camp Marshal were both roughly six hundred miles away as the Enfield flew, and Snarl could cover that distance in fewer than ten hours at top speed. Even at his average flying speed, he could have made that journey in under a day. There was only one reason he would have been delayed: Lord Eidan had kept him close at hand to send a message to the Duke.

Sure enough, a piece of parchment lay rolled within Snarl's message tube. Drawing it out, Aravon opened the note and read. The words scrawled on the parchment froze the blood in his veins.

No!

In an instant, Aravon was on the move. He leapt into his saddle and, shouting the command word for Snarl to follow, turned his horse's head back toward the trail. His heels dug into the charger's flank and he rode hard, crashing through the underbrush in his hurry to catch up to the Duke. He didn't care who heard or saw—he had to relay Lord Eidan's message *now*.

Aravon's heart hammered in time with the pounding of his horse's hooves as he galloped up the hunting trail. Mind racing, Aravon bent low over the horse's neck and urged it to greater speed.

Skathi and Belthar whirled as Aravon came pounding up the trail behind them. The Agrotora lowered her bow, but worry sparkled in her eyes.

Aravon thundered past, racing alongside the column and reining in beside the Duke's enormous black charger. "Your Grace, you must see this at once!"

Duke Dyrund reined in his horse and snatched the message from Aravon's outstretched hands. Blood drained from his face as he read Lord Eidan's words. "Impossible!"

Aravon shook his head. "I expected they'd regroup in the marshlands, maybe try another assault on Rivergate. But this…" He grimaced beneath his mask. "That's one hell of a problem, sir."

"What's a problem?" Lord Virinus' nasal voice echoed from his place behind the Duke.

"The Eirdkilrs that attacked with the Jokull were spotted returning south." Duke Dyrund repeated Lord Eidan's message, his tone somber. "They crossed the Westmarch fifty miles south of Hammer Garrison." He crumpled the note in his fist, a snarl twisting his lips. "Two hundred and fifty of the bastards disappeared into Deid lands yesterday."

"Which means they're ahead of our position," Aravon said. "Between us and Storbjarg."

All along the line, mercenaries reached for their weapons, their expressions growing grim. Skathi's grip tightened on her bow and Belthar's on his axe. Zaharis and Rangvaldr's eyes darkened and they exchanged somber glances. Two hundred and fifty Eirdkilrs was a serious threat even to a full Legion battalion, much less a company of fewer than twenty hired swords.

Before anyone could speak, the sound of drumming hoofbeats echoed to the south. Aravon whirled toward the noise, and dread sank like a stone in his gut as he spotted Noll racing up the trail toward them.

Noll pulled up just in front of the head of their column, his fingers flashing before he'd come to a full stop. "Eirdkilr tracks, dead ahead!"

Chapter Thirty-Five

Aravon drew in a sharp breath. Before he could respond, Colborn burst into view around the trail to the southeast. From the way the Lieutenant bent low in the saddle and spurred his horse to a gallop, Aravon knew he'd found tracks as well.

"Which way do the tracks lead?" Aravon's fingers flashed before Colborn reined in.

Colborn didn't lose a beat. *"Northeast from our position, around Cold Lake toward Godahus."*

A fist of iron clenched in Aravon's gut. Godahus was one of the smaller Deid villages, built a short distance from the southeastern edge of Cold Lake. If the Eirdkilrs had penetrated this deep into Deid territory, it could mean they headed for Saerheim, north of the vast lake. The shadow in Colborn's eyes told Aravon the Lieutenant had reached the same grim conclusion.

"How old?" Aravon spoke aloud, for the benefit of the Duke's party. If they were to face a company of Eirdkilrs, best they all knew to be ready for it.

"A day, maybe more." Colborn's tone was grim.

Aravon stifled a curse. *If they passed this way a day ago, we could be too late. Saerheim could already be surrounded, or destroyed.*

Yet that didn't seem quite right. He'd seen no sign of Eirdkilrs around Cold Lake, no indication that Saerheim on the northern shore was under siege. Unless the enemy was preparing to spring a trap, they could have simply gone raiding the smaller village—both for supplies and to send the same message to the Deid that they'd delivered to the Eyrr clan at Oldrsjot.

But it was more than that. According to Lord Eidan's note, the Eirdkilrs had crossed the Westmarch fifty miles south of Hammer Garrison. Their journey from the Jokull lands had led them nearly three hundred miles through hostile lands. Yet there had been no hint of any attacks on Deid villages.

Why would they skirt the Deid west of the Westmarch, only to double back north toward a small Deid village near one of the Deid's largest cities? Are they so hard up for supplies that they'd risk attacking allied clans this close to a Legion stronghold? Hammer Garrison stood fewer than thirty miles from the southwestern shore of Cold Lake.

It made no sense, but the Eirdkilr strategy had been wildly unpredictable of late. *If their assault on Rivergate proves anything, it's that we need to start expecting the unexpected.*

Aravon turned to the Duke. "Your Grace, permission to follow the trail?"

Hesitation flashed across the Duke's face.

"Your mission leads south, Your Grace, and I will send two of my best to guide you." His fingers moved in the silent hand signals for Noll and Rangvaldr to accompany the Duke. "But if the Eirdkilrs are planning an attack on the Deid, we owe it to our allies to help. Even if we're too late to help Godahus, we may be able to summon reinforcements or bring word of warning in time for the Deid warband or the nearest garrison to send troops."

Duke Dyrund growled a curse. "You're right. I've got to get to the meeting with the Hilmir at once, but you and yours can afford a few hours' detour." He raised a warning finger. "I expect you to do nothing but scout and follow. *Find* the enemy, if you can, but only engage if there is no other choice, understood?"

Aravon snapped a Legion salute. "Your Grace." Turning to Belthar, Skathi, and Zaharis, he signed. "*We move out. Follow Colborn!*"

Silent nods met his wordless command, and the three spurred their horses to follow Aravon past the head of the column, toward where Colborn had already begun turning his mount's head to ride back the way he'd come.

"Swordsman be with you!" Duke Dyrund called after them. "Until we meet in Storbjarg!"

Whenever that will be, Aravon thought. Last time, he'd gone riding off in pursuit of Eirdkilrs, he'd barely arrived in time to prevent the enemy from killing the Duke. This close to enemy territory, he hated the idea of leaving Duke Dyrund with so few men to guard him. Noll's scouting and Rangvaldr's knowledge of Fehlan woodcraft made them the best choices to guide the Duke to Storbjarg, but even with nine Black Xiphos mercenaries and Lord Virinus, Aravon wouldn't stop worrying until he once again rode at the Duke's side.

Yet now, the matter of the Eirdkilrs demanded his attention. Those two hundred and fifty warriors had traveled a long way from Jokull lands, likely enraged at the loss of their comrades and the recapture of Rivergate. If they *were* headed for Godahus, they would likely be out for blood—allied Fehlan in lieu of Princelander.

Colborn set a fast pace, pushing the *Kostarasar* chargers to the limits of their speed and footing on the muddy hunting path. The specially-bred horses could cover ground far faster than any mounts Aravon had ever encountered, yet it felt as if they moved at a walk. Every thundering hoofbeat tightened the knots straining his spine. Every gust of icy wind rolling off Cold Lake to the north added to the chill running through his veins.

Godahus was close to twenty miles northeast of their current position. They'd reach the village in less than two hours at this pace. But that could be far too late.

Images of Oldrsjot flashed through his mind. *Smoke still rose from the charred debris of the Fehlan longhouses. The fire had melted the wattle and daub walls, leaving only the smoldering beams, like the ribs of a grotesque obsidian monster. In the center of Oldrsjot, shards of marble had been crushed into fine gravel, as if someone had pried up the very stones of the village's main square. The bodies of Eyrr men, women, and even children lay strewn like refuse littering the ground. Their blood turned the boot-churned earth to a crimson mud.*

Horror churned in Aravon's gut. The sight had sickened him, even after a decade and a half of combat and bloodshed. *Is that what we'll find in Godahus? More charred corpses and ruined lives?*

Slowly, one pounding step at a time, they closed the distance to Godahus. Twenty miles became fifteen, then ten. Aravon's gaze darted to the forest looming on either side of the path, searching for enemies. Two hundred and fifty Eirdkilrs out for revenge after their loss at Rivergate. Vengeance they would extract from innocent Deid men, women, and children.

Eight miles. Five. Three miles, then two. Sweat streamed down Aravon's back and his legs ached from the horses' punishing pace. Yet he didn't dare slow, not with the fate of Godahus resting in the balance.

Please let us be in time to do something! The silent prayer to the Swordsman did little to shake loose the knowledge that the Eirdkilrs had likely come and gone hours earlier. Yet, it gave him something to cling to as he raced toward the Deid village.

His gut twisted as he caught the familiar whiff of wood smoke. The same scent that had presaged the utter destruction of Oldrsjot. His heart sank. *We're too late.*

At that moment, they crested a hill and the forest thinned, giving way to a broad swath of cleared land that surrounded a small village.

The village of Godahus was small, barely a dozen longhouses surrounded by a smattering of wooden buildings. Sheep and cows grazed in the hillside, watched by dozing shepherds and barking sheepdogs. Farmers labored in the nearby fields, their wives and children toiling at their sides. Smoke rose from every longhouse—smoke produced by villagers burning wood to smoke meat, cook their meals, and stay warm in the winter chill.

All was peace and calm in Godahus.

Chapter Thirty-Six

Confusion hummed within Aravon's mind. He barely managed to stop his horse as Colborn reined to a sudden halt.

"What in the fiery hell?" Belthar rumbled. "I thought the Eirdkilr tracks led—"

"This way." Colborn had ridden a short distance up another smaller trail that led due north, skirting the village of Godahus entirely.

Something else, something that had nagged at the back of Aravon's mind for the last two hours, made even *less* sense.

"Wait!" he called after Colborn. "This isn't right."

The Lieutenant turned his horse and trotted back to where Aravon, Skathi, Zaharis, and Belthar sat. His eyes narrowed behind his mask. "What are you thinking, Captain?"

"The tracks." Aravon scrunched up his face in thought. "Noll said they led from the south, heading northeast toward Godahus, yes?"

Colborn nodded.

"And how many Eirdkilrs would you say made those tracks?"

"Two to three hundred, easy." Colborn cocked his head.

"But why?" Aravon's brow furrowed. "If they *were* intending to attack Godahus, why did they need so many warriors? And the fact that they left such visible tracks is unlike them."

Colborn seemed to understand the direction of Aravon's thought. "With that many men, it's impossible for even Fehlans and Eirdkilrs to move through the forest undetected. So if it *was* just a supplies raid on Godahus, they'd take a smaller party—small enough that they would leave no trace of their passing."

"Precisely." Aravon let out a long breath. "And, add to that the fact that they bypassed Godahus entirely, it means their attack wasn't a simple raid." He frowned in thought. "Which means…"

He sucked in a breath as Captain Lemaire's words flashed through his mind. *Could it be?* There was only one reason to send so many men to attack a seemingly random target.

"Captain?" Skathi asked. "A silver half-drake for whatever just popped into your head."

"Silver is right!" Aravon whirled toward his four companions. "This many Eirdkilrs so deep in allied Fehlan territory, yet not going for easy pickings like Godahus or attempting an assault on Saerheim. It's like Silver Break Mine all over again!"

Four pairs of eyes widened. "A mine?" Confusion echoed in Colborn's voice. "I've never heard of any Deid-controlled mines this far south."

"Just like you'd never heard of Silver Break Mine," Aravon answered. "Precisely because the Eirdkilrs would try to capture it and cut off the Prince's resources."

The eyes of his comrades darkened. They all knew what awaited them if the Eirdkilrs had passed by here a day earlier. Yet they had no choice but to ride *toward* the danger, toward whatever lay ahead.

"Ride," Aravon told Colborn in a quiet voice. "Guide us to wherever the Eirdkilr tracks lead."

With a solemn nod, Colborn spurred his horse to the north. Aravon followed, but not before shooting a silent glance toward Godahus. The men, women, and children of the Deid village appeared to have no idea the grim fate they'd been narrowly spared. But somewhere ahead, others—Princelanders or Fehlans, Aravon couldn't know yet—had not been so fortunate.

The horses splashed their way across the shallow channel feeding into Cold Lake, up a steep incline, and through dense woodlands, heading northeast. Aravon had no idea where Colborn led them, but he trusted the Lieutenant to follow the Eirdkilr tracks to their destination. Wherever that was, and whatever they'd find.

Fifteen minutes of hard riding turned to twenty, the miles between them and Godahus lengthening as they followed the Eirdkilrs' trail northeast, deeper into the wetlands east of Cold Lake. Aravon's gut tightened as they raced through the thickly-forested lands. If the Eirdkilrs lay in wait, they could be riding into another ambush. The five of them couldn't hope to defeat even a quarter of the enemies that had come this way. Yet Aravon could only tighten his grip on the spear strapped to his saddle and pray that the Swordsman sharpened Colborn's eyes and kept them safe.

Then he saw the thick cloud of crows circling high above the forest. A cloud of gray smoke darkened the afternoon sky, tingeing the air with the stink of burning wood, rope, and canvas.

They were too late.

The smell reached him long before the grisly scene came into view. The stench of death and decay, bodies left to rot beneath the Fehlan sun. Destruction, total and ruthless, with only silence to welcome Aravon and his companions.

The mining camp was laid out much the same as Silver Break Mine, a sea of wooden shelters and canvas tents spread out in an ever-widening circle around the base of a stone-covered hill. Yet these appeared far more permanent. Solid walls of wood and wattle-and-daub, with thatched roofs to keep out the rain and chill. Proper picket lines for the horses and paved stone loading areas for wagons and carts. Only two were visible, empty and abandoned, with no oxen or draft animals in sight. Someone had even painted a sign. "Gold Burrows", it proclaimed in bright yellow letters.

But where Silver Break Mine had been utterly devoid of life, this camp was filled with death. Bodies lay scattered around the camp, skulls crushed in, limbs shattered, flesh carved to gruesome ribbons. Women lay beside their children, arms wrapped protectively around bodies that had been hacked and slashed by Eirdkilr weapons. Men run through by enemy spears, arms and legs sheared through by enormous axes. Charred corpses in a pile of blackened flesh and bone.

The Eirdkilrs had slaughtered them all. The blood of these miners ran thick, turning the ground to a gruesome red-tinged muck.

Aravon's stomach twisted and threatened to disgorge its contents, but he clenched his jaw hard. "*Skathi,*" he signed, "*head east, search for survivors. Zaharis, west. Belthar, guard our backs.*"

The archer and Secret Keeper responded with silent nods and turned to obey Aravon's command. Belthar pulled his horse to a stop and dismounted, his movements slow, burdened by the horror surrounding him. Metal *creaked* as Belthar loaded his crossbow, the sound echoing eerily loud in the utter stillness of the camp.

In grim silence, Aravon rode with Colborn deeper into the sea of burned homes and shattered bodies.

The corpses grew thicker on the ground as they approached the mouth of the mine. Picks, trowels, and shovels lay beside the bodies of men and women who had fought in vain to defend themselves and their loved ones. Carrion birds pecked at unseeing eyes, tore at flesh long ago gone cold, feasted on the silent dead. Naught but the occasional *caw* of a crow or the rustle of the wind whispering in the trees broke the all-encompassing stillness of death.

But the Eirdkilrs hadn't only slain unarmed miners. Before the mouth of the mine, a thick line of fur-clad bodies lay sprawled in the crimson muck. Fehlan shields and swords were scattered among the axes, clubs, and spears of the Eirdkilrs. Colborn's face turned ashen as he studied the fallen warriors.

"Deid?" Aravon asked.

Colborn nodded mutely.

Aravon hesitated a moment. "Did you…know any of them?"

Colborn turned toward him, eyes gaunt, hollow. After a long moment, he shook his head, but offered no more.

Aravon let out a long breath. "Though it's little consolation, at least they died a warrior's death."

Huge figures with blue-stained faces and clad in icebear pelts lay among the slain Deid warriors. Thirty Fehlans had fallen, but they had taken nearly two dozen Eirdkilrs with them.

"Aye, so they did." Bitterness echoed in Colborn's voice. "And see what good that did them."

"Stay here." Aravon dismounted and strode toward the mouth of the mine. He gave the pile of bodies a wide berth, careful not to disturb the silent dead. Bloody, reeking mud squelched beneath his boots, and the stink of rotting flesh hung in a thick miasma around him.

Stooping, Aravon retrieved a burned-out torch from where it had fallen beside a Deid warrior. With quick, deft movements, he struck sparks with his Legion-issue flint. Long seconds passed before the mud-covered torch caught flame. Drawing in a deep breath, Aravon stepped into the mine, torch held high.

The light of a million stars glimmered in the pitch black heavens inside the mine. No, not stars, Aravon realized. Gold. A kingdom's worth, waiting to be harvested from the walls, floors, and ceilings. Everywhere the torchlight touched, gold sparkled and glinted back at him from a sea of stone blacker than onyx.

Yet the sight of such wealth did little to drive back Aravon's horror. The smell within the mine was stronger, yet far less rank. The underground chill had preserved the two dozen corpses that lay scattered around the mines. Picks, carts, and shovels lay abandoned beside crushed, hacked, and ruined bodies of miners. Dark-haired Princelanders and blond, bearded Deid lay side by side, brothers in death.

The miners had clearly been caught at work, toiling to free the precious gold from its stony black prison. Yet no overstuffed sacks lay nearby. The hand-carts stood empty, overturned in the fight. The Eirdkilrs had made off with not only the gold, but the ghoulstone that Captain Lemaire had called "worthless".

Turning, Aravon strode back out into daylight and into fresh air. *Fresher* air, where the icy afternoon wind carried away the reek of slowly-decomposing bodies, and the smell of smoke hung like a funeral shroud atop the remains of Gold Burrows Mine.

Outside, Colborn had dismounted and now crouched over the body of a fallen Deid warrior. His hand trembled only slightly as he closed the man's eyes, bowed his head, and whispered something in Fehlan too quiet for Aravon to hear. Perhaps a prayer to *Olfossa*, god of the Deid, commending the warriors to *Seggrholl*.

Aravon gave Colborn his space, instead climbing into his saddle and riding a few dozen yards south, back the way they'd come. Back into the midst of the carnage, the thick carpet of savaged bodies and bloody mud. He ignored Belthar, who stood with his enormous crossbow shouldered and ready to fire. Instead, his eyes roamed the death and destruction that surrounded him, so at odds with the eerie stillness of Silver Break Mine.

Why was this attack on the mine different? Aravon's brow furrowed. *Why did they leave no trace of their passing in Eyrr land, but leave such death and destruction here?*

He glanced over his shoulder, toward the line of Deid bodies arrayed in front of the mine. Had *their* presence caused the massacre? In Silver Break Mine, there had been no defensive force—the mine was kept a secret by limiting the number of Fehlans and Princelanders that knew of its existence. If the Eirdkilrs had descended upon the mine and met no resistance, they could have simply…

What, exactly? Confusion swirled in Aravon's thoughts. *They could easily have killed the miners, just as they did here. But instead of leaving a camp filled with bodies, they left nothing. Not a trace of where they'd come from or where they'd gone.*

Yet that realization led to another grim thought. *What if their true purpose was not only to capture the mine, but the miners?*

Silver Break Mine had been a relatively new endeavor, yet the miners working there had been experienced laborers. Judging by the sturdy construction of the shelters alone, Gold Burrows had been in existence for at least a few years.

Dread settled in his stomach at the thought of Princelander, Deid, and Eyrr in the clutches of the Eirdkilrs. *What the hell do they want with miners?* At best, the Eirdkilrs would enslave them to work in the mines they had recaptured in the south of Fehl, perhaps even some in the Sawtooth Mountains and beyond. He didn't want to think about the worst-case—the Eirdkilrs could be savage and bloodthirsty in battle, but he'd heard enough stories about their ritual sacrifices and tortures to wish a speedy death on the captive prisoners.

The sound of pounding hoofbeats snapped him from his pondering. Skathi cantered back from the eastern edge of the camp, shaking her head. "*Nothing,*" she signed. "*Nothing but more bodies.*"

A flash of orange fur caught Aravon's eye. Snarl had sunk his teeth into a leather boot, gnawing at the tough hide, unaware of the severed foot that still lay within. Gut twisting, Aravon blew his whistle and Snarl came running. Aravon scooped the little Enfield up and held him in his arms, heedless of Snarl's insistent whining to be let go. The creature seemed not to understand what had happened here, but Aravon did, and he hated the knowledge. Only monsters could do something so bestial, so inhumanely murderous.

Zaharis appeared from the west a few minutes later. Unlike Skathi, however, he hadn't returned empty-handed. He rode with a sack slung across his saddle, and his horse's slow trot set the rocks within clacking against each other.

"*Found a dead Eirdkilr,*" Zaharis signed. "*He was carrying this.*" With a grunt of effort, he lifted the sack from the saddle and dropped it to the ground. It landed with a loud *thump* and *splash* in the crimson muck, and the heavy contents within split the seams. Among the black stone that spilled across the ground, shards of gold gleamed bright in the afternoon light.

"Keeper's teeth!" Belthar whistled. "That's a bloody lot of gold!"

Zaharis nodded. "*A fortune, by Princelander standards.*"

"Enough to pay a full company's wages for a week," Colborn put in.

Aravon frowned down at the sack. "So they came for the gold, but when they found the Deid warriors defending the mine, it turned into a battle."

"A one-sided battle," Skathi growled. The fingers of her right hand toyed nervously with the feathered fletching of the arrow that lay nocked across her short horsebow. "Poor bastards never stood a chance against so many."

"And that explains why the Eirdkilrs brought such a large force." The wheels had begun to turn in Aravon's mind. "They wanted to not only haul away all the gold, but they were taking prisoners, too."

Four pairs of eyes narrowed at him. "*Prisoners?*" Zaharis signed. "*That's not the Eirdkilrs' style.*"

"Until now." Aravon quickly recounted his train of reasoning. "If, and I know this is a big if, the Eirdkilrs decided that they wanted to extract the resources from the mines they control in the south, they wouldn't waste warriors on it."

"They'd simply raid the Fehlans and *take* the miners as slaves." Colborn's expression grew grim. "That was ever the Fehlan way, before the Einari settled the north. Still is, among many of the southern clans."

"Though what the Eirdkilrs could want with all that gold," Skathi put in, "makes no sense to me." She gestured around her. "I can see them cutting into the Prince's supply, cut him off so he can't afford to support the Legions he's got here, much less bring more across from the mainland. But to mine their own? What use could they possibly have for gold?"

Aravon frowned. Long moments passed before he shook his head. "I don't know."

"Then there's the matter of the prisoners," Skathi continued. "Unless you plan to murder them all, you've got to make sure they're fed, housed, clothed. Even as slaves, they'd need basic living conditions to survive."

Aravon drew in a deep breath. Skathi made a valid point. The Eirdkilrs had never taken prisoners until now because they had no use for them. They never surrendered in battle, so there was no need to exchange or ransom prisoners.

277

They considered the Eird, the "half-men", little better than animals. They could be used as slaves, but as Skathi had said, slaves consumed resources. Resources that the ever-roaming Eirdkilrs had always hunted, stolen, or pillaged from southern Fehl. Even a few hundred slaves would hinder mobility and steal food from the warriors' bellies.

Yet Aravon couldn't deny the evidence of his eyes. The camp was large enough to house three hundred, yet a quick count of the corpses revealed little more than *half* that number. That meant at least a hundred Princelanders and Fehlans had survived—either fleeing into the Deid lands or captured by the Eirdkilrs. The fact that there had been no news of the attack on the mine hinted at the latter.

The Eirdkilrs had more than a hundred prisoners.

"*What bothers me is how the Eirdkilrs knew about this,*" Zaharis signed. "*Even if, as you and the Duke believe, there is a traitor among the Prince's Council feeding them the information, I still don't understand how this particular band of Eirdkilrs got that information. And if they were fresh off the march from Jokull lands, why they came this way in the first place.*"

Aravon nodded. "You're right. All of you." He fixed his four companions with a solemn gaze. "Too much about this doesn't make sense. Just like so much of what the Eirdkilrs have done in the last few weeks. It's more than just a traitor in the Princelands—there is something new at play here, something cleverer than any Eirdkilr we've known in the past. They've changed their strategy, and until we figure out exactly what they're after, what their end game is, they're going to keep catching us off-guard."

Silence and grim looks met his words. His four companions exchanged glances, hesitation written in their eyes.

"I don't expect any of you to have an answer now." Aravon shook his head. "But from here on out, we've got to stop treating them like the enemy we've faced for years. We've got to start thinking of them as a new enemy, a colder, more cunning one. And *everything* we see, everything they do, it's going to factor into their new strategy somehow. It's up to us to figure out what."

"Then to figure out how to put an arrow in the eye of whatever bastard's calling the shots!" Skathi patted her bow.

"Aye," Belthar rumbled, adjusting his grip on his enormous crossbow.

Aravon turned to Colborn. "Find which way the Eirdkilrs left. We'll follow their tracks back to wherever they've gone."

Colborn nodded as he climbed into his saddle. "If they are carrying prisoners, they'll leave a trail broad enough for even Noll to follow."

Skathi snorted and muttered something derisive under her breath.

"Trampled brush, back that way," Zaharis signed, jerking a thumb to the west. *"Plenty of tracks where I found the dead Eirdkilr."* His eyes dropped to the sack spilled in the muddy ground, where shards of gold-rich ore lay gleaming among the pile of black ghoulstone. *"And what do we do with that?"*

"Leave it." Aravon gave a dismissive wave. "It's not ours to take, and it's not our problem to deal with."

The mask hid Belthar's face, but a sudden tension knotted his shoulders, as if he prepared to argue the point.

"It'll just slow us down," Aravon said, shaking his head. "And when we rejoin the Duke, he'll make sure to send word to the right people to come take care of...this."

His gesture included the corpses. He wanted to bury them, to give them a send-off to the afterlife far more dignified than this. Yet they couldn't afford the time. They were fortunate to have found the Eirdkilr tracks a day after the enemy had passed; if they delayed, they could lose the already faint trail.

"We ride," he ordered. "Follow the tracks, see if we can catch up to the Eirdkilrs." A tiny hope, he knew, but he had to try for the sake of the captive Deid and Princelanders.

In silence, Colborn dug his heels into his horse's flanks and trotted west, in the direction Zaharis had indicated. Zaharis followed, but not without a look back at the abandoned sack—unusual for the Secret Keeper, who had never shown any interest in gold or wealth.

"Snarl!" Aravon said as he fell in behind Colborn. "Follow!"

The Enfield leapt from Aravon's arm and took wing, quickly gaining altitude until he joined the crows circling Gold Burrows. His angry barking dispersed the carrion birds, but only for a few seconds. All too soon, the dark black shapes returned to their feast.

Aravon debated whether or not to send Snarl with a message. After a moment's contemplation, he decided against it. They'd catch up to Duke Dyrund with a few hours of hard riding. News of the massacre could wait until then. He was better off keeping Snarl close in case he had to send an urgent message.

279

Belthar and Skathi rode close on Aravon's heels, bringing up the rear of their small column. They seemed only too glad to leave the carnage behind.

Even with his rudimentary tracking skills, Aravon could make out the trail the Eirdkilrs had left as they marched out of the mining camp. Trampled grass, snapped bushes, bent leaves, ground stained with blood. Bootprints had churned the ground to mud as dozens, or hundreds of prisoners were led away from the corpses of their friends and families.

The trail led southwest for half a mile before it reached a broad, fast-flowing stream. Aravon's heart sank as he approached the bank and found the Eirdkilr tracks ended there. Or at least his inexperienced eyes couldn't detect any sign of the enemy's passing.

Aravon turned toward Colborn, but the half-Fehlan Lieutenant was already riding north along the stream, scanning the far bank. He kept riding north until he disappeared into the forest. Dread sank like a stone in Aravon's gut when Colborn rode back toward them and pursued the stream farther south.

Anger burned brighter and brighter in Aravon's chest as he waited for Colborn to return. Belthar and Skathi shifted in their saddles, gripping their weapons tighter and scanning the forest around them with wary eyes. Zaharis sat with his eyes unfocused, as if deep in thought, turning something over and over in his fingers. Aravon's brow furrowed at the sight of the black chunk of stone the Secret Keeper had retrieved from the wagon in Rivergate. The same black stone, it seemed, that had filled the sack of gold taken by the Eirdkilrs.

Before he could ask Zaharis about it, Colborn rode back toward them. "River ran high last night," he growled. "Churned the banks to mud, covered any tracks. I could cross, but—" He shook his head. "We'd lose hours trying to find them, much less catch up to them."

Aravon's chest tightened. *Damn it!* It should have been impossible— hundreds of Eirdkilrs and their prisoners couldn't simply disappear. Yet they had at Silver Break Mine, and now here. If Colborn had lost the Eirdkilr trail, it was well and truly lost.

"What now, Captain?" Skathi asked, piercing green eyes fixed on him. "Go after the prisoners, or rejoin the Duke?"

The burden of command weighed heavy on Aravon's shoulders, as it always did when faced with a difficult choice. Much as he ached to help the Fehlans and Princelanders captured by the Eirdkilrs, he knew that the five of them had little hope of catching up, much less freeing the prisoners. Pursuit

280

would only increase the risk of their being captured behind enemy lines. And the Duke needed his protection as he rode into the Fjall lands. This close to Eirdkilr-held territory, Aravon's place was at the Duke's side.

With a frustrated growl, Aravon turned his horse southeast. "To the Duke," he snarled. "And Storbjarg."

They might have been too late to save the miners at this camp, but the Fjall capital held their best hope of peace and an end to the Eirdkilr cruelty.

Chapter Thirty-Seven

"Gold Burrows Mine?" Duke Dyrund's eyebrows pulled together, a deep scowl creasing his forehead. "Keeper damn them!" He drove his clenched right fist into his open left palm with a resounding *smack*. "I thought Silver Break was likely an isolated incident, but I never would have imagined…" His expression grew grim. "A hundred or more miners taken prisoner?"

Aravon nodded. "That was our best guess, Your Grace, given the size of the camp and the number of casualties." The word "casualties" felt cold, far removed from the truth—slaughtered women, children, and men were far from just numbers on an after-battle report—yet years in the Legion had taught Aravon that he couldn't allow himself to *feel* every death in war. If he did, he'd drown beneath a torrent of sorrow at the wanton cruelty. Not only fellow Legionnaires and soldiers taking up arms, but the Fehlans and Princelanders that suffered as a result of war.

He swallowed the surge of emotion and continued. "We lost their trail at the *Smar* River, but they'd passed more than a day earlier. By now, they're likely deep in Fjall territory."

"Out of our reach, for now." The Duke's voice dropped to a growl. "Once we have the Hilmir and the Fjall warband on our side, by the Swordsman, we'll make the bastards pay!"

Aravon cocked his head. "You expect Throrsson to accept the Prince's terms?"

"He'll claw for every inch of ground, protest that we need them more than they need us." The Duke shook his head. "But, in the end, we have what he needs. And the Fjall have as much reason to hate their southern neighbors as

283

we do. More, seeing as the Eirdkilrs have made their home in Fjall lands ever since the Vigvollr. Swordsman only knows how much the smaller Fjall villages and towns have suffered from Eirdkilr raids."

Again, the image of Oldrsjot flashed through Aravon's mind. The Eirdkilrs wouldn't burn and destroy their Fjall neighbors; they needed the farmers, shepherds, and herders alive to keep raising the food they would steal. But in the end, they would bleed the Fjall dry, leaving them as dead as the Eyrr they had slaughtered. Indeed, starvation made for a far crueler killer than Eirdkilr steel.

"The fact that the Hilmir reached out to us means he's desperate," the Duke continued. "He knows his warband's not large enough to deal with the Eirdkilrs alone, and Wraithfever's making his hold on his lands even more tenuous. Doubtless, the only reason the Eirdkilrs haven't taken advantage of the Fjall's weakness is because of Legionnaires stationed in Dagger Garrison and the Bulwark. But if the illness persists, Throrsson's army will only grow weaker. The Hilmir's not going to let Eirdkilrs rip away everything he's worked for." The Duke's expression grew grim. "He'll make a deal, Captain, one way or another."

"For all our sakes, I pray to the Swordsman that you're right."

The Duke fixed Aravon with a piercing stare. "So do I," he said in a quiet voice.

Once again, Aravon was struck by the shadows around Duke Dyrund's eyes, the wrinkles that had grown deeper, more prominent in the last few weeks. The weight of responsibility weighed heaviest on those who wielded the most power.

"Go," the Duke said quietly. "Check on your men. Once I get a message off to Lord Eidan, I'll join you."

Without a word, Aravon saluted, turned on his heel, and strode back through the trees toward the camp.

He and his company of five had caught up with Duke Dyrund's party at the second hour before midnight. The Duke had made camp in a shallow dell, where a short hill and a thicket of hazel trees offered shelter from the wind and prying eyes. Indeed, Aravon might have ridden past had Colborn not spotted one of the Duke's mercenaries hiding in the bushes beside the narrow hunting path. The man, Scathan, had been posted to guide them to the well-concealed camp—one Aravon suspected had been chosen by Rangvaldr and Noll.

The little scout was nowhere in sight; he'd drawn the second watch of the night, and he'd taken up position on the narrow path that led back to the main trail. Rangvaldr, however, lay sleeping on the soft grass covering the gentle slope, his feet propped up on a protruding root. He seemed perfectly at home among the Fehlan wilds—no great surprise, for he *was* Fehlan, a warrior of the Eyrr, born and raised in the forests and hills around his home.

Lord Virinus had curled up in his heavy fur cloak, though he hadn't ceased tossing and turning in an unsuccessful effort to find a comfortable position on the hard ground. The Black Xiphos mercenaries, save for the two on watch with Noll, busied themselves sharpening their black-handled weapons, checking their gear, munching on their cold meal, or sleeping while they could.

But the four that had accompanied Aravon to Gold Burrows Mine appeared anything but relaxed. The faint light of their meager fire cast dark shadows across their masked faces, painting the snarling greatwolf features with a looming sense of menace tinged with cold dread.

Skathi sat in silence, her fingers unmoving, the un-fletched shaft of an arrow abandoned between her feet. Belthar ran an oiled cloth up and down the head of his axe. It had long ago passed gleaming—the Odarian steel could blind its enemies, given its brilliant sheen of polish—and still his hands moved, as if operating independently of his mind. A mind lost in memories of the slaughter at Gold Burrows Mine.

Zaharis' fingers hadn't stopped moving since leaving the mine. He toyed with the black stone, turning it over, over, and over so many times it nearly appeared smooth. His eyes shifted from an unfocused, distant gaze to narrowed scrutiny of the stone, then back again.

The heavy darkness of the Fehlan night had nothing on the cloud of gloom that hung over Colborn. The Lieutenant hadn't spoken a word since losing the Eirdkilr tracks. Though the mask concealed his face, the hunch of his shoulders, the stiffness of his spine, and the hollow look in his eyes spoke of brooding.

Those were his people, Aravon realized. *Even if he didn't know them personally, they were his clan.*

Aravon had a good sense of what Colborn was feeling; he'd felt the same torment of emotions when he awoke to find the corpses of Sixth Company scattered across the Eastmarch. Men he'd marched beside, commanded, and shared food and drink with for years, butchered by the Eirdkilrs. Those men of

Sixth Company had been "his people" just as much as the slain Deid miners and warriors at Gold Burrows Mine were Colborn's.

A sense of helplessness descended over Aravon. *What could I possibly say to make him feel better?* Any words he could summon would sound and feel trite.

Yet he had to try. Colborn's quiet words in Bjornstadt had helped Aravon cope with the losses of Sixth Company, the guilt he felt over their deaths. He owed the man at least the effort of attempting to help.

He strode toward Colborn, his mind racing as he tried to figure out what to say. But, before he could reach the man, Belthar set aside his axe and stood. "*A word, Captain?*" the big man signed.

Aravon hesitated a heartbeat, caught between his duty to Colborn and his need to hear whatever Belthar had to say. One look in Belthar's eyes, however, made the decision. Belthar emanated uneasy reluctance, yet grim resolve glimmered there as well. Whatever Belthar had to say, it had taken the big man effort to work himself around to speaking up.

"*Of course.*" Aravon's fingers flashed and, with a glance at the brooding Colborn, he gestured for Belthar to follow him into the shadows a short way away from the fire.

Once they were far enough away that Aravon didn't have to worry about being overheard, he turned to Belthar. "I'm listening."

Belthar remained silent a long moment. Everything about him was defensive, from his posture to the way he leaned away from Aravon to his wandering gaze. Yet, finally, it seemed he summoned up the courage to speak.

"I wanted to say something back in Rivergate, but I didn't get a chance, what with Turath's death and the race to join the Duke. After that…" Belthar hung his head, shame flashing in his eyes.

"It's okay, Belthar." Aravon reached up and placed a hand on the big man's shoulder. "Whatever it is, you can speak without fear of judgement. From me, or any of the others."

Belthar's shoulders tensed and his gaze darted toward the campfire. Toward Skathi. His reluctance doubtless stemmed from fear over what his companions would think of him, but her most of all. Again, he seemed to wrestle with some inner turmoil before he continued.

"Back in Rivergate, you saw those wagons parked next to the bridge, yes?"

Aravon raised an eyebrow. "I did."

"Did you ever find out what they were for?" Belthar's voice held a depth of meaning Aravon didn't quite understand.

"Silver from a secret mine deep in Jokull territory," Aravon replied. "The second load."

"And the first," Belthar's words were slow, made ponderous by his rumbling voice, "what happened to it?"

"Vanished overnight, according to the Captain." Aravon's curiosity blazed. *Where's he going with this?*

Belthar nodded. "So it's true." His huge shoulders knotted tighter, his spine stiffening. "It's the Brokers."

Aravon's eyes narrowed at the unfamiliar name. "The Brokers?"

"Smugglers," Belthar said, his voice quiet. "Best in the Princelands."

Suddenly, the meaning behind Belthar's words dawned on Aravon. "Smugglers." He drew in a breath. "The sort of men who would use a secret tunnel out of Ironcastle."

Belthar gave a single, curt nod, but nothing else.

"Should I ask about how you know all this?" Aravon cocked his head. "How you knew the tunnel was there, and how you're certain the Brokers are the ones who spirited away the wagons of silver?"

"I…" Belthar hesitated, his eyes dropping away. "I knew my fair share of 'em, years ago. A past lifetime, before I joined the Duke's regulars at Hightower."

Again, the big man's words held a hidden depth of meaning. Aravon might not understand precisely what Belthar was keeping secret, but he had no doubt the man *was* hiding something. Something important, something that filled him with such shame he didn't want the rest of his company to find out the truth.

"Back in Oldcrest, I asked you if your past would affect our mission." Aravon kept his voice neutral, calm. "Knowing your…history with these Brokers, I have to ask again."

"No." Belthar shook his head, then seemed to think better of it. "Or at least, it shouldn't. Not out here, away from the Princelands. The Brokers know better than to venture south of the Chain."

Aravon wanted to press the man, wanted to know how Belthar had such insight into a group of smugglers. But, like Zaharis' past with the Secret Keepers, it didn't matter right now. Their mission was ahead, to the Fjall and the south. When the time came that it *could* affect their tasks, Aravon would bring it up again. Giving Belthar a chance to tell his secrets in his own time would earn the man's trust, but if push came to shove, the big man would find no one shoved harder than Aravon when his soldiers' lives were on the line.

"Thank you, Belthar." Aravon nodded. "I'll let the Duke know." He held up a hand as Belthar stiffened. "Not about you, but about the Brokers in general, and the fact they're involved with the silver flowing through Rivergate."

If smugglers *were* tangled up with the mines in Jokull lands, it could speak of malfeasance. After all, the Prince undoubtedly had his own people to manage the transportation of the mined wealth. Unless he relied on smugglers—always a possibility, given the lengths to which Prince Toran had gone to keep mines like Silver Break a secret—the Duke needed to know so he could set Lord Eidan to investigating the matter.

"Yes, Captain." Belthar seemed to relax, and the worry in his eyes diminished as he turned to go.

"But, Belthar..." Aravon's voice stopped the big man in his tracks. Belthar glanced back, anxiety written in every muscle of his huge body. "Remember what I told you. The time's coming, sooner rather than later, when you'll have to trust us. Without that trust, we've got no chance of surviving what we're certain to face out there."

The big man's eyes darkened. "I know, Captain. You're right, but..." He let out a slow breath. "Way I grew up, trusting the wrong person got you dead. What others don't know can't come back to bite you in the arse."

"Until it does." Aravon stepped closer, lowering his voice. "Look at what happened with Zaharis in Rivergate. He was blindsided by Darrak. If he hadn't been the faster, better fighter, that could have put an end to our mission then and there." He shook his head. "A wise man once told me, 'Secrets are like trench foot; eventually, they'll turn everything rotten, and ignoring or concealing it only destroys you faster.'"

Belthar gave a harsh chuckle. "Colorful."

"Soldiers tend to be." Aravon smiled, but it was filled with sorrow at the memory of Naif, Sixth Company's Lieutenant. His friend, who had fallen in the ambush on the Eastmarch. The pain of that loss still hadn't faded completely, but hung like a weight on his shoulders. With effort, he pushed it aside...for Belthar's sake. "The message still rings true. Eventually, when we return to the Princelands, it's going to come out. Just like it did with Zaharis."

"*If* we return to the Princelands." Belthar's voice echoed with a note of gloom. "No telling what'll happen to us out here, so close to the enemy."

"Not if, Belthar." Aravon raised a clenched fist. "We *are* returning home, all of us."

He couldn't imagine a life where he didn't see Mylena and his sons once more. Everything he'd sacrificed thus far, everything he'd had to endure, it had all been for the sake of ending the war. An ending he intended to live long enough to see, and his men with him.

"The sooner you let others help you carry the burden, the sooner it stops dragging on you." He gripped the man's huge bicep. "After all we've been through, I think the others have earned your trust."

"Aye, they have." Belthar nodded his huge head. "And I don't want to ruin that."

"Nothing you say will ruin it." Aravon fixed the man with a solemn gaze. "You're our brother, our comrade. No matter what's in your past, we can handle it. I promise."

A long moment of silence elapsed before Belthar finally responded. "Yes, Captain." His voice was quiet, burdened, yet a hint of hope sparkled in his eyes. "I'll give it some thought, sir."

"We're here for you, Belthar. All of us." Aravon's gaze darted to Skathi. "Right now, you've both got your secrets, and holding onto them will just keep that wall between you impassable. The best thing you can do is let her see who you really are. After that…" He shrugged. "The rest is up to her. If she's not interested in what you've got to offer, you owe her the respect of honoring her wishes. But if you want to have any chance, telling her the truth is the only way she'll start to trust you."

Belthar ducked his head. "Speaking from experience, sir?"

Aravon laughed. "Hard-won, let me tell you. If Mylena hadn't come out and told me exactly what I was doing wrong with her, I might not be the man I am today." He rested a hand on the man's shoulders. "Good soldiers learn from their mistakes, but the best learn from the mistakes of other poor idiots."

Belthar's rumbling chuckle echoed from beneath his mask. "I'll keep that in mind."

"Good." Nodding, Aravon clapped Belthar on the back. "Now, get some rest. We're back on the road at first light."

Belthar saluted—*he's getting better,* Aravon noted, *his movements crisper*—and returned to his place before the campfire. He said nothing, simply leaned forward and stretched out his hands to the meager warmth of the flames, yet Aravon sensed he'd gotten through to the man. As with so much else, it would take Belthar time to come around, but when he finally did, their small company would be better for it.

A burden settled on Aravon's shoulders. After a long few days and the butchery at Gold Burrows Mine, he needed a few hours of rest before his early morning watch. But not before he spoke with Colborn. He had to make sure his Lieutenant was—

His brow furrowed as he glanced to where Colborn had been sitting. The half-Fehlan was gone. Rangvaldr, too, Aravon realized. The two men had slipped away during his conversation with Belthar. Colborn's watch was in three hours with Aravon, and Rangvaldr had already stood his shift.

A faint hope blossomed within Aravon. Rangvaldr wasn't just a brave warrior of the Eyrr; he was also *Seiomenn,* a priest, loremaster, and wiseman of his people. He had faced the same self-doubt over raising his hands against his own kind, and he, too, had lost brothers and fellow clansmen. If anyone could help Colborn through his grief and inner turmoil, it would be Rangvaldr.

Aravon let out a long breath and strode toward his pack and bedroll. He'd check on the Lieutenant in the morning, once he got a few hours of sleep. That morning watch would come all too soon.

* * *

"Captain." A hand shook Aravon's shoulders gently, but Aravon was up and alert in a second, spear held at the ready. Soldiers who slept too deep couldn't always count on wakening. More than once, Eirdkilrs had attempted to creep past unwary sentries to slit Princelander throats. Aravon, like all good Legionnaires, learned to sleep light.

Yet, as he took in the camp around him, he realized that light had already begun filtering through the canopy. The early morning mists hung thick in the brightening sky.

I slept through my watch!

He spun toward the one who had awoken him. Rangvaldr had stepped back to evade him as he leapt to his feet, and a hint of humor glinted in the deep green eyes behind the leather mask.

"Good to see you up," Rangvaldr signed in the Secret Keeper hand language. *"We were all sure Belthar's snoring would rouse you. Drove away the wildlife for a mile in all directions."*

Aravon's heart hammered. *"Why wasn't I roused for my shift?"* he demanded. His gaze darted to Noll, who was busy stuffing his belongings into his pack. The scout was supposed to get him up for his turn at watch.

"We took a vote, decided it was best to let you sleep," Rangvaldr answered. *"Figured we needed your mind sharp when we ride into Storbjarg today."*

Aravon narrowed his eyes. *"You should have awoken me."* His fingers flashed, his sharp movements mirroring the irritation that flared within him. *"I'm just as capable as—"*

"Don't bother finishing that." Rangvaldr shook his head and gave a dismissive wave. *"It was not a matter of doubting your abilities. You bear the heaviest burden of all, that of command. Consider it our way of lightening the load the best way we know how."* He winked. *"Take it as a compliment from your soldiers."*

Aravon drew in a breath. The *Seiomenn's* words soothed the burning flare of annoyance, filled him with a quiet pride. It felt good to know his men didn't just follow him because they were ordered to, but that they *cared* enough.

"Besides," Rangvaldr continued, *"Zaharis wasn't going to get much sleep anyway, so he's the one who took your shift."*

Aravon looked for the Secret Keeper. Zaharis was already mounted up, his pack and small wooden chest strapped in place behind his saddle.

"Thank you," Aravon signed.

Zaharis inclined his head, but his fingers remained silent—too occupied turning that chunk of black stone over and over. A new nervous habit, it seemed.

Memories of the previous night washed over Aravon. He turned to Rangvaldr. *"You talk to Colborn?"*

Rangvaldr gave a slow nod. *"He's solid. Troubled, certainly. Dealing with things in his own silent way, but solid."*

"Whatever you said to him, I can only hope it helped as much as your words helped me." A smile broadened Aravon's face. *"Another of those stories of yours, yes?"*

291

"No story this time." Rangvaldr chuckled. *"I've learned to save those for special conversations."*

Aravon shrugged. *"The way the Saga of Gunnarsdottir helped at Rivergate, I'm of the opinion you can tell us a tale anytime you want."*

"Careful, Captain, or I might hold you to that." Rangvaldr laughed and, clapping Aravon's shoulder, turned to pack his belongings.

Aravon worked quickly, rolling up his bedroll, tying it behind his saddle, and stowing his pack in place atop the blankets. The action, completed by rote as it had been so many mornings before, worked the kinks and knots from his muscles. Even after fifteen years in the Legion, he hadn't mastered the delicate art of finding a comfortable spot on the hard ground. Judging by Lord Virinus' stiff, jerky movements, the nobleman had suffered far worse.

Just as he finished packing his gear, the snort of a horse sounded behind Aravon. Turning, he found Belthar sitting in his saddle, with Aravon's mount beside him. The big man held out the reins. "Captain," he rumbled.

Aravon met Belthar's eyes. Gone were the shadows from the previous days, and he was much more like the lighthearted, jovial man he'd first met at Camp Marshal. Yet, as Aravon had seen in the days since Ironcastle, that happiness had been nothing more than a façade to conceal whatever dark past weighed on Belthar's soul. This version of the man, troubled but resolved, was more real, and Aravon welcomed the change.

"Thank you," he signed. He had to be careful about using his voice around Lord Virinus. Though he'd never met the man, there still existed a chance that the Icespire nobleman would recognize him. Lieutenant Naif had always said Aravon's voice rang with the same steel that filled General Traighan's, though without the harsh edge of a Drill Sergeant.

Belthar nodded and turned his mount to join Skathi and Zaharis at the rear of the Duke's column. The Duke himself and most of the mercenaries were already mounted, with Scathan, Barcus, and two others cleaning away the last traces of their camp. Aravon saw no sign of Colborn—likely he'd ridden out early to scout the way south, make sure no enemies stood between them and the Fjall lands. Given the Eirdkilr presence so far into Deid territory, it was better to be safe.

Aravon paused a moment, long enough to say a silent prayer. *Guide our steps and guard our backs, mighty Swordsman. Bring us safely to the lands of the Fjall where, by your grace, we will find a way to put an end to the war.*

He didn't know if the Swordsman heard him—the god of heroes never spoke back—yet he felt better for it.

With a nod to his men and the Duke, Aravon touched his heels to his horse's flank and the beast broke into a run. Southward, to the Fjall and a hope for the future of Fehl.

Chapter Thirty-Eight

Aravon whistled quietly as he crested the rise and saw the Fjall's capital spread out below him. After more than a hundred miles of empty forests and hilly grasslands, Storbjarg seemed far more massive than anything he could have imagined.

Storbjarg deserved its reputation as the largest and strongest of the Fehlan cities. No mere village or town, but a thriving hub of commerce, trade, and Fjall military power as large as Hightower, Ironcastle, or Wolfden Castle, dwarfed in size only by Icespire itself. Though Duke Dyrund's spies had never managed to get an accurate count of the population, judging by the city's size, Aravon estimated close to eighty thousand.

Thousands of longhouses, huts of wattle-and-daub, and multi-storied buildings of stone and wood sprawled across five square miles of flat land. Roads of paved stone intersected the city from the four points of the compass, merging at a massive open-air plaza at the heart of Storbjarg. Even from a mile away, Aravon could hear the hubbub emanating from the bustling city.

Most impressive of all was the high stone wall that surrounded Storbjarg. Somehow, despite the fact that the Fjall stonemasons could never rival the skill of Princelander or Einari artisans, they had managed to build a wall fully thirty feet tall to ring the entire city within a barrier of solid stone. The Fjall had also cleared back the forests to the east and south, providing a clear line of sight in all directions.

"Impressive, isn't it?" The Duke's voice echoed from Aravon's elbow.

"Yes, sir." Aravon answered in the deep voice he adopted for the "Captain Snarl" persona. "Such a feat is unheard of south of the Chain."

"Storbjarg has always stood apart from the rest of Fehl." The Duke shot him a wry smile. "From the day the Bastard Bearhound defied the first Eirdkilrs."

All on Fehl, even Princelanders, knew the tale of Jorund Ofeigsson, Throrsson's great-grandfather, who led his warband to battle at Vigvollr. The ill-fated battle had caused monumental losses on both sides of the field—more than twenty-five thousand Eirdkilrs and Fjall had bled and died there.

"That fierce, stubborn streak was always a hallmark of the Fjall." Rangvaldr, who had ridden up on the Duke's other side, spoke in a quiet voice. "A trait that has made the Fjall warband the best on Fehl. Were it not for Vigvollr, it is likely they would control far more territory. Perhaps everything south of the Chain."

"A dream that didn't die with the Bastard Bearhound, it seems." The Duke's expression grew pensive. "Why else would Throrsson adopt his great-grandsire's title of Hilmir and restore his warband?"

"If that's the case," Aravon asked, "why haven't the Eirdkilrs moved against them? Stopped them from growing strong?"

"Because the Hilmir is a clever man," Duke Dyrund replied. "For years, he has promised to lend aid to the Eirdkilrs in their attempts to subjugate Fehl and drive out the Princelanders. During that time, he has sent his warband raiding south, east, and west."

"To 'blood' them in preparation for battle." Rangvaldr nodded. "Only a warrior who has slain an enemy, endured a winter in Ornntadr, and sired a son may stand in the shield wall. To the Fjall, war is not just a duty—it is their sacred calling. A Fjall warrior seeks death in battle, the only fitting tribute to *Striith*, their god."

Not too unlike the sermons preached by recruiters for the Legion of Heroes, Aravon thought. He had joined the Legion to honor his father, but not before the silver-tongued men had plied him with speeches about grand heroics, brave warriors, and duty to Prince and country. *Wide-eyed young Fjall are just as susceptible to stirring rhetoric as Princelanders and Einari.*

"Surely the Eirdkilrs can't be that naïve," Aravon pressed. "The existence of the Fjall warband would constitute a threat they couldn't ignore."

"Indeed." The Duke inclined his head. "But, with the Legion forces so close at hand, the Eirdkilrs cannot afford to shatter their tenuous peace with the

Fjall. They require the Fjall's silent acceptance of their presence, even if they cannot demand their full support."

"A precarious position for Throrsson to find himself in." Aravon shook his head. "Enemies on all sides, both demanding they help attack the other. Forces decimated first by battle, and now by disease."

"The fact that he has navigated it so well thus far proves that the Hilmir could well be worthy to bear the title he has claimed." Duke Dyrund tugged at his beard, which seemed to hold more gray than dark brown these days. "Indeed, were it not for Wraithfever, he might have taken the battle to the Eirdkilrs—or, Swordsman forbid, to the Legion—on his own, and triumphed. Cruel and callous as it may sound, this illness is the best thing that could have happened for us."

The Duke was right: it *did* sound cruel and callous. But at least the Duke hadn't come to prey upon the Fjall weakness, as the Eirdkilrs would. At least, not in the same fashion. The Eirdkilrs would subjugate the Fjall, while Duke Dyrund came with an offer of alliance, a hope for restoration. Aravon clung to that small distinction—it was all that separated men like the Duke and Prince Toran from the enemy he despised.

"Any idea how far it's spread?" Aravon asked. "Or if the Fjall have found a cure for it?"

The Duke shrugged. "I have had no word from within Storbjarg since the Hilmir's request for a meeting. But I trust that Lord Eidan would have sent word if the situation had changed."

Duke Dyrund had grasped the unspoken meaning beneath Aravon's question. If the reports of Wraithfever were a pretense or no longer a concern, they could be riding into a trap. Throrsson could have easily arranged to sell out the Prince's highest-ranked councilor and one of the most powerful men in the Princelands. The promise of a peace treaty would suffice to lure the Duke here, where he'd be surrounded by Fjall warriors. Even a fool would expect some sort of subterfuge or treachery, and the Duke was no fool.

But if he believed the situation hadn't changed, then Aravon could only operate based on the Duke's collected intelligence. That didn't mean he'd let down his guard—if anything, it only served to heighten his wariness of what lay ahead—but he would trust the Duke's judgement.

"Come." The Duke touched his heels to his horse's flanks. "Whatever lies ahead, we face it sooner rather than later."

Aravon kicked his mount into motion, following the Duke down the hill toward the gates of Storbjarg. Noll and Colborn appeared from the east and west, signaling that the way was clear—at least, they had found no sign of a trap or Eirdkilrs lying in wait around the city. That did little to ease the nervous tension that set Aravon's nerves twanging like a bowstring. He slid his hand to the spear strapped across his right leg. Danger could lie within Storbjarg, hidden among the wooden longhouses, huts, and houses. No matter what came, he'd be ready.

Noll and Colborn fell into position at the front of their column. Aravon and Rangvaldr rode on either side of Duke Dyrund, with four sellswords fanning out to flank them. Behind the Duke rode Zaharis, Lord Virinus, and two of the Black Xiphos mercenaries. The last three rode behind the Icespire nobleman, followed by Belthar and Skathi at the rear. A small company, yet, Aravon knew, one strong enough to face far superior numbers. The skill of his soldiers and his trust in the Duke's judgement was all that kept him riding toward Storbjarg when every instinct screamed at him to retreat, to take up a secure position within the forest.

You are no longer a Legionnaire, he told himself. *Gone are the days of standing the shield wall. Now, you fight a different sort of battle, even if that battle leads you into the jaws of the enemy.*

The Fjall had never been overtly hostile to the Princelanders—aside from frequent raids on their Fehlan allies—yet until now, all attempts at negotiation had been rebuffed. Aravon wasn't quite ready to trust that the Hilmir intended them no harm.

"*Eyes sharp, weapons ready,*" Aravon signed to Rangvaldr, Skathi, and Belthar. He turned in his saddle to glance at Zaharis. "*Got a surprise ready in case they try anything, Magicmaker?*"

Zaharis' eyes narrowed behind the leather mask, and Aravon had little doubt his bearded face creased into a scowl. "*Rangvaldr created that code name in jest, Captain.*"

"*We've all seen the magic you make, Zaharis.*" Despite the tension in his shoulders, Aravon couldn't help smiling. "*And we all agree that it's the perfect name for you.*"

Zaharis' fingers signed something far too crude and insulting for Aravon to bother translating, though he ended his tirade with, "*…but if they try anything, I've got a little treat to shove so far up their arses they'll taste knuckles.*"

298

Chuckling, Aravon turned back to face forward. He'd seen what Zaharis' "little treats" could do. The Secret Keeper's knowledge of alchemy had proven invaluable far too many times to count.

The gates of Storbjarg swung open at their approach, five men struggling against the weight of each enormous, iron-banded steel door. Up close, the city walls were even more impressive—thirty feet tall but nearly ten feet thick, built from river-hardened stones held together by a mortar so dark gray it nearly appeared black.

Inside, the city of the Fjall shared a great many similarities with the Eyrr—only the number of longhouses, huts, and houses outnumbered Bjornstadt's dwellings by a factor of hundreds. Muddy streets radiated outward from the north-south paved stone avenue, and a thick layer of dust seemed to cover the walls, doors, windows, and thatched roofs.

Yet dirt or no, there was nothing dull or faded about Storbjarg's flags. Every Fehlan clan had their own flag, but few bothered displaying it anywhere outside their chief's longhouse. Here, however, Fjall pennants flew from every house, every turret atop the stone wall. A black raven with a serpent's tongue and outstretched claws holding a longsword and shield, atop a field of brilliant red—the *Reafan* of *Striith,* symbol of the Fjall warband.

The flags fluttered in the wind, *snapping* so loud the noise echoed above the din of the busy Fjall city. Yet as the Duke's column passed, men, women, and children paused in their duties and errands to gawk at the newcomers. Even clad in Fehlan-style furs and leather armor, no one would mistake Duke Dyrund, Lord Virinus, or the Black Xiphos mercenaries for anything but Princelanders. Aravon and his six masked, mottle-armored companions earned a multitude of stares both curious and suspicious.

Aravon's shoulders tightened as they rode deeper into Storbjarg. He scanned the upper-floor windows for enemy archers, peered into every shadowed alley in search of warriors lying in wait, studied the sea of Fjall faces for any indication that the wool-and-fur-clad people around them intended the Duke harm. His jaw ached from clenching, his knuckles whitened around the haft of his spear. He forced himself to relax his body, but his mind never stopped working, never stopped analyzing the city around him for threats.

Yet, as long minutes passed and the muddy streets of Storbjarg passed, no attack came. No arrows sped toward the Duke. No Fehlan or Eirdkilr reavers leapt onto their horses. No wild war cries shattered the din of a bustling city. Everything was simply…normal.

299

Then they reached the open square at the heart of the city, and Aravon drew in a quiet breath at the dazzling black stone that stretched for two hundred yards in every direction. He'd seen the stone before, at Bjornstadt, where it had been used for the raised platform from which Chief Ailmaer greeted them. Yet here in Storbjarg, the entire plaza was tiled in the stone. Darker than onyx, with an appearance like liquid shadow and a depth that threatened to draw his eyes and mind into its murky vastness.

And there, standing in the heart of the sea of black, was the man that could only be Eirik Throrsson. Tall, nearly as tall as Belthar, with shoulders broadened by years of wielding a sword and shield, the Hilmir wore enough furs to cover three Fehlan black bears, with a coarse black beard that hung in two thick braids down to his waist. His hair, dark as the ravens on his standard, had been pulled back into three loose tails, revealing a high brow, strong cheekbones, and a square jaw.

A warrior, every inch of him.

Aravon stared into the man's eyes, and was surprised to see the glimmer of cunning there. Letters, numbers, and other knowledge valued in the Princelands meant nothing to the Hilmir; his intellect was devoted to the only expertise that mattered to the Fjall: battle and bloodshed.

The Hilmir said nothing, but stared at the men riding into his city's square. He remained silent as the Duke reined in, dismounted, and crossed the three steps to stand before the Fjall leader. Aravon, Colborn, and Rangvaldr hurried from their saddles and kept pace with the Duke, an honor guard to match the fifty Fjall warriors at Throrsson's back. The Fjall chief seemed not to notice them. His ice-blue eyes locked on Duke Dyrund's face, his gaze piercing and intense. Even though he stood only a few inches taller than Duke Dyrund, the breadth of his shoulders and his heavy furs made him appear to loom.

Yet the Duke seemed not at all intimidated by the hulking warrior before him. He simply gave the Hilmir a bow, extended a hand, and said in perfect Fehlan, "Do you think fifty is a large *enough* greeting party to keep you safe? I could wait if you want to summon more."

Aravon froze; he couldn't imagine the Duke addressing Prince Toran in such a tone. His grip tightened on his spear and he prepared to leap to the Duke's defense if necessary.

Long moments passed in tense silence. All in the square seemed to hold their breaths in nervous anticipation of the Hilmir's reaction.

Then a smile broke out on the Fjall chief's face, and booming laughter echoed across the open-air plaza.

"Duke Dyrund of Eastfall." The Hilmir returned the grip, his massive hand encircling the Duke's forearm and squeezing hard. "For a second, I worried your Prince had sent one of his weak-spined noblemen to speak with me." His gaze darted past Aravon to where Lord Virinus sat in his saddle, swathed in furs that now appeared far less grand when compared to Throrsson's own. "But a man who greets a former enemy with such confidence, it fills me with hope for some of you, at least."

The Duke inclined his head and, after taking back his arm from the Hilmir's crushing grip, reached into his cloak. "A gift from my Prince."

Aravon's eyes widened as the Duke drew out the glass bottle filled with dark red liquid. He couldn't believe the Duke had opened the negotiations by giving the Hilmir the cure to Wraithfever—even with his limited understanding of statecraft and diplomacy, he knew that sort of leverage was intended to *seal* the bargain. A coup de grâce should Throrsson prove stubborn.

Throrsson shook his head, sending his braided beard and hair whipping around his face. "Fjall do not drink your puny Princeland wines! Only the finest mead for the true sons of *Striith*."

"The contents of this bottle are worth far more than even the strongest *braggot* from the mead halls of Ornntadr." The Duke's voice rang with confidence. "Let us share the *Drekka,* then I will share with you the secret that will save your people."

The Hilmir's eyebrows rose as the Duke spoke. "A Princelander who speaks of Ornntadr *braggot* knows to ware his words." His eyes narrowed slightly. "Yet, perhaps, he, too, knows the value of such words. Words that a wise chief would at least hear before making up his mind."

He stepped down from the raised platform and gestured to the enormous longhouse that fronted the square's western side. "Come, Duke. We will share the *Drekka,* if you are man enough."

The Duke chuckled. "My Prince would not have sent a *prottdrykkr* to negotiate with the Hilmir."

Aravon's brow furrowed at the unfamiliar words. He'd learned Fehlan from Colborn, but Rangvaldr's Eyrr language had slight variations that Colborn hadn't taught him. The word "prott" sounded similar to the word Aravon knew for "feeble", but *drykkr* was new to him. Considering they were speaking of mead, Aravon guessed it had something to do with drinking.

Duke Dyrund fell in step beside Throrsson and, together, the two men strode toward the timber, thatch, and wattle-and-daub longhouse. Aravon's silent signal brought Skathi, Belthar, Zaharis, and Noll out of their saddles, followed a moment later by the mercenaries and, at the last, Lord Virinus. Before the Duke had gone five steps, the seven of them had formed an honor guard beside and behind Duke Dyrund—a match for the ten Fjall warriors flanking their Hilmir.

As the Duke and Throrsson reached the entrance to the longhouse, the Hilmir turned to the Duke. "As is the Fjall custom, we enter alone."

Aravon tensed. The Duke, going into the dark longhouse alone? Throrsson could have men hiding in wait inside, ready to pounce on the Duke. For that matter, the Hilmir himself could simply turn and kill the Duke himself. While Duke Dyrund was a formidable warrior in his own right, Aravon had little doubt Throrsson was the superior fighter.

"All that mead has gone to your head, it seems." Again, Duke Dyrund's answer surprised Aravon. "Fjall custom dictates that honored guests share the *Drekka* not alone, but with two seconds-in-command standing guard."

A wry smile spread across the Hilmir's face. "Of course." He chuckled, a deep, throaty sound, and patted his stomach. "Hunger can make a man forgetful."

Aravon relaxed. *It was another test.* The Hilmir might appear the warrior, but he was proving far more cunning than Aravon gave him credit for. Everything since the moment they'd arrived had been a test to determine the Duke's intelligence, understanding of Fjall culture, and mettle. Apparently, Duke Dyrund had done his homework.

Eirik Throrsson turned to the warriors at his side. "Gyrd," he barked. "Grimar."

The first man who stepped forward had threads of gray dotting his beard and braided hair, his face lined and tanned by the sun. Yet he stood tall, confident, and strode into the longhouse ahead of the Hilmir. The Fjall who followed was no less a warrior, though twenty years his junior, with only two bead-and-bone-laden braids in his platinum-blond beard.

"Captain Snarl," the Duke said in Fehlan, using Aravon's code name.

Eirik Throrsson's bushy eyebrows rose as Aravon moved toward the longhouse door. "Captain Snarl, eh?" Curiosity rumbled in his voice. "A curious name for a man who hides his face behind a wolf's bared teeth."

Aravon met the man's ice-blue eyes. He stood only an inch shorter than Throrsson, and the breadth of his shoulders would never rival the Hilmir's. Yet he, too, met the man's gaze with calm. He sensed no hint of threat from the man, only that same assessment.

"Even the mighty bear may fall to those fangs," he said. "Wolves hunt where they will, and a wise bear knows to make peace with the pack." He had no idea where the words had come from—doubtless some trite piece of poetry read to him during his youth—but they brought a smile to Throrsson's lips.

The Hilmir's chuckle rumbled from deep within his belly. "So it is." A hint of approval flashed across the man's strong, black-bearded face.

Turning, Aravon strode into the longhouse, spear held at his side yet ready to strike if needed.

The longhouse had a narrow antechamber barely ten feet wide and long, with an opening on the far end covered by thick hides. Beyond the fur curtain was a massive room filled with benches and tables, the walls adorned by shields, swords, axes, spears, helmets, and the mounted heads of animals both predatory and prey. A firepit occupied the heart of the longhouse, and within a fire blazed bright, filling the longhouse with radiant warmth and illumination. Fur rugs and bear pelts lay strewn across the earthen floor, and beneath the thick smell of wood smoke that filled the room, Aravon caught the scent of meat cooking somewhere in the shadows to the rear of the longhouse.

Beyond the far end of the firepit, two chairs stood opposite each other across a short wooden table. Gyrd had taken up position behind one fur-covered chair—the larger of the two, clearly intended to make Throrsson loom over whoever sat opposite him—so Aravon moved to stand behind the other. He locked eyes with the Hilmir's second-in-command, a moment of silent scrutiny passed between them as they measured each other.

A moment later the Hilmir entered, followed by Duke Dyrund and Lord Virinus, with the Fjall warrior Grimar bringing up the rear. The two leaders strode to their chairs and sat, facing each other. Lord Virinus took up position behind the left side of the Duke's chair, while Grimar took a similar position opposite Aravon.

303

"Let us share the *Drekka*." Throrsson turned to Grimar with a nod, and the warrior turned toward one of the wooden tables against the wall. A small barrel—the size of a Princeland beer rundlet—sat atop it, with two drinking horns. Unstoppering the barrel, Grimar filled the horns, which he brought to the table and handed to Duke Dyrund and his Hilmir.

The two men brought the horns to their lips. But, instead of drinking, they both spat into the horns. Once, twice, three times.

Throrsson held up his horn to Gyrd, who stepped forward and took it from his Hilmir. Aravon hurried to do the same with the Duke's horn and, imitating the Hilmir's second-in-command, offered the horn to Throrsson. With a nod, the Hilmir took the horn and raised it, spittle and all, to his lips. Aravon's stomach churned as the Duke swallowed the honey-colored liquid, still frothed with the Hilmir's spittle. To his surprise, neither Throrsson nor the Duke simply stopped after a long draught. Instead, the two men continued to drink deep.

Aravon's eyes widened. *A drinking contest?* The *Drekka* was, it seemed, yet another test.

His gaze snapped to Duke Dyrund. The Duke's horn was held a little lower than Throrsson's, and the Hilmir's jaw worked as he downed the mead. Thin streams of yellow liquid trickled down Throrsson's bearded chin, sliding off the furs around his neck and chest. With a loud gasp of delight, he slammed the horn down on the table.

"*Skaal!*" His shout echoed off the timber rafters.

A heartbeat later, Duke Dyrund's horn slammed onto the table and his "*Skaal!*" reverberated through the room.

Throrsson's broad face creased into a grin. "No *prottdrykkr*, indeed."

Aravon had seen the Duke share drinks with his men in Camp Marshal, or savor a goblet of fine Nyslian wine at Icespire soirees. He'd never believed it possible that a former Legionnaire would be a lightweight, yet to finish that entire horn of mead—and *Fjall* mead, at that—was a feat that even Belthar would find difficult.

He stifled a chuckle. *The Prince has, indeed, sent the right man for the job.*

"You know a great deal of our customs, Princelander." Throrsson's expression grew wry. "Then again, I would expect no less from the Duke of Eastfall."

"Then you know, Hilmir of the Fjall, that I would not come with hollow promises or empty hands." Once again, the Duke drew out the glass vial and set

304

it on the table. The dark red liquid within seemed to glow in the firelight. "But before I make my Prince's offer, I must know that you are serious."

The Hilmir's eyebrows lowered and a scowl creased his forehead. "After we have shared the *Drekka,* you still doubt?" He tugged at his braided beard. "Perhaps you do not know our customs after all."

"I know that men are men, no matter what clan they call their own." The Duke sat straighter in his chair. "I know that the Hilmir bears a burden of duty to his warband and his people. I know that, in the end, men will do whatever they must for the sake of those they hold dear."

"If you know that," Throrsson said, "then you will know that I would never violate the sanctity of the *Drekka.*"

"Oh, of that, I have full confidence." The Duke gave a dismissive wave. "I have no fear for my life within these halls. But it is what happens *after* I leave, after I return to my people, that I question."

Eirik Throrsson stood and threw back his bearskin cloak, revealing glittering chain mail atop a thick coat of padded leather armor. The sword that hung at his side had to weigh as much as a Voramian greatsword, and three white bone-handled daggers protruded from his belt. Aravon tensed as the Hilmir drew a long seax, but Throrsson made no move to attack; instead, he raised his left hand and dragged the blade across his palm. Blood welled from the cut and splashed to the table.

"By the iron fist of *Striith,* I pledge that I enter into this negotiation in good faith as Hilmir of the Fjall." The solemn words echoed off the longhouse's mud walls, seeming to ring for long seconds before falling silent.

"That will suffice." The Duke inclined his head. "Then, under the eyes of the Watcher, god of justice, I vow that I enter into this negotiation in good faith, as representative of Prince Cedenas Toran of Icespire, ruler of the Princelands." He gave a little chuckle. "I hope you don't mind that I keep my dagger sheathed. At my age, a man's better off keeping as much blood in his body as possible."

Chuckling, the Hilmir gave a dismissive wave and took his seat once more. "So tell me, Duke Dyrund, what is in this bottle of yours that could be so valuable? The sacred mead of *Upphiminn*? *Striith's* tears, perhaps, or the immortality-giving waters of *Seggrholl*?" A sarcastic smile broadened his face.

The Duke didn't rise to the bait. Instead, he picked up the bottle and held it out in one hand. "I offer you the cure to Wraithfever, and hope for your people."

A startling transformation came over the Hilmir. In that moment, the blustering warrior disappeared, replaced by a cold-eyed, cunning man staring with naked suspicion at the Duke.

"Impossible!" Throrsson spoke in a rumbling whisper. "My own *gyoja* can find no cure."

"Our healers have access to knowledge that yours do not." The Duke spoke it not as a boast, but a statement of fact. "But this—" He tapped a fingernail against the glass bottle. "—this is what you seek, I swear by the Swordsman."

The Hilmir's eyes narrowed. "I put no trust in your god, Princelander. I trust only the proof of my eyes."

"Then I will prove it." The Duke's voice was calm. "This vial contains enough cure for *one* person. Man, woman, child, it will suffice." He leaned forward. "Choose who you will, and let me administer it to them. When you see I speak the truth, we will talk of peace between the Princelands and Fjall."

Throrsson's face went hard as stone, yet something dark flashed in his eyes, some inner, unspoken turmoil that pierced his attempt at concealing his true feelings. Long moments of silence passed as the Fjall chief stared at Duke Dyrund—no, Aravon realized, the Hilmir's eyes were fixed on the Duke, yet he saw nothing but the thoughts whirling inside his own mind.

"A cure for one." A bitter edge tinged the Hilmir's words. "You offer me hope for my people, then snatch it away in the next breath?" He threw himself to his feet, a flurry of motion that had Aravon instantly on the defensive. "What use is a cure that will only save *one?*" he roared.

The Duke didn't flinch. "The best I could do on short notice," he answered, his voice calm and quiet. "I received your message and hurried here at all haste, and my healers could only craft this much of the cure in the short time I gave them."

The Hilmir was a hurricane of movement, whirling to stomp around his throne. Gyrd's face revealed nothing, but Grimar's hand hovered close to the long Fehlan sword hanging on his belt, his eyes fixed on his pacing chief.

"But more is coming, Hilmir," the Duke pressed. "Even now, my healers are loading wagons with the cure and bringing it to Silverhill, where they await

306

my word." He stood, a wall of calm in the face of Throrsson's storm. "The moment the Fjall align with the Princelands, I will send word and your people will have the cure within a week."

"A week?" Throrsson roared. "Do you know how many more of my warband will fall ill and wither away in that time?"

"Scores." The Duke nodded. "Perhaps hundreds, and thousands of your people with them. But that would have happened had I not arrived. Your only hope, Hilmir of the Fjall, is to make peace."

"Peace!" The Hilmir threw up his hands. "You call it peace, but to my people, it means war." His lip curled up into a snarl. "War with an enemy far deadlier and closer to home than the Legion ever was."

"I understand what we are asking," the Duke replied. "Which is why I came to do the asking in person. As the voice of the Prince, his personal envoy, out of respect for the decision you must make." He stepped toward the Hilmir, the fingers of his right hand motioning for Aravon to stay. "I have no desire to hold the future of your people as leverage to convince you to join us, but you know that if the Fjall do not join us, the future of *my* people is at stake. But together, Hilmir, with Fjall fighting beside Princelander, there is hope for both our peoples. That is what I offer here." He raised the bottle. "A hope for all of Fehl. A Fehl free of the *Tauld* and their cruelty."

A torrent of emotions passed through the Hilmir's eyes, and anger darkened his face. Yet he remained silent for long moments, his heavy brow furrowed, deep in thought.

"Gyrd," he said without looking away from the Duke. "Bring Bjarni."

"Hilmir—" The graying Fjall warrior began.

"Now." Throrsson's quiet voice echoed with an edge of steel that brooked no argument.

"Yes, Hilmir." The man hurried into the shadows at the rear of the longhouse.

Aravon's eyes narrowed as he watched Gyrd go, then turned back to study Throrsson. The man's face had grown tight, his expression strained. The Hilmir's huge jaw muscles worked and his hands tightened on the back of his wooden chair.

Gyrd reappeared a few minutes later, and in his arms he carried a young man. Fever brightened the young man's lightly-bearded cheeks, which had grown gaunt, as hollow as his glassy, unfocused eyes. Sweat streamed down his face, yet even through the thick blankets and furs bundling him, shivers wracked his body. He mumbled incoherent words in Fehlan, his mind tossed on the currents of fever nightmares.

Aravon's gut clenched. Despite the young man's sallow appearance, he had the same strong features, black hair, and solid build as Throrsson.

"Give it to him." Something broke in the Hilmir's voice as he turned and rested a hand on the young man's forehead. "Heal my son. If you can do that, you will have your peace."

Chapter Thirty-Nine

Aravon's mouth felt suddenly dry. He hadn't expected the Hilmir to simply accept the Duke's word that the cure would work without demanding proof. But to test it on his *son*? That raised the stakes far beyond anything Aravon had imagined.

If the cure fails or, Swordsman forbid, makes the Wraithfever worse, we won't just fail to make the alliance. Aravon's fingers tightened on the ash shaft of his spear. *The Hilmir will kill us for killing his son.*

Duke Dyrund's calm façade cracked for a single heartbeat—little more than a sidelong glance at Aravon, a flash of worry in his eyes, flitting by so fast that Aravon only recognized it because he knew the man so well—but the sight of that apprehension added to Aravon's nervousness. The Duke had sounded confident when speaking of the Wraithfever cure, yet there was no such thing as "foolproof" alchemy or healing remedies.

With the Hilmir's son's life on the line, Aravon had to hope that the Duke's confidence was well-founded. The fate of Fehl sloshed within that tiny glass bottle.

The Duke hesitated only a moment before nodding. "Of course, Hilmir." Without a hint of tremor in his hands, he reached for the bottle. The *pop* of the cork echoed loud in the longhouse. Aravon held his breath as the Duke stepped toward the feverish young man and, with Gyrd's help, emptied the contents into the youth's open lips.

For long seconds, it seemed nothing would happen. The young man's eyes remained glassy, unfocused, sweat streaming down cheeks tinged bright red with fever. He seemed beyond protest, barely capable of swallowing the dark red liquid sliding down his throat.

Eirik Throrsson leaned forward eagerly, eyes locked on his son, his huge hands flexing and relaxing. Aravon recognized the frustration of a helpless man—Swordsman knew he'd felt the same during the long hours Mylena had spent laboring in childbirth. Only at the end of his wife's struggle, new life had come into the world. Throrsson's waiting could very well be shattered by his son's death.

Yet as seconds turned to a minute and still no sign of effect, Throrsson's helpless frustration gave way to irritation, then towering anger. He whirled on the Duke, fury flashing in his eyes. "Your healers are no better than ours! Worse, they do not promise—"

"Hilmir!" Gyrd's gasp snapped Throrsson back around.

The flush of fever had diminished, the dark red in Bjarni's cheeks slowly giving way to a healthy pallor. Slowly, the young man's eyes focused, fixed on the Fjall chief. "F-Father?"

Bjarni's voice was little more than a croaking whisper, weakened by the Wraithfever. Yet the brilliant glow of delight and relief set the Hilmir's heavy face glowing. He crossed the distance to his son in two huge steps and swept him up into an embrace, clutching him tight against his barrel chest.

"My boy," he rumbled, pressing a fierce kiss to his son's tangled black locks. "My valiant *herknungr.*"

For long minutes, the two remained locked in the embrace, weakened son upheld in the arms of his father, the most powerful man in southern Fehl. A chieftain, a warrior, and a father filled with indescribable joy at finding his son returned to him from certain death.

A lump rose to Aravon's throat at the sight, and a sudden desire to turn away gripped him. Despite his relief to find the Duke's healing draught worked, he couldn't help the surge of resentment burgeoning in his chest. *If only my father cared that much.*

He tried to banish the thought, to push down the stone that had settled like a lead weight in his stomach. Yet he could not. For twenty-five years, since the death of his mother, the burden had never truly lifted. He'd ignored it, thrown himself into caring for the soldiers by his side and under his command. But it always came back, eventually. That feeling of anger, resentment, the biting acid that surged in his stomach, whenever he thought of General Traighan.

"Thank you!" Throrsson's hoarse voice pierced Aravon's maudlin thoughts. He looked up to find the Hilmir staring at the Duke, gratitude burning in his ice-blue eyes. "Truly, man of the Princelands, I owe you a father's gratitude. You have given me a gift I could never repay."

The words drove the bitter dagger deeper into Aravon's gut. He could never imagine his own father saying such a thing to anyone.

"There is no debt between us, Hilmir." Duke Dyrund's voice was calm, yet it echoed with confidence. "I could not stand by while your people suffer." His gaze went to the young man still crushed to Throrsson's chest. "Your son's life is but the first of those that will be saved if you join us against the Eirdkilrs. Princelander and Fehlan alike, our land will only know peace and plenty once the *Tauld* are driven back across the Sawtooth Mountains."

Throrsson's expression grew somber, and he released his son back into Gyrd's waiting hands. In just the few minutes since he'd received the draft, already Bjarni had begun to appear healthier, his fever waning, the sweat drying on his forehead. He even managed to stand upright, tottering weakly alongside Gyrd as the Hilmir's second-in-command led him from the room.

Eirik Throrsson gestured for the Duke to sit, and resumed his own seat. "Your remedy, you say it could be delivered within a week?" He clasped massive hands across his thick stomach and leaned back in his chair. "No sooner?"

The Duke mirrored the Hilmir's posture. "The wagons already sit waiting at Silverhill, but it is a journey of many miles, and through territory plagued by enemies." He shook his head. "I will give instructions for my people to travel with all haste, yet—"

Throrsson held up a hand. "So be it, Duke of Eastfall. Speak your Prince's terms, and you will have my answer."

"The terms are simple," the Duke replied. "Join us against the Eirdkilrs, and send your warband to fight beside the Legion and our allies. Once the *Tauld* have been pushed back across the Sawtooth Mountains and our Legionnaires once more hold Snowpass Keep, our only request is that you permit us to re-establish the defensive garrisons along the Westmarch and Eastmarch."

Throrsson's eyes narrowed. "*Solely* to prevent the Eirdkilr return, no doubt." His voice held a mocking edge.

The Duke shrugged. "Prince Toran has no desire to claim Fehlan land. Once the war is ended and peace returns to Fehl, the Fjall and every other clan

311

are free to do as they please." He leaned forward. "My Prince *will*, however, continue to maintain friendly relationships with the Deid, Eyrr, and other clans that have valuables worth his interest."

"You Princelanders and your mines!" The Hilmir snorted. "I have never understood why you hold those gleaming metals in such high regard."

Aravon cocked an eyebrow. Throrsson wore three heavy torcs—two bearing the likeness of the *Reafan*, and one with the snarling face of a bear—all made from glimmering gold and silver.

"The garrisons require men to maintain them, and men must be paid in coin," the Duke replied simply. "But the garrisons in Fjall land will be manned by no more Legionnaires than are required to keep them operational and to maintain a close eye on the Eirdkilrs and their allies among the southern clans."

The Hilmir's face creased into a wolfish grin. "And if the Fjall move to…control the clans that sided with our enemies?"

Duke Dyrund turned his palms up. "Prince Toran will see it as a service to peace and prosperity on Fehl, of course."

"Of course." Throrsson's rumbling chuckle echoed in the longhouse. "Peace and prosperity."

Aravon's eyebrows rose behind his mask. With a few simple words, Duke Dyrund had made the Prince's position clear: should the Fjall attack northward, the Legion would side with their Fehlans allies. However, he'd also given the Hilmir free rein over the south of Fehl—the fractious Bein, Myrr, and the smaller clans to the west. The Legion would never be able to subdue them and maintain tight control on their territory. Throrsson and his warband would have no oppositions to the expansion of their territory—a desire the man had made plain by adopting his great-grandfather's title of Hilmir—by crushing the clans hostile to the Princelands.

Damn! Aravon whistled silently. *That's a bargain where both parties came out ahead.*

The Prince had chosen his envoy well.

At that moment, Gyrd returned to the meeting room. The tightness in his face seemed to have relaxed slightly, and his posture behind the Hilmir had grown far less wary and hostile.

Throrsson's smile didn't waver, but neither did it grow warmer. The Hilmir fixed the Duke with a piercing scrutiny, the same look that Snarl adopted when hunting a particularly juicy mouse. Long moments of silence passed before he spoke.

"I have heard your Prince's terms, and I find them agreeable. However…" He held up a huge finger. "I must first consult with my *Seiomenn*, hear what *Striith* would have us do in this matter."

"Of course, Hilmir." Duke Dyrund inclined his head. "My men and I await your pleasure."

"I shall not be long." Throrsson stood and gestured to Gyrd. "In the meantime, allow me to offer you the hospitality of Storbjarg."

The Duke stood as well as bowed from the waist. "May your god speak clearly to you, Hilmir. And may his guidance lead down the path that is best for your people and mine both."

With a nod, Throrsson strode deeper into the shadows of the longhouse and disappeared through the hanging wall of furs.

Chapter Forty

The longhouse prepared for them certainly didn't look like much—walls of mud daub and sod, a heavy odor of oxen and cattle, the haze of wood smoke hanging thick around the firepit—yet Aravon had learned enough of Fehlan customs to understand that the Hilmir had shown them a high honor by placing them here. The building stood opposite the Hilmir's, second largest in size to the chief's longhouse—a place for distinguished guests.

Yet even as that thought flashed through his mind, he was assessing the interior for vulnerabilities, hidden threats, and escape routes. Noll and Colborn pushed through the door first, fanning out to the right and left, searching the shadows. The two men disappeared through the hanging furs at the far end of the longhouse, then returned a moment later.

"*All clear,*" Colborn signed.

Aravon strode deeper into the longhouse, analyzing the layout to find the best defensive positions should the need arise. It was only *after* he'd formulated a plan for holding the structure that he paid attention to the crackling fire radiating warmth and light, the platter of food sitting on the table, and the half-sized barrel with its collection of drinking horns.

The Duke nodded to Grimar, who had served as their escort and guide. "Thank you."

Throrsson's second-in-command grunted. "The Hilmir will summon you when he is ready." It was all the answer he gave before turning and striding from the longhouse.

Duke Dyrund gestured to the table. "Captain Snarl, Lord Virinus, let us refresh ourselves."

Lord Virinus gave a little sniff, pressing a hand to his nose. Yet he managed to hold his tongue at the simplicity of their accommodations and the heavy smells. Taking a seat across the table from the Duke, he picked at a chunk of roast lamb delicately.

"My lord, far be it from me to question your wisdom," Lord Virinus said, in a tone that held immeasurable doubt, "but wasn't revealing the Wraithfever cure so early in the negotiation giving up a crucial advantage? Reserving it to the end would have allowed you to extract as much from Throrsson and his Fjall as the Prince desires."

"Perhaps." The Duke took a bite of suckling pig and chewed thoughtfully. "But a man like Throrsson does not negotiate like a Princelander. He responds better to a more direct, forthright approach. You see, Myron, the Fjall are warriors at heart, dedicated to…"

Aravon stopped listening as the Duke spoke about the Fjall's warlike customs and culture. Instead, he turned to his men.

"Any other way out than the back door?" he asked.

"No," Colborn signed with his right hand, his left gripping a fire-roasted chicken leg. *"Fehlan longhouses are sealed against the cold winters, so there are only ever two entrances."*

"Cellars?" Aravon signed.

Noll shook his head. *"Nothing underground."*

Aravon nodded. *"Good."* The meeting with the Hilmir had gone far better than he'd expected—he'd almost believed Throrsson would agree to the Duke's terms on the spot—but that couldn't cause him to let down his guard. This close to Eirdkilr-held territory, he had to be wary for spies, assassins, and enemies on all sides. If the Eirdkilrs had managed to plant a spy or turn a traitor in the Prince's Council, it wasn't a stretch to imagine that they'd done the same among their Fehlan neighbors.

"Belthar," he signed to the big man, *"post up by the front door. Show off that axe of yours, yeah?"*

Gathering up a handful of nuts, fruits, and meat, with a drinking horn full of mead, Belthar strode over to the main entrance to the longhouse and settled to the ground right in front of the opening. He leaned his massive crossbow against the wall, drew his axe, and set about sharpening it. The long, loud strokes of his whetstone were only occasionally interrupted as he snatched a bite of his meal—a task that proved difficult, given the heavy leather mask. He, like all of them, had to loosen the lower strap and lift the mask to put the food in his mouth. Yet it was the only way to conceal their identities from Lord Virinus and the Black Xiphos mercenaries scattered around the longhouse.

"*Colborn, Noll, north and south walls,*" Aravon signed. "*Skathi, dead center, arrows handy.*"

The three moved to their designated positions. Colborn and Noll settled into the shadows against the walls, out of the dim light of the fire burning in the firepit. There, they could remain undetected while keeping an eye on the front and rear entrances. Skathi's short horsebow would be far more maneuverable indoors, and her position at the center of the longhouse meant she could shoot in both directions in an instant.

Rangvaldr and Zaharis, he kept with him near Duke Dyrund. Even with nine mercenaries and Lord Virinus, he wouldn't trust the Duke's personal safety to anyone else.

Two of the sellswords remained outside the front door, with two more posted as guards at the rear entrance. The man Scathan sat at the Duke's left hand, Barcus at Lord Virinus' right. The remaining three were scattered around the longhouse, eating and drinking yet never relaxing their wary vigil.

Satisfied, Aravon took his seat on the Duke's right hand, rested his spear against the table's edge, and picked at the meal.

"...understand, my lord." Lord Virinus was saying. "Thank you for clearing that matter up for me."

"Of course, Myron." Duke Dyrund nodded. "Diplomacy, at its core, is about finding a way for both sides to get what they want."

Lord Virinus' expression was pensive as he stood and turned to refill his drinking horn. A loud *squelching* sound echoed in the longhouse, and the reek of cow dung rose from the dark brown pile beneath his foot. The nobleman growled and shook his foot, trying to kick free the ordure clinging to his costly leather boots. "Bloody savages," he muttered beneath his breath.

Not the most diplomatic diplomat. Aravon shook his head. The elderly Lord Aleron Virinus must have had significant pull at court to convince the Prince to send his second son along on this mission. A mission for which he seemed far less than ideally suited.

But isn't that always the way of Princeland politics? Aravon snorted inwardly. *Men using their wealth and influence to grow even more powerful.*

317

He'd always hated the courts of Icespire, the backbiting, deceit, and treachery inherent in matters of statecraft—one of the primary reasons he'd joined the Legion of Heroes at such a young age. A soldier's life had its share of dangers, yet he would stand a shield wall far more eagerly than dance at the Wintertide formal or engage in the saccharine repartee of the high nobility. Polite conversation had never been his forte, a trait he'd inherited from his father.

A bitter sneer twisted Aravon's lips. *Conversation of any sort was out of the General's realm of expertise.* Barking orders came easy to his father, the result of years spent commanding Legionnaires. Yet Aravon couldn't think of one meaningful exchange he'd shared with the man. Or, at least one that hadn't involved his father shouting, raging, or cursing at him. Even on those occasions when his "bloody disappointment of a son" hadn't been the true target of the General's anger, proximity made Aravon the most convenient victim.

"Captain Snarl." Duke Dyrund's quiet words brought Aravon's attention back to the present. "A word." He inclined his head toward the wall of furs at the rear of the longhouse.

Curious, Aravon pushed back his meager meal and followed the Duke into the privacy of the back chamber—little more than bare walls, piled furs, and a wool-stuffed armchair set beside a smaller firepit.

"Sir?" Aravon asked as the Duke turned to him.

"How is he?" Duke Dyrund signed.

Confusion twisted Aravon's brow for a moment, until the Duke's eyes snapped to where Colborn sat against the north wall. Evidently, he hadn't missed the cloud of gloom that hung over the Lieutenant, no matter how preoccupied he was with matters critical to the Princelands.

"Rangvaldr spoke to him," Aravon replied, careful to keep his hands out of Colborn's line of sight. *"Troubled by what happened at Rivergate and Gold Burrows, but solid."*

A puzzled frown creased the Duke's face. *"What happened at Rivergate?"*

"He killed Jokull. First time he's gone against his own."

"Ahh." Understanding gleamed in Duke Dyrund's eyes. *"That'd take a toll on anyone, even a man as strong as our Lieutenant. Finding the Deid warriors slaughtered at the mine would just compound things."*

Aravon cocked his head. *"You knew he was Deid?"*

318

The Duke's shoulders gave a little twitch. *"That's half the reason I recruited him. The Deid are our closest allies, and some of the best huntsmen on Fehl. And, given his history..."* His fingers remained motionless for a long moment. *"He needed a change, to get away from the Legion, and I needed a man like him for our mission. Two Eirdkilrs, one arrow."*

Aravon nodded. He'd learned precious little of Colborn's past, but what the Lieutenant had told him made it clear Colborn had few ties binding him to the life he'd lived before joining their company.

"A word of advice from someone who's spent his life around soldiers." The Duke gave him a wry grin. *"Give him space, but don't leave him adrift."*

"Words at once cryptic and poetic." Aravon snorted. *"You'd have made one hell of a Lectern, Your Grace."*

Duke Dyrund rolled his eyes. *"What that means is that men like Colborn need time to clear their heads. But, if they spend too much time in their heads, they start to feel alone, like a boat cast adrift."*

Aravon inclined his head. *"I've been there, more than once."* A part of him wished he could call Snarl, that he hadn't had to order the Enfield to hide in the woods out of sight of Storbjarg. The little Enfield had brought him back from the depths of his gloom. That, and the camaraderie of men like Duke Dyrund, Colborn, and the rest of his company.

"So let him think, let him feel." The Duke nodded. *"But not too long, and not alone. Be there for him, even if he thinks he'd rather face it on his own. Once he comes out the other side, he'll be grateful for it."*

"Thank you, sir," Aravon signed. *"For the advice, and for caring."*

The Duke seemed genuinely surprised by the words. *"Is that so foreign an idea, Aravon?"*

"Just..." Aravon hesitated a long moment. *"Just not the sort of thing he's had much of."*

A knowing look entered the Duke's eyes. *"Or you, either, eh?"*

Aravon's gut clenched. He'd tried to deflect to Colborn's struggles, but ever since seeing the Hilmir embrace his son, he hadn't been able to push back the bitterness burning a hole in his stomach.

The Duke leaned forward, placing a hand on Aravon's shoulders. *"Traighan's many things, Aravon,"* he signed one-handed, *"but he's not a monster, and he's not made of stone.*" A frown creased his face. "*He…might not have always known how to show it, but he cares. In his own way.*"

Aravon felt the anger simmering deep, deep down threatening to rise to the surface, the way it always did when the matter of his father came up. "*Of course.*"

"*No, truly.*" Duke Dyrund searched his eyes. "*Before his…illness, every time I spoke with him, he would tell me about your latest promotion, some new posting you'd gotten, or some new triumph of yours.*"

Aravon's eyes widened. That sounded nothing like the cold, stony man he'd lived with—on the occasions his father had been home, of course, which grew ever more infrequent after the death of his mother—and even less like the roaring, swearing, drunken Legionnaire smashing the wooden furniture of their kitchen, living room, and sitting room to pieces.

"*Even now, in his moments of lucidity, he's proud of you, Aravon.*" The shadow of pain and sorrow glimmered in the Duke's eyes. "*Proud of the man you'd become. The Legionnaire, Mylena's husband, father to your sons.*"

A fist of anger squeezed at Aravon's heart. "*Then he should have said something before I died.*"

"*He wanted to.*" The Duke's face fell. "*If he'd known how, he would have. But men like the General…*" He drew in a deep breath. "*It doesn't come easy to them.*"

"*It should!*" Now the anger boiled over. Aravon felt like shouting, like leaping to his feet and raising his voice so loud it would set the mud walls rattling. Yet he wouldn't, wouldn't let it get the better of him as it had gotten the better of his father so many times before. He wouldn't be the raving, shouting madman who had turned his son's home into a nightmare.

His muscles clenched so tightly his hands trembled as he signed. "*It couldn't have been that hard to say the words. Swordsman knew he said them often enough when giving grand speeches to his Legionnaires. But no.*" He shook his head. "*That would have been too much for his soldier's pride.*"

"*Perhaps.*" The Duke gave a little nod. "*But that doesn't change how he feels. Nothing ever will, not even his illness. His mind may be leaving him, but he will never forget his love for you.*"

Aravon bit back an angry retort. The Duke's kindness stood at such sharp contrast with his father's aloofness. A part of him—a small, quiet part that Aravon rarely allowed to give voice, even in his thoughts—had often wished that the situation had been different. That he'd had a *different* father. A better

320

father, one more like Duke Dyrund rather than the cold, hard block of granite that was General Traighan.

He raised his hands to reply in the silent hand language, but a sound from outside the longhouse snapped his attention around. The voice of Urniss, one of the two mercenaries guarding the front entrance, echoed loud, though Aravon couldn't make out the Fehlan words.

In an instant, he was through the curtains and racing back to the table to snatch up his spear. "Stay behind me, Your Grace," Aravon called, retreating toward the Duke.

Zaharis and Rangvaldr were on their feet before the Black Xiphos mercenaries. Belthar all but leapt upright, and the *creak* of Skathi's bow filled the longhouse. Noll and Colborn pressed deeper into the shadows, weapons held at the ready.

But it was only Gyrd who pushed through the wall of furs and strode into the longhouse. The graying Fjall warrior seemed unperturbed by the multitude of weapons arrayed against him—if anything, he seemed *amused* to find the Hilmir's guests ready for an assault.

A small smile tugged at his thin lips. "Come, men of the Princelands." The warrior motioned toward the door. "The Hilmir has your answer."

* * *

Aravon had heard of the Fjall's sacrificial temples—the *Blotahorgr*, or "the place of blood and worship"—but never seen one in person. As with the wall of Storbjarg, he found himself impressed by the sheer size and scope of the construction.

Built from the same stone as the city wall with the same near-black mortar, the *Blotahorgr* was a massive dome that stood fully thirty feet high and sixty feet across. While many Princelander priests adorned their temples with marble, gold, or precious stone, the exterior of the Fjall's temple was a glittering surface of black. The ghoulstone seemed even darker now that the sun had set, and the light of flickering torches reflected off the temple, casting eerie shadows.

Yet it was the temple's interior that stood as the true marvel. The entire surface of the floor was paved with the same deeper-than-black ghoulstone, and the wooden pillars and support beams had been stained red—doubtless with the blood of slaughtered victims, enemies, or sacrificial animals. Suspended

321

from the rafters hung hundreds, perhaps thousands of swords. Copper, bronze, iron, and steel blades, their sharp tips dangling over the heads of the five men who stood within the *Blotahorgr*.

Gyrd took his place at Throrsson's left hand, with Grimar standing a step behind and to the right of the Hilmir. Throrsson's right arm was wrapped around the shoulder of his son, Bjarni. Though the young man's fever had broken, he still appeared gaunt, weakened by the disease. Yet he stood tall, clad in a warrior's furs and chain mail, sword on his belt. In his eyes glimmered the same warrior's spirit Aravon had seen among so many Legionnaires before— walking wounded determined to stand in the shield wall and fight the enemy beside their comrades, pain or injury be damned.

Behind the sacrificial altar stood a man, doubtless the *Seiomenn* of Storbjarg, with a beard and braided hair of pure white that had been dyed into long, lank streaks of red, black, and purple. Aravon glanced to the man's neck, expecting to see a holy stone similar to Rangvaldr's, but found none. It seemed not all Seiomenn had magical gemstones—perhaps that explained why Wraithfever had spread so widely among the Fjall.

The Seiomenn pounded an animal-hide drum and he chanted in an unfamiliar language—one that sounded like Fehlan, but far older, with a poetic intonation that flowed with the beat of the music, the clacking of the myriad bones entwined in his beard. The mélange of sounds echoed off the stone floors, rising to fill the temple and mingling with the thick haze of smoke that emanated from a stone bowl atop the sacrificial altar.

"You come to us with talk of peace, men of the Princelands." The Hilmir's voice rang in the temple, a deep, booming cadence that harmonized with the ceremonial music and chanting. "Yet we do not bandy our words, do not waste our breath on clever tricks of the tongue!"

The sudden tightening of Aravon's stomach had nothing to do with the reek of smoke or the bloody décor. The deal had been all but sealed. Bjarni's presence at Throrsson's side should have been the end of negotiations. Yet the way the Hilmir spoke, it almost sounded as if he intended to reject the Duke's offer.

Eirik Throrsson's eyes flashed with anger. "The Fjall are men of war, warriors of *Striith*, descended from the first men to walk the lands of Fehl. To us is given the gift of battle and death." He raised a clenched fist. "We bring those gifts to *any* who seek to take from us what is rightfully ours!"

Aravon tightened his hold on his spear, ready for anything. Had Throrsson taken offense at the Duke's request to let Legionnaires enter Fjall lands? Had he seen their offer as nothing more than a ploy to encroach on his territory, take advantage of his weakness?

Yet, as Aravon caught sight of the Duke's face, he recognized the familiar glint in the man's eye. Triumph, the same look he'd gotten every time he defeated Aravon at Nizaa.

"And so it shall be!" Throrsson roared. "Let us bestow those gifts upon our enemies. Let battle and death once more flood our lands, and let the *Tauld* know the true meaning of Fjall courage, resolve, and steel. By the will of *Striith*, let it be so!"

"By the will of *Striith*!" echoed Gyrd, Grimar, Bjarni, and the *Seiomenn*.

"By the will of *Striith*," the Duke intoned.

Relief coursed through Aravon. The Fjall had joined their side. Their mission had been a success.

Thus far, Aravon reminded himself. *Now comes the hard part.*

The Hilmir had agreed to lead his men into battle, but many, many Eirdkilrs and Fjall would die before this was all over. It was up to him, the Duke, and Throrsson to find a way to tip the scales as far in their favor as possible.

Chapter Forty-One

"We cannot engage the *Tauld* directly, not yet." The Hilmir shook his head, setting his braided beard and hair whipping about. "Only once the warband is at full strength can we truly be confident of winning."

"Waiting could be a mistake." Duke Dyrund frowned across the wooden table at the Fjall chief. They, along with Aravon, Lord Virinus, Gyrd, and Grimar, had returned to the Hilmir's longhouse, sharing another horn of mead before diving into the discussion of tactics and strategy. A discussion that had, until now, proven only *partially* productive. Throrsson was nothing if not stubborn and self-assured.

"Right now," the Duke continued, "the Eirdkilr forces are divided, locked in a siege of the Eastmarch garrisons." He snapped his fingers and Lord Virinus stepped forward, passing him the canvas map of Fehl. The Duke unrolled the map across the Hilmir's table and bent over it, tapping on the black squares indicating Dagger Garrison and the Bulwark. "At last report, close to six thousand of them, committed to an assault they had no chance of winning."

Both strongholds were strong, well-supplied, and each home to a full battalion and a half of Legionnaires, along with their cavalry, attached Agrotorae, and auxiliaries. Six thousand Eirdkilrs could only hope to capture the stone fortresses through a surprise attack, as they had at Anvil Garrison and Rivergate. The fact that the Legion retained control of both meant the gates had been closed in time and the garrisons fortified. The men of Pearl, Sapphire, and Diamond Battalions could withstand an Eirdkilr siege for two full months before their supplies ran low.

Eirik Throrsson's huge brow furrowed. "So I have heard. A strange strategy, yet since the arrival of Tyr *Farbjodr*, the *Tauld* have been anything but predictable."

Aravon raised an eyebrow behind his mask. He recognized the name "*Farbjodr*" from the Saga of Gunnarsdottir; it was the name given to the monstrous beast that plagued the icy wastelands beyond the Sawtooth Mountains.

The Duke pursed his lips. "I have heard the name spoken, but beyond the fact that he commands the Eirdkilrs, I have uncovered little more." Frustration echoed in his voice. "What can you tell us about him?"

"I can only share what I have heard from the rumors spread among the southern clans." Eirik Throrsson gave the Duke a wry grin. "It is whispered that he strode naked from the icy wastes in which no man can survive, clad only in snow and stone. In his hand, he wielded a sword made of blood, a blade that gleamed with the light of death. And with it, he fought his way to claim command of first one village, then more, until all the *Tauld* marched beneath his black banner."

Aravon resisted the urge to snort. Rumors and legends tended to be *highly* exaggerated—he knew firsthand, for he'd heard the *true* account of the Battle of Stormcrow Pass, where his father and Duke Dyrund had slain thirty Eirdkilrs between them, not three hundred as the Legion stories held.

"He called himself Tyr, and *Farbjodr* was the name given to him by the men who serve him." Eirik Throrsson's expression grew grim. "For he is as ravenous as the monster Gunnarsdottir faced, and he will stop at nothing until the Eird are driven from their lands."

The Duke narrowed his eyes. "Sounds like a real charmer."

Throrsson chuckled. "I have not met him, but the stories of the savagery unleashed on his defeated rivals are matched only by the reports of his cunning and strategy. For fifteen years, he has commanded the *Tauld*, and in that time, their reach has grown long, their foothold in my lands strengthened."

Fifteen years. Right around the time the Eirdkilrs had attacked Highcliffe Motte and attempted to storm the eastern passage through the Sawtooth Mountains. That was when the Eirdkilr battle strategy had changed, grown more difficult to predict. In that time, Prince Toran had been forced to triple the number of Legionnaires on Fehl just to hold the fortresses and stave off attacks on allied Fehlan lands.

The Duke leaned forward. "So he is the one we need to take down to put an end to the war?"

"His word guides the *Tauld*," the Hilmir replied, "but it is said he never ventures north of the Sawtooth Mountains. Instead, he sends his loyal chieftains to carry out his orders."

Anger flared hot and bright in Aravon's chest. "Men like Hrolf Hrungnir," he growled.

Throrsson's eyes snapped to him, and a shadow flashed across his face. "The *Blodhundr* chief numbered among one of Tyr *Farbjodr's* most capable leaders. And the cruelest." He fixed Aravon with a piercing stare. "Far too many of my people suffered under his heel before he was defeated at *Brotna Hamarr*, what you call Broken Canyon. No Fjall will mourn his sudden, mysterious disappearance."

The Duke inclined his head. "Nor will the Princelands." He gave the Hilmir a sly smile and raised his horn of mead. "And the Eyrr will rest more soundly for his absence."

Curiosity blazed in the Hilmir's eyes. The Duke hadn't just taken credit for Hrolf Hrungnir's death; he'd also hinted at a relationship with the Eyrr, thereby solidifying the Princelands' hold over northern Fehl. A reminder to Throrsson that they may be in Fjall territory, but the Prince wielded far more power on the continent than the Hilmir.

"However, the *Blodhundrs'* defeat was likely little more than a momentary setback in Tyr *Farbjodr's* plan." Throrsson spoke in a slow, thoughtful voice. "The *Blodsvarri* still controls the *Tauld* in the west."

Aravon's eyebrows drew together. *Blood Queen?* A rough translation, given the differences in Fehlan dialects, but one that seemed suitably fierce for an Eirdkilr leader. *But a queen? Would the Eirdkilrs follow a woman?*

"This *Blodsvarri*," the Duke said, "what is she like?"

"As crafty and ruthless as Hrolf Hrungnir ever was," the Hilmir continued, stroking his braided beard with a heavy hand. "More so, according to the stories of her subjugation of the *Haugr* and *Hafr* clans."

Haugr and *Hafr* were two of the eight smaller clans that occupied the southeasternmost corner of mainland Fehl, just north of the Sawtooth Mountains. Those clans were little more than roving bands of reavers, locked in an endless series of blood feuds and violent disputes that kept them fighting each other—no real threat to their neighbors, the Fjall to the north and Bein to the east.

"It is said she slit her husband's throat to take Tyr *Farbjodr* as her mate." Throrsson's face twisted in a grimace. "They rutted atop his corpse, bathed in his blood and entrails."

The Duke snorted. "A match made in a dark, twisted hell." His expression grew pensive. "Yet the fact that she leads the Eirdkilrs speaks volumes."

"Aye." Throrsson nodded. "I have met her, have stared in her eyes." A dark look flashed across his face. "I am no *Seiomenn*, but even I know the legends of the *Hveorungr*. There is no life within her, only death. Death and a thirst for blood. Fehlan, *Tauld*, and Princelander, it makes no difference to her. Defeating her will be no easy task."

The Duke inclined his head. "But you would not be the Hilmir if you did not have a plan." A smile tugged at his lips. "So I would hear it, and perhaps there is a word or two of counsel I might lend."

Throrsson fixed him with a narrow-eyed stare. "Sometimes, Princelander, you know far too much for your own good."

The Duke chuckled and swept a little bow from his seat. "That is, after all, my job."

"Of course." Throrsson gave a dismissive wave. "Without my full strength, I cannot be assured of success against the *Blodsvarri*. My warband is reduced to six thousand, and she has ten thousand *Tauld* at her back—six thousand committed to the sieges on your garrison, and four thousand at her back. A prouder Hilmir might insist that his men are worth two of their enemies, but Thror Arvidsson did not raise a boastful fool." His face broadened in a wry grin. "Well, not a fool, at least."

The Duke smiled in return, but said nothing, only gestured for the Hilmir to continue.

"The *Blodsvarri* knows the strength of my warband," Throrsson said. "I have made certain that she does. Since the plague struck—" His expression darkened, his eyes growing shadowed. "—I have ensured that her demands for Fjall assistance are met with protests about our weakened condition. A fact that I intend to capitalize on."

The Duke leaned forward. "Go on."

"I have arranged a meeting with the Blood Queen at the Waeggbjod, when the sun is at its peak, the day after tomorrow."

Aravon stiffened. *A meeting, with the Eirdkilrs?* Only the Duke's calm demeanor kept him from stepping forward or leveling his spear at mention of such treachery.

"Waeggbjod." The Duke seemed to chew on the word. "*Walled field*, yes?"

Throrsson nodded. "Once, the place where feuding Fjall chieftains met to settle the fate of their clans in single combat."

Aravon's eyes narrowed, his tension giving way to incredulity. "You plan to challenge her to a duel?" That was the sort of thing mainlanders did—courtly duels were all the rage in the Praamian and Voramian courts, and had come into fashion in the Princelanders as well. He couldn't imagine an Eirdkilr bound by the rules of polite dueling etiquette, especially not one with the name "Blood Queen".

"No." Throrsson shook his head. "For the last two hundred years, the Waeggbjod has been a sacred meeting ground. It is there that the first Hilmir was crowned, and where I will one day be likewise, with *Striith's* blessing."

Now it was the Duke's turn to look suspicious. "And why will the Blood Queen agree to meet you there?"

Throrsson leaned back in his chair. "Because I sent word that I desired to speak of joining the *Tauld*."

"Traitorous savage!" Lord Virinus' nasal, piercing shout echoed in the longhouse. The Icespire nobleman leapt to his feet, gilded sword half-drawn, his face red and eyes fixed on Throrsson.

Aravon's blood ran cold. The Hilmir's words had taken him by surprise, and even the Duke seemed puzzled. Yet Lord Virinus' reaction was the violent, knee-jerk outburst of a fool—the sort of foolish officer who committed his men into battle without first hearing his scouts' reports.

Worse, the explosive tantrum could provoke Throrsson's ire or cause offense. If the nobleman drew steel on the Hilmir, Virinus could very well end up dead—or, at the very least, shatter any chance at reaching an agreement.

Aravon moved on instinct drilled into him over years as a Legionnaire and weeks at Camp Marshal. He danced forward, moving light on his feet like he'd seen Zaharis do a thousand times, and seized the nobleman's wrist in a firm grip. With Virinus' hand locked in place, Aravon wrapped his arm around the nobleman's neck, seized his chin, and pulled him around and backward.

The attack, taught to him by Zaharis, could snap a man's neck with a quick wrench. Aravon, however, had no intention of killing Lord Virinus, outburst or

329

no. His move simply dragged the man off-balance and twisted his head around, silencing his explosive words. A quick twist of his hips and he sent the nobleman to the ground—hard enough to knock the wind from his lungs. Aravon knelt atop the man's chest and drove a knee into his solar plexus.

"Shut up and stay still!" he growled.

A breathless, wide-eyed Lord Virinus stared up at Aravon. Stunned surprise soon gave way to outrage, but he could not suck in air to form words.

"Lord Virinus!" The Duke's voice cracked like a whip. "Control yourself!"

The nobleman labored to draw breath. "B-But…he…"

Duke Dyrund stood, strode to where Aravon knelt atop the prone nobleman, and spoke in a low voice. "Only a fool speaks before he knows all the facts. Consider this your first lesson in diplomacy, and thank the Swordsman that Captain Snarl got to you before your sword cleared its sheath."

Virinus' eyes snapped to Aravon, and the burning indignation flared bright on his slim face.

"Had you drawn, you would have challenged the Hilmir to single combat." The Duke shook his head. "And how do you think *that* battle would have gone?"

The blood drained from the nobleman's face, and he gave a labored gasp.

At the Duke's nod, Aravon stood from Lord Virinus' chest. The slight man drew in a breath, wincing as he struggled to sit upright.

"The Prince promised your father that you could listen and learn." The Duke's eyes narrowed to angry slits. "So, like Captain Snarl said, shut up and stay still, or I send you back to Icespire tonight. Understood?"

After a moment, the nobleman bobbed his head. "Yes, Your Grace," he said in a voice that barely stopped short of a sullen pout.

The Duke straightened and turned back to the still-seated Throrsson with an apologetic smile. "Pardon his rudeness, Hilmir. Some Princelanders fail to learn how different things are among their southern neighbors."

Throrsson's eyes were fixed on the nobleman. Steel glinted there, not anger, but a disdain for Lord Virinus that bordered on distaste.

"No apology needed," he finally rumbled, turning back to the Duke. "This is, after all, my finest shirt." He gestured to his lamb-skin vest and the roughspun tunic beneath. "It would have been such a shame to ruin it with his blood."

It was no boast, no jest, a simple statement of fact. Aravon had little doubt that a man that could lead the Fjall, the toughest and largest of the Fehlan clans, would be a mighty warrior in his own right.

The Hilmir's gaze traveled to rest on Aravon, and his lips pursed slightly, a hint of amusement tugging at his lips. After a moment, he shrugged and returned his attention to the Duke. "As I was saying, I have made arrangements to meet the *Blodsvarri* at the Waeggbjod. There, on the sacred grounds, we will lay down our weapons and speak of peace between the *Tauld* and Fjall."

Duke Dyrund steepled his fingers before his face. "To what end?"

Grim humor twinkled in the Hilmir's eyes. "To lure the Blood Queen into my trap, of course!" He leaned back, a smile of utter confidence brightening his face. "A trap that our friends of the Deid will be ready to spring."

Aravon sucked in a breath. *The Deid?* The Fjall had never been on friendly terms with the Deid, even before the Eirdkilrs began launching raids into Deid lands from Fjall-controlled territory.

Throrsson's beaming grin widened. "The Fjall have called for a peaceful parley with the *Tauld* leader, and the *Blodsvarri* will come because she knows that I would never break the sanctity of the Waeggbjod. She and I will enter alone, and there we will remain until one of us declares the discussion concluded—either with the promise of peace or a declaration of war."

"You, of course, will speak of peace, yes?" The Duke raised an eyebrow.

"Of course." Throrsson nodded his shaggy head. "What better way to throw the Blood Queen off-guard than to promise her precisely what she wants?"

"And, because you are arranging for it to be held on the sacred ground," the Duke continued, "she will believe your offer is genuine."

"Right up until the Deid launch their surprise attack." Throrsson's bushy eyebrows rose. "As they are not *my* warriors, but the warband of a clan that has, until now, been hostile to the Fjall, there will be no oaths broken, the sanctity of the Waeggbjod unsullied."

"A cunning plan." The Duke nodded approval.

"But not without one major flaw," Aravon put in.

Throrsson turned a curious gaze on him. "And what is that, wolf man?"

"Killing the Blood Queen will chop the head off the snake," Aravon said. "Yet it doesn't account for the ten thousand Eirdkilrs at her command. Even if

331

you discount the six thousand arrayed against the Legion garrisons, that still leaves four thousand."

"By the end of the attack, that number will be fewer than three." A smug smile played on the Hilmir's face.

Aravon cocked his head. "I'm listening."

"In the days when the Waeggbjod was a battleground," Throrsson said, "only two men entered alone to draw swords and spill blood. Yet there were always warriors who stood watch to ensure neither side played false. Each clan would summon one thousand, one hundred, and eleven of the strongest men and women of their warband to stand testimony before *Striith*. The *Haelvitni*, they were called. Witnesses of death."

Understanding dawned on Aravon. "So your eleven hundred and eleven will face an equal number of *Tauld*, but with the Deid warband launching a sneak attack to throw the enemy off-guard."

Throrsson nodded. "The *Blodsvarri* will be the first to fall, and the two thousand men of clan Deid will force the *Tauld* to split their forces. The momentary confusion will suffice to give us the advantage." He raised a finger. "As will the two thousand additional Fjall warriors that will be waiting a mile from the Waeggbjod."

Five thousand Fehlans against eleven hundred Eirdkilrs. Aravon nodded. *Now that's the sort of odds I can get behind.*

"Gyrd will be leading a company two hundred strong, the fleetest warriors of the Fjall tasked with the duty of hunting down any *Tauld* that escape the battle." Throrsson raised a clenched fist, and defiance glittered hard as ice in his blue eyes. "None will survive to bring word of warning of the *Blodsvarri's* death to their fellows. They will not be expecting it when the Fjall warband swoops down upon them and drives them from our lands once and for all!"

Aravon played over the strategy in his mind. If they *could* defeat the Blood Queen at Waeggbjod, that left fewer than three thousand Eirdkilrs to face more than twice that number of combined Fjall and Deid warriors. The Duke had already sent Skathi riding out of Storbjarg to call Snarl and send word of their concord with the Hilmir to Lord Eidan in Icespire and his agents in Silverhill. Within a week, the wagons would arrive bearing the Wraithfever cure, and the Hilmir's warband would be restored to near-full strength—minus however many warriors succumbed to the illness in that time.

A week, Aravon thought. *Eight thousand Fehlan warriors should be able to hold their own against three thousand Eirdkilrs that long.* If the Hilmir could use his knowledge of Fjall lands to launch surprise attacks on the Eirdkilrs, they had a real chance of reducing their numbers further, until the fever-ridden warriors recovered enough for one final push. With six thousand Eirdkilrs focused on besieging Dagger Garrison and the Bulwark, Throrsson had a real chance of shattering the enemy's grip on his lands.

By the Swordsman, he's actually got a chance of pulling this off! Hope surged within Aravon, lifting a weight off his shoulders. What had once seemed impossible now drew within their reach.

Yet, even as the thought passed through his mind, a figure raced into the longhouse. Skathi, masked and armored, horsebow in hand and longbow slung over her shoulder, ran straight to the Duke's side and thrust out a small strip of parchment.

In silence, the Duke took the message from her and read it quickly. His face grew gray, new lines forming around the corners of his eyes and mouth. When he turned to hand the note to Aravon, shadows darkened his eyes.

As Skathi retreated from the longhouse, Aravon turned over the note and read the words scrawled in Lord Eidan's neat hand. The words drove a spike of ice into his belly.

"Last night, the Eirdkilrs broke off the siege of Dagger Garrison," the Duke said. "Three thousand of them, marching in this direction even as we speak."

Chapter Forty-Two

Throrsson leapt to his feet. "What?" he roared, his eyes blazing. "Impossible!"

"If only that were so." The Duke's voice was grave. "But my watchers have never yet fed me false information."

"The impossibility is that you *know* of such an action." Throrsson narrowed his eyes. "Not even the fastest horse can travel that distance in a single day."

A smile played on Aravon's masked face. *Snarl can outrace a horse any day.*

An Enfield flying at full speed could cover the distance from Dagger Garrison to Icespire in twelve hours, with another twelve to fifteen hours for a second, fresh messenger to deliver the report.

The Duke gave Throrsson a knowing grin. "The Princelanders and Fjall both have our secrets, Hilmir." Then his mirth faded and expression grew serious. "But regardless of how we came by the knowledge, what matters now is that we *have* this intelligence. We know that three thousand Eirdkilrs abandoned the siege and march in this direction even now. We must decide what to do about them, not waste time with pointless questions."

After a long moment, the Hilmir seemed to accept the Duke's words. "So be it." His frown deepened to a pensive scowl, his eyes darkening. After a moment, he looked up. "I cannot believe that the *Blodsvarri* knows of my plans. I have shared them with no one but my most trusted warriors." He gestured to Gyrd and Grimar, who stood silently behind him. "Even then, only a select few know the full extent."

Aravon raised an eyebrow. *Just like only a handful of people on the Prince's Council knew of the mines.* The Eirdkilr battle strategies had grown more cunning in the last few years; it wasn't impossible to expect they'd adopt similar tactics in other aspects of the war, including intelligence-gathering. The fate of Gold Burrows and Silver Break were proof enough.

The Duke shook his head. "Our holy men teach that coincidences exist, but nothing happens at random. However, far be it from me to offer the Hilmir of the Fjall—"

Throrsson cut him off with a wave. "Speak your thoughts plainly, Princelander." His eyes narrowed. "My father taught that a wise Hilmir heeds the counsel of experienced men."

Duke Dyrund inclined his head. "The fact that she broke off her siege leads me to believe she sees *you* as a larger threat than the Legionnaires holding Dagger Garrison. If there is even a slight chance that the Blood Queen knows what you intend for her, you must act accordingly."

The Hilmir's frown deepened. "Continue."

The Duke leaned forward. "Your plan is predicated on taking her by surprise and overwhelming her forces before she can retreat or summon reinforcements. But if she suspects, she will have her own warriors lying in wait, ready to spring a trap of her own. Which means that meeting her at the Waeggbjod is...inadvisable." He tugged at his graying brown beard. "Not only will you be walking into whatever she has planned, but you will now have three thousand more enemies marching through your lands. That threat cannot be ignored."

Anger blazed in Throrsson's eyes. "You suggest we abandon the plan?"

"Not abandon." The Duke shook his head. "Change it up. Give her what she's expecting, but use those expectations against her."

Now the Hilmir leaned forward, interest flashing across his suntanned face. "I'm listening."

Duke Dyrund drew in a breath. "No one knows Fjall lands like you do. No one, perhaps, except the enemy that has claimed that land as their own. Which means that the *Blodsvarri* will likely know the Waeggbjod as well as the surrounding countryside. If she is half as cunning as you believe, she'll already have scouts positioned where they can keep watch."

The Hilmir nodded. "Scouts that Gyrd and his men will deal with before the meeting."

336

"Which will, in itself, lead her to suspect something is amiss," the Duke continued. "Either she will call off the meeting or she will simply spring her trap *before* she ever steps foot onto sacred ground." He raised an eyebrow. "Do the *Tauld* hold your rituals and customs in the same high value as you and your warriors?"

"No," Throrsson replied without hesitation. "But the *Blodsvarri* will honor the ritual. She cannot afford to have the Fjall as her enemy."

"Unless she already suspects that you *will* join forces with us." The Duke's expression grew pensive, and his fingers toyed with the sharp bone tip of his drinking horn. "In which case, those three thousand Eirdkilrs marching from Dagger Garrison are intended as a clear threat. A promise of what she will do to you if you do *not* sue for peace."

Throrsson's bushy eyebrows knitted together in thought.

"If your roles were reversed," the Duke pressed, "if you went to such a meeting with an old enemy that finds its position weakened, its forces thinned, would you not do likewise? With those three thousand Eirdkilrs at your back, she would hold the *tyna* position, force you to call *daudr* and cede the victory."

Surprise registered on Throrsson's face. "You know *hnenfatafl?*"

The Duke inclined his head. "I have long been a student of such games of strategy. Not only our own Nizaa, but your games as well. A much more direct, warrior's approach than Nizaa—an admirable insight into the mind of a *Fehlandr* warrior."

A small grin tugged at the Hilmir's lips. "Another lesson my father taught me, one I learned well." He gestured to a side table, upon which sat a wooden board and carved ivory pieces very similar to the Einari game of Nizaa. "Perhaps, one day soon, we will have to play a game, you and I."

"One day soon." The Duke smiled. "After the *Tauld* have been dealt with and peace restored to your lands and ours."

"Indeed." Throrsson's grin faded, and his expression grew somber once more. "Your counsel is wise, Duke of Eastfall. I can understand why the Prince sent *you* in his stead."

Duke Dyrund bowed in his seat. "The Hilmir does me a great honor." Genuine warmth echoed in his voice—the shared respect between powerful men who understood and perhaps even liked each other.

"This message of yours," Throrsson said, gesturing to the parchment in Aravon's hand, "it said the three thousand *Tauld* broke off their attack last night?"

Aravon nodded. "Yes."

The Hilmir ran a hand through his heavy, braided black beard. "That is more than two hundred of your miles away. Even if they ran all day and all night, they would require nearly three days to reach the Waeggbjod." His expression grew pensive. "My meeting with the *Blodsvarri* takes place at noon, the day after tomorrow. Long before those additional warriors pose any threat."

The Duke's expression never wavered, but Aravon noticed a sudden tightness in the man's shoulders. "Perhaps not at the Waeggbjod, but to Storbjarg, certainly."

Throrsson nodded. "A valid concern, Duke Dyrund, but with three thousand of my own warriors holding the walls, the Blood Queen's threat will lack any real bite." He bared his teeth in a savage grin. "The walls of Storbjarg have never been captured, and as you saw at your garrisons, the *Tauld* have little hope of victory if it comes to a siege. No, Princelander, we have no need to worry about Storbjarg."

"And what of the villages they pass?" the Duke asked. "The Eirdkilrs could—"

"The *Tauld* would not be that foolish." The Hilmir shook his head. "They raid and pillage, but if they *destroyed,* they would suffer as much as my people. For it is our crops, our livestock, our furs, our lumber, and our goods they steal." Anger darkened his face, and a stormcloud brewed in his eyes. "They cannot live off the land *and* make war on your Legions, and they cannot afford to turn us against them."

"But you are already turning against them," the Duke protested. "The *Blodsvarri* has to know that, else she wouldn't have pulled back those three thousand warriors from the siege to threaten your land."

"She may *suspect,*" Throrsson retorted, "but she cannot know for certain. She may be a cunning bitch, but she cannot truly see the hearts and thoughts of men."

"You say there's *no* chance that she could have learned of your true plan?" The Duke raised an eyebrow, his tone bordering on incredulous.

"None." Throrsson's jaw took on a stubborn cast. "Gyrd traveled alone to the meeting with Chief Runolf of the Deid. My warband has been quietly preparing for battle, but even *they* do not know what battle they will fight, not until the hour when I lead them out of Storbjarg." He slammed a clenched fist onto the wooden arm of his throne-like chair. "The *Blodsvarri* will have her suspicions, but there is no way she can *know.*"

The Duke drew in a deep breath, remaining silent for a long moment. Aravon had a good idea of what the man was thinking. Someone high in the Prince's confidence had leaked important information to the enemy, so it wasn't impossible to believe that the Eirdkilrs had eyes and ears among Throrsson's people. Yet pushing the matter would only insult the Hilmir, strain their fledgling relationship with the man. Unless he had proof that someone in Throrsson's confidences was a traitor, saying so would do little to endear the Duke to the Fjall chief.

"So be it." The Duke gave a little half-bow from the waist. "You know your men as only a warrior and Hilmir could."

"Precisely why I believe that my plan *will* succeed." Throrsson's heavy, bearded face creased into a snarl. "With half my warband to hold Storbjarg and the other half by my side, we will put an end to the *Blodsvarri*. Even if the *Tauld* do lay siege to Storbjarg, our walls are high, our gates strong. We have supplies enough to last for months. And, with the warriors of the Deid marching at our side, we will take the fight to them."

A new problem presented itself to Aravon. "If the enemy lays siege to Storbjarg," he said, "how will your people receive the Wraithfever cure?"

That stopped Throrsson cold. His expression grew hard as stone, his jaw muscles working. After a moment of silence, he shook his head. "*If* the *Tauld* surround Storbjarg, they will only make our task of defeating them easier. They will be trapped between our walls and the five thousand men at my command."

"If it were *just* three thousand," Aravon pressed, "I'd lay good odds on you winning that battle. But that doesn't account for the other four thousand Eirdkilrs under the *Blodsvarri's* direct command. Seven thousand enemies against your five thousand and the three thousand holding Storbjarg. Odds far worse than golden, even for the Fjall."

Throrsson's stony expression deepened slowly into a scowl.

"Consider this alternative, Hilmir." The Duke spoke quickly. "Three weeks ago, General Vessach marched out of Icespire at the head of Onyx Battalion, reinforcements for Dagger Garrison and the Bulwark. When news of the sieges reached him, the General intended to hold them at Hammer Garrison, plan a

339

counterattack to break the Eirdkilrs one stronghold at a time. But with the siege abandoned, that leaves an entire battalion to join the assault on the Eirdkilrs in Fjall lands. And, with the Eirdkilrs focused to the south, there is a chance we could free up men—perhaps as many as *two* thousand—from the northernmost Eastmarch garrisons and bring them here to help drive out the *Tauld*."

Throrsson's eyes narrowed. "Two thousand of your Legion, in my land." His expression soured, as if he'd just swallowed a mouthful of Noll's cooking.

"The combined forces of the Princelands, Fjall, and Deid would outnumber the Eirdkilrs," the Duke pressed. "With our shield walls and your warriors' courage, the enemy would have no chance of standing before us. The Legion could march the Wraithfever cure straight to Storbjarg, driving back the Eirdkilrs and delivering healing to your people at once." He raised a clenched fist, and excitement filtered into his voice. "Such a defeat would cost the enemy dearly. Not just *crippling* them, but perhaps even pushing them from your lands altogether."

For a moment, a glimmer of hope flickered to life within Aravon. The Hilmir's expression was pensive, yet it actually seemed as if he'd concede to the Duke's plan.

"Change the rendezvous with the *Blodsvarri*." Duke Dyrund's voice held an insistent edge. "Send word that the Wraithfever has weakened your warband so much that you cannot risk pulling your men far from your city for fear of Princelander attack. Instead, change it to a meeting place nearer Storbjarg, someplace where you hold an even greater advantage. Not just a tactical advantage, but close enough to the men here in the city that you could summon reinforcements if the battle turns against you. And, with the Deid to attack from the rear and the Legion marching to your aid, your victory is all but assured."

The momentary hope died within Aravon as Throrsson's face hardened, grew somber. "There is nowhere else."

Chapter Forty-Three

"What?" The Duke's eyebrows shot up.

"To the south of Storbjarg and beyond the forests to the east and west, the terrain is little more than flat grasslands. To the north, plenty of hills and forests, but nowhere to hold a pitched battle." Throrsson shook his head. "The Waeggbjod is the *only* place for fifty leagues that offers any sort of tactical advantage. The high mountains offer ample hiding places to conceal not only my men, but the Deid warband as well. With just one way to march men in and out, it is the *only* place where we can trap the *Blodsvarri* and her warriors."

Anxiety twisted in Aravon's gut. The Duke's plan *had* been good, but his ignorance of the local terrain worked against him.

"And we may be aligned in our mutual enmity against the *Tauld*," Throrsson continued, his voice barely above a growl, "but as my great-grandfather and his fathers before him, I will *not* permit your soldiers to enter my lands. For far too long, where your Legions marched, they conquered and controlled." Anger darkened his eyes. "Your garrisons on the Eastmarch and Westmarch already infringe on the boundaries of what was once Fjall lands. I have permitted them because they keep the *Tauld* occupied and, given our new alliance, I will continue to permit them. But I would rather be dragged through the burning *Helgrindr* into eternal darkness than let your Legionnaires invade my lands."

"With all due respect, Hilmir—" the Duke began.

"There will be no discussion!" Throrsson roared, rising to his feet. Fury blazed in the warrior's eyes and his teeth bared in a snarl. For a moment, his wrath and hulking form bore an undeniable resemblance to the ferocious

Fehlan black bear whose pelt he wore. "My warband will push back the *Tauld*, with the help of *true* sons of Fehl. Your Legionnaires will remain north of my borders, or by *Striith*, you will taste Fjall steel."

"You believe you can push them back across the Sawtooth Mountains?" the Duke asked in a quiet voice. "Even with your warband at full strength, the Eirdkilrs outnumber you. And they fight beside the Myrr and Bein."

"Savages in name and spirit!" Disdain twisted Throrsson's face and he turned a wrathful glare on Lord Virinus. "Brutes, flesh-eaters, and cave dwellers, just as you Princelanders label *all* of us."

The humiliated nobleman had remained silent all this time but now, singled out by the enraged chief, shrank back. His face paled and he seemed to wilt beneath the Hilmir's fury.

The anger in Throrsson's eyes lessened, though didn't truly fade, and he turned back to the Duke. "You offer the salvation of my people and speak of invasion in the same breath. Were you anyone else, Duke of Eastfall, I would have you eviscerated and slain in the *Blotahorgr* as a blood sacrifice to *Striith*. Yet, I give you warning, there will be no talk of Princelander soldiers in Fjall lands."

The Duke's face had gone as rigid as his spine, yet he showed no fear in the face of Throrsson's fury. "So be it." His voice was stiff, controlled. "You are the Hilmir, and my Prince wishes only to make peace with the Fjall. Your terms are acceptable."

Aravon knew the Duke well enough to recognize the unspoken "for now". Even with the support of the Deid warband, the Fjall wouldn't suffice to drive the Eirdkilrs back across the Sawtooth Mountains. Though the Hilmir's plan could cripple the enemy, if it succeeded, it would only set the Eirdkilrs back a year or two. But Fehl would never truly know peace until the Eirdkilrs were soundly defeated and the stronghold at Snowpass Keep rebuilt and guarded.

Yet Duke Dyrund was far too savvy to drive that point home, at least in this meeting. He would wait until the Fjall found themselves in more dire circumstances before offering Legion assistance once more. *Let's just hope Throrsson and his people don't lose too much before he's willing to consider it.*

Aravon's mind flashed back to the carnage and death at Gold Burrows Mine, the corpses of the Deid warriors and miners piled high. The Jokull had lost nearly half their warriors in the space of a single night, and the Eyrr had nearly been destroyed by Hrolf Hrungnir. Too many Fehlans had suffered at the hands of the Eirdkilrs—thousands of Princelander and Einari Legionnaires as well. The suffering would only end once the Eirdkilrs had been destroyed or thrown back beyond the Sawtooth Mountains.

"I *would*, however, ask a favor of the Hilmir." The Duke's voice was calm, with no trace of the frustration he doubtless felt.

"A favor?" Throrsson raised a bushy black eyebrow, resuming his seat once more.

"No one on Fehl would doubt the courage, strength, and skill of the Fjall warband," the Duke said, "but the ebb and flow of battle can be impossible to predict. If, by some twist of grim fate, the *Blodsvarri* were to survive your trap at the Waeggbjod, the consequences could prove...disastrous. After all, the success of your plan hinges on first eliminating her, then falling upon a disorganized, leaderless enemy, yes?"

Throrsson's eyes narrowed and he leaned forward. "What is this favor?" he growled.

To Aravon's surprise, the Duke gestured to *him*. "Permit Captain Snarl and his men to lay a trap of their own at the Waeggbjod. One that will end with an arrow in the Blood Queen's heart."

Aravon's grip tightened on his spear. He had no desire to leave the Duke's side, especially with the enemy marching toward them. Yet he couldn't fault the Duke's plan. Skathi was the best archer Aravon had ever known—even Noll and Colborn admitted it, though not without a good deal of begrudging on Noll's part. She could put an arrow into the *Blodsvarri's* eye from two hundred yards. Sending her would be the best way to ensure the Hilmir's plan succeeded and the Blood Queen never left that meeting alive.

Throrsson seemed to reach the same conclusion. "Blood may not be spilled on the sacred ground," he rumbled, his voice slow and pensive, "but the moment she leaves the Waeggbjod, your men may spring their trap."

A wry smile twisted his lips. "My great-grandfather might have considered your plan the coward's way. *Mine* as well, for that matter. But the Bastard Bearhound is long dead and buried, and the world has changed since his days." He stood, nodding. "We must change with it, for it is the only way that we can defeat our enemies."

The man's words struck Aravon as surprisingly...enlightened. Many Princelanders saw Fehlans as stubborn savages, clinging to rituals that men like Lord Virinus saw as "barbaric" or "primitive". But men like the Hilmir were proof that those Princelanders were wrong. The people of Fehl were as intelligent and perceptive as the savviest men of Icespire. The only difference lay in their priorities; Fjall, Deid, Eyrr, and every other Fehlan saw life through eyes no one from outside their cultures could truly understand. That realization was the first step toward finding common ground with men like Eirik Throrsson.

"Thank you, Hilmir." The Duke stood as well, reaching out a hand to Throrsson. "For being willing to speak of peace with we who have been your enemies for hundreds of years."

"You saved my son, offered salvation to my people." Throrsson's voice was quiet as he clasped the Duke's forearm. "The *Tauld* demand blood and servitude. I prefer your way."

"I'd certainly hope so!" The Duke snorted. "Now, I hear that a cask of exquisite Ornntadr *mjod* has been tapped in the great hall. I believe that is something even an uncultured Princelander like me can enjoy."

"Aye, so it is!" Excitement gleamed in the Hilmir's eyes and he patted his broad belly. "My Asleif has been instructed to keep a goat roasting on the spit for us." He stopped at the door. "But, for the sake of what we face, I would ask you remain in your *langhus*. We cannot risk the *Blodsvarri's* eyes and ears sending word of a Princelander feasting with the Fjall."

"Of course, Hilmir." The Duke gave a little bow. "I must speak with my men and make final arrangements regarding the Wraithfever cure."

"I will seek you out before I march on the morrow," the Hilmir said. He made to leave, but stopped and turned back, his gaze darting to Aravon. "Tell me, Captain Snarl, why do you not remove your mask, even now? After all, men who fight together must know each other's faces. Else how will they tell friend from foe?"

The question caught Aravon off-guard. The Hilmir hadn't seem bothered by it since the moment they rode into Storbjarg, yet now suspicion stained his face, echoed in his question.

"Surely you are not so monstrous that you fear revealing your face to the world?" The smile on Throrsson's lips didn't reach his eyes.

"Handsome or hideous, my face matters not." Aravon shook his head. "All that matters is the strength of my arm and the sharpness of my spear." He straightened, met Throrsson's gaze without hesitation. "A spear that now fights at your side, Hilmir of the Fjall. The wolf's fangs and the bear's claws. When

344

you see this mask, be it mine or the warriors that ride with me, you will know that you battle beside a friend against any foe."

The skepticism in Throrsson's eyes didn't quite fade, but he seemed to accept the words. "So be it." He nodded, then turned to the Duke. "Until tomorrow, Duke Dyrund."

Duke Dyrund bowed, but Throrsson had already turned and strode off into the depths of his longhouse, disappearing through the curtain of furs. Aravon shot a glance at Grimar and Gyrd, the Hilmir's seconds-in-command. Both had remained silent throughout the proceedings, watching him, Lord Virinus, and the Duke with wary eyes. Neither spoke as Aravon gave them a nod and followed Duke Dyrund from the longhouse, the slight Lord Virinus at his heels.

The Duke set a brisk pace, striding across the black-paved square toward the longhouse assigned him. Aravon hurried to match the Duke's fast walk. Behind him, Lord Virinus' voice echoed in protest.

"Y-Your Grace, I must speak with you at once." The nobleman's words rang with a distinctively plaintive edge. "When my father sent me on this mission, he never intended I end up in harm's way. If we are to ride to battle, I-I must insist I remain behind, w-with a guard to—"

"Silence!" Duke Dyrund rounded on the young man, eyes flashing. Lord Virinus shrank back. "You will be in no danger, *my lord.*" He spat the honorific like an insult. "You will remain here, in Storbjarg, at my side, where it is *safe.*" The word came out in a half-sneer, half-snarl. He shook a finger in the nobleman's face. "But know that when I return to Icespire, I will include a full report to the Prince and your father on your diplomatic tact. Or lack thereof."

Lord Virinus blanched, a look of utter horror on his face.

Before the young man could speak, Duke Dyrund turned on his heels and stalked away. Aravon hurried after the Duke.

He waited until the Duke put a few dozen strides between himself and the still-stunned Lord Virinus—time enough for his anger to cool, hopefully—before speaking in the silent hand language.

"*I can have my company ready to move out by midnight, Your Grace,*" he signed. Most of his soldiers had remained in the longhouse, content to relax after weeks spent traveling and battling. Rangvaldr, however, had wanted to minister to those stricken by Wraithfever. "To offer them Nuius' healing grace," he'd said.

Aravon had wanted to let the Seiomenn go, but prudence held him back. After using his holy stones in Bjornstadt and at Rivergate, Rangvaldr had been exhausted. Here, he could use all of his strength and it would heal only a handful of the *thousands* dead or dying from the Wraithfever. They'd need Rangvaldr in fighting shape for the battle to come.

And they couldn't risk the Seiomenn's identity being discovered. If the holy stones *were* unique to the Eyrr holy man, using them here would immediately identify him as the Seiomenn of Bjornstadt. Word of that could escape Storbjarg and reach the Blood Queen, or any other Eirdkilr chieftain. They had just finished saving the Eyrr—the discovery of Rangvaldr's presence among their company could put the northeastern clan at risk of utter annihilation once again.

He'd said as much to Rangvaldr, and the Seiomenn had agreed, albeit reluctantly. It was in his nature to provide healing and comfort, so the idea of sitting back and doing nothing while others died went contrary to everything he stood for.

Aravon studied the Duke from the corner of his eye. *"Are you sure it's wise to send all of us? And why are you staying in Storbjarg, what with those three thousand Eirdkilrs—"*

"Aravon!" Duke Dyrund cut him off with a sharp gesture. *"My safety is not your primary mission. I have Scathan and his men for that. Your job is to make sure the Blodsvarri falls in that battle, and that the Fjall and Deid have a real chance of winning. That is the true reason you are here."*

The Duke's words took Aravon by surprise, and his step faltered a moment. The Duke's initial message had made it clear that he wanted Aravon and his company to watch his back so close to enemy territory, but now…

Aravon caught up with the Duke. *"You knew there'd be a battle?"* His fingers flashed in time with the *clacking* of his boots on the ghoulstone.

"I suspected," the Duke replied. He paused just short of the longhouse door and turned to Aravon. *"I didn't know the Deid had joined him, but everything I'd heard about the Hilmir made it clear he was a man of action. Which is why I needed your company on hand, to tip the scales in our favor no matter what the Hilmir decided."*

The Duke's foresight stunned Aravon. Duke Dyrund had known about Wraithfever long enough to not only have people produce a cure and prepare to deliver that cure, but to position himself in a place where he could take

346

advantage of his negotiations with the Hilmir. Which meant positioning Aravon and his specially-recruited warriors at hand.

"At least allow me to keep one of my men with you," Aravon pressed. *"Zaharis was the one who discovered Fetidroot, so he might be able to produce a cure before—"*

The Duke shook his head. *"If the battle goes bad, you'll want his bag of tricks handy."* He held up a hand to forestall Aravon's protest. *"Belthar's the one best-suited to fighting the Eirdkilrs hand-to-hand. Skathi's the best shot you've got, but you'll need Noll and Colborn in case anything happens to her. And the two of them are critical for getting you past enemy scouts and navigating the terrain. You can't go without a healer, and I know there's no way you'll send your men out into hostile territory without you there. And I need your eyes and mind at that battle. I heard what you did with Jade Battalion at Broken Canyon, and again at Rivergate."* His face set in a stubborn cast, his expression growing as hard and unyielding as the stone beneath his feet. *"I need all of you there."*

"And you?" Aravon asked. *"At least consider retreating to Saerheim or Jarltun, out of the path of the Eirdkilrs marching this way."*

"I cannot." The Duke's expression grew grim. *"To leave Storbjarg would be an insult to the Hilmir. A signal that I expect his plan to fail."* His jaw muscles worked. *"I must stay here, Aravon. It is my duty as the Prince's envoy."*

"Then at least promise that you'll keep at least one man watching the enemy at all times," Aravon insisted. *"Scathan's a decent tracker and scout. So's Torin. Use them so you've got a warning if the enemy turns this way."*

The Duke nodded. *"I will, Aravon."* With a wry smile, he tapped the bone whistle hanging from his neck. *"And just because I'm here in Storbjarg, that doesn't mean I'm cut off from communication with the Princelands. I'll be sending word to General Vessach to hurry his ass up and get Onyx Battalion to Dagger Garrison. And something along the same lines to the Commanders of Hammer and Sentry Garrisons. Even if the Hilmir's not going to let us march two thousand Legionnaires into Fjall lands just yet, I'll be damned if I let our men sit idle when they can be ready to make a difference in this fight."*

Aravon opened his mouth to argue, but it would do no good. The Duke had his mind made up and nothing short of divine intervention from the Swordsman himself would change that. And, Aravon had to admit, the Duke *was* right. He had enough to worry about with taking down the Blood Queen; he'd have to leave the Duke's safety up to the men brought specifically for the task.

"Stop worrying about me, Aravon." The Duke gave his shoulder a reassuring squeeze. *"You've got the bigger fight to face, and you need to make sure your men are all there."* Worry flashed through his eyes. *"And that you're all there."*

The memory of his earlier conversation with the Duke flashed through Aravon's mind. The anger had dimmed—it always did, after a time, though it never truly left, but remained a hard knot deep within the core of Aravon's being—and he had the task ahead to focus on. But the paternal concern in Duke Dyrund's gaze brought back the feelings of longing. How different his life might have been had he been raised by a man like the Duke rather than his own father.

Drawing in a breath, Aravon pushed down the worry for the Duke's safety, the ball of emotion burning in his chest. *"We've got this, Your Grace."* The mission was all that mattered now. *"The Blood Queen will never know what hit her!"*

Chapter Forty-Four

A thick wall of chilly mist hung over the forest, ghost-gray, filling the world with a dense silence that seemed to swallow all sound. Not even the thundering of seven huge horses racing along the hunting trail seemed to break the eerie stillness; if anything, the fog only muffled the noise of their passage, deadening it and painting green-and-brown forest around a drab, colorless void.

Aravon tried to shake the gloom that hung over him. *At least the mists give us cover.*

The mist obscured the terrain for more than ten yards on all sides, making it near-impossible to calculate their speed, but Aravon guessed they were riding at close to ten standard Princeland miles per hour. As long as the fog remained thick enough to obscure them from potential enemies hiding among the trees, he could let the *Kostarasar* chargers set the pace. They had to hurry to reach their designated spot for the ambush, but they had to be wary for any enemies. Even the allied Deid warriors lying in wait northeast of the Waeggbjod might be in a mood to attack first, ask questions later.

Once they approached the Waeggbjod, however, they'd be forced to slow their pace, likely leave their horses a mile or two back to avoid being spotted by Eirdkilr lookouts or ambushers. The Hilmir had made it clear that the enemy would almost certainly be expecting a trap and have men lying in wait. It was up to Colborn, Noll, and Rangvaldr to spot the Eirdkilrs and take them down silently to avoid alerting the *Blodsvarri* of what Aravon had planned for her.

Which meant that they couldn't take the same direct route that the Hilmir would march to the Waeggbjod. Most of the land between Storbjarg and the ritual grounds was level, wide-open expanses broken only by the occasional hills or copses of short, broad-leafed trees. Unlike the land of the Deid and Eyrr to the north and west, Fjall territory was mostly grasslands and fields. The terrain turned mountainous farther to the south, with thick forests growing to the east and frozen marshes to the west, but the heart of the Fjall demesne was flatlands.

Thus, Aravon and his company found themselves riding northeast, back across the border and into Deid territory. There, the thick forests would provide ample concealment from any Eirdkilr scouts searching for enemy troops. Ten hours and a hundred miles from Storbjarg, Colborn had finally turned them down a small hunting trail that led east. They'd travel east for another seventy or so miles before turning southwest to come up on the Waeggbjod from the rear.

According to Gyrd, the Hilmir's second-in-command, the Deid warband would be waiting ten miles northeast of the ritual grounds. At dawn, they would begin a slow, silent move through the dense woodlands surrounding the rocky hills upon which the Waeggbjod sat. But while the Deid would skirt the western edge of the hill to get into position for a flanking attack on the ritual ground, Aravon and his company would go straight up. Even with the cover of the trees that grew up the slopes of the hill, they'd likely have to take the ascent at a snail's pace to avoid or eliminate Eirdkilr watchers.

Thankfully, they were making good time. Aravon guessed they'd rendezvous with the Deid warband shortly after midnight, which gave them twelve hours to cover ten miles and get into position. No easy feat, but if anyone could pull it off, it was the six highly-skilled warriors under his command.

Time seemed to stand still around him. No matter how far they traveled, they could not escape the mists. The dense, gray clouds blotted out the sun overhead and trapped them within a radius of limited visibility barely more than twenty yards across. Aravon had no way to tell if they were traveling in the right direction; he'd have to trust Colborn and Noll to keep them on track.

Aravon searched out Colborn, leading their small column. Noll rode forward scout somewhere fifty yards ahead of their position, which left the half-Fehlan Lieutenant as their eyes and ears in the front.

Much as he wanted to, he hadn't had a chance to speak with Colborn. With the Duke's orders ringing in their ears, the seven of them had hurried to pack their gear, load up on supplies—courtesy of the Fjall—and ride out. Midnight had found them three miles from Storbjarg. None of their small company had spoken a word since riding out, but Colborn's silence spoke of more than just concentration on the mission. He was as alert as ever, his head on a swivel, his fingers toying with the shaft of a nocked arrow, but the gray clouds seemed to hang thickest about him, his mood dark.

The Duke's words flashed through his mind. *"Give him space, but don't leave him adrift."*

They wouldn't stop to rest until after their rendezvous with the Deid, but when they did, Aravon would make time to pull the Lieutenant aside. He had to be certain Colborn was focused on what lay ahead.

Twisting in his saddle, Aravon glanced at the four riding behind him. Rangvaldr was his usual calm self, and Zaharis' mood had improved the moment they rode south of the Chain—worries about Darrak and the Secret Keepers left far behind. The shadows hadn't quite left Belthar's eyes, but the big man seemed fractionally more relaxed than before his conversation about the Brokers. Aravon didn't know if he'd come out and told anyone—Skathi, Colborn, the others—but his brooding anxiety had waned.

As for Skathi…well, she was still a mystery to him. He'd only ever managed to draw her into *one* real conversation, three days before the assault on Rivergate. In those few minutes, he'd gotten a glimpse at the woman beneath the mask—not only the leather wolf mask they all wore, but the fierce façade that she, like so many other Agrotorae, donned around the Legionnaires beside whom they marched, fought, and died.

He knew so little of her—her past before and during her years of service, her thoughts of the future—and, truth be told, he hadn't done much to learn more. He had been so consumed by his own concerns and those of the others in his company that he hadn't put much effort into it.

But damn it, she deserves better from me. Fiery hell, she deserves better from all of us. She's as much a part of our company as all the others.

The problem was that Aravon had never felt truly confident around women. Like most young Princelanders, he'd certainly *pretended* confidence—the swaggering arrogance of a soldier, son of one of Icespire's most famous Generals. Yet that façade had only gone skin deep.

He'd gotten lucky with Mylena. She had made things so easy for him, had come out and *told* him what she wanted from him. In a way, that had helped him to grow more confident. Not only as a man, but as a husband, a father, and a soldier.

But he still felt uncertain of how to approach Skathi. He'd spent his life around men like Belthar and Noll, and he'd known many with qualities in common with Colborn. Rangvaldr was much like Duke Dyrund, and with Zaharis, he always knew where he stood.

Yet, just because Skathi proved a trickier nut to crack, that didn't mean he could avoid it. It was his duty as her commanding officer—and, as he hoped, a genuinely decent human being—to help her feel comfortable among them, able to open up to the men who were her brothers-at-arms.

The "how" of that eluded him, but he determined to work at it. She deserved to find the same camaraderie in her company that the rest of them had.

Likely, that would begin with Aravon having a conversation with Noll and Belthar. None of the others had shown Skathi any unwanted attention—Colborn had dealt with her as any Lieutenant treated the soldiers under his command, and both Rangvaldr and Zaharis had developed a rapport as easy and open as she had permitted. But Noll had begun his relationship with Skathi in the worst possible fashion, and he hadn't put much effort into improving it. And Belthar's…fascination had earned her ire on more than one occasion. Thankfully, the big man had ceased his misguided, if good-intentioned, attempts at protecting her. At least, Aravon hadn't heard anything after the Battle of Rivergate, so he could only hope Belthar learned his lesson from Bjornstadt.

But, as with every one of the soldiers under his command, Aravon had to ensure she felt at ease around her comrades. Skathi could more than handle her own battles, but it would be far better if all those battles came from *external* sources, not within her company.

One more matter for him to deal with. All part of commanding capable, strong-willed soldiers.

With no way to mark the passage of time, nothing beyond endless walls of gray, the hours seemed to drag by. Miles passed in a blur of ceaseless motion: the rise and fall of the horse's back beneath Aravon, the swaying of his mount's head, the blood pounding in his ears, the burn of muscles far too tired from not enough rest. The only break in the monotony came when Aravon's growling stomach insisted it was time to eat.

They ate in their saddles, never slowing the horses' steady pace. Aravon had to admit the Fjall made their travel rations far tastier than the Legion—the strips of deer jerky had cracked peppercorns as well as the salt used for drying. Yet it *was* still tough, rangy meat, and the tepid water in their waterskins did little to help to wash it down. Finally, he could stomach no more and fed the last

352

piece to Snarl, who had descended from flying high overhead to run alongside his horse. The little Enfield gave a bark of delight and leapt to snatch the meat from Aravon's hand, his sharp teeth making quick work of the morsel.

Colborn turned them south at some point during what Aravon guessed to be the late afternoon. The hunting trail gave way to a proper wagon-width road, complete with deep ruts carved by heavy wheels. On the broader path, they could push their horses to greater speeds, and the rapid, rolling gaits of the *Kostarasar* chargers ate up the miles.

Day turned to night slowly, the endless gray darkening around them. A hint of color pierced the dull fog, and Aravon caught his first glimpse of sky as they rode out of the mist to find the sun already descended beneath the western horizon. The shadows grew quickly long, deepening to blackness beneath the thick canopy of the dense forest through which they traveled.

Noll joined them then, slowing his pace to match the column's speed. With night fallen and the darkness of the forest to conceal them from the enemy, he had no need to range so far ahead. Their only eyes and ears were Snarl, who Aravon sent flying overhead to watch for signs of danger.

Hours passed in silent riding. Aravon grew more wary with every mile, aware that they approached both the Deid warband and whatever scouts or skirmishers the *Blodsvarri* had watching the northern approach to the Waeggbjod. The knots in his shoulders tightened and his hand strayed more and more toward the spear strapped to his saddle.

An hour before midnight, Colborn slowed his horse to a walk and gave a quiet hiss. *"Deid,"* his fingers flashed. *"Ten, to the west."*

"Five more, east of us," Noll signed. *"Archer or two."*

Nervous tension stiffened Aravon's spine, yet he forced himself not to reach for his spear. Instead, he drew in a calming breath and raised empty hands. *"Heil og sael,"* he called, the traditional Fehlan greeting.

"We come in peace." Rangvaldr spoke up, also in the Fehlan tongue. "With greetings from Storbjarg for Chief Svein Hafgrimsson of Jarltun."

At Colborn's quiet insistence, Aravon had designated the *Seiomenn* the speaker for their interactions with the Deid. He'd said it was because Rangvaldr had the best Fehlan of any of them—Noll was banned outright from speaking, and even Aravon had to be careful not to let his Princelander accent show—but Aravon was all but certain Colborn didn't want to risk being recognized by the people of his clan. From his words, their treatment of him, an outsider, a bastard Princelander, had been far from kind.

"Identify yourselves," came the call from the forest. Aravon could see no sign of the warriors hidden among the trees, but he hadn't expected to. Fehlan camouflage was so good Zaharis had adopted it for their alchemically-treated armor.

With slow, cautious movements, Aravon reached down and unslung from his saddle the leather-bound bundle Gyrd had given him. He untied the leather thongs holding it closed, opened the wrappings, and drew out a thick, heavy object: the sharp horn of a male musk-ox, dyed a deep, bloody crimson and the mark of a black raven burned into its surface.

"From the Hilmir himself," Rangvaldr called in Fehlan. "The situation has changed, and he has sent us to relay the news to your chief."

Long moments of silence passed before the voice echoed again. "Ride on until you reach the fork, then follow the eastern trail for a mile. There you will find Chief Hafgrimsson."

"*Takk, min brodr.*" Rangvaldr, assuming the role of commander, gave the signal to advance. Aravon shifted his horse to the left, opening space for the *Seiomenn* to move ahead, and fell back beside Zaharis.

Less than five minutes later, they reached the fork in the wagon road. The eastern path was little more than a hunting trail, yet even with his rudimentary tracking skills, Aravon could see the underbrush bordering it had been freshly trampled beneath a multitude of booted feet.

Aravon spotted the Deid's makeshift campsite only a few seconds before he rode right into the first Fehlan warrior. A hundred Deid leapt up at their approach, leveling weapons and shouting for them to identify themselves. Yet, once Aravon held up the Hilmir's horn, the warriors let them pass, one guiding them to where the Deid chief sat among his trusted warriors.

Svein Hafgrimsson was a big man by Fehlan standards, though he failed to match Throrsson's towering bulk. Yet he still had an impressive, looming air about him, amplified by the heavy wolf pelts slung over his shoulders. He wore no helmet, but the snarling fangs and skull of a greatwolf protected his head. Chain mail rings *clinked* as he stood and stepped forward to greet them.

Rangvaldr drew up his horse. "*Heil,* Chief Svein Hafgrimsson." He dismounted and strode to clasp arms with the man. Aravon leapt down to join him, carrying the crimson horn with its raven—the mark of the Hilmir himself—to present to the Deid chief.

"You are not of the Fjall warband," Hafgrimsson rumbled. His eyes narrowed and he stroked the thick, red locks of his braided beard. "Yet there is no trace of the Princelands in your voice. Who are you and why do you hide your faces? Only cowards wear masks; true warriors meet death face to face."

"All due respect, Chief Hafgrimsson," Rangvaldr replied in a calm voice, "but my face is not important. What matters is that I bring word from the Hilmir, as you can see." He gestured toward the horn in Aravon's hand. "And for the sake of what we prepare to face, Fjall and Deid alike, I will forget that you called my men and me cowards."

Svein Hafgrimsson harrumphed, but accepted the proffered horn without further insult or question. "What word from Storbjarg?" His voice was a deep, rumbling bass, like thunder rolling across foothills. "Does the Hilmir, too, march to battle? Long have the *Tauld* plagued our lands and slaughtered our brave warriors. My sword grows dull waiting to taste the blood of my enemies!"

"The Hilmir has sent us with news of great importance, Chief." Rangvaldr's words echoed with a solemn, almost ceremonial tone. "The enemy has abandoned their siege of the Legion's Dagger Garrison, and now three thousand of them march south to join the *Blodsvarri.*"

"Dire news, indeed." A low growl issued from the Deid chief's throat and he narrowed his eyes. "Few would call Eirik Throrsson a coward, but if he plans to withdraw from the battle ahead—"

"The Hilmir will be at the Waeggbjod at noon tomorrow." Rangvaldr shook his head. "But he insisted that you know the threat we will face. Those three thousand *Tauld* will soon be deep in Fjall lands, and if tomorrow's attack fails, there will be enemies to the south, west, and north of Storbjarg."

"Then the attack *must* succeed," Svein Hafgrimsson rumbled. "And the Deid will make certain it does!" He gestured to the men clustered around him. "More than two thousand of the finest warriors on Fehl, clad in armor with shield, sword, and spear eager to taste enemy blood. Our faces will be the last thing the Blood Queen sees before we send her screaming through the flames of *Helgrindr.* Our war cries will shatter the *Tauld's* courage, our swords and axes carve their flesh for the crows. Tomorrow, the Deid repay in kind the suffering that they have heaped upon us for so long."

355

"The Hilmir will be pleased," Rangvaldr replied. "Long has he desired peace between the Fjall and Deid, and now it has come to pass."

"Tomorrow's battle decides the fate of our peoples," Svein Hafgrimsson replied. "We shall see if the vaunted Fjall warband can hold their own, or if the Hilmir's boasts are simply that."

"May *Olfossa* strengthen your shields and guide your swords," Rangvaldr intoned.

"And may our enemies crumble beneath Her strength!" Hafgrimsson finished the ceremonial words.

"Until we stand side by side on the field of battle, Chief Hafgrimsson." Rangvaldr bowed, and Aravon followed suit. The Deid chief responded with a grunt and a dismissive wave.

Aravon and Rangvaldr mounted up and, at Rangvaldr's shouted order of "Ride!", their small column of seven headed south. They still had ten miles to go to reach the northern slope of the hill upon which the Waeggbjod stood, and only twelve hours to slip past or eliminate Eirdkilr watchers and get into position.

Aravon didn't need to see Colborn's face to recognize the storm brewing in the man's mind. The Lieutenant rode hunched over, his shoulders tight, his eyes darker than the midnight shadows. Being among the Deid—his *own* people—had had a marked effect on him. Aravon nearly stopped their ride to speak to Colborn, but doubted singling the man out would improve his mood. He'd have to find a chance to take the Lieutenant aside sooner rather than later.

They made slower progress as they rode south toward the Waeggbjod. Colborn and Noll kept them off the hunting trails and pathways, pushing them through the thinnest sections of underbrush to make as little noise as possible while avoiding any Eirdkilr watchers. Moonlight dappled the forest and cast the trees in dense shadow. Aravon had no idea how Colborn, Noll, or Rangvaldr could move with such confidence when he could barely see. Yet he had only a few weeks of training in the marshlands—the three of them had spent their lives moving through the darkness, scouting, hunting, and tracking. Experience had instilled in them an innate skill he doubted he'd ever match.

It was approaching the third hour after midnight when Colborn called for a halt. "*We're two miles away,*" he signed. "*We go on foot from here.*"

The seven of them dismounted and removed their packs, weapons, and other necessary gear from their horses. While Belthar and Zaharis set about tethering the horses, Aravon slipped toward Colborn, who was preparing to lead them on their hike toward the Waeggbjod.

"Colborn—" Aravon began in a low voice.

"Captain, we need to move." Even quiet, the Lieutenant's words held a sharp, strained edge. "Eirdkilrs could be all over the mountainside."

Aravon opened his mouth to respond, but hesitated. "Give him space," Duke Dyrund had said. Judging by the stiff defensiveness of Colborn's posture, the Lieutenant wasn't yet ready to talk. Pushing him now would only push him *away*.

"Understood." Aravon nodded. "We're right behind you and Noll."

Colborn slipped into the forest without a backwards glance, Noll a few steps behind. Zaharis, Belthar, and Skathi followed, with Snarl padding along silently at the archer's side.

Aravon hung back to speak to the *Seiomenn*. "Rangvaldr, why didn't you tell Hafgrimsson of the fate of their warriors at Gold Burrows Mine?"

"I considered it." Rangvaldr gave a slow nod. "But I decided against it."

Aravon cocked his head. "Why? They need to know what happened to their people."

"They do," Rangvaldr replied, again with a nod. "But not tonight, the night before battle."

Aravon ground his teeth. "Damn it, Rangvaldr, they—"

"Tell me, Captain." The *Seiomenn's* words echoed with a quiet ring of steel. "Had you marched off to fight the same night you heard of your father's health, how do you think you would have fared?"

Aravon's retort died on his lips. That last evening in Camp Marshal, he hadn't slept more than a few hours. "I see your point."

Rangvaldr placed a hand on Aravon's shoulder. "You are a good man, Aravon, and I know you believe it to be the right thing to tell them the fates of their fellows. But such a distraction would only make it harder for them to fight. And, given what they face tomorrow, they need their full attention focused on bringing down the enemy."

Aravon wanted to protest, but a part of him knew the *Seiomenn* was right. "So be it." He let out a long breath. "I just hope we did the right thing."

After a moment of silence, Rangvaldr said, "By the grace of Nuius."

Aravon raised an eyebrow. Was that uncertainty he heard in the *Seiomenn's* voice? Rangvaldr had always been so assured, with years of experience as a warrior and holy man of the Eyrr guiding his decisions. Yet there had been a note of hesitance to his words, as if he, too, doubted his decision.

But Rangvaldr said no more, simply turned and slipped into the woods after the rest of their company. After a moment, Aravon shrugged and followed. *If he can live with the decision, I owe him the respect to trust him.*

The trek through the dense woods proved even more nerve-wracking than the ride through the fog or their approach on the Deid camp. Back then, they'd known they *might* face enemies; here, it was all but certain. Aravon was willing to gamble that any Eirdkilr that Eirik Throrsson described as "cunning" wouldn't walk into a meeting with a potential enemy unprepared. Even a semi-competent commander knew to post scouts to watch for ambush or trap.

Aravon's heart beat faster with every step deeper into the forest. Sweat streamed down his brow and the muscles of his legs, spine, and shoulders ached from the slow, cautious pace, controlling every step and movement. He did his best to imitate Noll, Colborn, and Rangvaldr, moving in a low crouch and scanning the ground before he placed his feet. The effort only added to the tension mounting within him. His mouth grew parched, his throat drier than a Westhaven drought. A primal part of his brain wanted to leap at every shadow, twitch at every sound. He *knew* enemies waited in the shadows—the only question was where and how many?

Yet as one mile became two and they reached the base of the hill, no enemies appeared. The forest was quiet, the stillness broken only by the rustling of the wind in the leaves and the rush of Aravon's pulse. Drawing in a deep, quiet breath, Aravon pushed away the nervous anxiety. It seemed the *Blodsvarri* hadn't had the presence of mind to leave guards. She *wasn't* expecting an attack at the Waeggbjod.

Which means the Hilmir's plan has a damned good shot at working. A hint of hope brightened his spirits, eased the tension in his muscles. *If she's not preparing for any surprises, she'll be expecting Throrsson to actually accede to the Eirdkilrs' demands.*

His heart slowed its hammering beat, and Aravon felt his confidence growing. His movements came easier, his steps lighter. He darted from tree to tree smoothly, matching Colborn's steady ascent of the hill.

Aravon did quick calculations on the rest of their trek. The climb was only half a mile or so, which meant they'd have plenty of time to get into position for their noon ambush on the Blood Queen. *Fiery hell, I might even get a nap out of this.* A grin split his lips. *I could use a few minutes to—*

A hand gripped his arm and pulled him flat to the ground. Aravon barely caught himself before his face slammed into the leaf-strewn side of the hill.

Beside him, Colborn's face was grim, his eyes wide. *"Eirdkilrs,"* he signed, *"dead ahead!"*

Chapter Forty-Five

Every muscle in Aravon's body went rigid and he froze, not daring to move, to make a sound. The fact that the enemy hadn't cried out was good—he hadn't been spotted. Yet the Eirdkilrs' presence sent a pang of worry down his spine.

So the Blood Queen is expecting an ambush. Aravon's mind raced. *Either that, or she's planning to attack the Hilmir in the sacred grounds.* Both options left him nervous, and the fact that he didn't know *which* added to his discomfort. The *Blodsvarri* was more duplicitous than the Hilmir anticipated—the question remained to find out just *how* much of his plan she had foreseen and made preparations to counter.

Slowly, Aravon rolled over onto his back, careful not to set the leaves rustling beneath him. He continued rolling until he reached a thick oak tree, with a heavy root system sprouting from the side of the hill. Once safely behind cover, he glanced around and let out a quiet breath of relief. Between the darkness and the mottled pattern on their armor, he could see no trace of his five companions.

Movement from behind a heavy boulder caught his attention. "*Orders?*" Colborn signed slowly.

"*Where are they?*" Aravon asked.

Colborn peered out from behind the rock. "*First one, twenty yards up and to the left, behind the fist-shaped pile of rocks. Two more behind the twin ash trees, thirty yards up and off to the right. Last one's thirty feet up the big cottonwood, fifty yards straight up the hill. The one that looks like Belthar's knees.*"

Aravon cautiously poked his head out of cover. He had no trouble making out the twin trees that grew thirty yards above them, and had he not been a heartbeat from battle, he might have laughed at the sight of the knobby, bulbous trunk of the cottonwood tree Colborn had indicated. Yet he could find no pile of rocks shaped like a fist.

"*You take the one at the rocks,*" Aravon signed. "*Arrows or dagger?*"

After a moment's hesitation, Colborn reached for the blade at his belt. "*Give me ten minutes to get in place. Blow a blast on that whistle when the others are ready.*"

Nodding, Aravon turned back toward the hill they'd just climbed. He'd moved up in the column during the trek, climbing a few yards behind Colborn with Belthar and Skathi behind him, Zaharis, Rangvaldr, and Noll bringing up the rear. The darkness was far too thick and all-encompassing to make out, with only faint hints of moonlight streaming through the forest canopy and dappling the leaf-carpeted floor. Yet he had to trust the others were watching him for instructions.

"*Four enemies,*" he signed into the darkness. "*Two at the twin trees, thirty yards and to the right of my position. Third one's up in the knobby tree straight ahead. Colborn's got the last one.*"

Skathi's strong hand appeared in a patch of moonlight between a pair of slender silver-birch trees. "*Plan?*" her fingers signed.

"*I'm going up, try to get around behind them and cut off any escape.*" Aravon would have rather sent Noll, but he needed the scout's aim. "*Skathi, Noll, when I blow the whistle to get their attention, bring them down. Belthar, take the one in the tree, thirty feet up. Signal to confirm.*"

A long moment of tense silence passed before Skathi's hand reappeared in the silvery moonbeam. "*Belthar's got no shot. Bad position.*"

Aravon snarled a silent curse. "*You got the one in the tree?*"

"*Can't see him,*" Skathi signed. "*Noll's going to try to get a better angle, but no way Belthar can load the crossbow quietly.*"

Tension knotted Aravon's shoulders. With Colborn dealing with the enemy behind the pile of rocks, he was the only one in a position to sneak up on the enemy.

"*Noll, take the one in the tree,*" Aravon finally signed. "*Skathi, take the one behind the left-hand tree. Belthar, stay put. Zaharis?*"

"*Close by,*" Skathi signed.

"Tell him to break out the quickfire lamps, twenty minutes. Give the bastards something to look at. The minute they poke their heads out from behind the trees, take them down."

Skathi shot him the signal for "understood", then her hand disappeared back into the darkness. Once again, the silence of the forest pressed in around him, and he marveled at their ability to move without making a sound. Knowing Skathi, she'd nocked an arrow and held her bow ready to draw. Noll, too.

That just left him and Colborn, and he *knew* the Fehlan would take care of his man.

Slow and quiet, he told himself, drawing in a deep breath. *Just like back at Camp Marshal.*

He replayed Colborn's lessons on stealthy movements through dense forests or marshlands. Noise came in two forms: debris and objects trod underfoot or brushed up against, and the sounds made by clothing, gear, weapons, and the human body. Zaharis' alchemical treatment had taken care of the noise made by leather armor, and Aravon slowly stripped off his pack and left it behind the tree. After a moment, he left his spear as well. He couldn't risk a glimmer of moonlight reflecting off the Odarian steel head. That left him only his Fehlan longsword and belt dagger. The smaller, lighter blades stood far less chance of punching through Eirdkilr furs, chain mail, and leather armor. But this was no shield wall, no military charge. Speed, surprise, and superior-quality weapons gave him an edge.

Aravon moved in a stalking crouch, lifting his feet high, placing the outside ball of his foot down first, rolling to the inside ball of his foot, then lowering toes and heels. A strange, awkward walk, but one Colborn had insisted on practicing four to six hours a night back at Camp Marshal. Aravon hadn't yet mastered it, but he could move well enough to cover ground without fear of making too much noise.

Yet all of Colborn's lessons failed to prepare him for the jangling of his nerves, the anxious hammering of his heart, the shrieking voice in his mind that told him to charge as he'd trained to for years. *This* was the hardest part of new skills like woodcraft—so much of what he'd learned during his weeks in the Duke's special company went against the instincts honed as a Legionnaire. He could no longer forward-march in a straight, orderly line, not with enemies hiding somewhere ahead of him. If he wanted to survive this new mission, he had to become a new man.

363

The soft, springy ground made it easier to keep a steady pace, yet the thick grass and the heavy carpet of leaves forced him to move slowly. A single dried leaf or twig *crunched* underfoot would alert the Eirdkilrs to his presence. Clenching his jaw, he steadied his nerves and willed his muscles to maintain a glacial forward speed. As long as he clung to the shadows and kept his movements slow, he could do it.

Sweat dripped down his forehead and stung his eyes, soaking his leather face mask, turning his tunic sodden. Suddenly, the world around him swam into crystal clarity. He heard every tiny sound—the rustling of leaves, the wind rattling branches against each other, his own breathing, far too loud in his ears. The smells of damp, mold, and fresh plant life filtered into his nostrils. His eyes locked on the shadows of the twin trees ahead and to his right.

One step at a time! He growled a silent curse. Thirty yards became twenty-five, then twenty. *How long have I been at this?* It felt like hours, yet it couldn't have been more than two or three minutes. Fifteen yards, ten, five. Closer, so close he could hear the Eirdkilrs' quiet breathing. Aravon fought the instinct to hold his own breath—the resulting *gasp* of air would be far more noticeable than a slow, steady flow of oxygen in and out of his lungs.

Even from three yards away, he couldn't see the man hiding in the deep shadows. All that mattered was that he could hear the Eirdkilr. And that the Eirdkilr didn't hear or see him until it was too late.

Slowly, Aravon slithered the last ten feet toward the twin trees and crouched beneath the exposed, dangling roots. The scent of earthy loam and dripping roots filled his nostrils, yet he could only think of how close he was to the Eirdkilr. Close enough that if he made one wrong move, the Eirdkilr would see and hear him.

It took every ounce of self-control to keep his movements ice-slow as he reached for the hilt of his Fehlan-style longsword. He couldn't draw until the last minute, but when the moment came—

An Eirdkilr appeared between the trees. Moonlight shone on the blue-stained face, the hard, bearded features, the hooded eyes that stared over Aravon's head and straight downhill. With a quiet grunt, the Eirdkilr drew the attention of his comrade to something down the hill.

Something hissed through the darkness, followed by a meaty *thunk*. In that instant, Aravon ripped his sword free and drove it up between the gap in the two trees. The thick, razor-sharp point sliced through the Eirdkilr's tangled beard and into the underside of his chin. Aravon leapt to his feet as he thrust upward, driving the tip home into the barbarian's brain until it struck skull. Hot, warm blood gushed down his hand as he tore the blade from the enemy. Like a felled oak, the Eirdkilr toppled to the ground with a resounding *thump*.

Above and to Aravon's left, a faint gurgling sound split the silence. Moments later, something heavy crashed through the branches of the knobby cottonwood tree and slammed into the ground.

Heart hammering, Aravon reached for Snarl's whistle and gave a short, sharp blast. Higher up the hill, behind a pile of rocks, the sound of a scuffle broke out. Men grunted, steel *clanged* off stone, and the loud *smack* of a fist striking flesh resounded in the darkness.

Aravon had no idea what had happened, but suddenly he was on his feet and racing up the hill toward the rocks. If Colborn hadn't managed to surprise the Eirdkilr—

A huge, bearded figure with blue-stained face and a thick fur cloak darted out from behind the pile of rocks. Aravon wound up to throw his spear, only to remember he wielded his sword, the spear left behind. Horror thrummed within him as he caught sight of the blood staining the Eirdkilr's knuckles. Even as he leapt over the gnarled roots of an ash tree, he couldn't help fearing for Colborn. He couldn't know what had happened—if the Lieutenant was dead or bleeding out onto the soft, damp hillside.

But the Lieutenant wasn't his priority. He had to take down that Eirdkilr, stop him from getting word of their presence back to the Blood Queen.

Yet, try as he might, he couldn't close the gap to the fleeing enemy. The Eirdkilr's legs were longer, and he fled across level ground, while Aravon raced uphill toward him. Dread sank like a stone in his gut. He couldn't hope to match the Eirdkilr's speed.

I can't let him get away!

The next instant, an arrow sprouted from the man's neck. A second and third followed in rapid succession, slamming into the Eirdkilr's left leg and side. The force of the impacts hurled the barbarian head-first into a tree. His steel skullcap collided with a solid walnut trunk and he rebounded, staggered backward, and toppled with a wet, gurgling sound. Even as Aravon closed the distance, the fallen Eirdkilr's frantic twitching movements slowed, then stilled. A huge, bloodied hand fell away from the arrow shaft embedded in the huge vein beside the dead man's throat.

Without slowing, Aravon whirled to the right and charged the pile of rocks behind which the Eirdkilr had been crouched. Anxiety turned to horror as he caught sight of a helmetless Colborn sprawled face-down on the ground.

Chapter Forty-Six

No!

Aravon threw himself into a crouch beside the Lieutenant, scrabbling at the man's heavy form and struggling to roll him over. Blood glistened in the moonlight, streaming from a gash in Colborn's forehead just above the edge of his mask and staining the sharp edge of a nearby rock. The Lieutenant's eyes were wide, dazed. Yet relief surged within Aravon as Colborn sucked in one ragged breath, then another.

Thank the Swordsman!

The tension drained from his muscles and his movements slowed. He ran hands over Colborn's neck, down his chest and sides, but mercifully the man bore no other wounds. *We're lucky the Eirdkilr decided sending a warning was more important than finishing off his enemy. Otherwise…*

He shoved aside the thought. He didn't want to think about that, didn't want to entertain the image of Colborn lying on the ground with his skull shattered, his neck snapped, or his guts spilled across the forest floor. He'd already lost too many of the men under his command; he could only count himself and Colborn lucky that the Lieutenant wouldn't be another name to add to the burden on Aravon's heart.

At that moment, Colborn groaned and blinked. "C-Captain…"

"Easy, Colborn." Aravon spoke in a low voice; he couldn't be certain they'd finished off *all* the Eirdkilrs in the area, but he doubted Colborn was clear-headed enough to speak in Zaharis' sign language. "Give it a moment. You took a hard hit."

"Bastard heard me coming," Colborn muttered, wincing as he pressed a hand to his forehead. "Knocked me back before I could take him down."

Aravon raised an eyebrow. *Heard Colborn?* None of them, not even Fehlan-born Rangvaldr, could match Colborn's stealth in the wilds. Either the Lieutenant had gotten unlucky, or…

"Take it easy." He helped Colborn sit up and lean against the boulder. The man's face twisted in pain, but shame burned in his eyes.

"Did we get them all?" Colborn asked.

Aravon nodded. "Quick and quiet, like you trained us."

"Good." Shadows played across his face, but anger blazed bright in his ice-blue eyes.

A quiet rustling sounded off to their right, and Aravon spun, sword gripped tight and raised to strike. He stopped at sight of Zaharis' snarling wolf mask appearing from the darkness. *"How bad?"* the Secret Keeper signed.

"Hard hit to the head," Aravon replied. *"Not too bad, but have you got anything to get him back on his feet?"*

"Rangvaldr's a few steps behind." Zaharis jerked a thumb over his shoulder. *"Those Eyrr holy stones ought to help."*

Aravon shook his head. *"Can't risk the glow giving us away."*

"That's not what you said a moment ago." A playful glint shone in Zaharis' eyes.

"Good work on that." Aravon nodded. *"I'll let Rangvaldr work his magic if we get a chance later. For now, can you do anything?"*

Zaharis hesitated a moment, then his shoulders drooped slightly. *"Sorry, Captain,"* he signed. *"Last of my painkillers were left with Darrak. I haven't had a chance to restock supplies or go foraging."*

"No matter." Aravon shrugged it off. *"He's a soldier. He's taken harder hits before. He just needs a few minutes and he'll be back on his feet."*

Zaharis nodded. *"First chance I get, Captain, I'll see what I can scrounge up."* He looked around him. *"Never been this far south before, so it'd be interesting to look around, find out what sort of plants grow down here."*

"Maybe you'll get lucky." Aravon shot Zaharis a knowing look.

Something flashed in the Secret Keeper's eyes—hope, dread, remorse, a combination of all three?—but he nodded. *"Maybe."* His encounter with Darrak had been a fresh reminder of what he'd given up in his quest for the ice saffron.

368

At that moment, two more figures appeared from the bush—Skathi and Rangvaldr, who held out Aravon's spear and pack, retrieved from where he'd left them.

With a grateful nod to the *Seiomenn*, Aravon turned to Skathi. *"Good shooting,"* he signed. *"Though you cut it bloody close with that last one!"*

The archer shrugged. *"Couldn't get a clear shot."* Her gaze flitted past Aravon to Colborn. *"He going to need attention from Stonekeeper?"*

"Once we're somewhere the glow won't attract attention, yes." Aravon nodded. *"For now, I'll give him a moment to shake it off, then get him back on his feet and keep climbing."* He glanced up the hill. *"We're almost halfway up. Get Noll and Rangvaldr out in front, eyes sharp for any more hiding in the shadows."*

"We'll clear the way." A savage light blazed in the archer's eyes, and she raised a clenched fist, revealing two bloodstained arrows—arrows she'd stopped to dig out of the bodies of her kills.

"Get up top and find someplace to get a clear shot at the Waeggbjod. You, Noll, and Belthar, three different vantage points."

"Want we should find a nest for him, too?" Skathi asked. *"Or you think he'll be too woozy to shoot straight?"*

Aravon pondered a moment. *"Three's enough for now. If he feels up to it, we'll get him in position a bit later."* He glanced up through the thick forest canopy at the sky; the first glimmers of daylight brightened the eastern horizon. *"But the rest of you need to move now. We'll follow as soon as we can."*

Skathi gave him the Agrotorae salute and turned to relay Aravon's orders to Belthar and Noll, who had joined them on the trail.

Aravon's eyes went to Rangvaldr. The *Seiomenn's* hand clutched the holy stone at his neck.

"Later," Aravon told him. *"Once we're not in danger of being spotted or hunted."*

Rangvaldr inclined his head and lowered his hand. *"We'll give you a moment, Captain."* He shot Aravon a knowing look before joining the other four. Within less than half a minute, they disappeared into the woods, Noll and the *Seiomenn* in the lead, followed by Skathi, Zaharis, and the heavier, noisier Belthar at the rear.

Turning back to Colborn, Aravon rested his spear against the stone and took a seat against a stone opposite the Lieutenant. Colborn had removed his mask to wipe the blood from his face and forehead, leaving dark streaks across

369

his ruddy skin and staining his blond beard. Aravon did likewise, setting the leather mask in his lap and toying with its textured surface.

"Can't believe he heard me," Colborn muttered, his voice so quiet Aravon almost missed it. "That's never happened before."

Aravon shrugged. "We all have bad days. Just happens you've had a few in a row."

Colborn's face grew as hard as the stone behind him. "Bad days get men killed, Captain. Nearly did me in."

"All it means is that you're human." Aravon raised an eyebrow. "Might help if you say whatever it is aloud. This about Rivergate or Gold Burrows?"

"Neither. Both." Colborn hesitated, but pain tugged at the corners of his eyes. Finally, he let out a long breath. "Ever since Rivergate, I can't get their faces out of my head."

"The Jokull?" Aravon asked.

Colborn nodded. "Then, when I saw the bodies at the mine, it all came crashing back on me. Like *I* was the one that killed them."

Aravon's eyebrows shot up.

"I know, insane, right?" Colborn gave a bitter shake of his head. "Rangvaldr tried to talk me through it the night after, and his words helped. Some…"

"But?" Aravon asked.

For long moments, Colborn said nothing, simply stared at the ground. "But I can't stop. Can't stop feeling guilty, angry, ashamed. Just like *him.*"

Aravon's eyes narrowed. *He's talking about his father?* He'd seen the deep-rooted pain glimmering in Colborn's eyes the night after the Battle of Rivergate. Some wounds cut to the bone and never fully healed, no matter how much a man tried to push past them.

"Like him, how?" Aravon pressed, gently.

Colborn gestured to his face. "Every time he shouted at me, every time he beat me, he wasn't actually mad at me. He was mad at himself. At his weakness. With my mother. A Fehlan, the thing he claimed to hate most in the world. I was a reminder of every moment of weakness he had. Not once, not twice, but for months. All his life, his father had hammered into him that Fehlans were savages, little better than animals. So how was he any better than them when he did what he did to her?"

Aravon's gut clenched. He'd seen men's appetites drive them to extremes—drink, drugs, carnal pursuits, and more—but this…this was far more than anything he could have imagined.

"He hated himself—more than anything in the world, he *hated* what he'd done—and took it out on me." Anger glimmered in Colborn's eyes. "When you're young, you hear you're a worthless piece of Fehlan shite long enough, you eventually start to believe it. Hard to shake it, no matter what you do or where you go. It may go quiet, leave you alone for a while, but it always comes back. It always comes back."

Aravon remained silent. He could find no words, but he needed none. As the Duke had said, Colborn wrestled with this alone, but just knowing Aravon was there, that he cared, was enough for the Lieutenant.

"That's what's got me shaken, Captain." Colborn fixed Aravon with a haunted look that had nothing to do with his head wound. "That I'm going to hate myself so much for what I did that I'm going to turn out like him. A self-hating bastard that turns every bit of good in his life to piss."

That was the last thing he'd expected to hear from Colborn, an experienced soldier, an officer in the Legion, a man who'd fought and killed for years. Yet he, too, knew how long and dark a shadow fathers could cast over their sons.

"The last time I spoke with my father," Aravon said in a quiet voice, "he said I was 'the greatest disappointment in his life,." He shook his head, a bitter snarl on his lips. "I heard that all my life, more so after my mother died of the Bloody Flux. Imagine that, the son of the great General Traighan, a disappointment."

Colborn's eyebrows rose. "Damn, Captain! I had no idea."

"Not exactly a great story for around the campfire, is it?" Aravon gave a harsh chuckle. "But, yes, I know what you mean. That voice doesn't ever really go away." He leaned forward. "Want to hear something I've never told anyone else?"

Colborn nodded.

"When I was ambushed on the Eastmarch, when the Eirdkilrs wiped out the entire Sixth Company, you want to know what my last thought was?" Aravon clenched his fists. "*Not* that I'd never see my sons or my wife again, but it was the look of disappointment in my father's eyes. That my death had been the last of a long line of failures. And then, when I woke up buried beneath the corpses of my men, I realized *that* was the last failure. My men had died but I'd lived. I had failed them and survived."

Surprise flashed across Colborn's face. "A harsh truth for any man to live with."

"Indeed." Aravon inclined his head. "So, like you, when the Duke offered me a chance to stay dead, the General was one of the reasons I accepted it. For the good of the realm, certainly. But also so I didn't have to see the look in my father's eyes when he found out that *I* was the only man of Sixth Company that didn't die a soldier's death." He gave a bitter laugh. "Heroic and noble, isn't it?"

Colborn's expression was pensive, and he remained silent for long seconds. "Maybe." He shrugged. "But in the end, sometimes the 'why' doesn't matter half as much as the 'what'. What you do to prove him wrong."

Aravon's lips twisted into a cold smile. "Followed in his footsteps and joined the Legion."

"And in doing so, saved how many lives?" Colborn tilted his head. "Not just at Rivergate, and Bjornstadt, and Broken Canyon, and everywhere else we've been. But during your fifteen years as a soldier and an officer *before* all this. That's what I've been telling myself since I came back and joined the Legion. That I was proving my father wrong, showing him I wasn't that worthless piece of Fehlan shite that he believed I was."

"And that's why you're never going to turn out like him." Aravon poured genuine warmth and concern into his voice. "You don't hate yourself because of something you've *done*, but because of something someone else told you that you *are*. Everything you do proves that you're right, that you are worth far more than he could have ever imagined. A soldier. A leader." He stood and held out a hand. "A friend."

Emotion glimmered in Colborn's eyes as he clasped Aravon's hand.

Aravon pulled Colborn to his feet. The Lieutenant was unsteady at first, his eyes losing focus as the blood rushed to his wounded head, and Aravon supported him until he found his feet.

"When the Sixth fell," Aravon said in a quiet voice, "I tried to find a reason for their deaths, and for why I'd lived. But eventually, I realized that there was no reason. As a wise archer we know once said, 'All's shite in love and battle.'"

Colborn chuckled, wincing at the pain in his head.

"And, as a friend of mine once told me, 'You did what you had to. Saved the Legion.'" Those were Colborn's words, spoken after Aravon's mad dash to sound the retreat that prevented the Eirdkilrs from slaughtering Jade Battalion. "I don't know if that'll make it easier to live with, but it's all the wisdom I've got for one night. You want more, go have a talk with the Duke or Rangvaldr."

Colborn chuckled, a bright sound that had lost much of its previous melancholy and rancor. "We'll save the speeches for another day, yeah?" He grinned at Aravon. "For now, we've got an Eirdkilr queen to kill."

* * *

To Aravon, it felt as if the sun had never traveled so slowly across the sky. It seemed a week had passed in the four hours he'd spent hiding among the stones surrounding the Waeggbjod. Life as a Legionnaire had hammered patience into him, but he *hated* the interminable wait before battle.

For the tenth time in the last hour, he scanned his surroundings. No sign of Colborn, even though he knew where he was crouched beside Zaharis and Rangvaldr on the northeastern corner of the standing stone square. Aravon had insisted Colborn rest, even after taking Zaharis' hastily-prepared alchemical remedy—a few roots and twigs the Secret Keeper said would diminish the discomfort but not much more.

Noll and Skathi were hidden to the east and west, tucked out of sight among the tall menhirs surrounding the Waeggbjod. If he squinted hard enough, he could just make out the six-foot-long arms of Belthar's enormous crossbow protruding from between two huge stones at the northwestern corner. Hiding anything that size, much less the massive man holding it, was near impossible, and a testament to the Fehlan camouflage Zaharis had painted onto their leather armor.

To Aravon's right, Snarl lay on his belly, wings curled up against his furry body, eyes closed. Yet Aravon knew the Enfield would leap to action the moment he was needed.

Confident his company was in place, Aravon studied the field of battle. Again.

The Waeggbjod was a flat grassy expanse fifty yards wide and long, a near-perfect square surrounded by a wall of towering menhirs. Aravon couldn't tell if the standing stones had been carved by human hands or simply placed there, but the Fehlan runes etched into the stones proved the Fehlans had had a hand in building the ceremonial place.

As the name suggested, the Waeggbjod was hemmed in on all sides by the standing stones, forming a solid barrier that no army could pass. Even after spending the better part of two hours circling the stone ring, Noll and Skathi had found only four openings large enough for Belthar—or an Eirdkilr—to slip through. Throrsson had been right when he said there was no way to launch a surprise attack from the north, south, or east.

To the west, however, an opening in the stone wall provided a clear view of the Fjall lands spread out around the base of the hill upon which the flat ceremonial grounds sat. A single broad sinuous path wide enough to march ten men across ascended to the Waeggbjod.

Up that path marched the eleven hundred and eleven warriors of the Fjall. Tall, broad-shouldered men with black, red, brown, and blond beards tied into tight braids and strung with colorful beads, bones, and bits of steel. Sunlight glinted off thousands of steel skullcaps, chain mail, swords, and axes. The red-painted shields of the warriors proudly bore the glistening black Reafan of the Hilmir. The sea of furs, pelts, and hides resembled a pack of hunting animals, but with fangs and claws of sharp steel instead of bone.

The Fjall marched for war, and Eirik Throrsson led them. The Hilmir was resplendent in his glimmering chain mail, his black hair seeming wilder and thicker than ever in the bright light of day. His helmet bore the face of the snarling black bear—doubtless the same one to which his bear fur cloak had belonged. When he drew his sword, he seemed to shimmer with a brilliance almost as dazzling as Rangvaldr's holy stones.

Aravon shot a glance up at the sky. *One more hour until noon.* By now, Chief Svein Hafgrimsson and his Deid warriors should have taken their positions for the ambush. Somewhere over one of the hills north of the Waeggbjod, just out of sight, two thousand more Fjall warriors lay in wait. *One more hour until the war for the Fjall lands begins in earnest.*

Since hearing the Hilmir's plan, a faint hope had taken root deep within Aravon. The Hilmir's strategy was sound, his preparations as thorough as any Legion commander or general. No battle plan survived a clash with the enemy, but Eirik Throrsson had done as much as any man could to mitigate the risks, to stack the odds in his favor. With three thousand warriors holding the city walls and more than five thousand here, they had the best possible chance of victory here.

374

Victory, and the death of the *Blodsvarri*. That would be the first step into what Aravon hoped would be a successful—and short—campaign to drive the Eirdkilrs out of Fjall lands.

Aravon's gaze went to the horizon southeast of the Waeggbjod. At any moment, the seven-foot Eirdkilrs would appear over the gentle hill two miles from the ritual grounds. A crushing tide of filthy icebear pelts, blue-painted faces, and fury. Enemies that sought only to maim, kill, and destroy—not only the "half-men" that had invaded their lands, but their own people. Ruthless, bloodthirsty, a force of death and destruction and a blight on the land of Fehl. And at their head, the Blood Queen herself.

Their appearance would herald the beginning of the end for the Eirdkilrs and their sanguinary leaders.

Yet, as the minutes slowly passed and the horizon remained empty, worry began to gnaw at Aravon's stomach. Faint, quiet, and subtle at first, like a mouse chewing at a galleon's ropes. Then more noticeable, deeper, like acid eating into flesh. Every beat of his heart echoed in his ears, his pulse pounding an anxious rhythm.

Another glance at the sky, and Aravon's brow furrowed. *Noon, but still no sign of them.* Only a horizon of gently rolling hills, a sea of verdant grass unbroken by savage, brutish figures. The sun that should have stared down on a scene of battle and blood filled the air with a strangely beautiful warmth that made the utter silence all the more uncanny.

Instinct screamed at Aravon. *Something's not right.* His mind raced. *She should have been here by now.*

The worry within his chest hardened to a dagger of ice as he caught the first threads of gray rising on the horizon. His breath caught in his throat, dread freezing the air in his lungs.

Smoke. And it came from Storbjarg.

Chapter Forty-Seven

Fear drove an icy dagger into Aravon's gut. *Duke Dyrund!*

In an instant, Aravon leapt to his feet and whirled toward the spot where he knew his men waited among the menhir. "Zaharis, Noll, back down the hill and get our horses. Bring them around. We've got to get to Storbjarg now!"

Stones clattered and tree branches rustled, and Aravon caught a hint of movement as Noll abandoned his hidden position among the stones. Within seconds, the scout and Secret Keeper were scrambling down the steep hill, back to where they'd left their horses. It would be a three-mile journey, then another five or more to circumnavigate the base of the hill. Yet none of his companions questioned his order; doubtless, they'd all seen the same plume of gray rising in the distance.

"Rangvaldr, get Colborn ready for battle," Aravon called.

"I'm fine, Captain," Colborn's voice drifted from his hiding place. "Just—"

"Shut up and let Rangvaldr do his thing," Aravon snapped. "We need your head healed and your mind sharp. If there's a fight, we're going to be ready."

No protest came from Colborn's position. Even as Aravon picked his way toward the nearest opening in the wall of menhirs, a blue light glowed bright between the standing stones. Aravon had seen what the Eyrr holy stones could do in the *Seiomenn's* hands. Though he didn't understand the magic—fiery hell, until a few weeks ago, he'd never have imagined such a thing possible—all that mattered was that the healing stones would deal with Colborn's wounds, any lingering trace of concussion. He couldn't have his Lieutenant keeling over as they raced to battle.

"Belthar, Skathi, with me!" With effort, Aravon squeezed himself through the boulders and onto the flat, grassy Waeggbjod. Loud grunts echoed from Belthar's position as the man did likewise. His broad shoulders made it difficult, and it took a full minute for him to find an opening large enough for his bulk. Skathi slithered through the close-packed menhirs with a lithe agility even Snarl would envy, padding onto the grass from the east.

But even as Aravon broke free of cover, the Hilmir was on the move. "*Blodsvarri* bitch!" His roar echoed across the Waeggbjod. He tore his sword free of its sheath and waved it over his head. "*Striithlid,* to Storbjarg! The treacherous *Tauld* will taste Fjall steel!"

Throrsson's words set the Fjall surging toward the path descending from the Waeggbjod to the flat lands below. Before Aravon crossed the first ten yards, the Hilmir had begun a sprinting dash down the hill. His warriors streamed behind him, clogging the narrow trail, a tide of fur-and-steel-clad bodies driven by fury at their enemy's treachery.

Heart sinking, Aravon slowed his mad dash. He'd never reach the Hilmir on foot now. No way he'd get through that crush of warriors on that narrow path. And even if he could somehow shoulder through, what were the odds Throrsson would actually listen to him? The sight of the smoke had whipped the Fjall warriors into a frenzy; it would take a miracle to stop their mad dash back to Storbjarg.

Aravon couldn't blame them. He wanted nothing more than to race back to the Fjall capital, to find out what had happened. Duke Dyrund was within the walls of Storbjarg, facing whatever enemy forces had surrounded the city—or, and the sight of the smoke made him assume the worst, somehow stormed the wall. It took every shred of self-control to remain in place when every instinct shrieked at him to run the seventy miles between the Waeggbjod and the Duke.

But remain he did. Though every minute of inaction grated at his nerves, he forced himself *not* to join the tide of warriors stampeding down the narrow path. He couldn't waste his energy on a frantic footrace back to Storbjarg; Noll and Zaharis would catch up with their horses before he'd covered even a fraction of the distance. And, as he'd learned from hard experience and centuries of military history, such haste could lead even the best-trained army down a path to disaster.

Fear made men throw caution and common sense to the wind. Aravon *had* to hope the Hilmir hadn't lost his good sense in the face of his rage and worry for his people. The minute their horses arrived, the seven of them would mount up and pursue the Hilmir, try to talk him into a slower, more deliberate approach to Storbjarg. A faint hope, but he had to cling to it.

"Captain?" Belthar's voice rumbled from behind and to Aravon's left. "What do we do?"

Aravon glanced over his shoulder; worry twisted the big man's features and darkened Skathi's forest green eyes. Belthar's huge fists were white on the oaken stock of his crossbow, and Aravon caught a twitch of Skathi's normally rock-steady fingers on her bow—the only sign of anxiety he'd ever seen from the archer. Their thoughts had to be with the Duke, just like his.

Yet, he couldn't let worry for Duke Dyrund stop him from thinking clearly.

"We wait." Aravon forced his lips to form the words, though they went against every instinct. "Until Noll and Zaharis bring the horses, we'll only waste our strength chasing the Hilmir or racing to Storbjarg. Now, we take time to think, to plan."

"A wise decision." Rangvaldr's voice drifted from behind them. Aravon turned and found the *Seiomenn* striding toward them at a steady pace, Colborn at his side.

"Assess the situation, evaluate what we know, and act accordingly." Colborn nodded. The Lieutenant moved easier, his steps more certain than when Aravon had helped him ascend the hill hours earlier. The fact that he once more wore his mask and helmet proved Rangvaldr's holy stones had worked their healing magic.

"*That's* pretty damned clear," Belthar growled, thrusting a finger at the pillar of gray smoke.

"Is it?" Aravon shook his head. "Not long ago, we watched water burning outside of Rivergate. That smoke could be a ruse just the same, something to throw the Hilmir off-balance and do exactly *this*." He gestured to the tide of Fjall warriors surging down the hill, spilling across the plains east of the Waeggbjod. "If she *did* suspect that he planned something here, no way she'd allow Throrsson to pick the spot. Military strategy at its most fundamental: always be the one to choose your battleground."

"Damn!" Colborn groaned. "Which could mean those Eirdkilr watchers were nothing more than a tethered goat to draw the Hilmir in."

Aravon's brow furrowed beneath his mask, setting the leather *creaking*. He followed the process that led Colborn to reach that conclusion. *The Hilmir would believe she suspected him, but the Blood Queen would want to lure him into believing he had the advantage. So her scouts were confirmation that she was suspicious of Throrsson, as well as proof that she intended to come to the Waeggbjod anyway.*

Tactics and battle strategy often amounted to guesswork that could make an Illusionist Cleric's head spin, based on a commander's understanding of his enemy and the information at his disposal. It seemed the Hilmir had been *mostly* right in his prediction of the Blood Queen's behavior, but she had been one step ahead of him.

"Swordsman's beard!" Aravon swore. He began to pace, his mind working. "The last the Hilmir told us before we left Storbjarg indicated that the Eirdkilrs *were* marching this way." He thrust a finger to the southeast. "His scouts placed the Blood Queen somewhere around Harbrekka, a hundred miles south of Storbjarg, east of the Jarnhaugr Mountains."

"And the Eirdkilrs from Dagger Garrison?" Colborn asked.

Aravon's brow furrowed. "Moving at top speed, they couldn't have reached Storbjarg before tonight. And not even the Eirdkilrs can sprint all day and night without stopping."

Hrolf Hrungnir and his *Blodhundr* had run a hundred and twenty miles through dense Eyrr forests and across rivers to reach Bjornstadt. They'd made the journey in just over a day—a pace that *any* armed force, Fehlan or Princelander, would find impossible.

"So what's going on?" Skathi's eyes narrowed. "If the enemy was so far away, how in the bloody hell did they get to Storbjarg without the Hilmir's watchers noticing them?"

"I don't know, and that's what bothers me!" Aravon clenched his fist. "Not only were there *no* enemies reported anywhere near the Fjall city, but there should have been three *thousand* Fjall holding the walls. From what I know of the Hilmir, I'm confident he ordered the gates closed the moment his warband marched out of the city. Which means there's no way that the enemy should have gotten into Storbjarg."

"Leading you to suspect a ruse," Rangvaldr offered.

"It's the only explanation that makes sense." Aravon nodded. "Start a fire near Storbjarg, force the Fjall into a hurried retreat back to Storbjarg, then…" He sucked in a breath. "Then hit them on the road back to the city!"

380

Four pairs of eyes widened, and the five of them whirled toward the east, where the last of the Fjall warriors had descended from the Waeggbjod and joined the mad dash back to Storbjarg.

"We've got to warn the Hilmir!" Colborn shouted.

Aravon had no time to wait for the horses. Noll and Zaharis would arrive within less than an hour, but in that time, the Fjall warband could be locked in battle with the Eirdkilrs. A well-placed ambush, launched at the right time, with the Fjall in such a hurry—the results could be devastating. Even with experienced scouts to guard his flanks and search for enemies, the Hilmir might not see the trap until its steel jaws snapped shut on his throat.

"Let's go!" Whirling, Aravon sprinted toward the narrow path, racing down the steep incline and leaving the Waeggbjod behind. He didn't turn back to see if his men followed; the sound of their booted feet pounding along behind him was proof enough, even if he hadn't had full confidence in them. Colborn, the fastest of their company, caught up to Aravon and fell into step beside him before he'd descended thirty yards. Rangvaldr's healing stones had worked their magic, indeed, for Colborn had no trouble matching Aravon's breakneck speed down the hill.

The descending path zig-zagged back and forth, but Aravon dared not take the direct route down the steep, rocky hill. The distance seemed interminable, his heart hammering against his ribs, yet it couldn't have been more than five minutes before the path leveled out and rejoined the dusty road cutting through the gentle-hilled grasslands.

Only then did Aravon slow. "Belthar, Rangvaldr," he gasped, struggling to control his breathing, "wait here for the others."

Both men appeared ready to protest, but Aravon cut them off with a slash of his hand. Between Belthar's enormous crossbow, his heavy muscles, and the ponderous steel axe he wielded, he'd never keep up. And he needed Rangvaldr for *another* critical task.

Aravon sucked in a deep breath, his lungs burning. "Belthar, get Noll and Zaharis up to speed, then ride with Zaharis to catch up to us. Rangvaldr, take Noll and get to Chief Svein Hafgrimsson. He's going to need to know why the battle horn never rang, and it's up to *you* to convince him to join battle." He shook his head. "We can only pray to the Swordsman that it's not too late."

The two men nodded after only an instant's hesitation.

381

Turning, Aravon broke into a run and raced off to catch up to the fast-moving Fjall band, which had already covered nearly a mile in their breakneck dash back to Storbjarg. Fehlan warriors trained to move far faster than heavily-armored Legionnaires, and Aravon had always envied Colborn's impressive endurance when running. And these weren't *any* Fehlans, but Fjall warriors, running toward their home through terrain they knew far better than Aravon or his men.

Aravon risked a glance toward his companions. At his side, Colborn moved with the same easy, loping run, no sign of the exhaustion that dragged on Aravon's limbs. Behind them, Skathi's arrows clattered and rattled in their quiver, but the fleet-footed archer matched Aravon's pace without complaint.

A part of Aravon wanted to order Colborn to run ahead, to catch up to the Hilmir and try to talk sense into him, yet he discarded it a moment later. Throrsson *might* respond to Colborn's attempts to reason with him, but it was unlikely. Aravon wasn't even certain the Hilmir would accede to him as the Duke's second-in-command.

So he ran, as fast as he could, eking out every shred of strength and endurance from his body. Sweat soaked his tunic and streamed down his face, but Aravon only gritted his teeth against the stinging in his eyes and forced himself to keep running. It was the only way to reach the Hilmir in time.

With every pounding step, the nagging worry gnawed deeper into his belly. He had a Legionnaire's endurance, legs strengthened by years of riding a saddle and marching in a shield wall. But the Legion's fast-march could *never* match the pace of a Fehlan warband. And, even at the peak of Aravon's physical conditioning, his endurance paled compared to Colborn's and the men of the Fjall.

Jaw clenched, Aravon struggled to control his breathing—it had already grown heavy, labored. Fire raced through his leg muscles and the spear seemed terribly heavy in his hand, his palms slick with sweat. Every minute's delay meant a greater chance that the Fjall warband walked into a trap. He had nothing but suspicions and the Hilmir's evaluation of the Blood Queen, yet years of experience and education had honed his intuition. He couldn't ignore the feelings in his gut any more than the evidence of his eyes.

Worry for Duke Dyrund gnawed at Aravon's belly, weighing on his tiring muscles. The Duke *could* be in far more danger than the Hilmir, stone walls or no, and had only a small force of hired swords at his side. No telling what could be happening in Storbjarg, and Aravon couldn't rest easy until he reached Duke Dyrund and made personally certain the man was safe.

Grim images flashed through his mind. The streets of Storbjarg churned to bloody mud as the Eirdkilrs carved their way through the Fjall warriors, then cut down the Duke himself amidst his Black Xiphos mercenaries. Charred corpses, the Duke and his companions burned within the longhouse. A hundred more dire outcomes, his fear for the Duke's safety flooding him with ghastly visions.

With effort, Aravon pushed back the worry, forced himself to focus on the Fjall warband. *One problem at a time.*

Yet, even as Aravon forced his legs to keep moving, he could see the gap between him and the Fjall warband widening. Already, the Fjall had reached the first of the hills to the southeast. Throrsson and the foremost warriors had streamed out of sight, the rest of the warband close in pursuit. Every muscle in Aravon's body cried out for rest, his lungs shrieking for air, but he couldn't slow. If he did—

A new sound pierced the hammering of his pulse in his ears. He almost didn't recognize it through the frantic beating of his laboring heart. Yet, as realization dawned, hope surged within him.

Hoofbeats!

He risked a glance back and beheld the most glorious sight: Belthar and Zaharis, crouched low over the necks of their *Kostarasar* chargers, racing toward him. Behind the pair came three more horses with empty saddles.

Yes!

Aravon slowed and turned as the two men came pounding up beside him. He shot a glance to the northwest as he clambered into the saddle, and was rewarded with a glimpse of two smaller figures galloping off to where Chief Hafgrimsson would be waiting for the Hilmir's signal to strike. The Deid would be warned; Aravon had to hold out hope that Rangvaldr could convince them to march in time to make a difference.

But he had his own mission to stay focused on. Digging his heels into his horse's flanks, he spurred the beast to a gallop. Spear gripped tight, heart hammering against his ribs, Aravon raced after the Fjall warband. Behind him rode Colborn, Skathi, Belthar, and Zaharis, bent lower over their mounts' necks, urgency gleaming in their eyes.

Turning back to the land ahead, Aravon gritted his teeth and clutched the reins tighter. He was so close to the Fjall—just a few dozen more yards and he'd catch up to the rear of their column. The horses would reach Throrsson at the head of his men in less than five minutes, and Aravon *would* stop that column, even if he had to duel the Hilmir single-handedly. He couldn't let Throrsson race into the Blodsvarri's—

At that moment, he crested a rise and came face to face with two battle lines drawn up. Warriors of the Fjall, clad in bright chain mail, stood surrounded by a host of blue-painted, seven-foot-tall Eirdkilrs.

Horror clutched Aravon's heart in a fist of iron. He was too late.

The Blood Queen's trap had been sprung.

Chapter Forty-Eight

Aravon took in the scene in a heartbeat. The Fjall stood clustered in a long, ragged line of men, more a disorganized mass of warriors than any real battle formation. Even the best-trained Legionnaires struggled to maintain rank cohesion when moving at such a hurried pace, and the Fjall had thrown order to the wind in their mad dash home.

Yet discipline and years of battle experience quickly reasserted itself. Before Aravon brought his horse to a complete stop, the Fjall shield wall had already begun to form. Steel, iron, and wood clattered as the warriors joined together, round shields interlocked, into a solid, wide line. Men gripped swords, shields, and axes tighter, faces turned toward their enemy.

Yet the sight of the Eirdkilrs set Aravon's heart plummeting into his stomach. The towering figures in fur pelts and chain mail armor formed a long line that stretched from a thicket of trees off the Fjall's left flank, down the hill in front of them, and to the small pond beside their right flank. A line five ranks deep, which stretched half a mile wide.

Ice ran down Aravon's spine. *Blessed Swordsman!* Eleven hundred and eleven Fjall, with Eirik Throrsson at their head, faced more than three times as many Eirdkilrs.

A hand grabbed at Aravon's reins, pulling his horse around and back down the hill. Aravon, stunned by the sight of the enemy, barely had the presence of mind to cling to his horse's mane as Colborn pulled him down the decline and out of sight of the forces arrayed below.

Aravon's mind cleared quickly, and he shot Colborn a nod of thanks. He had no desire to sit idle while the Fjall faced an enemy that far outnumbered them, but the lieutenant was right to pull him back. Their best chance of doing something, anything, to turn the tide of battle in the Hilmir's favor was to remain undetected.

Yet in that moment, a nagging dread seeped into his bones, chilled him to the marrow. What hope did they have against so many?

Pushing back his dismay, Aravon leapt from his saddle and ran in a low crouch toward the top of the rise. Skathi and Belthar moved to his right, Colborn and Zaharis to his left. As they reached the hill's gentle crest, he lowered himself onto his belly and crawled upward until he could peer through the thick ryegrass and study the scene below.

Neither side had moved. The solidified Fjall shield wall stood defiant, Throrsson at its front and center. For once, the Eirdkilrs' war cries remained silent. The giants stood without a sound, a sea of blue-painted faces that stared with naked enmity at the enemy arrayed before them. An enemy that, Aravon knew, they would crush. Nothing short of a miracle would save the Fjall warband.

He turned to Zaharis. *"Anything you can do?"* he signed.

The Secret Keeper shook his head, a shadow darkening his eyes. *"Not against that many."*

Aravon ground his teeth and turned back to the battlefield. The Blodsvarri had chosen her terrain well. The Fjall could retreat up the hill, yet that would not save them. The Eirdkilrs had them surrounded on three sides, and it wouldn't take more than a few minutes to fully engulf the Fjall shield line. And they had the men to do it. Save for the thicket of trees to the south and the small pond to the north, there was nothing the Fjall could use for any battleground advantage.

How in the bloody hell did they manage to sneak up behind the Fjall? The question nagged at Aravon. *Throrsson had to have his scouts keeping an eye on the enemy, not to mention the two hundred with his second-in-command.*

His answer came a moment later.

A figure broke from the front ranks of Eirdkilrs. Tall, taller even than most of the seven-foot giants in the Eirdkilr line, she had hair of deep brown that hung in seven long braids down her back and around her neck. Skulls and bones dangled from those braids, rattling with every step. She had a heavy, blunt jaw, cheeks, and nose, somehow made all the fiercer by the lack of a beard. That, and the thick layer of blood smeared across her features. The blood shone bright crimson on the pale skin of her right cheek and turned a deep, grisly purple atop the intricate, swirling lines of blue dye that stained the left half of her face.

Aravon sucked in a breath. *The Blodsvarri.*

In her right hand, she carried a spear longer than she was tall, with a steel head the length of her forearm. But instead of a standard circular shield, she carried only the end of a thick hempen rope in her left hand. A grim smile twisted her bloodstained lips and she gave a vicious yank on the rope. A figure lurched into view between a gap in the Eirdkilr line, staggering toward the *Blodsvarri,* the rope tied in a noose around his neck.

Gyrd.

Blood trickled from the man's forehead, streamed from two split lips, and stained the graying hair of Gyrd's beard. Throrsson's second-in-command had endured a brutal beating, which left both of his eyes swollen shut and his nose shattered and twisted to one side. Yet his jaw was set in a stubborn cast, his bleeding lips pressed tightly together. He refused to cry out, even when the *Blodsvarri* knocked him to the ground with a vicious punch to the face.

Howls of gleeful laughter echoed from the Eirdkilr ranks, and more of the blue-painted, fur-clad barbarians broke from the line. They, too, hauled at heavy ropes, dragging forty struggling, snarling prisoners out in front of their ranks. With savage blows of their clubs, axes, and spears, the Eirdkilrs beat their prisoners to the ground. Yet the barbarians took care to avoid killing the Fjall warriors. Not out of mercy, Aravon realized.

They're going to make a spectacle of it.

"Eirik Throrsson, Chief of the Fjall!" The Blood Queen's voice echoed across the sixty-foot gap separating her and her captives from the front ranks of the Hilmir's shield wall. She spoke with the harsh, guttural accent of the Eirdkilrs—even with Aravon's comprehensive grasp of Fehlan, understanding her words proved challenging. "He who calls himself King!"

"Blood Queen." Throrsson's voice was calm, controlled despite the overwhelming odds arrayed against him, the rage that doubtless burned within him at the sight of his men so mistreated. "Is this your idea of honoring the Fehlan customs? Failing to present yourself at the sacred grounds, then attacking and taking my warriors captive? Such actions reek of treachery!"

"Said the serpent to the scorpion!" The *Blodsvarri* hissed. "Or do you deny that you entertained the very Eird I seek to destroy in your city not two days ago?" Her use of the word "half-men" was tinged with spittle and venom. "The same Eird that break bread and drink mead in your longhouse?"

Aravon's gut clenched. *So the Hilmir's suspicions were correct. She does have spies among his people.*

"The Eird offered me a cure for my people." Still, Throrsson seemed at ease. "So I accepted their offer under false pretenses to *lure* them into my stronghold, where they are at *my* mercy."

Ice slithered down Aravon's spine. *Duke Dyrund!* His fingers dug into the grass beneath him; was the Duke, even now, lying dead or captive in Storbjarg?

No. With effort, Aravon forced down the acid roiling in his stomach. *The Duke would have known if the Hilmir was deceiving him.* Few men in the Princelands were as perceptive as Duke Dyrund, which was the reason the Prince had chosen him as personal advisor and unspoken leader of his Council. He wouldn't make such an error in judgement.

And I looked in the Hilmir's eyes, Aravon thought. *There was no deceit there, no treachery aimed at the Princelands.*

The Duke had given Throrsson back his son, heir to the crown he hoped to one day wear. The Hilmir's gratitude had been real, no doubt about it.

Even then, if the Hilmir *had* intended to betray the Duke, he would have done it the day they rode into Storbjarg. It would have been a simple matter of surrounding the longhouse in which he'd quartered the Duke, then ordering the six thousand healthy warriors at his command to take them down. Or, simply burn the longhouse to the ground.

No, I can't believe he means it. Aravon's eyebrows shot up as realization dawned. *He's stalling for time!*

The Deid warband hadn't been the only force waiting in ambush for the Blood Queen's arrival. In addition to the eleven hundred and eleven men with Throrsson and the two hundred at Gyrd's side, the Hilmir had set another two thousand of his warband in waiting for the signal to attack.

Aravon rolled onto his side, shooting a glance at Colborn. "*Go!*" he signed. "*Find the Fjall ambushers and get them here now!*"

Colborn seemed to have reached the same conclusion, for he was already moving, scrambling backward low along the ground until he could rise to his feet, out of sight of the enemy below. Within seconds, he had sprinted the short distance to their horses, leapt into his saddle, and clapped his heels to the charger's flanks. Grass and clods of dirt flew beneath the horse's hooves as it

388

galloped off to the northeast, toward the dried-up riverbed where Throrsson had said his warriors would be awaiting the signal to attack.

A faint hope took root within Aravon. *With the Deid hopefully already on the way, there's a chance we can turn this around!* He scanned the grasslands to the north. The slopes of the Waeggbjod rose high into the morning sky, the thick forests surrounding its north and eastern edge. Yet he saw no sign of Noll, Rangvaldr, or Chief Svein Hafgrimsson at the head of the Deid warband bursting from those trees.

They'll come, he told himself as he turned his attention back to Throrsson and the Blood Queen. *They have to!*

"...what it takes to prove that I desire to join the *Tauld*," Throrsson was saying, "I will tear the Eird Prince's envoy apart with my bare hands." He jabbed a finger toward Gyrd, lying beaten and bloodied at the Blood Queen's feet. "But there can be no accord until you release my men."

From his position, Aravon saw the strange dance of emotions that flitted across the *Blodsvarri's* blunt, bloodstained features. Mockery mingled with incredulity, turned to disgust, then disdain. "I hold the advantage, *Hilmir.*" She sneered the word. "I have no need to *speak* of peace. I command it!"

The Blood Queen was still and speaking one moment, a violent explosion of movement the next. She spun the long-bladed spear above her head once, twice, setting the steel head glinting in the sunlight, and drove it point first into Gyrd's throat. The Fjall warrior's eyes flew wide and he gasped, bound hands flying to his neck, pawing at the wound.

But the *Blodsvarri* was far from done. She leaned on her spear, driving it deeper into Gyrd's neck and the ground beneath. The Fjall warrior's hands fell slack, his movements limp and spineless. With a bark of gleeful laughter, the leader of the Eirdkilrs stooped, seized the dying man, and hauled him high into the air. She held him aloft, like a trout skewered on a fishing spear, and leaned her head back as Gyrd's blood gushed from the tear in his throat and bathed her.

"By the Watcher!" Belthar's low curse echoed from beyond Skathi.

Aravon was unable to tear his gaze from the grisly scene. Gyrd's eyes had gone even wider, his face growing pale as he bled out, his body hanging above the *Blodsvarri's* head. The woman's muscles trembled not an inch at the exertion of holding the full-grown, lightly-armored Fjall warrior. Crimson stained the Blood Queen's face, soaked into her dark brown hair, dripped off her face and trickled from furs, leather, and chain mail coat. She reveled in the gush of blood, closing her eyes to relish the sensation.

Acid rose to Aravon's throat. It was clear where she'd gotten her name. The ruthlessness of Hrolf Hrungnir and his *Blodhundr* paled in comparison to her callous, sanguinary cruelty.

Slowly, Gyrd stopped gurgling, gasping for breath, the last drops of blood draining from his body. He hung limp on the Eirdkilr's spear, his eyes agape and empty. With a sneer, the *Blodsvarri* threw the corpse to the side, spraying droplets of crimson across the green grass carpeting the hillside.

"*I command it!*" the Blood Queen screamed again.

The Eirdkilrs behind her threw back their heads and took up a howling war cry, a long, keening sound that curdled Aravon's blood. Those holding the captive Fjall raised clubs, axes, and spears. Forty Fehlan warriors died in seconds, butchered like calves at a barbaric ceremonial feast, their deaths underscored by the savage ululations of their enemies.

Now the *Blodsvarri* turned back to Throrsson. Blood dripped from her blue-stained face, and her eyes gleamed with a wild light. "Kneel, *Hilmir!*" she hissed. "Throw down your weapons and face the *Tolfraedr* like *true* men of Fehl." A snarl curled her lip. "I will even give you the mercy of going first, spare you watching your men suffer."

"You call that mercy?" Throrsson's voice was strong, only a hint of a quaver. "*Tauld* ritual butchery?"

"The *Tolfraedr*," the Blood Queen hissed, "or I will keep you alive long enough to watch every man that marches at your back torn limb from limb. I will give your arms, legs, and manhood to the *Bein,* so they may consume your flesh before your very eyes. Then you, the *Hilmir* of all Fehl, will bear witness to the total destruction of your precious Storbjarg as my soldiers burn every longhouse, tear down every stone of the wall of which you Fjall are so proud. You will live, Eirik son of Thror, a long life of suffering, and you will see what the *Tauld* do to every town, village, and farm under your rule, then to every clan that allies with the Eird!"

The Eirdkilr leader stepped forward and pointed her spear, still stained with Gyrd's blood, at the Hilmir. "And only then, only once we have destroyed everything you hold dear, everything you cherish, then you will be permitted to die. A slow death of festering wounds and old age. A coward's death. Even in your afterlife, *Striíth* will spit on your maimed, putrid corpse and cast you through the *Helgrindr* into eternal darkness!"

For long moments, Throrsson remained silent.

Aravon narrowed his eyes. *Could he actually be considering her offer of surrender?* He had no idea what the *Tolfraedr* was, but knowing the Eirdkilrs...

"The Fjall do not kneel!" Throrsson's voice rang out across the open ground. He slammed his sword against his shield, setting the metal singing. "To no man or woman, Princelander or *Tauld!*" Again, the flat of his blade *thumped* against his shield. "Death holds no fear!"

More of his warriors took up the chant. "Death holds no fear!" They clashed swords on shields, a rhythmic sound that swelled as the entire Fjall warband joined in. The sound of steel striking wood echoed louder, louder, until it seemed to reverberate from the distant hills, the trees, even the blue sky above.

"Do your worst, queen of blood!" Throrsson raised his sword above his head and shouted over the cacophony. He raised his voice. "We are Fjall, mightiest warriors of Fehl, and by *Striíth,* we do not kneel!"

The Fjall warband took up the rhythmic chant. "*Striíth! Striíth!*" Their voices echoed in time with their clashing weapons, and Aravon felt as if the ground rumbled beneath his belly.

Yet when three thousand Eirdkilr throats echoed a war cry, it drowned out the Fjall's chant. The Blood Queen's left arm rose, fist clenched above her head, and in her right, she lowered her spear at the Fjall shield wall.

The Eirdkilrs charged.

Chapter Forty-Nine

Aravon had stood in the Legion ranks and faced an Eirdkilr charge many times in his life. It never grew easier to stand strong in the face of such overwhelming force.

The seven-foot barbarians surged toward the Fjall, a tide of furs, glimmering chain mail, leather armor, braids, and blue-painted skin. The force of their charge rumbled in Aravon's bones, the pounding of their feet deafening in his ears. His right hand tightened on his spear, as if in memory of gripping his shield and sword in that breathless, gut-wrenching moment before the clash. The seconds between life and death, when only open air and ground stood between him and enemies howling for his death.

There was no strategy to this battle, no cohesive ranks or lines of archers to soften the Fehlan shield wall. None was needed. Three thousand Eirdkilrs, thrice as many as their enemies, swept across the grass, up the dirt-rutted wagon track, and down from the thicket of trees to crash into the Fjall.

Flesh, wood, and steel met in a thunderous clash. Not a single clash, but dozens. Hundreds. Thousands, all at once. Booming, shrieking, thundering as warrior slammed into warrior. Spears thrust through gaps in shields. Axes bit deep into flesh and clubs crushed helmets. Bright steel swords filled the air with blood and death. Crimson misted in the air, sprayed from gaping wounds, deluged the ground as Fjall and Eirdkilr locked in battle.

Aravon more than heard the screams of pain; he *felt* them, every one of them, deep in the core of his being. He'd screamed like that before, in terror, agony, and rage as he faced the savage Eirdkilrs. His muscles twitched, going through the motions. Block, strike, deflect, block again.

393

Steel sang a song of death. Leather-covered shields shattered, wood splintered beneath heavy clubs that crushed heads, shattered arms, and stoved in chests. Mud grew thick and slippery as booted feet trampled grass and blood soaked into the earth. Gasping, crying, screaming, shouting. Warriors, trapped in a struggle that could only end in death. Death to friend and enemy alike.

Aravon found himself gasping for breath, as if *he* stood in the shield wall. With effort, he pulled himself back from the battle, back from the memories of seeing nothing but the enemy intent on spilling his blood.

He blinked, hard, and suddenly he was back on the hill overlooking the battle, watching the Fjall struggle to hold off the Eirdkilrs.

Hope came hard.

The Fjall had lost a fifth of their number in the initial clash, borne down beneath the weight of the towering, charging barbarians. The cohesion of the shield wall held, barely. The battle had disintegrated into a chaotic, swirling mess of bodies. Fjall and Eirdkilr stood chest to chest, face to face. Weapons trapped by their sides or against their chests, they drew daggers or lashed out with bare hands. Stabbing. Chopping. Hacking. Digging fingernails into eye sockets and tearing at throats. Pressed too tight together to bring skill to bear. Strength and the weight of numbers would carry this battle.

The Eirdkilrs had both on their side.

Aravon whirled on Zaharis. *"We have to help!"*

The Secret Keeper had already unpacked half his pouch, and he was pawing through his alchemical supplies, his movements frantic. Yet he shook his head, dismay ice cold in his eyes. *"I'm out of everything!"* He hadn't had a chance to restock since Rivergate. They'd been on the move so much he'd found no time to replenish his supplies from nature's bounty.

Aravon growled a frustrated curse and rolled over, facing Belthar and Skathi. Belthar's wide eyes were locked on the battle below, his huge hands balled in tight fists. At his side lay his enormous crossbow, forgotten and abandoned, his axe still strapped to his back.

"Skathi!" Aravon's fingers flashed. *"Can you take down the Blood Queen from here?"*

The archer's eyes narrowed. She turned back to the battle for a moment, then slowly shook her head. *"Too far, even for my longbow."*

In desperation, Aravon scanned the battlefield once more, searching for something, anything he could do to give the Hilmir a chance. If not to win, at least to retreat, to pull as many men out of this battle alive as possible. Yet, as his eyes went back to the Fjall warriors, the Eirdkilrs closed the circle behind them. The Hilmir's men had turned to face the enemy that surrounded them, shields locked, faces set and grim. Courage meant little against such impossible odds.

Aravon wanted to shout—no, he wanted to leap to his feet and rush down the hill, throw himself onto the enemy. It didn't matter that they weren't *his* men, his fellows of the Legion. They had come to the Fjall lands because the Hilmir's warband was their best hope of defeating the Eirdkilrs.

And now, that warband was being torn to shreds not two hundred yards from where he lay.

Aravon shot a glance back over his shoulder. *Please, mighty Swordsman, let them come!*

The flat grassy plains behind him were empty, devoid of life. The bright sun filled the air with a golden light, and a gentle wind set the grass swirling gracefully. The serenity felt horrifyingly eerie in contrast with the tumultuous symphony of blood and death that raged below their hilltop perch. No sign of the Deid. Or Colborn with the two thousand Fjall warriors. Nothing, but silence and serenity.

Dread settled like a stone in Aravon's gut. Much as he wanted to help, he *knew* he couldn't. Only a suicidal fool would rush down and join such an impossible battle. The smart play here was to wait, to watch for any opportunity to help the Hilmir. Or, to hope that the stubborn Throrsson surrendered before his warband was slaughtered to a man.

Yet "smart" meant sitting by in silence, watching good men—men he'd hoped would join their battle against the Eirdkilrs—die. Fjall warriors in the prime of their strengths died beneath flashing Eirdkilr spears and axes. Skulls crushed, faces caved in, limbs shattered. Blood, so much blood, spilled across the grassy field.

Eleven hundred and eleven men had dwindled to fewer than seven hundred. Six hundred and fifty. Six hundred. There was nowhere Throrsson's men could run. No escape from the Eirdkilrs. Men died by the dozens, hemmed in on all sides by implacable foes with faces stained blue and dripping crimson. Towering, fur-clad enemies that howled for their deaths.

The Blood Queen's piercing, high-pitched laughter echoed beneath the Eirdkilr war cries. She stood behind her embattled warriors, her eyes wild as she watched her warriors tear the Fjall to shreds. A savage smile twisted her lips and she leaned forward, eager to see the proud Hilmir brought low.

Throrsson roared for his men to fight, to stand strong. Fehlan warriors shouted to *Striith*, called to comrades, spat hatred into their enemy's faces.

And still they died. In twos, threes, tens and twenties. Surrounded, trampled, crushed, and stabbed. Eyes gouged out and throats slashed by enemy spears. Limbs and necks hewn, helmets shattered.

The sight of so much death, the cries of dying men, and the coppery tang of blood filled Aravon's senses. It made him sick.

Five hundred. Now four hundred. In any other battle, the Fjall would have abandoned the field or thrown down their weapons. But there was no escape. Their only hope lay in the Hilmir bending the knee, something the proud, defiant chief would never do.

Throrsson went down, lost somewhere beneath the crush of bodies. Slain by an Eirdkilr axe or spear. A hundred Fjall faced more than twenty times their number. Grim, defiant, bold, their faces creased in snarls. They gave as good as they got. All the Fjall had. The Eirdkilr ranks had been reduced to barely more than two thousand. Yet in less than a minute, the last hundred fell.

Fell, but not to lie still and silent forever. Fehlan warriors groaned, wept, or cried in agony among the bodies of their comrades. Some cradled shattered limbs or sat in numb, dazed silence, blood leaking from head wounds and crushed chests. Missing arms and legs, or eyes, noses, even lips and ears. Men torn to shreds by the savagery of the Eirdkilrs, yet somehow alive.

Aravon didn't know whether to rejoice or grimace as a still-living Eirik Throrsson was dragged from beneath a pile of Eirdkilr and Fehlan corpses. Kicking, snarling Fehlan curses, he bled from a half-dozen wounds. Three towering enemies wrestled him to the ground, bound his hands and legs with ropes, and hauled him before the Blood Queen.

"Remember," her hiss carried up the hill to where Aravon lay watching, "I offered you the *Tolfraedr*. Now, all who live will face the culling. And you will watch it!"

"Savage bitch!" Throrsson spat a mouthful of blood in her face.

The *Blodsvarri* laughed and wiped the blood from her cheeks, licking it off one callused finger. "Good. Save that spirit, *Hilmir*." The word dripped mockery. "You will need it to sustain you through the night."

A hiss from beside Aravon brought him whirling to his right. He blinked, almost surprised to find Skathi and Belthar there. He'd gotten so lost in the carnage, the swirl and chaos of battle, that he'd forgotten the soldiers beside him.

"*Colborn,*" Skathi signed, and jerked a thumb over her shoulder.

Aravon craned his neck, and a dagger of steel drove into his gut. A single rider raced toward them. No Fjall warband or Deid warriors. No army four thousand strong. Just one man riding a massive charger, alone.

There would be no salvation for Throrsson and his men.

Aravon glanced back down the hill toward the scene of battle. The Eirdkilrs had begun digging through the Fehlan bodies. But instead of dispatching survivors quickly, they pulled any still living out of the crush of corpses. Wounded, bleeding, and dying men were dragged to one side and bound with strips of cloth, fur, leather, and rope cut from the bodies of their comrades. Screaming, weeping, or groaning, they lay on the grass, their blood staining the earth around them. Some with intestines spilling from gaping wounds or severed limbs hanging from shredded flesh. Many with wounds more debilitating than mortal.

The ones who fell in battle had the better fortune, of that Aravon had no doubt.

Turning, he scrambled down the hill toward Colborn. The Lieutenant reined in his horse and leapt from his saddle with a grim shake of his head.

"I found tracks leading back to Storbjarg," Colborn reported, "but they were at least two hours old."

Two hours? Aravon's eyebrows shot up. *Has it really been that long since we first spotted the smoke?* The rush of battle and the threat of death could play strange tricks with time—speed it up to a frantic, blistering pace one moment, and slow it to a glacial crawl the next.

Gritting his teeth, he forced himself to think clearly, to pull his mind from the chaos of battle.

That's a good thing for Storbjarg, he realized. *With two thousand men to join the three thousand holding the walls, there's no way the Eirdkilrs can take the city. If they hadn't already, of course. And if they have, there's a chance it can be reclaimed.*

Hope for Storbjarg, however, meant nothing for Eirik Throrsson and the still-living Fjall warriors below. Aravon tried to formulate a plan, tried to evaluate his next steps, but it seemed impossible to come up with anything that didn't wind up with the five of them dead.

His eyes went to the northeast. Still no Deid. *Where in the frozen hell are they?*

But it no longer mattered. Two thousand Deid could never defeat an equal number of Eirdkilrs in open combat. Even if Noll and Rangvaldr rode up with Chief Svein Hafgrimsson 's men that very minute, there would be no hope for Eirik Throrsson's men.

The battle had been lost. Now, it was time for Aravon to re-adjust, formulate a new plan. *Preferably one that didn't end up with them all dead. And, Swordsman willing, one that gives us a chance to save Throrsson.*

That was when the screaming began.

Chapter Fifty

The densely packed leaves of the hickory trees did little to drown out the sounds of screaming, weeping, and dying Fjall warriors. A shudder ran down Aravon's spine as the next man was dragged, bound and bleeding, from the ranks of captives. Even after fifty deaths—slow, torturous deaths, each carried out by the *Blodsvarri* herself—the Eirdkilrs hadn't sated their lust for blood.

Aravon hated himself, hated the helplessness, but he knew he could do nothing. Nothing but watch from cover of the thicket and wait until his chance to strike back came.

Until then, more Fjall would die.

The Blood Queen wasn't content to open their throats or remove their heads. One by one, she had the captive Fjall bound to stakes her Eirdkilrs had driven deep into the earth. Then she went to work with her knives. Slow, almost tender strokes of her blades carved two runes into their flesh. The first, the Fehlan rune for *Tauld;* the second, a complex symbol that stood for "traitor". Deep into the soft flesh of their bellies the *Blodsvarri* etched those cruel words, her knives slicing through skin, muscle, and organs. Organs that she pulled out with bloodstained hands. Yanking, dragging on the lengths of intestines, tearing until the warriors died from loss of blood or sheer overwhelming agony.

Always died, always screaming. Yet no amount of suffering seemed to dim the Blood Queen's savagery. When one died, another was hauled forward. Sunset hadn't put an end to the torment—she had simply ordered torches lit and fires made, then continued her tortures under the watchful eyes of the rising moon. The darkness seemed to make the cries of agony echo louder.

The Tolfraedr. Colborn had paled at mention of the Blood Queen's words. Now Aravon knew why.

Aravon had always believed the Legion cruel for its practice of executing every tenth man in a mutinous company—a sentence that hadn't been carried out on Fehl for more than fifty years. Yet the dispassionate beheadings of disloyal Legionnaires could never truly compare to the deliberate cruelty being inflicted upon Eirik Throrsson and his warriors. The Blood Queen reveled in her orgy of blood, death, and anguish, her warriors looking on with delight burning in their eyes.

And through it all, the Hilmir had been forced to watch. Tears streamed down his huge, bearded face, his lips pressed so tight they had gone pale beneath the blood caking his skin. With his bloodied arms and legs bound to stakes driven deep into the ground, guarded by ten Eirdkilrs at all times, Throrsson had had no choice but to bear witness to his men's suffering. Hear their screams, watch their entrails ripped out, and their blood and bile stain the grassy field.

Aravon had never been squeamish—he'd fought in the shield wall, killed hundreds of enemies in hand-to-hand combat, sat beside men as Legion healers and physickers hacked off shattered and rotting limbs. Yet he turned away as the Blood Queen began her tortures anew. He could watch the brave warriors suffer no more.

And not for much longer! Fists clenched, he shot a glance at the sky. The sun had descended behind the western hills more than an hour earlier, and the moon had yet to rise. Even once it had ascended, it would be little more than a sliver among the stars twinkling in the heavens. A perfect night for stealth and subterfuge.

The Eirdkilrs had anticipated the darkness and set fires and torches blazing around the perimeter of their makeshift campsite, established a few yards from the dead slain in battle. Even from a hundred yards away, the stench of the corpses and the metallic tang of dried blood grew thick enough to twist Aravon's stomach. Yet, he dared not move out from the shadow of the hickory thicket. He couldn't risk approaching the fires. At least, not yet.

His eyes darted to his right, toward the hill where he and his comrades had watched the battle. The hill was empty, he knew, and his comrades long ago gone to follow his orders. Belthar and Skathi, ridden off to hunt down the two thousand Fjall who had marched on Storbjarg and to observe the situation in the Fjall capital. Skathi would send Snarl winging off to the Princelands,

400

carrying news of Storbjarg and the Hilmir's losses here to Lord Eidan and the Prince. Colborn had gone to meet with Rangvaldr, Noll, and the Deid forces, to update them on the outcome of the day's battle.

And Zaharis was preparing a surprise for the Eirdkilrs, one that would give Aravon the chance he needed. One chance, little more than a few seconds, but he'd have to make it work.

If he didn't, every captive warrior of the Fjall and the Hilmir would die screaming.

A pang of fear and worry flashed through Aravon's chest. Somewhere in the darkness to the east, Duke Dyrund was in danger. Either trapped within Storbjarg, hiding or fleeing from the Eirdkilrs. With effort, he swallowed the anxiety, forced himself to calm.

The mission comes first, he told himself. *This mission.*

Belthar and Skathi would worry about the Duke—they'd take stock of the situation in Storbjarg, figure out the best plan to get Duke Dyrund and his companions out safely. Aravon had to focus on the impossible task at hand.

Come on, Zaharis! Aravon gripped his spear tighter. The two of them had taken shelter in the small thicket just before the Eirdkilrs sent out skirmishers to collect any Fjall stragglers, and the cover offered him ample concealment from the barbarians below.

And he *needed* the dense shadows within the trees to keep him out of sight. Though the majority of the Eirdkilrs basked in the Blood Queen's gruesome spectacle, a hundred stood watch to the northeast, their eyes locked on the land in the direction of Storbjarg against any counterattack by the Fjall.

Yet it seemed a mere formality—the Blood Queen seemed confident in the total success of her ambush on the Hilmir's forces. The absence of any counterattack after the Hilmir's defeat only bolstered her belief that she had triumphed this day.

And she was right. No one would march to the Hilmir's rescue. The Fjall two thousand had raced back to their burning capital, and the Deid wouldn't assault a larger group of Eirdkilrs on their own.

Which left the fate of Eirik Throrsson and his men in Aravon's hands. With only Zaharis nearby, he *had* to pull this off right, else he would join the Hilmir and his men under the Blood Queen's cruel knives.

Then it came. The signal—in true Zaharis fashion, an unmistakable spectacle that drew all eyes.

Fire shot up from the surface of the pond, a brilliant wall of red and orange that reached flaming fingers high into the night sky. A thunderous *whooshing* of air drowned out the piercing shrieks of the dying Fjall warrior, the *Blodsvarri's* delighted laugher. The darkness of the evening burst to blinding brightness as the pillars of fire grew taller, stretched across the length of the pond.

The Eirdkilrs reacted immediately. Hands dropped to weapons, men turned to face the blazing light and crackling flames, and those nearest fell back from the burning pond. Shouts of alarm, fury, and terror echoed from the Eirdkilrs' camp. Hundreds of enemies surged toward the eastern edge of the camp in anticipation of a Fjall attack. Cries of stunned surprise mingled with their war cries echoed loud—they had never seen *water* burning, and the "magic" awed and terrified them. Just as it had been intended to.

And it bought Aravon precious seconds to move.

Silent as a wraith, furtive as a shadow, he darted out of the tree cover and dashed down the hill toward the captive Fjall. The Eirdkilrs holding them hadn't abandoned their posts, but their eyes were turned away, facing the new threat. That light, so brilliant crimson and orange, didn't just draw their attention—it blinded them to deep darkness of the evening.

Blinded them to the figure in mottled armor that flowed like liquid shadow down the hill. With the stealth of a stalking greatcat, Aravon crossed the distance to the nearest cluster of prisoners and threw himself to the ground behind their kneeling forms. He crawled on his belly, inching his way close enough to draw his dagger—coated with mud to conceal the gleam—and slash the ropes holding them bound.

Five were freed in the space of ten seconds. Then ten, fifteen, twenty. The sharp Odarian steel blade sliced through coarse Eirdkilr-made ropes with a single stroke, cutting away bonds and freeing the captive warriors. Aravon had chosen the warriors that appeared *least* injured; they bore a collection of bruises and bleeding wounds, but their limbs remained unbroken by their enemies. They had struggled most fiercely when watching their comrades dragged to the *Tolfraedr.*

That strength gave them a chance for freedom. And for vengeance.

Aravon reached the first Eirdkilr guard, one of the thirty who had been assigned to watch the captives. The man held an enormous axe in a thick-fingered hand, the huge steel head resting on his right shoulder. The weight of that axe would shear a Fjall's neck—or Aravon's—in a single stroke. But only if he could bring it to bear.

That instant of distraction meant everything. With his eyes fixed on the burning pond, the Eirdkilr never saw Aravon creeping up beside him. Never saw the long, sharp blade of a spear driving up toward his neck. The man didn't so much as turn as Aravon rose to his knees and thrust his spear at the Eirdkilr's throat in one smooth move. Odarian steel sliced through the barbarian's beard, punched through the side of his neck, and severed his spine in the space between heartbeats. The body had barely *thumped* gently to the grassy hillside before Aravon snatched the axe from his lifeless fingers.

Whirling, Aravon thrust the haft of the enormous weapon into the hands of one large, broad-shouldered Fjall warrior. The man gave him a savage grin and, seizing the weapon, charged another of the Eirdkilrs holding the captives. Steel glinted in the alchemical firelight, blood sprayed, and another Eirdkilr fell, never to rise.

But Aravon hadn't come to kill Eirdkilrs. He'd exhausted precious seconds racing down the hill, freeing the Fjall, and taking down the first enemy. The nearest guards would begin to notice the liberated captives at any second, and the Fjall would find themselves fighting for their lives.

He had to get to the Hilmir.

Aravon darted back, out of the circle of firelight, and raced south around the Eirdkilr encampment. The barbarians, still mesmerized and incensed by the mysterious and magical fire, had turned eastward to face the new threat. Never bothering to look backwards and see the figure darting through the shadows.

Zaharis hadn't yet run out of surprises.

BOOM! Earthshakers, the Secret Keeper had called them, and rightly so. One moment the Eirdkilr ranks were clustered tightly across the southeastern road, the next a brilliant burst of orange light erupted in their midst with such fury it set the ground trembling. The explosion hurled a dozen backward and scores more fell with shrieking cries, scythed down by an invisible hand.

The Blood Queen shouted orders to her men, abandoning her torments and racing toward the line of warriors facing the invisible enemy. The Eirdkilrs surrounding the bound and bloodied Hilmir loped alongside her, leaving Throrsson guarded by only five enormous warriors.

Aravon raced toward them. Five Eirdkilrs against one of him. *Rubbish odds on the best of days, but this is anything but.*

Confused and enraged shouts echoed from the camp's northern edge, accompanied by the clash of steel. The Eirdkilrs had discovered their captives freed and armed. Shouts of "For *Striith*! For the Hilmir!" pierced the darkness, adding to the turmoil within the Eirdkilr camp.

The Eirdkilrs guarding the Hilmir drew their weapons and formed a line between their prisoner and the Fjall captives.

Precisely what Aravon had hoped they'd do. Racing through the shadows, he slipped around the Eirdkilrs and ducked behind the posts to which the Hilmir was bound. Four quick strokes of his dagger severed the ropes holding Throrsson in place. The Fjall chief sagged with a groan, falling to the ground. Exhaustion, pain, and thirst dragged at his limbs, and blood loss had turned his skin pale in the light of the burning alchemical blaze. Yet as Aravon pressed his own longsword into the Hilmir's hand, Throrsson's grip tightened around the hilt, and a savage growl rumbled in his throat.

Aravon leapt past the still-kneeling Throrsson and brought his spear whipping around in a slashing blow. The blade, heavy enough to cut as well as thrust, slashed across the hamstrings of the three nearest Eirdkilrs. Odarian steel sliced through furs, leather, chain shirts, and flesh. The men fell with a cry, half-turning in their shock. Aravon thrust twice in quick succession, opening two barbarian throats. Before the third could bring his enormous club around, Aravon slammed the iron-shod butt of his spear into the side of the barbarian's head. The man went down, hard, skull crushed.

Something dark hurtled past on Aravon's left. The Hilmir, a blur of rage and motion, struck out at the startled Eirdkilrs. The blade in his hand—the finest mainlander steel forged in the style of a weighty Fehlan longsword—sheared through one enemy's neck and buried deep into the second man's chest. Aravon was there in an instant, driving his spear into the man's throat to silence his cry of alarm and agony. The Eirdkilr gave a quiet, wet gurgle and toppled backward. Crimson gushed from the ragged tear in his neck, seeping into the ground and mingling with the blood of the tortured and slain Fjall warriors.

Aravon whirled on the Hilmir. "*We leave, now!*" he hissed in Fehlan.

"My warband—" Throrsson began.

"Fight for their freedom." Aravon thrust a finger toward the battling captives. Less than a minute had elapsed since Zaharis set the pond ablaze, and in the confusion of the burning water and the sudden explosive blast within their midst, only a handful had turned toward the freed prisoners. None had noticed Aravon and the Hilmir…yet. "But *you* must escape!"

The Hilmir's jaw set. "I will not leave my men."

"You *must!*" Aravon took a step toward the man. "For the sake of your people, you must live to fight another day."

Shouts echoed from the east, and more Eirdkilrs tore their eyes away from the wall of fire to join the battle against the liberated Fjall warband. Fully a hundred of the once-captive warriors had taken up arms—ripped from the hands of their slain enemies or fallen comrades—and hurled themselves at the nearest Eirdkilrs. Mayhem held the Eirdkilr camp in a fist of iron, yet Aravon knew it would only last a few minutes at most.

"Now, Hilmir!" Aravon seized the man's arm and dragged him away from the torn and eviscerated corpses of his fellow warriors. "While the enemy is distracted." And before the decimated Fjall succumbed to their wounds, exhaustion, and superior numbers.

Throrsson was a big man, and strong. For a long second, he refused to budge, his gaze fixed on his men, bloodstained sword gripped in knuckles gone white with fury. Yet, another explosive *BOOM* from the darkness, accompanied by the screams of dying and enraged Eirdkilrs, seemed to snap him out of it. When he turned, Aravon recognized the look in his eyes: the look of a commander who *knew* he was condemning men to die, yet had no choice but to do so.

It was the same look that had haunted General Traighan all of Aravon's life.

Reluctance etched deep lines of sorrow into his strong face, yet the Hilmir nodded. "Go!" he growled. Fire blazed in his ice-blue eyes. "We live to avenge their sacrifice."

Chapter Fifty-One

Without hesitation, Aravon slung the Hilmir's arm over his left shoulder and hurried up the hill as fast as the wounded Throrsson could manage. Away from the carnage and death howling through the enemy camp. Away from the screams of wounded Fjall, dying Eirdkilrs, and the *Blodsvarri's* shrieking cries to "Bring down the traitors!" Into the welcoming embrace of the shadows and hope of escape for Throrsson, even if it cost the lives of every man left behind them.

The fifty yards seemed to stretch on forever, and it felt like an eternity before Aravon and the gasping, staggering Throrsson dove into the shadows of the hickory thicket. The shouts grew louder, the clash of steel ringing high and piercing in the night. Aravon paused only long enough to risk a quick glance backward.

Fjall warriors had reclaimed their captured weapons or ripped them from their captors' hands; now, men that lived and breathed battle fell upon their enemy. The enemy who had tortured their comrades to death, who had massacred nearly one-tenth of the Fjall warband. Cries to the Fjall god and shouts of "For the Hilmir!" echoed loud through the darkness.

Yet Aravon had to turn away before the slaughter began in earnest. Zaharis' fire was dazzlingly bright and mysterious, but no enemy had appeared from the southeast. Now, the full might of the Blood Queen's remaining warband flooded toward the freed Fjall captives.

Pain etched every line of the Hilmir's face—not only from the wounds suffered in battle and at the *Blodsvarri's* hands, but from the knowledge of his warriors' fates. He limped as fast as he could, gasping for air, struggling to bite back a cry as blood trickled from a dozen lacerations in his arms, face, and bared chest. Yet, without a word, he stubborned on, hurrying along beside Aravon as best he could.

They couldn't stop, not until they had left the enemy far behind. The moment the Eirdkilrs discovered the Hilmir's absence, the Blood Queen would flood the surrounding land with her hunters. The enemy wouldn't rest until Throrsson lay dead or bound at the *Blodsvarri's* feet once more.

With deft movements, Aravon unwound his horse's reins from the hickory tree. "Get on," he hissed at Throrsson. "We need to cover ground quickly."

Throrsson shook his head. "The Fjall do not ride." A hard, stubborn tone edged his words. "A true warrior meets death on his feet."

"And a King does whatever the bloody hell it takes to live!" Aravon gestured to the horse. "The only way we're going to get out of here before they come looking for us is if you get on. You can't cover ground fast enough in your condition."

He'd lost a great deal of blood from the wounds sustained in battle, and the Blood Queen's knives had done their terrible work on his body. He'd run himself into the ground long before they escaped the Eirdkilrs.

And Throrsson knew it. With a reluctant growl, he strode toward the horse and tried to mount. A grunt burst from his lips at the pain of trying to pull himself into the saddle. The effort re-opened wounds that had scabbed or crusted over, and fresh blood trickled anew. Finally after a few fruitless attempts, Aravon settled for shoving the heavy Fjall warrior onto the horse, not bothering to be gentle with his wounds. His effort elicited a growl from the Hilmir but Aravon had no time for polite decency. Every second's delay could cost them their chance at escape.

Aravon gripped the horse's reins and shot a glance up at the mounted Throrsson. The man looked supremely uncomfortable and unsteady, like a first-time swimmer thrown into the riptides of Icespire Bay. "Hang on," he growled.

Before Throrsson could raise a protest, Aravon tugged the reins and pulled the horse into a slow trot. He broke into a jog, then a run as the horse gained speed. Down the southwestern slope of the hill they ran, away from the Eirdkilr camp and the din of battle—a din that had grown steadily louder, now tinged with the cries of Fjall warriors dying beneath the Eirdkilr onslaught.

Urgency thrummed in Aravon's bones, fueled his muscles. The day's exertions dragged on his limbs yet fear of what lay behind them forced him onward. He couldn't slow, not for the Hilmir's sake and certainly not for his own. He *had* to keep running, had to put as much ground between them and the Eirdkilrs before—

A savage, piercing howl split the night behind them, echoed a heartbeat later by a thousand throats. Ice slithered down Aravon's spine. The Eirdkilrs had discovered the Hilmir's absence. Now, the giant barbarians were coming for them.

Gritting his teeth, he leaned into his run, forcing his tired legs to greater speeds. He shot a silent prayer of thanks to the Swordsman for the grassy hills hiding them from the Eirdkilr camp. The sliver of moon had just appeared over the horizon, giving him faint threads of light to guide his steps. Yet one wrong step and he—or, worse, the horse—could break something, and their chances of escape would be shattered.

Throrsson's growl echoed from the horse's saddle. "Where…are…you…going?" His words burst out in time with the horse's bouncing gait. "Why…do we…head…south?"

"It's the last place the enemy will look for us!" Aravon gasped. His lungs begged for air, his legs burned from the exertion, but his mind was clear.

Most of the southern Fjall lands were held by the Eirdkilrs. It made the most sense for the chief to flee northeast, back in the direction of Storbjarg and his warband. If not back to his capital, then toward one of the larger Fjall towns to the east or northwest. Perhaps even to the safety of the Deid lands to the north.

But the Eirdkilrs would *never* expect the Hilmir to flee south, deeper into land they controlled. They'd send scouts to search in that direction, no doubt about it, but their efforts would be far more concentrated to the north, east, and west.

It's our best chance of getting out alive. Aravon shot a glance over his shoulder at the Hilmir. Throrsson sat awkwardly in the saddle, swaying and unsteady, hunched over in pain. Exhaustion lined his face, dragged at his limbs. Aravon growled a silent curse. The man wouldn't get far in his condition.

But until Throrsson actually collapsed or Aravon's strength gave out, they would keep moving, keep putting as much distance between them and their enemies as possible. Zaharis would find his way back to Colborn and the others—that left Aravon alone in hostile territory with an injured Hilmir.

First we find a place to rest, Aravon decided, *then we figure out how to get back to Fjall lands.*

Yet as one mile became two, the terrain to the southwest of the Eirdkilr camp grew more rugged, the ridges steeper and taller, the ground uneven. Trees grew thicker along the spiny ridges of cliffs, and the grasslands gave way to stony hills. Hope surged within Aravon as he spotted the meandering bed of a dried-up river cutting through a deep gully directly west.

Yes! They could at least get out of sight there, make it harder for the Eirdkilr pursuers to find them. Or, if they had no choice but to fight, have at least a chance of getting out alive. *It's better than being out in the open!*

"Captain...Snarl." The Hilmir's voice drifted toward Aravon, weak, so faint he nearly missed it.

Aravon glanced over his shoulder and up at the mounted Fjall. Throrsson swayed like a drunken scout, his hands locked around the horn of his saddle and his face pale from exhaustion and blood loss. As Aravon slowed the horse, the Hilmir's eyes rolled up in the back of his head and he toppled to the side.

Whirling, Aravon leapt to the man's side just in time to stop him from falling out of the saddle. Throrsson blinked down at him, his eyes unfocused, glazed over.

"Hold on, Hilmir," Aravon growled, pushing the big man back upright on the horse and holding on until Throrsson found his balance. "We just need to get there, out of sight."

The Hilmir squinted into the darkness, blinking hard. "*Hellir,*" he muttered.

Aravon's brow furrowed. The Fehlan word was unfamiliar. Perhaps it wasn't a word at all, but a name. Throrsson wouldn't be the first warrior to see the faces of dead enemies, friends, or loved ones floating before his eyes, his weakened mind hallucinating.

"Don't you die on me, you bastard!" Aravon tightened his grip on the Hilmir's blood-soaked leather belt and held him upright. "We'll get you to safety, but you've got to hang on."

Throrsson muttered something Aravon didn't quite hear. Yet the words were drowned out a moment later by the howling of the Eirdkilrs behind him. Aravon cast a glance backward, and his gut clenched at the sight of torches shining in the darkness. The Eirdkilr pursuers were catching up.

410

"Come on!" Aravon released his hold on the man's shirt and, scooping up the reins, took off at a fast run. He could *never* hope to outrun the Eirdkilrs, but he was close enough to the gully to get out of sight.

Aravon's heart hammered in his chest, beat a frantic tattoo against his ribs. Sweat stung his eyes and his mouth begged for water just as his lungs cried out for air. Fire ran through his legs, up and down his spine. Yet he ran, desperate to reach safety before the Eirdkilrs found them.

The war cries grew nearer, so near Aravon almost imagined he could hear the footsteps of heavy boots pounding across the grasslands toward him. It didn't matter that the enemy was the better part of half a mile behind them—he and the mounted Hilmir would be plainly visible moving across the flat grasslands, bathed in the faint silvery light of the quarter-moon.

Come on! Aravon gritted his teeth and forced himself to run faster, to keep a tight grip on the horse's reins. His pulse pounded so loud in his ears it drowned out the soft padding of the horse's hooves on the grass. The race to the gully seemed interminable, the distance so vast Aravon imagined he raced across the Frozen Sea with lead weights dragging at his limbs.

Then the horse's hooves clattered on hard earth, and Aravon's booted feet scrambled over stone-strewn ground. The gully loomed large in front of Aravon and he dropped down the steep side. His boots dug into soft ground and he fell, hard, sliding for a few feet before he caught his balance. To his relief, the horse and the mounted Throrsson managed the descent with far more grace.

The dried-up riverbed made for tricky going, and Aravon had to move more slowly to avoid stepping on loose stones or stumbling on the uneven ground. His relief at reaching the gully was short-lived. The faint moonlight shone on high earthen walls of the hill, with only sparse shadows to conceal them from their enemies. Once the Eirdkilrs caught up, no way they'd miss the huge shape of the horse and two men hiding in the gully.

Keeper take it! Grinding his teeth, Aravon turned back the way he'd come and tried to scramble back up the gully's earthen walls, but stopped short. The first of the Eirdkilr torches appeared to the south, less than a quarter-mile from the gully. His only hope was to push through the gully, to keep running with the exhausted Hilmir. If they followed the trail of the riverbed, there was a chance, however faint, that they could find shelter somewhere to the north.

"*Hellir.*" Throrsson's muttered word reached his ears once more.

Aravon whirled toward the Hilmir. "What is it?"

"Cave." The word was faint, little more than a whisper.

Aravon's eyebrows shot up. "Where?"

Throrsson lifted a weak finger. "Deeper into…gully."

Aravon's hope renewed. With speed born of desperation, he seized the horse's reins set north along the gully. The clatter of stones and the sound of the horse's hooves on the dried-up riverbed echoed loud in his ears, so loud he feared their pursuers would overhear. Yet if the Hilmir was right and there *was* a cave farther along the gully, it gave them a faint hope of surviving the night.

The gully curved sharply to the west, the steep earthen walls rising twenty feet over Aravon's head and blocking out the faint moonlight. Yet there, in the deep shadows, was a man-height radius of black so profound it could only be the opening to the cave.

He hauled on the horse's reins and hurried toward the blackness. His questing hands found damp earth walls that gave way to an opening taller than his head and wider than his shoulders.

Elation bloomed within Aravon. *Yes!*

He whirled back toward his horse to help Throrsson down. Not a moment too soon. The Hilmir sagged and Aravon barely had time to reach out to catch the falling man. A grunt of effort burst from his lips; his exhausted muscles strained from the effort of supporting the heavily-muscled warrior. He dragged the Hilmir from the saddle and into the cave, pausing long enough to tug on the horse's reins.

The scent of damp earth hung thick within the pitch blackness of the cave, accompanied by the fetid rotted-meat reek of mushrooms and mold. Aravon felt his way along the tunnel one-handed, the other struggling to hold the slumping Hilmir upright. Finally, his muscles and Throrsson's legs gave out and he dropped the heavy warrior to the ground. Throrsson hit the soft earth with a loud *thump* and groaned.

Something bumped Aravon's back and he whirled, only to find himself face to face with his horse's wet nose. He pushed the beast aside and slipped back toward the narrow opening of the cave. His heart pounded a nervous rhythm as he crouched in the darkness, eyes fixed on the shadowed gully beyond.

Had the Eirdkilrs spotted them before they reached the gully? Did they know of this cave's existence? He gripped his spear tighter and prepared for anything.

412

Knots tightened his shoulders as a faint noise echoed through the night beyond. A moment later, the sound coalesced to the familiar *clatter* of stones, the heavy tread of Eirdkilr boots on the hard-packed earth of the parched riverbed. The night grew brighter, the stink of burning torches drifting past on the chilly breeze.

Damn it! If the Eirdkilrs searched the gully with their torches, there was no way they'd miss the cave. Aravon slipped backward, deeper into the shadows, until he bumped up against his horse's flank. He could retreat no more, so the time had come to fight. The narrow opening would force the enemies to come at him one at a time, but the desperate flight from the Eirdkilrs' camp had left him drained.

Yet fight he would, no matter how exhaustion weighed on his limbs. He'd fight until his last breath for a chance to get out of here alive—and to bring the Hilmir back alive with him. The future of Fehl depended on it. If Throrsson and the Fjall fell, nothing would stop the Eirdkilrs from dominating the southern half of the continent. The Deid alone couldn't stand against them, and the Legion had few men to spare in the defense of their allies.

Aravon gripped his spear tighter, forced himself to draw in calm, slow breaths. He couldn't get ahead of himself, couldn't let his mind run rampant with images of doom and gloom.

He clenched his jaw. *We will get out of here!* One way or another, even if he had to fight through a horde of Eirdkilrs alone.

A quiet groan shattered the silence and drove a dagger of ice into Aravon's gut. The triumphant shouts from outside the cave left him with no doubt. The Eirdkilrs had heard Throrsson, and now they were coming. The night outside grew steadily brighter, the flickering glow of the Eirdkilr torches dispelling the shadows.

Gritting his teeth, Aravon gripped his spear in both hands and prepared to meet the attack. Within the cave, he had little room to maneuver. It would take just *one* enemy to summon reinforcements; he couldn't hold out forever.

Yet he'd be damned if he let the Blood Queen take him alive. He would fight until his last breath, no matter how many of the blue-painted savages came for him.

Chapter Fifty-Two

Light blazed blinding and bright in the cave as an Eirdkilr burst through the narrow opening, torch in one hand, spear in the other. He let out a howl of delight at the sight of Aravon and drew his spear back for a thrust.

But Aravon was ready. He struck first, driving his weapon forward, slamming the Odarian steel head home in the man's chest. Chain mail links *snapped* beneath the force of the blow. The bright blade punched through leather, tunic, and flesh, sliding between the man's ribs. Dark red blood poured from the wound and the Eirdkilr stumbled back. Spear and torch fell from numb fingers and he gasped once, twice, three times, before slowly toppling backward.

Aravon tore the spearhead free of the dead Eirdkilr and whipped it back toward the narrow entrance, splattering the stone walls with blood. Taking a step back, he braced himself for the impending onslaught.

It never came. Two loud *crunches* echoed from outside the cave, followed by the audible *snap* of shattering bone. Wet, weak gurgling accompanied three thumps. Then silence.

Aravon's heart hammered a rapid beat, but he stood firm, forcing in one deep breath after another. Whatever was out there—

A familiar figure stepped into the faint light of the dropped torch. "*Good to see you, Captain.*"

Aravon's jaw dropped. "Zaharis?"

A grin broadened the Secret Keeper's unmasked face. "*Seems I got here just in time, eh?*"

"I'll say!" Aravon lowered his spear and let out a long breath. Tension drained from his shoulders and his muscles uncoiled. "But what are you doing here? I sent you to join Colborn and find the others."

Zaharis shrugged. "*I figured you needed a hand,*" he signed. "*We do this as a unit, right, Captain?*"

A warm glow suffused Aravon's chest, tingling down his spine. "Thank you, truly." A feeling of gratitude nearly overwhelmed him. "If you hadn't gotten here when you did…" He trailed off, his brow furrowing. "How *did* you get here?"

Zaharis stooped to retrieve the torch and leaned it against a nearby rock where it could burn unimpeded. "*After setting the blaze, I began circling around south to rejoin you. Figured you might need someone to cover your getaway. When the Eirdkilrs began hunting, I had to take to my horse and get out of there. South seemed the most logical choice. Less chance of being found. Imagine my surprise when I found you thinking the exact same thing.*"

Aravon couldn't help smiling. "Wise minds think alike."

Zaharis chuckled, a sound made harsh, rasping without a tongue. "*I knew what I was looking for, so it was easy to spot the two of you. I followed, though the Eirdkilr hunters forced me to take a longer way around, else I might have gotten here sooner.*"

Aravon threw up his hands. "No complaints from me."

Zaharis jerked a thumb toward the dead Eirdkilr. "*I only found this spot thanks to our noisy friends.*" He looked around the cave. "*Good hiding place. His idea?*" His eyes darted past Aravon to where the Hilmir lay.

"Yeah." Aravon turned to Throrsson. In the faint light of the Eirdkilr torch, he could see the Hilmir's face had gone pale, pain twisting it into a grimace. A circle of blood leaked from a deep wound in his right side. "Shite!"

He crossed the distance to Throrsson in a single bound and knelt beside the quietly groaning Hilmir. Crimson seeped through a long, ragged tear in his flesh, just beneath his lowest rib.

"Damn." Aravon's jaw clenched. "This looks bad."

Zaharis pushed in beside him, and worry furrowed his brow. "*Hit an organ, you think?*"

"Possibly." Aravon studied the blood trickling down Throrsson's side. "Even if not, he'll die if he keeps bleeding like this." He glanced up at Zaharis. "Tell me you've got something for this."

Zaharis' expression grew pensive. *"I'm no Mender or Seiomenn, but…"* He dug into his pouch and drew out a single slim saw-toothed blade of grass. *"This ought to at least stop the bleeding."*

Aravon cocked an eyebrow. "What is it?"

"Dragon Thorngrass," Zaharis replied one-handed. *"The last of what I collected before Rivergate."*

Aravon's eyes widened and he stared down at the plant. It appeared so *innocuous,* yet Aravon had seen what it could do—first in the flaming wall outside Rivergate, then again a few hours earlier. That little blade of grass had caused water to burn and bought the Hilmir time to escape.

"The oil burns hotter than the fiery hell, even when floating on water," Zaharis explained. *"But we won't get more than a few drops out of this."* He shrugged. *"Hopefully enough to cauterize his wound."* From his pack, he drew out his small pestle and mortar, along with a small pouch that contained shriveled, dried-up roots of some plant Aravon didn't recognize.

"Chew on this." The Secret Keeper thrust the root toward Aravon. *"But whatever you do, don't swallow!"*

Aravon hesitated, eyes narrowing. "This isn't going to kill me, is it?"

Zaharis shook his head. *"Make things awfully uncomfortable next time you squat behind a tree, though."*

Aravon took the root but made no move to put it in his mouth.

"Look," Zaharis signed, *"as long as you don't swallow, you'll be fine. But we need that root nice and moist so it'll mix with the Dragon Thorngrass oil. Together, it'll form a crust, similar to hardened maize starch."*

Aravon chewed with caution, careful not to swallow. He grimaced at the taste, little better than mud with a hint of stick and rotted leaves. The treacle-like consistency was worse. It coated the inside of his mouth and threatened to slide down his throat despite his best attempts. Thankfully, only a few seconds passed before Zaharis held out the small stone mortar, and Aravon could spit the foul-tasting muck. He spat again on the ground to clear the taste from his mouth, and found lips and tongue gone slightly numb.

Zaharis busied himself mashing the chewed-up root together with the crushed Dragon Thorngrass. He worked for long, silent minutes, until he finally seemed satisfied. *"Here."* He held out the mortar to Aravon. *"Apply this to the wound."*

As Aravon worked the paste onto the tear in Throrsson's side, Zaharis drew his dagger and held it over the torch. The Odarian steel blackened, then slowly brightened to a glowing red. Without a word, he held out the torch to Aravon and gestured for him to make room. Aravon moved out of the way for the Secret Keeper to kneel next to the pale-faced, unconscious Hilmir.

"*Better cover his mouth,*" Zaharis signed one-handed. "*This might sting a little.*"

Setting down the torch, Aravon lowered one knee onto Throrsson's right shoulder, leaned a hand on his chest, and pressed the other over the Hilmir's mouth. The last thing they needed was Throrsson's screams to alert any nearby Eirdkilrs, or his agonized thrashings to make the wound worse.

"Do it." He nodded to Zaharis.

With only a moment's hesitation, the Secret Keeper pressed the glowing tip of the knife against Throrsson's side. Flesh sizzled and crackled, and the reek of burning meat and scorched swamp grass grew thick in the cave. Throrsson's eyes snapped wide and his muffled screams sounded terribly loud, reverberating off the stone walls. The Hilmir jerked and thrashed, forcing Aravon to lean all his weight on his knee and hand to keep the Fjall warrior still for the long, agonizing seconds Zaharis spent searing the wound closed.

"*Done!*" Zaharis pulled the blade away, leaving behind scorched flesh and a blackened, crusted mess of crushed root and grass.

Slowly, Throrsson's writhing diminished, his movements weakening as the agony retreated, and he soon fell still. Pain twisted his face, but already Aravon could see a hint of color returning to his pale cheeks. His eyes closed and he lay back, gasping for air, yet his breathing came easier.

"Here." Aravon drew out his waterskin and tilted it up to the man's lips. "Drink."

Throrsson took a few sips, barely swallowing a mouthful before falling unconscious once more.

Aravon seized the opportunity to give the Hilmir a quick examination. The wound in his side was the worst, though he bore nearly twenty lacerations on his chest, face, and arms from the Blood Queen's knives. Those would heal, in time, and the deepest wounds would be those on his soul. Watching his warriors tortured to death would weigh on him heavily, Aravon knew. Such horrors could shatter even the strongest spirit. How the Hilmir emerged from this trial remained to be seen. Either the *Blodsvarri's* cruelty had broken him, or it had lit a fire of fury and vengeance in his chest.

Aravon turned to Zaharis. "Even with that wound closed, he's still in bad shape. Anything you can do for him?"

"*Sorry, Captain.*" Zaharis' expression grew strained, tight. "*I left everything I had for pain back...*" His eyes dropped, and it took him a moment to continue. "*...back at Rivergate.*"

Aravon understood the meaning for his hesitation. Zaharis had left the pouch beside Darrak.

For the first time, he got a clear look at the cave that had proven their salvation. It was wide, more than ten feet across, but barely long enough for the *Kostarasar* charger to fit. Roots dangled from the ceiling, reaching tendrils down through the ground above in search of water. Hundreds of mushrooms in varying shades of white, brown, and even a few hints of red sprouted to the soft earthen walls.

"Maybe there's something in here?" Aravon asked.

"*Most are little more than a light snack, but a few are unfamiliar to me. There's a chance one of them will do some good.*"

As Aravon's eyes roamed over the mushrooms, he spotted something else. At the rear of the cave, just a few feet from where the Hilmir lay, a small aperture burrowed deeper into the earth. *A tunnel?*

He snatched up the torch and held it up to the hole. Sure enough, though it was only wide enough for a grown man to crawl through, it opened up onto another similarly large cave beyond.

Aravon turned back to Zaharis. "Try in there. You go deeper in, see what you can find. I'll take care of the bodies." Standing, he shook his head. "Can't have anyone stumbling across the dead Eirdkilrs and finding our hiding place."

For answer, Zaharis nodded, a shadow darkening his eyes. Drawing out his quickfire globes, he got on his hands and knees and began crawling through the opening.

Aravon turned and, leaving the torch within the cave, squeezed through the narrow opening into the night beyond. Darkness hung like a heavy blanket over the gully, broken only by the flickering, guttering light of a fallen Eirdkilr torch. The wind carried the metallic reek of blood and the stench of bowels loosened in death.

Three enormous Eirdkilrs lay dead on the rocks covering the dried-up riverbed. One's skull had been stoved in, his face slashed by the spikes of Zaharis' mace. Another's head was twisted at a grotesque angle, and the last

419

barbarian's eyes were wide, his hands still clutched around his crushed windpipe. Not for the first time, Aravon couldn't help marveling at the Secret Keeper's skill and lethality.

Thank the Swordsman he's with us. The display of combat mastery between Darrak and Zaharis had left him stunned.

Stooping, Aravon seized one of the dead Eirdkilrs by the ankles and dragged the body into the shadows beside the cave. The seven-foot giant weighed far more than any man ought to, and the weight of his heavy fur cloak, chain mail, and helmet only made the task more difficult. Aravon was breathing hard and sweating harder by the time he set about hauling the third corpse out of sight. Any Eirdkilr marching up the gully would doubtless see the bodies, but they'd be invisible from above—the best he could do to conceal their presence.

Ice slithered down his spine as a cry echoed from deep within the cave. High, piercing, a cry that he'd only heard once before. Whirling, Aravon released his grip on the dead Eirdkilr, snatched up his spear, and raced into the cave, in the direction Zaharis had gone. He scooped up the torch to light his way and scrambled through the narrow tunnel into the cave beyond. His spear led the way and he found his feet in a heartbeat, ready for whatever he'd find within.

The second cave was nearly twice the size of the first, and rose in a near-perfect dome with hundreds of root tendrils dangling from the rounded earthen roof five feet above Aravon's heart. Mushrooms by the thousands clung to the walls, filling the torch-lit cavern with a myriad of shades of brown, white, and red.

Yet Aravon had eyes only for Zaharis, who knelt in the heart of the open space, hunched over a small mound of soft, damp earth.

"Zaharis?" Aravon tensed, ready for anything. "What's the—"

Zaharis spun, a wild light in his eyes. His fingers formed no words in the silent hand language, simply pointed to the single pale blue flower growing from the mound.

Aravon's eyebrows shot upward. "Is it…*ice saffron?*" He scarcely dared breathe the words.

Zaharis gave no reply. His gaze was locked on the little blue flower, his fingers twitching as he held the glass light globes up to its petals and studied it. He seemed frozen in time for a long moment, the only sound his breath coming in shallow, excited gasps. Yet, as the seconds dragged on, Aravon saw the tightening of the Secret Keeper's shoulders, the hunch in his spine. Zaharis' head drooped and, closing his eyes, he let out a long, shuddering breath.

Without looking up at Aravon, his fingers signed, *"It is not."*

Aravon recalled the description Zaharis had given him. *Pale blue flowers with crimson threads, growing in a cluster on thick stems that can grow up to two feet long.* The threads of this flower were a brilliant gold, and the stem was thin, spindly.

Sorrow thickened Aravon's throat. The hunt for ice saffron meant so much to the man, and this was the *third* time he'd nearly found it, only to be disappointed by cold, hard reality. He rested a hand on the Secret Keeper's shoulder. "You'll find it, Zaharis."

"Will I?" Zaharis whirled on him, his eyes blazing yet tears streaming down his face. *"Ten years, Captain. Ten years I've spent hunting this damned plant. Something that everyone else has told me doesn't exist. I've lost friends, loves..."* His fingers faltered, fell still, and he shook his head fiercely. *"I've given up everything for this, Captain. And all I've got to show for it is this!"*

He ripped the flower savagely from the mound of earth and crushed it in his fist. *"Nothing but empty hands and crushed hopes."*

"Not nothing." Aravon moved around to crouch in front of the man. "You've got us. We may not be Secret Keepers, but we're as much your family and friends as anyone in your Temple of Whispers." He gripped Zaharis' shoulder tighter. "You've saved our lives a dozen times over. Not just us, but thousands more. Princelanders, Fehlans, even Einari. Everything you do makes a difference in this war. Even if you haven't yet found the ice saffron, no one could ever say that your life meant nothing."

Zaharis stared at him, yet his eyes were unseeing, glazed over. The look of a man that had lost much and bore the burden of painful memories. Aravon had seen that same expression in the mirror, and in the eyes of thousands of Legionnaires before. Many men never recovered fully from whatever had shattered their spirits.

But Aravon couldn't let that happen to the Secret Keeper. His friend.

"Here's the truth." He fixed Zaharis with a solemn stare. "I don't know whether you'll ever find what you seek. I don't know if you'll ever solve the mystery of the Elixir of Creation or unlock the Serenii's secrets. But that won't matter. Not to me, not to the Duke, to Rangvaldr, or anyone else in our company. Because we're all better off just for knowing you and fighting beside you. Your life, your actions and choices, they're the only reason we're still alive. Remember that, Zaharis. Remember what you mean to *us*."

The sorrow didn't fully leave Zaharis' eyes, but he managed a smile midway between sadness and gratitude. *"Thank you, Captain."* Distaste twisted his face and he stared down at his hands. The sap of the blue flower turned his hands sticky, making it difficult to form the hand signals. Yet curiosity blazed in his eyes, and he moved his hand closer to his face to sniff at the liquid. A slow smile tugged at his lips. *"Turns out it wasn't such a waste, after all."*

Aravon cocked his head.

"In my hunt for ice saffron, I've read about this plant. Winter's Mist, it is called." He scooped up the crushed blue petals with caution. *"Mixed with the grapes fermenting for icewine, it makes a heady brew—one a friend of mine jokingly called the Elixir of Destruction."* His smile turned wry, yet for a moment, the sadness retreated. *"Hangovers that not even Drunkard's Salvation can cure."*

"Your Secret Keepers learned from hard experience?" Aravon chuckled.

"More often than not, yes." Zaharis stood, cradling the delicate, bruised petals in his hand. *"But on its own, it can be a potent painkiller and cleansing agent. Speeds up healing, too."*

"Hah!" Aravon clapped the Secret Keeper on the back. "The gods provide."

Zaharis nodded, slowly. *"Aye, so they do,"* he signed one-handed. *"Give me half an hour, and I'll mix up something that'll have the Hilmir back on his feet by daybreak."*

Hope surged within Aravon. "Best news I've heard all night, my friend."

Chapter Fifty-Three

Throrsson sputtered and coughed, gagging as the contents of Zaharis' quickly-brewed remedy slid down his throat. Yet, as his eyelids fluttered open, color returned to his cheeks and his eyes were bright, alert. He even managed to sit up with Aravon's help, and leaned back against the cave wall with only a little groan of pain.

"What…?" Confusion twisted his face as his eyes darted around. He seemed surprised to find himself in a cave, and his perplexity deepened at the sight of Aravon and Zaharis crouching over him. Then his confusion gave way to dark shadows of sorrow, anger, and dismay. "My men."

"Fought with the bravery and skill for which the Fjall are renowned." Aravon spoke in a quiet voice, his tone gentle. "When this is over, all of Fehl will know that your men died as *true* warriors. Not bound and butchered by the *Blodsvarri*, but on their feet with steel in their hearts and hands."

Throrsson's expression hardened. "Who are you, Captain Snarl?" His ice-blue eyes drilled into Aravon. "What manner of man risks his life as you did?"

"A man who knows that the Hilmir's life is worth more than a hundred of the finest Fjall warriors," Aravon replied without hesitation. "Not because of his skill at arms, but because of his mind, his courage." He leaned forward. "And what he represents to his men: hope, strength, and the promise of a better future. It is what Kings have *always* been. That, Hilmir, is more powerful than the sharpest sword and the strongest shield."

"Wise words. Words I would expect from the Duke of Eastfall." Throrsson's lips quirked into a wry smile. "I can see why he brought *you* and your comrades." His eyes darted to Zaharis, who sat nearby grinding the pale blue petals of the Winter's Mist flowers to a paste in his mortar. "Tell me that what I saw back there, the wall of fire and those thunderclaps loosed by *Striith* himself, that was not simply my imagination."

Aravon chuckled. "You've our Magicmaker there to thank for that display." The stiffening of Zaharis' shoulders only made Aravon smile broader; Rangvaldr truly *had* chosen the Secret Keeper's code name well.

"And you to thank for my life." Throrsson reached out a hand, with only barely a wince. "Your actions prove you have the courage of any Fjall."

Aravon gripped the Hilmir's forearm. "An honor."

"And the foolhardiness of a Princelander." Throrsson shook his shaggy head. "I'd have beaten that behavior out of my warriors long ago."

Zaharis snorted. *"If only he knew what other antics we've pulled,"* he signed.

Aravon chuckled and turned back to the Hilmir. "Let's just say the risk was worth the reward. We've got you out of the *Blodsvarri's* clutches. Now, all we need to do is get you back to your warband and—"

"What of Storbjarg?" Throrsson growled. "Have you heard anything of my city?"

Aravon's eyes darkened. "No." He hadn't heard from Skathi on the fate of the Hilmir's city...or Duke Dyrund. That worried him. "But my people should already be there now. They'll assess the situation and send a report on the situation."

Throrsson tried to climb to his feet. "I must go to them," he rumbled. Yet he'd barely risen halfway before his knees gave out and he wobbled, collapsing against the wall.

Aravon caught the huge warrior just before he toppled to the side. "Not a good idea right now, Hilmir." He pushed Throrsson back down to a sitting position—a task made easy by the man's exhaustion and weakness from loss of blood. "You need food, drink, and rest before you try to travel."

"I cannot fail my city, too." Throrsson's voice was firm, his spirit strong despite his physical weakness.

"Then stay alive." Aravon gripped the man's shoulder hard. "Live long enough to collect your warband and march with the Deid to face the *Blodsvarri* in proper battle. That is how you honor the warriors who fell yesterday."

Throrsson's jaw muscles worked, setting his braided beard twitching, yet he relented and leaned back against the earthen wall.

"Here." Aravon drew out his waterskin and the small bundle of rations remaining to him. Throrsson hesitated, but Aravon insisted. "Eat, drink, and recover your strength. You will need it. As soon as you feel up to it, we're moving out."

Zaharis caught Aravon's attention with a snap of his fingers. "*I'll have another dose of this brew ready in an hour. Longer infusion time will make it more potent. Should help with the pain and keep him on his feet as we head out.*"

"Good." Aravon turned back to the Hilmir. "My man will have something ready soon. His brew will keep you going until we can get back to safety."

Throrsson's brow furrowed as he studied Zaharis crushing the blue petals. "You know, if my *Seiomenn* was here, he might believe that flower to be *Reginkunnr.*" He gave Aravon a wry smile. "But it cannot truly be the Flower Divine."

Zaharis was immediately on full alert. "*Ask him what he's talking about!*" Excitement sparkled in his eyes.

"What is this flower?" Aravon asked.

"An ancient legend of the Fjall, nothing more." Throrsson gave a dismissive wave, sending crumbs of the hard tack in his hands flying. "A plant given to mankind by *Striith*, a test of courage and a chance at immortality."

Zaharis glanced at Aravon, hope etched into every line of his face.

"And your legends," Aravon pressed. "Did they say where to find it, this Flower Divine?"

Throrsson shrugged. "The *Reginkunnr* was said to grow only in the bitterest cold, yet for those brave enough to travel the wastes of Fehl, it offered a reward fit for the gods themselves." He shook his head. "But that was long ago, in the days when the old, deep ice covered the lands. The days of Gunnarsdottir and Asvard Giantsbane. Even if such a legend *was* true, no one on Fehl has seen the Flower Divine."

The momentary excitement in Zaharis' eyes died, the darkness returning to his eyes.

"Such legends are a thing of the past," Throrsson said. "We must look to the future—a future that we will never see if the Blood Queen has her way. She would see the Fjall destroyed, would claim our lands as her own." He sat straighter, raised a clenched fist. "Not as long as I draw breath and have strength to swing a sword!"

425

Aravon nodded. "You know where we are, yes?" he asked. "How far we will have to travel to rejoin your men and the Deid warband?"

"These are *my* lands!" Throrsson's eyes flashed. "The *Tauld* may have laid claim to them, but my people have fought and died for them since the days of the first *Grimafaegir* brotherhood. I know them as well as I know my own city."

"Good." Aravon turned to Zaharis. "*Think that'll keep him going long enough to rejoin the others?*"

"*It'll dull the pain for a few hours, at least,*" Zaharis signed. "*If I get a chance to forage a bit, especially in dense forests, I ought to be able to come up with a few things to keep him on his feet.*"

"Excellent." A plan had already begun to formulate in Aravon's mind. "As soon as Zaharis is done, we're out of here. What's the nearest place we can get out of the flatlands and find decent cover?" he asked Throrsson.

"*Blarskogr*, the Grim Forest, ten miles north of here."

Aravon grimaced. *That's a long way to run.* No way they could ride double— the weight of two full-grown men would tire out even the hardy *Kostarasar* chargers. He and Zaharis would have to switch off riding and running, and they'd cover far less ground than if they'd had a third horse. But, at the moment, they had little choice.

"So we use the cover of darkness to make for the forest," Aravon continued. "Once there, we take shelter in the trees, and I'll send word to my people. Get a report on Storbjarg, the Deid, and the Fjall warband. *Someone* will be keeping an eye on the Blood Queen." Colborn, Noll, and Rangvaldr would all be awaiting word from him, but they wouldn't be caught sitting on their arses. "We regroup with the others and make plans on how to hit back at the enemy."

"Hit back?" Throrsson raised an eyebrow. "With nearly five thousand of my warband dead or ill with Wraithfever, that leaves far too few to face the *Tauld*."

"We have the Deid," Aravon said. "And the Legion at Dagger—"

"No!" Throrsson shook his head.

Aravon bit down on an angry retort. Now wasn't the time for such stubbornness, but shouting at Throrsson would do little good. He needed to think and talk like the Duke. Diplomacy and tact could convince the Hilmir. "All due respect, but you said it yourself. You have too few to face the enemy, even with the Deid."

"I will not hear of it." Throrsson set his jaw, stubborn, his blunt features growing mulish. "The Legion will not step foot on Fjall lands as long as I still live!"

Aravon clenched his teeth, but forced his voice to sound calm. "So be it." He didn't give up on the thought, simply tucked it away for later. It was more than likely the Hilmir would find himself forced to change his mind as the situation demanded. "We regroup, plan a new offensive, and strike the Blood Queen where it hurts most. She might have anticipated your ambush at the Waeggbjod, but she *couldn't* have known about the Deid." If she had, she wouldn't have remained at the site of battle and indulged in her torturous fantasies.

"And," Aravon continued as a new thought struck him, "she couldn't have known about the two thousand Fjall lying in wait." The realization brought a measure of hope. "That means she won't know how many men are holding Storbjarg, or that fully one-fifth of your warband is somewhere they can strike at her. We've got an advantage, one we can use to put some serious hurt on her at the right time and place."

Throrsson's eyes narrowed. "I see the Duke didn't bring you solely for your skill with that spear." He thrust his chin at Aravon's weapon. "Again I ask, who are you, Captain Snarl? Your mind is not that of a hired sword, or a nobleman like that fool who rode beside the Duke. You are a soldier, a commander of men. You have an authority that any leader would recognize."

Aravon inclined his head. "I *was* an officer in the Legion of Heroes, until the Eirdkilrs slaughtered my men." That bit of information couldn't hurt; Eirik Throrsson couldn't possibly know him by name or face, though his father had a reputation among the Fehlans on both sides of the conflict. "But the Duke chose me to lead his hand-picked soldiers because he trusts me to look beyond the shield wall. I may not bear the title of Hilmir, but with our minds together, we can come up with a plan that the *Blodsvarri* will never be able to predict."

Throrsson's expression grew pensive. "Indeed." Long moments of silence passed as the Hilmir studied Aravon. Finally, he nodded. "Any man who could pull off such an impossibility as you did tonight is a man worth listening to. So speak freely, Princelander, and I will listen." He held out a hand. "As you say, together, we can turn bitter defeat into a triumph so resounding the *Tauld* will never recover."

"You've got a deal." Aravon clasped Throrsson's hand and pulled him to his feet. "Now, to formulate the plan, tell me everything I need to know about the Fjall lands *north* of Storbjarg."

* * *

Aravon heard the quiet *flap* of wings a moment before a furry figure plummeted toward him. He had only a moment to brace himself before Snarl's furry body crashed into his chest. Even still, he nearly went down beneath the force of the impact. Exhaustion dragged at his muscles, and he barely caught Snarl.

The Enfield yipped and barked in delight, his paws scrabbling on Aravon's muddy armor, and his pink tongue flashed out to lick Aravon's muck-stained mask.

"Hey there!" Aravon gave a tired laugh and reached up a hand to scratch the scruff of Snarl's neck. "Good to see you, boy. Did you miss me?"

Snarl gave another loud *yip* and leapt from Aravon's arms, taking to flight and soaring up through the canopy once more.

"An Enfield?" Surprise echoed in Throrsson's voice. "They have not been seen on Fehl in two hundred years."

Aravon turned back and found the Hilmir staring at him through narrowed eyes. He shrugged. "Turns out there still a few flying around."

Throrsson gave a tired *harrumph*. "I'd wager my finest barrel of mead that your Duke Dyrund has found a way to make them useful." His eyes widened a fraction. "Is *that* how you knew of the *Tauld* breaking off their siege?"

Again, Aravon shrugged, but said nothing. He was too tired to do more than turn back and keep marching northward along the narrow forest trail. *If Snarl's here, that means—*

"Captain!" Delight sparkled in Noll's eyes as he slipped out from behind the broad beech tree where he'd made his perch. "Keeper's teeth, you had us worried there."

Despite the bone-deep exhaustion dragging at his muscles, Aravon couldn't help smiling at the little scout's enthusiasm. "Truth be told, *Foxclaw*—" He used Noll's codename for the sake of Throrsson, who sat mounted on Aravon's horse. "—it was bloody close more often than not."

428

"Wait until you hear what the Captain had us do to get through that Grim Forest unnoticed." Zaharis' fingers flashed. *"If I never taste peat again, it'll be too soon!"*

Aravon grimaced beneath his mask. He still had mud in places he didn't know he had places, and every muscle in his body ached from the effort of the last three days of travel. His jaw ached from chewing on the gnarled Spiceroot, dirt still trapped between his teeth. Yet the root worked as Zaharis had explained—even now, nearly two days after the food had run out, he felt no hunger, only a deep, inescapable thirst. He wanted nothing more than a chilled glass of wine, a hot bath, and two long nights of rest.

But, as Skathi's latest message indicated, the situation was dire. Even now, Snarl would be winging back toward the archer—following the scent of the cloth Skathi had given Aravon—at her position just outside Storbjarg, where she'd remained for the last day and a half. She needed to know what he and the Hilmir—with a few of Zaharis' more *oblique* tactical additions—had cooked up for the Blood Queen.

Throrsson grimaced as he climbed down from the saddle, hunching over the still-healing wound in his side. The myriad of cuts inflicted by the Blood Queen's knives had gone stiff, the skin tender. It would take a miracle to get him in fighting shape—or a touch of Eyrr magic.

"Get Stonekeeper," Aravon snapped an order. "The Hilmir could use a healing hand."

"Yes, Captain!" With a crisp salute, Noll turned and raced up the path.

Aravon tried to ignore his tired feet and aching legs as he followed the scout into the forest. Thirty-six hours with only fitful snatches of sleep when Throrsson was too tired to continue. Fifty miles traveling across flat grasslands, through dense forest and one very muddy peat bog, dodging Eirdkilr hunters all the while. Once, when the enemy had caught up with them, they'd had no choice but to turn and fight. The wound in Throrsson's side had reopened and bled anew, weakening the Hilmir and slowing their journey further. What would have taken them a day or less on horseback had been a three-day trek, with no food and limited access to water. Only Zaharis' on-the-go foraging had spared them from starvation and exhaustion.

Spiceroot proved a double-edged sword. The root sent a jolt of energy coursing through their muscles, driving back hunger and fatigue, yet the resulting "crash" had nearly cost their lives. The Secret Keeper had only given it to them when they were on the verge of collapse, and even then sparingly.

But now they had reached safety.

Aravon rounded the bend in the forest trail and relief flooded him at the sight of the Deid war camp spread out below. Hundreds of tents and thousands of fur-clad warriors, all armed and prepared for battle. The Hilmir had his warband—or at least the *first* of the warriors that they would use to strike back against the Blood Queen. The time would soon come when the Eirdkilrs would feel the full wrath of the Fjall. The Hilmir *would* have vengeance for his tortured and slain warriors.

Yes, the desire to rest was overwhelming, but a greater desire burned within him, one he'd ignored since the moment he first spotted smoke over Storbjarg.

He needed to see the Fjall city with his own eyes, needed to witness the destruction and carnage firsthand. And, if Duke Dyrund truly *was* dead as Skathi feared, Aravon needed to be there to figure out how to exact a heavy toll in blood on the bastards who had killed him.

Chapter Fifty-Four

Even with all of Colborn's Fehlan-bred woodcraft, night had nearly fallen by the time Aravon and the Lieutenant drew within sight of Storbjarg. They'd seen the billowing columns of dark gray smoke in the Deid war camp, heard the clash of steel and the Eirdkilrs' howling from a mile away. Yet nothing could have prepared him for the turmoil and bloodshed that consumed the city.

Even now, four days later, the battle for Storbjarg raged on. Fjall warriors shouted to their god or hurled insults at the Eirdkilrs, who answered back with their shrieking, ululating war cries. The stink of burning wood and sod tinged the air, the fumes scorching Aravon's lungs. Pillars of black smoke rose to block out the first stars appearing in the darkening sky, the settling haze so thick around Storbjarg Aravon could barely see the city's towering stone walls. A thick, reeking night had descended upon the Fjall's capital—a night of death and destruction at the hands of the Eirdkilrs.

"Captain."

Aravon tensed at the quiet, rumbling voice that came from less than an arm's length to his right. Belthar was all but invisible in the hazy, smoke-thickened twilight—he would have been even without the cape of camouflaging branches and leaves he wore atop his mottled leather armor. Beneath the pandemonium of battle echoing from inside Storbjarg, they had no fear of being overheard.

Aravon slipped closer to the big man. "Situation report."

"Gone to shite, sir." Worry twisted Belthar's shoulders. "Gotten worse since Skathi and I arrived two days back."

431

Branches rustled and a figure dropped from the tree, landing beside him with the light-footed grace of a mountain lion.

"It's bad, Captain." Skathi's green eyes were dark behind her leather mask, and she barely paid attention to Snarl, even as the Enfield rubbed against her legs. "Real bad. The Eirdkilrs are in the city."

Aravon's gut tightened. He had no clear view into the city, but the screaming of women, the terrified shouts of children, and the enraged battle cries of Fjall warriors defending their homes and families painted a perfectly clear scene.

"How in the Keeper's name did they pull that off?" Aravon demanded. "What happened to the Hilmir's warband?"

"Best worst guess, Captain?" Worry echoed in Skathi's voice. "Something happened at the south gate." She jerked a finger toward the southern end of the city. "I circled around, got as close a look at it as I could, and it looked like someone or something tore it off its hinges."

Aravon's eyes widened. The gates of Storbjarg should have withstood a dozen battering rams.

"When we got here, all I saw was lots of fire and smoke, and someone was raising hell inside." Skathi shook her head. "I've done laps around the city, tried different vantage points to get a clear look inside. Nearly got caught in the process. But the Eirdkilrs are inside the city, no doubt about it. Walls don't mean shite when the gate's open. Can't be certain, but I'd say all three thousand of the bastards that marched from Dagger Garrison are hacking their way through Storbjarg."

"Keeper's teeth!" Aravon's blood ran cold. *So many!* "And the warband?"

"Holding their own," Skathi replied. "At least they were, until the reinforcements showed up."

Aravon's mind raced. He tried to think of how the Blood Queen had managed to get men into Storbjarg while committing so many of her forces to the attack on Throrsson. The Hilmir had said she commanded four thousand men directly, and only three thousand had been present for the attack on Throrsson's eleven hundred. That left one thousand Eirdkilrs unaccounted for—plus the three thousand marching from Dagger Garrison. Had the walls remained intact, the Fjall's three thousand should have been able to hold. Yet with the gate destroyed, Throrsson's men fought a losing battle.

432

"Smoke's too thick to get a clear view, Captain." Skathi's eyes were dark. "But it's not sounding good. I don't hold out much hope for those inside."

With as many as four thousand Eirdkilrs rampaging through Storbjarg, it would be impossible for Throrsson's men to hold the city and protect the citizens. Seventy thousand Fjall men, women, and children were now at the mercy of the merciless Eirdkilrs.

"And the Duke?" Aravon forced himself to say the words. He'd dreaded this moment since he first spotted the rising smoke. In the three days since, his dread had grown. Now, he had no choice but to face the grim truth.

Skathi hesitated, shot a glance at Belthar. The big man's spine went rigid. Their silence told Aravon everything he needed to know.

The world whirled around him, his head spinning wildly. Dark gray tendrils of smoke enveloped him in their hazy embrace and drove sharp, biting fingers into his mind, his heart. Acid scorched his lungs and the breath clutched in his chest. He struggled to draw in air, to think beyond the silent admission. Yet he could not marshal his wildly spinning thoughts, couldn't suck in a single gasp of smoke-tinged oxygen.

"Captain!" Colborn's hiss echoed from his side…or a thousand leagues away, Aravon couldn't tell. Strong hands supported him, lowered him slowly to the ground. He sat hard, leaning against the tree, trying desperately to regain control over his leaden limbs, his pounding heart, and the ache gnawing in his belly.

"I-I'm fine," Aravon managed to gasp out. "Just…hard time…breathing. The smoke."

He didn't dare meet the three worried pairs of eyes staring down at him—if he did, if he saw the sorrow reflected back at him, the tears would flow. So he clenched his jaw and balled his fists so hard his hands trembled.

"Here." Colborn pressed a waterskin into his hands, his voice as gentle as his movements. "You've been pushing yourself hard, Captain. Take a breath." A knowing look shone in his eyes, yet he said nothing as he turned away.

Belthar and Skathi turned back toward Storbjarg, giving Aravon a respectful moment of peace.

Aravon drained the waterskin, but it did little to wash away the sorrow that threatened to burst from within his chest.

He couldn't believe the Duke was dead. Didn't want to. Hated the very idea that the man he respected—who he had grown to admire...to love—could be gone.

The world suddenly seemed a cold, empty place. The Duke had been there when he awoke after the ambush on the Eastmarch, had been the voice of calm reassurance when Aravon wanted to join his men in death. He'd *always* been a solid, comforting presence in Aravon's life. The proud friend that had stood beside General Traighan as Aravon marched off to his first Legion posting. A smiling face on the days when Aravon hid out in the stables to avoid his father's drunken wrath. Quietly supportive as Aravon struggled with his first commission in the Legion—and his new mission for Prince Toran.

And now he was dead. Slaughtered with the Fjall, betrayed by one of the Hilmir's warriors.

No! Aravon's mind recoiled from the truth. *He can't have died. He's smart, he'll find someplace to hide.* He latched on to that faint hope like a drowning man clung to driftwood.

The Duke would have made himself scarce, taken refuge someplace safe the moment he heard of the attack. He and his mercenaries would likely be hidden in Storbjarg, away from the Eirdkilrs.

Yet the thought lacked conviction. He had no idea what happened to the Duke, if he'd fallen under the initial wave, taken up defense of the city, or found refuge someplace safe. Worse, he couldn't risk himself or his unit on a mission to sneak into Storbjarg to find out. At that moment, the only way to give the Duke a fighting chance of survival—if he'd somehow managed to survive this long—would be to carry out the plan he'd hatched with the Hilmir and Zaharis.

A desperate, dangerous plan. One that could get every Fjall and Deid warrior killed with a single misstep. But for the sake of the Fjall trapped within Storbjarg and the rest of the Hilmir's lands, they had to try.

So, despite every part of Aravon that wanted to lie down and curl up—from exhaustion, hunger, and the burden of sorrow—he forced himself to rise to his feet. Still woozy and wobbling, but leaning on his spear and the trunk of a thick hazel for support.

He had to stand, had to fight. It was all he could do now. If he didn't, he'd crumble beneath the strain. The mission was all—it would keep him going until he could process the torrent of emotions roiling within him.

As he stood, Colborn turned, and a silent signal from the Lieutenant brought Skathi and Belthar around as well.

"Orders, Captain?" Colborn asked.

"You three, stay here and keep watch. Anything changes, you let me know at once."

Belthar and Skathi nodded, but Colborn cocked his head. "You sure about this, Captain? You know that favorite military proverb about keeping your plans simple."

"Aye." Aravon inclined his head. Colborn was *right* to question the strategy he and the Hilmir had concocted on their desperate flight north—it was his job as Aravon's second-in-command. "But the Blood Queen's proven that simple's not going to work. Our only chance of pulling this off is to do the last thing she's expecting."

A long moment of silence passed, then Colborn nodded. "Swordsman guide your steps, Captain."

"And you." With a Legion salute to the three of them, he turned and slipped back into the forest, back toward his horse and the journey to the Deid war camp.

Chapter Fifty-Five

"Are you insane?" Chief Svein Hafgrimsson leapt to his feet. "You plan on doing *what?*"

"Attacking Storbjarg." Exhaustion weighed heavy on Aravon's muscles, dragging at his limbs, and it took all his effort to stand straight. Yet he forced himself to stand tall, to meet the Deid chief's scorn with cool calm. "It's the last thing the *Blodsvarri* will expect."

"Because it's madness!" Chief Svein Hafgrimsson rolled his eyes and threw up his hands. "I will not risk my warriors on your foolhardy plan."

"Good." Aravon nodded. "Because we need the Deid here." He tapped on the crude map he'd drawn in the loamy soil. "Lying in wait beside the *Fornbryggja.*"

The Deid chief narrowed his eyes. "An ambush at the Ormrvatn crossing?"

"Precisely." Aravon gestured to Throrsson, who sat regally on a fur-covered stump a short distance away. "The Hilmir will lead his men in an assault on the walls, but *if* he should prove unsuccessful in retaking Storbjarg, the Fjall warband will need ground to hold against the four thousand enemies within the city. Plus, the two thousand that the Blood Queen has marching at her side, and however many more she'll have brought up to reinforce her position."

The words sounded grim. Two thousand Fjall and two thousand Deid against nearly six thousand enemies—that he knew of. Even with the perfect position, they'd be fortunate to get out of a battle alive, much less triumphant. Zaharis could only tip the odds so far in their favor. In the end, it would come down to a knock-down, drag-out battle between the Fehlans and Eirdkilrs. Their best hope would be to whittle down the Blood Queen's forces as much as possible before that happened.

That culling would begin in Storbjarg.

"Tell me you have a better plan than this, Hilmir!" Chief Svein Hafgrimsson rounded on Throrsson. "This cannot be the best choice."

"It is the *only* choice." Hard, grim resolve echoed in Throrsson's voice, sparkled in his eyes with a glitter of steel. He stood, slowly, ponderous as a great bear, his face twisted in pain at his still-healing wounds. Yet, when he drew up to his full height, he was once more the commanding Fjall chief, leader of the largest and most powerful warband on Fehl. Or what *had been* until three days earlier. Now, Aravon couldn't be certain how many of the Hilmir's men remained. Yet that uncertainty did little to diminish the man's authority, his commanding presence.

"This is *my* plan." Throrsson's words echoed across the clearing. "And it is the only way that we stand a fighting chance against the *Blodsvarri.*"

With most of his warband dead, embroiled in a bitter battle for Storbjarg, or weakened by illness, the Hilmir knew the impossibility of the battle they faced. Yet that only served to strengthen his determination. That desire for vengeance against the Blood Queen for what she had done to his men and to his city burned like a bonfire in his chest—a fire that would drive him to fight until his last breath, his last drop of blood.

"This plan forces the Blood Queen's hand," Aravon pressed. "She cannot leave the Hilmir alive, so she will have no choice but to commit."

"And when she does," Throrsson said, stepping close to the Deid chief. "The Deid will be there to bring down *Striith's* mighty hammer."

The words appeared to mollify Chief Svein Hafgrimsson . After a long moment, he threw up his hands. "So be it," he growled. "The Deid will hold the *Fornbryggja.*"

Hope surged within Aravon. That was just a *part* of their plan to defeat the Blood Queen, but a critical one.

"Long has it been since Fjall and Deid marched together." Throrsson spoke in an almost ceremonial tone. "Let the old alliances be rekindled, the old resentments laid to rest. Let our clans stand shoulder to shoulder as it was in the days of the *Grimafaegir,* once more the chosen warriors of *Striith* and *Olfossa* joined in common purpose." He thrust out a huge, hairy hand toward the Deid chief.

"As you say, Hilmir of the Fjall." Chief Svein Hafgrimsson clasped Throrsson's hand. "The forgotten oaths of our people are renewed until such a time as the *Tauld* no longer threaten our lands."

With a nod, he turned away and marched off into his war camp, barking orders to his men. The Deid warriors exploded into a flurry of motion, pulling down tents, stowing bedrolls, and preparing to move out.

The moment Chief Svein Hafgrimsson strode out of view, Throrsson gave a little groan and sank back into his chair.

"Hilmir!" Aravon hurried to the man's side.

"I am fine." Throrsson waved a huge hand, dismissing Aravon. "Nothing a mug of fine mead and a night of rest cannot cure."

Aravon raised an eyebrow, an expression lost beneath his mask.

"But perhaps *you* might consider taking care of yourself, Captain Snarl." Throrsson leaned forward. "Do not think your exertions of the last few days have gone unnoticed. The last thing we need is for you to collapse before the battle has even begun."

Aravon forced a tired chuckle. "I look that bad?"

"No, which is to your credit." Throrsson gave him a wry smile. "One would almost think you a man of the Fjall warband."

Aravon inclined his head. "High praise from the Hilmir."

Eirik Throrsson gave a dismissive wave. "Praise means nothing to a dead man. Rest while you can. Tomorrow, we march to battle."

"As you say." Aravon gave a little bow and turned to leave.

"If I asked how you find yourself in the company of a *Seiomenn*, would you answer?" Throrsson's comment stopped Aravon in his tracks. When Aravon turned back to the Hilmir, a sly smile tugged at his lips, and his teeth shone white against his thick black beard. "Holy stones are not so common as to be found simply lying around Fehl. Yet, knowing your Duke Dyrund, the answer to that question is as forthcoming as to who you are behind that mask, is it not?"

Aravon hesitated a moment. "If my Stonekeeper wishes to tell you his story, he will do so. Otherwise…" He shrugged. "We wear these masks to protect not ourselves, but those we love."

"A fact that has not escaped me." The Fjall chief pursed his lips. "Yet, were the Duke here, I might press him for answers. A Hilmir's curiosity, you understand."

Mention of the Duke brought back the burden of sorrow, and Aravon's shoulders drooped beneath the weight. His throat thickened and he could find no words to reply.

"Do not despair, Captain Snarl." Throrsson's voice was surprisingly gentle, a kind look in his blue eyes. He stepped up to Aravon and rested a huge hand on his shoulder. "At the first sign of danger, Asleif would conceal him alongside herself and Branda."

Aravon cocked his head. The Hilmir had mentioned his wife, Asleif, but the other name was unfamiliar. "Branda?"

A shadow flashed across Throrsson's eyes. "My daughter." His face darkened, his expression growing grim. "She, too, was cursed by the Wraithfever."

Aravon sucked in a breath as his mind flashed back to the night Duke Dyrund offered Throrsson the Wraithfever cure. The Hilmir had chosen his son, Bjarni, to receive the cure. The realization of the choice Throrsson had made staggered Aravon. He couldn't imagine doing the same—if both Rolyn and Adilon fell ill, how could *any* father make such a decision?

Throrsson seemed to understand Aravon's reaction. "The burdens of command, Captain Snarl." He appeared tired once more, and he stood, his shoulders stooped beneath a great weigh. "At least I can console myself with the knowledge that Bjarni lives, and he will fight beside me as we attack Storbjarg tomorrow. I owe your Duke his life, at least."

With that, he shuffled off into the war camp, toward the section where his Fjall warriors—and Bjarni, his son—had pitched their tents.

Aravon watched the Hilmir go and a wave of fatigue crashed atop him. He felt drained, too exhausted to move, to think. It took every shred of effort to rise to his feet and ascend the short hill toward the patch of forest where Noll, Rangvaldr, and Zaharis had set up their little camp.

The Fjall would march to battle within the hour, and he'd be beside them when they did. But first he needed a few moments of rest and a bite to eat. Anything to stop his stomach from gnawing itself from the inside out, to restore strength to limbs that felt little better than soggy ropes.

The smell of cooking food reached him twenty yards away from the campsite. Aravon drew in a tired breath, the scent of fresh herbs, spices, and venison stew set his mouth watering.

Noll spotted him first. "Captain!" Leaping to his feet, the scout scooped up a bowl and filled it with a generous portion of the thick, meaty stew.

Aravon took the bowl with a nod of thanks and settled against a nearby tree. He nearly wept tears of relief at the first bite of the rich, perfectly-spiced meal—doubtless Zaharis' handiwork, for Noll could *never* produce anything beyond barely edible and Rangvaldr's culinary skills didn't extend beyond skinning and dressing animals. It was the best thing he'd eaten in what felt like an eternity.

The clamor and clatter of the departing Fehlan warriors faded into the background as Aravon lost himself in the meal—the first simple comfort he'd enjoyed since…he couldn't remember when. He stretched out his legs, and a lump rose in his throat as he remembered that he'd left Snarl with Skathi. She'd need the Enfield to send word if the Eirdkilrs abandoned Storbjarg or the city fell. But that left Aravon feeling lonely—so, terribly alone, burdened by his sorrow over the Duke's death—and miserable, even after a bowl of Zaharis' delicious stew.

"Zaharis was just telling us about the battle." Rangvaldr's eyes were dark behind his mask, his shoulders tight. "The *Tolfraedr* is an antiquated cruelty, one I believed even our southern cousins had given up long ago."

"This Bloody Bitch really is a piece of work, ain't she?" Noll shook his head. "Get me within bowshot, and I'll plant a pair of arrows in her eyes."

With effort, Aravon pulled himself out of his shell of misery and sorrow. "If we get the chance," he said quietly, "I expect you to take it. But no unnecessary risks. We're going to need all hands alive and ready if we're to pull this off."

"Aye, Captain." Reluctance echoed in the scout's voice. "Shame I wasn't there." He turned to Zaharis, excitement echoing in his voice. "I'd love to have seen what those Earthshakers could do."

As if by magic or truly dexterous sleight of hand, the Secret Keeper made two small iron orbs, the size of apples and studded with knobby spikes and deep notches, appear in his palm. "*I didn't use them all,*" he signed one-handed. "*With what's ahead, it's likely you'll get a chance to see them in action yet.*"

"Hah!" Noll burst out laughing. "Let me carry one. Nothing like the heat of battle to give me cover enough to sneak up on the Blood Queen and shove them so far up her arse she'll be spitting metal."

The Secret Keeper made the Earthshakers disappear as quickly as they'd appeared. "*I wouldn't trust you with a pair of pointy sticks, Noll, much less something with this much boom!*"

"Careful," Noll retorted, "or I'll be forced to put two of my *pointy sticks* in your backside." He shook a pair of steel-tipped arrows at the Secret Keeper. "I could use a bit of target practice."

In the second that Aravon glanced down at his bowl, he missed Zaharis' response. When he looked up, however, Noll's sharp gesture and snarled "Bah! Keeper take you, then" made it clear Zaharis' sharp wit had won this verbal exchange.

Aravon almost managed a smile...almost. This sort of banter had been sorely lacking over the last few days. It didn't matter that tomorrow their company marched into battle against a superior foe that far outnumbered them—as long as his men could bicker and snap at each other, they were alive.

"You good?"

Rangvaldr's quiet question brought Aravon's head around. The *Seiomenn* was staring at him, a worried look in his eyes, his right hand toying with the gemstone hanging at his neck.

"Yeah." Aravon nodded. "Nothing needing healing. Just a bit tired, hungry, sore, muddy, thirsty...and did I say tired?"

That elicited a chuckle from Rangvaldr.

"I'm good," Aravon replied. "A bit of rest will do me good."

"Your body, yes." Rangvaldr inclined his head. "But your heart will be heavy still. The Duke was more than just your superior officer. I saw as much every time you spoke to him. And when he spoke of you as well."

The lump returned to Aravon's throat. "The Hilmir's confident that his wife got the Duke into hiding." It took effort to form the words, and his voice came out raspy, strained. The sight of the Seiomenn's healing stone filled him with a twisting pang of sorrow. Had he known Eirik Throrsson had a daughter, it might have been worth revealing Rangvaldr's true identity long enough to heal Branda. Saving both his son and daughter would have immediately convinced the Hilmir of the Duke's honorable intentions.

"Perhaps." Rangvaldr's tone was musing. "Asleif isn't only renowned for her mead and the beauty of her flaxen locks. She is as much to credit for the Hilmir's ambition and success as Throrsson himself. It is likely she had the presence of mind. And yet…" He trailed off, shrugging. "Storbjarg burns, and the enemy rampages in its streets. Many a man would find it hard to hold out hope for the one he loves."

Aravon's stomach twisted. He forced himself to say the words aloud. "I *have* to hope," he said, barely above a whisper. "And to keep fighting no matter how I feel about it. If he really is gone, I will have time to mourn when this is all over."

"Wise words," Rangvaldr said, not unkindly. "But sometimes the heart knows truths the lips cannot speak." He reached over and rested a hand on Aravon's leg. "I, too, pray to Nuius for the Duke. And for you, if the worst comes to pass."

Aravon swallowed hard, swallowed again. "Thank you," he managed to croak out.

"If you have need of me, you know where to find me." Rangvaldr removed his hand and, with a little nod, turned back to the fire and Zaharis' silent conversation with the noisy, protesting Noll.

Aravon paid the two little heed. Rangvaldr's words hung heavy on his heart, a weight that pressed on his chest and pushed him down to the ground. He lay down, not bothering with a bedroll, missing the warmth and comfort of Snarl's presence, too tired and burdened to move. It was all he could do not to curl up and wallow in misery.

He *wanted* to hold out hope. To believe the Duke was, in fact, still alive. Yet a part of him knew that was only delaying the inevitable. He'd have to come to terms with the painful truth sooner or later. If he didn't, it would drive him mad.

But not tonight. Not with the threat of battle looming over him. Tomorrow was another day, a day when they would take the fight to the Eirdkilrs. The *Blodsvarri* would taste defeat, would watch her men slaughtered. Even if Throrsson didn't have the numbers to retake Storbjarg and eliminate the Eirdkilrs entirely, by the Swordsman, he'd make them bleed!

Chapter Fifty-Six

Aravon snapped awake at the sound of a stealthy footfall a few paces from where he lay. He was halfway to his feet, spear ready to strike, before he recognized Noll's compact form, mottled pattern armor, and masked face.

"Tried to let you sleep as long as I could, Captain." Noll sounded apologetic. "But we need to move now if we're to be in position by daybreak."

Aravon blinked the last vestiges of sleep from his eyes and rolled the kinks from his muscles. A fresh, dewy scent filled his nostrils. The world around him was still dark, the chill of night hanging over their small forest camp. Yet the air was filled with the anticipation of pre-dawn, a stillness that settled over nature just before the first threads of morning light appeared on the eastern horizon.

The total absence of sound felt eerie. The previous night, more than two thousand warriors had camped a short distance away, the clamor of their movements and marching resounding through the forest. Now, only dense , oppressive silence pressed in around him.

He and Noll were alone.

"Zaharis and Rangvaldr?" Aravon asked.

Noll nodded. "Off to their posts an hour ago. Knowing Colborn, he, Belthar, and Skathi will be in position as well. All that's left is for us to get in place when the show starts." He gestured to Aravon's horse, which he'd evidently fed, watered, and saddled before waking Aravon.

"Thank you, Noll." Aravon clapped the little scout on the shoulder.

"We've all got our roles to play, Captain." Noll hitched up the quiver of arrows slung over his back. "Truth be told, after Rivergate, I don't mind being

445

on the sidelines at the beginning. Things…" His brow furrowed. "Things got nasty back there."

Aravon struggled to mask his surprise. Noll had never shown anything short of utter confidence, the same blustering ego common to so many experienced soldiers. Yet now, with no one around but Aravon, none of his companions to judge him, he felt free to open up and reveal the truth beneath the swaggering façade.

"I'd have died if not for the *Seiomenn*. And you, Colborn, Skathi, and everyone else." Noll shook his head. "Not the first time I've stared the Long Keeper in the face, but every time I do, it makes me think about what really matters."

"And what's that?" Aravon asked gently.

Long moments of silence passed before Noll spoke. "My family."

The words sent a jolt of ice down Aravon's spine. "Family?"

"Three sons and a daughter." Noll nodded, his voice heavy, laden with heartache. "In Lochton. Haven't seen them in the better part of a decade. Their mother's idea." His shoulders drooped and his eyes couldn't meet Aravon's. "Kicked me out. Wanted nothing to do with me."

Aravon's eyebrows rose. "I had no idea."

"Not the sort of thing a man shares with strangers. Or commanding officers." Noll gave a harsh chuckle. "Makes a man look bad, you understand."

Aravon laughed. "I can understand that."

Noll nodded, gaze downcast. "It's why I got into this. The Duke's mission, working with you and the others." He drew in a deep breath. "I owed a few debts, and the Duke promised to settle them all, keep my family fed and clothed as long as I served."

"As noble a reason as any other." Aravon shrugged. "We've all got a duty to our families." His thoughts flashed to Mylena and his sons, Rolyn and Adilon. He'd taken on this mission for their sakes—to protect them from the war that had been a part of his life for as long as he could remember.

After a long moment of silence, Noll sighed. "Kind of a cruel joke that I'm a better father to them dead than alive, isn't it?"

Aravon shook his head. "One day, when this is all over, you'll go back to them. If the last weeks are any kind of proof, I've no doubt you'll be the sort of man that makes their lives better, not worse."

Noll swallowed, but gave a slow nod. "Thanks, Captain. Here's hoping." He turned away, but not before Aravon caught a hint of moisture in his eyes. When he turned back, his voice was once again gruff, edged with his usual sharpness. "Now, if you're done napping, maybe we ride out and get into position. This battle ain't going to win itself."

* * *

The first gentle swirls of reddish-gold painted the eastern sky as Aravon hauled himself up and into position beside Colborn. The Lieutenant glanced over from his camouflaged perch on a branch forty feet up an enormous red beech tree and nodded.

"Captain," the Lieutenant muttered in a low voice. "Had me worried you'd sleep through the fun."

"I thought about it." Aravon shrugged. "Figured I'd better be here, make sure none of you messed up my careful battle plans."

"You ever hear that old saying about battle plans?" Colborn shook his head. "Only useful until—"

"Some idiot buggers it up." Aravon chuckled. "Best we can do is hope the idiot's on the other side of the battlefield, yeah?"

Colborn chuckled, then turned his attention back toward the thick haze of smoke shrouding Storbjarg. "The Hilmir?"

"Knows his part to play," Aravon replied. "It's half his plan, after all."

"With just enough Zaharis thrown into the mix to give the Eirdkilrs a nasty surprise." Noll's voice held a wicked edge. The scout had joined Aravon and Colborn in the tree, sitting comfortably on a branch thicker than his head, as relaxed as a man taking an afternoon nap. A sharp contrast to the acrid wall of smoke, the shouts of fighting Eirdkilrs and Fjall, and the crackling of burning buildings echoing from within Storbjarg.

Let's just hope Zaharis can find what he needs, Aravon thought, but didn't say. The Secret Keeper had run dangerously low on his alchemical supplies; his distraction to free Throrsson had literally burned through the last of the Dragon Thorngrass he'd collected at Rivergate. Now, he was dependent on what he could find in the Fjall forests.

447

Aravon turned his attention back to Storbjarg, what little he could see of it. The fires had dimmed in the Fjall's enormous city, making it near-impossible to peer through the thick, choking wall of smoke that hung like a funeral shroud over the Hilmir's capital. The sounds of battle within had also diminished—as with all urban battles, the fighting had doubtless degenerated to short, sharp clashes among the muddy alleys and back streets. Any Fjall warriors still in Storbjarg would likely be hunkering down, searching for the best chances to ambush their enemies or flee the city with their women and children. Against three, perhaps four thousand Eirdkilrs, the Hilmir's warband had little chance of victory.

Again, the overwhelming burden of sorrow descended on Aravon's shoulders. The Eirdkilrs had set Storbjarg to the torch, and according to Skathi's reports, they held both the north and south gates. Unless the Duke *had* managed to escape before the initial assault, he was somewhere within the blackened remains of the city. Alive or dead, Aravon couldn't know for sure, yet the dark parts of his mind filled his thoughts with images of the Duke's corpse—hacked to pieces by Eirdkilr axes, burned to nothing but charred flesh in the fires that consumed the city.

"Here they come." Breathless excitement echoed in Colborn's words, and he thrust a finger toward the south.

Aravon pushed back against the emotions, locking them away down deep, forcing himself to focus on the mission. He squinted in the direction indicated. Between the faint threads of morning light and the thick pall of smoke, Aravon could barely see a flicker of movement from the forest bordering the southern road. But if *he* had a hard time spotting the Hilmir's men, and he was looking for them, they'd be all but invisible to the Eirdkilrs in Storbjarg.

Tension coiled in his stomach, knots tightening his shoulders. His hand tightened around the ash shaft of his spear. He hated standing by and watching, but for this part of the battle, he needed to be an observer. He'd come face to face with the enemy soon enough.

The attack came so silently it took Aravon by surprise. No shout of "For *Striith*!" broke the silence. No battle horn echoed off the walls of Storbjarg. From where he crouched in the bushes, Aravon heard only a faint *clanking* of shields and swords, the metallic whisper of *clinking* chain mail, and the soft footfalls of a thousand Fjall warriors padding across the grassy expanse surrounding the city.

Eirik Throrsson, Hilmir of the Fjall, raced at the head of his men, a towering figure clad in gleaming chain mail, a massive brown bear pelt, and plain steel skullcap. Like the tip of a spear, he drove straight toward the open south gate, fury driving him and his warband to breathtaking speed.

Time seemed to slow, and Aravon's breath caught in his lungs. Fifty yards to the city gate. No shout of alarm from within. Thirty. Twenty. Still no sign the enemy had caught sight of the approaching force. Ten yards. Five.

A bellowing roar shattered the silence. Throrsson gave voice to his fury now, a wordless battle cry taken up by a thousand Fjall throats. The deafening wall of noise rolled across Aravon and set his flesh prickling. That battle cry held a depth of rage and defiance sufficient to drive fear into the hearts of any foe.

The Hilmir charged through the gate, his warriors streaming after him, and disappeared into the thick wall of smoke. The sounds of clashing steel echoed through the haze of smoke, and Eirdkilr howls turned to cries of agony as the Fjall hit them hard.

Then, through a momentary gap in the gray haze, Aravon caught sight of the Hilmir and his men locked in furious battle with the Eirdkilrs. Only a few dozen of the towering barbarians, barely enough to slow the tide of the assault. The surprise attack had caught the enemy off-guard. So consumed were they by the battle inside Storbjarg that they couldn't mount a proper defense against this new threat.

Throrsson and his thousand Fjall rolled over the first scattered bands of Eirdkilrs like a giant sea wave crashing onto the banks of Icespire Bay. A dozen, two dozen, fifty, then a hundred fell. Cut down by furious Fjall, trampled into the bloody mud by booted feet that never slowed their furious advance. Skulls crushed, bones shattered, crimson darkening their filthy icebear pelts, the Eirdkilrs died howling, screaming, or weeping in agony. Fifty of Throrsson's men tore off to the west, hunting down Eirdkilrs flooding the back streets of southern Storbjarg. Another fifty charged east, but the bulk of the Hilmir's force surged down the long, straight avenue that led into the heart of the city.

Aravon's fists tightened on his spear until his knuckles turned white. *Come on, Throrsson! Don't abandon the plan.*

The Hilmir knew the danger of getting bogged down, trapped within the streets of Storbjarg. His meager force of one thousand could never hope to defeat the three thousand or more holding the city.

449

Yet in the heat of battle, even the coolest-tempered man could lose his head. Surrounded by the burning wreckage of their homes, the corpses of their friends and loved ones. Aravon had felt that rage many times—the burning, all-consuming desire to tear an enemy's throat out with bare hands, to hack and slash at a foe until nothing remained but bloodied ribbons of flesh and shattered bones. But if the Hilmir and his men gave in to it, they'd lose the battle before it even began.

Aravon's gloved fingers worried at the smooth ash shaft of his spear, anxiety twisting in his stomach. The Hilmir's forward thrust hadn't lost momentum; if anything, it had gained speed as the Fjall warband crushed groups of scattered, disorganized Eirdkilrs. More enemies fell to the surprise assault, swallowed beneath a roaring wave of Fehlan rage and steel.

But the farther into Storbjarg they went, the greater the risk. *Damn you, Throrsson. Not so far!*

Aravon leaned so far forward he nearly toppled from his perch. A sense of helplessness tightened his chest, set his nerves jangling. He should have been there, should have helped lead the charge to prevent the Hilmir and his men from losing their heads. Any farther and they might not be able to retreat when—

The howling war cries of the Eirdkilrs grew deafening as they spilled out of the back alleys and down the main avenue. Through the haze of smoke, Aravon caught sight of scores, then hundreds of towering figures with blue-stained faces, filthy icebear pelts, and enormous weapons surging through the streets toward the Hilmir's warband. In a matter of seconds, the Fjall warband would crash with an ever-growing tide of Eirdkilrs.

"Pull back!" The shout burst from Aravon's lips before he could restrain himself. It was lost beneath the roar of battle, the crackling of the still-burning city. It would do no good, anyway. Throrsson was committed, driven by his rage and bloodlust. And Aravon was too far away to do anything but watch as the Hilmir charged his men toward a rapidly solidifying wall of enemies.

Then the racing Throrsson came within sight of the Eirdkilrs. Aravon sucked in a breath as the Hilmir slowed. *Sound the retreat! Pull out while you still can.*

His hope died in the next heartbeat. The Fjall chief raised his sword high and with a roar of "For *Striith!*" drove straight toward the center of the Eirdkilr line.

450

Chapter Fifty-Seven

No!

The thunderous crash echoed off the walls of Storbjarg, pierced Aravon's bones and filled him with dread. The howling war cries of the Eirdkilrs mingled with the shouts of the Fjall, the *clangor* of steel on steel, the screams of dying men. The enemy line buckled beneath the force of the charge, pushed backward, but held. Even as Throrsson's warriors hacked, slashed, and chopped at the enemy crushed up against them, the Eirdkilr line grew, thickened, and solidified. With every passing second, more and more of the Fjall warband committed to the attack, and more Eirdkilrs streamed from the streets to join the fray. The Eirdkilr battle line stretched across the main avenue, while the Hilmir drove his spear-tip formation straight into the center—a center far too thick to punch through.

Keeper take you, Throrsson! Aravon whirled and scrambled toward the trunk of the tree, then began climbing down to the ground. The Hilmir had lost his head, had succumbed to the rage of battle and the horror at seeing his city destroyed. Emotion had burned away all rationale. Throrsson fought for his city, his people.

And doing so would get his people killed.

It fell to Aravon to salvage the battle. He had to find a way to get the Fjall to pull back, to get out while they still could. Every passing second brought more Eirdkilrs to the battle. At any moment, the tide would turn and the enemy would engulf Throrsson's men.

If they don't get out now, they'll—

The sound of a battle horn pierced the din of chaos. A glorious, ringing blast that carried across Storbjarg and echoed off the high stone walls. Hope surged within Aravon as the horn blew again, then a third time. *Three blasts!* The Fjall signal to retreat.

Yes!

The icy fingers uncurled from around Aravon's heart, and he scrambled back up toward his perch beside Colborn.

"They're pulling out." Relief echoed in Colborn's voice.

Sure enough, as Aravon regained his vantage point, he found the rearmost Fjall breaking off the battle. Warriors had turned to flee, racing back down the muddy street toward the twisted, ruined remains of the south gate. Scores, then hundreds of the Fjall, abandoning the battle.

Yet not the Hilmir. Throrsson and a handful of his men remained locked in combat. Steel war axes flashing, swords biting, shields slamming into Eirdkilrs or absorbing the brutal punishment of their enemy's enormous weapons. A bestial roar rumbled from the Hilmir's throat as he battled the barbarians who had destroyed his home.

Damn it, Throrsson, get the bloody hell out of there!

Superior Eirdkilr numbers exacted a heavy toll on Throrsson's warriors. Fjall fell beneath the stronger, larger enemies. Blood spattered filthy white icebear pelts and faces stained blue as the Eirdkilrs bit back, hard, against the Fjall. Fehlan warriors died beneath the renewed assault. Crimson sprayed in the air, the screams of pain echoing in time with the pounding of Aravon's heart. The Eirdkilrs pushed the Hilmir's shield wall back one step, then two. With every inch of ground, more Fjall fell. Brave warriors never to rise again.

Aravon swallowed the acid that rose to his throat. This was the most dangerous part of the battle, and if Throrsson didn't disengage now, the Eirdkilrs would engulf the few men remaining beside him. Already, the outer flanks of the Eirdkilr line had begun to push inward, forcing the Hilmir's line to bow inward. In seconds, it would collapse in on itself, and the battle would be—

Then came the horn, a single piercing blast. The signal the Hilmir was waiting for. With a furious shout, the Fjall leaned into their shields, swung their weapons with every shred of rage. The Eirdkilrs were thrown back by the ferocity. In that instant of pause, Throrsson and his men broke off, turned, and raced after their men. A dozen Fjall fell as they abandoned the fight, but the

452

abruptness of their flight caught the enemy off-guard. For a heartbeat, an eerie silence hung where the sounds of battle and death had once held the city of Storbjarg in an iron grip.

The calm was shattered a moment later by the Eirdkilrs' howling war cries. Fierce, bloodthirsty, and bestial, the giant barbarians raised their voices in triumph and gave chase to their fleeing foes. Slowly at first, like a boulder just beginning to roll down a mountain, then faster and faster, gaining momentum as the flood of enormous, fur-clad figures pursued the Hilmir. They had their prey in their sights. He wouldn't escape *again*.

Aravon gasped, blew out the breath he hadn't realized he'd been holding. Blood flowed in his veins once more and he could move, no longer frozen by the nervous tension of battle. His eyes darted south of the rushing Eirdkilrs, to where Throrsson and his fleeing warband thundered through the streets of Storbjarg.

Just a few more steps! Aravon's heart hammered a staccato beat against his ribs. The pounding quickened as the Fjall disappeared once more behind the wall of smoke hanging over the city.

Then the first of the Fjall warriors streamed through the gate. Disorganized, chaotic, yet only in appearance.

Suddenly, Aravon understood Throrsson's actions. They needed to make the assault on Storbjarg convincing, else the Eirdkilrs would never believe their retreat and flight genuine. That was why Throrsson had pushed the advance so far, kept his men locked in battle until the last moment.

They *had* kept to the plan.

And now it's my turn!

Aravon scrambled down from his perch. "Let's go!" he called to his men.

Leaves and branches rustled as Colborn and Noll clambered down the tree above him. Aravon's breathing quickened at the urgency humming within him, and it seemed an eternity before he reached the ground. Without waiting for his companions, he sprinted the twenty yards to where they'd left the horses. He untethered all three horses and hauled himself into his saddle as Noll and Colborn burst through the bushes. Noll leapt onto his horse's back without slowing, and Colborn was only a step behind. Sawing on his horse's reins, Aravon turned the mount's head east. Toward the place where he knew the Hilmir would lead the Eirdkilrs.

Branches whipped at his face and head as he thundered through the dense woods, and he bent low over his horse's neck, digging in his heels to spur the horse into a gallop. Though the forest floor was uneven, he trusted his fleet-footed charger. He had mere minutes to ride nearly two miles and get in position for the second phase of his plan.

He didn't bother glancing to the south; the thick forest bordering Storbjarg would hide the Hilmir's fleeing men and their Eirdkilr pursuers. But it didn't matter. The Hilmir had proven that he could stick with the plan, even amidst the blazing ruins of his home. He'd keep the Eirdkilrs engaged long enough to get them where they needed to be.

Come on! Time seemed to drag at a snail's pace as Aravon and his two companions raced through the forest. His mouth was dry, his palms sweaty as he clutched his horse's reins. He knew what awaited him beyond the woodlands—he just needed to *get there* before the Eirdkilrs did.

Then he saw it: blue sky between the trees, the western edge of the dense woods. *Yes!* Jaw set and grim, Aravon raced through the woods, darting between the trees, and charged out onto the grassy hill beyond the tree line.

There, on the narrow wagon road leading northwest, three hundred of the Fjall warband had formed into a solid line. The warriors' red-painted shields displayed the glistening black *Reafan* of the Hilmir, and a gleaming forest of steel axes, spears, and swords bristled all along the Fjall battle line. Three hundred broad-shouldered warriors clad in heavy furs, chain mail, and spike-tipped bowl helmets, glaring defiance at the still-empty road to Storbjarg.

Aravon shot a glance over his shoulder. *"To your places!"* he signaled to Colborn and Noll.

Instantly, the two broke away from him and rode south along the tree line. They had their own roles to play in the battle to come.

Aravon turned his attention back to the Fjall warband formed up for battle. A pitiful force compared to the enemy that even now raced toward them. Yet with the Fjall lands so flat, *this* was the best place to lure the Eirdkilrs into battle.

Spurring his horse down the hill, Aravon galloped toward the middle of the line. He sought out the brown-bearded Fjall warrior in command—Sigbrand, who had led the force of two thousand awaiting the ambush at the Waeggbjod.

Aravon reined in his horse in front of the man. "They're coming!"

A fierce grin split Sigbrand's face, revealing teeth as yellow as the amber beads braided into his beard. "You hear?" he turned and roared to his men. "The *Tauld* have taken the bait. Today, they learn the true measure of Fjall bravery!"

Three hundred throats loosed a defiant shout, and the air echoed with cries of "For *Striith*!" and "For Storbjarg and the Hilmir!"

With a nod, Aravon wheeled his horse and galloped back along the lines, circling around behind the line of warriors. He would be of little use locked in the Fjall shield wall—he had no experience fighting in the Fehlan-style battle line—but from the rear, seated in his saddle, he had a clear vantage of the battlefield. He'd be in the best position to act should the tide of combat turn against them.

Grim resolve hardened in his gut as he drew his spear and tucked it under his arm in a lancer's grip. He'd never ridden into battle—he'd lived and breathed infantry during his fifteen years in the Legion—but his officer's training had involved a basic understanding of the couched lance charge. And, with the speed, mobility, and weight of his horse, he stood the best chance of inflicting serious punishment on the enemy.

A wry smile twisted his lips. *A mighty cavalry charge of one. Commander Oderus would have loved this.*

He reined in behind the line, turning his horse to face the road up which the enemy would soon appear. Tension hung thick over the shield wall, a nervous silence that seemed to thunder in Aravon's ears. Nervous sweat rolled down his spine and his heart hammered in anticipation of the battle to come. This was always the worst part: the waiting before the battle.

Aravon turned to the only one who could help him now. *Strengthen our arms and guide our swords, mighty Swordsman,* he prayed. As always, the silent plea brought a measure of peace, stilled the anxiety twisting like worms in his gut. He drew in one long breath, exhaled. A cold calm settled onto his shoulders and lifted the burden of worry. He would do everything he could to affect the outcome of battle—the rest was up to his god and the men fighting at his side.

Then the first of the Fjall warriors appeared from the south. First a trickle, a few dozen, but that number grew to fifty, eighty, a hundred, and still more. Running, hair and braided beards flying in the wind, armor clanking and boots *pounding* up the hard-packed earth of the wagon path. A streaming mass as chaotic as any fleeing army.

At their rear, the Hilmir and the last of his retreating warriors. A black-haired young man raced at his side. Aravon let out a slow breath at the sight. Bjarni, Throrsson's son, had survived the clash in Storbjarg.

But not all of the Fjall warriors had been so fortunate. Aravon's quick count estimated closer to nine hundred remaining of the original thousand that entered the Fjall capital at the Hilmir's side. Even with their surprise assault, Throrsson's warband hadn't escaped without casualties.

The Fjall appeared to be fleeing in a disorganized rout, gripped in the chaos of defeat. Yet as they reached their formed-up comrades, they swirled around and to the sides, joining the shield wall in fives and tens. Wider and thicker the wall grew as one hundred, then two hundred, then five hundred of the Fjall warband locked shields with their fellows. Within the space of a few minutes, all nine hundred of the Hilmir's warriors joined the shield wall, with Throrsson, Bjarni, and Sigbrand holding front and center.

Then came the Eirdkilrs. They *were* a haphazard, howling mass of warriors streaming up the road hot in pursuit of their fleeing foe. Their charge faltered a heartbeat as they caught sight of the Fjall shield wall. Yet there were barely more than a thousand Fjall, and Aravon estimated this first wave of Eirdkilrs—those closest to the escaping warriors—numbered at a thousand. More joined them with every passing second.

The Eirdkilr charge stalled only for a few seconds, little more than a stutter in their headlong pursuit of the fleeing Fjall. Howling war cries split the air, the fury and volume redoubled as they saw their enemy close at hand. With a cry of *"Death to the traitors!"*, they charged.

In Aravon's experience, the Eirdkilrs typically opened a battle with a flurry of arrows. Their powerful longbows could punch a steel arrowhead deep into Legion shields. Yet, here, with the abrupt sneak attack and flight, those gathered hadn't managed to form cohesive ranks or any real battle strategy. A few unlimbered their bows and sent shafts hurtling toward the Fjall shield wall, but most simply bulled headlong into melee. Within seconds, the foremost Eirdkilrs had drawn so close that the archers couldn't loose shafts for fear of hitting their own.

That was *precisely* what Aravon and Throrsson had counted on. The round Fehlan shields were sturdier then Legionnaire shields, but they only covered half a man's body. Eirdkilr arrows would do serious damage to the Fjall's ranks, so they'd needed a plan that suckered the enemy into a head-on charge.

456

The Eirdkilr charge ate up the ground at a breathtaking speed. Two hundred yards closed to a hundred and fifty seemingly within the space of a heartbeat. A hundred. Eighty. Seventy. Sixty. Fifty. Aravon drew in a breath and braced himself for the impending crash.

Then another horn sounded. Two long, sharp blasts. A savage grin split Aravon's lips at the glorious sound for which he'd waited.

The Eirdkilrs never saw the ambush coming.

Chapter Fifty-Eight

Before the sound of the horn faded into the horizon, ten arrows streaked from the forest west of the Eirdkilrs' position. Red-fletched shafts plunged into the mass of enemies. Skathi's unerring accuracy wasn't necessary; the enemy stood so tightly-packed that she couldn't miss.

A moment later, a single crossbow bolt three feet long and as thick as Aravon's spear slammed into the center of the Eirdkilr's force. The missile slammed into one barbarian, punched through his side, and hurled him into the enemies marching beside him. The flapping, flailing Eirdkilr took four of his comrades to the ground with bone-jarring force, and the five were drowned and crushed beneath the stampeding feet of their comrades.

Loud hissing filled the air, and the sky west of the Eirdkilrs darkened. A savage grin split Aravon's lips at the sight of a hundred darts hurtling toward the enemy. Unlike their southern cousins, the Fjall used no ranged weapons in their attacks. Due to the darts' short range—as far as a strong man could hurl them—they were used primarily from the defensive vantage point of a tall city wall.

But not today. The Fjall had collected every dart they could scrounge up—just two hundred, scavenged from the town of Ingolfsfell to the northwest—and distributed among the warband. Now, half of those missiles rained down on the unsuspecting Eirdkilrs from their right. Caught by surprise, the barbarians had no time to raise their massive circular shields before the forearm-length darts plunged toward them. Barbed metal tips punched through chain mail, leather armor, furs, and flesh. Scores of Eirdkilrs fell beneath the hail of sharpened iron.

Then came the Fjall warband. Four hundred warriors crested the narrow rise to the west with a cry of "For *Strúth!*" and charged down the short, shallow hill toward the clustered enemy.

A furious howl rose from the force of Eirdkilrs, and a third of their number wheeled toward the new attackers.

The horn sounded again, double clarion calls that echoed across the grasslands. From the forests east of the Eirdkilrs, a hundred more darts—the last of the Fjall missiles—darkened the sky. Arrows loosed by Colborn and Noll joined the swarm of death that rained down on the enemy's backs. More Eirdkilrs fell, hammered to the earth by an invisible hand. Screams, cries, and howls of rage echoed loud as the remaining four hundred of Throrsson's warband marched into view.

Anger curled tight and hot in Aravon's stomach. *Got you, you bastards!*

The suddenness of the simultaneous attacks from both sides threw the Eirdkilrs into disarray. Any sense of cohesion they might have maintained during their headlong pursuit of the Fjall warband shattered. When the Hilmir sounded the charge a heartbeat later, he and his warriors hammered a staggered, confused enemy, little better than a rabble.

Throrsson's shield wall struck first. A thunderous *crash* of steel and wood striking flesh set the ground trembling, and the Fjall cries of rage and vengeance echoed loud. At their head, the Hilmir fought beside his son, Bjarni, with his trusted Sigbrand at his left and the proud warriors of Fjall surrounding him. Throrsson battled like a man possessed. His sword hacked, bit, thrust, and chopped, spraying crimson and felling Eirdkilrs beneath the force of his rage. He fought for his people, avenging the deaths of those within Storbjarg. And the Eirdkilrs paid a heavy price in blood.

Yet, in the seconds it took the remaining eight hundred Fjall to reach the enemy, the Eirdkilrs had managed to form a semblance of a shield wall. Massive, heavily-muscled figures clad in icebear pelts locked shields and waved enormous axes, clubs, and spears at the enemy. When the four hundred from the west and four hundred from the east slammed into the Eirdkilrs, they inflicted far lighter casualties. Barely a few score fell beneath the charge. The Fjall flank attacks were stalled nearly instantly, crashing against a solid force of prepared and organized enemies.

From his seat in the saddle, Aravon took in the battle scene at a glance. Throrsson's twelve hundred hammered the Eirdkilrs hard, and the enemy fell back beneath the superior numbers. But the four hundred attacking from the east was having a hard time of it. Their shield wall was too long, their ranks too thin. Whoever commanded that force had overestimated the impact their charge would have. Facing a line of formed-up Eirdkilrs, the Fjall were so focused on trying to surround the enemy from the south and east that they failed to anticipate the failure of their charge.

The center of their shield wall buckled beneath the Eirdkilrs' ferocity. The southernmost warriors, in particular, struggled to corral the Eirdkilrs. Their attempts to encircle the enemy was failing and they took heavy losses. Worse, they found themselves beset from the south by a steady trickle of enemies streaming from Storbjarg.

Ice slithered down Aravon's spine. *They're going to break!*

Without hesitation, Aravon dug his heels into his horse's ribs and spurred to a gallop. The sound of battle faded around him as his eyes fixed on the too-thin battle line. His heart hammered terribly loud in his ears and he gripped his spear tighter. *Hold on, damn it!*

A heartbeat before he arrived, the shield wall broke. The right flank, beset from the south and too thin to hold back the Eirdkilrs, crumbled. Five towering giants pushed through the gap in the line, trampling fallen Fjall, and fell upon the shield wall from the side and rear. The gap widened one dying Fehlan at a time, until the Eirdkilrs threatened to stream through.

With a roar, Aravon drove his spear into the first Eirdkilr's chest. The force of his thrust, backed by the weight of the charging horse, punched the steel head through armor, leather, and flesh and hurled the Eirdkilr backward. The dying barbarian stumbled, arms flying wild, and his huge club smashed into the face of another Eirdkilr behind him. The two went down and for a the space of a single heartbeat, their enormous bodies blocked the gap.

In that instant, Aravon leapt from his horse and threw himself into the breach. Spear whirling, steel flashing in the sunlight, he slammed the iron-shod butt into one Eirdkilr's forehead and sliced another's throat with a single spinning motion. Took down another with a thrust to the chest. Ducked a high axe slash, knocked aside a club, and drove his spear up into the fork of the barbarian's legs. The Eirdkilr fell with a groan, and Aravon finished him off with a slash to the face.

An Eirdkilr club smashed into him from the side. Pain flared through his right shoulder and he was hurled backward, off-balance. He would have fallen had he not crashed into a Fjall warrior beside him. The man went down but Aravon regained his balance in time to dodge the crushing club blow. The metal-capped butt of his spear crushed the enemy's knee. Sagging, screaming, the Eirdkilr swiped at Aravon. The wild blow struck with rib-shattering force, and only the alchemically-treated surface of Aravon's armor kept him alive. More pain in his side, dull and aching. Breath burst from his lungs and he gasped for air.

An arrow slammed into the Eirdkilr's face, knocking him onto his back. The next instant, Colborn was beside Aravon, his Fehlan-style longsword flashing, his shield batting aside enemy strikes. With a roar, Colborn threw himself into the Eirdkilrs surging through the gap. Blood sprayed as Odarian steel slashed throats, sheared heavy limbs, or punched through chain mail.

Aravon drew in one ragged breath, then another. Pain faded beneath the rush of battle. Pushing off his spear, he rose to his feet and hurled himself into the gap beside Colborn. Together with the Fjall warriors, they threw back the Eirdkilrs and, one bloody step at a time, closed the gap in the shield wall.

A hand gripped Aravon's shoulder and dragged him backward, away from the re-forming Fjall warriors.

"Trying to get yourself killed?" Colborn shouted over the din of battle.

Aravon was too winded to do more than shake his head. He'd acted on instinct, throwing himself into the gap to repel the enemy. If the Eirdkilrs had managed to break out, they could have done far worse damage. With the forces arrayed against them, the Fjall warband couldn't afford heavy casualties, not yet. The time would come to slug it out with the Eirdkilrs, but for now, they had to rely on lightning attacks, ambushes, and surprises to carry the day.

From his vantage a few yards behind the shield wall, Aravon could see the Fjall's plan to encircle the Eirdkilrs to the south had worked. Mostly. A few dozen of the Hilmir's warband had turned to face the steady stream of Eirdkilrs racing to join their comrades. Already, those warriors were beset by a near-equal number of enemies—a number that grew with every passing heartbeat.

Aravon stifled a grunt of pain as he clambered into his saddle. He needed to get up high, to see the battle more clearly.

Hope surged within him as he caught sight of the Hilmir locked with the Eirdkilrs. The initial charge had winnowed the enemy's forces, and the ferocity of Throrsson's assault whittled the number to less than half of the original thousand. The remaining four hundred fought with the bloodthirsty ferocity for which the Eirdkilrs were feared, yet against so many, beset from all sides, they had little chance.

Keeper's teeth, we might actually pull this off! Eliminating so many of the Blood Queen's men in this initial assault would go a long way toward evening the odds when it came time to battle. *All we've got to do is finish them off before—*

His hopes died in that moment. A short, lithe figure in mottled armor galloped toward him, bent low over his charger's neck.

No! Aravon's breath clutched in his chest. *It's too soon!*

Yet Noll's presence could only mean one thing.

Reinforcements are coming.

Aravon rounded on Colborn. "Go! Find the bugler and sound the retreat!"

Colborn hesitated, anger blazing bright and hot in his eyes. Aravon knew exactly what he was thinking—he felt the same. *We were so close! So close to wiping out this force here and now.*

Yet if they delayed, if they continued fighting in an attempt to eradicate the remaining four hundred Eirdkilrs, they would find themselves surrounded by the Eirdkilrs who had marched from Storbjarg.

"Now, Colborn!" Aravon roared.

The Lieutenant snapped to action, digging his heels into his horse's ribs and wheeling it toward the eastern forest, where the Fjall bugler and the fifty warriors remaining in reserve hid among the trees.

Aravon's heart sank as he caught sight of the approaching Eirdkilr force. By his count, nearly eleven hundred Eirdkilrs had streamed from Storbjarg in pursuit of the fleeing Hilmir. A thousand had been caught in their ambush, and the remaining hundred had come upon the Fjall from the rear in twos and threes.

Yet the force that surged up the road toward them numbered more than three thousand. Either the Eirdkilrs had abandoned Storbjarg in their desire to bring down the Hilmir, or…

Icy feet danced down Aravon's back at the sight of the figure leading the enemy. A tall, brown-haired woman with a bloodstained face clad in a filthy icebear pelt dyed rusty crimson by the dried blood of her victims. The Blood Queen herself, come to finish what she'd started near the Waeggbjod three days ago. At her back marched two thousand Eirdkilrs, shaggy-haired giants that filled the air with their howling war cries. Sunlight glinted off the steel swords, chain mail coats, and skullcaps, and the ground trembled beneath the force of their feet.

Added to the Eirdkilrs still within Storbjarg, that set more than four thousand enemies arrayed against them. If they joined battle here, the Hilmir and his Fjall warriors died. Their only hope of survival now was to pull back.

The horn rang, three high, sharp blasts that pierced the din of battle. Yet even with the retreat sounded, combat continued unabated. A few of the Fjall warriors broke off from the rear of the shield walls, but the bulk remained committed.

This was the most dangerous part of their desperate plan. Disengagements always took a bloody toll on those trying to break off battle. Whether they turned to flee or simply retreated, that moment when warriors *stopped* fighting gave the enemy an opening to exploit. For a few heartbeats, the Fjall took heavy losses as the shield walls struggled to disentangle themselves from the enemy.

It was only by the Swordsman's grace that the Eirdkilrs were too few to take advantage of the disengagement. The Hilmir's ambush had whittled their numbers to fewer than two hundred, and most of the Eirdkilrs were too occupied fighting for their lives to do more than stagger forward, stunned at the sudden cessation of battle. The gap between the retreating Fjall and the off-balance Eirdkilrs grew wider with every passing heartbeat, the casualties dwindling.

"Captain!" Noll's shout snapped Aravon's attention to the south. "They've got archers!"

Ice slithered down Aravon's spine. The Eirdkilrs beside the *Blodsvarri* had slung bows and nocked arrows. Even from nearly three hundred yards away, their heavy longbows could punch arrows through Fjall armor, shields, and flesh. In the precious seconds it would take for the Hilmir to get out of range, the Eirdkilrs could inflict bloody punishment on the fleeing Fehlans.

In horror, Aravon realized he and Noll were within bowshot. Sawing at his horse's reins, he spun the beast to the north. "Ride!" he shouted.

The two horses broke into a gallop, racing away from the approaching Eirdkilrs. Yet, as Aravon glanced over his shoulder, he saw the enemy drawing back their bows to fire.

If they loosed, they wouldn't just strike the retreating Fjall; she'd cut down the two hundred warriors still clustered around the site of battle.

Aravon sucked in a breath. *She wouldn't!*

She did.

At the *Blodsvarri's* snarled command, a thousand Eirdkilr longbows *twanged* in unison. The sky darkened behind a hail of black-shafted arrows. Sharp steel arrowheads gleamed in the morning light, singing a song of death as they arced through the air and plummeted toward the slowest of the Fjall. And the two hundred remaining Eirdkilrs.

Arrows clanked and banged off the raised Fehlan shields or slipped through the narrow gaps between, a symphony of death that scythed down Fjall by the scores. The Eirdkilrs, backs turned to their approaching reinforcements, never saw the hail of missiles speeding toward them. Three-quarters fell beneath the first volley. The heavy steel-tipped arrows of their comrades punched through icebear pelts, chain mail, and flesh. The screams of dying Fjall and Eirdkilrs mingled, the battlefield turning red with Fehlan and barbarian blood alike.

A few arrows whipped past Aravon, one close enough to glance off his leather pauldron. Yet they were at the extreme end of the longbows' range, too far for the enemy to loose with any semblance of accuracy. Within a few heart-pounding seconds, the last of the missiles wobbled past or fell short as Aravon, Noll, and Colborn rode out of bowshot.

Only then did Aravon risk a glance back, and acid surged to his throat. Too many of the Fjall had joined the Eirdkilrs pinned to the earth by the black-shafted arrows. A hundred, perhaps more; Fehlans too slow to retreat or helping the wounded flee.

Anger mingled with the sorrow and worry burning in Aravon's gut. He'd always known they'd take losses—heavy losses, given the enemy's superior numbers. Yet this many, so early in the battle? They could ill-afford the casualties.

It didn't matter that the Blood Queen had lost nearly fifteen hundred of her warriors in the space of an hour. More than four thousand marched at her back, and the Hilmir had only the two thousand of his warband. Closer to seventeen hundred when the retreat was sounded. The clash in Storbjarg had cost Throrsson, and the battle here hadn't been entirely one-sided. With a single cruel command to slaughter her own men, the *Blodsvarri* had whittled down the Fjall warband to just sixteen hundred.

And however many more are still alive in Storbjarg, Aravon tried to console himself. The city hadn't fully fallen yet. Sounds of battle had still rung out

465

within the walls an hour earlier. The Hilmir's warriors fought with dogged tenacity, holding on to their city and protecting their people to the bitter end.

But even if all three thousand remained alive—an impossibility, given the fact that they had faced an equal number of Eirdkilrs—they would have their hands full trying to hold or recapture the city. That left only the few with Hilmir to defeat the four thousand marching with the *Blodsvarri,* and however many more she could summon from the Eirdkilr-held lands.

Aravon gritted his teeth and bent lower over his horse's neck. *We're hurt bad, but not out of this fight yet!* He glanced left, spotted Colborn keeping pace just beyond the edge of the forest. A few hundred yards off to the right, Belthar and Skathi were mounted and galloping north as well. *And we're all still alive.*

The battle had just begun, the opening move played. Though they had taken a beating, their ranks thinned, Aravon had to hold out hope that they still had a chance.

As Aravon charged past the retreating Fjall, he sought out Throrsson among the body of warriors. He caught the Hilmir's gaze and the man shot him a grim nod. Blood stained Throrsson's armor and exhaustion lined his face, yet a grim determination blazed within his eyes. He and his Fjall were far from being out of the fight.

Aravon spurred his horse faster, and within a few minutes, pulled far ahead of the fast-moving Fehlan column—little more than a ragged string of warriors struggling to outrun their pursuers. Yet they did not have far to run.

Aravon's gaze roamed the terrain to the north, and his heart leapt as he spotted the first trees rising in the distance. Three miles away, the next step of his plan awaited. They just had to hope the Fjall reached it before the Eirdkilrs caught up.

Gritting his teeth, Aravon bent lower in his saddle and fixed his eyes on the bridge ahead. The *Fornbryggja* was the only way across the broad, deep Ormrvatn River for ten miles to the east or west. That single ribbon of water was the Fjall's best hope of not only holding off the Eirdkilrs, but by the Swordsman's grace, defeating them altogether.

But only if Zaharis and Rangvaldr played their parts.

The *Fornbryggja,* called the Immortal Bridge, had stood for as long as any Fjall could remember. Eirik Throrsson had spoken of the bridge as a marvel of ancient Fehlan construction, a landmark that all on Fehl recognized by name if not by sight.

466

Compared to some of the stone bridges built by Legionnaires—Rivergate Bridge, for example—the *Fornbryggja* was far from an architectural masterpiece. One hundred and fifty yards long and wide enough to march ten men abreast, it was a flat, solid construction of oaken planks set atop vast redwood beams. Legends held that it could bear the weight of a thousand men without crumbling. The fact that it had stood for more than five hundred years—as far back as the Fjall's historical records remembered—was the true marvel. The wood had been sealed against water and the elements by an ancient mixture of oils and resins that no Fehlan alive today could replicate.

So Aravon had set Zaharis to studying the bridge and finding a way to bring it down.

It had taken two full days to convince the Hilmir to let him enact his plan, but finally Throrsson had agreed that the dire nature of their situation demanded such…extremes. Yet Aravon knew that the act would pain the Hilmir as deeply as if Aravon had watched the gleaming Icespire itself torn down.

The horses' hooves *clattered* atop the solid oak planks as he and his four companions thundered across the *Fornbryggja*. Aravon glanced at the Ormrvatn River flowing beneath the bridge—sharp rocks protruded from the riverbed, churning the fast-moving water to white. Even the Eirdkilrs wouldn't risk that crossing without the bridge.

Hope surged within him as he reached the far side of the crossing and reined in his horse. The ground beyond was flat, the wagon road wide and dry, with only a few ruts left by iron-banded wheels. They'd have a good position to hold.

He turned to scan the trees clustered bordering the road to the east and west, searching for any sign of Rangvaldr or Zaharis. It was up to them to prepare the ground for their next battle—the most critical strike of the day, one that could finally give them a real advantage over the Blood Queen.

Yet the sparse forests were empty. Aravon saw no sign of either man.

"Captain?" Confusion echoed in Belthar's rumbling voice. "Shouldn't they be here?"

Aravon's brow furrowed. *What in the bloody hell?* In Zaharis' case, that likely meant he was still busy putting the finishing touches on his surprise. But Rangvaldr should be in place, waiting for them to arrive.

467

"Stonekeeper!" Aravon's shout echoed through the woods. Silence answered him. Not so much as a leaf or branch stirred within the forest. *Where in the Keeper's name are they?*

Aravon whirled to face his four companions. "Fan out," he ordered. "Find them."

Worry gnawed at Aravon's belly, doubt digging sharp claws into his mind. *Something's wrong.*

He whirled northward at the sound of approaching hoofbeats. A single figure rode a massive *Kostarasar* charger. No Fehlan warriors marched at his back or slithered among the trees. Only Rangvaldr, alone, with his heavy sword and round shield slung over his back.

Aravon's brow furrowed, his apprehension deepening with every pounding hoofbeat of the *Seiomenn's* horse. Rangvaldr was riding from the north, far beyond the place where he should be waiting.

"Captain!" Rangvaldr drew his horse to a halt in front of him. "They're gone!"

Aravon sucked in a breath, and a fist of ice closed around his heart.

"Svein Hafgrimsson and the Deid warband." The *Seiomenn* shook his head. "They've abandoned us."

Chapter Fifty-Nine

"What?" Aravon snapped. "What in Keeper's name happened?"

Rangvaldr's eyes darkened. "Word came of Gold Burrows Mine."

Aravon's stomach bottomed out. His breath caught in his chest, and the realization set his mind spinning. His and the Hilmir's battle strategy, carefully orchestrated and planned to the minutest detail, had just crumbled before his eyes.

"And they just…left?" Colborn sounded incredulous.

Rangvaldr nodded. "Hafgrimsson said to tell the Hilmir, 'If you cannot protect your own lands, how can we trust you will take care of ours?' I've spent the last hour riding alongside them, trying to convince him to change his mind. Nothing."

Bitter fury echoed in Colborn's voice. "Cowards!"

Aravon felt the burning anger, the frustration at the Deid fleeing at the most inopportune moment, but he could understand the Deid's actions. That same fear for home and family had led the Hilmir into the Blood Queen's trap.

Worse, he felt guilty. Had he spoken up earlier, he might have been able to avert this disaster. He fixed Rangvaldr with a piercing stare. "I should have told them."

The *Seiomenn* shook his head. "No, that burden rests with me." His shoulders tightened, his posture stiffening. "For the last four days, I have broken bread and shared the fire with the Deid, knowing the truth of what happened to their lands, their warriors." He drew in a breath. "I carry the blame for this."

"Much as I'm all for hearing someone *else* cocked everything up," Noll interjected, "no pity party's going to solve our current problem."

Aravon swallowed the emotions surging within him, pushed back the anger, guilt, and frustration. Biting sarcasm aside, Noll was right. "We've got to figure out how to deal with this."

"And quickly." Colborn's voice was solemn. "The Hilmir's almost here."

Chaos whirled in Aravon's mind and he struggled to marshal his thoughts, to formulate a new tactic on the go. A glance toward the southern horizon revealed the foremost Fjall racing toward them. He had *minutes*—ten, maybe fifteen at most—before the Hilmir's warriors reached them, the Eirdkilrs hot on their heels. He needed to figure out how to pull this back from the edge of defeat.

Thoughts racing, Aravon turned back to his comrades. "Rangvaldr, how's your aim with a bow?"

The *Seiomenn* shrugged. "I was a passable hunter during my days as an Eyrr warrior."

"Good." Aravon rounded on Skathi. "Give him your horsebow and a quiver of arrows."

The Agrotora hesitated, her eyes darting to the three quivers hanging from her saddlehorn. One was all but empty, and the other two held only sixty arrows between them.

"Half a quiver, and that's an order." Aravon's tone brooked no argument.

With visible reluctance, the archer handed her short horsebow to the *Seiomenn* and passed a fistful of arrows to the near-empty quiver.

Rangvaldr accepted bow and arrows with a nod. "I will treat them with the respect I show my own weapons."

Skathi inclined her head, but Aravon didn't need to see beneath her mask to sense her displeasure. In a way, she was *right* to conserve her ammunition. *Swordsman knows we'll run out of arrows long before we run out of enemies.*

But for his plan to work, he needed as many archers as possible. At the moment, he had just five.

"Skathi, Colborn, get into the trees on the west," Aravon commanded. "Belthar, Noll, Rangvaldr, take the east. When the enemy starts crossing the bridge, let loose on them as fast as you can. Rate of fire over accuracy, got it?"

Colborn's eyes narrowed behind his mask. "The five of us?"

Aravon shrugged. "It's all we've got for now." He turned to Belthar. "Get off one shot with your crossbow, then it's up to you to make enough noise to convince the Eirdkilrs we've got an army waiting in the woods."

"Aye, Captain." Belthar cleared his throat loudly. "Been a while since I've been able to bellow properly."

"Now's your chance." Aravon clapped him on the shoulder.

"All due respect, Captain," Colborn interjected, "but you want us to start shooting *while* they're crossing, not after?"

Aravon nodded. "Even experienced archers loose their missiles prematurely."

"That's what every woman ever has said about Noll," Belthar muttered, earning a scowl from the little scout.

Aravon ignored the gibe. "We want them to hesitate before they cross that bridge, *expecting* the ambush we planned to have lying in wait for them."

Noll scooped up the horses' reins and led them out of sight, deeper into the sparse woods west of the wagon road. Belthar saluted and, unhooking his crossbow from his horse's saddle, followed Noll and Rangvaldr to their designated positions under cover of the trees. Skathi left as well, after shooting a look of mild irritation at the departing *Seiomenn*. Aravon knew better than to separate an Agrotora from her bows, but he had little choice in their present circumstances. She *was*, after all, the only one who carried two bows with her.

And it's not like I had anyone touch her longbow. That conversation would have gone *very* differently. The Agrotorae were vicious in the defense of their longbows, masterpieces on par with the finest sword or shield. Skathi would have put an arrow into Rangvaldr's chest before letting him touch her prized possession and weapon of war.

"What are you thinking?" Colborn's voice sounded from beside him.

Aravon turned to the Lieutenant. "You know our plan for this bridge, yeah?"

Colborn nodded. "Lure a portion of the enemy across, then have Zaharis work his magic on the bridge." He chuckled at the use of "magic"—he knew as well as the rest of them how testy the Secret Keeper got when anyone used the forbidden word in reference to his alchemical sciences. "With the bridge gone, there'd be a thousand or so of the big bastards trapped on our side, between the Fjall and the Deid."

471

"But without the Deid," Aravon said, "we've got no way to spring the trap. Not the way we originally intended." He drew in a long breath, resisted the urge to remove his helmet and run a hand through his sweat-soaked hair. "But if we make them *think* there's a trap waiting for them, the *Blodsvarri's* going to think carefully about how to approach the crossing. Either she pulls back and we have a bit of time to breathe—"

"Or she'll come across all nice and organized-like. Neat little rows of Eirdkilrs all dressed up for battle." Colborn whistled. "Then, when the Magicmaker does take the bridge down, they take heavier losses."

"Precisely." Aravon appreciated and respected Colborn's quick grasp of his thinking; the Lieutenant had proven he had a mind as sharp as any officer Aravon had met. He'd never have advanced within the Legion due to his Fehlan heritage, but not his lack of skills.

A fact we're bloody well going to change, if we get a chance. I'll take it to the Duke myself if...

The thought died half-formed. Sorrow welled within him at the thought. After seeing the Eirdkilrs' thorough destruction of Storbjarg, even the most willfully stubborn fool would have trouble clinging to the hope that Duke Dyrund still lived. Even the Hilmir's reassurance couldn't keep the grim truth at bay. No way the Duke would have escaped that towering inferno or survived the Eirdkilr assault. If he had, he'd have found a way to reunite with them by now.

With effort, he pushed the bleak thoughts aside and pulled his mind back to the matter at hand. *I'll take it to the Prince,* he amended, shooting a pensive glance at Colborn. *If that's what he wants, of course.*

Once, Aravon himself had desired nothing more than to rise to rank of Battalion Commander, perhaps even to General someday. Yet now, given everything that he'd endured since the death of Sixth Company, he wasn't certain what lay in his future. A part of him wanted nothing more than to return home to Icespire, to live the rest of his days in quiet comfort with Mylena. To watch Rolyn and Adilon grow into strong, capable men. To live in a version of the Princelands that wasn't consumed by battle and war.

Yet none of that would happen—not for him, and not for Colborn, if his heart ran in the same direction as Aravon's—until the Eirdkilrs were defeated. That defeat began here, now.

"The Hilmir's not going to like the change," Aravon said, "and Keeper knows he's going to be spitting fire and venom when he hears about the Deid. But we've got no time to catch him up. We'll have to trust that he'll handle his part and keep the Eirdkilrs occupied. Hopefully, between the Fjall and our arrows, we'll have enough to pull the Blood Queen across, into our trap."

"By the Swordsman's grace." Colborn shrugged. "Best get to it, then." With a quick salute, he turned and raced after Skathi, deeper into the woods.

Aravon shot a hesitant glance toward the south. The retreating Fjall covered ground as only running Fehlans could, and they'd reach the bridge within ten minutes. That gave him just enough time to get down to Zaharis and make sure the Secret Keeper knew the change in plans.

Swordsman, have mercy on us, Aravon prayed silently. *Please help us pull this off.*

Courage bolstered a fraction, he hurried toward the bridge and slipped down the hill beside it, using his spear to steady himself on the steep incline.

"Zaharis?" he called out as he reached the heavy redwood supports holding up the ancient wooden *Fornbryggja.*

The Secret Keeper poked his head out from his perch, just beneath the spandrels under the bridge. "*Captain?*" he signed. "*What's the matter?*"

Aravon explained the situation in a few brief sentences. "Whatever you're doing to bring down the bridge, I need you to make it...bigger, more lethal."

"*About that...*" Hesitance flashed in Zaharis' eyes.

Aravon's gut tightened. *That can't be good.*

"*Foraging didn't turn up anywhere near enough to do real damage here.*" He thrust a mud-covered finger toward small patches of what looked like drying reddish-brown clay dabbed onto the underside of the bridge, where the wooden support pillars met the girders that formed the base of the *Fornbryggja's* deck. "*Truth be told, I'm not even sure this will be enough to bring it all down, much less inflict any serious punishment.*"

Aravon stifled a growl of frustration. *Damn it!*

"*Sorry, Captain.*" Zaharis' eyes darkened. "*I know how important this is. It's just that...*" He blew out a breath. "*Lots of unfamiliar plants in the Fjall lands, and no time to test what they can do. Best I could come up with on short notice was—*" His fingers signed a name Aravon didn't recognize, likely the name of the plant or plants he'd used for his alchemical concoction. "*It's just too damned long and wide to bring down without the proper supplies.*"

Aravon studied the underside of the bridge, and his mind flashed back to the Rivergate Bridge. "What if you concentrated it all right there?" Aravon pointed toward a section just shy of the middle of the bridge. "Bring just the center section down."

Zaharis squinted up at the wooden structure, at his alchemical concoction, then back at the bridge. After a long moment, he nodded. "*Should work. Might even take a few Eirdkilrs with it.*" He glanced back at Aravon. "*But that's just a short gap. Five, maybe ten yards long at best. Nothing a few logs won't bridge.*"

"That's fine." Aravon gave a dismissive wave. The wheels had begun turning, his mind working at the new problem. "In fact, that might actually be a *good* thing."

Zaharis cocked his head. "*Now this I have to hear.*"

Aravon shook his head. "I can't exactly predict what the Blood Queen will do. But I think that if we piss her off badly enough, she'll be itching to follow us, even if she has to waste a few hours felling trees. And it'll pull them farther from Storbjarg."

If the Duke *was* still alive, drawing the Blood Queen away from the Fjall capital gave him a fighting chance at survival.

"*So be it.*" Zaharis nodded. "*Give me ten minutes to get this all in place.*"

"You've got five!" Aravon turned and scrambled back up the slope. "Watch for my signal to bring it down."

He didn't glance over his shoulder for Zaharis' response; none was needed. The Secret Keeper would handle his business, just as the rest of his men would. Now, it was up to Aravon to deal with his part of the problem. A simple matter of figuring out how to defeat four thousand Eirdkilrs with only sixteen hundred of the Hilmir's men.

His conversation with Zaharis had sparked the beginnings of a plan. Desperate, with an outcome as unpredictable as anything he'd ever attempted, yet with the Deid abandoning the field, it was the best they could hope for. He wasn't certain how or where, but they had time to figure it out.

Later. He pushed the ruminating thoughts to the back of his mind. *One problem at a time.*

Aravon scrambled up the steep, muddy riverbank and onto the flat ground, racing toward the forest bordering the eastern side of the bridge. Close enough that he could see Zaharis working frantically beneath the wooden structure, yet out of sight of the approaching Fjall and their blue-painted pursuers.

The Fjall moved with speed born of desperation. Throrsson and his men, exhausted from the battle and night spent maneuvering into position, couldn't hope to outrun the Eirdkilrs over a long distance. Their Eirdkilrs pursuers could race a trotting horse and sustain that eight-mile-per-hour pace for hours on end.

In truth, the Hilmir's only salvation was the Blood Queen's wary caution. After Throrsson's trap and slaughter of more than eight hundred of her men, she wasn't taking any chances with the pursuit. The *Blodsvarri* had to know her forces outnumbered the Hilmir's nearly three to one—terrible odds on the best of days. Yet only a fool would charge headlong at the same enemy who had just suckered them into an ambush an hour earlier.

Aravon and Throrsson had counted on that caution to give the Fjall warband time to retreat to the bridge. The *Blodsvarri* couldn't possibly know of Zaharis' alchemical wonders, which gave them an advantage in their current position at the *Fornbryggja*. The fact that they'd had two thousand Deid to set the ambush made the bridge crossing even more favorable.

Now, however, they'd have to make the best of a rubbish situation. A storm of arrows and Belthar's bellowing wouldn't be nearly as good as the Deid warband, but it would suffice. All they had to do was slow the Blood Queen down, make her think twice before committing to the crossing. That'd give Zaharis a chance to work his alchemical wonders.

The harder we bite her, the more she'll want to bite back. His plan hinged on the Eirdkilrs' lust for blood and vengeance.

Then the first of the Fjall streamed across the bridge, their boots pounding on the wooden planking in a cacophony that echoed the grim desperation of the situation. Less than a quarter-mile behind, barely a few hundred yards away from the rearmost of the fleeing Fehlans, the Eirdkilrs filled the air with their war cries. They moved at a steady pace, a match for the desperate flight of the Fehlan warriors, inexorable, implacable, relentless.

Aravon's heart sank as he recalled the Hilmir's original plan. The Fjall's instructions had been to race into the forest then, under cover of the trees, re-form into a shield wall and serve as the anvil to the Deid's hammer once Zaharis brought down the bridge.

But that won't work now!

Heart hammering, Aravon leapt out of his hiding place and raced toward the bridge. He burst from tree cover just as the first of the Fjall warriors thundered across the *Fornbryggja* and stepped onto the northern bank of the Ormrvatn River.

"Stop!" he shouted in Fehlan. "Hold here! Form a shield wall!"

The first warriors slowed, curiosity twisting their heavy-bearded faces. Yet, as more and more of the Fjall streamed past, not stopping at Aravon's shouts, the rest joined suit.

No!

Aravon shouted for the Fehlans to form up, to stand. They *had* to hold the bridge, had to hold the enemy here.

Yet nothing he did stopped the Fjall from fleeing past. He was no warrior of the *Striithlid*, no Fehlan chieftain to give commands. The warband simply flowed around him, following their Hilmir's original instructions.

Aravon's heart sank as any hope of success trickled away like sand through his fingers. If the Fjall didn't form up here, it wouldn't matter if Zaharis brought down the bridge. The Eirdkilrs would have a foothold on this side, and they'd be locked into a fighting retreat. They'd never cover enough ground with the enemy snapping at their heels.

He shouted until his voice grew hoarse, his throat ragged and raw. In vain. The Fjall paid him no heed. In desperation, Aravon seized one racing warrior in an attempt to slow him. The man simply shoved Aravon, sending him staggering, and sprinted onward.

Then Aravon caught sight of a towering, black-bearded warrior. The Hilmir himself raced across the bridge, his son Bjarni at his side.

"Hilmir!" Aravon shouldered his way through the press of charging warriors. "Hilmir!" The cry set his hoarse throat aching, but he refused to stop. He *had* to turn the Fjall around before it was too late.

Throrsson was so intent on reaching his rally point deep in the woods that he barely noticed Aravon in time to avoid a collision. Anger flashed in his eyes as he skidded to a halt. "What are you doing, Captain Snarl? The plan was—"

"The plan's gone to shite!" Aravon snarled. "You need to form your shield wall here, *now!*"

"What are you talking about?" Throrsson's eyes narrowed. "What has happened?"

"Just trust me," Aravon insisted. "We need to convince the Blood Queen that we're holding this bridge."

476

A heartbeat of tense silence passed as Throrsson's ice-blue eyes locked on Aravon. Searching, burrowing deep into him, the wheels in his mind turning. Finally, after what seemed an eternity, he nodded. "By *Striith*, we hold!"

Whirling to his fleeing men, he raised his voice to a roar. "*Striithlid*, shield wall!" His booming timbre echoed loud above the tumult of the fleeing Fjall warriors. "By *Striith*, we hold the bastards here!"

A handful of Throrsson's men slowed at his call, heeding his command with an alacrity any Legion commander would envy. One by one, they formed up the shield wall, until two became five, then twenty, then a hundred and still more. With every heartbeat, the Hilmir's shouts brought more and more of his fleeing men back around to rejoin their comrades until the Fjall line solidified into a cohesive mass of warriors. Gasping, bloodied, and exhausted warriors, many bearing wounds or supporting injured companions. Yet warriors no less ready for battle.

The sight rekindled Aravon's hope. "Hold them!" he shouted to the Hilmir. "You'll know what to do!"

Throrsson growled a wordless response and turned back to his men. Though many had already fled out of sight, enough remained to form a solid shield wall. By the time Aravon returned to his place in sight of Zaharis, the Fjall battle line had swelled to fully three hundred warriors, shields locked, swords, spears, and axes held at the ready.

Triumph surged within Aravon as the Blood Queen responded precisely as he'd hoped. The Eirdkilrs slowed and stopped short of the bridge, just out of arrow range of the trees on the northern riverbank. Like any clever commander, she sensed a trap. The position was *too* perfect—a bottleneck with ample concealment to hide an army. The presence of the Fjall's shield wall formed up just north of the bridge *had* to confirm it for her.

Come on! Aravon sucked in a breath. He could almost see the *Blodsvarri's* mind working, her eyes narrowing in suspicion.

For long moments, nothing happened. The Blood Queen studied the wooden bridge, the Fjall shield wall, the sparse woods bordering the wagon road. Her Eirdkilrs remained motionless, their war cries falling silent, until it seemed the entire world stood still.

One agonizing breath, then another. Silence, so thick and oppressive Aravon felt it crushing in on him.

Take the bait, damn you!

The *Blodsvarri* moved. Without looking away from the bridge, she barked out an order, one he couldn't overhear. This was the moment of truth. Either she gave the command to fall back, or she let the tantalizing allure of the Fjall's presence entice her onward.

The Eirdkilrs moved. A single, slow step north, toward the bridge. Toward Aravon's trap.

Chapter Sixty

Triumph surged within Aravon, but he forced himself not to give in to the elation. *We still haven't pulled it off.* His eyes darted to Zaharis. The Secret Keeper still worked beneath the bridge, scraping away the reddish-brown clay and re-applying it to the supports he intended to bring down. His movements were frantic, driven by a desperate urgency to complete his task in time.

You've got this! Aravon willed Zaharis to move faster. It did no good, but it helped to ease the tension mounting within him.

The first Eirdkilr stepped onto the bridge. Silence from the Fjall warband, save for the clattering of armor and shields. More followed, ten, twenty, thirty, crossing in clusters of threes and fours. Even their towering, seven-foot-tall frames seemed dwarfed by the enormous bridge.

Just as they reached the middle of the *Fornbryggja*, the first of Skathi's arrows whistled from the cover of the forest. Two red-fletched missiles flew before Colborn's joined in and Noll answered from the opposite side of the wagon road. Before the lead Eirdkilr fell to Skathi's first missile, a dozen more arrows—including a few from Rangvaldr—sliced through the air.

Ten arrows found their marks, and eight Eirdkilrs dropped with screams, grunts, or wet, gurgling cries. A moment later, Belthar's enormous crossbow bolt sped toward the enemy and punched into them from the side. Without shields raised, packed so tightly together, the three-foot missile plowed devastation through their ranks. Five more fell beneath the hail of arrows.

Then came Belthar's roar, a mighty bellow that echoed from the trees and set the ground rumbling. That cry was echoed by hundreds of Fjall throats, and the Hilmir's warband clashed swords and axes on their shields.

Thank you, Swordsman! With the Fjall taking up the cry, the *Blodsvarri* wouldn't know that one big man with a powerful set of lungs was the only *army* baying for their blood.

The surviving Eirdkilrs on the bridge raised their massive shields against the hail of arrow fire, and quickly pulled back out of range. Aravon's jaw dropped. He'd never seen the Eirdkilrs retreat, no matter the odds. It seemed the *Blodsvarri* was far less prone to bloodlust and impulsivity than he'd given her credit for. Instead of simply throwing her men across in endless waves, she'd given the order to pull back.

His eyes sought out the Eirdkilr's leader. Her heavy, blunt features were twisted in a pensive half-snarl, half-frown. *Now what are you going to do?*

Every muscle in his body coiled tight, his breath hitching in his chest. Her actions now would decide the outcome of this battle.

For long moments, the Blood Queen remained motionless, her gaze roving across the assembled Fjall warband and the trees lining the riverbank. Aravon imagined he *felt* those eyes resting on him, but dismissed it as simply his imagination. She couldn't possibly see him in his mottled armor, tucked away behind a thick oak tree.

Come and get us, you savage!

With a snarl, the Blood Queen thrust a finger at the Fjall. "Death to the traitors!" she shouted in the guttural Eirdkilr dialect.

The howling war cry split the air, and thousands of blue-stained Eirdkilr faces twisted into barbaric snarls. Slowly, the huge figures lumbered forward, picking up speed as they crossed the hundred yards of grasslands to reach the *Fornbryggja*.

For an instant, Aravon held out hope the Blood Queen would lead the charge in true Eirdkilr and Fehlan fashion. Yet she remained unmoving, holding her place while her warriors charged past. Aravon's estimation of her rose a fraction higher. She might be an Eirdkilr, as savage and ruthless as any of her kind, yet that didn't stop her from being cautious and cunning.

That's going to make this battle a whole damned lot harder to win!

As the foremost Eirdkilrs thundered onto the wooden planks of the *Fornbryggja*, they raised shields in anticipation of the arrow storm. It never came. Doubtless Skathi had—wisely—chosen to conserve her arrows, a fact that Colborn, Noll, and Rangvaldr appeared to agree with. As did Aravon. Their actions had fulfilled their purpose.

480

The clamor of booted feet grew to a thundering roar as the Eirdkilrs raced across the bridge, setting the ground trembling. Closer they drew, packed in a tight mass of shouting, snarling, howling giants. The steel heads of two thousand axes and spears glinted bright in the sunlight, so brilliant it nearly blinded Aravon. Yet their approach held no fear for Aravon, only grim satisfaction.

Keep on coming. Aravon's eyes fixed on the bridge, on the Eirdkilrs charging across. To his surprise, the giant barbarians slowed as they reached the middle of the bridge. Instead of a headlong charge, they moved slowly, purposefully, with a cohesion any Legion company would envy. They had no need to rely on the brute force of a stampede, not against an enemy far inferior to them. Though the Hilmir's shield wall had swelled to nearly a thousand, stretching across the entire wagon road, more than four times that number marched toward them.

Aravon's gut clenched as the first Eirdkilr stepped off the bridge, onto the northern bank of the Ormrvatn River. They seemed almost *surprised* to find themselves unassailed by the army lying in wait in the forest or the Fjall warband.

One turned to two, then five, then ten, and still more. The number of Eirdkilrs swelled to fifty, a hundred, every heartbeat bringing additional reinforcements across.

Aravon's eyes snapped to Zaharis. The Secret Keeper was still moving frantically, his hands a ceaseless blur of motion as he re-applied the alchemical clay to the bridge.

It's taking too long!

Too many Eirdkilrs had already crossed the bridge. Two hundred grew to three hundred, approaching four hundred, and still Zaharis worked at a feverish pace.

Aravon waited for the Secret Keeper to turn, to seek him out for the signal, but the man was too focused on his task, leaping from spandrel to spandrel with the agility of a sailor clambering through ship's rigging. With every second, more Eirdkilrs streamed across the bridge and spread out, forming an ever-widening solid shield wall in front of the Fjall battle line.

Finally, Aravon could wait no longer. "Do it now, damn it!" he roared in Fehlan.

The Secret Keeper whirled at the sound of his voice and shot him the signal for "All good!" Then, turning back to the wooden bridge, he drew out a firestriker, lit the wooden stick, and touched it to the nearest patch of reddish-brown alchemical clay. In a heartbeat, clay caught alight, and Zaharis slithered beneath the spandrel and slid down the nearest wooden column, dropping into the water just short of the muddy riverbank.

But the Secret Keeper wasn't the only one who heard his signal. The Eirdkilrs tensed, scores of them glancing in his direction. They whirled toward the west and formed a solid wall of shields against the expected attack.

The Hilmir heard his command as well. With a roar of "For *Striith*!", he set his warband surging toward the Eirdkilrs.

The Eirdkilr shield wall—all but those who had turned to face Aravon—was ready. They met the Hilmir's charge with howls of delight and a solid wall of steel, flesh, and bone. Shields clashed on shields and the Fjall staggered, repelled by the unmoving giants, then threw themselves at the Eirdkilrs once more. Swords struck and blood sprayed. Enormous axes sheared limbs and clubs crushed helmeted skulls. Eirdkilrs' spears punched through Fjall armor and found flesh beneath. Fjall warriors hurled curses and screams at their enemies as they hacked, chopped, and thrust. The cohesion of the Hilmir's shield wall shattered in an instant. The battle degenerated to a frenzied thrashing of men crushed against each other, stabbing, punching, biting, spitting. Chaos and bloodlust reined before the *Fornbryggja*.

Aravon's eyes snapped back to the bridge's support. Zaharis was nowhere in sight, but where he'd been, a thin stream of fire trickled upward toward—

BOOM!

Fire blossomed in the bright morning light, tongues of brilliant orange and red flame that consumed a five-yard section of bridge and blasted away the supports holding up the *Fornbryggja*. Wood splintered or crumbled away to ash. The massive structure groaned beneath the weight of the Eirdkilrs. One burned plank broke away from the bridge, then a second. Gaps opened in the bridge and Eirdkilrs fell, screaming, through the opening. More and more of the *Fornbryggja* gave way, a girder collapsing without its redwood support beam. Then, like a sandcastle in the face of the ocean's waves, the center of the bridge sagged and collapsed.

Those Eirdkilrs caught atop the crumbling section fell and splashed into the fast-flowing Ormrvatn River. Crashed atop the sharp stones, spraying blood and shattering bones. Screaming, crying, shouting, they were sucked under the current and dragged downriver.

The weight of the Eirdkilrs atop the bridge brought down larger sections, and dozens more, locked in step with their companions, plummeted into the icy river or onto the jagged rocks. Rivulets of red threaded the white-churned surface of the Ormrvatn, a grisly companion to the fur-clad, armored bodies being towed away and dashed against the river's stones.

But Zaharis' alchemical fire hadn't just brought down the bridge. The concussive blast staggered the Eirdkilrs nearest the explosion, sending them stumbling into their companions. Those on the southern side of the ruined bridge simply fell, bringing down the Eirdkilrs marching behind them, or toppled off the crumbling wooden planks. Those on the north side jostled their comrades in the shield wall facing the Fjall, throwing them off-balance. For a heartbeat, the cohesion of the Eirdkilr line shattered.

That moment was all the Hilmir needed. With a roar, he drove forward into the gap, hewing about him with his steel longsword, bashing in Eirdkilr faces with his shield. Blood sprayed around him, misting in the air as he opened Eirdkilr throats and sheared limbs. Beside him, Bjarni and Sigbrand hurled themselves into the momentary opening, widening the gap. More and more Fjall warriors seized the moment. The Eirdkilrs, caught off-guard by the blast and crumbling bridge, faltered. The ferocity of Throrsson's attack pushed them back a single step. A step that cost the rearmost their lives. Eirdkilrs were shoved off the crumbled bridge by their retreating companions. Another step, and more fur-clad barbarians fell to be swept away by the fast-flowing current or drowning in the river's icy embrace.

Black-shafted arrows whistled across the river and rained down onto the Fjall—and the backs of the last surviving Eirdkilrs. Hundreds of Eirdkilr archers loosed shafts, turning the air dark. Steel-tipped missiles clattered into the earth, *thunked* into the trunks of the trees, or found Fehlan flesh. Men screamed and died on both sides of the battle.

But the Blood Queen's fury lacked real teeth. Fewer than a dozen of the Hilmir's warriors fell before they locked shields, forming a defensive carapace— a tactic they'd adopted from the Legion of Heroes. Clattering chaos rang out across the river as the Eirdkilr arrows thumped into upraised Fehlan shields, punched through leather or *spanged* off iron and steel rims. Even as the Eirdkilrs on the northern side of the bridge fell to the plunging fire, the Fjall warriors slowly gave ground, retreating from the bridge, out of range of the Eirdkilr bows and into the safety of the trees.

The Eirdkilrs' howls of rage echoed loud across the Fjall grasslands, the *Blodsvarri's* loudest of all. Yet the cries rang hollow, an empty waste of breath beneath the glow of victory that burned bright within Aravon. The Fjall answered back with insults and jeers, raising their voice in the Fjall song of triumph.

Aravon sought out the *Blodsvarri* and found her eyes locked on him. Even from this distance, he could feel the hate emanating from within her.

Smiling beneath his mask, Aravon swept a bow that would have been at home in Prince Toran's court. When he straightened, the anger in her wild, frenzied eyes burned brighter than Zaharis' alchemical explosion.

That made victory all the sweeter.

Chapter Sixty-One

"The cowards!" Eirik Throrsson roared. He slammed a fist into a nearby sapling. Wood splintered beneath the force of the blow and the trunk snapped, bringing the young alder tree crashing down at his feet. "The eel-spined, limp-kneed, white-livered, dung-swilling cringelings!"

"Sounds like he's winding down," Colborn signed behind the Hilmir's back.

Aravon's lips twisted behind his mask, but he said nothing. The Hilmir's tirade against the Deid had lasted for the better part of five minutes, and his shouts doubtless echoed all the way back to Jarltun deep in Deid territory. Perhaps even those south of the Sawtooth Mountains had overheard the diatribe of Fehlan curses—many far too creative for Aravon's grasp of the language to comprehend.

And his rage was justified. The Deid's retreat had cost them a critical opportunity. Instead of taking down a quarter of the Blood Queen's forces as originally planned, the Eirdkilr casualties had numbered fewer than eight hundred. The attack at the *Fornbryggja* had cost the enemy, but the Fjall paid a steep toll as well. Close to one hundred and fifty of the Hilmir's warriors lay dead at the bridge crossing, felled by Eirdkilr axes, spears, clubs, and arrows. Only Zaharis' alchemical marvels had prevented what should have been a decisive victory from turning into bloody defeat.

But now, with fewer than fifteen hundred soldiers—five hundred of whom bore wounds, many grievous—the Hilmir found himself in a dire predicament. A predicament from which Aravon hadn't yet figured a path to escape, even now, an hour after the sun had set and evening descended on the Fjall forests.

"Get me close enough to that gutless Hafgrimsson," Throrsson raged, "and I will snap his spine, rip it from his body, and feed it to him up the arse. Then maybe he'll begin to understand what a damned fool he was to pull back when we had the Blood Queen by the short-hairs!"

"But at least the day's attack was not an utter failure, Father." Bjarni spoke up from where he sat nursing a shallow wound on his left shoulder. "The *Tauld* suffered far heavier losses than we did." He wiped away a trickle of blood leaking from a gash in his forehead—the wound had already begun to purple, but his face was a stoic mask that revealed no pain. All trace of the Wraithfever had gone as well. The Duke's cure had worked.

The rage burning in Throrsson's eyes didn't fade, but at least his invectives slowed to a growling trickle. Finally, he let out a long breath and turned to the young warrior. "You are right, my son. Not a complete loss." He turned to Aravon. "How high do you estimate the enemy's casualties?"

Aravon frowned in thought. "Between the attack on Storbjarg, the ambush on the road, and the bridge collapse," he said after a moment, "I'd say they lost more than two thousand. Perhaps as many as twenty-five hundred."

"Hmmph." The Hilmir's grunt almost sounded pleased. "It could have gone worse."

Aravon seized on the momentary lull in the Hilmir's anger. "Unless the *Blodsvarri* can summon reinforcements from deep within *Tauld*-held lands," Aravon said, "she's got only the three thousand or so marching at her back." He'd estimated her total strength at close to thirty-five hundred. "And, given the situation at Storbjarg, I feel confident to say that she *won't* risk pulling out the men holding the city."

"Indeed." Throrsson's bushy eyebrows bunched together, a frown deepening his brow. "If she tried to pull those men out of Storbjarg, they would have my warband snarling at their backs."

What's left of it, Aravon thought, but didn't say. Invading cities was bloody work, and the aggressors always paid a high cost in lives when trying to take well-fortified cities. Doubtless the Blood Queen's casualties had been high, the Fjall forcing them to bleed for every inch of ground they gained. Yet four thousand Eirdkilrs faced only three thousand Fjall—even fighting for their homes and families, the Fehlan warriors battling in the city streets would take heavy losses. Setting fire to the city created havoc and forced the Fjall to try and protect the citizens as well as repel the Eirdkilr invasion. The Eirdkilrs had

486

burned Storbjarg to confound the defenders, and now, there was no sign of the warriors the Hilmir had left to guard his city.

We're on our own, Aravon thought, a grim mood settling onto his shoulders.

"The Blood Queen's forces *only* outnumber us two to one." Throrsson's voice was a growl, as bestial as the black bear to whom his fur cloak had once belonged. "All because of the craven Deid!"

"So we start evening the odds." Aravon spoke quickly before the Hilmir could unleash another long-winded tirade against Hafgrimsson and his warriors. "We whittle down their forces, one man at a time, if we have to. Fight like *they* do."

Throrsson narrowed his eyes. "Battle from the shadows." He stroked his braided beard with one huge, hairy hand, setting the beads and bones rattling. "Ambushes and traps."

"Precisely." Aravon paced around the small camp, his mind working at the problem. "My men are watching the Blood Queen's men at the bridge, and they tell me she'll be across by midnight." He shot a glance at Colborn, who nodded confirmation. "So when she gets across, let's make sure she follows us. And that she bleeds every step of the way."

"Follows us to *where?*" The Hilmir scowled. "Our plan to meet her in open battle at Dreyrugrakr only worked because we had the Deid at our backs. And it relied on the enemy taking heavier losses at the *Fornbryggja.*"

Aravon frowned. Their original strategy would have ended with a pitched battle at the broad, flat expanse known as the Bloodstained Field, where the superior numbers and maneuverability of the combined Deid and Fjall forces gave them a fighting chance against the Blood Queen. Yet now, with only the Fjall, they couldn't hope to meet twice their number of Eirdkilrs out in the open. At least, not at Dreyrugrakr.

The problem was, Aravon didn't know the Fjall lands well enough to suggest an alternative battle site. Throrsson's question made it clear *he* didn't have a better solution, either.

To Aravon's surprise, Colborn spoke up. "I know a place."

Aravon and Throrsson both turned to face the Lieutenant. "Where?" Aravon asked.

"*Banamadrhaed.*" Colborn's voice was solemn, his expression grave.

Aravon frowned. *Why do I know that name?* He could have sworn he had encountered it in his lessons of military history, but its significance escaped him.

"Or," Colborn said quietly, "as it is known among the Princelanders, Hangman's Hill."

Aravon's eyebrows shot up. *Of course!*

All in Fehl knew of Hangman's Hill, but it held special significance to the Deid and Fjall in particular. It was there, on the steep slopes of *Banamadrhaed* that the Deid stood in open battle against the Fjall and, for the first time in more than a hundred years, carried the day. Aravon's father and Duke Dyrund had been at Hangman's Hill that day—as privates in their first proper battle—as the Legion fought on the side of their Deid allies. Together, Princelanders and Deid carried the day, though not without heavy losses on both sides. So heavy, in fact, that Throrsson's grandfather, Arvid Jorundsson, hadn't had enough of his warband to protect his southern lands from the Eirdkilr attacks.

Throrsson's jaw muscles worked. "Hangman's Hill." His face tightened at the name, as to be expected from a proud Fjall warrior. As the Duke had explained on their travels, that loss at *Banamadrhaed* was considered by the Fjall to be the worst defeat in recent history—worse even than the Battle of Vigvollr.

Yet mention of the battleground set Aravon's thoughts churning. He went over everything he'd read about the battleground, the tactics employed by the Fjall, Deid, and Legionnaires. Though he had never been there in person, Lectern Harald had referred to it numerous times when teaching Aravon the power of small-force tactics. In fact, it was a small company of Legion cavalry— less than a hundred strong—that had turned the tide of battle. A fact the Lectern had drilled home during his lessons back at Camp Marshal.

It didn't matter that he'd never seen the battlefield with his own eyes— he'd heard it described and depicted so many times he knew every inch of that hillside and the surrounding marshlands, forests, and the river at its back. And it came with an added bonus: it was disputed territory, claimed by both the Fjall and Deid.

Aravon's mind raced. "The steepness of the hill *would* give us an advantage. And, with the marshes on our left flank and the river at our back and right flanks, we wouldn't have to worry about being encircled."

"There would also be no way of escape should the battle turn against us." The Hilmir's eyes were dark, grim. "We could not retreat."

488

One of Lectern Harald's lessons on battle strategy flashed through Aravon's mind. "And the Blood Queen will know that," Aravon said. "A fact that we'll use against her."

Raising an eyebrow, Throrsson leaned forward. "Explain." He tugged at his beard, running his fingers through the braids as he listened.

"The only way we get to choose the battleground is if we make the *Blodsvarri* think *she* chose it." A wry grin twisted Aravon's lips behind his mask. "My wife loves to remind me that all of my best ideas are, in fact, *her* ideas, simply presented in a way that I believe that they originated with me."

Despite the burning intensity in his eyes, the Hilmir actually chuckled. "My Asleif says that she is 'the fist of iron wrapped in ermine fur'." A smile cracked his solemn facade. "Even the mightiest warrior may find his actions directed by the invisible hand of a clever woman."

Aravon pushed back against the feelings of homesickness that came whenever he thought of Mylena, the desire to see her once more, to sweep her and his sons, Rolyn and Adilon, into a fierce embrace. He had no time for the sorrow and longing; they had battles to plan, enemies to defeat.

"Precisely." Aravon nodded. "So we're going to make the Blood Queen think she's pushing us back, forcing us to retreat. Farther and farther north, until we are left with no choice but to make a desperate last stand."

Throrsson's eyes narrowed. "Clever." He tugged at one of his beard braids, pulled lose a twig that had been stuck there for hours and cast it aside. "And, by harrying her advance every step of the way, we force her to keep following us. Keep pushing us backward."

"Many an army's advance has been turned to ruin by an active defense." Lectern Harald's words echoed in Aravon's mind. "They'll be moving quickly, trying to catch up to us, which gives us multiple opportunities to hit them hard with counterattacks and ambushes." He glanced at Colborn. "We keep them on their heels, keep the initiative in our favor, force them to advance more slowly. All the while, we keep the *Blodsvarri* engaged and focused on us while we set up a proper defense at Hangman's Hill."

Colborn remained silent a long moment, his eyes narrowed in thought. Finally, he nodded. "It'll take more than just a few small sneak attacks to keep the Blood Queen hot on our heels. We'll need to make it look like we're desperate, throwing everything we can in an attempt to slow her down."

"How many men, Ghoststriker?" Aravon used Colborn's code name.

Again, a moment of contemplative silence before Colborn answered. "Five, maybe six hundred."

"That is nearly half my warband!" Throrsson growled. "Dividing our forces is a risky gamble against so many enemies."

"But what would *sigra* demand in a match of hnenfatafl?" Colborn straightened, facing up to the Hilmir. He was only an inch shorter and equally broad in the chest, his blond beard and hair a stark contrast to the Hilmir's shaggy black locks. Yet his voice rang with the conviction and confidence of a Legion officer—of a man like Duke Dyrund. "A true victor takes decisive action in the face of impossible odds."

Throrsson met the Lieutenant's eyes, their gazes locked. For a moment, Aravon was struck by the Hilmir's resemblance to the black bear whose pelt he wore, just as Colborn's strength and leather mask appeared like a snarling greatwolf. Two powerful men in a silent battle of wills—neither enemies nor friends, but two warriors and equals.

Long seconds of tense silence stretched on, but finally Throrsson nodded. "It is a good plan."

"And I'll need two hundred more to watch our flanks," Colborn said without hesitation, "to stop the *Blodsvarri's* scouts from getting around our position."

"Anything else?" Throrsson snorted. "Perhaps a night in the Hilmir's bed or a seat of honor at the head of my table?"

"I'll settle for your son." Colborn's voice held a note of quiet self-assurance.

Throrsson's bushy eyebrows shot up, his face going purple. He opened his mouth, doubtless to unleash his rage on Colborn, but the Lieutenant spoke first.

"The Blood Queen needs to believe our defensive assaults are real." Colborn gestured to Bjarni. "She knows you're wounded, so it would make sense that your son stands in your place."

A sly plan took shape in Aravon's mind. "And we *convince* her that you're too weak to fight." He rounded on Colborn and Bjarni. "Let ambush and counterattack ring with cries of vengeance for the Hilmir's death."

Surprise flashed across Throrsson's heavy face. Then, a slow laugh boomed from his massive chest. "I have always wondered how my men would feel after my death."

"We will be suitably infuriated and aggressive, Father." Bjarni's grin mirrored Throrsson's. "I will personally lead the assault to claim the Blood Queen's head."

"Between the fighting retreat and the greatly exaggerated rumors of your death," Aravon said, "the Blood Queen will believe her victory all but assured." He turned to Bjarni. "After all, she will believe herself far more cunning than the Hilmir's young son."

"Especially if we sell it," Colborn added. "A few ambushes that don't quite go off without a hitch, or a counterattack that gets bogged down just a second or three too long." He shot Bjarni a confident glance. "Think you can pull off 'enraged hothead'?"

Bjarni drew himself up to his full height, his expression grandiose. "I am my father's son." A smile cracked his hauteur. "To hear my mother speak, enraged hothead should be the family emblem."

"Careful, Bjarni," Throrsson growled. "You are not so strong and I am not so old that I will hesitate to lay you across my knee and thrash you as I once did." He gestured around. "There is a convenient abundance of willow switches at hand."

Bjarni didn't exactly flinch, but his jests at his father's expense fell silent.

Aravon and Colborn exchanged amused glances.

"Think you can pull it off?" Aravon signed in the Secret Keeper hand language.

"Have to try, don't I?" Colborn replied. *"Only way we get through this alive."*

"Then let it be so." Throrsson's booming voice echoed through the forest clearing. He clapped a huge hand on his son's shoulders. "Take Sigbrand, my son. He will guide and guard you in the battle to come."

"Thank you, Father." Bjarni turned to face his father. "For trusting me to do this."

Throrsson embraced his son. "You have already returned from certain death once. If *Striith* chooses to take you now, I will send you to *Seggrholl* knowing you were a true man of the Fjall."

Bjarni returned the fierce hug. "I will make you proud."

A lump rose in Aravon's throat and his eyes slid away. The sight brought back memories of his own father and Duke Dyrund—painful for two entirely different reasons.

491

He swallowed his emotions as Bjarni left his father's side and hurried toward the hastily-erected Fjall torchlit war camp to gather his men.

Throrsson turned to Colborn. "Sigbrand is a proud warrior and a true son of the Fjall, but if I instruct it, he will accede to your orders."

"Thank you, Hilmir." Colborn held out a hand to the Fjall chief. "I'm honored by your trust."

Throrsson clasped Colborn's hand. "It is a shame that not all men of the Deid are like you, Ghoststriker."

The words froze Colborn. He seemed paralyzed, unable to move or speak—likely due to Throrsson's identifying him as Deid.

"Your father must have been a true warrior to produce a man like you." The Hilmir gave Colborn a warm smile. "If only *you* had led the Deid warband in place of Hafgrimsson, perhaps we would not find ourselves in such dire straits."

Aravon saw the slight tightening in Colborn's armored shoulders, the sudden stiffness of his spine. When he broke off the clasp, a shadow turned his eyes dark. "Thank you, Hilmir." The words were courteous, but ice tinged Colborn's voice at the mention of his father. What Throrsson intended as praise was nothing but a reminder of the cruel bastard that had tormented and hated Colborn his entire life.

Throrsson's eyes narrowed as he watched the Lieutenant stalk through the camp. "Strange to find such a compliment causing offense." He shot a curious glance at Aravon. "Is he *not* of the Deid? His words and accent—"

"He is Deid, but…" Aravon hesitated, uncertain how much of Colborn's story to share. Not only because of the secrecy of their existence, the reason they wore the leather masks, but also because it was Colborn's story, not his. If the Lieutenant wanted Throrsson to know, he would have spoken up.

Throrsson raised a knowing eyebrow. "Ahh, a complicated history, yes?"

Aravon nodded.

The Hilmir chuckled. "Not all men are born into this world fortunate. Some to poverty, others to hunger, others to infirmity." He gave a bitter shake of his head. "Others to men who were *never* meant to be fathers."

Aravon turned a surprised look on Throrsson. That was the last thing he'd expected to hear from a man like the Hilmir, the most powerful warrior and chief on Fehl.

Throrsson gave a little shrug. "Taking on the title of Hilmir was not my only way to cast off my father's shadow." He cast a glance after Bjarni, who had disappeared into the camp. "Every day, the memory of Thror Arvidsson reminds me that I must be better. A better man, a better warrior, and a better father to my children." Darkness clouded his face, his lips twisting into a frown. "Both of them."

Aravon could *feel* the pain radiating from the huge Fjall warrior. Such a difficult choice—to use the Wraithfever cure to save his son *or* his daughter, but not both—would be enough to weigh heavy on even the strongest of men.

"A choice no one would envy." Aravon rested a hand on the Hilmir's massive shoulder. "Yet only a true father, a true *man,* feels that pain."

The Hilmir turned a sad look on Aravon. "I never had a chance…" He swallowed. "A chance to tell Branda I was sorry. For choosing Bjarni."

"She knew." Aravon's voice was quiet, kind. "She *had* to."

A moment of silence stretched between them, broken when Throrsson roughly brushed a hand across his face—scrubbing away tears Aravon purposely *didn't* see. "Well, Captain Snarl, I must find Sigbrand and speak with him, relay my orders regarding your Ghoststriker. Tired or not, my men and I march to Hangman's Hill within the hour." He held out a hand. "Give us two days, and we will be ready for the Blood Queen. The bitch will pay for every Fjall life she has claimed."

Aravon clasped Throrsson's forearm. "Two days, Hilmir. Until we meet in battle once more."

With a chuckle, the Hilmir turned and strode away—off to make the preparations that would mean the difference between triumph or defeat at Hangman's Hill.

493

Chapter Sixty-Two

"Ghoststriker!" Aravon caught up to Colborn at the southern edge of the Fjall camp. The Lieutenant was mounted, his bags packed and tied to his saddle.

Colborn looked back at the sound of his code name and reined in. "Captain?"

"A word." Aravon thrust his head toward the dark, empty forest a short distance away.

Colborn's eyes narrowed but, without a word, he dismounted and followed Aravon a few dozen yards into the wood. Only once they had traveled out of sight of the Fjall war camp did Aravon stop. Reaching up, he untied the straps that held his leather mask in place. "Swordsman's grace, that's good!" He sighed in relief and scratched the itch that had been bothering him through the entire conversation with the Hilmir.

Colborn cocked his head. "What is it, Captain?"

Aravon gestured to the man's leather mask. "Take it off."

"Sir?"

"The mask, Colborn." Aravon insisted. "We need to talk face to face."

With stiff, slow movements, Colborn removed his mask. His face was a stony mask, his eyes flat and hard.

"Are you up for this?" Aravon asked.

"Of course, Captain." Irritation flashed in Colborn's eyes. "I don't know why you'd a—"

"With everything that's been going on," Aravon said, "I haven't had a chance to talk since the night before the Waeggbjod."

Colborn's jaw muscles worked, his brow furrowing.

Aravon shook his head. "I'm not doubting you. That's not what this is." He fixed the Lieutenant with a piercing gaze. "Everything else going on, if you take it with you, it could get you or the others killed. Just tell me your mind's on the mission and your head's on straight, and we're good."

Colborn hesitated, but only for a heartbeat. "Eyes sharp, mind clear, Captain."

Aravon searched the man's eyes, the hints of emotion revealed by the tightness of his expression. Despite the shadows that darkened his eyes, the result of the Hilmir's intended compliment, Colborn seemed less troubled than he had before the Waeggbjod. It seemed that night on the hill had given him a measure of closure, brought peace to the turmoil raging within him.

"Good." Aravon nodded and clapped the man on the shoulder. "That's all I needed to know."

Colborn's eyes narrowed. "And you, sir?" he asked quietly. "You got everything in hand? We're all worried about the Duke, but..." He trailed off with a shrug. "Your plan's solid, but I figured I'd ask."

Aravon opened his mouth to reply, to reassure Colborn, but stopped. He spent a moment in internal analysis, probing his own emotions and feelings on all that had happened. The soldiers under his command deserved the respect of a truthful answer.

"Honestly," he finally said, "I've kept my mind focused on the matter at hand just to keep myself from thinking about the Duke. I haven't let myself believe that he really *could* be dead somewhere in Storbjarg, and I won't until this battle's done." He let out a long breath, trying to expel the dread growing within him. "Best I can do is promise to try not to let it cloud my judgement or make me do anything stupid."

A little smile tugged at Colborn's lips. "Best any of us could ask for, Captain."

With a nod, Aravon replaced his mask. "Then let's go rejoin the others. We've got a Blood Queen to piss off."

* * *

496

Aravon crouched in the shadows of the forest, his eyes fixed on the Eirdkilrs hard at work repairing the *Fornbryggja*. *Keeper's teeth!* He growled a silent curse. *They'll have that finished and start crossing before midnight.*

The Eirdkilrs had hewn logs—backtracking south the better part of two miles for lumber—and hauled the materials to the crumbled wooden bridge. Their "repair" was crude at best, little more than massive trunks bound together with rough hempen rope and strips of hide. Yet even crude proved effective. Zaharis' destructive blast had only brought down a section of the bridge twenty yards long. The towering cypress trees more than spanned the gap, which meant the attack had only stalled the Eirdkilrs, not stopped them.

He clung to the hope that the Blood Queen would cross her entire force of thirty-five hundred before marching after the Fjall, which meant the bulk of her forces wouldn't set off until nearly daybreak.

But, even if the main Eirdkilr body didn't march immediately, doubtless they'd send scouts or skirmishers in pursuit of the Hilmir and his men. It was Aravon's job to make sure that advanced force found only the Fjall warriors marching with Bjarni and Sigbrand. A force that even now was working with Colborn to prepare a nasty surprise two miles north of the bridge.

Aravon turned to his men. "*Skathi, Belthar,*" he signed, "*stay here and keep an eye on things. Colborn will have Fjall up here to cover for you in an hour. When they arrive, get to the ambush spot and see what needs doing.*"

Both nodded and returned to watching the Eirdkilrs.

"*Zaharis,*" Aravon found the Secret Keeper crouched in the shadows beyond Skathi, "*Colborn needs you for, as he said, 'something bloody devious'. Follow the trail and take the first fork to the east. You'll find him at the stream two miles north.*"

"*Yes, Captain.*" With barely a rustle of leaves, Zaharis slipped into the forest and out of sight, hidden in the deep shadows of darkness.

"*Noll, Rangvaldr, with me.*" Aravon jerked his head to where the horses stood waiting, their reins looped around a low-hanging birch branch.

Exchanging curious glances, the little scout and the *Seiomenn* broke from cover and followed him back to their mounts. Once well out of enemy earshot, Aravon filled the two in on the plan to lure the Blood Queen to Hangman's Hill.

"Sounds like a good plan." Rangvaldr nodded. "I visited Hangman's Hill once, many years ago. A good place to make our stand."

497

"Especially if we can whittle them down a lot at a time." Noll rubbed his hands together. "I can't wait to see what sort of fun Colborn's got Zaharis cooking up for them."

Aravon shook his head. "Sadly, you'll miss out on the show. For us to have any hope of survival, I need the two of you for very specific tasks."

Chapter Sixty-Three

Just a little closer. Aravon's eyes tracked the small company of Eirdkilr skirmishers slipping through the early morning mists. The towering barbarians kept low, creeping swiftly through the ravine, careful to avoid the water trickling among the smooth stones that littered the creek bed. The mud walls sloped upward only ten feet from the creek, offering easy concealment for the fast-moving barbarians.

A mile west of their position, Bjarni, Sigbrand, and five hundred of the Fjall were making enough noise on their retreat that the blindest, deafest cretin on Fehl could follow them. Even from this distance, Aravon could hear the enraged shouts as the Hilmir's son sold the ruse of his death from battle wounds. The cunning *Blodsvarri*, wary of more surprises after yesterday's battle, had sent teams of skirmishers and scouts to flank the Fjall position and assess the Hilmir's forces.

Unfortunately for the Eirdkilrs sneaking along beside the creek below, Colborn had expected the maneuver. At any minute, the Lieutenant would be springing his own trap on the scouts sent to circle the western edge of Bjarni's force. It fell to Aravon to ensure this particular ambush went off without a hitch.

Ten yards, he counted silently. *Five. Four. Three, two, one.*

"Now!" he roared in Fehlan.

The Eirdkilrs were no fools or cowards caught off-guard. All forty whirled toward the sound of Aravon's voice, shields raised, boots splashing in the creek as they turned to face the enemy. Raising shields, spears, axes, and clubs, they braced for the charge.

But Aravon's position on the western bank of the ravine was just one more ruse. Fifty Fehlan warriors burst from the eastern bank and hurled fist-sized stones at the enemy below. Rocks, hurled with all the force of the Fjall's fury and strength, pelted the Eirdkilrs' backs, legs, and helmeted heads. The massive, blue-painted barbarians staggered beneath the onslaught from the rear. Ten fell, stunned and dazed.

With a roar of "Avenge the Hilmir!", the Fjall warriors threw themselves into the ravine. Down the muddy walls, sliding and skidding, straight into the off-balance Eirdkilrs. The barbarians barely had time to turn and raise shields before the Fjall hit them.

Fehlan and Eirdkilr shields *clashed* as the smaller warriors threw themselves against their larger, less numerous enemies. The Eirdkilrs, off-balance, struggled to recover and mount a cohesive defense. A dozen fell in the initial vicious onslaught, cut down by Fjall axes and swords. Even as the survivors raised weapons and struck back, the Fjall spread out to encircle them.

Aravon leapt out of his hiding place and raced south along the ravine. He had none of Zaharis' tricks to deal with this group—Colborn had needed the Secret Keeper's help setting up a particularly vicious ambush—which left him, Skathi, and Belthar to deal with any surprises.

Despite being caught off-guard, the Eirdkilrs held their own. The lumbering warriors stood a full head taller than their Fehlan cousins, their weapons far heavier and backed by the force of powerful Eirdkilr muscles. Shouts, cries, and Eirdkilr war cries resounded through the forest. Blood sprayed, men screamed, and blue-stained faces split into savage grins as the first Fjall warriors fell. Axes *crunched* through Fehlans shields, one shattering the arm beneath. An Eirdkilr spear found an exposed Fehlan throat and crimson misted in the morning air. In the space of ten seconds, the stream grew red with Eirdkilr and Fjall blood, the ravine's walls churned to gruesome mud beneath heavy boots.

But the initial assault had taken a heavy toll. The ten brought down beneath the hail of stones never rose—five Fjall warriors with sharp spears saw to that. More fell as the Fjall surrounded them, like a pack of wolves nipping at enormous wasteland icebears. One Eirdkilr corpse splashed into the creek, then another. The howling, barbaric cries grew quieter as fewer throats remained to take up the call. Less than a minute after Aravon's shout, only fifteen Eirdkilrs still stood, facing forty-five determined Fjall.

Crouched behind a thick alder tree, Aravon watched the battle in the creek with one eye and the ravine to the south with the other. He wouldn't put it past the *Blodsvarri* to send a second company of skirmishers close behind the first, or set more scouts to watch. They couldn't take *any* chances with this fight.

Then came the high-pitched whistle he'd dreaded. *Keeper's teeth, I hate being right!*

Two figures burst from the trees on the opposite bank of the ravine.

"Forty more, two hundred yards back," Skathi signed as she raced north, the huge Belthar hot on her heels. *"They're coming fast!"*

"Be ready," Aravon signed.

With a nod, the archer ducked into the trees and disappeared from Aravon's view. Belthar, however, didn't follow. Instead, the big man raced northward, stopping only ten yards south of the embattled Fjall and Eirdkilrs. In the shadows of a huge, brightly-colored maple tree, he knelt and set about cocking his enormous crossbow.

Of the six Odarian steel-tipped bolts he'd brought from Camp Marshal, only two remained in Belthar's quiver. Skathi's superstition seemed to have rubbed off on him; he'd insisted that the archer help him fashion new bolts—little more than wrist-thick sticks three feet long, with crude fletching and fire-hardened tips—rather than loose his last missile. Yet, in this battle, he wouldn't need accuracy over a long range. Power was all that mattered in such close proximity.

The sound of splashing grew louder, accompanied by the clatter of weapons and the high-pitched *clinking* of chain mail shirts. Aravon glanced to the south, spotted the huge figures racing up the creek toward him. Behind him, the cries of the dying Eirdkilrs mingled with the enraged shouts of the Fjall warriors. When Aravon turned, he found the Fjall had all but finished off their enemy. Five Eirdkilrs remained, surrounded by forty of the original fifty Fehlan warriors. A quick glance revealed five Fjall down for good—throats slashed, skulls crushed, or limbs sheared—with another five bearing wounds ranging from slashing cuts to, in the case of one unlucky Fjall, a caved-in chest.

Aravon's jaw clenched, knots of tension forming in his stomach. *This had better work!* If it didn't, the Fjall would find themselves outnumbered, with no easy escape.

His eyes tracked the Eirdkilrs' movement. Closer they came, picking their way along the ravine, leaping over water-smoothed stones and muddy patches of ground. They broke into delighted howls as they spotted the Fjall, howls that grew angry at the sight of the Eirdkilr corpses piled in the ravine.

The Fjall turned to face the new threat, and they, too, gave voice to their rage. Rage at the loss of their home, the "death" of their Hilmir, and the suffering they'd endured at the hands of the Eirdkilrs for years. Clashing swords and shields, they charged south down the ravine toward the oncoming barbarians.

Aravon's gut clenched. *Slow it down!* The Fjall were running as fast as they could, covering ground quickly in their haste to close with their enemy. His eyes snapped to the bend in the river that had been set as the mark. A few quick calculations, and dread sank like a stone in his stomach.

They're moving too fast. Yet he could do nothing but watch, trapped in his position, as the Fjall and Eirdkilrs closed.

Finally, he could wait no longer. The foremost Eirdkilrs drew within spitting distance of the designated spot, and Aravon *had* to strike. If he didn't, the Fjall would end up caught in their own trap.

He didn't shout—he trusted Skathi to analyze the situation and react as he did—but simply whirled and struck. His spearhead glinted in the dappled forest light and Odarian steel sheared through rope, bit into wood with a loud *thunk*. A moment later, an ear-splitting *crack* echoed through the forest. One crack turned to two, then five, then more, growing louder as the pre-sawn tree collapsed.

Right on top of the Eirdkilrs. The immense weight of the oak tree slammed atop the enormous fur-clad figures, crushing them to the ground with pulverizing force. Ten Eirdkilrs were turned to pulp beneath the toppling tree.

But the trap hadn't been sprung without a hitch. The oak slammed into the front of the line, not the center as he'd intended. Instead of splitting their line into even halves, five Eirdkilrs were cut off by the trees behind them to face the charging Fjall, while more than twenty remained south of the collapsed tree.

Skathi's oak tree collapsed a heartbeat later, crushing another five Eirdkilrs at the far rear of the line. Far too few. The ambush, intended to demolish the rearmost Eirdkilrs and leave the foremost twenty arrayed against the Fjall's forty, had only slowed the Eirdkilrs and taken a few casualties. Nowhere near enough. The five Eirdkilrs north of the felled trees died beneath the Fjall's onslaught, but twenty-five trapped between the two fallen oaks were unharmed.

Five arrows whistled from the forest in quick succession, slamming into the clustered Eirdkilrs. One took an Eirdkilr in the throat and the huge barbarian fell, blood gushing over his filthy white icebear pelt. Another collapsed with an arrow driven deep into his eye socket. But the remaining three slammed into upraised Eirdkilr shields or *pinged* off their steel skullcaps.

Then Belthar charged out of the forest. Five lumbering steps, then he knelt, aimed his massive crossbow, and pulled the trigger. The loud *whomph* of the bow's arms snapping forward was followed a moment later by a piercing shriek as the three-foot bolt drove through an Eirdkilr shield and deep into the chest of the man beneath.

But more Eirdkilrs remained—blocked from reaching the Fjall by the huge oaks, yet unharmed. Aravon's gut clenched as their battle cries split the air and they surged up the shallow, muddy walls of the ravine. Right toward Belthar.

With slow, deliberate movements, the big man set down his crossbow and unslung the enormous axe from its hook on his back. The snarling wolf mask hid his face, but Aravon would have sworn a smile broadened Belthar's face as he rolled his head and loosened his shoulder muscles.

"Avenge the Hilmir!" he shouted in thickly accented Fehlan.

He met the first charging Eirdkilr with cool calm. The double-bladed head of his enormous axe knocked aside a thrusting spear and bit deep into the side of the barbarian's neck, plowing devastation through the man's collarbone and ribs. Blood sprayed as he tore the axe free, spun, and slammed the crimson-stained edge into the next Eirdkilr's shield. The barbarian cried out as Odarian steel chopped through tough hide, wooden planks, and the fur-covered arm beneath. A savage kick to the Eirdkilr's chest sent him stumbling backward.

Then the first of the Eirdkilrs clambered up the ravine walls on Aravon's side. Tearing his spear free of the tree, Aravon raced the three steps to where the barbarian was hauling himself up onto the grassy bank. With a snarl on his lips, Aravon drove the sharp spearhead straight into the man's chest. Chain links *snapped* beneath the thrust. Steel sliced through leather, furs, flesh, and bone. The Eirdkilr gave a weak gasp and fell back, dark red gushing from his chest.

Two more Eirdkilrs scrambled out of the ravine and onto firm ground before he could tear his spear free. Bestial howls of delight burst from their throats as they swung enormous, iron-studded clubs at him. In desperation, Aravon ripped his spear from the Eirdkilr's corpse and leapt back, barely avoiding the skull-crushing blows. His foot caught on a mound of earth and he fell, hard. Acting on instinct, he threw himself into a backward roll and came to his feet. Barely in time to bat aside a club swinging for his head. Too slow to dodge the low strike.

Pain flared through his thigh. The force of the blow sent him staggering to the side, off-balance. He slammed into a solid tree trunk hard enough to knock the breath from his lungs, rebounded, and lashed out with a wild, slashing strike of his spear. The sharp tip tore a gouge out of one Eirdkilr's cheek and bit through the other's ear, *spanging* off his skullcap.

The wounds did nothing to slow the Eirdkilrs. With savage ferocity, they swung their heavy clubs at his head, chest, legs, arms, spear—anything to bring him down. It was all he could do to dodge and duck the strikes; without a shield to block, he had only his spear for defense. He had to regain his balance, take control of the combat before one of those crushing blows landed.

Another desperate strike, and this one struck home in an Eirdkilr's throat, tearing flesh and cartilage. The barbarian gurgled, gasping as blood gushed from the torn vein in his neck. Hot, wet crimson pelted his mask and splattered the face of the second Eirdkilr. In the instant the barbarian blinked to clear the blood from his eyes, Aravon brought the iron-shod butt of his spear around and slammed it into the man's knee. Bone *crunched* and the Eirdkilr shrieked in agony. Before he could fall, Aravon whirled the spear around once and drove the sharp tip up, beneath the man's chin, into his brain. The screams fell silent. The Eirdkilr flopped to the ground, limp, eyes wide and lifeless.

A loud cry from a few feet away brought Aravon whirling around, in time to find the Fjall warriors finishing off the last of the Eirdkilrs. The smaller, more compact Fehlans had scrambled out of the ravine far faster than their enemies. On the far side of the ravine, a panting, bloodied Belthar tore his axe free of an Eirdkilr's skull.

Aravon's mind raced. *Let's hope that's the last of—*

A shout of alarm from behind Belthar shattered his thoughts. Loud *crashing* sounds, like heavy bodies stampeding through dense forests, echoed from the east. A moment later, Skathi's armored figure appeared racing among the trees, straight toward the ravine. "A third company on their way!" she shouted in Fehlan. "Half a minute out and closing fast!"

Chapter Sixty-Four

Ice slithered down Aravon's spine. *Another company?* The *Blodsvarri was* smart. She hadn't just sent a second group of skirmishers to follow the first—the cunning commander had sent three, maybe more. *Who knows how many more are out here, hunting us? And now they know where we are!*

"Fall back!" he shouted, also in Fehlan. He had to sell the deceit that the Hilmir's forces were in retreat, but in this case, it was no ruse. Going up against a *third* company of Eirdkilrs here wasn't part of the plan. They had to pull back, find another spot to set up an ambush.

The Fjall had already clambered out of the ravine to deal with the Eirdkilrs. Aravon's cry sent them racing for the woods west of the ambush, back to Bjarni's main body of warriors.

Skathi had just broken from the tree cover when she pitched forward, as if hurled by an invisible hand. The archer fell, hard, rolled once, and *smashed* into the trunk of one of the two felled oak trees.

"Skathi!" The shout tore from Belthar's lips. Instantly, he was a blur of motion, his bulk moving with impossible speed as he took four huge steps to where the archer lay in a heap in the shadow of the oak.

Aravon was on the move as well. Ignoring the twinges of pain shooting up and down his leg, he leapt onto the nearest downed tree and scrambled across the improvised log bridge.

Right into the teeth of an arrow storm. A dozen Eirdkilr missiles whistled out of the trees. One slammed into his pauldron and spun off over his right shoulder. A second struck his helmet a glancing blow, and two more skittered through the branches mere inches from his legs. Agony exploded in his chest as an arrow slammed into his breastplate. Dead center. The impact knocked the air from his lungs and slowed his forward momentum. Gasping, staggered, Aravon nearly slipped off the log and plummeted into the rock-strewn ravine.

Somehow, impossibly, he managed to keep his balance and throw himself onto the western bank beside Belthar. Every breath sent waves of pain radiating through his torso, but at that moment, he couldn't worry about that.

"She's out cold, Captain!" Belthar shouted. The big man knelt over Skathi, his body and his huge double-headed axe a shield from the Eirdkilr arrows. Only the dense cover of the surrounding trees kept the Eirdkilrs from riddling them with shafts, but the moment they broke through the underbrush and got within view, he, Belthar, and Skathi would be vulnerable in the open.

"The...arrow?" Aravon gasped. "Bad?"

"No," Belthar shook his head. "Armor held."

"Good!" Relief flooded Aravon, but it died as the Eirdkilr howls echoed in the trees. So close, maybe forty or fifty yards west of them. And closing quickly. It sounded as if a herd of stampeding oxen crashed through the forest. They had *seconds* before the Eirdkilrs reached them, and their Fjall comrades were on the far side of the ravine and retreating fast.

A dozen options, each more suicidal than the last, flashed through Aravon's mind in the space between heartbeats. Plans considered and discarded. He couldn't just think of how to get out of this skirmish alive, but how to keep their plan on track. The plan that would put an end to the Blood Queen and turn the tide of battle.

"Go!" he shouted to Belthar. "Get her out of here. Pull the Fjall back."

Without hesitation, Belthar scooped up Skathi's limp form, careful to collect her quiver and longbow as well. He cradled the archer in his arms, his enormous bulk shielding her from the arrows hissing past. "What about you?" Belthar asked, then ducked as a missile slashed the air an inch from his head.

"Let's see how these Eirdkilrs fare at a game of 'catch the Legionnaire'!"

Whirling, Aravon sprinted straight into the forest east of the ravine. He crashed through the dense underbrush, making as much noise as he could manage as he sprinted northeast. Forty Eirdkilr ambushers would move in a fairly tight formation—both for unit cohesion and maximum impact when striking at their enemies—and the storm of arrows had given him a rough idea of the enemy's position. He could only hope none of the Eirdkilrs had gotten too far ahead of their fellows, or he was in for a nasty surprise.

506

"Hey, goat-buggers!" Aravon shouted one of the Fehlan insults Colborn had taught them—at Noll's insistence, of course. "I'm over here!"

The tumult of the approaching Eirdkilrs grew louder, and huge, lumbering figures appeared through the woods. Their shaggy icebear pelts gave them the appearance of towering forest monsters with slavering fangs and faces stained a hideous blue. They moved far too fast for such enormous men, bursting through bushes, cracking branches, and trampling anything that stood between them and their prey.

Aravon couldn't outrun them on flat terrain, but in the woods, with his mottled armor and the woodcraft skills Colborn had hammered into them all, he stood a chance.

And he *had* to pull the Eirdkilrs away from Belthar and Skathi. He had to give his men a fighting chance.

Pain lanced his chest and radiated in throbbing waves through his entire torso. That arrow might not have punched through his alchemically-treated armor, but it would leave one hell of a bruise. And as Aravon ran, he found it increasingly difficult to draw breath. The ache constricted his lungs, preventing him from pulling in enough air. Coupled with the sharp, stabbing pain in his thigh, Aravon knew he had *minutes* to lose his pursuers.

Aravon half-expected enemies to leap out at him. But he'd gotten lucky, chosen a path that led him in front of the enemy. A faint hope surged within Aravon—he might actually pull this off!

He caught sight of a flash of orange fur winging through the trees above him. Snarl had followed him, circling high overhead. Aravon felt a sense of relief, and gratitude. He'd almost forgotten about the Enfield, hidden away in the bushes, keeping out of sight of the Fehlan warriors. But Snarl hadn't forgotten him. He'd stayed close on Aravon's heels, watching out for his fellow pack mate.

Come on, boy! Aravon gritted his teeth against the pain and forced himself to run faster. *Let's give these bastards a proper chase!*

* * *

Aravon hadn't felt so tired in…well, he was too tired to remember. And muddier than a prized Princelander pig. The long hours of running, walking, and climbing had helped to ease the pain of his leg—or he'd simply pushed his

507

muscles so hard he'd gone *through* the discomfort period—but the ache in his chest had grown with every long, weary mile.

Yet a quiet elation burned within him. It had taken the better part of twenty miles, but he'd finally given the Eirdkilrs the slip. He'd headed northeast, cut back sharply south through a thicket of blackthorns, and snuck around behind the Eirdkilr pursuers. The same narrow creek he'd used to trap the Eirdkilrs had served to conceal his presence—he'd crossed far downstream where the current was faster, the water deep enough to hide his bootprints.

With Snarl as his guide, he had no trouble keeping out of sight of the enemy and finding his way back west to where Colborn and the rest of his company waited with Bjarni and Sigbrand's Fjall warriors. If he was reading the terrain right, he was a mere half-mile away from the camp. And, hopefully, a fire where Zaharis brewed up a half-decent meal and something to help with the pain.

Mist slowly settled over the land as darkness blanketed the forests. The gray haze had a chilly edge that seeped into Aravon's mud-soaked armor, sending a shiver down his spine. With the deep shadows of the forest pressing in around him, it was hard not to imagine enemies hiding in the darkness, ready to leap out at him.

He distracted himself from his fatigue by going over the day's mission. A success, no doubt about it. Eighty Eirdkilrs dead, with only a handful of Fjall casualties. *That ought to be enough to keep the Blood Queen seeing red.*

The Fjall ambush would send the *Blodsvarri a* clear message that the Hilmir—or his son, now that Throrsson was "on his deathbed"—wasn't going down without a fight. Yet, as the small size of the counterattack and the quick retreat indicated, the Fjall didn't have enough warriors to mount a proper defense.

By Aravon's best guess, the Blood Queen would continue to send the bulk of her forces at the main Fjall warband, but use skirmishers like she had today to keep Bjarni on the defensive, retreating. That suited Aravon just fine. As long as the Fjall kept the Eirdkilrs from circling around behind them, they could maintain the steady retreat. Let the *Blodsvarri* think *she* was herding them toward Hangman's Hill, rather than the other way around.

Aravon tensed as a shadow appeared in the gloom, but relaxed at the sight of orange fur, gleaming yellow eyes, and dark wings. Snarl padded up to him and dropped something at his feet with a quiet *yip* of delight.

Kneeling, Aravon scooped up the object. A fat rabbit, with blood staining its brown fur where Snarl's teeth had closed around its now-snapped neck. The little Enfield stared up at Aravon with an eager light in his eyes.

"Thanks, boy," Aravon whispered, chuckling, and stroked Snarl's fur. "You eat it." He held the rabbit out to the Enfield. "I've got my own meal waiting back at camp."

After only a moment's hesitation, Snarl snatched the rabbit in his teeth and tore into it. Aravon couldn't help smiling at the Enfield's gesture; Snarl was becoming more and more a part of their "pack". He'd taken not only to Aravon and Skathi, but to everyone in their company. Rangvaldr, certainly, though that likely had to do with the bits of meat the *Seiomenn* kept sneaking him. Snarl seemed to tolerate even Noll, though he gave the occasional growl whenever Belthar moved too close to Skathi at the campfire. He was protective over every member of his pack. Not just their messenger, but part of their odd little company.

Aravon's stomach growled as he watched Snarl devouring the rabbit. He'd left his pack and rations on his horse, which meant a long day with no food and only a few mouthfuls of water. He was all too eager to get back to the camp and get something hot and warm in his belly. He needed enough energy for what lay in store for them—

Snarl dropped the half-eaten rabbit and his head perked up, ears twitching. The little Enfield's fox body tensed, his posture stiff, amber eyes alert. A low barking growl rumbled in his throat.

Aravon tensed as well. Only one thing could make Snarl react like that. *Enemies in the night!*

Snarl slunk into the bushes, padding between the trees, his eagle's claws near-silent on the soft, damp forest floor. Aravon followed in a low crouch, one eye on the slinking Enfield and the other on the surrounding forest.

Deep shadows hung thick in the forest, the mist blotting out any starlight that seeped through the dense canopy. Yet, in the darkness, Aravon heard the sound of *clanking* armor, the quiet *thump* of booted feet on soft earth, and the harsh breathing of men.

Aravon froze as a figure appeared through the mist. Tall, broad-shouldered, wearing shaggy furs with a round shield slung over his back. Then another, and a third, and more. Ten, twenty, fifty, more. Moving slowly, slipping quietly through the trees.

Straight toward the place where Bjarni's forces made camp.

Ice slithered down Aravon's spine. *The Eirdkilrs are going to launch a sneak attack!*

Chapter Sixty-Five

Aravon tightened his grip on his spear, his mind racing. The Fjall, exhausted from a day spent locked in a fighting retreat, would be resting in shifts. Yet with the dense mists providing cover, the Fehlan sentries would be hard-pressed to see the approaching enemy.

Not if I have any say about that! Drawing in a deep breath, he opened his mouth to shout a warning.

Yet something stopped him before he raised his voice. Something about this was...wrong.

Then a figure moved right in front of him—so close Aravon could reach out and tap the warrior's shoulder with the tip of his spear. His eyebrows shot up as he realized what had stopped him.

They're too small to be Eirdkilrs. The figures were strong, tall warriors clad in furs, carrying rounded shields—the same shields carried by the Fjall warband and the Eirdkilrs. But they were no hulking behemoths with blue-stained faces. Their furs had come not from wasteland icebears, but Fehlan brown bears, reindeer skins, otters, and other smaller animals found *north* of the Sawtooth Mountains.

Aravon's eyes fell on a figure moving at the front of the clustered warriors, and his eyebrows shot up. *Grimar?* He recognized the Fjall—the blond hair and beard pulled into two tight braids, his broad jaw and heavy brows—from the day they first arrived in Storbjarg. The man had been in command of the three thousand warriors left to guard Storbjarg. *How in the fiery hell did he get here?*

Straightening, Aravon broke into a jog. "*Heil,* Grimar!" he called out.

The Fjall warrior spun at the sound of his name, and the warriors surrounding him did likewise. A bristling forest of axes, spears, and swords sprang to life in a vicious, edged circle surrounding Aravon. Aravon held his hands out and made no threatening move. After a moment of squinting into the shadows, Grimar seemed to recognize him.

"Captain Snarl?" he asked. "Is that you?"

"In the flesh," Aravon replied in Fehlan. "How are you here? Yesterday morning, Storbjarg was in flames, and the Eirdkilrs roamed its streets freely."

"It is the fate of Storbjarg that brings me here." Darkness hid Grimar's expression, but sorrow echoed in his voice. "And now, with the Hilmir fallen, I must bring news of the capital to the Hilmir's son at once."

Aravon raised an eyebrow. *They heard the shouts, did they?* The Fjall warband had raised an unholy clamor; the sound must have reached Grimar and his men as they crept around, behind, or through the Eirdkilr lines.

"Where is he?" Grimar asked. "Where is Bjarni Eiriksson?"

"I don't know." Aravon shook his head. "I've spent the day leading the enemy on a merry chase. But if he is in camp, we will find him under Sigbrand's watchful eye."

The first Fjall scouts greeted Aravon and Grimar with shouts to identify themselves, but those quickly turned to cries of elation at the sight of their comrades still alive. The news traveled through the camp so quickly it took less than five minutes for Bjarni and Sigbrand to make an appearance.

"*Fraendi!*" The dancing torchlight set delight sparkling in Bjarni's blue eyes, and a smile broadened his strong face. "We have been so worried about you and the others."

Grimar pulled the Hilmir's son into an embrace, then pounding Sigbrand on the back in true Fehlan warrior fashion. "It does my heart good to find you alive and well, *Brodrbaurn*, despite everything that has happened." His expression grew grave, his features heavy. "I only wish I came bearing better tidings."

Bjarni's eyes darkened, a look of solemnity that bore a strong resemblance to the Hilmir. "Storbjarg?"

"Fallen." Grimar shook his head. "Set to the torch by the *Blodsvarri's* men."

Bjarni's face grew ashen. "And my mother, my sister?"

Grimar's dark expression and his silence spoke volumes.

Bjarni appeared torn between sorrow and stunned horror. "By *Striith!*" His face twisted into a grimace. "What happened? How did the enemy get in? When my father marched out, did he not command the gates to be locked?"

"Aye, and so they were." Grimar tugged at his braided beard, shame burning in his eyes. "Yet the *Tauld* came upon us so quickly and with such force that even the gates of Storbjarg could not withstand them. Once inside, they set fire to every *langhus* they could, used the smoke as cover for their assault."

Bjarni bowed his head, as if to hide his anguish over the loss of his mother and sister.

Grimar's shoulders seemed to droop beneath a heavy weight. "We tried to hold them back, but there were too many. Against their three thousand, we fought a losing battle, to save our homes, protect our people, and repel the enemy."

Bjarni raised his head, tears still in his eyes, and placed a hand on Grimar's arm. "*Fraendi*, you cannot—"

"No!" Grimar whirled on Bjarni, a snarl twisting his lips. "It is my eternal shame that *I* am to blame for the loss of the Fjall's greatest city. Now, nothing but ashes remains. The *Tauld* have ripped up the very stones of Storbjarg's heart, torn down the *Blotahorgr*, and hauled away the remains. When we finally made our escape, they had set to work on the walls of Storbjarg. They intend to set an example for all of Fehl."

Worry twisted a dagger in Aravon's gut. He desperately wanted to ask about Duke Dyrund, but Grimar and his warriors were exhausted, muddy, bloodied, and beaten—physically and emotionally. They needed rest and food.

But it wasn't only thoughts of the Fjall that kept Aravon from voicing the question. A part of him didn't want to know what had happened; there was a very real chance their answer, the *truth* of the Duke's fate, would be too heavy to bear. With everything they'd face over the next few days, it would be better to carry a weight of uncertainty instead of the ponderous burden of knowing he'd never see the Duke again.

"I not only lost the city," Grimar was saying, "I *abandoned* it." He straightened, set his jaw in a hard line and squared his shoulders. "My men are not to blame for such cowardice. They only followed my command, so any punishments my Hilmir deems worthy will—"

Bjarni cut the warrior off with a shake of his head. "My father has always told me that there is no shame in withdrawing from an impossible battle." He collected himself, schooled his expression, and clapped Grimar on the back. "But it is good that you are here. How many men with you?"

"Two hundred and fifty." Grimar's face twisted into a frown. "There may be more of our warriors roaming the lands to the north and east of Storbjarg, but this small force is all I could gather with me." Reaching out a hand, the Fjall warrior gripped Bjarni's shoulder hard. "Your father's attack on the city gave us a chance to escape out the north gate while the *Tauld* were distracted. We owe him our lives. A debt we intend to repay by standing here, with you." He hung his head. "If you will accept the service of a shamed and dishonored warrior."

"My father's trusted companion!" Bjarni's voice echoed with noble certainty, his tone warm with reassurance. "We would be honored to have you join us in our fighting retreat."

"Retreat?" Grimar's eyes narrowed.

A grin broadened Bjarni's face. "We buy my father time to prepare the true field of battle."

Grimar sucked in a sharp breath. "Your father?" Surprise flashed across his face. "The Hilmir…lives? Your shouts of vengeance for the Hilmir's death have rung loud enough to be heard in every corner of Fehl."

"A ruse." Bjarni shot Grimar a sly wink. "To deceive the *Blodsvarri.*"

"*Striith* be praised!" The Fjall warrior turned his palms and face skyward. "My men and I, we will march to him with all speed!"

Bjarni's face fell. "But you said you have come to join *us*. To help us hold the enemy in the retreat."

Grimar gripped Bjarni's shoulder. "It would be an honor to fight by your side, *Brodrbaurn*, but knowing my Hilmir as I do, he has entrusted you with enough men to see your mission through. Yet if he is preparing the field of battle, then I have no doubt he will welcome more hands to work."

Bjarni's expression was pensive. He shot a glance at Sigbrand, who gave a little shrug. Then he turned to Aravon. "What do you say, Captain Snarl?" the young Fjall asked. "My father placed his full faith in your advice, and it is *your* men who lead our warriors to keep the *Blodsvarri* following our retreat. Where are Grimar's men most desperately needed?"

The question surprised Aravon, almost as much as hearing Bjarni say that Throrsson trusted his counsel. Yet, after a moment to recover, Aravon's mind set to work on the problem at hand.

Without speaking to Colborn, he couldn't know the outcome of the western ambush. But, given the results *his* mission had achieved, he wasn't certain adding two hundred and fifty warriors to their part of the plan would yield exponential results. It would make their position a bit more secure, give them a few more shields to hold the fighting retreat, but little more.

Aravon's brow furrowed in thought. "As Grimar rightly said, your father entrusted you with a force large enough to keep the Blood Queen in pursuit." He glanced at Sigbrand. "How heavy were your losses today?"

Sigbrand grunted. "Light."

"Thirty-five wounded, twenty gone to feast with *Striith* in *Seggrholl.*" Bjarni's jaw muscles worked and his fists clenched at his side. Aravon recognized that expression—the burden of command would weigh heavy on one so young.

"The decision is yours, son of the Hilmir," Grimar said. "We march under your father's banner. Either by his side or yours."

Bjarni nodded. "I would hear Captain Snarl's counsel, still."

Finally, Aravon inclined his head. "If you don't think you'll need them here, I'm certain your father could use a few more hands."

Bjarni remained silent a long moment, his expression thoughtful as he contemplated Aravon's words. "Go, Grimar. Join my father at Hangman's Hill, and bring him word that his plan works as he hoped." He lifted his head and stood taller, a look of regal confidence on his handsome, lightly bearded face. "When the sun rises on Fehl the day after next, it will find the Fjall warband ready for battle."

"With steel in our hands and defiance in our hearts!" Grimar clapped the young man on the back. "We march within the hour."

"Not until you have eaten." Bjarni glanced at the exhausted, mud-covered, battered warriors surrounding Grimar. "You look famished."

"Our flight from Storbjarg gave us little time to grab provisions," Grimar shook his head, "and forage this far north has never been abundant."

"Then come, *Fraendi.*" Bjarni wrapped an arm around the man's shoulder. "By the grace of *Striith*, we may find a few drops of decent Ornntadr mead to wash the smoke and dust from your throat."

Grimar chuckled. "To that offer, *Brodrbaurn*, you will never hear argument from me."

Chapter Sixty-Six

"How is she?" Aravon frowned down at Skathi. The archer lay on her bedroll, covered in a blanket that looked suspiciously like Belthar's. In the meager light of their small campfire, her unmasked face looked pale, the wound on her head darkening to a deep purple bruise.

"Sleeping," Belthar rumbled. In the privacy of their small camp, set twenty yards north of the main Fjall encampment, he'd removed his own mask as well, revealing a face stained by mud and blood and darkened by worry. "Been in and out of consciousness all day."

Worry twisted in Aravon's empty stomach. Zaharis had taken great pains to disabuse him of the "fanciful, idiotic notion" that sleeping after a serious head wound could lead to brain damage—in fact, the Secret Keeper emphasized that rest helped the brain to recover from the injury. Yet fifteen years of heeding the wisdom of temple-trained Menders was hard to shake. "Has Zaharis been by to see her?"

Belthar shook his head. "Haven't seen him. Or Colborn."

That only added to Aravon's growing nervousness. *They should have returned by now.* He had no idea what could delay them; *they* hadn't had to outrun Eirdkilrs as he did. *So where in the fiery hell are they?*

He forced himself not to voice the question—it would do no good to add to Belthar's worries over Skathi. Instead, he removed his mask and sat on a fallen log a few yards from the big man.

"She'll be fine, right, Captain?" Belthar's quiet question held a depth of genuine concern.

"I'm no Mender, Belthar, but if I know Skathi, she'll be back on her feet and snapping at you by morning." Aravon pulled off his helmet and ran a hand through his sweat-plastered hair. It felt utterly marvelous, better than the freshest linen sheets or a cool Frozen Sea breeze on the hottest summer days. "But as soon as Zaharis and Colborn get back, we'll—"

"Feed them a feast fit for Kings?" Colborn's voice echoed from behind Aravon. "Give us the Prince's comfiest bed and a week to sleep?"

Aravon whirled, so fast he nearly toppled off the log. A smile broadened his face as two very bedraggled, muddy, leaf-covered figures in leather armor shuffled into their campsite.

"Keeper's teeth!" Aravon whistled through his teeth. "You go swimming in a mud hole?"

"This, from the picture of elegance and grace?" Colborn gestured at Aravon's armor.

Aravon glanced down. He hadn't yet had a chance to wash off, either, and the mud caking his armor made it feel twice as heavy. "Spent the afternoon playing 'capture the Legionnaire' with the Eirdkilrs. Still the reigning champion, even if it meant taking a little slush bath."

Colborn removed his mask and was about to retort, but stopped when he caught sight of Skathi. Worry blazed in his ice-blue eyes and he hurried to crouch over Skathi. "What happened?"

"Took an arrow to the back," Belthar rumbled. "Her armor bore the brunt, but the hit to the head's the real problem."

"*Move aside, you big oaf!*" Zaharis' fingers flashed, and he gave Belthar a little shooing gesture. Once the big man made way, he crouched beside Colborn and frowned down at the sleeping Skathi. "*Before she slept, was she awake, alert, talking?*"

Belthar nodded, his jaw muscles working and his face strained. "Enough to shout at me for nearly cracking her longbow with my 'big, clumsy bear paws'."

"Got anything to speed things up?" Aravon asked. "Like what you gave me at Camp Marshal?"

Zaharis shook his head. "*Ran out of that at Rivergate. Haven't had a chance to brew up more.*"

Aravon stifled a frustrated growl. They'd need their archer in fighting shape for the fight at Hangman's Hill. A few well-placed arrows could turn the tide of battle.

"But, I think I saw some Fire Daisies just west of camp." With a tired sigh, he pushed himself to his feet. *"Let's go, Belthar. Your arms will hold a lot more than mine."*

Belthar hesitated. His gaze fixed on Skathi, and reluctance hardened his broad, heavy features. He clearly didn't want to leave her side.

Aravon placed a hand on the big man's shoulder. "We'll keep an eye on her."

"Of course, Captain." Belthar blushed and rose to his feet in a hurry, his thick fingers fumbling at the straps of his leather greatwolf mask.

"I'd take a bit of whatever pain-killing herbs you find," Aravon said. The pain in his leg had mostly diminished, but the throbbing ache of his bruised chest seemed to have set in to the bone.

Zaharis cocked his head. *"You take a beating?"*

Aravon grimaced. "Glancing club blow to the leg. Arrow to the chest." He scraped away the mud crusting his leather breastplate, revealing a deep gouge in the material, courtesy of the Eirdkilr arrowhead. "This alchemical coating of yours does wonders to keep us alive, but not much to soften the punch."

Zaharis shrugged. *"Nothing's perfect, Captain."*

"No complaints from me." Aravon shook his head. "Just need to be around and on my feet tomorrow, and the next day for Hangman's Hill."

Zaharis flashed him the signal for "understood" and, snapping his fingers at Belthar, turned and hurried westward through the camp.

"You sure you're okay, Captain?" Colborn's quiet voice radiated a concern that was mirrored in his eyes. "Arrow to the chest's going to leave a bloody big bruise."

Aravon drew in a long breath—*yes, still hurts like a donkey kick to the bollocks*—and let it out slowly. "Won't be dancing shirtless in an Icespire henhouse anytime soon, but you don't have to worry about me keeling over in the middle of a battle."

Colborn raised an eyebrow. "Icespire *henhouse?*" His expression grew incredulous. "Do I want to know?"

Heat suffused Aravon's face, his cheeks burning. He couldn't believe exhaustion had loosened his tongue so much—that was one secret of his youth he'd intended to take to his grave. He changed the subject, quickly. "Mission report?"

"Success." Colborn sat beside the sleeping Skathi, leaned against the tree with a groan of delight. "A hundred Eirdkilrs gone to worms, with fewer than a dozen friendly casualties. Few wounds here and there, but nothing serious." He shook his head, his expression amazed. "I swear, I still can't get over the crazy magic Zaharis can conjure up, almost out of thin air. No matter how many times I see it, it's still bloody impressive."

Aravon leaned back against a nearby tree, propped his boots up onto the log beside him. After the day he'd had, he welcomed a few minutes of doing absolutely nothing.

"He's come through for us a lot, hasn't he?" Aravon nodded. "If being around him has taught me anything, it's that even the tiniest things can make the biggest difference. Like those Earthshakers Noll was fiddling with. Nearly made the Eirdkilrs piss their breeches when they went off!" A wry laugh burst from his chest. "I can only thank the Swordsman they don't have Magicmakers of their own."

Colborn chuckled, yet his smile faded. "Speaking of magic, where's Rangvaldr?" His brow furrowed. "Shouldn't *he* be dealing with Skathi's wounds?"

"He's not back yet," Aravon said. "Mission's taking him longer than he expected."

Colborn growled. "Damn the stubborn bastards!" To the Lieutenant, it went beyond simply the needs of their situation—it was personal.

"Give him time." Aravon sighed. "If anyone can talk sense into them, it's Rangvaldr."

"If not, we're well and truly fucked." Colborn's lip curled up into a snarl.

"Have faith, Colborn." Aravon tried to sound more confident than he felt. Since the ambush on Throrsson's men, he'd found himself struggling to keep up the belief that he could outthink, outmaneuver, or outfight the *Blodsvarri*. The Eirdkilr leader had proven herself far more devious than he'd expected, and even with his understanding of military history, he'd felt like a drowning man struggling to keep his head above water more than once.

Yet he couldn't let the soldiers under his command *see* that self-doubt. They needed to believe in him, which meant he had to believe in himself. And those who fought at his side. "Have faith in the Hilmir and his Fjall, in Rangvaldr and Noll. Without faith, we've got nothing left but the promise of certain death."

"A real ray of sunshine, aren't you?" Skathi muttered from where she lay curled on her bedroll.

Instantly, Colborn and Aravon leapt to their feet. The Agrotora had made no move to sit up, but the fact that she was speaking filled Aravon with hope.

"How are you feeling?" he asked.

"Like the Eirdkilrs are howling inside my skull." Skathi grimaced, blinked hard. But instead of getting up, she closed her eyes and nestled deeper into the blankets. "'F'its all the same to you, Cap'n, I'll just go back to…" Her sentence trailed off unfinished and her breathing grew deep, steady once more.

"At least we know the thump to her head didn't mess with her sunny disposition." Colborn gave Aravon a wry grin.

"Clear sign she'll heal up just fine." Aravon let out a relieved sigh and, taking a seat, leaned back against the tree trunk once more. Snarl padded from the darkness and curled up in Aravon's lap. The Enfield's presence was soothing, and Aravon ran a hand down Snarl's furry head and back.

"She's got the right idea, though." Colborn yawned, his voice heavy with fatigue. "It'll be time to get up and at it before too long. Best we take the opportunity to sleep while we can."

"Aye." The word was all Aravon could muster. Exhaustion dragged at his limbs, which had grown too heavy to move. His eyelids drooped and he felt sleep settling over him. With Snarl's warm, heavy body pressing against his legs and stomach, Aravon allowed himself to drift off into the peaceful void of well-earned sleep.

* * *

"Fall back!" Aravon shouted in Fehlan, waving his spear to get the Fjall's attention. "Back!"

The last of the Fjall broke off from the ambush, but not before leaving ten of their comrades lying on the ground amidst the Eirdkilr bodies littering the bloodstained, muddy ground. They had hit the enemy hard—after Colborn's hastily dug spike pits and spear traps softened them up. The pile of felled trees had funneled the Eirdkilrs straight into their chokepoint, and the forty Fjall with them had taken down the first group of enemies before they knew what hit them.

But the Blood Queen had learned her lesson. Within half a minute of springing the trap, three more companies, each forty or fifty-strong, had appeared from the south.

Colborn raced up beside him, gasping. "The enemy's too close, Captain!" Blood trickled from a shallow cut along his right cheek, staining his white-blond beard a deep crimson. "A fourth group's circling west and they'll hit us in seconds. The *Blodsvarri's* throwing everything she can to push us back."

"It means she's doing what we want!" Aravon leapt toward an Eirdkilr that had managed to force his way through the fallen trees. He blocked the wild swing of the enormous axe, shattered the barbarian's knee with the iron-shod butt of his spear, and drove the blade through the man's throat. "She's keeping us penned in, stopping us from breaking out. She's got her sights set on trapping us in at Hangman's Hill."

Colborn threw himself into the gap beside Aravon, his shield *clanging* beneath the impact of an Eirdkilr club. "Think she'll be kind enough to give us a night off…" Colborn grunted as another blow crashed against his shield. "…before she cuts us down?" He punctuated his words with a hard thrust of his longsword. The sharp Odarian steel blade punched through the Eirdkilr's chain mail and deep into his chest.

"Let's hope so!" Aravon kicked the dying Eirdkilr backward, sending his corpse flying into the barbarians pushing through the gap behind him. "She's got a lot more men than we do, but they'll be pretty exhausted by now, too. Even the Eirdkilrs can't fight forever."

For a moment, the Eirdkilr's huge form blocked the gap, like a cork in a bottle keeping the barbarians behind him from getting through. Aravon spun toward the figure crouching in the shadows of a felled tree. "Do it!"

Zaharis moved quickly, lighting his alchemical firestriker and touching its burning end to a thick trail of sap that oozed from the pine tree. The highly flammable resin, mixed with a few drops of an oil Zaharis had extracted from the Fire Daisies, caught alight in an instant. Bright orange flames licked along the length of the felled trees and leapt toward the Eirdkilrs caught in the brambles.

The conflagration lacked the alchemical violence and ferocity of the fire wall outside Rivergate, but it served its purpose nonetheless. Aravon, Colborn, and Zaharis scrambled backward as the blistering heat washed over them.

Screams, high-pitched and tinged with agony, echoed from within the inferno but quickly fell silent as the fire consumed the Eirdkilrs.

Aravon grimaced at the reek of burning flesh, the terrible *crackling* of the billowing flames. Yet he couldn't help feeling relieved as well. The Eirdkilrs wouldn't be using this gulch to circle around the Fjall's eastern flank. This was the last place where the *Blodsvarri* could have cut off their retreat to Hangman's Hill. With the Hardrfoss River guarding their eastern flank and the marshlands to their west, her only way to hit the main Fjall forces would be straight down the middle. By cutting the Eirdkilrs off here, they had bought Bjarni's men a few hours—precious time to rest and recover from nearly three consecutive days of fighting.

As Aravon slipped back through the trees to where they'd left the horses tethered away from the battleground, he called to mind the crude map of the Fjall lands the Duke had shown him back at Storbjarg and did quick calculations. *We've marched nearly a hundred and thirty miles northeast from Storbjarg. That puts us just ten miles from Hangman's Hill.*

The Fjall would have to cover that distance on foot—at least half a day's march, given their exhaustion—but Aravon and his small company had horses that could make the journey in the space of two hours. *As long as the Blood Queen doesn't push her exhausted Eirdkilrs too hard, we'll have time to recover. Maybe even send Zaharis and Belthar on a flower-picking mission. Keeper knows we could use some of his alchemical marvels tomorrow.*

The Secret Keeper's supplies had all but run out, and his marvelous wooden chest seemed to have reached its bottom. The latest ambush had *only* succeeded thanks to the resinous pine trees growing around the gulch and Zaharis' search for painkilling Fire Daisies the previous evening.

But unless he somehow managed to re-stock tonight, he'd have nothing to use for their battle tomorrow. It would come down to the courage of the Fjall in the face of Eirdkilr savagery and strength. Throrsson's preparations against the Blood Queen's cunning.

We've done all we can, Aravon told himself as he climbed into the saddle and turned his horse back toward their camp. *Now it's up to Eirik Throrsson and his men to achieve the impossible.*

Chapter Sixty-Seven

A nervous silence hung over their small camp. The coolness of the cave Belthar had managed to find seemed almost chilly, made even more tense by the occasional *crack* of their merrily burning fire and the harsh rasp of whetstones on steel. Aravon and Colborn worked at their weapons, and Belthar was hard at work turning his collection of birch branches into arrows. Zaharis tended to the bubbling pot that hung suspended from his portable iron cookframe over the fire. The stew smelled marvelous—they would all have eaten it then and there had the Secret Keeper not insisted that it needed a few more minutes.

Aravon's eyes darted toward Skathi. The archer sat against the stone walls of the cave, bundled up in her bedroll. The bruise on her face had darkened since the previous night, spread from her forehead to purpling circles around her left eye and down to her ear. Even with Zaharis' painkilling remedy—which, the Secret Keeper himself admitted would do little more than dull the discomfort, not heal it—she still winced every time she moved.

Her face pinched with discomfort as she shifted in her seat, trying not to disturb Snarl curled around her feet. When she reached for one of the birch branches she'd worked at earlier, she sagged, her eyes wobbling, and barely managed to catch herself before falling.

Belthar dropped his arrow and reached toward her. "Let me—"

"Don't!" Skathi snapped. "I'm fine!"

Belthar froze, then quickly retreated. His expression darkened and his face grew hard. Yet not inscrutable. The big man had hidden secrets of his past, but he had never been good at concealing his emotions. Pain glimmered in the eyes he turned back toward the unfletched arrow shaft.

Aravon exchanged glances with Colborn. *"Flower-picking?"* he signed.

Colborn raised an eyebrow. *"Need a moment alone?"*

Aravon nodded.

With a theatrical groan, Colborn stood. "Ahh!" he sighed. "Feels good to work the kinks out of my muscles."

Zaharis ignored the Lieutenant, focused on stirring the stew. Skathi didn't bother looking up, and Belthar was too busy being miserable to tear his gaze from the stick in his hands.

"You know, Zaharis," Colborn pressed, "I could *swear* I spotted a little patch of white flowers on our way back today. Could they be the ice saffron you're looking for?"

Zaharis shook his head without looking up. *"Ice saffron have blue petals, not white. Probably nothing more than lilies."*

"They didn't smell sweet," Colborn said. "I'm no expert on plants, but maybe there's a chance you can use them to cook up something unpleasant for the Eirdkilrs tomorrow?"

A long moment passed, then Zaharis sighed. *"Sure, why not?"* He stood slowly—even though he slept no more than a few hours a night, the last few days had taken an equally heavy toll on him. *"Stew needs another ten minutes to cook, so we've got time."*

"Give us a hand, Belthar," Colborn said, turning to the big man. "If they *are* useful, the more we've got, the better."

Belthar said nothing but, after a darting glance at Skathi, stood and followed Colborn and Zaharis into the darkness beyond the cave mouth.

Aravon watched the three men go, waited until they were well and truly gone before—

"Spit it out, Captain."

Skathi's steel-edged words took Aravon by surprise. "What?"

"Oh, please!" Skathi rolled her eyes. "Colborn's a damned good tracker, but I've seen alley cats give more convincing performances." She gave a little snort. "And remember, I speak the hand language as well as you."

Aravon gave her a wry grin. "At least your eyes are still as sharp as ever, head wound or no."

"That's what this is about?" Skathi's jaw clenched, her fingers tightening around the stick she'd been working on so tight it creaked in her grip. "You think because I'm a woman, a bump like that's going to suddenly make me useless?" Anger burning bright and hot in her eyes as she leaned forward and thrust the sharpened stick at Aravon. "Belthar collects wounds like a miser with gold coins, but when *I* get hit, you—"

"Enough, Skathi!" Aravon's voice cracked like a whip.

The archer fell silent, yet her fury remained undiminished. Aravon could sense it simmering beneath the surface, as it *always* had since the moment she joined their company. The time had come to put that to rest. Or, at least, put it behind them.

"Yes, I'm worried about your head wound." Aravon nodded. "Same way I'm worried about this damned bruise on my chest every time it hurts to breathe. But no, that's *not* what this is about."

"Then, like I said," Skathi growled, "spit it out."

Aravon bit back an angry retort. It would do no good to lash out in frustration. He drew in a deep breath, filling his lungs with the cool air to regain his calm.

"Since Bjornstadt, I've had a chance to talk to everyone, except you." He chose his words carefully. "For that, I owe you an apology."

His words had an instant effect. Skathi's anger cracked, replaced by a flash of surprise. "A-Apology?"

"Yes," Aravon said. He drew in a deep breath. "Since the first day you joined our company, it's been clear how you feel about a few of us." His brow furrowed. "I know that Noll's gotten on your nerves, and Belthar...well, that's a different snarl of yarn."

Snarl perked up at the sound of his name, but when no offer of food or order to fly was forthcoming from his two packmates, he settled down around Skathi's feet once more.

Skathi snorted. "Understatement of the decade."

"I'd offer to talk to them about it—" Aravon began.

"I can handle my own business," Skathi snapped.

"And *that's* what this is about." Aravon leaned forward. "You seem to think that just because you *can* handle your business alone somehow means you have to."

Skathi's eyes narrowed and she leaned back, strong arms crossed in front of her defensively.

"You're a part of our company, Skathi." Aravon gestured around. "You've earned your place here as much as any one of us." He cocked an eyebrow. "Hells, probably more than most. Your skill and courage has saved all our arses as many times as Zaharis' magic or Colborn's woodcraft."

The tightness in the archer's broad shoulders diminished slightly. Just a fraction, yet enough that Aravon held out hope that his words would reach her.

"But it's up to you to actually *become* a part of the company," he continued in a quiet voice. "Not to watch from a safe distance."

The tension returned. Stone walls went up in Skathi's eyes, the lines of her face growing tight.

Aravon drew in a deep breath. "I don't know what history you have with people like Noll, or Belthar, or even me." He shrugged. "And I'm not going to push. I *want* you to feel comfortable enough that you can talk about what's going on. What's bothering you, what you want or need, even if it's not mission-critical. Maybe not with everyone, but with me, at least. My job as your commanding officer isn't just to give orders and expect you to follow them. It's also on me to make sure you're in the right state, heart and mind, to do what needs to be done."

Skathi stiffened and clenched her jaw. Aravon could *see* her mind working, her lips forming a sharp retort.

He spoke before she could. "It's *never* me doubting you." He fixed her with a piercing gaze. "It's concern for you, one of my soldiers. Just like I'm concerned for Colborn, Belthar, Rangvaldr, or any of the others. That's what this is about. Me doing my damnedest to prove that you're as important to this company as everyone you march with."

For a moment, it seemed his words had fallen on stony ears. Skathi remained motionless, her posture defensive and the angry light burning in her eyes. But as the seconds grew long, she seemed to relax, the stiffness draining from her spine and shoulders, her face softening a fraction. "Understood, sir."

"So, again, I'm going to ask, you up for this?" Aravon said in a quiet voice. "Tomorrow's battle is going to be a bloodbath. That head wound would have *me* questioning if I should fight or not, and the way you're wincing every time you move your right arm, I'm not sure you should be drawing a bow. But if you say you're solid, I'll take you at your word. You've more than earned my respect and trust."

Skathi remained silent a long moment. Something akin to gratitude and pride flashed in her eyes. Only for an instant, so fast Aravon almost thought he'd imagined it. But the ghost of a smile on her lips spoke volumes. "I'll be there, Captain," she said. "Might be a bit shaky thanks to this." With her left hand, she gestured to her forehead. "But when the time comes that you need my arrows, you'll have what's left of them."

Aravon shot a glance at her quiver. Fewer than twenty of Polus' arrows remained, with another dozen of the scores she'd fashioned along the journey south. Yet in her hands, those few could affect the tide of battle.

"Good." He nodded. "Then I'll find a place where you can do the most damage. Maybe even get a shot at the Blood Queen herself."

"Damn right!" Skathi growled and sat up, wincing slightly. "I'll bloody her nose good and well, Captain."

"I know you will," Aravon said, a smile tugging at his lips. "And Skathi, if there's *ever* anything going on, I need you to know that I won't think any less of you for it."

Skathi frowned, yet she nodded.

"We all carry around the weight of our pasts." Aravon leaned forward. "But as my father always told me, shared burdens grow lighter."

"Yes, Captain." Something dark and ugly flashed across Skathi's face, as if at a painful memory. "Don't take this the wrong way, but you're not like most Legion officers I've had the misfortune to work with."

"Oh?" Aravon's eyebrows rose. "How so?"

Her eyes reflected the depth of meaning ringing in her words, but she gave him a little smile. "You care. I think that's what has kept us all going, even when things go to shite. What's kept us alive this long, impossibility be damned."

Aravon chuckled. "I just wish we had a barrel of good ale. I could drink to that!"

Skathi laughed. "Next time we find ourselves in the Princelands, Captain, the first drink's on me."

"You know I'll be collecting on that offer." Aravon grinned. It felt good to smile after what seemed like days of endless fighting and worrying. And to see Skathi smile, to know she could feel comfortable around him.

With a sigh, Aravon leaned back against the cave wall and stretched out his legs. The tension in the enclosed space seemed to have fled, and now the crackling of the fire and the rich, herb-heavy smell of stew filled him with a sense of peace, an all-consuming calm. For a few precious minutes, the chaos of the previous days and concerns for the future faded and Aravon felt truly relaxed.

Then Snarl started growling. The little Enfield leapt upright, his posture stiff and his ears twitching, amber eyes locked on the entrance to the cave.

Instantly, Aravon was on full alert. He scrambled to his feet and scooped up his spear, all fatigue and pain forgotten. Wood clattered as Skathi nocked an arrow to her bow, but didn't pull.

Aravon wanted to call out to Colborn, Belthar, and Zaharis, but dared not. The nearby enemies might not have seen or heard them yet, but drawing attention to them eliminated any hope that they had evaded detection and could come to their aid.

"*Eyes sharp,*" he signed to Skathi. "*Watch my back.*"

Nodding, Skathi sat straighter and twisted to aim her bow at the darkness beyond the cave entrance.

Aravon padded closer to Snarl. "Go!" Aravon spoke the command word. He had no idea what Snarl had sensed, but the alertness in the Enfield's posture, the sudden tension in his little body couldn't be good.

With a little *yipping* bark, Snarl darted toward the entrance. The sound confused Aravon. It wasn't the same growl that had warned him of the Fjall warriors the previous night. No, it sounded…joyful.

Aravon raced after Snarl, bursting out of the cave and into the night beyond. Snarl's eagle claws *clacked* as he scrambled over the rocks littering the bank of the nearby river. His yipping grew louder, eager, delighted.

What in the bloody hell?

The Enfield raced the twenty feet toward the river's edge and threw himself into the water, splashing around a dark shape draped over a large, smooth stone. Moonlight shone on heavy furs and what could only be sodden fabric. The bundle gave a weak groan and shifted, but its movements fell still and it slumped back into the water.

Aravon closed the distance to where Snarl stood over the body. A man, Aravon realized, as he caught sight of the broad shoulders and dark beard. With cautious movements, he reached down and turned the man over onto his side.

Moonlight shone on the man's face, and Aravon's blood turned to ice. *It can't be!*

But there was no mistaking the dark hair, graying beard, and angular features of Duke Dyrund.

Chapter Sixty-Eight

Aravon blinked, twice, three times, his mind refusing to accept the evidence of his eyes. His breath caught in his lungs. It had to be a trick of some sort.

Then the Duke stirred. Barely more than a flutter of his eyelids, a twitch of his fingers, but in that instant, hope blossomed in Aravon's chest.

He's alive! He barely stopped himself from shouting in elation.

Snarl splashed around the Duke's body, leapt up onto the rock, and licked his face. Turning his amber eyes to Aravon, he gave a happy *yip*.

Aravon wrapped his arms around the Duke and scooped him up. He turned and scrambled back toward the cave as fast as he could manage, his own pains forgotten in the joy of finding the Duke alive. Yet even as he raced across the smooth river stones, he sensed something wrong with Duke Dyrund. The Duke was a tall man, strong, a warrior in flesh as well as spirit, but at that moment, he weighed next to nothing. He shivered weakly in Aravon's arms but radiated a heat as intense as the burning pine trees.

"Skathi!" Aravon called out as he stumbled toward the mouth of the cave. "It's the Duke!"

No arrows greeted him as he entered, only Skathi's look of wide-eyed surprise. "Fiery hell!" Skathi cursed. "How is he—"

But Aravon didn't hear the rest of her question. In the light of the flickering campfire, the Duke's face appeared gaunt, hollow. Dark circles formed around eyes that had grown deep-sunken. Aravon couldn't tell if the moisture on the Duke's forehead was sweat or water from the river, but there was no mistaking the feverish shivers wracking his body or the bright red hue to his cheeks.

Horror twisted a biting dagger of acid in Aravon's gut. *Wraithfever!*

The Duke's eyelids opened, sluggish. Eyes gone glassy and fever-bright fixed on Aravon. "A…ra…von?" a whisper, faint and weak, escaped the Duke's lips.

"It's me, Your Grace." Aravon's voice cracked, his throat thick. "I'm here." Kneeling, he set the Duke's body gently on the earthen floor as close to the fire as he dared.

"A…ravon." A little gasp, and the Duke's eyelids drooped closed once more.

Aravon glanced over his shoulder. Snarl had run into the cave, his *yipping* barks echoing loud in the enclosed space. Aravon didn't know if there were Eirdkilrs somewhere out in the darkness and at that moment, he didn't care. He had to save the Duke, and there was only one man who could do it.

Without hesitation, he rose to his feet, spun, and raced the few steps toward the mouth of the cave. "Zaharis!" he shouted into the night. "Zaharis, get over here!"

Not waiting to see if the Secret Keeper had heard his call, he returned to his place kneeling beside the Duke.

"What's the matter?" Skathi asked.

"Wraithfever." Aravon clenched his jaw. "He's burning up. We need to get it under control."

At that moment, Zaharis burst into the cave, Colborn hot on his heels and Belthar a few lumbering steps behind. The three of them reacted with the same shocked surprise as Skathi.

"Wraithfever!" Aravon called to the Secret Keeper. "Tell me you've got something for this, Zaharis!"

Zaharis scrambled to his pack and pawed through its meager contents, a frantic look on his face. He finally drew out a small pouch, tearing at the drawstrings so violently he nearly ripped them. From within the pouch he produced a single gnarled, dried root and whirled on Belthar. *"Drop the Bonesets!"* he signed.

Belthar dumped his armload of pure white flowers onto the ground in front of Zaharis and, sparing only a single worried glance at Skathi, frowned down at the Duke. "Will he live?" he rumbled.

Zaharis had no answer; his hands moved so quickly, crushing the white flowers into the mortar, he couldn't spare a moment to sign a response. Digging into his pack, he drew out a few of the bright yellow Fire Daisies and added them into his mortar. "*Water!*" he signed in Colborn's direction without looking up from his pestle-work.

Colborn snatched the near-empty waterskin from his belt and, tearing out its stopper, thrust it into Zaharis' hand. The Secret Keeper drained the meager contents into his stone mortar a few drops at a time, using the pestle to crush the leaves, stems, and white and yellow blossoms into a thick sludge. A bit more water, and he poured the concoction into a small wooden cup he always carried.

"*Make him drink this.*" The Secret Keeper held the cup out to Aravon. "*It'll slow the fever, but not by much.*"

Once Aravon took the cup, Zaharis leapt to his feet. "*Belthar, get to the river and fill this.*" He thrust the waterskin out toward the big man, who took it and disappeared outside in a moment.

Zaharis frowned down at the Duke. "*No lie, Captain, this is bad. The cold water of the river kept the Wraithfever at bay, but he'd have died from the chill soon enough. Without Fetidroot, I can't even begin to mix up a proper cure. I'm low on supplies, and the best I can hope for is to find a bit of feverfew, some elderflower, and maybe, if the Mistress smiles on us, a bit of Violet Coneflower.*"

"Just do whatever you can!" Desperation burst from Aravon's chest and rang in his words. His mind raced. He turned to call Snarl—he could send the Enfield to Lord Eidan, have him bring back a dose of Wraithfever cure in his message tube—but paused.

"How long does he have?" he asked Zaharis.

The Secret Keeper's eyes darkened. "*If I can find a way to break the fever, he might have a day.*"

Aravon's gut twisted. *Not enough time!* Sending Snarl to Lord Eidan would take the better part of half a day, and Lord Eidan's presence in either Icespire or Camp Marshal meant Snarl would then have to fly to Hightower to collect the cure, then race back to where they now sat. He'd never make it in time.

But there *was* someone who could. "We just need to keep him alive until we can get Rangvaldr to him!"

Zaharis gave a quick nod before turning and sprinting off into the forest. Aravon cradled the Duke's head in his lap, pulling his mouth open gently to pour a trickle of Zaharis' concoction between his lips. The Duke, unconscious, seemed too weak even to swallow.

"Here, let me." Colborn knelt beside him gently massaged Duke Dyrund's throat. Long seconds passed before the Duke finally managed to swallow the few drops.

Come on, Duke Dyrund! Aravon's heart hammered against his bruised ribs, anguish burning a fiery path down his throat and stomach. *Fight, damn it! Just stay alive long enough for us to get Rangvaldr here!*

Rangvaldr's holy stones *had* to work. If the Seiomenn had believed they would cure the Fjall stricken by the plague, it meant they could save the Duke's life.

He tried again, and this time the Duke managed to swallow on his own. One tiny sip, then another. Barely a few drops at a time, but Aravon didn't stop until he had emptied the contents of Zaharis' cup down the Duke's throat.

His eyes locked on the Duke's face. In the glow of their small campfire, the Duke's fever-bright cheeks contrasted sharply with the near-white pallor of the rest of his skin. He shuddered in Aravon's arms, his eyelids fluttering open and closed.

Time slowed to a crawl as Aravon watched, powerless to help the Duke. He gripped the Duke's shiver-wracked frame as if trying to wring the fever from his body. Yet nothing seemed to happen.

It's not working! The effects on Bjarni had been nearly instantaneous, but that had been a proper cure. Not the crude, hastily-mixed remedy comprised of random flowers.

No! Aravon clung to the Duke's body and to the faint hope. *It'll work!*

Duke Dyrund was a strong, stubborn man—*fiery hells, the fact that he somehow got all the way here from Storbjarg is proof of that!* It didn't matter that Wraithfever had already killed fifteen thousand Fjall, including hundreds of the Hilmir's warband. If anyone could fight through the illness, it was the Duke.

Please, Aravon begged silently. He no longer wore the silver Swordsman's pendant, so he clutched the Duke's arm tighter instead. *Please, don't let this be the end. Bring him back to me.*

A torrent of emotions washed over him—all the feelings he'd kept bottled up from the moment he first saw the smoke rising over Storbjarg. He'd forced himself to remain focused on the mission, to put the needs of the Princelands and Fehl over his personal concerns for the Duke's safety. The life of one man, even a man as valuable as the Prince's personal counselor and envoy, meant little compared to the tidal wave of bloodshed that would engulf Fehl if the Eirdkilrs defeated the Fjall.

Yet at that moment, he didn't care what happened beyond the circle of firelight. A fist of iron gripped his heart, squeezing so tightly he felt his chest would burst. His lungs refused to draw breath and his thoughts whirled in a chaotic jumble. He hadn't felt like this since he sat at his mother's bedside. Since he held her hand and watched the Bloody Flux consume her soul, wither away her spirit until nothing but a husk of the bright, smiling woman remained. Then the husk had become a corpse, cold and pale, eyes unseeing.

The loss of his mother had nearly broken him—it had certainly shattered a part of General Traighan's spirit, left him a broken shell of the man he'd once been. Years had passed before Aravon could bear to remember his mother without tears flowing. Only after Mylena had he been able to visit her grave in Icespire Memorial Gardens. The sight of her name carved into the headstone would have broken him had Mylena not been there to hold his hand. He didn't know if he could endure this loss, not after so many others.

The Duke wasn't just his commanding officer, even his mentor; the man had been more like the father figure he'd needed. Far more a father than the cold, distant General Traighan had ever been. A man without whom life would be a crueler, darker place.

He clutched the Duke's forearm tighter and prayed a silent, wordless plea to the Swordsman. Time lost its meaning, and the world seemed to whirl by around Aravon, leaving him alone with the Duke in a bubble suspended in that single moment between life and death. Aravon saw nothing, heard nothing— nothing else mattered but the Duke. All he knew was the beating of his heart, the gentle rise and fall of the Duke's chest, and the tears burning in his eyes.

A hand on his shoulder shattered his trance. Aravon blinked, found himself staring into Zaharis' eyes. When had the Secret Keeper returned? And Belthar, too, with his waterskin full to bulging.

Zaharis' fingers moved, but Aravon's numbed mind refused to grasp the meaning. He looked at the Secret Keeper, unseeing, uncomprehending.

"Captain." Colborn's voice sounded distant, as if he spoke from a mile away, though he stood at Aravon's side. "You need to let him go."

Aravon wanted to protest, to shout that the Duke still lived, that he wasn't ready to give up. But as he caught sight of Skathi moving her bedroll to make a place beside the fire, he understood the meaning of the Lieutenant's words. He released his death-grip on the Duke's arms, letting Colborn and Belthar lift Duke Dyrund from his leaden, numbed hands.

They're taking care of him. With effort, Aravon forced himself to rise from his seated position, to move muscles and limbs that had gone numb from remaining motionless for so long. With movement and the return of blood flow came sensation, a thousand pins and needles prickling along Aravon's spine, arms, and legs. Yet that discomfort pushed back his stupor and his heart seemed to beat once more, his thoughts slowing, coalescing from whirling chaos into something approaching rational thought.

Zaharis knelt over the Duke and tipped the wooden cup up to his lips. Wisps of steam rose from the thick, dark-green liquid within—had Aravon truly been so focused on the Duke that he hadn't noticed Zaharis return and set to work heating up whatever he was now using to treat the fever?

The Secret Keeper emptied the cup into the Duke's mouth, and for a moment it seemed the world stood still. Silence hung thick, tense in the cave. No one breathed, no one moved. All eyes fixed on the Duke, waiting, hoping.

A sound shattered the silence: a ragged, faint inhalation of air. The Duke's chest expanded, and the burning red faded from his cheeks.

Aravon nearly wept with relief. He scrambled to a position kneeling in the dirt beside the Duke, a rush of emotions swelling within his chest as the color returned to the Duke's pale skin, the shivers stopped, and his eyelids ceased fluttering. The Duke breathed easier, rested comfortably.

Aravon's eyes snapped up to Zaharis' face. "Thank you!" The lump in his throat turned his words hoarse. He wanted to throw his arms around the man, to let the tears of joy flow free. He hadn't felt this happy or relieved in what felt like forever.

Zaharis nodded, but his expression was grim. *"I got lucky finding Violet Coneflower back there. Mixed with these Fire Daisies and a bit of white willow bark, it'll slow the fever, stop it from overheating his body and damaging his brain. He's got a chance of holding on a little longer. Hopefully long enough until we can get him to Rangvaldr."*

Mention of the *Seiomenn* snapped Aravon's mind back to reality. The numbness faded and gave way to the memories of their dire situation, the impending battle, and the looming threat of the Eirdkilrs. His worries returned and with them, a burden of guilt.

He'd been so consumed by his concern for the Duke, the overwhelming grief and hopelessness, that he'd nearly lost himself. In that moment, he had a better understanding of his father. Of how his father had become the man Aravon remembered.

He shot a glance at Colborn. "How long?"

The Lieutenant cocked an eyebrow.

"How long was I…" Aravon hesitated, grimacing. "…out of it?"

"Hour. Maybe a little more."

Keeper's teeth! Aravon's jaw clenched. He could easily have drowned within that chasm of emotions. He'd forgotten everything, everyone. At any other time, it could have gotten him killed. Him, or the soldiers under his command.

He stared at his four companions. Guilt and shame brought a flush of heat to his cheeks. "I-I'm sor—"

"Not needed, Captain." Skathi cut him off with a shake of her head. "We know how much the Duke means to you. We've got your back."

Aravon's gaze went to Belthar, and the big man nodded. Colborn and Zaharis likewise. There was no condemnation, no recrimination in their eyes. Only understanding, compassion. Each of them had suffered their own losses, felt crushed by the same burdens of sorrow that weighed on him. That shared pain was what bound them together.

Gratitude surged within his chest. "Thank you," he choked out. He looked at each in turn, at the reassurance on their faces. "Truly."

Belthar grinned. "We're your faceless company, Captain. Your Grim Reavers. No matter what."

Aravon smiled at the name, given them by the men of Rivergate. It felt wonderful to know they cared for him as much as he cared for them. That friendship, that bond of brotherhood, *that* was what made them strong as a team. A bond no enemy could shatter.

A weak moan escaped the Duke's lips, and his eyelids fluttered open once more. "A-Aravon?"

Aravon whirled toward the Duke. "I'm here, Your Grace." He scooped up the Duke's hand; the heat rolling off his skin had diminished, though not gone altogether. "I'm here."

The Duke blinked, struggled to focus on Aravon's face. Slowly, lucidity returned to his eyes as the flush of fever drained from his cheeks. "Where...?" He swallowed, grimacing. "Water!" he croaked.

Before Aravon could ask, Skathi thrust her waterskin toward him with a wince at the pain but no protest. Aravon nodded thanks and, unstoppering the skin, tilted it up to pour a trickle of water into the Duke's mouth. Duke Dyrund swallowed, coughed, and swallowed again. When Aravon tried to give him more, the Duke gave a weak shake of his head.

"Just...had to wash out...the taste...of Zaharis' hogwash."

The Secret Keeper snorted. *"Fine way to say thank you, Your Grace."*

Aravon laughed. The Duke's joke was a clear sign he felt better, at least for now. Zaharis' remedy had bought them a day—hopefully time enough to return with Rangvaldr and his holy stones.

He finally voiced the question he'd been dying to ask since he first found the Duke lying on the riverbed. "How are you here? How did you get out of Storbjarg?"

"Asleif," the Duke croaked. "Underground tunnel...from the Hilmir's longhouse."

Relief flooded Aravon. The Hilmir had been right to place trust in his wife's capabilities.

"The Hilmir's wife...hid us...with her daughter." The Duke gasped for breath as he struggled to sit upright. The fever had left him weak, though his voice grew stronger with every breath. "When the time...came to flee...I helped carry Branda."

Memories of his last conversation with Eirik Throrsson flashed through Aravon's mind. The Hilmir's guilt at not giving his daughter the cure for Wraithfever—fever that had now spread to the Duke.

"Where are they now?" Aravon asked. "The Hilmir's wife and daughter?" Throrsson would want to know—hope and relief at discovering his family alive would spur him to fight, but so would a desire for vengeance.

"Gone." The Duke shook his head. "Asleif...fell in the flight. Captured by Eirdkilr skirmishers."

Aravon's jaw clenched. "And Branda?" He'd never forget the remorse that darkened the Hilmir's eyes, the burden of knowing he'd chosen to let his daughter die.

"Sent north...with Lord Virinus."

Aravon's eyebrows shot up. "What?"

The Duke swallowed, coughed, and swallowed again before speaking. "We found a way...to slow the Wraithfever."

"You found Fetidroot this far south?" Zaharis signed.

The Duke shook his head. "Feverfew, elderberry, something Asleif called yarrow. Bought her a few more days." This time, he managed to push himself upright, his strength returning as the fever retreated. "I tried to send for help—" His hand went to his neck. "—but my bone whistle got lost in the fighting as we fled..." He broke off into a spell of coughing. "Couldn't call Skyclaw to bring...the cure!"

He gasped and coughed again, a deep hacking that brought up phlegm from his lungs, and only recovered after a drink of water. "Lord Virinus has instructions to bring her to Saerheim. Safely out of Fjall territory, and Lord Eidan is sending a dose of the Wraithfever cure there with a fast rider."

Relief lightened the burden on Aravon's shoulders. Throrsson would be glad to hear that his daughter had a chance of living.

The Duke's eyes flew wide and he clutched at Aravon's shirt. "Storbjarg!" he gasped. "The Hilmir was betrayed!"

Blood turned to ice in Aravon's veins. "Betrayed? By whom?"

"I don't know!" The Duke shook his head weakly. "But when the Eirdkilrs attacked, someone threw the gates open for them. Let a small force inside and to set fire to the city and hold the gates long enough for the three thousand from Dagger Garrison to arrive."

They had known of the Eirdkilrs marching from Dagger Garrison, a force that shouldn't have arrived until after midnight the day of the Waeggbjod ambush. But with the *Blodsvarri* marching to spring her trap on the Hilmir, where had that "small force" come from?

Horror seeped ice cold into Aravon's bones. *It can't be!* The very idea seemed an impossibility, and yet...

"How small a force?" He demanded. "How many?"

"A few hundred, I don't know. Not enough to take the city, but certainly enough to destroy the gates and throw Storbjarg into confusion." The Duke shook his head. "I never saw them, but Asleif said they *weren't* the Blood Queen's warriors."

541

Aravon felt as if he'd just taken a warhorse's hoof to the gut. He sat back heavily, his breath catching in his lungs. *By the Keeper!*

"Captain?" Confusion echoed in Colborn's voice.

Aravon turned to the Lieutenant. "The Eirdkilrs from Rivergate."

Colborn's eyes flew wide, and both Belthar and Skathi sucked in sharp breaths. "What?" Skathi demanded.

A grim chill settled into his body. "We knew they had crossed the Westmarch, but we never found their tracks."

"But Gold Burrows Mine—" Belthar rumbled.

"The attack on the mine came from the southwest." Colborn's mind was clearly working along the same lines as Aravon. "The *Blodsvarri's* warriors!"

Aravon nodded glumly. "If she had someone within the Hilmir's warband, she'd have to know that Throrsson had reached out to the Deid." The sheer breathtaking scope of her cunning and foresight staggered him. "That attack wasn't just about the gold. She wanted to send a clear message to the Deid."

"Get them to abandon the fight, just like they did." Colborn's bushy blond eyebrows knitted together.

"What?" The Duke's eyebrows shot up. "The Deid have abandoned the Hilmir?"

Aravon filled the Duke in on everything that had happened since they rode out of Storbjarg—the Hilmir's defeat and loss of his eleven hundred men, the attack on Storbjarg and the ambush on the Blood Queen, the *Fornbryggja* and the fighting retreat. "We've managed to turn back everything she's thrown at us, but no matter what we do, in the end it comes down to the fact that she's just got too many damned men. We're on our final play, our last hope. The Hilmir's digging in at Hangman's Hill right now." Aravon shot a glance at the cave mouth—the sky outside had already begun to brighten. "We should already be on our way there. He's expecting an enemy to attack just after dawn. With Bjarni's eight hundred and the two-hundred fifty men under Grimar, that'll put his forces at…"

He trailed off, fresh horror driving a dagger of ice deep into his spine. "Grimar!" The word burst from his mouth with explosive force. "Grimar was one of the only Fjall who knew the Hilmir's plan. *He* was the one left to guard the gates of Storbjarg."

"*He* is the traitor," Colborn breathed.

Chapter Sixty-Nine

Aravon's gut clenched. *Bloody hell!* The warrior's shame and remorse had all been an act. If he *was* the traitor, he could have been sent by the Blood Queen to strike down Bjarni. That explained his surprise at finding the Hilmir still lived—the Eirdkilrs had to have believed the Fjall's rage at Throrsson's death.

And we just sent him marching straight toward the Hilmir.

The *Blodsvarri's* insidiousness knew no bounds. A sudden betrayal at the right moment in the impending battle could not only turn it into a rout—it would lead to the death of the Hilmir, Bjarni, and every Fjall loyal to Throrsson. Those two hundred and fifty Fjall warriors with Grimar were a sharp knife poised to drive into the Hilmir's back.

Aravon leapt to his feet. "We've got to warn the Hilmir!"

Colborn, Belthar, and Zaharis were a heartbeat behind him, and even Skathi struggled upright, wincing at the pain in her head and shoulder.

"Colborn, Belthar, with me!" Aravon snapped. "Skathi, you're with Zaharis."

Anger blazed in Skathi's eyes. "I already told you, Captain, I can fight!"

"I'm counting on that!" Aravon's jaw clenched. "I need Zaharis to do everything he can to keep the Duke's fever at bay until we can get Rangvaldr. Which means I need *you* to watch his back."

Skathi's expression hardened, her eyes going flat, cold. Aravon had a good guess what was going through her mind—he'd felt the same after the ambush on the Eastmarch, a need to earn the respect of the men beside whom he

543

fought, to show he wasn't weak despite his injuries. But this wasn't the time for that. He needed her to *obey*, for her sake as well as the Duke's.

After a long moment, her features softened. "Understood, Captain." She nodded, the icy look leaving her eyes.

Relief flooded Aravon. That answer spoke volumes about the change in Skathi. She'd taken his words to heart. She *was* one of the team, with no need to prove anything to anyone.

Colborn spoke quickly. "The Eirdkilrs shouldn't be coming this way, but just in case—"

"*We'll keep out of sight,*" Zaharis signed. "*Wait for you to send word that all's clear.*"

"Aravon." Duke Dyrund's voice drifted up from where he sat.

Aravon turned to kneel beside the Duke. "I've got to go, Your Grace, but Zaharis will get you fighting fit in no time." He shot a glance up at Skathi. "As soon as we can, I'll send Snarl with a place to meet us, where Rangvaldr can do his thing."

Skathi nodded. "I'll be watching." She knelt and reached a hand under Snarl's neck to scratch his scruff, earning a delighted *yip* from the little Enfield.

"Be safe, Aravon." The Duke reached out to clasp his hand. "You've accomplished so much more here than I could have ever imagined. Know that no matter what happens today, I could not be more proud of you."

A lump rose to Aravon's throat. "Thank you, sir." It was the first time he'd ever heard those words…from anyone. "You just worry about healing up, and leave the battle to us."

He locked gazes with the Duke, saw the pride and respect glimmering there. Tears burned at his eyes and he felt an overpowering urge to embrace the Duke. But he settled for squeezing the Duke's hand.

"We'll be back before you know it."

The Duke gave him a little smile and a nod, but his words were interrupted by a fit of coughing.

Aravon stood quickly—if he didn't go now, he might not be able to bring himself to leave the Duke's side—and turned to Zaharis. "Take care of him, Zaharis."

"*Aye, Captain,*" the Secret Keeper signed. "*Split some Eirdkilrs heads for me, yeah?*"

With a grim chuckle, Aravon strode past the Secret Keeper. "Colborn, Belthar, we ride now."

Colborn moved toward his pack and set about stowing his gear without a word. Belthar hesitated only an instant, casting a glance at Skathi.

"Get out of here!" Skathi growled. "It's just cruel to rub in the fact that you get to have all the fun!" Her tone was angry, but humor sparkled in her eyes.

"Want I should send a few this way?" Belthar asked. "I can always paint a big sign in Eirdkilr runes saying, 'The cave of wonders—get your arrows here'!"

Skathi chuckled. "Eirdkilrs can't read, you big idiot!"

"Oh, yeah." Belthar shrugged. "Next time, then."

As Belthar turned to his pack, Aravon slung his own satchel over his shoulder and fixed Zaharis with a stern gaze. "Keep him alive, no matter what!"

"Go, Captain!" Skathi gave him a dismissive wave. "We've got this."

Aravon scooped up his spear and Odarian steel longsword and, with Snarl, Colborn, and Belthar on his heels, strode from the cave. The four of them slipped through the pre-dawn darkness of the riverbank to where they had left their horses grazing out of sight beneath a rocky outcropping.

They moved in silence, strapping their packs in place with deft movements and climbing into their saddles. At Aravon's wordless command, they wheeled their horses northwest, toward Hangman's Hill and the place where the Fjall would do battle with the Eirdkilrs.

"Go, Snarl!" Aravon shouted the command word. The little Enfield sprang into the air, snapping out its wings, and rose quickly into the slowly-brightening sky. He disappeared into the darkness to the north, a silent shadow that would watch over them from high above.

Grim resolve hardened within Aravon as he kicked his horse into motion. *Please don't let us be too late!*

Their pace was slow, the horses cautious as they picked their way over the smooth stones of the river. They'd chosen the cave not only for its location, out of the Eirdkilrs' path; it was also accessible from a single spot where the bluffs along the Hardrfoss River dipped low enough to descend to the rocky riverbank.

Aravon chafed at the slow pace, but he couldn't push the horses to run faster. He gritted his teeth and focused on figuring out how to prevent whatever

545

treachery Grimar intended. He had to get to the Hilmir *before* the battle and warn him of his second-in-command's betrayal.

Finally, after what seemed an eternity, they reached the dip in the bluffs, and Aravon spurred his horse onto the flat ground west of the Hardrfoss River. The Eirdkilrs would be traveling east of the river, heading straight toward Hangman's Hill. That meant the three of them could ride north along the Hardrfoss' western bank without fear of discovery. They'd have to find a place to cross over *before* reaching Hangman's Hill, but if they hurried, they might be able to reach it before the Blood Queen's men arrived.

"Hyah!" Aravon dug his heels into his horse's ribs, and the charger leapt forward into a gallop. The thundering of hooves filled Aravon's world as he crouched low over the horse's back, and the landscape flew past in a blur of dark and light grays. The sun hadn't yet risen, but his horse had far better night vision than any human eyes. The *Kostarasar* chargers, specially bred for long-distance running at high speeds, were as stable and dexterous as any prized Princeland racehorse.

He slowed his horse only long enough for Colborn to take the lead—the Lieutenant could read the terrain far better than he, making him better-suited to guide their desperate ride. Glancing back, Aravon found Belthar stubbornly clinging to his horse's back. The big man had never been the best rider, yet he had never slowed them down, either. He'd kept up through sheer force of will and physical strength.

Aravon's heart hammered in time with his horse's pounding hooves. Their little hidden campsite was less than ten miles from Hangman's Hill, mostly across flat or lightly-forested terrain. With the horses running at top speed—galloping for the first half-mile, then slowing to that smooth, rolling gait unique to their breed—they'd reach the battleground in less than an hour.

An hour. Aravon's gaze darted eastward. The first glimmers of light blue had begun to brighten the sky over the horizon. *It's going to be bloody close!*

Up hills, through thickets of towering birch trees and leafy alders, down gentle inclines, and across rolling grasslands. One thundering step at a time, their horses' hooves flying. Aravon's jaw ached from clenching, his teeth grinding in his gums. Fire scorched through his legs and down his spine, yet he only gripped his reins tighter and silently urged the horse to run faster.

We've got to get there in time!

If they didn't, Grimar would turn on the Hilmir and the Eirdkilrs—already vastly outnumbering the Fehlans—would win. The Fjall would be defeated, the most powerful warband south of the Chain destroyed. Without them, Fehl would fall to the Eirdkilrs.

I'll be damned if I let that happen, Aravon growled inwardly. He'd stop the treacherous Grimar, even if he had to put a dagger in the man's eye with his own hands.

Yet, as the eastern sky slowly brightened, the knots in Aravon's shoulders grew tighter. Nervous, anxious sweat rolled down his brow and soaked into his tunic and leather gloves. With every rib-pounding heartbeat, dawn drew nearer.

Then the first golden rays of sunshine peered over the treetops. In desperation, Aravon scanned the terrain ahead. The gleaming, white-tinged ribbon of the Hardrfoss River carved a sinuous path through the grasslands and forests to the north. The tree cover to the east remained unbroken, the grasslands west of the river empty and silent.

Aravon blessed the silence. Had the Eirdkilrs arrived, they'd already hear the clash of battle, the howling war cries, the shouts and screams of men bleeding and dying. As long as the terrain remained quiet, blanketed in a shroud of peace, he was still in time to reach the Hilmir.

Hope surged within him as he saw the Hardrfoss River curving sharply east and disappearing behind a hill. A hill that rose in a steep incline, and upon which stood hundreds of Fjall warriors clad in heavy fur cloaks and ringing chain mail, who carried swords, axes, and shields emblazoned with the black *Reafan* of the Fjall.

Hangman's Hill!

And still, silence hung thick in the air, broken only by the thundering of horses' hooves and Aravon's fast-beating heart.

We made it! He followed Colborn down the gentle hill that descended toward the river crossing just southwest of Hangman's Hill. They had arrived in time to warn the Hilmir of Grimar's treachery. They'd reached the battlefield before—

Then the first enormous figure lumbered out of the forest. Shaggy-haired, with a thick white icebear pelt slung over his shoulders, a steel skullcap crowning his head. He carried a shield four feet wide slung over his back, and his massive hands gripped a spear as long as Aravon was tall.

One Eirdkilr, then a second, equally massive and armed for battle. More followed, five growing to ten, then thirty, and still the barbarians emerged from the forest. One hundred, two hundred, five hundred, all forming up at the crossing, barring Aravon's path to the Hilmir.

The sight shattered Aravon's hopes and sent his heart plummeting into his stomach. They had arrived too late. The Eirdkilrs were here.

The battle for Hangman's Hill had begun, and there was no way he could warn the Hilmir of the traitor in the Fjall ranks in time.

Chapter Seventy

Colborn veered off sharply to his left, riding hard to the west and ducking into the sparse trees that grew a few hundred yards from the riverbank. Aravon, close on Colborn's heels, barely had time to realize what the Lieutenant was doing and spur his horse to follow. With Belthar at their back, the three of them raced through the towering birches, leafy alders, and nut-laden walnut trees.

He risked a glance east; the Eirdkilrs at the crossing hadn't turned toward them, gave no indication they'd realized the three riders were even there. Colborn's quick thinking had avoided a fight. Now it was up to them figure out how to get to the Hilmir.

They raced north, drawing abreast with the crossing and thundering past. Branches slapped at Aravon's helmeted head, shoulders, and face, forcing him to duck low. A grunt and *crack* from behind told him Belthar hadn't been so lucky. Yet, the pounding hooves of Belthar's horse remained close—the big man had managed to keep his seat.

Slowly, the forests thinned and gave way to berry bushes and thick shrubs. The gaps between the leafy branches widened and Aravon had a clearer view of the field of battle to the east.

Hangman's Hill had earned its Princelander name for the twin king oak trees that stood at its summit. The thick branches of the hundred-foot-tall trees had intertwined as the oaks grew, forming a square frame resembling the arms of a gallows. But the Fehlan name, *Banamadrhaed,* meant Executioner's Hill—a name that harked back to the ancient days of Fehl. Legends held that on *Banamadrhaed,* the mighty Asvard Giantsbane had forced *Bergrisi,* the giant from which it was rumored the Eirdkilrs had descended, to kneel in death or surrender. *Bergrisi* had chosen death by beheading, and his blood had watered the soil from which those enormous trees grew.

Aravon paid the legends little heed. To him, it mattered only as a defensive position—as ideal a location as the Hilmir could have chosen. Dense marshlands and bogs guarded the Hilmir's eastern flank, while the Hardrfoss River provided defense to his west. The summit of the hill was close to a hundred yards wide, and the Fjall had more than enough men to hold it.

And Throrsson hadn't wasted a moment of the last two days. Heavy wooden barricades had been built around the bases of the two king oak trees, impassable spike-topped barriers intended to funnel the enemy toward three sections of the hilltop. The openings in the constructions were barely five yards across, and in those gaps stood the Fjall shield wall. A solid, unbroken line of fur-and-steel-clad warriors with gleaming steel helmets, bristling weapons, and shields displaying the black-on-red *Reafan* of the Hilmir. Front and center, at the head of his men, stood Throrsson himself, resplendent in chain mail that seemed to shimmer in the daylight.

To reach him, the Eirdkilrs would have to charge straight up two hundred yards of steep, muddy slope. The altitude also limited the effectiveness of the Eirdkilr archers. And, if the Hilmir was half the tactician Aravon believed, he would have used every minute of the last two days planning for the inevitable Eirdkilr charge.

The enemy had pushed him into a corner, and now the Hilmir set his back against a wall and bared his fangs at the *Blodsvarri's* army.

As Aravon drew abreast of the field's southern edge, he caught sight of the ever-growing ranks of Eirdkilrs forming their own wall at the base of Hangman's Hill. Thousands of them, huge figures in shaggy icebear pelts, faces stained dark blue. Weapons far too large for any Fehlan or Princelander to wield, clutched in hands that could crush skulls and tear out throats.

Yet the towering barbarians made no move to attack. They had no need to hurry—their enemy was within their grasp, with no way of escape. Though the Fjall held the high ground, they had nowhere to retreat. The Hardrfoss River circled northward, curling around behind Hangman's Hill and cutting off any avenue of escape. Once the Eirdkilrs closed with Hilmir's men, there would be no way out. Death or victory—given the number of Eirdkilrs arrayed at the base of the hill, the latter was next to impossible.

550

Their plan to lure the Blood Queen to battle here had paid off. Now, the Eirdkilrs would have to assault the Fjall, dug into a position of advantage. All their efforts over the last few days—whittling down the Eirdkilr forces in bite-sized chunks and preparing for this fight—was just the preamble. Neither the Hilmir nor Aravon had doubted it would come to battle. Eirdkilr and Fjall locked shield wall to shield wall. The outcome rested on the courage, skill, and determination of the Fjall warband.

Not if Grimar springs his trap!

Aravon reined in his horse just within the cover of trees and scanned the ranks of Fjall warriors, desperately searching for the treacherous Fjall warrior. Behind their locked shields, with bright steel helms covering their faces, Aravon had no way of telling Grimar and his warriors apart from the rest of the warband. The treacherous Grimar could be standing at Throrsson's side, ready to turn on his Hilmir at a crucial moment in battle.

"Shite!" Colborn's curse echoed from beside Aravon. The Lieutenant had pulled up and circled back toward him. "What's the plan, Captain?"

Aravon forced himself *not* to look at the enemy preparing to attack, but instead study the terrain. Tension knotted his shoulders as his eyes followed the land northward. The western bank of the Hardrfoss River rose as steeply as Hangman's Hill, but the river was too broad to ford anywhere but the shallow crossing—the crossing now guarded by more than six hundred Eirdkilrs.

Even if they followed the river's course, they wouldn't find a way across. The Hardrfoss circled in a tight horseshoe bend toward the northeast of Hangman's Hill, then cut sharply northward in the direction of Cold Lake and Saerheim.

Yet something nagged in the back of Aravon's mind. A memory from Lectern Harald's story of the battle between the Fjall, Deid, and Legionnaires.

He whirled to Colborn. "You remember the Battle of Hangman's Hill, yeah?"

Colborn nodded, eyes narrowing behind his mask.

"Is it just me, or was there mention of a *bridge* in that story?"

"Of course!" Colborn's eyes widened and he sucked in a breath. "A narrow footbridge, used by pilgrims come to visit the site of the Giantsbane's victory!"

"That's the one." Aravon's mind raced. "The Legion used it to reinforce the Deid's position on the hilltop—"

551

"—sending three full companies across, until...." Colborn's excitement faded. "Shite!"

Then Aravon remembered why he hadn't bothered to include that bridge in his battle plan: it had crumbled beneath the weight of the Legionnaires. Half a Legion company had died in that collapse, drowned in their armor, dashed against the rocks, or swept downstream by the current.

Keeper's teeth! There *was* no bridge. In the aftermath of the battle, the Fjall and Deid had both claimed the land as their own, which meant neither had rebuilt the crossing. Nothing remained but the weathered, rotted wooden supports that had given way and nearly lost the battle.

Aravon's momentary hopes shattered. With the Eirdkilrs holding the ford and no way to get across the Hardrfoss, he'd never get to the Hilmir in time to warn him of Grimar's treachery.

Despair loomed heavy in his mind, a weight that threatened to drag him down. He gritted his teeth and pushed back against the burden. The setback couldn't stop him from reaching Throrsson *before* the battle was lost.

"Belthar, with me!" Aravon ordered. "Colborn, head south along the Hardrfoss, see if you can find us any kind of way across." He turned his horse's head northward.

"Where are you going?" Colborn called after him.

"To see about that bridge!" Memories of Rivergate flashed through Aravon's mind. There, too, the bridge had been destroyed, but they'd built a way across. "If I'm not back in a quarter-hour, that means I've found a way." It was a faint hope, but anything was better than nothing.

"Aye, Captain!" Colborn's voice echoed through the trees behind him.

Aravon raced northward, keeping to the tree cover to conceal his position from the Eirdkilrs to the east. He bent low over his horse's neck, both to avoid the branches whipping past and to remain balanced. Every chance he got, he risked casting glances at Hangman's Hill.

The Eirdkilrs hadn't charged. Yet. Their battle cries filled the morning air, piercing howls that rang off the steep slopes of the hill. The Fjall remained silent, defiant, unmoving. Aravon didn't need to see their faces to know that every man on that hilltop was feeling the nerves before battle. Jaws clenching, fists tightening around weapons, hearts hammering in Fjall chests. Even the bravest warriors suffered that instinctive fear in the minutes before the enemy charge, the clash of weapons and shields.

Then the Eirdkilrs fell silent. So suddenly, as if all sound had been sucked out of the world, leaving only a void of utter stillness. Even the pounding of the horses' hooves seemed to grow quieter in that lull.

Aravon risked a glance eastward in time to see a single figure break free of the pack. Long, dark hair hung in myriad braids around the *Blodsvarri's* blue-tattooed, blood-crusted face. Spear in hand, a snarl on her lips, the Blood Queen marched a few feet up the hill. Her voice rang out in the distance—too far for Aravon to hear what she said, but he had little doubt as to her message. Insults to the Fjall, threats of death and torture, promises of the suffering she'd heap on the families of every man who stood in that shield wall.

The Blood Queen's snarling shouts continued for long minutes, her guttural Eirdkilr words ringing out with a burning ferocity that sent an instinctive shiver down Aravon's spine. A part of his mind, a part deep down within him, almost gave in to the belief that she *would* win. Her forces not only outnumbered the Fjall two to one, but she had the traitor hiding in Throrsson's ranks. Two hundred and fifty traitors.

And Aravon could do nothing to warn the Hilmir of the danger.

Chapter Seventy-One

Gritting his teeth, Aravon gripped the reins tighter and dug his heels into his horse's flanks, pushing the charger to a gallop. His racing path led north and east, circling around behind *Banamadrhaed*. As he drew abreast of the hill's summit, he got a clear view of the Hilmir's forces arrayed behind the barricades. The Fjall stood in three spearhead formations, the sharp tips thrust through the openings in the bulwarks and growing wider until they joined into one solid, unbroken line of warriors. A strong, well-anchored position—as long as they held the hilltop.

Hope bloomed radiant as Aravon caught sight of the bridge on the hill's northern slope. It *had* been destroyed in the Battle of Hangman's Hill, but someone had rebuilt it. The construction was as crude as the Eirdkilrs' repair of the *Fornbryggja*, little more than logs lashed together with rope. It was barely wide enough for two men to cross abreast. Yet its presence meant *everything* for the battle ahead.

Throrsson, you bloody genius!

Aravon's eyes snapped upward toward the Hilmir's ranks, and he counted quickly. Something about the shield wall had struck him as off, and now he knew what it was.

There are two hundred Fjall missing!

The Hilmir had taken seven hundred and fifty men to prepare the battle at Hangman's Hill. Bjarni had lost a hundred-twenty of his original eight hundred men in the last two days of ambushes and fighting retreat. With Grimar's two hundred and fifty to swell the Hilmir's ranks, the Fjall warband formed up on the hill's summit ought to number close to eighteen hundred. Yet, Aravon estimated fewer than sixteen hundred stood in the Fjall shield wall.

So where the hell are those other warriors?

As Aravon approached the crudely-repaired bridge, he caught sight of bootprints leading off north and west into the sparse forests. His mind raced.

If the Hilmir had sent two hundred of his warriors to the west, it meant he planned to take advantage of the crossing southwest of Hangman's Hill—the same one now held by the Eirdkilrs. Such a small force would inflict few casualties on a solid wall of enemies, but once the Blood Queen had committed her men to the charge…

Hit them from the back hard, take advantage of their eyes locked on the hill.

But the genius wasn't in just the flanking attack. With the bridge restored, Throrsson had an avenue of retreat. He'd pay a heavy toll in Fjall blood if he yielded the hill, but Aravon knew the Hilmir well enough by now to know he'd *only* do it in extremis.

Given what they're facing, that may be all too soon!

As if on cue, the Eirdkilrs took up the howling war cries again. The Fjall responded now. Defiant shouts, cries of "For *Striith!*", and the deafening clash of swords and axes on steel-rimmed shields. A cacophony of fury and contempt, a challenge to the enemy arrayed against them. Daring them to charge and taste the full force of the warband's might.

The tumult set acid churning through Aravon's stomach. He had to hurry to reach the Hilmir before—

The Eirdkilrs' howls rose in volume and, with a shrieking cry from the *Blodsvarri*, the giant barbarians charged. A thundering tide of warriors that set the ground trembling as they lumbered up the hill toward the Fjall position.

Damn it!

Then the land west of the Hardrfoss dipped, and the rising ridge of Hangman's Hill hid the charging enemies from view. But not their cries, those eerie, bestial howls that rolled over the warriors clustered among the hilltop and rang around the empty land around Aravon.

Come on!

Aravon raced the last two hundred yards toward the repaired bridge and drew his horse to a skidding, panting halt. He leapt from the saddle before his charger came to a full stop and spun toward the two figures that had followed him.

"Belthar!" he shouted. "Get back to Colborn and tell him the Fjall are going to hit the Eirdkilrs at the southwestern crossing. The two of you, find them and lend a hand."

"You can't go alone, Captain!" Belthar protested. "Not with Grimar waiting to strike."

Aravon opened his mouth to snap a retort, to *order* Belthar to obey. Yet, the words died on his lips unformed. The big man was right. Those two hundred Fjall warriors were an arrow in the Hilmir's strategic quiver, but their rear attack wouldn't matter if the main Fjall force crumbled.

"Go!" Aravon thrust a finger back the way they'd come. "Get to Colborn, tell him the plan, then get across and join me on the hill! We're going to do our damnedest to keep the Hilmir alive."

"Yes, sir!" Belthar sawed savagely at his horse's reins, turning the beast's head back the way they'd come. He dug his huge heels into the charger's ribs and set off at a gallop in the direction of where they'd left Colborn.

That left Snarl. The Enfield had dropped out of the sky and landed on the grassy hill beside him, amber eyes gleaming in the bright morning light.

"Go!" Aravon shouted the command word and thrust a finger at the tree cover. "Hide!"

Snarl gave a little whine and padded closer to Aravon.

"No." Aravon shook his head. "You can't fight, not here."

The Enfield had saved Noll and Rangvaldr in the battle at Rivergate, but here, in broad daylight, he'd be too visible and a target for Eirdkilr arrows. Aravon wasn't willing to risk Snarl's life.

The bright yellow of Snarl's eyes darkened and the Enfield sat on its haunches, staring up at Aravon and filling the air with its whining barks.

Aravon knelt beside Snarl. "Go," he whispered. "Stay safe, Snarl!"

Snarl nuzzled against him, his fur soft on Aravon's neck, his body warm and comforting. His trust filled Aravon with confidence and hope—they could *do* this!

He gave the Enfield a gentle push. "Go!" he shouted the command word. "Hide!"

Snarl obeyed this time, turning and racing toward the trees a hundred yards away. Aravon had little doubt the Enfield would watch the battle, watch over him, but as long as Snarl was safe, he could focus on doing what needed to be done.

Whirling, he raced the few steps toward the bridge and leapt onto the rope-bound logs that stretched across the wooden supports. The logs groaned and shifted beneath his boots, but the Hilmir's construction held.

The howling of the Eirdkilrs echoed loud enough for Aravon to hear clearly, even with the hill between them—clear enough that he could hear the cries change, from glee at finding their enemy trapped to ringing notes of pain and surprise.

A defiant grin split Aravon's face. *Give them hell, Throrsson!*

The hastily rebuilt bridge was no architectural masterpiece, but it would suffice if the Hilmir had cause to use it. More than that, it gave Aravon a way across—and with it, hope for the battle. Aravon just had to reach Throrsson before it was too late.

The Eirdkilrs' howls of agony redoubled as Aravon leapt off the bridge onto the reverse slope of Hangman's Hill. He dashed the twenty yards up the steep incline and crested the sharp ridge.

Just in time to see hundreds of Eirdkilrs stumble and fall. The barbarians' cries of agony rent the air as they raced across a stretch of hillside strewn with jagged rocks. Similar to Legion-made caltrops, the debris slowed the enemy charge. Eirdkilrs staggered or collapsed, ankles snapped, and the rocks sliced the Eirdkilr boots to ribbons. The thundering charge slowed as the enemy stumbled and fell.

Slowed, but didn't stop. With no archers or darts to throw, the Fjall could do nothing to take advantage of the Eirdkilrs' stalled momentum. The jagged rocks would inflict a handful of casualties at best, force the Eirdkilrs to pick their way across the uneven terrain, but the Hilmir had no way to bite back.

The Eirdkilrs, however, had archers aplenty. The thousand warriors surrounding the *Blodsvarri* raised their massive longbows, drew, and loosed. Hundreds of black-shafted arrows darkened the brightening southern sky, filling the air with a terrible hissing. Missiles driven by the powerful Eirdkilr longbows arced high, slowed, and plunged toward the Fjall shield wall.

"Shields!" came the Hilmir's roar. In a single smooth motion, the wall of red-and-black-painted shields swiveled upward, locking together to form a carapace as solid as a tortoise's shell—a Fjall tactic the Legion of Heroes had imitated when conquering Fehl centuries earlier.

Aravon spared the arrows a single glance—they'd fall short, he knew. The Eirdkilrs had underestimated the steep angle of the hill and the distance.

Yet as he raced toward the rearmost ranks of the shield wall, he knew the Fjall wouldn't get lucky with the second volley. Only the specially-trained Agrotorae exceeded the skill of Eirdkilr archers.

"Hilmir!" Aravon shouted in Fehlan. His voice was drowned beneath a hailstorm of steel and stone-tipped arrows *thumping* into the grassy hillside just beyond the Fjall's front ranks.

Before he could shout again, the second wave of missiles rained down around him. The Eirdkilr archers had found their range.

Aravon threw himself under cover of the Fjall's upraised shields. Heavy Eirdkilr arrows thumped into shields made of hide-reinforced wooden planks banded with steel. Screams echoed along the Fjall lines as arrows slipped through tiny gaps, punched into chain mail or sliced exposed flesh. Pain flared through Aravon's neck as one slammed into his aventail. The arrow that would have plunged into his throat bounced off the alchemically-treated leather, but not without impact. Sharp, stabbing twinges radiated down his neck and into his left shoulder.

The rain of arrows had barely slowed before Aravon risked moving again. He darted out from beneath the Fjall shields and raced along the rear of the shield wall toward Throrsson's position at the center of the line.

"Hilmir!" he shouted, in a vain hope Throrsson could hear him over the clattering of arrows and the Eirdkilr howls.

Legion Commanders directed the battle from the rear, trusting their Captains, Lieutenants, and Sergeants to lead the individual squads and platoons that made up their companies and battalions. But a Fehlan shield wall was a beast of a very different nature. Instead of fighting in individual, independent companies, Fjall warriors formed a single, solid line that stretched across the hilltop. The leader of the warband *always* fought at the front and center of the battle line, his trusted seconds to his right and left, flanked by the most skilled and heavily-armored of his warriors.

That position made it near-impossible for Aravon to reach him with warning of Grimar's treachery.

A fourth volley of arrows forced Aravon to take cover once more. He gritted his teeth in frustration as he waited for the rain of missiles to slow. The thunderous *clanking* and *banging* of arrows striking shields, armor, and helmets deafened him, made it difficult to think clearly. Adrenaline surged in his veins, narrowing his field of vision to the panting, grunting warriors around him, the stink of blood, the metallic taste in his parched throat.

Aravon blinked hard, pushing back the fog of battle. He risked a glance out from beneath the shield cover and gauged the distance to Throrsson's position. The bridge stood at the northeastern corner of Hangman's Hill, fully fifty yards from the center of the Fjall line. He'd crossed barely half that distance, and at the rate the Eirdkilrs kept firing, it'd take him at least a half minute to cover the rest. Far too long.

A lot could happen in thirty seconds.

Screw it! Gritting his teeth, Aravon abandoned the protective carapace of shields and raced along the rear of the line. Arrows rained down around him, *thumping* into the ground, *clanging* off shields and helmets, or *thudding* into flesh. Fjall warriors shrieked, grunted, or cried beneath the torrent of missiles. One man immediately in front of Aravon toppled backward, a black-fletched shaft protruding from his throat. Blood gushed from his neck and stained the grass dark crimson.

Aravon had an instant to react. No time to dodge, so he leapt over the slumping body. Pain raced up his left shoulder as an Eirdkilr arrow clipped his pauldron. The impact spun him half around and he hit the ground hard, staggered, thrown off-balance. A clod of dirt gave way underfoot and he went down. Soft grass slammed into his right side, shoulder, and face, setting his head spinning. For a moment, the world whirled wildly around Aravon, and pain raced through his neck and shoulders.

With effort, he levered himself upright and struggled to rise. His eyes flew wide as he saw the arrow embedded in the ground a hand's breadth from where he'd lain. Pushing back the instinctive surge of fear at his near-death, he rose to his feet and hurried onward.

Yet as he placed his weight on his right foot, a sharp twinge of pain raced up and down his leg. His ankle had been twisted, slowing him down. The throbbing in his shoulders and neck spread up to his head, and pounding that settled in his skull. Aravon gritted his teeth and forced himself to hobble onward, down the line, toward the Hilmir.

I've got to get there in time to warn him!

The Eirdkilrs' howling war cries redoubled, the piercing shrieks adding to his splitting headache. Through a gap in the upraised shields, Aravon caught sight of the huge fur-clad figures resuming their charge up the hill. A murderous tide of shaggy furs, filthy leather and gleaming mail, blue-stained faces, hatred blazing in their eyes.

Suddenly, the foremost ranks of Eirdkilrs seemed to drop out of sight. Hundreds fell from view, as if swept over the edge of a waterfall. Muffled screams of pain echoed from where they had been a heartbeat earlier.

"Enjoy the taste of those spikes, you bastards!" one of the nearby Fjall warriors roared at the enemy.

Pain or not, Aravon couldn't help a fierce smile. *Well done, Hilmir!* Spike pits were primitive, the sort of hunting traps used to snare prey, but highly effective. They required far more time and effort to build than the Legion cared to invest—far better to build earthen mounds to slow an Eirdkilr charge long enough to rain arrows down on them or unleash a swarm of ballista bolts. But without missile weapons, the Hilmir had been forced to use the terrain against his enemy. No supplies were needed to dig pits, and the forest below offered an abundance of wood to use for spikes.

Slowly, the pain in Aravon's ankle faded and he picked up speed. Thirty yards closed to twenty, then fifteen, ten, and five. Hope surged within his chest as he caught sight of a familiar broad-shouldered, black fur-clad figure at the front of the Fjall ranks.

"Hilmir!" Aravon waded into the densely-packed Fjall, shoving his way through the press of men. The rearmost of the eight ranks were formed more loosely, but he couldn't get past the fifth rank. The warriors standing shoulder to shoulder, pressed against each other in their determination to hold the opening in the barricade. His attempts to push through were met with snarls, curses, and strong arms that shoved him backward.

Desperate, Aravon raised his voice as loud as he could. "Hilmir!"

Throrsson never turned. At the head of his warriors, flanked by his son and Sigbrand, with his eyes locked on the enemy, the Hilmir would be seeing nothing but the battle ahead, the Eirdkilrs coming for his blood. That unbreakable focus, the sharpness of mind and clarity of thought, was a warrior's greatest blessing and most dire curse. Time slowed in combat, the world narrowing until all that was the enemy ahead and the solid feel of weapons in one's hands.

Damn it! Aravon couldn't let himself be drawn into the battle focus—the strength of the warriors at his side, the hammering of his heart, the cries and shouts of the warriors in the shield wall, the smell of blood in the air. He had to stay back, keep an eye on the big picture.

At that moment, that meant warning the Hilmir. He could keep trying to force his way through to the Hilmir's side, but without a shield, he'd only weaken the defensive line. Without hesitation, he turned and pulled back, shouldering his way out of the tightly-packed ranks of Fjall warriors. Behind the lines, free to move once more, he could plan his next move.

The spike pits had slowed the Eirdkilr advance and bought the Hilmir a few seconds. The enemy archers kept up a steady stream of fire, but now Aravon realized that it wasn't just the Fjall shields keeping the arrows at bay. Throrsson's wooden barriers sheltered his warriors from the Eirdkilr fury. The Blood Queen's archers couldn't shoot directly at the Fjall shield wall, but had to try for high-arching plunging fire. By the time the arrows slammed into the upraised shields, their energy had been all but expended.

Aravon spent those precious seconds deciding his next move. Throrsson was too lost in the heat of battle to be aware of Aravon. That meant Aravon would have to deal with the threat of Grimar himself.

He scanned the ranks of Fjall warriors, and breathed a sigh of relief. By the Swordsman's mercy, the traitor wasn't within striking range of the Hilmir. There existed a chance he'd planted one of his warriors in close proximity to Throrsson, but if Aravon could find and eliminate Grimar, he could prevent the man from giving his men whatever order the Blood Queen expected them to carry out.

He risked a glance downhill, and his gut tightened as he caught sight of the enemy. The Eirdkilrs had lost scores to the spike pits, but those behind the front ranks had no trouble skirting the traps. Their momentum had slowed for less than a minute. Now their furious howls split the air once more as the foremost warriors raced up the steep incline.

"Now!" Throrsson roared.

The Fjall warriors behind the barricades lowered their shields and, bending forward, lifted heavy poles from the ground. Poles they set against the topmost logs on their wooden wall. Dozens of Fehlans threw their weight to the task,

562

roaring with the effort. Slowly, the logs toppled off the barricades, and loud *thumps* echoed across the battlefield. A slow rumbling sound filled the air as the logs rolled down the hill.

Straight toward the Eirdkilrs picking their way between the spike pits.

Yes!

Hope surged within Aravon as the huge logs rolled into the tightly-packed ranks of enemies. Wood slammed into the Eirdkilrs with bone-shattering force, felling them by the dozens. Some were crushed beneath the weight of the rolling logs, while others were hurled backward into the spike pits.

Yet too few. Far, far too few. By the time the logs rolled through the ranks of Eirdkilrs, casualties numbered no more than a hundred and fifty. That left close to three thousand left to face the sixteen hundred arrayed beside the Hilmir. A few traps and snares wouldn't stop the Eirdkilrs.

The ululating war cries split the air as the massive figures charged up the hill. The ground trembled beneath the force of their pounding feet. Like a tidal wave of hideous flesh, bone, and filthy fur, they came on. Slowed by the steep incline, yet inexorable in their advance.

With effort, Aravon tore his eyes away from the charging Eirdkilrs and scanned the ranks of Fjall warriors. He couldn't hope to recognize the warriors from Storbjarg, but he *should* have a chance of picking out Grimar's blond hair and twin-braided beard from the Fjall ranks.

Come on!

Tension thickened the air as the Eirdkilrs' howls grew louder, the rumbling of their feet echoing like thunder in Aravon's ear. His heart hammered in his chest, his mouth gone dry, his palms sweaty. Instincts shrieked at him to wheel, to face the charging enemy, and it took every shred of effort to keep his eyes focused on the ranks of Fjall. To search for Grimar.

"Spears!" Throrsson's roar echoed along the shield wall.

This time it was the rearmost warriors that reacted. Stooping, they retrieved bundles of spears Aravon hadn't noticed between the thick press of men. Little more than long wooden shafts with sharp, fire-hardened tips, yet there were hundreds of them.

"For the Hilmir!" The Fjall raised their voices in defiance and hurled their spears. With the enemy less than a few yards away, accuracy meant little. The crude weapons leapt through the air and slammed into the charging Eirdkilrs. Blood sprayed and barbarians screamed as sharpened wood punched through

563

leather, armor, and flesh. Flailing, falling Eirdkilrs brought down their comrades or simply fell where they stood, gurgling, coughing, their shrieks and howls cut off in an horrible instant.

A second wave of spears flew, and more Eirdkilrs fell. More of the Eirdkilrs raced up the hill, only to find themselves faced with a third volley, this one far less cohesive. The rate of thrown spears slacked off as the Fjall's arms tired. All too soon, the last of the spears had been cast, and the Eirdkilrs' charge continued unabated.

Aravon's gut tightened as he scanned the Fjall ranks. *Where the bloody hell is he?* His eyes roved the steel helmets, the fur cloaks, the long braids of red, black, blond, and brown hair hung thick with beads, bones, metal, and trinkets. Fjall that looked like every other Fjall around them. Warriors clad for battle, nearly impossible to distinguish from the rest.

Then his eyes fell on the broad-shouldered, blond-haired man with two long braids hanging down his back, and hope blossomed in his chest.

There!

Grimar stood twenty yards to Aravon's right, at the center of what would be the Hilmir's eastern flank. He held the tip of the spear formation, holding the opening in the barricades against the charging enemy.

Aravon raced toward the man, mind racing. He had no idea how to stop Grimar—had no idea what the man intended—and there was little hope of reaching him at the front ranks of his warriors. But he had to figure out what to do before—

The Blood Queen and her traitor sprang the trap.

Chapter Seventy-Two

There was no warning, no signal to strike. Grimar simply turned and hacked down the warrior on his left. A heartbeat later, a dozen more swords and axes flashed in the shield wall holding the right flank. Blood misted in the air, stained heavy furs, spilled from slashed throats and shattered skulls. Men screamed and died, never realizing that their own comrades killed them. The warriors beside them turned stunned eyes on the traitors. Only to be cut down in the next instant.

Aravon never slowed in his frantic sprint, yet moved too slow to stop the traitor.

The entire right flank of Fjall warriors dissolved into a chaotic, swirling mess of bodies. The shield wall collapsed as men hacked, stabbed, and chopped at each other. Men that had been brothers and comrades before now slew each other. Fjall blood and bile thickened the ground, churned to mud beneath heavy booted feet. Men crushed up against each other, pressed too tight to do more than punch and bite, sought to bring down the enemies within their own ranks.

All up and down the line of warriors, the traitors turned on their comrades. Their strikes had no cohesion, but their attacks rippled outward, all along the length of the Hilmir's battle line. Warriors died beneath the axes, swords, and daggers of men they trusted to guard their backs. Shrieking, screaming, weeping, choking on their own blood, or dying without a sound. Packed so tightly together, there was no way for the Fjall traitors to swing freely.

Yet the true aim of the attack wasn't casualties, but disarray.

No! Acid surged in Aravon's throat as the Fjall shield wall writhed and squirmed beneath the assault from within. Two hundred and fifty warriors spread out among the entire hundred-yard line inflicted terrible damage. Worse, chaos rippled through the ranks of the Fjall. Fehlan turned against Fehlan, traitor and loyal Fjall warrior alike. Warriors fighting for their lives with no way of knowing who was friend or foe. Men cutting down all around them for fear of being cut down themselves.

That was when the Eirdkilr charge hit the line.

The giant barbarians crashed into the disordered Fjall, an inexorable tide of rage, fur, and steel. Howling, shrieking, screaming "Death to the traitors!". Steel glinted in the daylight and fury burned in eyes set in blue-stained faces. Straight toward the three tips of the triangular formations the Hilmir had waiting for them.

Or *would* have had waiting, if not for Grimar's treachery. The Fjall traitor had vacated his place at the tip of the spear formation on the Hilmir's right flank. As he struck, the treacherous warriors nearest him took a heavy toll on their comrades. When the howling mass of Eirdkilrs struck, the once-solid shield wall had disintegrated into swirling knots of embattled Fjall. Too focused on each other to stand against the oncoming enemy.

The shield wall crumbled before the Eirdkilrs' fury. Fjall warriors were thrown back by their comrades, stumbled over Fehlan corpses, or died beneath Eirdkilr axes, spears, and clubs. Crimson sprayed, bone *cracked,* wooden shields were turned to splinters, steel skullcaps groaned beneath dozens of impacts. The Fjall fell where they stood, trampled beneath Eirdkilr boots, crushed by clubs, hewn down by axes, impaled on sharp spears. Screaming, crying, shouting defiance and terror at friend and foe alike. The stench of loosening bowels, reeking urine, vomit, and blood hung like a pall over the swirling, chaotic knots of men.

Aravon's heart sank as the Fjall line buckled, sagged, and gave way. It didn't matter that the Eirdkilrs charged in a loose-packed mass rather than an organized formation—the Fjall's disarray was so widespread, Grimar's betrayal so complete, that the Fehlans couldn't hope to stand. The front ranks of Fjall died or were hurled backward, and the men behind them grunted, groaned, and roared as the Eirdkilrs punched deep into the disorganized third and fourth. All the while, Fjall traitors slaughtered their comrades, and warriors loyal to the Hilmir fell by the dozens.

The rearmost warriors pressed forward, only to be hurled backward by the giant barbarians. Axes flying, clubs swinging, the Eirdkilrs waded into the right flank. The entire eastern section of the Fjall's line descended into a chaotic orgy of carnage, agony, and death. Cohesion shattered, gaps in the ranks growing wider, the Fjall tried in vain to stem the tide of enemies.

Tried and failed. Paid with their blood, and still they could not push back the Eirdkilrs. Time slowed to a crawl as the seventh and eighth ranks splintered into knots of battling warriors, too occupied killing each other to pay attention to the Eirdkilrs.

They would break at any second, and Grimar's treachery would be the undoing of the Fjall warband.

With a roar of "For *Striith!*", Aravon launched himself at the nearest traitor. Sharp Odarian steel punched into the man's spine a heartbeat before he cut down another comrade. Blood sprayed as Aravon tore the spearhead free and brought it spinning around in a vicious slash that tore open another's throat.

But even as he cut down a third, another Fjall warrior struck at him. One of the Hilmir's *loyal* warriors. Aravon barely managed to deflect the slashing sword stroke, turning it aside before it punched into his chest. He drove the iron-shod butt of his spear into the man's chest. Hard enough to knock the breath from his lungs but not shatter bone. When the Fjall slumped to his knees, gasping, Aravon leapt around the man and raced toward the shattered right flank.

He searched in vain for Grimar. The traitorous Fjall had abandoned his place at the tip of the spear formation, and now Eirdkilrs drove deep into the opening. Without a cohesive shield wall to face them, the Fjall had little hope against their larger, stronger, fiercer cousins.

Aravon was about to throw himself into the chaotic battle line when something caught his eye. A warrior with twin blond braids and bloodstained sword had climbed onto the mound of earth supporting the barricade and scrambled east. Grimar's eyes were locked on the Hilmir, a snarl twisting his face.

No, Aravon realized, *not the Hilmir.* The traitor's sword would strike down the warrior on the Hilmir's right. *Bjarni.*

In the space between heartbeats, Aravon considered and discarded a dozen options, until only one remained. A desperate, foolhardy choice that could get him killed. He acted without hesitation. Reversing his grip on his spear, he brought it up over his head. Pain flared in his shoulder, neck, and bruised chest as his arm stretched back, but he ignored it and hurled his spear with every shred of strength and fury burning through him.

567

The spear flew true. The long, sharp blade punched through the side of Grimar's head, just beneath the rim of his helmet, and hurled the man into the barricade. Odarian steel buried deep into wooden logs, pinning the traitorous Fjall to the wall, like a butterfly mounted on display. Blood fountained from the tear in the massive vein in his neck, but the spear's tip severed Grimar's spine. He hung limp, twitching and gasping, as he bled to death.

Aravon had no time for satisfaction; drawing his longsword, he threw himself into the swirling, turbulent melee of the right flank.

"For *Striith* and the Hilmir!" he roared. He hacked down another traitorous Fjall, the marvelous steel of his heavy sword shearing fur, chain mail, muscle, and bone. He felt naked without his spear, but in the tight-packed ranks of the shield wall, he had little room to maneuver. This was work for a sword.

Desperation gripped Aravon's heart in an icy fist. He *had* to restore order to the shield wall. Only a fraction of the Fjall had managed to mount any semblance of defense against the Eirdkilrs. Yet they couldn't hope to stand against the towering enemies ahead and traitorous comrades cutting them down from behind.

Turning the tide of this battle would be near-impossible, but he had to try.

He fought like a Legionnaire, keeping his sword close at his side for quick, vicious thrusts. The crush of men gave him cover against the traitorous Fjall's wild swings, and the tip of his sword flicked out to turn aside spear thrusts. His slashing, stabbing, chopping blows brought down anyone who faced him. All the while, he kept up the calls of "For the Hilmir!"

The world narrowed in around Aravon, and for a moment, he lost himself in the chaos of battle. Duck a slashing strike, drive his sword into the man's chest. Drive a punch into one's face, turn aside a descending axe from another. Steel *clanged* off steel deafeningly close to his ear. A warrior grunted, spitting blood, falling with Aravon's sword in his throat. His own roars of "For the Hilmir!" seemed so distant, so faint beneath the screams, shouts, and clash of weapons.

Mud churned beneath his boots and he slipped, stumbled into a fellow warrior, and nearly went down. He caught himself on a Fjall's cloak, pulled himself upright. Turned aside a stab aimed at his chest and drove the pommel of his sword into a man's face. Shouted, roared with every shred of strength. Blood spattered his masked face, hot and warm on his neck. Reeking odors of bile, urine, and spilling entrails clogged his nostrils. His lungs burned, his shoulders and arm ached, his fingers clutched the hilt of his sword so tightly he lost sensation in his hand.

And still the enemies came on. Fjall seeking to cut him down—as traitor or loyal warrior, it didn't matter. Eirdkilrs breaking through the ranks one death at a time. Killing, filling the air with blood and chunks of brain matter spraying from their clubs and axes. Sharp steel edged crimson darting toward his face. Aravon twisted aside and the spear slid past his face, punching into a warrior behind him. Thrusting forward, he drove the tip of his sword into the Eirdkilr's throat.

A howling warrior came at him from the left, but Aravon had no time or space to turn. He could only watch, helpless, as the Eirdkilr club descended toward his head.

Only to be turned aside at the last minute by a Fjall shield. "For the Hilmir!" the warrior roared, and drove his sword into the Eirdkilr's groin. Another hacked down the slumping barbarian, then fell with his skull crushed by another Eirdkilr behind. Aravon deflected a thrusting spear, drove his shoulder into an Eirdkilr shield, and drove his sword up, under the steel-rimmed edge. Blood and intestines splattered his boots, thick and reeking, turning the ground muddy.

And still the Eirdkilrs came on. Huge figures that towered over the Fjall, their snarling, blue-stained faces filling Aravon's world and blotting out the sky. Shrieking, howling, chopping, slavering for his blood and death.

But Aravon no longer fought alone. His cries of "For the Hilmir!" now echoed from the throats of a dozen, then a score Fjall warriors formed up in the line beside him. Brave, strong men with bright steel weapons and solid shields. Shields that locked together to turn aside Eirdkilr strikes, and weapons that bit back against the enemy.

With a roar, the Fjall pushed back, shoving the Eirdkilrs back a single half-step. In that instant, with room to swing swords and axes, the Fehlans brought down the foremost barbarians. More came on, hurling themselves against the weakened shield wall. Huge bodies *crashed* against the shields, the sound of their charge thunderous, their cries savage and piercing. Aravon ducked a savage axe blow and drove the tip of his sword into the Eirdkilr's guts. The next enemy slipped, fell, and died beneath a savage thrust from the man on Aravon's right. That warrior fell, skull crushed by an Eirdkilr club, a moment later.

Aravon brought down the club-wielding barbarian and wheeled left, hacking through the forearm of an Eirdkilr about to strike down the Fjall guarding his side. The barbarian's agonized shrieks were lost beneath the din of battle, but as he stumbled backward, bleeding from the stump of his arm, a gap opened between Aravon and the next enemy. A moment to breathe, to take stock of the battle.

Time stood still, the thrill of combat running through his veins. The Fjall stood arrayed against the Eirdkilrs, a line twenty men wide and two deep, barely enough to hold the opening in the barricade. Yet that row of interlocked shields and bristling weapons was all that stood in the way of defeat. They *had* to hold—if the Eirdkilrs took the hilltop and shattered the right flank, they'd roll over the Hilmir's center and crush the warband.

Then the next Eirdkilr attacked, bringing his club swinging down toward Aravon's head. He barely managed to get his sword up in time to deflect it. Not far enough. Heavy wood *slammed* into his left shoulder. Pain exploded down his left arm, but his right struck back in the next instant. Driving the tip of his sword into the Eirdkilr's chest. The twisting motion sent sharp stabbing agony along his injured left side, but he managed to recover in time to meet the next attack.

And the next, and the next. The tide of enemy never seemed to slow. Aravon could barely snatch breath between barbarians. Killing one, then a second, and still more. Palms slick with sweat and blood seeping through his gloves, lungs burning, fire coursing through the knotted muscles of his right hand. But if he slowed even a fraction, he died.

Another Eirdkilr fell, and Aravon had another heartbeat to think. The crushing press of Eirdkilrs never slackened, only grew stronger, pushed harder, cut deeper as more and more enemies joined the attack. Yet the Fehlan shield wall had grown to sixty, thickened in front of the gap in the barricades. Impossibly, the right flank held.

A hand clamped on the collar of Aravon's armor and dragged him backward. Off-balance, it was all he could do not to fall as he was hauled out of the front line, through the swirling melee at the rear of the Fjall lines, and free of the crush of men.

That instant nearly cost the Fjall the victory. For a second, a gap opened in the ranks, and an Eirdkilr burst through. It took three Fehlans to beat him back, cut him down. It was only the dying giant's bulk that kept the enemy from surging through the opening. Trampling the Eirdkilr into the mud, the Fjall closed ranks, interlocked shields, and roared defiance at the enemy.

The hand released Aravon's collar, sending him stumbling. Aravon barely regained his footing before he fell, but whirled quick as a serpent, sword raised to strike.

And found himself face to face with Belthar.

Aravon caught himself before he lashed out. "Bloody good time!"

"Sorry about that, Captain!" Belthar shouted. "But without a shield, you're no good in the front line."

"Didn't have much choice!"

Movement from behind Belthar snapped Aravon's eyes to the right. A Fjall warrior raced toward the big man, axe upraised, eyes fixed on the back of Belthar's huge head.

Aravon had no time to figure out if the man was loyalist or traitor—he simply reacted. A smooth move. a fencer's graceful thrust. The tip of his heavy longsword slid past Belthar, a hair's breadth from his armored side, and punched into the Fehlan's chest. Belthar spun, swinging his huge elbow around to crash into the man's face. Yet his eyes flew wide at sight of the Fjall warrior that lay sprawled in the mud.

"Grimar's man?" he asked.

"No idea!" Aravon shook his head. "But we need to figure it out fast!"

Free of the battle and behind the line of warriors, Aravon had a moment to take stock of the situation. The right flank was still gripped in chaos. Swirling knots of warriors locked in combat, striking down friend and foe alike. A shield wall holding the barricade. Barely. Eighty men against five times their number of Eirdkilrs, a heartbeat from breaking yet fighting with every shred of courage and strength. Only the strong wooden barricades to their right and left prevented total collapse.

The Blood Queen's cunning had wreaked terrible havoc along the entire hundred-yard line. The right flank sagged, the formation pushed back, and only Aravon's intervention had kept it from collapsing completely. In the center, the Hilmir, Bjarni, and Sigbrand stood at the tip of their spear formation, shield wall strong and holding back the Eirdkilrs. Yet, behind them, knots of Fjall warriors still clashed in a desperate battle. Traitors who wore the same faces as the men they betrayed. Bewildered men killing their own comrades, comrades they had just watched cut down friends and brothers. The chaos of battle amplified a thousandfold by treachery.

To his relief, the left flank had held. Grimar's warriors had caused the least amount of damage there, and the strong formation had rebuffed the Eirdkilr advance.

Yet, one glance at the oncoming Eirdkilrs told Aravon the *Blodsvarri* had known where to strike. Grimar had purposely chosen to stand at the head of the right flank so the Blood Queen would see his position and exploit it.

At least half of the fifteen hundred Eirdkilrs committed to the attack were streaming toward the right flank, and more had begun the ascent of the hill. The Fjall's only salvation was that the two hundred-yard climb—over uneven rock-strewn ground and around logs and spike pits—prevented the Eirdkilrs from attacking en masse. With the Hilmir's barricades, they couldn't properly bring their superior numbers to bear. The thousand or more enemies streaming toward the left flank were clustered along the side of the cliff bordering the Hardrfoss River.

Damn, but Zaharis could have put a dent in them! He wasted no time with wishing; they'd have to win this battle without the Secret Keeper's alchemical marvels.

Then, through a gap in the lines, Aravon caught sight of the Eirdkilrs still at the bottom of the hill. His eyebrows shot up as he saw the two hundred Fjall warriors locked in battle with the Blood Queen's easternmost forces.

Aravon nearly wept. *Colborn, you beautiful bastard!*

Now he understood why the Blood Queen hadn't yet overrun their position. Grimar's attack had come at the perfect time for the *Blodsvarri's* plans, but Colborn, thinking quickly, must have thrown himself and the two hundred Fjall ambushers into the attack to prevent the Eirdkilr leader from committing the rest of her men. Nearly a thousand Eirdkilrs remained at the bottom of the hill. More than enough to rout Colborn's little force. Yet the Lieutenant had taken the gamble and bought Aravon and the Hilmir precious minutes.

"Belthar, pitch in here!" Aravon thrust a finger toward the right flank. "Hold that damned line, you hear!"

"Aye, Captain!" For once, Belthar didn't salute, but simply turned and threw himself into the shield wall with a roar. His huge axe gleamed brilliant in the sunlight—*Keeper's teeth, has the sun already risen so high?*—as he shouldered through the ranks of Fjall toward the front line.

If anyone could hold that position, it was Belthar. He towered a head taller than the warriors around him, his brawn a match for the Eirdkilrs he faced. With a shout of "For the Hilmir!", he threw himself against the Eirdkilrs about to break through the shield wall.

Aravon tore his eyes away from the right flank, his gaze traveling east across the battle line. He spared a glance for Grimar's limp corpse, still pinned in death to the barricades, dangling from Aravon's hurled spear. *Burn in the fiery hell, you bastard!*

In the center, the Hilmir still held the front of the line, but the ranks behind him had been thrown into chaos, a gap widening as men died. The Eirdkilrs had pushed him back a full two yards, forcing him to retreat from his position in the barricade opening. More and more of the giants streamed into the gap and hurled themselves against the Fjall shields.

Yet, even as Throrsson retreated beneath the Eirdkilrs' savage onslaught, the turmoil behind him, the clash of Fjall steel on steel, the shrieks and screams of Fehlan warriors, dimmed. Grimar had died, and his traitors had been brought down—at least *some*, enough for the center to reorganize. The Fjall knew their own. Slowly, one hammering heartbeat at a time, the center of the Hilmir's battle line, re-formed. Shields locked, men pressed shoulder to shoulder, driving forward to bolster Throrsson's line.

The Eirdkilrs fell back. Half a step, then a full step. One yard, two. Dying, killing, howling, screaming in agony. Blue-stained faces twisted in snarls of rage and expressions of torment as Fjall weapons chopped off limbs, punched through their armor, or carved into exposed skin. Hitting back, crushing Fehlan shields, massive weapons rending flesh. Yet slowly, inexorably, shoved backward by the Hilmir's roaring fury and the strength of his shield wall.

A faint hope blossomed deep within Aravon's mind. The Blood Queen's treachery hadn't killed them, hadn't shattered their line. They still held. By the Swordsman, they still held.

Then a new smell reached him. Sharper than the metallic tang of blood, deeper than the reek of blood, vomit, urine, and bowels emptying in death. An acrid smell, one that had filled the air around Storbjarg and hung thick among the ruins of Oldrsjot.

Smoke!

Aravon spun, and his heart sank as he saw threads of dark gray rising from the hill's reverse slope. From the northeast and Throrsson's crudely built bridge.

Heart in his throat, Aravon raced toward the bridge. Five Fjall warriors in blood-soaked furs and leather armor surrounded the bridge—three facing outward, facing Aravon, and two lowering torches toward the rope-lashed logs spanning the Hardrfoss.

Dread turned to rage that burned bright and hot in Aravon's chest. *Traitors!*

Down the hill he raced, ignoring the throbbing in his chest, the aches of his bruised shoulders and neck. No war cry escaped his lips. He gave the turncoats no warning, no time to react.

The first Fjall died before he could turn. Aravon's blade sheared through his neck and sent his head flying off the cliff to splash into the fast-flowing river. The second man half-turned, but Aravon's return stroke carved a deep gash across his chest, severed the muscles and tendons in his shoulder. Spinning, Aravon drove the tip of his blade three inches into the third warrior's belly. Blood sprayed as he ripped the sword free and gushed from the deep wound.

Instinct screamed in the back of his mind and he threw himself backward, retreating a quick step up the hill. The fourth Fjall's sword whistled a hair's breadth from his head. One of the torch-bearing Fjall had turned to face him, burning brand in one hand and longsword in the other. Crimson stained the edge of the blade—the blood of fellow Fjall.

"Traitors!" Aravon growled in Fehlan. "You betray your Hilmir and clan to the Blood Queen?"

The warrior spat. "No clan or King can stand before the *Tauld!* We chose to save our families, at any cost."

With a growl, Aravon rushed in for a high overhand chop. A feint. As the Fjall raised his sword to block, Aravon brought the sword low. Steel bit deep into leg muscle and shattered bone. The traitor fell with a scream. Spinning, Aravon deflected the vicious thrust from the second Fjall, knocking the longsword aside. A quick thrust and he tore the blade free. Blood gushed from the man's chest and he coughed, spraying crimson. Aravon whirled to the right and drove his sword home in the fallen Fjall's throat. The man stared up at him, wide-eyed in horror, and slowly toppled to the side.

Harsh, gurgling grunts echoed from Aravon's left. Spinning, he found one of the Fjall warriors still alive. Bleeding from the wound to his chest, drowning in his own blood, yet still living. Defiant, snarling curses as he scrabbled in the dirt for his torch.

574

Aravon leapt toward the man, sword flashing. Too late. The Fjall hurled himself onto the bridge, dropping the torch between two logs, then plummeted off the edge without a sound.

Even as the man's body *splashed* into the Hardrfoss, fire consumed the logs. Brilliant flames licked at the oil splashed atop the bridge, bursting upward in a pillar of shimmering heat so bright Aravon had to leap back to avoid being caught in the blaze.

Damn it! Aravon's heart sank as the oil-soaked logs burned. *No way out now.* The Blood Queen and her Fjall traitors hadn't just planned to destroy the Hilmir's battle line—they'd ensured Throrsson had no choice but to fight to the death, cut off from retreat and any hope of survival.

Heart sinking, Aravon scrambled back uphill. He crested the ridge in time to see the left flank bowing, the shield wall giving way before the Eirdkilr onslaught. The Hilmir's center had been pushed back a step, though it held, anchored by the roaring fur-clad figure of Throrsson himself. Belthar held the right flank by the skin of his teeth. His huge bulk and immense strength kept the Eirdkilrs from overwhelming the Fjall warriors. Barely. Even with the big man in the center of the line, it looked ready to buckle at any second.

At the bottom of the hill, Aravon caught sight of Colborn and the two hundred Fjall. Barely more than a hundred now. Slowly pulling back, forced to retreat beneath the Blood Queen's superior numbers. They'd have to abandon the crossing at any moment else risk being overrun. Yet they had done the impossible. They'd given Throrsson more time to fight.

And by the Swordsman, we'll fight!

Aravon had an instant to decide which way to go. The Eirdkilrs' howls of delight from the left flank made up his mind—he had to shore up that line before it crumbled.

He'd just taken his first steps to the left when the center line shattered. Eirik Throrsson fell, trampled beneath a tide of Eirdkilrs, and a broad gap opened in the shield wall. Towering barbarians surged into the gap with a roar of triumph.

As Aravon whirled, he saw Belthar pushed back, brought down by an Eirdkilr's club. The right flank began to give way, sagging in on itself, too weak to hold.

No! Ashes filled Aravon's mouth, and horror twisted an icy dagger in his gut. The Fjall battle line was crumbling, and not a damned thing he could do about it.

Then came the most beautiful sound in the world: the high, piercing cry of a battle horn.

Aravon's eyes snapped to the west. From the sparsely forested hills across the Hardrfoss River, hundreds of Fehlan warriors raced into view, spilling down the hill, surging toward the crossing where Colborn and the hundred Fjall struggled to pull back. At their head charged a broad-shouldered warrior clad in the furs, fangs, and skull of a gray Fehlan greatwolf. And beside him, a familiar figure clad in mottle-patterned leather armor, with a brilliant blue gemstone at his throat.

Aravon nearly wept at the sight. Rangvaldr and the Deid had arrived.

Chapter Seventy-Three

Yes!

Hope rekindled within Aravon as two thousand Deid warriors streamed down the hill toward the river crossing. The Eirdkilrs at the shallow ford had only a few seconds to break off the attack on Colborn's small group and re-form a solid shield wall before the Deid crashed into them. The tumult of that *clash* rang up the hill, echoed by the insistent, driving clarion call of Chief Svein Hafgrimsson's war horn.

The six hundred Eirdkilrs swarming across the ford found themselves facing more than thrice their number. Even their shields and strength couldn't hope to hold out against such overwhelming odds, against the rage that spilled from the throats of two thousand Fehlan warriors. The Deid knew the destruction visited upon their fellow warriors at Gold Burrows Mine. Now, with the enemy in their grasp, the time had come for vengeance.

A savage grin split Aravon's face at the sight of the Blood Queen's surprise. Her crimson-covered, tattooed features creased into a look of stunned shock. The Deid had come for her, and she had nowhere near enough men to stop them. Fewer than nine hundred Eirdkilrs remained at the base of Hangman's Hill, with another four hundred scattered across the hillside, picking their way over the jagged rocks or around the Hilmir's spike pits. Now it was the *Blodsvarri's* turn to scramble to get her men into position.

Yet, Aravon had no time to rejoice, or to watch the Deid roll over the Eirdkilrs holding the crossing. His own battle on Hangman's Hill had turned against him.

In an instant, his eyes darted between the Fjall's left and center. The left held, pushing back, and the center had managed to close the gaps in their ranks even after the Hilmir's fall. But the right, with Belthar gone down, was a heartbeat from collapsing.

Aravon raced toward the spot where he'd seen his man go down. He hadn't taken five steps before a massive figure in mottled leather armor roared up from beneath the tide of Eirdkilr and Fjall warriors. Belthar laid about him with great strokes of his axe, hewing off an Eirdkilr's head, crushing another's chest, hacking off a massive arm. Blood splattered his face and sprayed from the edge of his whirling axe. All the while, his shouts of "For the Hilmir!" echoed above the Eirdkilrs' howling war cries.

The warriors on the right flank's western edge cracked, and two Eirdkilrs surged into the gap. Fjall fell beneath their enormous weapons, helmets and skulls crushed, limbs shattered, flesh torn. The opening grew wider, wider, until five, eight, ten Eirdkilrs streamed through. Though the first two died before they'd taken three steps, the rest pushed through, deeper, punching a hole into the Fjall's weakened ranks. Three broke through the rearmost line and turned to fall on their enemies from behind. Their howls of delight split the air as they raised their bloodstained weapons.

Delight turned to agony as Aravon buried the tip of his sword into one giant's side. Blood gushed from the wound and the Eirdkilr slumped, spine severed. Tearing his sword free, Aravon spun and struck out at the next Eirdkilr. Odarian steel sheared through the wooden shaft of his massive axe. Even as the steel head spun away and the Eirdkilr's decapitated handle struck empty air, Aravon chopped through the braided beard, cartilage, and blood vessels in the man's throat. His war cries cut off in a gurgling, coughing spray of hot crimson.

The third Eirdkilr, however, was ready for him. Aravon's sword slammed into his upraised shield, the tip striking sparks on the metal boss at its center. The Eirdkilr behind the shield bared his teeth in a snarl and drove his spear at Aravon's chest. Aravon twisted aside, barely managing to avoid being run through. Yet even off-balance, his sword struck true. The sharp blade severed the man's right arm at the wrist and the spear clattered to the ground. The Eirdkilr howled, blood spraying from the stump of his arm.

Yet even that didn't stop him. The huge barbarian leaned into his shield and charged. Aravon, barely regaining his feet, had no time to react. The rounded metal boss slammed into his torso hard enough to hurl him from his feet. Pain exploded in Aravon's bruised chest, the air knocked from his lungs. He struck the muddy ground hard, and struck the back of his head. Though the helmet absorbed the impact to his skull, his armor did little to prevent the agony radiating from his already-injured breastbone. His back, spine, and shoulders ached from the impact and it was all he could do to suck in a breath.

A shadow darkened the sky over his head. The Eirdkilr loomed over him, blood dripping from his severed right wrist, shield held overhead. With a guttural curse, the barbarian brought the steel-rimmed edge of his shield down, straight at Aravon's head.

And missed. The heavy shield swung wide, the Eirdkilr staggering. Crimson trickled from the corner of his mouth, his eyes wide in pain. He toppled to the side and landed hard. A dark stain radiated outward from his belly, blood staining his chain mail, furs, and the mud beneath him. Stunned, he stared at Aravon, agony twisting his blue-stained face.

"May *Helgrindr* chew your soul and spit you into eternal darkness!" A Fehlan curse, growled by a familiar, furious voice.

Now it was Aravon's turn to be surprised. He stared up at the shaggy black hair and braided beard of Eirik Throrsson.

"Hilmir!" Aravon sucked in a breath—even that small movement had agony flaring through his chest, yet he struggled upright. "You're alive?"

"Looks like it." The Hilmir extended a hand to Aravon. "Feels like it, too." He winced and pressed a hand to a gaping wound in his right side, where an Eirdkilr axe had severed chain links, leather armor, padding, and the thick layers of fat and muscle beneath his ribs.

Aravon accepted the Hilmir's outstretched hand and, with a grunt, pulled himself to his feet. The pain in his chest settled deep into his bones, a throbbing ache that radiated outward every time he moved. Yet the fact that he was alive—and the Hilmir, too—did wonders to make that pain tolerable.

"Bjarni and Sigbrand got me out of there before the Eirdkilrs crushed me." He turned a scowl on his son and the brown-bearded Fjall warrior. "Nearly cost us the shield wall!"

"Your death would cost all the Fjall, Father!" Bjarni shouted over the din of battle. "But now, thanks to the Deid, we've got a fighting chance."

On his feet once more, struggling to catch his breath, Aravon had a moment to assess the battle. To his surprise, he found the swirl of combat atop the hill's summit had diminished. Fully a third of the Eirdkilrs had pulled back—doubtless at the Blood Queen's command—to protect her against the Deid. With the Fjall lines holding fast, the Eirdkilrs had lost the momentum for the battle.

Yet the Hilmir's men had paid a steep price. Of the sixteen hundred holding Hangman's Hill, fewer than half remained standing. The rest had fallen to the Eirdkilr assault—and to the weapons of their comrades. Perhaps some wounded, but until the battle ended, he *had* to assume that the men still locked in combat were all that remained to him. Enough to hold, that much he knew. With the Eirdkilrs pulling back to protect the Blood Queen, there were too few on the hilltop to force the position. The Hilmir's barricades and shield walls held.

By the Swordsman, we're still standing! Grimar's treachery cost the Fjall dearly, but it hadn't killed them outright.

"What in *Striith's* name happened?" the Hilmir demanded. "Grimar—"

"Was a traitor." Aravon quickly recounted what the Duke had told him. "The Blood Queen likely only agreed to let them go if they turned against you." His brow furrowed behind his mask—a mask that had grown thick, sticky, and crusted with drying blood. "One of the traitors said they did it to spare their families."

"Which means Storbjarg has fallen." Throrsson's eyes darkened. "And the rest of my warband slain."

"For that I am sorry, Hilmir, " Aravon replied. "But at least now, with the Deid's help, we've got a chance of carrying the day!"

As if on cue, loud cheers, jeers, and roars echoed from the Fjall's left flank. A moment later, the center took up the cry. The Eirdkilrs were pulling back. From *all* positions. They abandoned their assault on the right flank and raced back toward their embattled comrades.

Aravon's gaze darted downhill. The Deid's two thousand—accompanied by Rangvaldr, Colborn, and the seventy or eighty Fjall ambushers still standing—had rolled over the enemies holding the crossing. More than four hundred Eirdkilrs lay dead in the shallow waters, their blood turning the Hardrfoss River a grisly crimson. The Blood Queen fought just to stay alive long enough to pull her men back from their assault on the hill.

"I thought you said the Deid had abandoned us."

Aravon turned back to find Throrsson staring at him, suspicion in his narrowed eyes. "They did, but I've found that my *Seiomenn* can be surprisingly persuasive." He gestured at the hilltop. "And, the fact that we're now standing on Deid land gives them a good incentive to join."

Throrsson grumbled in his throat. "*Banamadrhaed* has been Fjall land since my ancestors first took up sword and shield. One victory does *not* give Hafgrimsson the right to claim it for his own."

Aravon shrugged. "Maybe save *that* dispute until after we win. For now, we regroup, re-form, and figure out how to make the most of this."

"First, we need to root out the traitors." The Hilmir raised a clenched fist. "Bjarni, Sigbrand, with me! Any man who stayed in Storbjarg surrenders or dies where they stand!" He turned and stalked into the mass of staggering, gasping, exhausted warriors.

Aravon let out a relieved breath. *He* might not be able to single out any of the traitors still living, but Throrsson knew each of his warriors personally. The Hilmir would sort out the matter.

In that moment, with the temporary cessation of the attack—on *their* position, at least—the adrenaline coursing in Aravon's veins retreated, giving way to the exhaustion and listlessness that settled in after battle. Every muscle in Aravon's body ached, and his chest throbbed, the pain radiating out toward his bruised shoulders and arm. His right hand refused to heed his commands to unclench, refused to release its death grip on his sword hilt. When he used his left hand to pry his fingers open, blood crackled where it had dried his glove to the leather wrappings. Fire coursed through his lungs, down his legs, and along his spine.

Yet the battle wasn't truly over. He couldn't give in to the aches and pains, the exhaustion, not yet. First, he had to make sure his men had survived.

He found Belthar kneeling and leaning on his axe, blowing for breath, his huge shoulders drooping with exhaustion. Dark crimson blood and mud stained his leather armor, along with chunks of bloody hair, gray matter, and bone shards. Yet, by all appearances, the big man had come out of the battle little worse for wear.

"Damn, Ursus, but you gave me a scare." Aravon shook his head. "Seems I'll have to remember to give you orders to *stay alive* next time."

Belthar straightened at the sound of his Captain's voice, rising to his feet quickly. "Right, Captain." Too quickly. He groaned and hunched over his right side. "Maybe send those orders to the enemy, too. They seemed damned determined to put me down."

Aravon chuckled. "Anything broken?"

"No." Belthar twisted his torso slightly, barely managing to stifle a groan. "Won't be dancing in the Icespire Royal Ballet for a few weeks, though."

"Good." Aravon clapped the big man on the back—carefully. "Find some water, take care of any wounds, and get ready for the next assault. The Deid bought us a few minutes, but if we want to finish this, we're going to have to push back, hard. That axe of yours won't stay clean for long."

"Understood, Captain." Belthar gave him a Legion salute.

Aravon grimaced, but said nothing. The Fjall around him were too exhausted, bruised, and battered to pay the two of them much heed.

All along the summit of Hangman's Hill, Fehlan warriors sat on the muddy ground, slumped against the wooden barricades, or—in the cases of the worst injured—lay where they had fallen. A few score had managed to keep their feet, forming up three lines in the barricade openings. Yet it was little more than a show of force; the Fjall had taken a heavy beating, and only barely survived the assault.

The clash of steel and the shouts, cries, and howls of battling warriors had fallen silent, but the screams of the wounded and dying filled the void. Men lay in the bloody muck, clutching at shattered limbs, gushing wounds, or trying desperately to keep entrails from spilling from their torn bellies. A few stumbled about, weaving like drunken men, their skulls and steel helmets crushed—they were already dead, but their brains simply hadn't yet caught up. The metallic reek of blood did little to cover the foul odors of loosed bowels or breeches stained with the sweat and piss of terrified men.

Aravon *felt* every scream, every weak gasp, every gurgling cry deep in the core of his being. It didn't matter that they weren't Princelanders—they were soldiers just like him, warriors that had stood strong in the face of an enemy that had come to kill him, too. In that moment, they were his brothers as much as any Legionnaire that had stood in a shield wall with him.

Yet, as he had in so many battles before, he forced himself to turn a blind eye to the suffering, to deafen his ears to the screams. Already, the least-injured Fjall had begun dragging the corpses out of the way, carrying the wounded to the hill's reverse slope and out of the way of the battle lines.

Though they'd survived the first clash, the fighting was far from over. The Deid's arrival had forced the Blood Queen on the defensive but, as he'd told

Belthar, only her death would end the clash here. At the moment, surrounded by more than a thousand Eirdkilrs, there was little chance of that happening.

A part of him regretted his decision to order Skathi to remain with Zaharis. One well-placed arrow could bring down the *Blodsvarri,* maybe even end this battle. But he pushed the fleeting regret aside. No matter how loudly she protested, he'd have been a fool to bring her into battle in her current condition.

Not that he was in much better shape. He had collected a grisly assortment of bruises, aches, and pains that seemed to grow worse with every breath, every hammering beat of his heart. Yet he had no time to give in to it. Like his father had taught him—at the end of his fist, hickory switch, or wooden training blade—he pushed back against the discomfort and bent his mind to the task at hand.

Lectern Harald's lessons flashed through his mind. *"Every army has its center of power, the critical point that, if destroyed or overrun, can collapse even the strongest point."*

In the Eirdkilrs' case, that "center of power" was with the Blood Queen, at the heart of the Eirdkilr lines. Unlike Hrolf Hrungnir and other Eirdkilr leaders he'd faced, the *Blodsvarri* didn't lead from the front. She approached battle like a Legion Commander, commanding her men from the rear. Surrounded and protected by her warriors, she was free to watch the ebb and flow of battle, to issue orders. A more effective strategy, one that would have carried the day if not for the Deid's timely arrival.

That'll also make it damn hard to get at her. Without archers, the Fjall's only chance at bringing down the Eirdkilr leader would be to charge downhill and close ranks. If they could drive a wedge into her forces, split them to the east and west, they could thrust right at the Eirdkilrs' heart. The Blood Queen's death might not break her army, but against two thousand Deid and nearly a thousand Fjall, the remaining force of fewer than two thousand Eirdkilrs had little chance of winning the battle here.

Aravon turned to find the Hilmir, to share his tactical analysis. His eyebrows rose as he found Throrsson, Bjarni, and a hundred of his warriors surrounding a group of fifty Fjall. Anger, hatred, and disgust blazed in the Hilmir's eyes, sentiments mirrored on the faces of every man at his back.

He had found the traitors.

Without a word, Throrsson stepped up to the first Fjall and buried his sword in the man's chest. The Fjall died in silence, with only a faint, gurgling gasp escaping his lips. The Hilmir ripped his sword free and hurled the traitor's body through the opening in the barricades and down the hill.

The second man opened his mouth to protest, but the Hilmir's sword opened his throat before he could get out a word. The Fjall holding the warrior released him and he slumped to his knees, gagging and drowning in his own blood.

"Please, Hilmir!" protested the third warrior as the Hilmir stepped up to him. "The Blood Queen threatened our families."

For an answer, Throrsson hacked off the man's head. "Fjall do not betray Fjall!" he roared. "We are chosen of *Striith*, chosen to live the lives of warriors and to die in glorious battle!"

He chopped down a fourth and fifth traitor with quick, savage strokes of his sword. Fire blazed in his eyes as he swung around to face the next men in line. "*Striith* will *never* know their names!" Blood dripped from his long blade, spattering the faces of the dead warriors as he thrust his sword at them. "They die with empty hands, no true warrior's death, and so they will never feast in *Seggrholl*, but will know only the torments of *Helgrindr* and eternal darkness! That is the reward their cowardice has earned."

The nearest men began to weep—not out of fear at the prospect of death, but for their immortal souls. For men like the Fjall warband, battle and death was a religion ingrained into every fiber of their being. Their highest hope was to join their god and fellow warriors at the hallowed feast tables of *Seggrholl*. Not die as cowards to be cast out and suffer an eternal afterlife of nothingness.

Throrsson knew that, knew the power it give him over their fates. "Yet I offer you a chance! I offer you *Seggrholl*." His voice echoed across the hilltop, carrying with a ferocity that rang out louder than the clashing Eirdkilrs and Deid at the base of the hill. He turned a grim expression on his warriors. "Choose. Die here, dishonored, cast out forever from *Striith's* embrace. Or take up your weapons and face the enemy like true Fjall. Die with sword and shield in hand as true warriors." He waved his bloodstained sword toward the Eirdkilrs. "Go, strike at the *Blodsvarri* who threatened your families. Earn back your honor and perhaps *Striith* will grant you an afterlife of *true* warriors."

Sigbrand and a dozen Fjall warriors dumped shields, swords, and axes at the feet of the traitors.

Throrsson thrust a finger at the weapons. "The choice is yours."

The forty-odd remaining warriors stared between the weapons and their Hilmir. A tense silence hung over the hilltop, and it seemed even the sounds of battle from below quietened as the traitors chose their fates.

One man knelt and reached for a sword and shield. "With this, I regain my honor as a true warrior of Fehl."

That opened the floodgates. Every man still alive retrieved weapons and turned to face the enemy. The ranks of Fjall parted, making way for the traitors to march through the lines of warriors, between the barricades, and down the hill.

"By the will of *Striith*," the Hilmir called as the ranks closed behind them, "fight and die like men!"

The traitorous warriors exchanged glances. They had expected to win, to defeat the Hilmir and serve the *Blodsvarri,* only to find themselves condemned by their cowardice and treachery. But, with this action, they bought back their chance at an afterlife.

To their credit, not a single one wavered. Down the hill they charged, moving in an easy, loping run. Silent, without cries to their god or in the name of the Hilmir they had betrayed. A grim band of Fehlan warriors marching to their death. Courageous in the face of certain doom, all for the hope of evading eternal damnation.

The Eirdkilrs saw them coming from thirty yards away. Contempt twisted the *Blodsvarri's* face as she spotted the charging warriors. At her barked command, a hundred Eirdkilrs swiveled to face the Fjall.

Yet the charge never slowed. Impossible odds or not, they had given their words and they would face death like men. A warrior's death in battle, as all Fjall craved. It didn't matter that they would never draw within striking distance of the Blood Queen—they would regain their dignities and die with honor.

The Eirdkilrs cut the fifty Fjall down in less than a minute. Aravon forced himself to watch the butchery, to not turn away until the last of the warriors fell. They had been traitors, but their final, courageous actions deserved his respect.

At the Hardrfoss River crossing, the battle had degenerated into swirling chaos. The Eirdkilr and Deid shield walls had broken apart, disintegrated into two lines of shoving, grunting, shouting, and howling warriors. Battering at each other with heavy axes, spears, swords, and clubs, clashing shields, filling the air with curses and war cries. Screams echoed like thunder as men killed and died.

Booted feet churned the water to mud, the river turning a gruesome crimson as blood thickened the water.

Yet the sight sent hope surging through Aravon. The Eirdkilrs had been pushed back at least ten yards, and the Deid had advanced onto the eastern riverbank, spreading out to envelop the enemy line, moving uphill to encircle them from the north. With the forest at their backs, the Eirdkilrs were off-balance.

"Hilmir!" Aravon called. "Now's the time for us to strike! We've got to help the Deid break the Blood Queen's back once and for all."

"Indeed." Eirik Throrsson turned to his men. "Come, warriors of the Fjall. Our enemy is on the defensive, and our brothers in arms battle alone. Let us show them the true might of Fjall courage and steel."

A voice rose from the crowd in a throaty roar. "Hilmir!" Within seconds, the rest of the Fjall took up the chant. "Hilmir! Hilmir!" Seven hundred and fifty warriors shouted, chanted, and cheered for their chief. Their King.

Aravon turned, found Belthar hovering at his back. With a nod, Aravon turned to join the flood of Fjall racing through the barricades and down the steep hill toward the Eirdkilrs.

Howling, piercing Eirdkilr war cries rent the air in that moment. But not from those arrayed around the base of Hangman's Hill. These came from the southeast, from across the river.

With a roar, Eirdkilrs boiled from the forests *behind* the Deid's position. A stampeding, thundering, screaming tide of blue-stained faces, filthy icebear pelts, and massive weapons. Scores, hundreds, then thousands of the towering barbarians spilled into the grasslands east of the river and charged the Deid warriors holding the crossing.

Chapter Seventy-Four

Aravon sucked in a breath. *Impossible!* He hadn't received word from Lord Eidan of enemies approaching from the east, and the Hilmir had insisted the Blood Queen's forces were limited to the men that now surrounded her. The only enemy force in Fjall lands that large was...

No! An icy dagger twisted in his spine. *They're from the Bulwark.*

The Blood Queen had pulled her besiegers away from Dagger Garrison to augment the forces assaulting Storbjarg. Knowing that she had the Hilmir on the run wasn't enough for her—she'd summoned fully two-thirds of that besieging force to guarantee that she crushed him.

Keeper take her! Aravon cursed himself. *She had to have summoned them days ago in case the Deid actually did end up joining battle.*

Neither he nor the Hilmir had expected her to abandon her siege of the Bulwark, much less expect or prepare for a Deid counterattack. Yet the fact that she'd raided Gold Burrows Mine to dissuade the Deid from joining battle proved that she could think far ahead—farther than either Aravon or Throrsson had realized before the ambush at the Waeggbjod. That degree of foresight was terrifying, and exactly what had made the Blood Queen such a fearsome opponent.

And Aravon's failure to anticipate her response cost the Deid dearly. Svein Hafgrimsson's horn blared, two sharp blasts, and the rearmost warriors at the crossing turned to face the rear assault.

Too late.

The Eirdkilrs barreled into them at a dead run. The giant barbarians picked up speed slowly, but like a boulder rolling down a mountainside, brought terrible force to bear when at full tilt. They crashed into the Deid warband with the momentum of a Legion cavalry charge. They lacked the weight and bulk of horses, but the blue-faced bastards more than made up for it in ferocity.

Enormous war axes flashed, sending heads spinning into the river or hacking through arms, cracking ribs, shearing off legs. Spears drove into the Deid, cutting through the tightly packed ranks as effectively as any company of lancers. Skulls crumpled and bones shattered beneath the blows of heavy clubs. Fehlan warriors collapsed or were hurled backward into their comrades as the Eirdkilrs drove their metal-bossed shields into their enemies.

The tide of Eirdkilrs washed over the Deid like a wave crashing into a sand sculpture. A tenth of the Deid warband died in the charge and initial clash, and the giant barbarians waded into their enemies with howling war cries, eyes blazing with hatred, and relentless savagery.

Swordsman's mercy! Aravon's stomach bottomed out. They'd been a heartbeat away from a victory they'd once believed impossible, only to have it all ripped away again by the *Blodsvarri's* cunning.

The Eirdkilrs pushed the Deid backward across the ford, spreading out to form a solid wall of flesh, muscle, and fury against the warriors Hafgrimsson managed to shout into formation. The Blood Queen's forces, reduced in number and a heartbeat from crumbling, greeted the reinforcements with howling cries that rang with sanguinary glee. They shoved back against the Deid, hurling them backward. Like an anvil striking a hammer, the two Eirdkilr armies closed in on Hafgrimsson's men from the west and east.

Deid fell by the hundreds. Bleeding, shrieking, gasping, clutching at torn throats and shattered limbs. The ferocity of the Eirdkilrs shattered their shields, arms, and the courage in their hearts. In an instant, their successful attack turned into a bloody rout.

Only the narrowness of the river crossing saved the Deid. The Eirdkilrs could only come at them forty or fifty at a time, with the main bulk of their force waiting until the foremost pressed the Deid far enough from the shallow ford that they could spill out onto the slopes of Hangman's Hill.

That's it!

A desperate plan formed within Aravon's mind. The Eirdkilrs couldn't *truly* surround the Deid at the crossing, but if the Deid tried to hold the ford, they'd be cut down from behind. Yet the Eirdkilrs *hadn't* cut off their way of escape. The Deid had pushed the Blood Queen's forces back enough to encircle them from the north, and they held the lowest twenty yards of the hill.

There's only one chance at getting them out alive. The Deid would suffer heavy casualties as they disengaged, but their losses would be far worse if they held fast. *We've got no choice!*

Whirling, Aravon sought out the Hilmir. Throrsson nodded. "We do what we can to cover them as they pull back up the hill!" Evidently, he'd come to the same conclusion as Aravon.

"We go now!" Aravon shouted in Fehlan. "They saved our arses. Time to return the favor!"

Raising his sword, the Hilmir roared. "For Fehl!"

Seven hundred and fifty Fjall warriors, less than one tenth of the Hilmir's once-proud warband, took up the cry. Swords and axes clashed against shields. Bloodied, battered, and wounded warriors exhausted from battle raised their voices in thundering war cries. Shouting, screaming, hurling their fury and spite at the enemy that had razed their homes, slaughtered their families and friends, and turned comrades traitor. Defiance blazed in their eyes and steeled their hearts. The ground shuddered beneath their pounding feet as they raced down the hill.

Aravon strode toward the center barricades and reached for his spear. With a savage yank, he tore the steel head free of the wood and Grimar's corpse. The traitor's body thumped to the ground and slid down the short earthen mound, his blood joining that of the Eirdkilrs and Fjall that had fallen there. Aravon didn't waste time on a curse for the man—he didn't deserve even that much.

Gripping the ash shaft of his spear tighter, Aravon turned to join the charge. Belthar's huge form appeared at his side. "I've got your back, Captain!" the big man shouted in his ear. His shoulders were tense, his axe held in white-knuckled hands, but a grim light of determination shone in his eyes.

Together, the two joined the stream of Fjall racing downhill. The current of fur-clad warriors broke into five long lines that threaded between the spike pits, hurtled the fallen logs, and pelted across the stone-strewn slope. Dozens stumbled over the uneven ground and died beneath the trampling feet of their comrades or brought down the warriors behind and beside them. The Fjall's charge slowed as they picked their way over the jagged rocks. Aravon managed to keep his feet, though he had to catch Belthar when the big man stumbled.

589

Yet in seconds, they had made it over the stones and resumed their charge down the last thirty yards of the hill.

"Hilmir!" The Fjall's roar echoed loud above the din of battle, and the *Blodsvarri's* eyes snapped toward them. Disdain flickered across her blood-encrusted face as she ordered her men to meet the charge.

Throrsson and his warriors smashed into the ranks of Eirdkilrs with a hundred deafening crashes. Shield struck shield, steel met flesh, bones shattered. Blood flowed freely as the Fjall hammered the Eirdkilr line. No longer a solid wall of shields, the Fjall were an unstoppable force of fury, with their Hilmir at the head of their formation—a driving arrowhead that punched into the Eirdkilrs arrayed against the Deid on the western edge of the hill.

The moment he passed the rocky ground, Aravon broke off from the main force and sprinted right, toward the embattled Deid. His eyes scanned the ranks of warriors for the familiar figure clad in mottled armor. Rangvaldr stood in the shield wall as if born to it. Three rows from the front, pressing forward, his sword thrusting, stabbing, hacking, and chopping over the heads and between the shields of his comrades. Yet unlike the warriors fighting at his side, the *Seiomenn* had managed to keep his head. At Hafgrimsson's side, he directed the flow of battle, keeping the encircled Deid warriors from collapsing.

"Stonekeeper!" Aravon had to shout over the din of battle. Belthar lent his prodigious, booming voice to the endeavor, and together they shouted to the *Seiomenn*. "Stonekeeper!"

Rangvaldr's snarling wolf mask swiveled toward the sound of his code name, and his eyes widened at the sight of Aravon and Belthar.

The fingers of Aravon's free hand flashed. *"Get the Deid up the hill. Stand with the Fjall."*

Rangvaldr nodded and swiveled to Chief Svein Hafgrimsson. An instant was all it took to convince the Deid chief to give the order. Hafgrimsson clapped the horn to his lips and blew four sharp blasts.

The warriors holding the hill had no trouble breaking off—with the steep riverbank at their backs and a reduced force arrayed against them, they could pull away without sustaining heavy casualties. But those crowded at the base of the hill and around the shallow crossing were harder-pressed to stay alive, much less disengage with any semblance of cohesion. Long seconds passed before the Deid even *began* to retreat up the hill. Hundreds fell in the space of a dozen hammering heartbeats, and still the warriors couldn't properly separate from their enemies.

Aravon's heart sank as he glanced to his left and found the Hilmir embattled, his seven hundred and fifty Fjall facing a force of twice as many Eirdkilrs. The downhill charge had driven the enemy back a few steps, clearing the way for the Deid's left flank to pull back. But his spear formation had punched too far into the Eirdkilr ranks. The force of Throrsson's downhill charge had driven a wedge deep into the Blood Queen's ranks. Too far.

He wanted to bring down the Blood Queen himself! Aravon realized.

Now, Throrsson found himself bogged down deep in his enemy's lines. His momentum slowed, he, Sigbrand, Bjarni, and the score of Fjall beside him struggled to hold their own against more than thrice their number.

Worse, the Eirdkilrs' superior numbers were beginning to take a heavy toll on the Fjall's formation. The barbarians at the Blood Queen's side had swung around and hammered at the Fjall from the west. Their thrust had pushed the middle of the Hilmir's formation back, and Throrsson's men in the lead were in danger of being encircled.

"Belthar!" Aravon shouted. He didn't wait to see if the big man followed—he simply raced the ten yards down the hill to where the Hilmir's warriors were locked in battle with the Eirdkilrs.

There was no shield wall, no densely-packed ranks of warriors to shove through. The Fjall line had splintered just as it shattered the Eirdkilr line. Now, barbarians and Fehlan swirled around in knots of combat. Men screaming, dying, and hurling curses as they clashed shields, locked swords, or howled defiance at their enemies.

Aravon raced across the ground, churned to bloody mud by a thousand feet, and leapt into the melee. Whirling his spear around his head, he slapped aside an Eirdkilr club, disemboweled the barbarian with a savage swipe, and drove the sharp tip into another's neck. The iron-capped butt of his spear crunched into an Eirdkilr with bone-shattering force and the man went down, screaming. Belthar's axe whistled past Aravon's head and split the Eirdkilr's steel skullcap, head, and neck in one powerful chop. Aravon knocked aside a spear thrust at Belthar's chest and drove his own spear through a leather-clad chest. The barbarian died, screaming and spitting crimson. Gore splashed across Aravon's face and soaked his hands. Hands that had once again clenched in a death grip on the blood-slicked shaft of his spear.

With Belthar at his side, Aravon carved his way through the battling warriors, surging toward the Hilmir and his warriors. The Eirdkilrs hadn't yet managed to push the Fjall back enough to encircle them, and Aravon would be damned if he let it happen. Thrusting, hacking, stabbing, slashing, and thrusting, he brought down any Eirdkilr that got in his way. All the while trusting Belthar would guard his back.

"Hilmir!" Aravon shouted over the din of battle. Clashing steel and screaming men drowned out his voice. His boots slipped on muddy ground and he fell, hard, only to be hauled to his feet by Belthar. Turned in time to drive his spear into the throat of the Eirdkilr that had come up behind the big man. Ducking as Belthar swung his axe to decapitate another barbarian on Aravon's left.

Aravon had no time to thank Belthar—he was too busy fighting for his life. For the life of the Hilmir, Bjarni, Colborn, Belthar, and every Fehlan and Princelander that faced the Eirdkilrs.

The world narrowed in around him, a red haze edging his vision. He saw nothing but the Eirdkilrs that stood between him and Throrsson. Thirty of them, hacking down the Fjall warriors surrounding the Hilmir. Blue-stained faces, blood-soaked furs, and rusting chain mail on bodies far too large to be fully human.

With a snarl, Aravon hurled himself toward the barbarians and unleashed every bit of pent-up rage and fury.

The Eirdkilrs had slaughtered his friends and comrades of Sixth Company to a man. They'd slain innocent Eyrr at Oldrsjot and killed half the warriors of Bjornstadt. Draian, their Mender. Hundreds of Princelander miners at Silver Break and Gold Burrows Mines. Three hundred and seventy-eight Legionnaires and Westhaven regulars at Rivergate. Thousands of the Hilmir's warband, tens of thousands of Fjall citizens. Men, women, and children that had done nothing wrong but strive to exist in the same world as the Eirdkilrs.

Duke Dyrund. Thoughts of the Duke's fever-bright face and gaunt frame set a blaze of fury in his chest. The Eirdkilrs had been the ones to blame for that. *They* had forced him into hiding, which had exposed him to the Wraithfever. Because of them, Aravon had nearly lost one of the most important people in his life.

And he'd be damned if they didn't pay for it.

His spear whirled, darted, struck, and stabbed, felling Eirdkilrs before they saw him coming. Rage burned in his veins, drove back his pain until nothing remained but the desire to kill. To make the Eirdkilrs suffer as they had made Gyrd and the Hilmir's warriors suffer near the Waeggbjod.

Then, so suddenly it staggered him, he had broken through the ranks of Eirdkilrs and drawn within two steps of Throrsson, Bjarni, and Sigbrand. "Hilmir!" he screamed. "We need to—"

Pain exploded in his right side. The blow hurled him backward and knocked him to the ground. A heavy boot stamped down hard on his right arm, pinning his spear to the ground. Stunned and reeling, Aravon barely managed to look up in time to see the Eirdkilr standing over him, axe upraised to strike.

Steel flashed and the barbarian's head spun from his shoulders. Blood sprayed over Aravon. Aravon managed to turn away in time to keep it from his eyes, but the hot, warm fluid seeped down his mask and into the collar of his leather armor. When he turned back, Belthar stood over him, legs spread in a defensive stance, protecting Aravon with his axe and his hulking body.

Aravon tugged at his right arm, found his spear trapped beneath the body of the headless Eirdkilr. With pain racing along his side, he rose to his feet and struggled to free his spear. He'd just torn it out from beneath the dead enemy and spun back to the battle when he caught sight of the Eirdkilr charging Belthar. The big man, so focused on protecting Aravon, never saw it coming.

Chapter Seventy-Five

"Belthar!" Aravon screamed.

The huge club *smashed* into the side of Belthar's huge head with bone-shattering force. The big man went down hard, sprawling in the bloody mud.

A wordless cry of rage burst from Aravon's lips and he drove his spear into the Eirdkilr's chest. So hard it punched through steel, ribs, organs, and out the barbarian's back. When he tore it free, the Eirdkilr collapsed forward, his huge body slumping atop Belthar.

Aravon had no time to see if Belthar still lived—no time to do anything but grab Belthar's arm with his free hand and set about dragging the man backward, up the hill. An Eirdkilr charged, forcing him to drop the big man's wrist and use both hands to turn aside the blow. Cutting down the man with a vicious slash of his spear, Aravon grabbed Belthar again and struggled.

In vain. Aravon was strong, but Belthar had to weigh nearly as much as a bloody horse, with the bulk of the dead Eirdkilr atop him.

Swordsman, help me!

Rangvaldr appeared at Aravon's side, seizing Belthar's other arm. Together, the two of them dragged the big man out from beneath the dead Eirdkilr, through the swirling knots of combat, and back up the hill.

"Fall back!" Eirik Throrsson's booming voice rang out from just ahead of Aravon. "Back!"

The Fjall broke off their combat as best they could, leaving dozens of corpses—Fehlan and Eirdkilr—sprawled on the muddy, blood-soaked ground. Throrsson's attack had bought the Deid a few seconds, time enough to pull back and retreat up the hill. Not without casualties. Fewer than two thousand Fehlans survived to join the shield wall forming on the slope forty yards above the Eirdkilrs' position at the crossing and the base of Hangman's Hill.

To Aravon's relief, the Eirdkilrs didn't give chase. The Blood Queen's remaining eight or nine hundred were exhausted from non-stop fighting for…*Keeper's teeth, has it already been two hours?*

Even the Eirdkilrs from the Bulwark seemed unwilling to pursue battle, for the moment. They'd traveled more than a hundred and twenty miles across Fjall lands to reach Hangman's Hill, doubtless setting a punishing pace to arrive in time. Ferocity and impossible strength and stamina aside, the Eirdkilrs were still human and as such, needed rest, air, and sustenance as much as any Princelander or Fehlan. Their war cries had given way to gasping, panting breaths, too exhausted to howl at their enemies.

But one look at the smug satisfaction that stained the Blood Queen's face told Aravon *exactly* what she was thinking. And she was right. She had them trapped. With her reinforcements once more holding the crossing and the bridge destroyed, the Hilmir had nowhere to run.

Worse. In saving the Deid, he'd given up the advantage of the steep hill, the barricades atop the summit, and his traps. Throrsson had relinquished anything that might have compensated for his reduced numbers. Even with the remaining fourteen hundred Deid joining ranks with the Hilmir's six hundred, the Eirdkilrs outnumbered them three to two.

Yet, to their credit, neither the Deid or Fjall warband faltered. Exhaustion lined their bloodstained faces, but not a one showed any sign of cowardice, any desire to retreat. They stood firm, shields locked together, Hafgrimsson's gray greatwolf beside the heavy black bear that was Eirik Throrsson. Defiance, hatred, and determination blazed in the eyes of every Fehlan in that line.

The Blood Queen was no longer simply a threat; she had murdered their people, destroyed their homes, and slain their comrades. The blood of brothers, kinsmen, and friends turned the ground to mud beneath their feet. Every man in the shield wall line would die here rather than surrender to the *Blodsvarri*.

Pride glowed within Aravon. They weren't Legionnaires, yet in that moment, there was no one beside whom he'd rather stand and fight. Men battling for their homes, their lives, and their futures.

He tensed as the Eirdkilr ranks parted and the Blood Queen strode forward.

"Eirik Throrsson!" Fire blazed in the *Blodsvarri's* eyes, a violent edge to her voice. "The might of the Fjall die here this day, and with them, their traitorous cousins of the Deid. Your collusion with the wretched Eird has doomed you."

"Save your venomous words, Vigdis Orridottir." Throrsson spat. "It will do you no good. Your power on Fehl is shattered, and it is *we* who have shattered it. Slink home to your master and tell him you have failed. Then we will see how Tyr *Farbjodr* rewards those who disappoint him!"

The Blood Queen's high-pitched laughter rang out, echoed off the steep hillside. "Proud words, Hilmir. Worthy of your great-grandfather. And you will die just as he did, a bearhound shorn of claws and stripped of fur. Only this time, there will be no one left to mourn you. Your warriors will face the *Tolfraedr,* even if I have to rip them from *Seggrholl* with my own hands. Their corpses will feed the Bein for years to come. And your proud head, Hilmir of the Fjall, will be mounted at—"

The Blood Queen's head suddenly snapped to the side, as if someone had driven a fist into her temple. No, not a fist. Aravon's eyes flew wide as he recognized the red fletching of the arrow that sprouted from the side of her neck. The woman toppled, gurgling, blood spraying from the torn vein beside her throat.

Aravon whirled to his right. A lone figure stood on the hill across the Hardrfoss. Clad in mottled leather armor and clutching a longbow, with a quiver of red-fletched arrows slung over his shoulder.

Yes! A defiant laugh burst from Aravon's lips as Noll drew another arrow, nocked, and raised his bow.

But the scout hadn't come alone. From the woods behind him, a full company of lightly-armored Agrotorae spilled out onto the hill. Arrows already nocked, they drew back and, at a command from the dark-haired woman in the lead, loosed. Two hundred and fifty arrows whistled through the air and rained down death onto the Eirdkilrs gathered at the ford.

Then came a new sound, like the rumbling of distant thunder, growing louder with every heartbeat. Two hundred warhorses clad in heavy plate armor burst into view from the western forest, a gleaming line of heavily-armored soldiers bearing long, steel-tipped lances. Lances that lowered toward the Eirdkilrs amassed at the Hardrfoss crossing. The column of glimmering steel closed the distance to the enemy in the space of a half-dozen heartbeats.

597

The Eirdkilrs, caught off-guard by the suddenness of the assault and their leader's death, barely managed to turn in time to face the new threat. The Agrotorae had kept up a steady rate of fire all the time, loosing ten shafts each in the time it took the cavalry to close. Yet with the precision that made them so damned effective in battle, the stream of arrows slacked off two seconds before the cavalry tore into the Eirdkilrs.

Even prepared, with their huge shields for protection, the Eirdkilrs could not stand before the towering warhorses and the force of that charge. Lances punched through wooden shields, chain mail, and barbarian flesh. Drawing long, heavy swords with a curved blade designed for slashing, the cavalry raked across the front of the Eirdkilr's hastily formed line. Barbarians died by the scores, their screams swallowed beneath the rumbling boom of the horses' hooves.

Then the cavalry was across the ford and splashing onto the flat land spread out at the base of the hill. Heavy sabers rose and fell, Eirdkilr blood sprayed, and the horses pounded past along the front of the line. Steel-clad mounts trampled the silent corpse of the Blood Queen into the crimson-tinged muck and mire. Down the wall of Eirdkilrs they raced, swords cutting down enemies by the dozen. Just before they got bogged down in the marshlands east of the hill, they wheeled left and pounded a few yards up the hill. With military precision, they circled back around to the west and galloped in front of the Fehlan line with a salute of their bloodied swords.

The Fjall and Deid roared, hurling insults not at the Legion horsemen, but at the stunned ranks of Eirdkilrs. Their cheers redoubled as shield-bearing Legionnaires marched out of the forest on the eastern side of the Hardrfoss. Hundreds, all bearing the black armor of Onyx Battalion, forming up quickly into shield walls of solid black. With the slow, determined pace of professional soldiers, they advanced toward the scattered, disorganized Eirdkilrs holding the crossing.

Aravon saw the look in the Eirdkilrs' eyes: their center of gravity was shattered, their forces in disarray, surrounded by far too many men to defeat. Exhausted from battle and long travel, bloodied by Fjall, Deid, and Legion attacks.

For the first time in Aravon's memory, the Eirdkilrs broke. With howls of rage, they turned and fled into the marshes to the west and the forests to the south. So swiftly, it seemed the barbarians were there one moment and gone the

598

next. But within less than thirty seconds, the Eirdkilrs were streaming out of sight and crashing through the trees and wetlands.

No Fjall or Deid gave chase. None of them so much as moved, doubtless as surprised as Aravon by the Eirdkilrs' flight. Yet after a long moment, cheers and shouts of triumph burst from Fehlan throats. Two thousand of the Hilmir and Hafgrimsson's men took up the cries, until the sound of their elation echoed off the hills and set the nearby forests trembling.

Realization struck Aravon like a hammer blow. *We won!* A triumphant laugh bubbled in his chest, and he let it loose. *By the Swordsman, we bloody did it!* Against all odds, in the face of certain defeat, they had defeated the Blood Queen.

A wave of exhaustion settled over Aravon like a leaden blanket. He was tired, so damned tired. He'd have fallen if he hadn't had his spear to lean on, would have dropped his spear had it not been resting against the ground. The injuries in his shoulders, chest, and side returned with a vengeance, setting every muscle in his body throbbing. He doubted he'd ever pry his right hand loose of his spear; his fingers had formed stiff claws, his glove caked in sticky, crusting blood.

Yet he welcomed the pain. It meant he was alive. Alive, and victorious.

Four horsemen splashed across the Hardrfoss and trotted up the hill toward them. The foremost, a man with the dark hair, manicured beard, and angular features common to mainlanders, wore the high-plumed helmet of the Legion Commander. To his right and left rode two Captains, likely his aides. And in the rear came Noll, his compact frame seeming even smaller on the enormous *Kostarasar* charger that towered over the Legionnaires' horses.

The Legion commander drew his horse to a halt before Throrsson. "*Heil og sael*, Hilmir," he said, his Fehlan bearing the heavy accent of the mainland city of Voramis. "I am Galerius, Commander of Onyx Battalion." He gave a crisp Legion salute and leaned forward in his saddle, grinning down at Throrsson. "Seems we arrived just in time."

Aravon's spine stiffened. The Hilmir's face revealed no trace of mirth, but his eyes had gone dark, angry. "I told your Duke the Legion was not welcome on Fjall soil," he growled.

Aravon snorted. "Technically, we're not on Fjall soil." He gestured to the hill behind them. "The Deid *did* claim this land in the Battle of *Banamadrhaed*."

"Aye, so we did!" Pride shone in Chief Svein Hafgrimsson's eyes. "And, as we proved today, the Deid are every bit the warriors the Fjall believe themselves to be."

Throrsson's jaw muscles worked, and his bushy eyebrows drew together. But to Aravon's relief, a slow smile played across his lips and he gave Hafgrimsson a curt nod. "Indeed." He held out a hand to the Deid chief. "And for that, you have our gratitude."

The Deid chief clasped his hand. "Save your gratitude. Send us a dozen casks of Ornntadr mead and we'll call it even."

Throrsson grunted. "We're not *that* grateful." With a shake of his head, he turned back to the Legion officer. "As for you, Commander Galerius of Onyx Battalion, perhaps, this *once*, I will not begrudge the Legion presence here."

"Generous of you." Sarcasm tinged Galerius' tone. "Now, Hilmir, if we're done with the pleasantries, it is time the Deid, Fjall, and Princelands speak of what to do about the three thousand Eirdkilrs that just abandoned the field. Not to mention , those still occupying Fjall lands."

"As long as you understand that the Legion is not welcome in my kingdom," Throrsson retorted, "we will have that conversation."

Aravon didn't bother listening to Commander Galerius' response. He'd fulfilled his duty to the Hilmir, and with the Duke opening the way for negotiations, Commander Galerius had a decent shot at convincing Throrsson to let the Legion and Hafgrimsson's Deid warriors lend a hand. And, though he'd never met Commander Galerius, Aravon knew of the man's reputation. A decent officer, respected among his fellow Commanders and the Legionnaires under his command, and a strategist on par with the best on Fehl. He would handle the negotiations and plans for the future well enough.

Now, Aravon had to focus on his own men. He turned to the scout sitting mounted behind the two Legion aides. "*You cut it awfully close, Noll,*" Aravon signed one-handed.

The Legion could cover upwards of thirty miles a day if pushed. Hammer Garrison, where Aravon had sent Noll to intercept Onyx Battalion, was little more than a hundred miles away. At top speed, they *should* have reached Hangman's Hill the previous night.

He shook his head. "*And here I thought you Legion scouts worked quickly.*"

Noll nudged his horse into a walk, moving around the conversing Hilmir, Hafgrimsson, and Commander Galerius. "*You know how I like to make an* entrance." He shrugged. *"Took the Commander a while to accept my bona fides, even with the Prince's insignia. And, it turns out Legionnaires march far too damned slowly for a scout like me."* A snort echoed from beneath his mask. *"I'm just glad Skathi didn't make the shot before I did."*

"She's not here." Aravon shook his head.

"And you're lucky she wasn't." Colborn's voice echoed from behind Aravon. As he came to stand on Aravon's right, he switched to the silent hand language, as well. *"She'd never let you hear the end of it for missing."*

"Missing?" The word burst from Noll's lips. The heads of the two Legion aides, Commander Galerius, and both Fehlan chiefs turned toward him.

Noll ducked his head and moved closer to Aravon, away from the conversing warriors behind him. *"I didn't miss,"* he said in the silent hand language. He thrust a finger toward the trampled, mangled corpse lying face-up in the grass. The red fletching of Noll's arrow still protruded from the Blood Queen's neck. *"I got her dead center."*

"Oh?" Colborn cocked his head. *"I'd have sworn you were aiming for her eyes."*

Noll's crude gesture wasn't suitable for even rough company, but Aravon was too glad to see the scout here to bother correcting him.

"Belthar and Rangvaldr?" Colborn signed.

Aravon's gut tightened, worry humming through his bones. Belthar had taken a bad head wound protecting him. He hadn't had time to check on the big man, but now that the battle was over…

He spun toward the spot where he'd left Belthar after dragging him out of the battle line. There, Rangvaldr knelt over the big man. The *Seiomenn* had removed Belthar's helmet, revealing an ugly, bloody mess on the side of Belthar's head. Rangvaldr had the Eyrr holy stone pendant pressed to his masked face. Slowly, the blue gemstone brightened, gleaming with an inner light, bathing him in a soft cerulean glow. Rangvaldr pressed the stone to the bloodied side of Belthar's head and remained kneeling, head bowed.

As Aravon had seen at Bjornstadt, the holy stones worked their magic instantly. The trickle of blood from Belthar's scalp slowed and stopped. Flesh re-knit before Aravon's eyes, the wound sealing itself, the bruises fading, though not disappearing altogether.

But the healing magic worked. Belthar's eyelids fluttered open, and his glassy eyes slowly focused on the faces of the four men standing over him.

Relief flooded Aravon, and he knelt at Belthar's side. "Welcome back, Ursus."

"Wha…" Belthar's voice was heavy, his word slurring. When he tried to sit upright, he groaned and his eyes wobbled.

"Easy." Aravon pressed a hand to the man's enormous shoulder. "That head wound's bad. Even with the Stonekeeper's magic, you're going to be out of it for a while."

"I-I'll be fine, sir." With laborious effort, Belthar shoved himself up onto one elbow, then managed to sit. "Just knocked a few bats loose in my attic."

"Magicmaker taught me a simple test to evaluate for damage to the brain." Colborn glanced up at Aravon. "With your permission, Captain."

Aravon nodded. "Do it."

Colborn waved a finger in front of the big man's face. "Follow my finger with just your eyes. No moving your head." After a few seconds, he nodded and lowered his finger. "Good. Now, answer these simple questions, yes or no. Got it?"

"Yes," Belthar rumbled.

"Are you in Rivergate?" Colborn asked.

"No." Belthar shook his head, wincing.

"Are you at Hangman's Hill?"

"Yes."

"Am I prettier than Noll?"

Belthar chuckled. "Horses are better looking."

"Damn, that head wound is *really* bad." Noll shook his head. "Probably fatal."

With a chuckle, Colborn stood and offered the big man a hand up. "Seems fine."

"Thank you." Aravon turned to Rangvaldr. "Your arrival couldn't have come at a better time. I and all the Fjall owe you our lives."

Rangvaldr gave a dismissive wave. "Just doing my job, right, Captain?" Humor sparkled in his eyes.
"But Hafgrimsson had the right idea about that Ornntadr mead."

"You'd betray your loyalty to Eyrr *ayrag?*" Aravon's eyebrows rose beneath his mask. "What would Nuius say?"

Rangvaldr shrugged. "Some men are fortunate enough to have *two* great loves."

"My flask's dry," Noll put in, "but I've got a bit of water left." He plucked the waterskin from his belt and thrust it out to Rangvaldr.

The *Seiomenn* took it. "That'll have to do." Uncorking the skin, he lifted his mask enough to place the opening to his lips and tilted back his head to drink. He'd gotten little more than a mouthful before he spat and sputtered. Lifting his fingers to his mouth, he plucked out a handful of what looked like muddy marsh river grass.

Noll dissolved in a fit of laughter. "Yes!" he howled. "I got you, you bastard!"

Rangvaldr was too busy spitting to form a reply.

Noll rounded on Aravon, triumph in his eyes. "It's like the old saying goes, Captain. 'Revenge is a drink best served tepid with a mouthful of swamp grass'."

Despite his exhaustion, thirst, and the pain radiating through every muscle in his body, Aravon couldn't help laughing.

Chapter Seventy-Six

By the Swordsman, we pulled it off!

Aravon stood halfway up Hangman's Hill, too tired to do more than sit and watch the men moving around the battlefield. Wounded Fehlans screaming, weeping, or suffering in grim silence. Limping men helping others with shattered arms and crushed skulls toward the base of the hill, where the injured were being tended to by their comrades or the Legion's Menders.

Far too many would never walk away from Hangman's Hill. Thousands slain in battle, with nearly as many succumbing to wounds, blood loss, pain, or infection. The sound of whirring bone saws and shrieking soldiers echoed from within the forest—the Legion surgeons would have a busy day. Almost as busy as the warriors set to collect the slain warriors of the Deid and Fjall warbands.

A full hundred-man company of Legionnaires had joined the Hilmir's men in cutting down trees to build the ceremonial biers for the Fehlan dead. The Eirdkilrs would be left to rot, their bones bleaching the marshlands where they had been dragged and discarded. But for the honored warriors that had died in battle—even the forty-odd former traitors—a fiery death and ceremonial farewell awaited. A tribute to their courage and strength. True sons of Fehl, each and every one.

And the blood. So much blood. Splattered across the bright green blades of grass, staining the churned mud a gruesome crimson, trickling along on the currents of the Hardrfoss. A metallic taint thickened the air, so heavy Aravon could taste it through his mask. It coated his armor, mask, gloves, and weapons, turning to a grisly crust as it dried. Among the blood, bits of shattered bone, locks of torn-off hair, and entrails spilled from torn-open bellies.

605

Aravon would *never* grow inured to that grim sight.

A few score Fjall and Deid moved among the fallen warriors, collecting weapons. On the western side of the hill lay a pile of Eirdkilr spears, axes, and clubs. In the center, near the funeral bier, the axes, swords, and shields of the slain Fehlans lay in a pile. Those weapons would be distributed among the dead and burned with their bodies—trophies to take into the afterlife, to hang on the walls of *Seggrholl* as they sat to feast with *Striith* and the Fehlan heroes gone before them.

The warriors still standing moved slowly, their eyes shadowed and faces gaunt, hollow with the horror of war. Even experienced warriors could know abject fear, feel the icy fingers of death clutching their necks. A battle like this left far deeper scars on the mind than on the body.

"It could have ended far, far worse." Eirik Throrsson's voice rumbled from Aravon's left.

Aravon shot a glance at the Hilmir. He hadn't heard the man approaching, but that came as no surprise. The battle had left him drained in mind as well as body. "Indeed."

The *Blodsvarri* had fallen, and the traitorous Grimar as well. The defeated Eirdkilrs were on the run. Their grip on the Fjall lands had been shattered.

Yet, the fate of the Hilmir's people still hung in a precarious balance.

Storbjarg had burned, its proud gates destroyed, and—if the traitorous Grimar had spoken truth—the walls torn down. The Fjall's once-mighty warband was all but annihilated; fewer than nine hundred had survived the battle, three hundred of whom were wounded. Many wouldn't live through the night, even with the Menders' aid.

"What will you do now, Hilmir?" Aravon asked. "What does the future hold for the Fjall?"

"I cannot say." Throrsson shook his head, setting his shaggy black hair flying the bones braided into his beard rattling. "Your Commander Galerius knows how to use a strategic position to his advantage. He presses me with the hope that, in my eternal gratitude for his timely arrival, I grant the Legion permission to enter my lands."

"Not the worst idea." Aravon shrugged. "You could use a few more swords to help drive out the Eirdkilrs in the south, hunt down the ones who fled now." He searched the Hilmir's eyes. "As the Duke said, the Princelands have no intention of conquering the Fjall. Our best hope is in alliance, in uniting against our common enemy."

Throrsson rumbled deep in his throat, a contemplative sound that held only a trace of anger. Long seconds of silence passed before he nodded. "I will consider it." He gave a dismissive wave. "But even with Storbjarg destroyed and my warband reduced, the Fjall are no weaklings."

"Of that, I have no doubt." Aravon chuckled. "You will rebuild, as you did after Vigvollr and *Banamadrhaed.*"

"Aye." Throrsson nodded slowly. "And we expect the Duke to come through on his end." He narrowed his eyes at Aravon. "I will expect the cure for my people to arrive as promised. To Ingolfsfell, where I will accompany them to Ornntadr."

Mention of Duke Dyrund and Wraithfever set worry panging through Aravon. The tiredness retreated beneath the urgency of getting Rangvaldr and his healing stone to the Duke's side.

"Of course." Aravon nodded. "You will have what you need to save your people. And your daughter."

"My d—" Throrsson cut off with a sharp breath, surprise staining his muddy, blood-caked face. "You mean…?"

"She lives," Aravon said. "The Duke personally carried her from Storbjarg beside your wife. Though your Asleif has gone to *Striith,* Branda still fights the Wraithfever." He leaned forward and spoke in a low voice. "The Duke has instructed a special dose of the cure to be delivered to her at Saerheim."

The Hilmir's eyes narrowed, his gaze darting around. "He sent her to the *Deid?*"

"They are allies to the Princelands, if not the Fjall." Aravon fixed him with a meaningful glance. "There, she will be safe until we can reach her. Until the *cure* can reach her."

Suspicion flashed across Throrsson's face. "And then what?" His jaw muscles worked and a snarl tugged at his lips. "Keep her as your hostage to ensure my…compliance?"

"Never." Aravon shook his head. "The Duke only gave that order to keep her out of harm's way. Once she is cured, he will ensure that she is brought safely to wherever you wish. Knowing the Duke, I'm certain he will task *us* with that mission."

For a moment, the wary light blazed brighter in Throrsson's eyes. But it quickly faded, and he gave a curt nod. "So be it, Captain Snarl." He held out a huge hand. "Find my daughter, heal her, and bring her safe to me. Seek me out in Ornntadr. There, we will raise horns of the finest *mjod* and speak of peace between Fjall and Princelander once more."

Aravon clasped the Hilmir's forearm. "By the will of *Striith*."

"A word of caution." Throrsson's words echoed in a low rumble. "The Blood Queen was just one of those leading the *Tauld's* attacks, and her death will only slow *Farbjodr's* plans, not stymie them completely. There is one, in particular, you would do well to watch out for when bringing my daughter south. A bastard of a man named Asger Einnauga. One-Eye, they call him. He commands the eight thousand *Tauld* that live among the Myrr and Bein. Though I have not heard rumors of his presence this far north for weeks, I have little doubt he will be the next arrow loosed from *Farbjodr's* quiver."

Aravon's brow furrowed. "Anything in particular springs to mind?"

Throrsson contemplated for a moment, then shook his head. "It is rumored that *he* was the one to plan the siege on your garrisons, but more than that, I could not say."

"Thank you, Hilmir." Aravon nodded. "I will make certain to keep a sharp eye out."

Throrsson grinned. "Of that, I have no doubt." He gave Aravon a little nod. "Until we meet again, Captain Snarl."

"Thank you, Hilmir." With a bow, Aravon turned and hurried down the hill.

His steps led toward the forest where the Fjall and Deid had taken their wounded. So many wounded. Men bleeding from shallow wounds and clutching gashes so deep bone shone white through their flesh. Warriors unconscious from pain or screaming to *Striith* and *Olfossa* for mercy, for relief from the pain. Proud, strong men of the Fjall and Deid warband reduced to tears, wordless sobs, or keening cries by grief, agony, and the burden of loss.

He found Rangvaldr sitting beside Sigbrand, pressing the holy stones to a long, jagged tear in the warrior's right arm. The wound was deep, the bone cracked, but the flesh slowly re-knit as the *Seiomenn* held out the glowing holy stones.

Aravon hurried toward him, but waited until the brilliant blue light diminished, the wound finished closing. "Stonekeeper," he called. "We need to go, now."

Rangvaldr nodded to Sigbrand and stood, slowly. Though the mask hid his face, Aravon saw the deepened wrinkles, the shadow that hung in the man's eyes. The *Seiomenn's* shoulders were slumped, burdened. "I would stay and help, Captain," he said. "There are many who could use Nuius' gift of healing."

"The Legion has Menders," Aravon insisted. "Besides, there is someone who has greater need of your aid." His fingers flashed the sign for Duke Dyrund.

Instantly, the *Seiomenn* was on full alert, his head snapping up. "What happened?"

"Wraithfever." Aravon's jaw clenched. "Magicmaker found a way to slow it, but—"

"Let's go!" Rangvaldr hurried toward him and, together, they strode out onto the flat, grassy expanse at the base of Hangman's Hill.

Just then, the thundering of galloping hooves echoed loud to their left, followed by loud *splashing* as Colborn and Noll rode across the shallow ford. Behind them came three huge chargers with empty saddles.

Colborn drew up in front of Aravon. "Captain." He dropped the reins of Aravon's horse and turned to scan the hillside until he found what he sought. "Ursus!" he called, and gave a loud whistle.

Belthar rose from his seat on the slope, his movements ponderous, still recovering from the head wound. Noll led the big man's horse up the hill and, with a grateful nod, Belthar clambered into the saddle.

Aravon cast a worried glance at the big man. On his back hung the huge crossbow—left carefully at the summit of the hill so as not to incur Polus' wrath on their next return to Camp Marshal—and he gripped his huge double-headed axe in his left hand. He seemed no worse for the serious wound sustained, though Aravon knew Rangvaldr would keep a close eye on him for the next few days. The side effects of that severe head injury could show up days after the battle ended.

But Belthar gave him a nod, his fingers flashing the hand signal for "*All good*". Aravon had to take the man at his word—Belthar deserved that much respect.

Aravon cast one last glance at the field of battle. The towering king oak trees cresting the hill. The wooden barricades splattered with the blood of Eirdkilrs and Fjall warriors. The deep crimson stains and swaths of ground churned to mud that covered the hillside. A place of death, yet for today, a place of triumph.

Grim satisfaction settled in Aravon's stomach as he turned his horse's head toward the east. He was glad to leave the battlefield, the blood and carnage, the reek of death far behind. Yet the knowledge of what they'd accomplished here left him hopeful, filled him with confidence.

They'd done the impossible, together. Because of today, there was hope for a better future for the Fjall, Deid, and all of Fehl—a future free of the Eirdkilrs.

Then he turned away from the battlefield and dug his heels into his horse's ribs, setting the charger into motion. Within five minutes, he and his companions had splashed across the ford and turned south along the Hardrfoss' western riverbank. Toward the cave where Skathi and Zaharis waited with the Duke.

We're coming, Duke Dyrund! Aravon gritted his teeth and spurred his horse to run faster. *Just hang on a little bit longer.*

The horses covered the first half-mile south in the space of five minutes, their smooth, rolling gait carrying them across the flat, grassy terrain with ease. Aravon waited until they were just far enough out of sight of the Legionnaires and Fehlans on Hangman's Hill before slowing and drawing out his bone whistle. Three short, sharp blasts were all he needed to summon Snarl.

Less than a minute passed before he caught sight of the furry, winged figure speeding through the crystal blue sky toward him. Snarl's orange-and-white coat gleamed in the sunlight, nearly as bright as the Enfield's amber eyes as he landed in front of Aravon's horse and raced toward him, yipping and barking in delight. Aravon had dismounted and now knelt to greet the Enfield, scratching Snarl's scruff and letting the little fox creature lick his face for a few seconds before drawing out the cloth that held Skathi's scent.

"Go!" Aravon said the command word. "Find her!"

Snarl sniffed the cloth and, with a delighted bark, leapt into the air, his wings flapping loudly as he climbed high above the treetops. By the time Aravon clambered into his saddle, the little Enfield had already dwindled to a fast-retreating shape on the southern horizon.

Aravon turned to find his four men looking at him, questions in their eyes. "Just in case," he said.

They seemed to accept it as an answer—or, at least Colborn did. The Lieutenant spurred his horse into motion, Aravon a heartbeat behind him. Belthar, Noll, and Rangvaldr kept pace so as not to be left behind.

Truth be told, Aravon didn't *need* to send Snarl ahead to the cave. They'd reach it in less than an hour at their fast pace. But he wasn't going to take risks, not with Eirdkilrs fleeing from the battle. There was a chance, however miniscule, that the retreating barbarians had spotted the cave and decided to take shelter there. With Skathi wounded and Zaharis looking after the Duke, Aravon wanted to be certain he spotted any surprises well ahead of time.

The minutes seemed to drag on, the terrain flashing by at a snail's pace. It didn't matter that the chargers were running at near full-speed; Aravon chafed at every second it took him to reach the Duke's side. Rangvaldr had to work his magic before the Wraithfever—

All thoughts faded as Aravon caught sight of Snarl speeding back toward him. The Enfield had been gone for less than five minutes. Dread settled like a stone in Aravon's gut. *That can't be!*

No way Snarl could have covered that distance in such a short time. Which meant something was truly wrong.

"Go!" he shouted and dug his heels into his horse's flanks.

Snarl swooped low, circled once with a high-pitched bark, and took off toward the south once more. Aravon followed as fast as he could, pushing his horse into a gallop until the Enfield flew into a dense stand of trees west of the riverbank. The thick branches, gnarled roots, and dense underbrush forced Aravon to slow his pace, which only added to the anxiety roiling within him. Worry settled into his bones; he couldn't put the sense into words, but every fiber in his being screamed at him that something terrible had happened.

He crashed through the trees headlong and burst into a small clearing amidst a circle of towering pine trees. He reined in, barely stopping in time before he plowed into Skathi. The archer stood with her feet planted, bow bent and an arrow nocked. Recognition flashed across her unmasked face as she caught sight of them, and she lowered her bow with a grimace. Yet there was no mistaking the worry that darkened her forest-green eyes.

Then Aravon saw the two figures behind the archer. Zaharis sat on the ground, his back against a tree, his face twisted in a look of sheer panic, cheeks white with horror and guilt. He rocked back and forth with a horrible, keening cry, hands clutching at the figure in his lap.

In that moment, all else faded around Aravon, and his eyes locked on the prone figure beside Zaharis. Duke Dyrund lay with his head on the Secret Keeper's leg. His eyes were wide, empty and unseeing, all flush of fever gone from his face. All hint of *color* fled as well.

The Long Keeper had gathered Duke Dyrund into his arms.

Chapter Seventy-Seven

No!

Aravon felt as if a mountain had just collapsed atop him, a thousand needles of molten iron driven into every nerve in his body. He half-fell, half-slid from his saddle and collapsed to his knees beside the Duke, seizing the man's hands. Cold, limp, hands that didn't grip back when Aravon held them tight.

"We tried to get him to you, Captain." Skathi's voice echoed as if from a thousand leagues away, so faint through the rushing blood that pulsed in Aravon's ears.

Tears stung Aravon's eyes, his breath freezing in his lungs. He couldn't breathe, couldn't think. Could only lift his blurred gaze to Zaharis.

"What happened?" The angry shout burst from his lips.

Zaharis seemed not to see Aravon. He rocked backward and forward, that eerie, keening cry rolling from his tongueless mouth. No tears spilled from his eyes, but guilt was etched into every line of his face.

"Zaharis!" Aravon gripped the Secret Keeper's shoulders and shook him hard, setting Zaharis' teeth rattling. "The Wraithfever, it was getting better!"

That seemed to snap Zaharis back to reality. His eyes fixed on Aravon and horror twisted his face. He seemed unable to lift his hand from cradling the Duke to sign the silent words. "*I did everything I could. The fever...*" He shook his head. "*It never fully broke. I had nothing...*"

Aravon could see no more through the blur of tears. A torrent of emotion burst from him in a single massive sob that wracked his shoulders. He tried to hold back the pain, the sorrow, but he could not. He could do nothing but sit at the Duke's side and clutch his pale, limp hand.

No! His heart seemed frozen between beats, his mind drowning in an overwhelming torrent of grief. Paralyzed, every fiber of his being screaming out in protest, Aravon felt as if he'd been hollowed out from the inside, his heart torn from his chest by a fist of iron. No, such a wound would kill him. This...this was far worse.

The pain deep within the core of his being eclipsed the mundane aches of his muscles, the throbbing of his wounds, the exhaustion at the day. He felt nothing, heard nothing. Simply sat, stunned and frozen in a paroxysm of anguish. It was as if a part of himself had died here. A part of his life that had been so important even if he hadn't known it all along.

That realization only made the heartache more painful. The Duke had been such a central figure in his life, the man who he turned to when he needed advice, a comforting voice when Aravon's father heaped scorn and disdain on his head. A friendly presence at his side after the horrors of losing Sixth Company, and again after the death of Draian.

But now, with the Duke gone, he had no one left. To the world, Captain Aravon was dead. Mylena and his sons believed him lost in the ambush. His father likely wouldn't remember him, even if he cared what happened to Aravon. Prince Toran knew, but he was the Prince, as far removed from Aravon as an eagle from a groundworm.

No. With effort, he forced back the thought. *I'm not alone.*

The darkness pressing in on his mind retreated, and he once more found himself sitting in that forest clearing, clutching the Duke's hand. Though it took every shred of willpower, he lifted his tear-blurred eyes to the six faces around him. Zaharis' pale, guilt-ridden face. Skathi's brow, furrowed with concern. The kindness in Rangvaldr's eyes, the empathy sparkling in Colborn's. The way Belthar hovered protectively over him, Noll's turning away to give him a moment of privacy.

I'm not alone...because I have them.

To the world at large, Aravon had died. Yet to these six people, these brave warriors that had chosen to join him in service to Duke Dyrund and the Princelands, he was very much alive. They *cared*—about his grief and pain, about his health, his safety. Belthar had risked his life to protect Aravon in the battle. Rangvaldr had set aside his desire to help his own people, all to heal the Duke.

614

Skathi had set aside her desire to fight so she could watch over the Duke and Zaharis—Zaharis, who had done everything in his power to keep the Duke alive. Colborn, who had the quiet support that bolstered Aravon's confidence when he doubted himself. Noll, who had somehow managed to look past his resentment over the deaths of his Sixth Company comrades to accept Aravon's command.

Without them, he had nothing, but with them, he had enough. The Duke's loss hit him hard, a burden that would not leave anytime soon, yet he couldn't wallow in his grief. For their sakes, he had to be strong.

He turned to Zaharis. "You did…everything you could." His words came out in a croak, his throat parched, but he forced his lips to form them. He swallowed. "Thank you, for trying."

Pain and guilt twisted Zaharis' face. That suffering, that regret could gnaw away at even the most unassailable confidence. The burden Zaharis now carried would make a good man go bad. It was Aravon's job as commander to take that off the Secret Keeper's shoulders. To take it upon himself. His decisions, his consequences. He needed his men free of those weights, free to do whatever was needed to fulfill their mission. He could bear the burdens—it was part and parcel of a commander's life.

The Duke had taught him that. Had shown him that a great leader did everything in their power to lighten the loads of those that followed him. And now it was Aravon's turn. His turn to live as the Duke would have, to honor his memory by being the man Duke Dyrund had always believed him to be.

That didn't dim the pain of loss, didn't lighten the burden of grief, but somehow, oddly enough, it gave Aravon the strength to bear up under the strain.

He tried to rise to his feet, lost his balance, and would have fallen if not for Colborn catching him. The Lieutenant held his shoulder, gripping it tight for a moment, until Aravon nodded. Instead of standing, Aravon rose to his knees and bowed over the Duke's body.

"Sing the song, Rangvaldr." His words came out in a whisper. "The song for the fallen heroes."

"Of course, Captain." Clearing his throat, Rangvaldr lifted his voice in the song he'd sung over the slain Eyrr, Draian, and the Duke's men that had died at Bjornstadt.

615

"In the hall of heroes,
Evermore to dwell
At the feast table of warriors and kings
Who in battle bravely fell

Enemies forever vanquished
Peace for time beyond breath
We mourn the sacrifice and laud the courage
Of those who died the glorious death."

Aravon closed his eyes, losing himself in the rise and fall of Rangvaldr's rich voice. The swell of the song, the ringing, mournful notes. A farewell—not a final farewell, but it would have to do until he brought the Duke's body back to Icespire for burial—yet fitting nonetheless.

When the last note was sung and Rangvaldr fell silent, Aravon lifted his head and opened his eyes.

"The Duke was many things to many people." He looked at the six solemn faces around him. "Duke of Eastfall. Lord of Wolfden Castle. Councilor to the Prince. Envoy to the Fehlans. Friend and companion to my father. To me…" His voice cracked.

Rangvaldr rested a hand on his shoulder. "To all of us." Sorrow gleamed in his eyes; he'd respected, even admired the Duke, which was why he'd joined the mission after Draian's death. "With his loss, the world grows a little colder, a little darker."

Aravon nodded gratefully to the *Seiomenn* and, swallowing hard, managed to find his voice. "Yet because of him, we are all united. United in purpose, a purpose he gave us. A mission to save the Princelands and Fehl from the Eirdkilrs. Because of him, the Fjall, Eyrr, and Deid still live. Because of him, Rivergate still stands." A sad smile twisted his lips. "That is a legacy that any man would be proud of."

"Aye," Belthar rumbled. "No better man than the Duke of Eastfall, that was what every regular in Hightower always said. Never thought I'd meet him outside a parade line. The day he chose me for this company, proudest day of my life."

"And mine." Noll had finished with the horses and now stepped up to join them. "Even when I was certain I'd never ride again, that I'd be of no use to anyone, he pushed me. It's thanks to him I'm here."

"Thanks to him we're *all* here." Something dark and dangerous gleamed in Skathi's eyes. "We'd be dead without him, no doubt about it."

"Then we do what he brought us together to do," Colborn spoke up. The Lieutenant had removed his mask, revealing his heavy half-Fehlan features, his braided beard, the ice-blue eyes that sparkled with grim resolve. "The battle here is won, but the Eirdkilrs are far from done for. So it's up to us to make sure the Duke's dream comes true. A dream of a peaceful Fehl, when Fehlans and Princelanders can live together."

"To the Duke's dream." Aravon's words rang out with far more strength than he felt.

"To the Duke's dream!" Five voices echoed in the clearing.

"*To the Duke's dream,*" Zaharis signed. "*And to living the life he expected us to.*"

Silence hung thick in the clearing for long moments. No one seemed eager to break the stillness, and Aravon couldn't think of anything to say. Everything important had already been said, for now.

Without a word, he settled back down beside the Duke and gripped the cold, lifeless hand in his own. He would come up with plans and clever strategies to defeat the Eirdkilrs later—now, he just needed a few moments to grieve. Not to lose himself or to wallow in misery, but to do as the Duke had said and "let himself think, let himself feel".

"Sir." Skathi's quiet voice echoed at his shoulder.

Aravon looked up and found only the archer hovered nearby—the rest, including Zaharis, had moved to the opposite side of the clearing and sat around silently cleaning their armor, sharpening weapons, and busying themselves in whatever tasks kept soldiers occupied. Giving him space to mourn in peace.

All but Skathi. The archer held out a small scrap of parchment to him. "He asked me to write it down, before…" She swallowed. "…before the fever got bad."

Aravon tried to form words of thanks, but none came. He could only nod, a lump thick in his throat, as he accepted the parchment and unrolled it.

The message, written in Skathi's hand, was brief. "*Aravon,*" it read, "*it was my greatest joy to know you. You have made us all proud. The future of the Princelands rests in the best hands I could hope for.*"

That was it. No poetic flourishes, no artful prose such as would be spouted by the bards and troubadours of Icespire. Just the simple, succinct note of a man who had been a soldier long before he became a politician and diplomat. In its own way, all the more powerful.

Moisture blurred Aravon's eyes once more, and his fist closed around the scrap of parchment bearing the Duke's final message. He made no attempt to hold back the flow of tears. For a few brief, quiet moments, he let the emotions wash over him. Not a tidal wave that threatened to crush him, but a river that cut deep, left a mark on his soul. As was right for a man like the Duke. Duke Sammael Dyrund had had a profound impact on Aravon all throughout his life. He would honor the man by carrying that mark forever.

Opening his eyes, Aravon rose to his knees. *Farewell, Your Grace.* He set the cold, lifeless hand gently on the Duke's chest, then laid the other atop it. A solemn, peaceful repose for a great man. *May you know the Swordsman's joy and peace in the Sleepless Lands forever more.*

He rose to his feet slowly, the pain of loss compounding the aches of his injuries and battle wounds. It would be a long while before that pain truly faded. Perhaps, like his improperly healed left arm, it would never be gone completely. So be it. He would bear the pain in honor of the man who had been a better, kinder, nobler father to him than his own father ever had.

The emotions retreated, and with them the numbness that had descended over him. The smell of the forest—rotting leaves, damp earth, the rich, resinous pine sap dripping from the nearby trees—and the sound of his companions' conversation filtered into his ears.

"…a damned good shot," Colborn was saying. "Three hundred, maybe three hundred and fifty yards."

"Not bad." Skathi inclined her head. "I'd say impressive, but—"

"Stick with impressive, yeah." Noll glowed.

A part of Aravon, the part recovering from his grief, was surprised by the conversation. Skathi hadn't snapped or snarled at Noll, and the scout hadn't responded with his usual salacity. A hint of pride glowed within him; they were truly becoming a company, as he and Duke Dyrund had dreamed. Death and battle had united them in a way that little else in the world ever could.

Aravon's eyes went to Zaharis. Misery, guilt, and sorrow etched into every line of the Secret Keeper's face. Aravon could feel his pain—it didn't matter that Zaharis wasn't a healer, didn't have magic stones or a Mender's knowledge.

618

He felt responsible for the Duke's death. His twitching fingers turned over the little chunk of black stone so quickly Aravon half-expected it to catch alight.

Aravon moved toward Zaharis, but Rangvaldr spoke before he'd taken a step. "What is that?" the *Seiomenn* asked.

"*Ghoulstone,*" Zaharis signed left-handed, the fingers of his right hand never slowing as he twirled the stone. "*Found it in Rivergate. More in Gold Burrows Mine.*"

"Let me see it." The *Seiomenn* held out a hand.

Zaharis hesitated. Aravon had seen the Secret Keeper's habit of fidgeting when nervous, worried, or, in this case, burdened by emotion. Zaharis clearly had no desire to relinquish his trinket—the self-soothing mechanism helped to keep him calm. But, after a long moment, he handed it to the *Seiomenn*.

"Never heard of ghoulstone," Rangvaldr muttered. "But I could swear I've seen stone like this before."

Zaharis didn't even look up. "*Where?*" he signed, his fingers sluggish.

Rangvaldr frowned down at the stone for a few long, silent seconds before speaking. "In the main square of Bjornstadt."

That caused Zaharis to look up. "*That was ghoulstone?*"

Rangvaldr tossed the little chunk of stone up and caught it. "Yes, I'm certain." He held it out to Zaharis. "Always been easy to find, stone like that. Too easy, to hear Ailmaer talk about it. Pretty-looking, but of little use. Too soft and easy to crack, which gave the chief a bellyful of grief every time he had to repair the main square."

Then his brow furrowed. "Come to think of it, I've seen it somewhere else, too." He reached up to touch the blue gemstone hanging at his neck. "The Eirdkilrs outside Rivergate, they wore them, too."

Aravon raised an eyebrow, but chose not to butt in to the conversation. Instead, he took a seat silently beside Colborn. As long as the *Seiomenn* kept Zaharis talking, it would give the Secret Keeper a chance to escape his feelings over the Duke's death. And knowing Zaharis, a puzzle was the best thing to divert his attention.

Rangvaldr's expression grew musing. "Funny thing is, a few of the Eyrr healers swore that it would stop certain poisons, but I always thought it was nothing more than—"

Zaharis leapt to his feet so abruptly the *Seiomenn* nearly fell backward. "*Poison!*" The Secret Keeper's fingers flashed. "*How did I not see it?*"

He rushed across the clearing and threw himself to one knee beside the Duke.

Aravon was a step behind the man. "What is it?"

Zaharis gave no answer; his hands were too busy pawing at the man's clothes, pulling up the Duke's leather armored vest, fur-lined undercoat, and the thin tunic beneath. The moment Zaharis caught sight of the Duke's exposed right side, a horrible keening sound burst from his tongueless mouth. His eyes darted toward Aravon, but instead of forming words, he thrust a finger toward a small, round mark just beneath the Duke's ribs.

Aravon frowned down at the tiny mark. Barely wider than a tailor's needle, it bore a strong resemblance to a black sun spot or mole. Yet at the sight of the raised, red flesh around the black mark, Aravon's eyes flew wide. "A wound?"

Zaharis nodded.

"From what?"

For answer, Zaharis turned toward the camp and snapped his fingers. *"My pack!"* he signed. *"Now!"*

Noll was the first to move, scooping up the Secret Keeper's pack and racing across the clearing. Zaharis snatched it from him and nearly tore the drawstring in his hurry to open it. He dug through the contents before pulling out a tiny glass vial of clear liquid. Popping the cork, Zaharis poured a single drop onto the black mark. Instantly, the liquid began to bubble, turning black and filling the air with a terrible odor.

Aravon bit back a cry at the sickening reek that rose from the Duke's side.

"Poison!" Zaharis' eyebrows flew up toward his hairline, his fingers flashing at lightning speed. *"No wonder my antidote remedies didn't work! The Duke's body wasn't just battling Wraithfever—it was trying to fight off the poison as well."*

Aravon sucked in a breath. "You're sure?"

Zaharis' face had gone pale, a look of utter revulsion in his eyes, but he nodded. *"This poison…I recognize it."* Horror tinged his expression. *"A Secret Keeper poison. From the Temple of Whispers in Icespire."*

Ice slithered down Aravon's spine. "You mean…the Secret Keepers wanted him dead? Why? If they didn't know that you were still alive on or Fehl—"

"No!" Zaharis shook his head. *"It's not the sort of poison we Secret Keepers would ever use. Ours are more…sophisticated."* Distaste twisted his lips into a sneer. *"The*

sort of poisons that would leave far less visible a trace. This." He gestured toward the Duke's body. "This is a poison we sell to the right kind of people with the right kind of coin. A lot of coin."

Aravon's mind raced. "I'd ask if you're certain, but—"

"I've seen this poison nowhere else but in the Princelands," Zaharis signed. "And it's made from ingredients found only within a ten-mile radius of Icespire."

Aravon's breath froze in his lungs. "So there's no way the Fjall traitors could have done it."

Zaharis shook his head. "Not unless they got it from a Princelander."

Realization drove a dagger into Aravon's gut. "The traitor!" The same traitor that had revealed the location of Silver Break Mine to the Eirdkilrs. "He had to have sent the poison with..." His eyes flew wide.
"With Lord Virinus or one of the Black Xiphos mercenaries."

The words had an instant effect on his six companions. They leapt to their feet, on full alert.

"The bastards!" Colborn growled.

"Backstabbing cunts!" Noll added his fury.

"We've got to hunt them down, Captain!" Skathi's fist tightened around the arrow she'd been fletching. "Just get me within range of them—"

"We'll string them up by the cullions and make them bleed," Belthar snarled.

"Damned right!" Anger blazed in Aravon's gut. "That's exactly what we're going to do." He turned a furious gaze on the six soldiers facing him. "We're going to find Lord Virinus and those mercenaries, even if we have to hunt them through every Keeper-damned mile between here and Icespire. And when we find them..." He cracked his knuckles loudly. "By the Swordsman, we'll find out who is truly the traitor to the Princelands once and for all."

End of Book 2

The Silent Champions return in:

Steel and Valor (The Silent Champions Book 3)

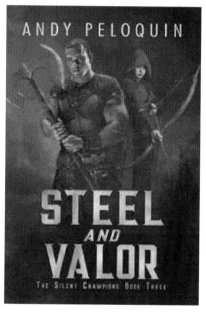

A hunt for a traitor. A desperate search for salvation. An uncovered secret that could destroy everything they hold dear.

Victory over an unstoppable barbarian horde and the salvation of an allied clan are distant memories for **Aravon and his Grim Reavers**. Now, they have a single objective: unmask the turncoat selling vital information to the enemy, and bring to justice the one guilty of murdering Aravon's mentor and surrogate father.

The noble quest throws the specially-trained champions directly in the path of a rampaging force of ruthless enemies. Scrambling to defend a precarious position, Aravon and his companions must rely on the courage and skill of mysterious masked warriors guarding a secret treasure.

But even with their forces bolstered, the soldiers have little hope of survival...much less victory.

Can Aravon defeat overwhelming odds to protect his people, or is his mission doomed to end in failure and death?

Steel and Valor is the third book in the epic Silent Champions military fantasy series. If you like intricate tactics, thrilling battle scenes, and brave soldiers fighting to their last breath, then you'll love Andy Peloquin's gripping series.

Buy Steel and Valor to join the war against the savage invaders today!

Enjoy More Series by Andy Peloquin

Plus, get backstory and insight into the epic world of Einan!

Queen of Thieves

Book 1: Child of the Night Guild

Book 2: Thief of the Night Guild

Book 3: Queen of the Night Guild

Traitors' Fate (**Queen of Thieves/Hero of Darkness Crossover**)

Hero of Darkness

Book 1: Darkblade Assassin

Book 2: Darkblade Outcast

Book 3: Darkblade Protector

Book 4: Darkblade Seeker

Book 5: Darkblade Slayer

Book 6: Darkblade Savior

Book 7: Darkblade Justice

Heirs of Destiny

Trial of Stone (Book 1)

Crucible of Fortune (Book 2)

Secrets of Blood (Book 3)

Storm of Chaos (Book 4)

Ascension of Death (Book 5)

The Renegade Apprentice (Book 6)

Different, Not Damaged: A Short Story Collection

About the Author

I am, first and foremost, a storyteller and an artist--words are my palette. Fantasy is my genre of choice, and I love to explore the darker side of human nature through the filter of fantasy heroes, villains, and everything in between. I'm also a freelance writer, a book lover, and a guy who just loves to meet new people and spend hours talking about my fascination for the worlds I encounter in the pages of fantasy novels.

Fantasy provides us with an escape, a way to forget about our mundane problems and step into worlds where anything is possible. It transcends age, gender, religion, race, or lifestyle--it is our way of believing what cannot be, delving into the unknowable, and discovering hidden truths about ourselves and our world in a brand new way. Fiction at its very best!

Join my Facebook Reader Group
for updates, LIVE readings, exclusive content, and all-around fantasy fun.
Let's Get Social!
Be My Friend: https://www.facebook.com/andrew.peloquin.1
Facebook Author Page: https://www.facebook.com/andyqpeloquin
Twitter: https://twitter.com/AndyPeloquin

Made in the USA
Coppell, TX
18 March 2020